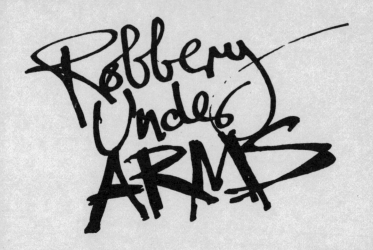

ROLF BOLDREWOOD

ANGUS
& ROBERTSON
PUBLISHERS

ANGUS & ROBERTSON PUBLISHERS

*Unit 4, Eden Park, 31 Waterloo Road,
North Ryde, NSW, Australia 2113, and
16 Golden Square, London W1R 4BN,
United Kingdom*

*First published in serial form
by the* Sydney Mail, *1881*
*First published in book form
by Remington, London, 1888*
*This edition by Angus & Robertson
Publishers, Australia, 1985*

ISBN 0 207 15181 4

*Printed in Australia by
The Dominion Press–Hedges & Bell*

How I Wrote "Robbery Under Arms."

By Rolf Boldrewood.

In writing novels, it has been my experience that the central idea is chiefly needed, everything else being comparatively unimportant. "The Squatter's Dream" and "The Miner's Right" had been published as serials in the "Town and Country Journal," when the late Mr. George Henry Cox, an old friend, happened to say, in conversation: "You ought to write a bushranger novel." I answered: "Well, I think I will." Nothing more passed at the time. This happened in 1880, when I was about to be transferred, as Police Magistrate and Warden of Goldfields, from Gulgong, in New South Wales, to Dubbo.

In those days the courthouse was not locked, the proximity of the gaol and police quarters being thought sufficient to deter petty larcenists. My friend's suggestion, meanwhile, had taken root. No outline of a plot had, however, been developed. Such was never my method. It was the summer season. Early rising had always been my habit; so, one February morning, I walked over to the court house, and wrote a fair instalment of the first chapter of "Robbery Under Arms," before returning to bath and breakfast.

I had been writing regularly for the "Australasian" and "Town and Country Journal." My friend, Mr. Gullett, then editor of the former paper, had, up to this time, accepted everything I sent him without comment. It may be imagined what a shock I received when he declined the first instalment of "Robbery Under Arms," though in a sympathetic manner.

The next attempt was on the "Town and Country." The manuscript was simply re-directed, without comment. Editor, probably busy. Not wholly discouraged, I sent it to the "Sydney Mail." With the "Sydney Morning Herald" I had had no previous literary connection, and much doubted that the "battle, murder, and sudden death" flavour would not find favour with the proprietary. But, rather to my surprise, it was accepted on my own terms, and the serial publication of "Robbery Under Arms" was commenced. It began to attract attention. All sorts and conditions of men, from bishops to boundary riders, read it with interest. People of all ages and both sexes delighted in it. If compliments were coins of the realm, I should have made a fortune, and retired from the profession of author then and there. "What a pleasure it must be to you!" says the enthusiastic reader. "How you must enjoy writing such delightful stories!"

Sympathetic Readers.

"Far from it, my dear young lady," I am often constrained to answer. "Reading gives me so much more pleasure, that I take up my pen with something like a groan when I shut up the book at the appointed hour." "Not fond of writing? Then how in the world do you do it?" queries the eager beginner, as yet innocent of the pains and penalties of authorship. "Well, I suppose I have a facile pen, and the story gets itself done. I never thought to have nearly twenty novels to my name, which the benevolent public is good enough to read and pay for."

One of the most original compliments which I remember receiving was from a squatter of the Queensland border. Returning by train from the direction of Bourke, he joined us at a roadside station. Starting the subject of the tale, he was much excited to find that I was the "real, live author" of "Robbery Under Arms."

"The mail comes in of a Saturday, y'know, and the station hands used to gather to hear me read the weekly chapter. There was a great to-do one night; the paper hadn't come! Been 'shook' on the road—like as not—there was nearly a riot. What d'ye think we did?"

"Don't know, I'm sure."

"Wired to the postmaster at the township to let us know how 'Starlight' had got on. It was a most important chapter."   ,

Who was "Starlight"?

Various conjectures have been hazarded as to the original of "Starlight,"—all were wide of the mark. If there was any lay figure from whom the chivalrous outlaw was limned, it was that of an undeveloped bushranger—part horse-thief—known as "Midnight," in the Gulgong and Dubbo districts. He "worked" between these localities and Queensland, bringing stolen horses from the latter State, and returning with similarly acquired animals from New South Wales. His real name was never known (the police told me), nor when he lay dying, mortally wounded, near Cunnamulla, would he divulge it. I used some of the incidents of his career in creating the character of "Starlight." He it was who stole "Locket," the racing mare with the white patch on her neck, and "Sir William," a thoroughbred, taken from a squatter's stable. He was riding the latter when the police, led by a blacktracker, came upon him. "Locket" was restored to her owner at Gulgong, but "Sir William," like his rider, was mortally wounded in the affray. "Midnight" was once nearly captured by the late Sergeant Wallings, of the Dubbo district police, when, with two troopers, he surprised him at daylight in a "shanty," near Wonbobbie, on the Lower Macquarie. He ran out of the back door, carrying a rifle, when the Sergeant rode at him, calling on him to surrender. But he stood fast, saying: "I don't want to shoot you, Wallings, but if you come on, by ———! I will."

Wallings, an intrepid fellow, had known men of his class surrender at the last moment, and took the risk. But the outlaw shot him through the body, and as he fell from his horse, mortally wounded, leaped into the saddle, and, riding for his life, distanced the troopers.

I saw "Rainbow"—a prominent character in "Robbery Under Arms"—win the "big money" at Gulgong, New South Wales, under the same circumstances as related in the book. His owner and he travelled in the same tent. A dried-up, withered-looking jock, scaling the weight to an ounce, he was leading his mount across the lower end of the course, in a leisurely way, when a steward rode up to him.

"You'll be late, old chap, if you don't hurry up."

"Never was late in my life," he croaked out, producing an old silver "turnip." "Don't yer start at your advertised time?"

The steward referred to his chronograph, and apologised. The old man, who had never altered his pace, crossed the dividing furrow, mounted, and took his place, no trace of excitement being visible on steed or rider. He won the race "hands down." A protest was lodged. The horse, evidently too good for his company, was alleged to have been entered under a wrong name; but no proof was forthcoming. The stakes were paid over by the stewards. The old man packed his tent and belongings and departed. As far as I know, he was never seen or heard of in that part of the country again. But I looked "Rainbow" well over, memorising him for future use. A lovely dark-brown, scarcely fifteen two inches in height, with a star in his broad, Arab-like forehead; perfectly shaped, and "fit to go for a man's life," as, in his time, he probably had done. Lord Rosebery wrote me a complimentary letter, after reading the book, when it came out, and inquired whether there really were horses of the type of "Rainbow" in Australia. I replied that such horses were rare in all countries, but that I had known several, in my lengthened equine experience, which fully answered the description. Had we been in Victoria, I should have judged him to be a relative of "Cornborough," or "Rory O'More," both brown horses, and sires of an illustrious progeny.

Statements have been made through the press, from time to time, by persons professing to identify "Starlight." As the character is chiefly imaginary, it is hardly necessary to say that such must be erroneous. I met, some years since, with a press notice of a bushranger who had raided stations on the Darling. He was a man of

education, who called himself, if I remember, "Frank Gordon," or
"Scott." At the time, I remarked: "If that fellow had turned out
before, instead of after I wrote my book, people might have said
that I had moulded 'Starlight' from him." And a year or two since,
when one "Pelly," who posed as "Major Pelly," and had a small
appointment in the Goldfields Department of Perth, died, every
press correspondent was certain that the long-lost "Starlight" had
been discovered. He may have been "Frank Gordon," for all I know,
but in no way did he enter into my tale.

Where Was Terrible Hollow?

In the same connection, bushmen in divers localities were confident that they knew the exact locality of "Terrible Hollow." That
weird fastness was drawn from a formation of "sunk country," in
the Gwydir district, New England, where in long past ages a sub-
sidence had taken place. The sandstone walls are stated to be three
thousand feet high. The area of grass country enclosed is fairly
large, with a creek running through it. It was described in the local
paper at Armidale, New England, when the police had just arrested
there a gang of horse and cattle stealers, about to start for Queensland with stolen stock.

With respect to the "Marstons"—father and sons—they were portraits drawn from the living model, with, of course, necessary altera-
tions in the matter of name and place. Bred and reared as I have
described, they bore eloquent testimony to the genial Australian
climate, as concerning the development of an Anglo-Saxon race.
Well above the ordinary standard of height, they were, as went the
old Scottish idiom, "pretty men," being good with all weapons of
which they had knowledge. Strong, active, enduring, intelligent,
"'t was pity of them" that so large an endowment of every manly
quality should have been diverted from the right path in life. Had
the South African War broken out before they were fatally com-
promised, none who knew them doubted that they would have
distinguished themselves at the front, as did so many of their
compatriots.

How the Tale Caught On.

The progress of the novel may be briefly alluded to as an un-
qualified success. Tens of thousands of copies have been printed,
reprinted, and sold in every English-speaking country. Under an
arrangement for royalty, it is now running as a serial in the "Montreal
Star." It has sold largely in the United States, as also in India,
where, at a mess dinner (given probably by the "White Hussars"),
at which a relative of mine was present, the conversation taking a
literary turn, the Colonel averred that "the novel 'Robbery Under
Arms,' written by some Australian 'Johnny,' was in his opinion
among the best he had ever read." My young friend secured temporary "kudos" by disclosing his relationship to the author.

Many have been the compliments bestowed upon the writer by the young and fair, the old and worn, schoolboys and sages, hardened editors and struggling scribes. So many, indeed, that but for the warning of "age, that brings the philosophic mind," the dangerous ailment of "swelled head" might have supervened. From such a visitation a merciful Providence has hitherto, I trust, preserved me. I may state that the question of fame never entered into my calculations. Possessing a lifelong experience of almost every Australian type, with a habit of observation, often unconsciously exerted, circumstances directed me, in middle life, to the path of literary work, in which, for the last thirty years, I have found employment for leisure hours. Beginning with "A Kangaroo Drive," in the "Cornhill Magazine," following up with "The Squatter's Dream," in 1870, and ending with the "Ghost Camp," published by Messrs. Macmillan, in October, last year, a list of eighteen novels stands to my credit, all more or less concerned with colonial life, besides short stories, sketches, and articles "too numerous to mention."

Old-time Bushranging.

Of the dramatic incidents of "Robbery Under Arms" I may state with confidence that they actually did take place, much after the fashion narrated in the tale. The names and localities are changed for obvious reasons. The late Mr. Keightley, whom I knew well, described the siege of his house at "Dunn's Plains," near Bathurst, to me personally. After a determined resistance, killing Burke, of the attacking party, he surrendered, but not before the ammunition ran out.

After the capture, two of the bushrangers took Mr. Keightley aside, intending to shoot him. They said, "Turn your back." He replied, "I have never done that to any man. Fire away!" facing them as he spoke. They raised their guns, when one of the men left in charge of Mrs. Keightley, and the other prisoners, called out to them to stop, for they had agreed to spare his life. Mrs. Keightley had, while imploring them not to kill her husband in cold blood before her face, promised them five hundred pounds to spare his life. This, after some demur, they accepted, knowing that her father, who lived at Bathurst, was a wealthy man. She proposed, if allowed to ride there with Dr. Pechey, to procure notes to that amount, and to send a messenger with the parcel to the "black stump," a fire-blasted eucalyptus within sight of their camp. To this arrangement they consented, and the lady started for the long ride, with her husband's life on the cards. It was Sunday afternoon when she rode into Bathurst. Her father at once called on the manager of a bank, who, under the circumstances, cashed Mr. R——'s cheque for the amount. The parcel, containing a hundred five-pound notes, was given to a trusty messenger, with, possibly, the old-fashioned injunction, "these with haste"—ride, ride, ride. He had a good horse—there were many such in the "City of the Plains." A hundred miles, "on a pinch," as a day's ride, was not unknown in that part of Australia.

On the next day the keen eyes of the watchers on the hilltop saw a horseman cross the levels below their camp, and ride towards the "black stump." They saw her messenger, for such he was, approach the well-known landmark, throw down a package, and retire. On examination, it was found to contain a hundred five-pound notes. The compact was kept. Within half-an-hour the prisoner was free, mounted on his own hackney, and making good time on the homeward route. It was always my opinion that the bushrangers sympathised with Mrs. Keightley, as being a native-born Australian, like themselves. Her beauty, and her tears—she was a very handsome woman—doubtless moved them to mercy.

Another sensational siege was that of the late Mr. David Campbell's station, "Goimbla." In that affair also the women (mistress and maid) showed unshaken courage. Mrs. Campbell carried ammunition to her husband, across the line of fire (the house had been attacked by night), when her neck was grazed by a bullet. The brave lady kept a close watch on the attacking party, and warned her husband of a man's approach. As he raised his head over the fence, Mr. Campbell killed him with a snapshot. Half an hour later, Mr. Campbell brought up men from the huts (they had abstained from interference), and made a search. They found the dead robber under a tree, where his mates had dragged him.

"Rolf Boldrewood."

The "nom de plume" under which nearly all my tales have been written was adopted early in my career as an author. A devoted admirer of Sir Walter Scott, I fell across these lines in the introduction to the first canto of "Marmion":

> And that Red King, who, while of old,
> Through Boldrewood the chase he led,
> By his loved huntsman's arrow bled.

The name took my fancy. So much so that, prefacing it with a Norse or Saxon one, I adopted it permanently. It has since been so thoroughly identified with my personality, that I frequently receive letters at my club, from distant realms, with no other address than "Rolf Boldrewood, Esq." It apparently serves the purpose.

In "My Run Home," partly fact and partly fiction, I adopted "Boldrewood" as the name of our "House." So that, in years to come, when the "weary pen" (as "Banjo" Paterson hath it) shall be laid by, permanently, the readers and riders of the Commonwealth, now in "statu pupillari," may hold reasonable doubt as to which feat of arms is to be credited to the hero, and which to the author.

"The incident of the theft of over a thousand head of cattle, related in 'Robbery Under Arms,' created a great stir in Queensland at the time. Bowen Downs Station, in central Queensland, was originally a cattle run, of an area equal in extent to three or four English counties, and carrying enormous herds, sometimes numbering 60,000 or 70,000. The brothers R——, hailing from New South Wales, were justly reputed to be the finest bushmen in Australia. They conceived, and carried out, the project of building stockyards on a remote part of Bowen Downs, where they mustered and drafted over a thousand head of cattle, including the imported bull, which led to their detection. They drove their haul through the back-blocks of Queensland and South Australia, and disposed of the cattle by public auction at Adelaide. Months afterwards, the manager of Bowen Downs noticed in an Adelaide auctioneer's circular the sale of a bull answering the description of their costly imported sire. Correspondence led to the arrest of the R——s.

"They were tried at Roma before Judge Blake. The clearest evidence was adduced against them. But the marvellous audacity of the wonderful droving feat appealed to the jury; they refused to convict. The judge gave them a piece of his mind, and the Assize Court Sessions at Roma were suspended for three years, only after much agitation to be reinstated. Nothing worse than cattle-stealing was ever ascribed to the R——s."

In defence of the accuracy of my portraits, I may state that, as I lived and went to school in Sydney, in the early "thirties," and but for one year's visit to Europe have lived in Australia ever since, I am fairly qualified to describe the men and manners of my adopted country. As a pioneer squatter, a Police Magistrate, and Warden of Goldfields, I have been necessarily brought into contact, official and otherwise, with all sorts and conditions of men. I may be excused for thinking that I know the "Australian native" "down to the ground." That he would ride well, fight well, march well, scout and forage well, more particularly the last, I have always held.

The Ethics of "Robbery Under Arms."

It has been urged, and may be conscientiously believed, that books like "Robbery Under Arms" have a tendency to injure the moral sense of boys who read them and contrast the lavish rewards and exciting adventures which accompany the outlawed life, with the slower gains and tame career of honest industry. But these are superficial deductions. Note Aileen's burning words, while denouncing the dishonest career of the Marstons. Jim had just said: "Who's fault's that? The dingo must live as well as the collie. He's not a bad sort, old dingo, and has a good time of it as long as it lasts."

"Yes! till he's trapped, or shot, or poisoned, some day, which he always is," said Aileen, bitterly. "I wonder that any man should be content with a wicked life, a shameful death!" And here she struck

CHAPTER I

My name's Dick Marston, Sydney-side native. I'm twenty-nine years old, six feet in my stocking soles, and thirteen stone weight. Pretty strong and active with it, so they say. I don't want to blow —not here, any road—but it takes a good man to put me on my back, or stand up to me with the gloves, or the naked mauleys. I can ride anything—anything that ever was lapped in horsehide—swim like a musk-duck, and track like a Myall blackfellow. Most things that a man can do I'm up to, and that's all about it. As I lift myself now I can feel the muscle swell on my arm like a cricket ball, in spite of the—well, in spite of everything.

The morning sun comes shining through the window bars; and ever since he was up have I been cursing the daylight, cursing myself, and them that brought me into the world. Did I curse mother, and the hour I was born into this miserable life?

Why should I curse the day? Why do I lie here, groaning; yes, crying like a child, and beating my head against the stone floor? I am not mad, though I am shut up in a cell. No. Better for me if I was. But it's all up now; there's no get away this time; and I, Dick Marston, as strong as a bullock, as active as a rock-wallaby, chock-full of life and spirits and health, have been tried for bush-ranging—robbery under arms they call it—and though the blood runs through my veins like the water in the mountain creeks, and every bit of bone and sinew is as sound as the day I was born, I must die on the gallows this day month.

Die—die—yes, die; be strung up like a dog, as they say. I'm blessed if ever I did know of a dog being hanged, though, if it comes to that, a shot or a bait generally makes an end of 'em in this country. Ha, ha! Did I laugh? What a rum thing it is that a man should have a laugh in him when he's only got twenty-nine days more to live—a day for every year of my life. Well, laughing or crying, this is what it has come to at last. All the drinking and recklessness; the flash talk and the idle ways; the merry cross-country rides that we used to have, night or day, it made no odds to us; every man well mounted, as like as not on a racehorse in train-ing taken out of his stable within the week; the sharp brushes with the police, when now and then a man was wounded on each side, but no one killed. That came later on, worse luck. The jolly sprees we used to have in the bush townships, where we chucked our money about like gentlemen, where all the girls had a smile and a kind word for a lot of game upstanding chaps, that acted like men, if they did keep the road a little lively. Our 'bush telegraphs' were safe to let us know when the 'traps' were closing in on us, and then —why the coach would be 'stuck up' a hundred miles away, in a different direction, within twenty-four hours. Marston's gang again! The police are in pursuit! That's what we'd see in the papers. We had 'em sent to us regular; besides having the pick of 'em when we cut open the mail bags.

And now—that chain rubbed a sore, curse it!—all that racket's over. It's more than hard to die in this settled, infernal, fixed sort of way, like a bullock in the killing-yard, all ready to be 'pithed.' I used to pity them when I was a boy, walking round the yard, pushing their noses through the rails, trying for a likely place to jump, stamping and pawing and roaring and knocking their heads against the heavy close rails, with misery and rage in their eyes, till their time was up. Nobody told *them* beforehand, though!

Have I and the likes of me ever felt much the same, I wonder, shut up in a pen like this, with the rails up, and not a place a rat could creep through, waiting till our killing time was come? The poor devils of steers have never done anything but ramble off the run now and again, while we—but it's too late to think of that. It *is* hard. There's no saying it isn't; no, nor thinking what a fool, what a blind, stupid, thundering idiot a fellow's been, to laugh at the steady working life that would have helped him up, bit by bit, to a good farm, a good wife, and innocent little kids about him, like that chap, George Storefield, that came to see me last week. He was real rightdown sorry for me, I could tell, though Jim and I used to laugh at him, and call him a regular old crawler of a milker's calf in the old days. The tears came into his eyes reg'lar like a woman as he gave my hand a squeeze and turned his head away. We was little chaps together, you know. A man always feels that, you know. And old George, he'll go back—a fifty-mile ride, but what's that on a good horse? He'll be late home, but he can cross the rock ford the short way over the creek. I can see him turn his horse loose at the garden-gate, and walk through the quinces that lead up to the cottage, with his saddle on his arm. Can't I see it all, as plain as if I was there?

And his wife and the young 'uns 'll run out when they hear father's horse, and want to hear all the news. When he goes in there's his meal tidy and decent waiting for him, while he tells them about the poor chap he's been to see as is to be scragged next month. Ha! ha! what a rum joke it is, isn't it?

And then he'll go out in the verandah, with the roses growin' all over the posts and smellin' sweet in the cool night air. After that he'll have his smoke, and sit there thinkin' about me, perhaps, and old days, and what not, till all hours—till his wife comes and fetches him in. And here I lie—my God! why didn't they knock me on the head when I was born, like a lamb in a dry season, or a blind puppy —blind enough, God knows! They do so in some countries, if the books say true, and what a hell of misery that must save some people from!

Well, it's done now, and there's no get away. I may as well make the best of it. A sergeant of police was shot in our last scrimmage, and they must fit some one over that. It's only natural. He was rash, or Starlight would never have dropped him that day. Not if he'd been sober either. We'd been drinking all night at that Willow Tree shanty. Bad grog, too! When a man's half drunk he's fit for any devilment that comes before him. Drink! How do you think a chap that's taken to the bush—regularly turned out, I mean, with a price on his head, and a fire burning in his heart night and day—can stand his life if he don't drink? When he thinks of what he might have been, and what he is! Why, nearly every man he meets is paid to run him down, or trap him some way like a stray dog that's taken to sheep-killin'. He knows a score of men, and women too, that are only looking out for a chance to sell his blood on the quiet and pouch the money. Do you think that makes a chap mad and miserable, and tired of his life, or not? And if a drop of grog will take him right out of his wretched self for a bit why shouldn't he drink? People don't know what they are talking about. Why, he is that miserable that he wonders why he don't hang himself, and save the Government all the trouble; and if a few nobblers make him feel as if he might have some good chances yet, and that it doesn't so much matter after all, why shouldn't he drink?

He does drink, of course; every miserable man, and a good many women as have something to fear or repent of, drink. The worst of it is that too much of it brings on the 'horrors,' and then the devil, instead of giving you a jog now and then, sends one of his imps to grin in your face and pull your heart-strings all day and all night long. By George, I'm getting clever—too clever altogether, I think. If I could forget for one moment, in the middle of all the nonsense, that I was to die on Thursday three weeks! die on Thursday three weeks! die on Thursday! That's the way the time runs in my ears like a chime of bells. But it's all mere bosh I've been reading these long six months I've been chained up here—after I was committed for trial. When I came out of the hospital after curing me of that wound—for I was hit bad by that black tracker—they gave me some books to read for fear I'd go mad and cheat the hangman. I was always fond of reading, and many a night I've read to poor old mother and Aileen before I left the old place. I was that weak and low, after I took the turn, and I felt glad to get a book to take me away from sitting, staring, and blinking at nothing by the hour together. It was all very well then; I was too weak to think much. But when I began to get well again I kept always coming across something in the book that made me groan or cry out, as if some one

had stuck a knife in me. A dark chap did once—through the ribs—
it didn't feel so bad, a little sharpish at first; why didn't he aim
a bit higher? He never was no good, even at that. As I was saying,
there'd be something about a horse, or the country, or the spring
weather—it's just coming in now, and the Indian corn's shooting after
the rain, and I'll never see it; or they'd put in a bit about the cows
walking through the river in the hot summer afternoons; or they'd
go describing about a girl, until I began to think of sister Aileen
again; then I'd run my head against the wall, or do something like
a madman, and they'd stop the books for a week; and I'd be as miserable as a bandicoot, worse and worse a lot, with all the devil's tricks
and bad thoughts in my head, and nothing to put them away.

I must either kill myself, or get something to fill up my time
till the day—yes, the day comes. I've always been a middling writer,
tho' I can't say much for the grammar, and spelling, and that, but I'll
put it all down, from the beginning to the end, and maybe it'll save
some other unfortunate young chap from pulling back like a colt
when he's first roped, setting himself against everything in the way
of proper breaking, making a fool of himself generally, and choking
himself down, as I've done.

The gaoler—he looks hard—he had to do that, there's more than
one or two within here that would have him by the throat, with his
heart's blood running, in half a minute, if they had their way, and
the warder was off guard. He knows that very well. But he's not a
bad-hearted chap.

'You can have books, or paper and pens, anything you like,' he
said, 'you unfortunate young beggar, until you're turned off.'

'If I'd only had you to see after me when I was young,' says I——

'Come; don't whine,' he said, then he burst out laughing. 'You
didn't mean it, I see. I ought to have known better. You're not one
of that sort, and I like you all the better for it.'

.   .   .   .

Well, here goes. Lots of pens, a big bottle of ink, and ever so
much foolscap paper, the right sort for me, or I shouldn't have been
here. I'm blessed if it doesn't look as if I was going to write copies
again. Don't I remember how I used to go to school in old times;
the rides there and back on the old pony; and pretty little Grace
Storefield that I was so fond of, and used to show her how to do
her lessons. I believe I learned more that way than if I'd had only
myself to think about. There was another girl, the daughter of
the poundkeeper, that I wanted her to beat; and the way we both
worked, and I coached her up, was a caution. And she did get
above her in her class. How proud we were! She gave me a kiss,
too, and a bit of her hair. Poor Gracey! I wonder where she is
now, and what she'd think if she saw me here to-day. If I could
have looked ahead, and seen myself—chained now like a dog, and
going to die a dog's death this day month!

Anyhow, I must make a start. How do people begin when they set to work to write their own sayings and doings? There's been a deal more doing than talking in my life—it was the wrong sort—more's the pity.

Well, let's see; his parents were poor, but respectable. That's what they always say. My parents were poor, and mother was as good a soul as ever broke bread, and wouldn't have taken a shilling's worth that wasn't her own if she'd been starving. But as for father, he'd been a poacher in England, a Lincolnshire man he was, and got sent out for it. He wasn't much more than a boy, he said, and it was only for a hare or two, which didn't seem much. But I begin to think, being able to see the right of things a bit now, and having no bad grog inside of me to turn a fellow's head upside down, as poaching must be something like cattle and horse duffing—not the worst thing in the world itself, but mighty likely to lead to it.

Dad had always been a hard-working, steady-going sort of chap, good at most things, and like a lot more of the Government men, as the convicts were always called round our part, he saved some money as soon as he had done his time, and married mother, who was a simple emigrant girl just out from Ireland. Father was a square-built, good-looking chap, I believe, then; not so tall as I am by three inches, but wonderfully strong and quick on his pins. They did say as he could hammer any man in the district before he got old and stiff. I never saw him 'shape' but once, and then he rolled into a man big enough to eat him, and polished him off in a way that showed me—though I was a bit of a boy then—that he'd been at the game before. He didn't ride so bad either, though he hadn't had much of it where he came from; but he was afraid of nothing, and had a quiet way with colts. He could make pretty good play in thick country, and ride a roughish horse, too.

Well, our farm was on a good little flat, with a big mountain in front, and a scrubby, rangy country at the back for miles. People often asked him why he chose such a place. 'It suits me,' he used to say, with a laugh, and talk of something else. We could only raise about enough corn and potatoes, in a general way, for ourselves from the flat; but there were other chances and pickings which helped to make the pot boil, and them we'd have been a deal better without.

First of all, though our cultivation paddock was small, and the good land seemed squeezed in between the hills, there was a narrow tract up the creek, and here it widened out into a large well-grassed flat. This was where our cattle ran, for, of course, we had a team of workers and a few milkers when we came. No one ever took up a farm in those days without a dray and a team, a year's rations, a few horses and milkers, pigs and fowls, and a little furniture. They didn't collar a 40-acre selection, as they do now—spend all their money in getting the land and squat down as bare as robins—a man with his wife and children all under a sheet of bark, nothing on their backs, and very little in their bellies. However, some of them do pretty well, though they do say they have to live on 'possums for a time. We didn't do much, in spite of our grand start.

The flat was well enough, but there were other places in the gullies beyond that, that father had dropped upon when he was out shooting. He was a tremendous chap for poking about on foot or on horseback, and though he was an Englishman, he was what you call a born bushman. I never saw any man almost as was his equal. Wherever he'd been once, there he could take you to again; and what was more, if it was in the dead of the night he could do it just the same. People said he was as good as a blackfellow, but I never saw one that was as good as he was, all round. In a strange country, too. That was what beat me—he'd know the way the creek run, and noticed when the cattle headed to camp, and a lot of things that other people couldn't see, or if they did, couldn't remember again. He was a great man for solitary walks, too—he and an old dog he had, called Crib, a cross-bred mongrel-looking brute, most like what they call a lurcher in England, father said. Anyhow, he could do most anything but talk. He could bite to some purpose, drive cattle or sheep, catch a kangaroo, if it wasn't a regular flier, fight like a bulldog, and swim like a retriever, track anything, and fetch and carry, but bark he wouldn't. He'd stand and look at dad as if he worshipped him, and he'd make him some sign and off he'd go like a child that's got a message. Why he was so fond of the old man we boys couldn't make out. We were afraid of him, and as far as we could see he never patted or made much of Crib. He thrashed him unmerciful as he did us boys. Still the dog was that fond of him you'd think he'd like to die for him there and then. But dogs are not like boys, or men either—better, perhaps.

Well, we were all born at the hut by the creek, I suppose, for I remember it as soon as I could remember anything. It was a snug hut enough, for father was a good bush carpenter, and didn't turn his back to any one for splitting and fencing, hut-building and shingle-splitting; he had had a year or two at sawing, too, but after he was married he dropped that. But I've heard mother say that he took great pride in the hut when he brought her to it first, and said it was the best-built hut within fifty miles. He split every slab, cut every post and wallplate and rafter himself, with a man to help him at odd times; and after the frame was up, and the bark on the roof, he camped underneath and finished every bit of it—chimney, flooring, doors, windows, and partitions—by himself. Then he dug up a little garden in front, and planted a dozen or two peaches and quinces in it; put a couple of roses—a red and a white one—by the posts of the verandah, and it was all ready for his pretty Norah, as she says he used to call her then. If I've heard her tell about the garden and the quince trees and the two roses once, I've heard her tell it a hundred times. Poor mother! we used to get round her

--Aileen, and Jim, and I—and say, 'Tell us about the garden, mother.'
She'd never refuse; those were her happy days, she always said. She
used to cry afterwards—nearly always.

The first thing almost that I can remember was riding the old
pony, 'Possum, out to bring in the milkers. Father was away somewhere, so mother took us all out and put me on the pony, and let
me have a whip. Aileen walked alongside, and very proud I was.
My legs stuck out straight on the old pony's fat back. Mother had
ridden him up when she came—the first horse she ever rode, she said.
He was a quiet little old roan, with a bright eye and legs like gate-
posts, but he never fell down with us boys, for all that. If we fell
off he stopped still and began to feed, so that he suited us all to
pieces. We soon got sharp enough to flail him along with a quince
stick, and we used to bring up the milkers, I expect, a good deal faster
than was good for them. After a bit we could milk, leg-rope, and
bail up for ourselves, and help dad brand the calves, which began
to come pretty thick. There were only three of us children—my
brother Jim, who was two years younger than I was, and then Aileen,
who was four years behind him. I know we were both able to nurse
the baby a while after she came, and neither of us wanted better
fun than to be allowed to watch her, or rock the cradle, or as a
great treat to carry her a few steps. Somehow we was that fond
and proud of her from the first that we'd have done anything in
the world for her. And so we would now—I was going to say—but
that poor Jim lies under a forest oak on a sandhill, and I—well, I'm
here, and if I'd listened to her advice I should have been a free
man. A free man! How it sounds, doesn't it? with the sun shining,
and the blue sky over your head, and the birds twittering, and the
grass beneath your feet! I wonder if I shall go mad before my
time's up.

Mother was a Roman Catholic—most Irishwomen are; and dad
was a Protestant, if he was anything. However, that says nothing.
People that don't talk much about their religion, or follow it up at
all, won't change it for all that. So father, though mother tried him
hard enough when they were first married, wouldn't hear of turning,
not if he was to be killed for it, as I once heard him say. 'No!' he
says, 'my father and grandfather, and all the lot, was Church people,
and so I shall live and die. I don't know as it would make much
matter to me, but such as my notions is, I shall stick to 'em as long
as the craft holds together. You can bring up the girl in your own
way; it's made a good woman of you, or found you one, which is
most likely, and so she may take her chance. But I stand for Church
and King, and so shall the boys, as sure as my name's Ben Marston.'

CHAPTER II

FATHER was one of those people that gets shut of a deal of trouble in this world by always sticking to one thing. If he said he'd do this or that he always did it and nothing else. As for turning him, a wild bull half-way down a range was a likelier try-on. So nobody ever bothered him after he'd once opened his mouth. They knew it was so much lost labour. I sometimes thought Aileen was a bit like him in her way of sticking to things. But then she was always right, you see.

So that clinched it. Mother gave in like a wise woman, as she was. The clergyman from Bargo came one day and christened me and Jim—made one job of it. But mother took Aileen herself in the spring cart all the way to the township and had her christened in the chapel, in the middle of the service all right and regular, by Father Roche.

There's good and bad of every sort, and I've met plenty that were no chop of all churches; but if Father Roche, or Father anybody else, had any hand in making mother and Aileen half as good as they were, I'd turn to-morrow, if I ever got out again. I don't suppose it was the religion that made much difference in our case, for Patsey Daly and his three brothers, that lived on the creek higher up, were as much on the cross as men could be, and many a time I've seen them ride to chapel and attend mass, and look as if they'd never seen a 'clearskin' in their lives. Patsey was hanged afterwards for bush-ranging and gold robbery, and he had more than one man's blood to answer for. Now we weren't like that; we never troubled the church one way or the other. We knew we were doing what we oughtn't to do, and scorned to look pious and keep two faces under one hood.

By degrees we all grew older, began to be active and able to do half a man's work. We learned to ride pretty well—at least, that is, we could ride a bare-backed horse at full gallop through timber or down a range; could back a colt just caught and have him as quiet as an old cow in a week. We could use the axe and the cross-cut saw, for father dropped that sort of work himself, and made Jim and I do all the rough jobs of mending the fences, getting firewood, milking the cows, and, after a bit, ploughing the bit of flat we kept in cultivation.

Jim and I, when we were fifteen and thirteen—he was bigger for his age than I was, and so near my own strength that I didn't care about touching him—were the smartest lads on the creek, father said —he didn't often praise us, either. We had often ridden over to help at the muster of the large cattle stations that were on the side of the range, and not more than twenty or thirty miles from us.

Some of our young stock used to stray among the squatters' cattle, and we liked attending the muster because there was plenty of galloping about and cutting out, and fun in the men's hut at night, and often a half-crown or so for helping some one away with a big mob of cattle or a lot for the pound. Father didn't go himself, and I used to notice that whenever we came up and said we were Ben Marston's boys both master and super looked rather glum, and then appeared not to think any more about it. I heard the owner of one of these stations say to his managing man, 'Pity, isn't it? Fine boys, too.' I didn't understand what they meant. I do now.

We could do a few things besides riding, because, as I told you before, we had been to a bit of a school kept by an old chap that had once seen better days, that lived three miles off, near a little bush township. This village, like most of these places, had a public-house and a blacksmith's shop. That was about all. The publican kept the store, and managed pretty well to get hold of all the money that was made by the people round about, that is of those who were 'good drinking men.' He had half-a-dozen children, and, though he was not up to much, he wasn't that bad that he didn't want his children to have the chance of being better than himself. I've seen a good many crooked people in my day, but very few that, though they'd given themselves up as a bad job, didn't hope a bit that their youngsters mightn't take after them. Curious, isn't it? But it is true, I can tell you. So Lammerby, the publican, though he was a greedy, sly sort of fellow, that bought things he knew were stolen, and lent out money and charged everybody two prices for the things he sold 'em, didn't like the thought of his children growing up like Myall cattle, as he said himself, and so he fished out this old Mr. Howard, that had been a friend or a victim or some kind of pal of his in old times, near Sydney, and got him to come and keep school.

He was a curious man, this Mr. Howard. What he had been or done none of us ever knew, but he spoke up to one of the squatters that said something sharp to him one day in a way that showed us boys that he thought himself as good as he was. And he stood up straight and looked him in the face, till we hardly could think he was the same man that was so bent and shambling and broken-down-looking most times. He used to live in a little hut in the township all by himself. It was just big enough to hold him and us at our lessons. He had his dinner at the inn, along with Mr. and Mrs. Lammerby. She was always kind to him, and made him puddings and things when he was ill. He was pretty often ill, and then he'd hear us our lessons at the bedside, and make a short day of it.

Mostly he drank nothing but tea. He used to smoke a good deal out of a big meerschaum pipe with figures on it that he used to show us when he was in a good humour. But two or three times a year he used to set-to and drink for a week, and then school was left off till he was right. We didn't think much of that. Everybody, almost, that we knew did the same—all the men—nearly all, that is —and some of the women—not mother, though; she wouldn't have touched a drop of wine or spirits to save her life, and never did to her dying day. We just thought of it as if they'd got a touch of fever or sunstroke, or broke a rib or something. They'd get over it in a week or two, and be all right again.

All the same, poor old Mr. Howard wasn't always on the booze, not by any manner of means. He never touched a drop of anything, not even ginger-beer, while he was straight, and he kept us all going from nine o'clock in the morning till three in the afternoon, summer and winter, for more than six years. Then he died, poor old chap— found dead in his bed one morning. Many a basting he gave me and Jim with an old malacca cane he had with a silver knob to it. We were all pretty frightened of him. He'd say to me and Jim and the other boys, 'It's the best chance of making men of yourselves you ever had, if you only knew it. You'll be rich farmers or settlers, perhaps magistrates, one of these days—that is, if you're not hanged. It's you, I mean,' he'd say, pointing to me and Jim and the Dalys; 'I believe some of you *will* be hanged unless you change a good deal. It's cold blood and bad blood that runs in your veins, and you'll come to earn the wages of sin some day. It's a strange thing,' he used to say, as if he was talking to himself, 'that the girls are so good, while the boys are delivered over to the Evil One, except a case here and there. Look at Mary Darcy and Jane Lammerby, and my little pet Aileen here. I defy any village in Britain to turn out such girls —plenty of rosy-cheeked gigglers—but the natural refinement and intelligence of these little damsels astonishes me.'

Well, the old man died suddenly, as I said, and we were all very sorry, and the school was broken up. But he had taught us all to write fairly and to keep accounts, to read and spell decently, and to know a little geography. It wasn't a great deal, but what we knew we knew well, and I often think of what he said, now it's too late, we ought to have made better use of it. After school broke up father said Jim and I knew quite as much as was likely to be any good to us, and we must work for our living like other people. We'd always done a pretty fair share of that, and our hands were hard with using the axe and the spade, let alone holding the plough at odd times and harrowing, helping father to kill and brand, and a lot of other things, besides getting up while the stars were in the sky so as to get the cows milked early, before it was time to go to school.

All this time we had lived in a free kind of way—we wanted for nothing. We had plenty of good beef, and a calf now and then.

About this time I began to wonder how it was that so many cattle and horses passed through father's hands, and what became of them.

I hadn't lived all my life on Rocky Creek, and among some of the smartest hands in that line that old New South Wales ever bred, without knowing what 'clearskins' and 'cross' beasts meant, and being well aware that our brand was often put on a calf that no cow of ours ever suckled. Don't I remember well the first calf I ever helped to put our letters on? I've often wished I'd defied father, then taken my licking, and bolted away from home. It's that very calf and the things it led to that's helped to put me where I am!

Just as I sit here, and these cursed irons rattle whenever I move my feet, I can see that very evening, and father and the old dog with a little mob of our crawling cattle and half-a-dozen head of strangers, cows and calves, and a fat little steer coming through the scrub to the old stockyard.

It was an awkward place for a yard, people used to say; scrubby and stony all round, a blind sort of hole—you couldn't see till you were right on the top of it. But there was a 'wing' ran out a good way through the scrub—there's no better guide to a yard like that—and there was a sort of track cattle followed easy enough once you were round the hill. Anyhow, between father and the dog and the old mare he always rode, very few beasts ever broke away.

These strange cattle had been driven a good way, I could see. The cows and calves looked done up, and the steer's tongue was out —it was hottish weather; the old dog had been 'heeling' him up too, for he was bleeding up to the hocks, and the end of his tail was bitten off. He was a savage old wretch was Crib. Like all dogs that never bark—and men too—his bite was all the worse.

'Go and get the brands—confound you—don't stand there frightening the cattle,' says father, as the tired cattle, after smelling and jostling a bit, rushed into the yard. 'You, Jim, make a fire, and look sharp about it. I want to brand old Polly's calf and another or two.' Father came down to the hut while the brands were getting ready, and began to look at the harness-cask, which stood in a little black skillion. It was pretty empty; we had been living on eggs, bacon, and bread and butter for a week.

'Oh, mother! there's such a pretty red calf in the yard,' I said, 'with a star and a white spot on the flank; and there's a yellow steer fat enough to kill!'

'What!' said mother, turning round and looking at father with her eyes staring—a sort of dark blue they were—people used to say mine and Jim's were the same colour—and her brown hair pushed back off her face, as if she was looking at a ghost. 'Is it doing that again you are, after all you promised me, and you so nearly caught —after the last one? Didn't I go on my knees to ye to ask ye to drop it and lead a good life, and didn't ye tell me ye'd never do the like again? And the poor innocent children, too; I wonder ye've the heart to do it.'

It came into my head now to wonder why the sergeant and two policemen had come down from Bargo, very early in the morning, about three months ago, and asked father to show them the beef in his cask, and the hide belonging to it. I wondered at the time the beast was killed why father made the hide into a rope, and before he did that had cut out the brand and dropped it into a hot fire. The police saw a hide with our brand on, all right—killed about a fortnight. They didn't know it had been taken off a cancered bullock, and that father took the trouble to 'stick' him and bleed him before he took the hide off, so as it shouldn't look dark. Father certainly knew most things in the way of working on the cross. I can see now he'd have made his money a deal easier, and no trouble of mind, if he'd only chosen to go straight.

When mother said this, father looked at her for a bit as if he was sorry for it; then he straightened himself up, and an ugly look came into his face as he growled out—

'You mind your own business; we must live as well as other people. There's squatters here that does as bad. They're just like the squires at home; think a poor man hasn't a right to live. You bring the brand and look alive, Dick, or I'll sharpen ye up a bit.'

The brand was in the corner, but mother got between me and it, and stretched out her hand to father as if to stop me and him.

'In God's name,' she cried out, 'aren't ye satisfied with losing your own soul and bringing disgrace upon your family, but ye must be the ruin of your innocent children? Don't touch the brand, Dick!'

But father wasn't a man to be crossed, and what made it worse he had a couple of glasses of bad grog in him. There was an old villain of a shanty-keeper that lived on a back creek. He'd been there as he came by and had a glass or two. He had a regular savage temper, father had, though he was quiet enough and not bad to us when he was right. But the grog always spoiled him.

He gave poor mother a shove which sent her reeling against the wall, where she fell down and hit her head against the stool, and lay there. Aileen, sitting down in the corner, turned white, and began to cry, while father catches me a box on the ear which sends me kicking, picks up the brand out of the corner, and walks out, with me after him.

I think if I'd been another year or so older I'd have struck back—I felt that savage about poor mother that I could have gone at him myself—but we had been too long used to do everything he told us; and somehow, even if a chap's father's a bad one, he don't seem like other men to him. So, as Jim had lighted the fire, we branded the little red heifer calf first—a fine fat six-months-old nugget she was—and then three bull calves, all strangers, and then Polly's calf, I suppose just for a blind. Jim and I knew the four calves were all strangers, but we didn't know the brands of the mothers; they all seemed different.

After this all was made right to kill a beast. The gallows was ready rigged in a corner of the yard; father brought his gun and shot the yellow steer. The calves were put into our calf-pen— Polly's and all—and all the cows turned out to go where they liked.

We helped father to skin and hang up the beast, and pretty late it was when we finished. Mother had laid us out our tea and gone to bed with Aileen. We had ours and then went to bed. Father sat outside and smoked in the starlight. Hours after I woke up and heard mother crying. Before daylight we were up again, and the steer was cut up and salted and in the harness-cask soon after sunrise. His head and feet were all popped into a big pot where we used to make soup for the pigs, and by the time it had been boiling an hour or two there was no fear of any one swearing to the yellow steer by 'head-mark.'

We had a hearty breakfast off the 'skirt,' but mother wouldn't touch a bit, nor let Aileen take any; she took nothing but a bit of bread and a cup of tea, and sat there looking miserable and downcast. Father said nothing, but sat very dark-looking, and ate his food as if nothing was the matter. After breakfast he took his mare, the old dog followed; there was no need to whistle for him—it's my belief he knew more than many a Christian—and away they went. Father didn't come home for a week—he had got into the habit of staying away for days and days together. Then things went on the old way.

CHAPTER III

So the years went on—slow enough they seemed to us sometimes—the green winters, pretty cold, I tell you, with frost and hail-storms, and the long hot summers. We were not called boys any longer except by mother and Aileen, but took our places among the men of the district. We lived mostly at home, in the old way; sometimes working pretty hard, sometimes doing very little. When the cows were milked and the wood chopped, there was nothing to do for the rest of the day. The creek was that close that mother used to go and dip the bucket into it herself, when she wanted one, from the little wooden step above the clear reedy waterhole.

Now and then we used to dig in the garden. There was reaping and corn-pulling and husking for part of the year; but often, for weeks at a time, there was next to nothing to do. No hunting worth much—we were sick of kangarooing, like the dogs themselves, that as they grew old would run a little way and then pull up if a mob came, jump, jump, past them. No shooting, except a few ducks and pigeons. Father used to laugh at the shooting in this country, and say they'd never have poachers here—the game wasn't worth it. No fishing, except an odd codfish, in the deepest water-holes; and you might sit half a day without a bite.

Now this was very bad for us boys. Lads want plenty of work, and a little play now and then to keep them straight. If there's none, they'll make it; and you can't tell how far they'll go when they once start.

Well, Jim and I used to get our horses and ride off quietly in the afternoon, as if we were going after cattle; but, in reality, as soon as we were out of sight of mother, to ride over to that old villain, Grimes, the shanty-keeper, where we met the young Dalys, and others of the same sort—talked a good deal of nonsense and gossip; what was worse, played at all-fours and euchre, which we had learned from an American harvest hand, at one of the large farms.

Besides playing for money, which put us rather into trouble sometimes, as we couldn't always find a half-crown if we lost it, we learned another bad habit, and that was to drink spirits. What burning nasty stuff I thought it at first; and so did we all! But every one wanted to be thought a man, and up to all kinds of wickedness, so we used to make it a point of drinking our nobbler, and sometimes treating the others twice, if we had cash.

There was another family that lived a couple of miles off, higher up the creek, and we had always been good friends with them, though they never came to our house, and only we boys went to theirs. They were the parents of the little girl that went to school with us, and a boy who was a year older than me.

Their father had been a gardener at home, and he married a native girl who was born somewhere about the Hawkesbury, near Windsor. Her father had been a farmer, and many a time she told us how sorry she was to go away from the old place, and what fine corn and pumpkins they grew; and how they had a church at Windsor, and used to take their hay and fruit and potatoes to Sydney, and what a grand place Sydney was, with stone buildings called markets for people to sell fruit and vegetables and poultry in; and how you could walk down into Lower George Street and see Sydney Harbour, a great shining salt-water plain, a thousand times as big as the biggest waterhole, with ships and boats and sailors, and every kind of strange thing upon it.

Mrs. Storefield was pretty fond of talking, and she was always fond of me, because once when she was out after the cows, and her man was away, and she had left Grace at home, the little thing crawled down to the waterhole and tumbled in. I happened to be riding up with a message for mother, to borrow some soap, when I heard a little cry like a lamb's, and there was poor little Gracey struggling in the water like a drowning kitten, with her face under. Another minute or two would have finished her, but I was off the old pony and into the water like a teal flapper. I had her out in a second or two, and she gasped and cried a bit, but soon came to, and when Mrs. Storefield came home she first cried over her as if she would break her heart, and kissed her, and then she kissed me, and said, 'Now, Dick Marston, you look here. Your mother's a good woman, though simple; your father I don't like, and I hear many stories about him that makes me think the less we ought to see of the lot of you the better. But you've saved my child's life to-day, and I'll be a friend and a mother to you as long as I live, even if you turn out bad, and I'm rather afraid you will—you and Jim both—but it won't be my fault for want of trying to keep you straight; and John and I will be your kind and loving friends as long as we live, no matter what happens.'

After that—it was strange enough—but I always took to the little toddling thing that I'd pulled out of the water. I wasn't very big myself, if it comes to that, and she seemed to have a feeling about it, for she'd come to me every time I went there, and sit on my knee and look at me with her big brown serious eyes—they were just the same after she grew up—and talk to me in her little childish lingo. I believe she knew all about it, for she used to say, 'Dick pull Gracey out of water'; and then she'd throw her arms round my neck and kiss me, and walk off to her mother. If I'd let her drown then, and tied a stone round my neck and dropped through the reeds to the bottom of the big waterhole, it would have been better for both of us.

When John came home he was nearly as bad as the old woman, and wanted to give me a filly, but I wouldn't have it, boy as I was. I never cared for money nor money's worth, and I was not going to be paid for picking a kid out of the water.

George Storefield, Gracey's brother, was about my own age. He thought a lot of what I'd done for her, and years afterwards I threatened to punch his head if he said anything more about it. He laughed, and held out his hand.

'You and I might have been better friends lately,' says he; 'but don't you forget you've got another brother besides Jim—one that will stick to you, too, fair weather or foul.'

I always had a great belief in George, though we didn't get on over well, and often had fallings out. He was too steady and hardworking altogether for Jim and me. He worked all day and every day, and saved every penny he made. Catch him gaffing!—no, not for a sixpence. He called the Dalys and Jacksons thieves and swindlers, who would be locked up, or even hanged, some day, unless they mended themselves. As for drinking a glass of grog, you might just as soon ask him to take a little laudanum or arsenic.

'Why should I drink grog,' he used to say — 'such stuff, too, as you get at that old villain Grimes's—with a good appetite and a good conscience? I'm afraid of no man; the police may come and live on my ground for what I care. I work all day, have a read in the evening, and sleep like a top when I turn in. What do I want more?'

'Oh, but you never see any life,' Jim said; 'you're just like an old working bullock that walks up to the yoke in the morning and never stops hauling till he's let go at night. This is a free country, and I don't think a fellow was born for that kind of thing and nothing else.'

'This country's like any other country, Jim,' George would say, holding up his head, and looking straight at him with his steady grey eyes; 'a man must work and save when he's young if he don't want to be a beggar or a slave when he's old. I believe in a man enjoying himself as well as you do, but my notion of that is to have a good farm, well stocked and paid for, by and by, and then to take it easy, perhaps when my back is a little stiffer than it is now.'

'But a man must have a little fun when he is young,' I said. 'What's the use of having money when you're old and rusty, and can't take pleasure in anything?'

'A man needn't be so very old at forty,' he says then, 'and twenty years' steady work will put all of us youngsters well up the ladder. Besides, I don't call it fun getting half-drunk with a lot of blackguards at a low pothouse or a shanty, listening to the stupid talk and boasting lies of a pack of loafers and worse. They're fit for nothing better; but you and Jim are. Now, look here, I've got a small contract from Mr. Andrews for a lot of fencing stuff. It will pay us wages and something over. If you like to go in with me, we'll go share and share. I know what hands you both are at splitting and fencing. What do you say?'

Jim, poor Jim, was inclined to take George's offer. He was that good-hearted that a kind word would turn him any time. But I was put out at his laying it down so about the Dalys and us shantying and gaffing, and I do think now that some folks are born so as they can't do without a taste of some sort of fun once in a way. I can't put it out clear, but it ought to be fixed somehow for us chaps that haven't got the gift of working all day and every day, but can do two days' work in one when we like, that we should have our allowance of reasonable fun and pleasure—that is, what we called pleasure, not what somebody thinks we ought to take pleasure in. Anyway, I turned on George rather rough, and I says, 'We're not good enough for the likes of you, Mr. Storefield. It's very kind of you to think of us, but we'll take our own line and you take yours.'

'I'm sorry for it, Dick, and more sorry that you take huff at an old friend. All I want is to do you good, and act a friend's part. Good-bye—some day you'll see it.'

'You're hard on George,' says Jim, 'there's no pleasing you to-day; one would think there were lots of chaps fighting how to give us a lift. Good-bye, George, old man; I'm sorry we can't wire in with you; we'd soon knock out those posts and rails on the ironbark range.'

'You'd better stop, Jim, and take a hand in the deal,' says I (or, rather, the devil, for I believe he gets inside a chap at times), 'and then you and George can take a turn at local preaching when you're cut out. I'm off.' So without another word I jumped on to my horse and went off down the hill, across the creek, and over the boulders the other side, without much caring where I was going. The fact was, I felt I had acted meanly in sneering at a man who only said what he did for my good; and J. wasn't at all sure that I hadn't made a breach between Gracey and myself, and, though I had such a temper when it was roused that all the world wouldn't have stopped me, every time I thought of not seeing that girl again made my heart ache as if it would burst.

I was nearly home before I heard the clatter of a horse's feet, and Jim rode up alongside of me. He was just the same as ever, with a smile on his face. You didn't often see it without one.

I knew he had come after me, and had given up his own fancy for mine.

'I thought you were going to stay and turn good,' I said. 'Why didn't you?'

'It might have been better for me if I had,' he said, 'but you know very well, Dick, that whatever turns up, whether it's for good or evil, you and I go together.'

We looked at one another for a moment. Our eyes met. We didn't say anything; but we understood one another as well as if we had talked for a week. We rode up to the door of our cottage without speaking. The sun had set, and some of the stars had come out, early as it was, for it was late autumn. Aileen was sitting on a bench in the verandah reading, mother was working away as usual at something in the house. Mother couldn't read or write, but you never caught her sitting with her hands before her. Except when she was asleep I don't think she ever was quite still.

Aileen ran out to us, and stood while we let go our horses, and brought the saddles and bridles under the verandah.

'I'm glad you're come home for one thing,' she said. 'There is a message from father. He wants you to meet him.'

'Who brought it?' I said.

'One of the Dalys—Patsey, I think.'

'All right,' said Jim, kissing her as he lifted her up in his great strong arms. 'I must go in and have a gossip with the old woman. Aileen can tell me after tea. I daresay it's not so good that it won't keep.'

Mother was that fond of both of us that I believe, as sure as I sit here, she'd have put her head on the block, or died in any other way for either of her boys, not because it was her duty, but glad and cheerful like, to have saved us from death or disgrace. I think she was fonder of us two than she was of Aileen. Mothers are generally fonder of their sons. Why I never could see; and if she thought more of one than the other it was Jim. He was the youngest, and he had that kind of big, frolicsome, loving way with him, like a New-foundland pup about half-grown. I always used to think, somehow, nobody ever seemed to be able to get into a pelter with Jim, not even father, and that was a thing as some people couldn't be got to believe. As for mother and Aileen, they were as fond of him as if he'd been a big baby.

So while he went to sit down on the stretcher, and let mother put her arms round his neck and hug him and cry over him, as she always did if he'd been away more than a day or two, I took a walk down the creek with Aileen in the starlight, to hear all about this message from father. Besides, I could see that she was very serious over it, and I thought there might be something in it more than common.

'First of all, did you make any agreement with George Store-field?' she said.

'No; why should I? Has he been talking to you about me? What right has he to meddle with my business?'

'Oh, Dick, don't talk like that. Anything that he said was only to do you a kindness, and Jim.'

'Hang him, and his kindness too,' I said. 'Let him keep it for those that want it. But what did he tell you?'

'He said, first of all,' answered poor Aileen, with the tears in her eyes, and trying to take hold of my hand, 'that he had a contract for fencing timber, which he had taken at good prices, which he would share with you and Jim; that he knew you two and himself could finish it in a few weeks, and that he expected to get the contract for the timber for the new bridge at Dargo, which he would let you go shares in too. He didn't like to speak about that, because it wasn't certain; but he had calculated all the quantities and prices, and he was sure you would make £70 or £80 each before Christmas. Now, was there any harm in that; and don't you think it was very good of him to think of it?'

'Well, he's not a bad fellow, old George,' I said, 'but he's a little too fond of interfering with other people's business. Jim and I are quite able to manage our own affairs, as I told him this evening, when I refused to have anything to do with his fencing arrangement.'

'Oh, Dick, did you?' she said. 'What a pity! I made sure Jim would have liked it so, for only last week he said he was sick and tired of having nothing to do—that he should soon lose all his knack at using tools that he used to be so proud of. Didn't he say he'd like to join George?'

'He would, I daresay, and I told him to do as he liked. I came away by myself, and only saw him just before we crossed the range. He's big enough and old enough to take his own line.'

'But you know he thinks so much of you,' she groaned out, 'that he'd follow you to destruction. That will be the end of it, depend upon it, Dick. I tell you so now; you've taken to bad ways; you'll have his blood on your head yet.'

'Jim's old enough and big enough to take care of himself,' I said sulkily. 'If he likes to come my way I won't hinder him; I won't try to persuade him one way or the other. Let him take his own line; I don't believe in preaching and old women's talk. Let a man act and think for himself.'

'You'll break my heart, and poor mother's, too,' said Aileen, suddenly taking both my hands in hers. 'What has she done but love us ever since we were born, and what does she live for? You know she has no pleasure of any kind, you know she's afraid every morning she wakes that the police will get father for some of his cross doings; and now you and Jim are going the same wild way, and whatever—whatever will be the end of it?'

Here she let go my hands, and sobbed and cried as if she was a child again, much as I remember her doing one day when my kangaroo dog killed her favourite cat. And Aileen was a girl that didn't cry much generally, and never about anything that happened to herself; it was always about somebody else and their misfortunes.

She was a quiet girl, too, very determined, and not much given to talking about what she was going to do; but when she made up her mind she was sure to stick to it. I used to think she was more like father than any of us. She had his coloured hair and eyes, and his way of standing and looking, as if the whole world wouldn't shift him. But she'd mother's soft heart for all that, and I took the more notice of her crying and whimpering this time because it was so strange for her.

If anyone could have seen straight into my heart just then I was regularly knocked over, and had two minds to go inside to Jim and tell him we'd take George's splitting job, and start to tackle it first thing to-morrow morning; but just then one of those confounded night-hawks flitted on a dead tree before us and began his "hoo-ho," as if it was laughing at me. I can see the place now—the mountain black and dismal, the moon low and strange-looking, the little water-hole glittering in the half-light, and this dark bird hooting away in the night. An odd feeling seemed to come over my mind, and if it had been the devil himself standing on the dead limb it could not have had a worse effect on me as I stopped there, uncertain whether to turn to the right or the left.

We don't often know in this world sometimes whether we are turning off along a road where we shall never come back from, or whether we can go just a little way and look at the far-off hills and new rivers, and come home safe.

I remember the whole lot of bad-meaning thoughts coming with a rush over my heart, and I laughed at myself for being so soft as to choose a hard-working, pokey kind of life at the word of a slow fellow like George, when I might be riding about the country on a fine horse, eating and drinking of the best, and only doing what people said half the old settlers had made their money by.

Poor Aileen told me afterwards that if she'd thought for a moment I could be turned she'd have gone down on her knees and never got up till I promised to keep straight and begin to work at honest daily labour like a man—like a man who hoped to end his days in a good house, on a good farm, with a good wife and nice children round him, and not in a prison cell. Some people would call the first, after years of honest work, and being always able to look everyone in the face, being more of a man than the other. But people have different ways and different ideas.

'Come, Ailie,' I said, 'are you going to whine and cry all night? I shall be afraid to come home if you're going to be like this. What's the message from father?'

She wiped away her tears, and, putting her hand on my shoulder, looked steadily into my face.

'Poor boy—poor, dear Dick,' she said, 'I feel as if I should see that fresh face of yours looking very different some day or other. Something tells me that there's bad luck before you. But never mind, you'll never lose your sister if the luck's ever so bad. Father sent word you and Jim were to meet him at Broken Creek and bring your whips with you.'

'What in the world's that for?' I said, half speaking to myself. 'It looks as if there was a big mob to drive, and where's he to get a big mob there in that mountainous, beastly place, where the cattle all bolt like wallabies, and where I never saw twenty head together?'

'He's got some reason for it,' said Aileen sorrowfully. 'If I were you I wouldn't go. It's no good, and father's trying now to drag you and Jim into the bad ways he's been following these years.'

'How do you know it's so bad?' said I. 'How can a girl like you know?'

'I know very well,' she said. 'Do you think I've lived here all these years and don't know things? What makes him always come home after dark, and be that nervous every time he sees a stranger coming up you'd think he was come out of gaol? Why has he always got money, and why does mother look so miserable when he's at home, and cheer up when he goes away?'

'He may get jobs of droving or something,' I said. 'You have no right to say that he's robbing, or something of that sort, because he doesn't care about tying himself to mother's apron-string.'

Aileen laughed, but it was more like crying.

'You told me just now,' she said—oh! so sorrowfully—'that you and Jim were old enough to take a line of your own. Why don't you do it now?'

'And tell father we'll have nothing more to do with him!'

'Why not?' she said, standing up straight before me, and facing me just as I saw father face the big bullock-driver before he knocked him down. 'Why not? You need never ask him for another meal; you can earn an easy living in half-a-dozen ways, you and Jim. Why should you let him spoil your life and ruin your soul for ever more?'

'The priest put that into your head,' I said sneeringly; 'Father Doyle—of course, he knows what they'll do with a fellow after he's dead.'

'No!' she said, 'Father Doyle never said a word about you that wasn't good and kind. He says mother's a good Catholic, and he takes an interest in you boys and me because of her.'

'He can persuade you women to do anything,' I said, not that I had any grudge against poor old Father Doyle, who used to come riding up the rough mountain track on his horse, and tiring his old bones, just "to look after his flock," as he said—and nice lambs some of them were—but I wanted to tease her and make her break off with this fancy of hers.

'He never does, and couldn't persuade me, except for my good,' said she, getting more and more roused, and her black eyes glowed again, 'and I'll tell you what I'll do to prove it. It's a sin, but if it is I'll stand by it, and now I'll swear it (here she knelt down), as Almighty God shall help me at the last day, if you and Jim will promise me to start straight off up the country and take bush-work till shearing comes on, and never to have any truck with cross chaps and their ways, I'll turn Protestant. I'll go to church with you, and keep to it till I die.'

Wasn't she a trump? I've known women that would give up a lot for a man they were sweet on, and wives that would follow their husbands about like spaniels, and women that would lie and deceive and all but rob and murder for men they were fond of, and sometimes do nearly as much to spite other women. But I don't think I ever knew a woman that would give up her religion for anyone before, and it's not as if she wasn't staunch to her own faith. She was as regular in her prayers and crossings and beads and all the rest of it as mother herself, and if there ever was a good girl in the whole world she was one. She turned faint as she said this, and I thought she was going to drop down. If anything could have turned me then it would have been this. It was almost like giving her life for ours, and I don't think she'd have valued hers two straws if she could have saved us. There's a great deal said about different kinds of love in this world, but I can't help thinking that the love between brothers and sisters that have been brought up together and have had very few other people to care about is a higher, better sort than any other in the world. There's less selfishness about it—no thought but for the other's good. If that can be made safe, death and pain and poverty and misery are all little things. And wasn't I fond of Aileen, in spite of all my hardness and cross-grained obstinacy?—so fond that I was just going to hug her to me and say, 'Take it all your own way, Ailie dear,' when Jim came tearing out of the hut, bareheaded, and stood listening to a far-off sound that caught all our ears at once. We made out the source of it too well—far too well.

What was the noise at that hour of the night?

It was a hollow, faint, distant roaring that gradually kept getting louder. It was the strange mournful bellowing that comes from a drove of cattle forced along an unknown track. As we listened the sound came clearly on the night wind, faint, yet still clearly coming nearer.

'Cattle being driven,' Jim cried out; 'and a big mob, too. It's father—for a note. Let's get our horses and meet him.'

CHAPTER IV

'ALL right,' said I, 'he must have got there a day before his time. It is a big mob and no mistake. I wonder where they're taking them to.' Aileen shrugged her shoulders and walked in to mother with a look of misery and despair on her face such as I never saw there before.

She knew it was no use talking to me now. The idea of going out to meet a large lot of unknown cattle had strongly excited us, as would have been the case with every bush-bred lad. All sorts of wonders passed through our minds as we walked down the creek bank, with our bridles in our hands, towards where our horses usually fed. One was easy to catch, the other with a little management was secured. In ten minutes we were riding fast through the dark trees and fallen timber towards the wild gullies and rock-strewed hills of Broken Creek.

It was not more than an hour when we got up to the cattle. We could hear them a good while before we saw them. 'My word,' said Jim, 'ain't they restless. They can't have come far, or they wouldn't roar so. Where can the old man have "touched" for them?'

'How should I know?' I said roughly. I had a kind of idea, but I thought he would never be so rash.

When we got up I could see the cattle had been rounded up in a flat with stony ridges all round. There must have been three or four hundred of them, only a man and a boy riding round and wheeling them every now and then. Their horses were pretty well knocked up. I knew father at once, and the old chestnut mare he used to ride—an animal with legs like timbers and mule rump; but you couldn't tire her, and no beast that ever was calved could get away from her. The boy was a half-caste that father had picked up somewhere; he was as good as two men any day.

'So you've came at last,' growled father, 'and a good thing too. I didn't expect to be here till to-morrow morning. The dog came home, I suppose—that's what brought you here, wasn't it? I thought the infernal cattle would beat Warrigal and me, and we'd have all our trouble for nothing.'

'Whose cattle are they, and what are you going to do with them?'

'Never you mind; ask no questions, and you'll see all about it to-morrow. I'll go and take a snooze now; I've had no sleep for three nights.'

With our fresh horses and riding round so we kept the cattle easily enough. We did not tell Warrigal he might go to rest, not thinking a half-caste brat like him wanted any. He didn't say anything, but went to sleep on his horse, which walked in and out among the angry cattle as he sat on the saddle with his head down on the horse's neck. They sniffed at him once or twice, some of the old cows, but none of them horned him; and daylight came rather quicker than one would think.

Then we saw whose cattle they were; they had all Hunter's and Falkland's brands on, which showed that they belonged to Banda and Elingamah stations.

'By George!' says Jim, 'they're Mr. Hunter's cattle and all these circle dots belong to Banda. What a mob of calves! Not one of them branded! What in the world does father intend to do with them?'

Father was up, and came over where we stood with our horses in our hands before we had time to say more. He wasn't one of those that slept after daylight, whether he had work to do or not. He certainly *could* work; daylight or dark, wet or dry, cold or hot, it was all one to father. It seems a pity what he did was no use to him, as it turned out; for he was a man, was old dad, every inch of him.

'Now, boys,' he said, quite brisk and almost good-natured for him, 'look alive and we'll start the cattle; we've been long enough here; let 'em head up that gully, and I'll show you something you've never seen before for as long as you've known Broken Creek Ranges.'

'But where are you going to take 'em to?' I said. 'They're all Mr. Hunter's and Mr. Falkland's; the brands are plain enough.'

'Are the calves branded, you blasted fool?' he said, while the black look came over his face that had so often frightened me when I was a child. 'You do what I tell you if you've any pluck and gumption about you; or else you and your brother can ride over to Dargo Police Station and "give me away" if you like; only don't come home again, I warn you, sons or no sons.'

If I had done what I had two minds to do—for I wasn't afraid of him then, savage as he looked—told him to do his own duffing and ridden away with Jim there and then—poor Jim, who sat on his horse staring at both of us, and saying nothing—how much better it would have been for all of us, the old man as well as ourselves; but it seemed as if it wasn't to be. Partly from use, and partly from a love of danger and something new, which is at the bottom of half the crime in the bush districts, I turned my horse's head after the cattle, which were now beginning to straggle. Jim did the same on his side. How easy it is for chaps to take the road to hell! for that was about the size of it, and we were soon too busy to think about much else.

The track we were driving on led along a narrow rocky gully which looked as if it had been split up or made out of a crack in the earth thousands of years ago by an earthquake or something of that kind. The hills were that steep that every now and then some of the young cattle that were not used to that sort of country would come sliding down and bellow as if they thought they were going to break their necks.

The water rushed down it like a torrent in wet winters, and formed a sort of creek, and the bed of it made what track there was. There were overhanging rocks and places that made you giddy to look at, and some of these must have fallen down and blocked up the creek at one time or other. We had to scramble round them the best way we could.

When we got nearly up to the head of the gully—and great work it was to force the footsore cattle along, as we couldn't use our whips overmuch—Jim called out—

'Why, here comes old Crib. Who'd have thought he'd have seen the track? Well done, old man. Now we're right.'

Father never took any notice of the poor brute as he came limping along the stones. Woman or child, horse or dog, it's the same old thing—the more any creature loves a man in this world the worse they're treated. It looks like it, at any rate. I saw how it was; father had given Crib a cruel beating the night before, when he was put out for some trifling matter, and the dog had left him and run home. But now he had thought better of it, and seen our tracks and come to work and slave, with his bleeding feet—for they were cut all to pieces—and got the whip across his back now and then for his pains. It's a queer world!

When we got right to the top of this confounded gully, nearly dead-beat all of us, and only for the dog heeling them up every now and then, and making his teeth nearly meet in them, without a whimper, I believe the cattle would have charged back and beat us. There was a sort of rough tableland—scrubby and stony and thick it was, but still the grass wasn't bad in summer, when the country below was all dried up. There were wild horses in troops there, and a few wild cattle, so Jim and I knew the place well; but it was too far and too much of a journey for our own horses to go often.

'Do you see that sugar-loaf hill with the bald top, across the range?' said father, riding up just then, as we were taking it easy a little. 'Don't let the cattle straggle, and make straight for that.'

'Why, it's miles away,' said Jim, looking rather dismal. 'We could never get 'em there.'

'We're not going there, stupid,' says father; 'that's only the line to keep. I'll show you something about dinner-time that'll open your eyes a bit.'

Poor Jim brightened up at the mention of dinner-time, for, boy-like, he was getting very hungry, and as he wasn't done growing he had no end of an appetite. I was hungry enough for the matter of that, but I wouldn't own to it.

'Well, we shall come to somewhere, I suppose,' says Jim, when father was gone. 'Blest if I didn't think he was going to keep us

wandering in this blessed Nulla Mountain all day. I wish I'd never
seen the blessed cattle. I was only waiting for you to hook it when
we first seen the brands by daylight, and I'd ha' been off like a
brindle "Mickey" down a range.'

'Better for us if we had,' I said; 'but it's too late now. We must
stick to it, I suppose.'

We had kept the cattle going for three or four miles through the
thickest of the country, every now and then steering our course by
the clear round top of Sugarloaf, that could be seen for miles round,
but never seemed to get any nearer, when we came on a rough sort
of log-fence, which ran the way we were going.

'I didn't think there were any farms up here,' I said to Jim.

'It's a "break,"' he said, almost in a whisper. 'There's a "duffing-
yard" somewhere handy; that's what's the matter.'

'Keep the cattle along it, anyway. We'll soon see what it leads to.'

The cattle ran along the fence, as if they expected to get to the end
of their troubles soon. The scrub was terribly thick in places, and
every now and then there was a break in the fence, when one of us
had to go outside and hunt them until we came to the next bit. At
last we came to a little open kind of flat, with the scrub that thick
round it as you couldn't hardly ride through it, and, just as Jim said,
there was the yard.

It was a 'duffing-yard' sure enough. No one but people who had
cattle to hide and young stock they didn't want other people to see
branded would have made a place there.

Just on the south side of the yard, which was built of great heavy
stringy-bark trees cut down in the line of the fence, and made up
with limbs and logs, the range went up as steep as the side of a house.
The cattle were that tired and foot-sore—half their feet were bleeding, poor devils—that they ran in through the sliprails and began to
lay down.

'Light a fire, one of you boys,' says father, putting up the heavy
sliprails and fastening them. 'We must brand these calves before
dark. One of you can go to that gunyah, just under the range
where that big white rock is, and you'll find tea and sugar and something to eat.'

Jim rushed off at once, while I sulkily began to put some bark and
twigs together and build a fire.

'What's the use of all this cross work?' I said to father; 'we're
bound to be caught some day if we keep on at it. Then there'll be
no one left to take care of mother and Aileen.'

He looked rather struck at this, and then said quietly—

'You and your brother can go back now. Never say I kept you
against your will. You may as well lend a hand to brand these
calves; then you may clear out as soon as you like.'

Well, I didn't quite like leaving the old chap in the middle of the
work like that. I remember thinking, like many another young fool,

I suppose, that I could draw back in time, just after I'd tackled this job.

Draw back, indeed! When does a man ever get the chance of doing that, once he's regularly gone in for any of the devil's work and wages? He takes care there isn't much drawing back afterwards. So I said—

'We may as well give you a hand with this lot; but we'll go home then, and drop all this duffing work. It don't pay. I'm old enough to know that, and you'll find it out yet, I expect, father, yourself.'

'The fox lives long, and gives the hounds many a long chase before he's run into,' he said, with a grim chuckle. 'I swore I'd be revenged on 'em all when they locked me up and sent me out here for a paltry hare; broke my old mother's heart, so it did. I've had a pound for every hair in her skin, and I shall go on till I die. After all, if a man goes to work cautious and runs mute it's not so easy to catch him in this country, at any rate.'

Jim at this came running out of the cave with a face of joy, a bag of ship-biscuit, and a lot of other things.

'Here's tea and sugar,' he said; 'and there's biscuits and jam, and a big lump of cheese. Get the fire right, Dick, while I get some water. We'll soon have some tea, and these biscuits are jolly.'

The tea was made, and we all had a good meal. Father found a bottle of rum, too; he took a good drink himself, and gave Jim and me a sip each. I felt less inclined to quarrel with father after that. So we drafted all the calves into a small penyard, and began to put our brand on them as quick as we could catch 'em.

A hundred and sixty of 'em altogether—all ages, from a month old to nearly a year. Fine strong calves, and in rare condition, too. We could see they were all belonging to Mr. Hunter and Mr. Falkland. How they came to leave them all so long unbranded I can't say. Very careless they often are on these large cattle-stations, so that sharp people like father and the Dalys, and a lot more, get an easy chance at them.

Whatever father was going to do with them all when he had branded 'em, we couldn't make out.

'There's no place to tail or wean 'em,' whispered Jim. 'We're not above thirty miles from Banda in a straight line. These cows are dead sure to make straight back the very minute they're let out, and very nice work it'll look with all these calves with our brand on sucking these cows.'

Father happened to come round for a hot brand just as Jim finished.

'Never you mind about the weaning,' he snarled. 'I shan't ask you to tail them either. It wouldn't be a nice job here, would it?' and father actually laughed. It wasn't a very gay kind of a laugh, and he shut up his mouth with a sort of snap again. Jim and I hadn't seen him laugh for I don't know how long, and it almost frightened us.

As Jim said, it wouldn't do to let the cattle out again. If calves are weaned, and have only one brand on, it is very hard for any man to swear that they are not the property of the man to whom that brand belongs. He may believe them to be his, but may never have seen them in his life; and if he has seen them on a camp or on the run, it's very hard to swear to any one particular red or spotted calf as you would to a horse.

The great dart is to keep the young stock away from their mothers until they forget one another, and then most of the danger is past. But if calves with one man's brand on are seen sucking another man's cows, it is pretty plain that the brand of the calves has been put on without the consent of the owner of the cows—which is cattle-stealing; a felony, according to the Act 7 and 8 George IV., No. 29, punishable with three years' imprisonment, with hard labour on the roads of the colony or other place, as the Judge may direct.

There's a lot of law! How did I learn it? I had plenty of time in Berrima Gaol—worse luck—my first stretch. But it was after I'd done the foolishness, and not before.

CHAPTER V

'Now then, you boys!' says father, coming up all of a sudden like, and bringing out his words as if it was old times with us, when we didn't know whether he'd hit first and talk afterwards, or the other way on, 'get out the lot we've just branded, and drive 'em straight for that peak, where the water shines dripping over the stones, right again the sun, and look slippy; we're burning daylight, and these cows are making row enough, blast 'em! to be heard all the way to Banda. I'll go on and steady the lead; you keep 'em close up to me.'

Father mounted the old mare. The dog stopped behind; he knew he'd have to mind the tail—that is the hindmost cattle—and stop 'em from breaking or running clear away from the others. We threw down the rails. Away the cattle rushed out, all in a long string. You'd 'a thought no mortal men could 'a kept 'em in that blind hole of a place. But father headed 'em, and turned 'em towards the peak. The dog worried those that wanted to stay by the yard or turn another way. We dropped our whip on 'em, and kept 'em going. In five minutes they were all a-moving along in one mob at a pretty sharpish trot like a lot of store cattle. Father knew his way about, whether the country was thick or open. It was all as one to him. What a slashing stockman he would have made in new country, if he only could have kept straight.

It took us an hour's hard dinkum to get near the peak. Sometimes it was awful rocky, as well as scrubby, and the poor devils of cattle got as sore-footed as babies—blood up to the knee, some of 'em; but we crowded 'em on; there was no help for it.

At last we rounded up on a flat, rocky, open kind of place; and here father held up his hand.

'Let 'em ring a bit; some of their tongues are out. These young things is generally soft. Come here, Dick.' I rode up, and he told me to follow him.

We walked our horses up to the edge of the mountain and looked over. It was like the end of the world. Far down there was a dark, dreadful drop into a sort of deep valley below. You couldn't see the bottom of it. The trees on the mountain side looked like bushes, and they were big ironbarks and messmates, too. On three sides of us was this awful, desolate-looking precipice—a dreary, gloomy, God-forsaken kind of spot. The sky got cloudy, and the breeze turned cold and began to murmur and whistle in an odd, unnatural kind of way, while father, seeing how scared and puzzled I was, began to laugh. I shuddered. A thought crossed my mind that it might be the Enemy of Souls, in his shape, going to carry us off for doing such a piece of wickedness.

'Looks queer, doesn't it?' says father, going to the brink and kicking down a boulder, that rolled and crashed down the steep mountain side, tearing its way through scrub and heath till it settled down in the glen below. 'It won't do for a man's horse to slip, will it, boy? And yet there's a track here into a fine large paddock, open and clear, too, where I'm going to put these cattle into.'

I stared at him, without speaking, thinking was he mad.

'No! the old man isn't mad, youngster,' he said; 'not yet, at least. I'm going to show you a trick that none of you native boys are up to, smart as you think yourselves.' Here he got off the old mare, and began to lead her to the edge of the mountain.

'Now, you rally the cattle well after me,' he said; 'they'll follow the old mare after a bit. I left a few cows among 'em on purpose, and when they "draw" keep 'em going well up, but not too fast.'

He had lengthened the bridle of the mare, and tied the end of a light tether rope that he had round her neck to it. I saw her follow him slowly, and turn down a rocky track that seemed to lead straight over a bluff of the precipice.

However, I gave the word to 'head on.' The dog had started rounding 'em up as soon as he saw the old mare walk towards the mountain side, and the cattle were soon crushed up pretty close to the mare's heels.

Mind this, that they were so footsore and tender about the hoofs that they could not have run away from us on foot if they had tried.

After "ringing" a bit, one of the quiet cows followed up the old mare that was walking step by step forward, and all the rest followed her like sheep. Cattle will do that. I've seen a stockrider, when all the horses were dead beat, trying to get fat cattle to take a river in flood, jump off and turn his horse loose into the stream. If he went straight, and swam across, all the cattle would follow him like sheep.

Well, when the old mare got to the bluff she turned short round to the right, and then I saw that she had struck a narrow path down a gully that got deeper and deeper every yard we went. There was just room for a couple or three calves to go abreast, and by and by all of 'em was walking down it like as if they was the beasts agoing into Noah's Ark. It wound and wound and got deeper and deeper till the walls of rock were ever so far above our heads. Our work was done then; the cattle had to walk on like sheep in a race. We led our horses behind them, and the dog walked along, saving his sore feet as well as he could, and never tried to bite a beast once he got within the walls. He looked quite satisfied, and kept chuckling almost to himself. I really believe I've seen dogs laugh. Once upon a time I've read of they'd have taken poor Crib for a familiar spirit, and hanged or burnt him. Well, he knew a lot, and no mistake.

I've seen plenty of Christians as he could buy and sell, and no trouble to him. I'm dashed if the old mare, too, didn't take a pleasure in working cattle on the cross. She was the laziest old wretch bringing up the cows at home, or running in the horses. Many a time Jim and I took a turn out of her when father didn't know. But put her after a big mob of cattle—she must have known they couldn't be ours—and she'd clatter down a range like the wall of a house, and bite and kick the tail cattle if they didn't get out of her way. They say dogs and horses are all honest, and it's only us as teaches 'em to do wrong. My notion's they're a deal like ourselves, and some of 'em fancies the square racket dull and safe, while some takes a deal kindlier to the other. Anyhow, no cattle-duffer in the colonies could have had a better pair of mates than old Sally and Crib, if the devil himself had broken 'em in special for the trade.

It was child's play now, as far as the driving went. Jim and I walked along, leading our horses and yarning away as we used to do when we were little chaps bringing in the milkers.

'My word, Dick, dad's dropped into a fine road through this thundering mountain, hasn't he? I wonder where it leads to? How high the rock-walls are getting above us!' he says. 'I know now. I think I heard long ago from one of the Crosbies of a place in the ranges down towards behind the Nulla Mountain, "Terrible Hollow." He didn't know about it himself, but said an old stockman told him about it when he was drunk. He said the Government men used to hide the cattle and horses there in old times, and that it was never found out.'

'Why wasn't it found out, Jim? If the old fellow "split" about it someone else would get to know.'

'Well, old Dan said that they killed one man that talked of telling; the rest were too frightened after that, and they all swore a big oath never to tell anyone except he was on the cross.'

'That's how dad come to know, I suppose,' said Jim. 'I wish he never had. I don't care about those cross doings. I never did. I never seen any good come out of them yet.'

'Well, we must go through with it now, I suppose. It won't do to leave old dad in the lurch. You won't, will you, Jim?'

'You know very well I won't,' says Jim, very soberlike. 'I don't like it any the more for that. But I wish father had broke his leg, and was lying up at home, with mother nursing him, before he found out this hell-hole of a place.'

'Well, we're going to get out of it, and soon, too. The gully seems getting wider, and I can see a bit of open country through the trees.'

'Thank God for that!' says Jim. 'My boots 'll part company soon, and the poor devils of calves won't have any hoofs either, if there's much more of this.'

'They're drawing faster now. The leading cattle are beginning to run. We're at the end of the drive.'

So it was. The deep, rocky gully gradually widened into an open and pretty smooth flat; this, again, into a splendid little plain, up to the knees in grass; a big natural park, closed round on every side with sandstone rock-walls, as upright as if they were built, and a couple of thousand feet above the place where we stood.

This scrub country was crossed by two good creeks; it was several miles across, and a trifle more in length. Our hungry weaners spread out and began to feed, without a notion of their mothers they'd left behind; but they were not the only ones there. We could see other mobs of cattle, some near, some farther off; horses, too; and the well-worn track in several ways showed that this was no new grazing ground.

Father came riding back quite comfortable and hearty-like for him. 'Welcome to Terrible Hollow, lads,' says he. 'You're the youngest chaps it has even been shown to, and if I didn't know you were the right stuff, you'd never have seen it, though you're my own flesh and blood. Jump off, and let your horses go. They can't get away, even if they tried; they don't look much like that.'

Our poor nags were something like the cattle, pretty hungry and stiff. They put their heads down to the thick green grass, and went in at it with a will.

'Bring your saddles along with you,' father said, 'and come after me. I'll show you a good camping place. You deserve a treat after last night's work.'

We turned back towards the rocky wall, near to where we had come in, and there, behind a bush and a big piece of sandstone that had fallen down, was the entrance to a cave. The walls of it were quite clean and white-looking, the floor was smooth, and the roof was pretty high, well blackened with smoke, too, from the fires which had been lighted in it for many a year gone by.

A kind of natural cellar had been made by scooping out the soft sandstone behind a ledge. From this father took a bag of flour and corn-meal. We very soon made some cakes in the pan, that tasted well, I can tell you. Tea and sugar, too, and quart pots, some bacon in a flour-bag; and that rasher fried in the pan was the sweetest meat I ever ate in all my born days.

Then father brought out a keg and poured some rum into a pint pot. He took a pretty stiff pull, and then handed it to us. 'A little of it won't hurt you, boys,' he said, 'after a night's work.'

I took some—not much; we hadn't learned to drink then—to keep down the fear of something hanging over us. A dreadful fear it is. It makes a coward of every man who doesn't lead a square life, let him be as game as he may.

Jim wouldn't touch it. 'No,' he said, when I laughed at him, 'I promised mother last time I had more than was good for me at Dargo Races that I wouldn't touch it again for two years; and I won't, either. I can stand what any other man can, and without the hard stuff, either.'

'Please yourself,' said father. 'When you're ready we'll have a ride through the stock.'

We finished our meal, and a first-rate one it was. A man never has the same appetite for his meals anywhere else that he had in the bush, specially if he has been up half the night. It's so fresh, and the air makes him feel as if he'd ate nothing for a week. Sitting on a log, or in the cave, as we were, I've had the best meal I've ever tasted since I was born. Not like the close-feeling, close-smelling, dirty-clean graveyard they call a gaol. But it's no use beginning on that. We were young men, and free, too! Free! By all the devils in hell, if there are devils—and there must be to tempt a man, or how could he be so great a fool, so blind a born idiot, as to do anything in this world that would put his freedom in jeopardy? And what for? For folly and nonsense. For a few pounds he could earn with a month's honest work and be all the better man for it. For a false woman's smile that he could buy, and ten like her, if he only kept straight and saving. For a bit of sudden pride or vanity or passion. A short bit of what looks like pleasure, against months and years of weariness, and cold and heat, and dull half-death, with maybe a dog's death at the end!

I could cry like a child when I think of it now. I have cried many's the time and often since I have been shut up here, and dashed my head against the stones till I pretty nigh knocked all sense and feeling out of it, not so much in repentance, though I don't say I feel sorry, but to think what a fool, fool, fool I'd been. Yet, fool, three times over—a hundred times—to put my liberty and life against such a miserable stake—a stake the devil that deals the pack is so safe to win at the end.

I may as well go on. But I can't help breaking out sometimes when I hear the birds calling to one another as they fly over the yard, and know it's fresh air and sun and green grass outside that I never shall see again. Never see the river rippling under the big drooping trees, or the cattle coming down in the twilight to drink after the long hot day. Never, never more! And whose fault is it? Who have I to blame? Perhaps father helped a bit; but I knew better, and no one is half as much to blame as myself.

Where were we? Oh, at the cave-mouth, coming out with our bridles in our hands to catch our horses. We soon did that, and then we rode away to the other cattle. They were a queer lot, in fine con- dition, but all sorts of ages and breeds, with every kind of brand and ear-mark.

Lots of the brands we didn't know, and had never heard of. Some had no brands at all—full-grown beasts, too; that was a thing we had very seldom seen. Some of the best cattle and some of the finest horses —and there were some real plums among the horses—had a strange brand, JJ.

'Who does the JJ brand belong to?' I said to father. 'They're the pick of the lot, whose ever they are.'

Father looked black for a bit, and then he growled out, 'Don't you ask too many questions, lad. There's only four living men besides yourselves knows about this place; so take care and don't act foolishly, or you'll lose a plant that may save your life, as well as keep you in cash for many a year to come. That brand belongs to Starlight, and he was the only man left alive of the men that first found it and used it to put away stock in. He wanted help, and told me five years ago. He took in a half-caste chap, too, against my will. He helped him with that last lot of cattle that you noticed.'

'But where did those horses come from?' Jim said. 'I never hardly saw such a lot before. All got the JJ brand on, too, and nothing else; all about three year old.'

'They were brought here as foals,' says father, 'following their mothers. Some of them was foaled here; and, of course, as they've only the one brand on they never can be claimed or sworn to. They're from some of Mr. Maxwell's best thoroughbred mares, and their sire was Earl of Atheling, imported. He was here for a year.'

'Well, they might look the real thing,' said Jim, his eyes brightening as he gazed at them. 'I'd like to have that dark bay colt with the star. My word, what a forehand he's got; and what quarters, too. If he can't gallop I'll never say I know a horse from a poley cow.'

'You shall have him, or as good, never fear, if you stick to your work,' says father. 'You mustn't cross Starlight, for he's a born devil when he's taken the wrong way. though he talks so soft. The half-caste is an out-and-out chap with cattle, and the horse doesn't stand on four legs that he can't ride—and make follow him, for the matter of that. But he's worth watching. I don't believe in him myself. And now ye have the lot.'

'And a d——d fine lot they are,' I said, for I was vexed with Jim for taking so easy to the bait father held out to him about the horse. 'A very smart crowd to be on the roads inside of five years, and drag us in with 'em.'

'How do you make that out?' says Father. 'Are you going to turn dog, now you know the way in? Isn't it as easy to carry on for a few years more as it was twenty years ago?'

'Not by a long chalk,' I said, for my blood was up, and I felt as if I could talk back to father and give him as good as he sent, and all for Jim's sake. Poor Jim! He'd always go to the mischief for the sake of a good horse, and many another 'Currency' chap has gone the same way. It's a pity for some of 'em that a blood horse was ever foaled.

'You think you can't be tracked,' says I, 'but you must bear in mind you haven't got to do with the old-fashioned mounted police as was potterin' about when this "bot" was first hit on. There's chaps in the police getting now, natives or all the same, as can ride and track every bit as well as the half-caste you're talking about. Some day they'll drop on the track of a mob coming in or getting out, and then the game will be all up.'

'You can cut it if you like now,' said father, looking at me curious like. 'Don't say I dragged you in. You and your brother can go home, and no one will ever know where you were; no more than if you'd gone to the moon.'

Jim looked at the brown colt that just came trotting up as dad finished speaking—trotting up with his head high and his tail stuck out like a circus horse. If he'd been the devil in a horsehide he couldn't have chosen a better moment. Then his eyes began to glitter.

We all three looked at each other. No one spoke. The colt stopped, turned, and galloped back to his mates like a red flyer with the dogs close behind him.

It was not long. We all began to speak at once. But in that time the die was cast, the stakes were down, and in the pool were three men's lives.

'I don't care whether we go back or not,' says Jim; 'I'll do either way that Dick likes. But that colt I must have.'

'I never intended to go back,' I said. 'But we're three d——d fools all the same—father and sons. It'll be the dearest horse you ever bought, Jim, old man, and so I tell you.'

'Well, I suppose it's settled now,' says father; 'so let's have no more chat. We're like a pack of old women, blessed if we ain't.'

After that we got on more sociably. Father took us all over the place, and a splendid paddock it was—walled all round but where we had come in, and a narrow gash in the far side that not one man in a thousand could ever hit on, except he was put up to it; a wild country for miles when you did get out—all scrub and rock, that few people ever had call to ride over. There was splendid grass everywhere, water, and shelter. It was warmer, too, than the country above, as you could see by the coats of the cattle and horses.

'If it had only been honestly come by,' Jim said, 'what a jolly place it would have been!'

Towards the north end of the paddock was a narrow gully with great sandstone walls all round, and where it narrowed the first discoverers had built a stockyard, partly with dry stone walls and partly with logs and rails.

There was no trouble in getting the cattle or horses into this, and there were all kinds of narrow yards and pens for branding the stock if they were clearskins, and altering or 'faking' the brands if they were plain. This led into another yard, which opened into the narrowest part of the gully. Once in this, like the one they came down, and the cattle or horses had no chance but to walk slowly up, one behind the other, till they got on the tableland above. Here, of course, every kind of work that can be done to help to disguise cattle was done. Ear-marks were cut out and altered in shape, or else the whole ear was cropped off; every letter in the alphabet was altered by means of straight bars or half-circles, figures, crosses, everything you could think of.

'Mr. Starlight is an edicated man,' said father. 'This is all his notion; and many a man has looked at his own beast, with the ears altered and the brand faked, and never dreamed he ever owned it. He's a great card is Starlight. It's a pity he ever took to this kind of life.'

Father said this with a kind of real sorrow that made me look at him to see if the grog had got into his head; just as if his life, mine, and Jim's didn't matter a straw compared to this man's, whoever he was, that had had so many better chances than we had and had chucked 'em all away.

But it's a strange thing that I don't think there's any place in the world where men feel a more real out-and-out respect for a gentleman than in Australia. Everybody's supposed to be free and equal now; of course, they couldn't be in the convict days. But somehow a man that's born and bred a gentleman will always be different from other men to the end of the world. What's the most surprising part of it is that men like father, who have hated the breed and suffered by them, too, can't help having a curious liking and admiration for them. They'll follow them like dogs, fight for them, shed their blood, and die for them; must be some sort of a natural feeling. Whatever it is, it's there safe enough, and nothing can knock it out of nine-tenths of all the men and women you meet. I began to be uneasy to see this wonderful mate of father's, who was so many things at once —a cattle-stealer, a bush-ranger, and a gentleman.

CHAPTER VI

AFTER we'd fairly settled to stay, father began to be more pleasant than he'd ever been before. We were pretty likely, he said, to have a visit from Starlight and the half-caste in a day or two, if we'd like to wait. He was to meet him at the Hollow on purpose to help him out with the mob of fat bullocks we had looked at. Father, it appears, was coming here by himself when he met this outlying lot of Mr. Hunter's cattle, and thought he and old Crib could bring them in by themselves. And a mighty good haul it was. Father said we should share the weaners between the three of us; that means £50 a piece at least. The devil always helps beginners.

We put through a couple of days pleasantly enough, after our hardish bit of work. Jim found some fish-hooks and a line, and we caught plenty of mullet and eels in the deep, clear water-holes. We found a couple of double-barrelled guns, and shot ducks enough to last us a week. No wonder the old frequenters of the Hollow used to live here for a month at a time, having great times of it as long as their grog lasted; and sometimes having the tribe of blacks that inhabited the district to make merry and carouse with them, like the buccaneers of the Spanish Main that I've read about, till the plunder was all gone. There were scrawls on the wall of the first cave we had been in that showed all the visitors had not been rude, untaught people; and Jim picked up part of a woman's dress splashed with blood, and in one place, among some smouldering packages and boxes, a long lock of woman's hair, fair, bright-brown, that looked as if the name of Terrible Hollow might not have been given to this lonely, wonderful glen for nothing.

We spent nearly a week in this way, and were beginning to get rather sick of the life, when father, who used always to be looking at a bare patch in the scrub above us, said—

'They're coming at last.'

'Who are coming—friends?'

'Why, friends, of course. That's Starlight's signal. See that smoke? The half-caste always sends that up—like the blacks in his mother's tribe, I suppose.'

'Any cattle or horses with them?' said Jim.

'No, or they'd send up two smokes. They'll be here about dinner-time, so we must get ready for them.'

We had plenty of time to get ourselves or anything else ready. In about four hours we began to look at them through a strong spyglass which father brought out. By and by we got sight of two men coming along on horseback on the top of the range the other side of the far wall. They wasn't particularly easy to see, and every now and then we'd lose sight of 'em as they got into thick timber or behind rocks.

Father got the spyglass on to 'em at last, pretty clear, and nearly threw it down with an oath.

'By ——!' he says, 'I believe Starlight's hurt somehow. He's so infernal rash. I can see the half-caste holding him on. If the police are on his tracks they'll spring the plant here, and the whole thing 'll be blown.'

We saw them come to the top of the wall, as it were, then they stopped for a long while, then all of a sudden they seemed to disappear.

'Let's go over to the other side,' says father; 'they're coming down the gully now. It's a terrible steep, rough track, worse than the other. If Starlight's hurt bad he'll never ride down. But he has the pluck of the devil, sure enough.'

We rode over to the other side, where there was a kind of gully that came in, something like the one we came in by, but rougher, and full of gibbers (boulders). There was a path, but it looked as if cattle could never be driven or forced up it. We found afterwards that they had an old pack bullock that they'd trained to walk up this, and down, too, when they wanted him, and the other cattle followed in his track, as cattle will.

Father showed us a sort of cave by the side of the track, where one man, with a couple of guns and a pistol or two, could have shot down a small regiment as they came down one at a time.

We stayed in there by the track, and after about half-an-hour we heard the two horses coming down slowly, step by step, kicking the stones down before them. Then we could hear a man groaning, as if he couldn't bear the pain, and partly as if he was trying to smother it. Then another man's voice, very soft and soothing like, trying to comfort another.

'My head's a-fire, and these cursed ribs are grinding against one another every step of this infernal ladder. Is it far now?' How he groaned then!

'Just got the bottom; hold on a bit longer and you'll be all right.'

Just then the leading horse came out into the open before the cave. We had a good look at him and his rider. I never forgot them. It was a bad day I every saw either, and many a man had cause to say the same.

The horse held up his head and snorted as he came abreast of us, and we showed out. He was one of the grandest animals I'd ever seen, and I afterwards found he was better than he looked. He came stepping down that beastly rocky goat-track, he, a clean thoroughbred that ought never to have trod upon anything rougher than a rolled

training track, or the sound bush turf. And here he was with a
heavy weight on his back—a half-dead, fainting man, that couldn't
hold the reins—and him walking down as steady as an old mountain
bull or a wallaroo on the side of a creek bank.

I hadn't much time to look him over. I was too much taken up
with the rider, who was lying forward on his chest across a coat
rolled round and strapped in front of the saddle, and his arms around
the horse's neck. He was as pale as a ghost. His eyes—great dark
ones they were, too—were staring out of his head. I thought he was
dead, and called out to father and Jim that he was.

They ran up, and we lifted him off after undoing some straps and
a rope. He was tied on (that was what the half-caste was waiting for
at the top of the gully). When we laid him down his head fell
back, and he looked as much like a corpse as if he had been dead a
day.

Then we saw he had been wounded. There was blood on his
shirt, and the upper part of his arm was bandaged.

'It's too late, father,' said I; 'he's a dead man. What pluck he
must have had to ride down there!'

'He's worth two dead 'uns yet,' said father, who had his hand on
his pulse. 'Hold his head up, one of you, while I go for the brandy.
How did he get hit, Warrigal?'

'That —— Sergeant Goring,' said the boy, a slight, active-looking
chap, about sixteen, that looked as if he could jump into a gum tree
and back again, and I believe he could. 'Sergeant Goring, he very
near grab us at Dilligah. We got a lot of old Jobson's cattle when he
came on us. He jump off his horse when he see he couldn't catch us,
and very near drop Starlight. My word, he very nearly fall off—
just like that' (here he imitated a man reeling in his saddle); 'but
the old horse stop steady with him, my word, till he come to. Then
the sergeant fire at him again; hit him in the shoulder with his pistol.
Then Starlight come to his senses, and we clear. My word, he
couldn't see the way the old horse went. Ha, ha!'—here the young
devil laughed till the trees and rocks rang again. 'Gallop different
ways, too, and met at the old needle-rock. But they were miles away
then.'

Before the wild boy had come to the end of his story the wounded
man had proved that it was only a dead faint, as the women call it,
not the real thing. And after he had tasted a pannikin full of brandy
and water, which father brought him, he sat up and looked like a
living man once more.

'Better have a look at my shoulder,' he said. 'That —— fellow
shot like a prize-winner at Wimbledon. I've had a squeak for it.'

'Puts me in mind of our old poaching rows,' said father, while he
carefully cut the shirt off, that was stiffened with blood and showed
where the bullet had passed through the muscle, narrowly missing
the bone of the joint. We washed it, and relieved the wounded man

by discovering that the other bullet had only been spent, after striking a tree most like, when it had knocked the wind out of him and nearly unhorsed him, as Warrigal said.

'Fill my pipe, one of you. Who the devil are these lads? Yours, I suppose, Marston, or you wouldn't be fool enough to bring them here. Why didn't you leave them at home with their mother? Don't you think you and I and this devil's limb enough for this precious trade of ours?'

'They'll take their luck as it comes, like others,' growled father; 'what's good enough for me isn't too bad for them. We want another hand or two to work things right.'

'Oh! we do, do we?' said the stranger, fixing his eyes on father as if he was going to burn a hole in him with a burning-glass; 'but if I'd a brace of fine boys like those of my own I'd hang myself before I'd drag them into the pit after myself.'

'That's all very fine,' said father, looking very dark and dangerous. 'Is Mr. Starlight going to turn parson? You'll be just in time, for we'll all be shopped if you run against the police like this, and next thing to lay them on to the Hollow by making for it when you're too weak to ride.'

'What would you have me do? Pull up and hold up my hands? There was nowhere else to go; and that new sergeant rode devilish well, I can tell you, with a big chestnut well-bred horse, that gave old Rainbow here all he knew to lose him. Now, once for all, no more of that, Marston, and mind your own business. I'm the superior officer in this ship's company—you know that very well—your business is to obey me, and take second place.'

Father growled out something, but did not offer to deny it. We could see plainly that the stranger was or had been far above our rank, whatever were the reasons which had led to his present kind of life.

We stayed for about ten days, while the stranger's arm got well. With care and rest, it soon healed. He was pleasant enough, too, when the pain went away. He had been in other countries, and told us all kinds of stories about them.

He said nothing, though, about his own former ways, and we often wondered whatever could have made him take to such a life. Unknown to father, too, he gave us good advice, warned us that what we were in was the road to imprisonment or death in due course, and not to flatter ourselves that any other ending was possible.

'I have my own reasons for leading the life I do,' he said, 'and must run my own course, of which I foresee the end as plainly as if it was written in a book before me. Your father had a long account to square with society, and he has a right to settle it in his own way. That yellow whelp was never intended for anything better. But for you lads' —and here he looked kindly in poor old Jim's honest face (and an honest face and heart Jim's was, and that I'll live and die on) — 'my advice to you is, to clear off home, when we go, and never come back here again. Tell your father you won't come; cut loose from him, once and for all. You'd better drown yourselves comfortably at once than take to this cursed trade. Now, mind what I tell you, and keep your own counsel.'

By and by, the day came when the horses were run in for father and Mr. Starlight and Warrigal, who packed up to be off for some other part.

When they were in the yard we had a good look at his own horse —a good look—and if I'd been a fellow that painted pictures, and that kind of thing, I could draw a middlin' good likeness of him now.

By George! how fond I am of a good horse—a real well-bred clinker. I'd never have been here if it hadn't been for that, I do believe; and many another Currency chap can say the same—a horse or a woman—that's about the size of it, one or t'other generally fetches us. I shall never put foot in stirrup again, but I'll try and scratch out a sort of likeness of Rainbow.

He was a dark bay horse, nearly brown, without a white hair on him. He wasn't above 15 hands and an inch high, but looked a deal bigger than he was, for the way he held his head up and carried himself. He was deep and thick through behind the shoulders, and girthed ever so much more than you'd think. He had a short back, and his ribs went out like a cask, long quarters, great thighs and hocks, wonderful legs, and feet of course to do the work he did. His head was plainish, but clean and bony, and his eye was big and well opened, with no white showing. His shoulder was sloped back that much that he couldn't fall, no matter what happened his fore legs. All his paces were good, too. I believe he could jump—jump anything he was ridden at, and very few horses could get the better of him for one mile or three.

Where he'd come from, of course, we were not to know then. He had a small private sort of brand that didn't belong to any of the big studs; but he was never bred by a poor man. I afterwards found out that he was stolen before he was foaled, like many another plum, and his dam killed as soon as she had weaned him. So, of course, no one could swear to him, and Starlight could have ridden past the Supreme Court at the Assizes, and never been stopped, as far as this horse was concerned.

Before we went away father and Starlight had some terrible long talks, and one evening Jim came to me, and says he—

'What do you think they're up to now?'

'How should I know? Sticking up a bank, or boning a flock of maiden ewes to take up a run with? They seem to be game for anything. There'll be a hanging match in the family if us boys don't look out.'

'There's no knowing,' says Jim, with a roguish look in his eye (I didn't think then how near the truth I was), 'but it's about a horse this time.'

'Oh! a horse; that alters the matter. But what's one horse to make such a shine about?'

'Ah, that's the point,' says poor old Jim, 'it's a horse worth talking about. Don't you remember the imported entire that they had his picture in the papers—him that Mr. Windhall gave £2000 for?'

'What! the Marquis of Lorne? Why, you don't mean to say they're going for him?'

'By George, I do!' says Jim; 'and they'll have him here, and twenty blood mares to put to him, before September.'

'They're all gone mad—they'll raise the country on us. Every police trooper in the colony 'll be after us like a pack of dingoes after an old man kangaroo when the ground's boggy, and they'll run us down, too; they can't be off it. Whatever made 'em think of such a big touch as that?'

'That Starlight's the devil, I think,' said Jim slowly. 'Father didn't seem to like it at first, but he brought him round bit by bit—said he knew a squatter in Queensland he could pass him on to; that they'd keep him there for a year and get a crop of foals by him, and when the "derry" was off he'd take him over himself.'

'But how's he going to nail him? People say Windhall keeps him locked up at night, and his box is close to his house.'

'Starlight says he has a friend handy; he seems to have one or two everywhere. It's wonderful, as father told him, where he gets information.'

'By George! it would be a touch, and no mistake. And if we could get a few colts by him out of thoroughbred mares we might win half the races every year on our side and no one a bit the wiser.'

It did seem a grand sort of thing—young fools that we were—to get hold of this wonderful stallion that we'd heard so much of, as thoroughbred as Eclipse; good as anything England could turn out. I say again, if it weren't for the horse-flesh part of it, the fun and hard-riding and tracking, and all the rest of it, there wouldn't be anything like the cross-work that there is in Australia. It lies partly between that and the dry weather. There's the long spells of drought when nothing can be done by young or old. Sometimes for months you can't work in the garden, nor plough, nor sow, nor do anything useful to keep the devil out of your heart. Only sit at home and do nothing, or else go out and watch the grass witherin' and the water dryin' up, and the stock dyin' by inches before your eyes. And no change, maybe, for months. The ground like iron and the sky like brass, as the parson said, and very true, too, last Sunday.

Then the youngsters, havin' so much idle time on their hands, take to gaffin' and flash talk; and money must be got to sport and pay up if they lose; and the stock all ramblin' about and mixed up, and there's a temptation to collar somebody's calves or foals, like we did that first red heifer. I shall remember her to my dying day. It seems as if I had put that brand on my own heart when I jammed it down on her soft skin. Anyhow, I never forgot it, and there's many another like me, I'll be bound.

The next morning Jim and I started off home. Father said he should stay in the "Hollow" till Starlight got round a bit. He told us not to tell mother or Ailie a word about where we'd been. Of course they couldn't be off knowin' that we'd been with him; but we were to stall them off by saying we'd been helping him with a bit of bush-work or anything we could think of. 'It'll do no good, and your mother's quite miserable enough as it is, boys,' he said. 'She'll know time enough, and maybe break her heart over it, too. Poor Norah!'

Dashed if I ever heard father say a soft thing before. I couldn't 'a believed it. I always thought he was ironbark outside and in. But he seemed real sorry for once. And I was near sayin', 'Why don't ye cut the whole blessed lot, then, and come home and work steady and make us all comfortable and happy?' But when I looked again his face was all changed and hard-like. 'Off you go,' he says, with his old voice. 'Next time I want either of you I'll send Warrigal for you.'

And with that he walked off from the yard where we had been catching our horses, and never looked nigh us again.

We rode away to the low end of the gully, and then we led the horses up, foot by foot, and hard work it was—like climbing up the roof of a house. We were almost done when we got to the tableland at the top.

We made our way to the yard, where there were the tracks of the cows all round about it, but nothing but the wild horses had ever been there since.

'What a scrubby hole it is!' said Jim; 'I wonder how in the world they ever found out the way to the Hollow?'

'Some runaway Government men, I believe, so that half-caste chap told me, and a gin[1] showed 'em the track down, and where to get water and everything. They lived on kangaroos at first. Then, by degrees, they used to crawl out by moonlight and collar a horse or two or a few cattle. They managed to live there years and years; one died, one was killed by the blacks; the last man showed it to the chaps that passed it on to Starlight. Warrigal's mother, or aunt or something, was the gin that showed it to the first white men.'

[1] A black woman.

CHAPTER VII

IT was pretty late that night when we got home, and poor mother and Aileen were that glad to see us that they didn't ask too many questions. Mother would sit and look at the pair of us for ever so long without speaking, and then the tears would come into her eyes and she'd turn away her head.

The old place seemed very snug, clean, and comfortable, too, after all the camping-out, and it was first-rate to have our own beds again. Then the milk and fresh butter, and the eggs and bacon—my word! how Jim did lay in; you'd have thought he was goin' on all night.

'By George! home's a jolly place after all,' he said. 'I am going to stay ever so long this time, and work like an old near-side poler—see if I don't. Let's look at your hands, Aileen; my word, you've been doing your share.'

'Indeed, has she,' said mother. 'It's a shame, so it is, and her with two big brothers, too.'

'Poor Ailie,' said Jim, 'she had to take an axe, had she, in her pretty little hands; but she didn't cut all that wood that's outside the door and I nearly broke my neck over, I'll go bail.'

'How do you know?' says she, smiling roguish-like. 'All the world might have been here for what you'd been the wiser—going away nobody knows where, and coming home at night like—like——'

'Bushrangers,' says I. 'Say it out; but we haven't turned out yet, if that's what you mean, Miss Marston.'

'I don't mean anything but what's kind and loving, you naughty boy,' says she, throwing her arms about my neck; 'but why will you break our hearts, poor mother's and mine, by going off in such a wild way and staying away, as if you were doing something that you were ashamed of?'

'Women shouldn't ask questions,' I said roughly. 'You'll know time enough, and if you never know, perhaps it's all the better.'

Jim was alongside of mother by this time, lying down like a child on the old native dogskin rug that we tanned ourselves with wattle bark. She had her hand on his hair—thick and curly it was always from a child. She didn't say anything, but I could see the tears drip, drip down from her face; her head was on Jim's shoulder, and by and by he put his arms round her neck. I went off to bed, I remember, and left them to it.

Next morning Jim and I were up at sunrise and got in the milkers, as we always did when we were at home. Aileen was up, too. She had done all the dairying lately by herself. There were about a dozen cows to milk, and she had managed it all herself every day that we were away; put up the calves every afternoon, drove up the cows in the cold morning, made the butter, which she used to salt and put into a keg, and feed the pigs with the skim milk. It was rather hard work for her, but I never saw her equal for farm work—rough or smooth. And she used to manage to dress neat and look pretty all the time; not like some small settlers' daughters that I have seen, slouching about with a pair of Blucher boots on, no bonnet, a dirty frock, and a petticoat like a blanket rag—not bad-looking girls either—and their hair like a dry mop. No, Aileen was always neat and tidy, with a good pair of thick boots outside and a thin pair for the house when she'd done her work.

She could frighten a wildish cow and bail up anything that would stay in a yard with her. She could ride like a bird and drive bullocks on a pinch in a dray or at plough, chop wood, too, as well as here and there a tree. But when she was in the house and regularly set down to her sewing she'd look that quiet and steady-going you'd think she was only fit to teach in a school or sell laces and gloves.

And so she was when she was let work in her own way, but if she was crossed or put upon, or saw anything going wrong, she'd hold up her head and talk as straight as any man I ever saw. She'd a look just like father when he'd made up his mind, only her way was always the right way. What a difference it makes, doesn't it? And she was so handsome with it. I've seen a goodish lot of women since I left the old place, let alone her that's helped to put me where I am, but I don't think I ever saw a girl that was a patch on Aileen for looks. She had a wonderful fair skin, and her eyes were large and soft like poor mother's. When she was a little raised-like you'd see a pink flush come on her cheeks like a peach blossom in September, and her eyes had a bright startled look like a doe kangaroo when she jumps up and looks round. Her teeth were as white and even as a black gin's. The mouth was something like father's, and when she shut it up we boys always knew she'd made up her mind, and wasn't going to be turned from it. But her heart was that good that she was always thinking of others and not of herself. I believe—I know—she'd have died for any one she loved. She had more sense than all the rest of us put together. I've often thought if she'd been the oldest boy instead of me she'd have kept Jim straight, and managed to drive father out of his cross ways—that is, if any one living could have done it. As for riding, I have never seen any one that could sit a horse or handle him through rough, thick country like her. She could ride barebacked, or next to it, sitting sideways on nothing but a gunny-bag, and send a young horse flying through scrub and rocks, or down ranges where you'd think a horse could hardly keep his feet. We could all ride a bit out of the common, if it comes to that. Better if we'd learned nothing but how to walk behind a plough, year in year out, like some of the folks in father's village in England, as he used to tell us about when he was in a good humour. But that's all as people are reared, I suppose. We'd been used to the outside of a horse ever since we could walk almost, and it came natural to us. Anyhow, I think Aileen was about the best of the lot of us at that, as in everything else.

Well, for a bit all went on pretty well at home. Jim and I worked away steady, got in a tidy bit of crop, and did everything that lay in our way right and regular. We milked the cows in the morning, and brought in a big stack of firewood and chopped as much as would last for a month or two. We mended up the paddock fence, and tidied the garden. The old place hadn't looked so smart for many a day.

When we came in at night old mother used to look that pleased and happy we couldn't help feeling better in our hearts. Aileen used to read something out of the paper that she thought might amuse us. I could read pretty fair, and so could Jim; but we were both lazy at it, and after working pretty hard all day didn't so much care about spelling out the long words in the farming news or the stories they put in. All the same, it would have paid us better if we'd read a little more and put the 'bullocking' on one side, at odd times. A man can learn as much out of a book or a paper sometimes in an hour as will save his work for a week, or put him up to working to better purpose. I can see that now—too late, and more's the pity.

Anyhow, Aileen could read pretty near as fast as anyone I ever saw, and she used to reel it out for us, as we sat smoking over the fire, in a way that kept us jolly and laughing till it was nearly turning-in time. Now and then George Storefield would come and stay an hour or two. He could read well; nearly as well as she could. Then he had always something to show her that she'd been asking about. His place was eight miles off, but he'd always get his horse and go home, whatever the night was like.

'I must be at my work in the morning,' he'd say; 'it's more than half a day gone if you lose that, and I've no half-days to spare, or quarter-days either.'

.   .   .   .

So we all got on first-rate, and anybody would have thought that there wasn't a more steady-going, hard-working happy family in the colony. No more there wasn't, while it lasted. After all, what is there that's half as good as being all right and square, working hard for the food you eat, and the sleep you enjoy, able to look all the world in the face, and afraid of nothing and nobody!

We were so quiet and comfortable till the winter was over and the spring coming on, till about September, that I almost began to believe we'd never done anything in our lives we could be made to suffer for.

Now and then, of course, I used to wake up in the night, and my thoughts would go back to 'Terrible Hollow,' that wonderful place; and one night with the unbranded cattle, and Starlight, with the blood dripping on to his horse's shoulder, and the half-caste, with his hawk's eye and glittering teeth—father, with his gloomy face and dark words. I wondered whether it was all a dream; whether J and Jim had been in it at all; whether any of the 'cross-work' had been found out; and, if so, what would be done to me and Jim; most of all, though, whether father and Starlight were away after some 'big touch'; and, if so, where and what it was, and how soon we should hear of it.

As for Jim, he was one of those happy-go-lucky fellows that didn't bother himself about anything he didn't see or run against. I don't think it ever troubled him. It was the only bad thing he'd ever been in. He'd been drawn in against his will, and I think he had made up his mind—pretty nearly—not to go in for any more.

I have often seen Aileen talking to him, and they'd walk along in the evening when the work was done—he with his arm round her waist, and she looking at him with that quiet, pleased face of hers, seeming so proud and fond of him, as if he'd been the little chap she used to lead about and put on the old pony, and bring into the calf-pen when she was milking. I remember he had a fight with a little bull-calf, about a week old, that came in with a wild heifer, and Aileen made as much of his pluck as if it had been a mallee scrubber. The calf baaed and butted at Jim, as even the youngest of them will, if they've the wild blood in 'em, and nearly upset him; he was only a bit of a toddler. But Jim picked up a loose leg of a milking-stool, and the two went at it hammer and tongs. I could hardly stand for laughing, till the calf gave him best and walked away.

Aileen pulled him out, and carried him in to mother, telling her that he was the bravest little chap in the world; and I remember I got scolded for not going to help him. How these little things come back!

'I'm beginning to be afraid,' says George, one evening, 'that it's going to be a dry season.'

'There's plenty of time yet,' says Jim, who always took the bright side of things; 'it might rain towards the end of the month.'

'I was thinking the same thing,' I said. 'We haven't had any rain to speak of for a couple of months, and that bit of wheat of ours is beginning to go back. The oats look better.'

'Now I think of it,' put in Jim, 'Dick Dawson came in from outside, and he said things are shocking bad; all the frontage bare already, and the water drying up.'

'It's always the way,' I said, bitter-like. 'As soon as a poor man's got a chance of a decent crop, the season turns against him or prices go down, so that he never gets a chance.'

'It's as bad for the rich man, isn't it?' said George. 'It's God's will, and we can't make or mend things by complaining.'

'I don't know so much about that,' I said sullenly. 'But it's not as bad for the rich man. Even if the squatters suffer by a drought and lose their stock, they've more stock and money in the bank, or else credit to fall back on; while the like of us lose all we have in the world, and no one would lend us a pound afterwards to save our lives.'

'It's not quite so bad as that,' said George. 'I shall lose my year's work unless rain comes, and most of the cattle and horses besides; but I shall be able to get a few pounds to go on with, however the season goes.'

'Oh! if you like to bow and scrape to rich people, well and good,' I said; 'but that's not my way. We have as good a right to our share of the land and some other good things as they have, and why should we be done out of it?'

'If we pay for the land as they do, certainly,' said George.

'But why should we pay? God Almighty, I suppose, made the land and the people too, one to live on the other. Why should we pay for what is our own? I believe in getting my share somehow.'

'That's a sort of argument that doesn't come out right,' said George. 'How would you like another man to come and want to halve the farm with you?'

'I shouldn't mind; I should go halves with some one else who had a bigger one,' I said. 'More money too, more horses, more sheep, a bigger house! Why should he have it and not me?'

'That's a lazy man's argument, and—well, not an honest man's,' said George, getting up and putting on his cabbage-tree. 'I can't sit and hear you talk such rot. Nobody can work better than you and Jim, when you like. I wonder you don't leave such talk to fellows like Frowser, that's always spouting at the Shearers' Arms.'

'Nonsense or not, if a dry season comes and knocks all our work over, I shall help myself to some one's stuff that has more than he knows what to do with.'

'Why can't we all go shearing, and make as much as will keep us for six months?' said George. 'I don't know what we'd do without the squatters.'

'Nor I either; more ways than one; but Jim and I are going shearing next week. So perhaps there won't be any need for "duffing" after all.'

'Oh, Dick!' said Aileen, 'I can't bear to hear you make a joke of that kind of thing. Don't we all know what it leads to! Wouldn't it be better to live on dry bread and be honest than to be full of money and never know the day when you'd be dragged to gaol?'

'I've heard all that before; but ain't there lots of people that have made their money by all sorts of villainy, that look as well as the best, and never see a gaol?'

'They're always caught some day,' says poor Aileen, sobbing, 'and what a dreadful life of anxiety they must lead!'

'Not at all,' I said. 'Look at Lucksly, Squeezer, and Frying-pan Jack. Everybody knows how they got their stock and their money. See how they live. They've got stations, and public-house and town property, and they get richer every year. I don't think it pays to be too honest in a dry country.'

'You're a naughty boy, Dick; isn't he, Jim?' she said, smiling through her tears. 'But he doesn't mean half what he says, does he?'

'Not he,' says Jim; 'and very likely we'll have lots of rain after all.'

CHAPTER VIII

THE 'big squatter,' as he was called on our side of the country, was Mr. Falkland. He was an Englishman that had come young to the colony, and worked his way up by degrees. He had had no money when he first came, people said; indeed, he often said so himself. He was not proud, at any rate in that way, for he was not above telling a young fellow that he should never be downhearted because he hadn't a coat to his back or a shilling in his pocket, because he, Herbert Falkland, had known what it was to be without either. 'This was the best country in the whole world,' he used to say, 'for a gentleman who was poor or a working man.' The first sort could always make an independence if they were moderately strong, liked work, and did not drink. There were very few countries where idle, unsteady people got rich. 'As for the poor man, he was the real rich man in Australia; high wages, cheap food, lodging, clothing, travelling. What more did he want? He could save money, live happily, and die rich, if he wasn't a fool or a rogue. Unfortunately, these last were highly popular professions; and many people, high and low, belonged to them here—and everywhere else.'

We were all well up in this kind of talk, because for the last two or three years, since we had begun to shear pretty well, we had always shorn at his shed. He was one of those gentlemen—and he was a gentleman, if ever there was one—that takes a deal of notice of his working hands, particularly if they were young. Jim he took a great fancy to the first moment he saw him. He didn't care so much about me.

'You're a sulky young dog, Richard Marston,' he used to say. 'I'm not sure that you'll come to any good; and though I don't like to say all I hear about your father before you, I'm afraid he doesn't teach you anything worth knowing. But Jim, there's a grand fellow: if he'd been caught young and weaned from all of your lot, he'd have been an honour to the land he was born in. He's too good for you all.'

'Every one of you gentlemen wants to be a small God Almighty,' I said impudently. 'You'd like to break us all in and put us in yokes and bows, like a lot of working bullocks.'

'You mistake me, my boy, and all the rest of us who are worth calling men, let alone gentlemen. We are your best friends, and would help you in every way if you'd only let us.'

'I don't see so much of that.'

'Because you often fight against your own good. We should like to see you all have farms of your own—to be all well taught and able to make the best of your lives—not driven to drink, as many of you are, because you have no notion of any rational amusement, and anything between hard work and idle dissipation.'

'And suppose you had all this power,' I said—for if I was afraid of father there wasn't another man living that could overcrow me— 'don't you think you'd know the way to keep all the good things for yourselves? Hasn't it always been so?'

'I see your argument,' he said, quite quiet and reasonable, just as if I had been a swell like himself—that was why he was unlike any other man I ever knew—'and it is a perfectly fair way of putting it. But your class might, I think, always rely upon there being enough kindness and wisdom in ours to prevent that state of things. Unfortunately, neither side trusts the other enough. And now the bell is going to ring, I think.'

Jim and I stopped at Boree shed till all the sheep were cut out. It pays well if the weather is pretty fair, and it isn't bad fun when there's twenty or thirty chaps of the right sort in the shearers' hut; there's always some fun going on. Shearers work pretty hard, and as they buy their own rations generally, they can afford to live well. After a hard day's shearing—that is, from five o'clock in the morning to seven at night, going best pace all the time, every man working as hard as if he was at it for his life—one would think a man would be too tired to do anything. But we were mostly strong and hearty, and at that age a man takes a deal of killing; so we used to have a little card-playing at night to pass away the time.

Very few of the fellows had any money to spend. They couldn't get any either until shearing was over and they were paid off; but they'd get some one who could write to scribble a lot of I O U's, and they did as well.

We used to play 'all-fours' and 'loo,' and now and then an American game which some of the fellows had picked up. It was strange how soon we managed to get into big stakes. I won at first, and then Jim and I began to lose, and had such a lot of I O U's out that I was afraid we'd have no money to take home after shearing. Then I began to think what a fool I'd been to play myself and drag Jim into it, for he didn't want to play at first.

One day I got a couple of letters from home—one from Aileen and another in a strange hand. It had come to our little post-office, and Aileen had sent it on to Boree.

When I opened it there were a few lines, with father's name at the bottom. He couldn't write, so I made sure that Starlight had written it for him. He was quite well, it said; and to look out for him about Christmas time; he might come home then, or send for us; to stop at Boree if we could get work, and keep a couple of horses in good trim, as he might want us. A couple of five-pound notes fell out of the letter as I opened it.

When I looked at them first I felt a kind of fear. I knew what they came from. And I had a sort of feeling that we should be better without them. However, the devil was too strong for me. Money's a tempting thing, whether it's notes or gold, especially when a man's in debt. I had begun to think the fellows looked a little cool on us the last three or four nights, as our losses were growing big.

So I gave Jim his share; and after tea, when we sat down again, there weren't more than a dozen of us that were in the card racket. I flung down my note, and Jim did his, and told them what we owed and to take change out of that and hand us over their paper for the balance.

They all stared, for such a thing hadn't been seen since the shearing began. Shearers, as a rule, come from their homes in the settled districts very bare. They are not very well supplied with clothes; their horses are poor and done up; and they very seldom have a note in their pockets, unless they have managed to sell a spare horse on the journey.

So we were great men for the time, looked at by the others with wonder and respect. We were fools enough to be pleased with it. Strangely, too, our luck turned from that minute, and it ended in our winning not only our own back, but more than as much more from the other men.

I don't think Mr. Falkland liked these goings on. He wouldn't have allowed cards at all if he could have helped it. He was a man that hated what was wrong, and didn't value his own interest a pin when it came in the way. However, the shearing hut was our own, in a manner of speaking, and as long as we shore clean and kept the shed going, the overseer, Mr. M'Intyre, didn't trouble his head much about our doings in the hut. He was anxious to get done with the shearing, to get the wool into the bales before the dust came in, and the grass seed ripened, and the clover burrs began to fall.

'Why should ye fash yoursel',' I heard him say once to Mr. Falkland, 'aboot these young deevils like the Marstons? They're as good's ready money in aul Nick's purse. It's bred and born and welded in them. Ye'll just have the burrs and seeds amang the wool if ye keep losing a smart shearer for the sake o' a wheen cards and dice; and ye'll mak' nae heed of convairtin' thae young caterans ony mair than ye'll change a Norroway falcon into a barn-door chuckie.'

I wonder if what he said was true—if we couldn't help it; if it was in our blood? It seems like it; and yet it's hard lines to think a fellow must grow up and get on the cross in spite of himself, and come to the gallows-foot at last, whether he likes it or not. The parson here isn't bad at all. He's a man and a gentleman, too; and he's talked and read to me by the hour. I suppose some of us chaps are like the poor stupid tribes that the Israelites found in Canaan, only meant to live for a bit and then to be rubbed out to make room for better people.

When the shearing was nearly over we had a Saturday afternoon to ourselves. We had finished all the sheep that were in the shed, and old M'Intyre didn't like to begin a fresh flock. So we got on our horses and took a ride into the township just for the fun of the thing, and for a little change. The horses had got quite fresh with the rest and the spring grass. Their coats were shining, and they all looked very different from what they did when we first came. Our two were not so poor when they came, so they looked the best of the lot, and jumped about in style when we mounted. Ah! only to think of a good horse.

All the men washed themselves and put on clean clothes. Then we had our dinner and about a dozen of us started off for the town.

Poor old Jim, how well he looked that day! I don't think you could pick a young fellow anywhere in the countryside that was a patch on him for good looks and manliness, somewhere about six foot or a little over, as straight as a rush, with a bright blue eye that was always laughing and twinkling, and curly dark brown hair. No wonder all the girls used to think so much of him. He could do anything and everything that a man could do. He was as strong as a young bull, and as active as a rock wallaby—and ride! Well, he sat on his horse as if he was born on one. With his broad shoulders and upright easy seat he was a regular picture on a good horse.

And he had a good one under him to-day; a big, brown, resolute, well-bred horse he had got in a swap because the man that had him was afraid of him. Now that he had got a little flesh on his bones he looked something quite out of the common. 'A deal too good for a poor man, and him honest,' as old M'Intyre said.

But Jim turned on him pretty sharp, and said he had got the horse in a fair deal, and had as much right to a good mount as any one else—super or squatter, he didn't care who he was.

And Mr. Falkland took Jim's part, and rather made Mr. M'Intyre out in the wrong for saying what he did. The old man didn't say much more, only shook his head, saying—

'Ah, ye're a grand laddie, and buirdly, and no that thrawn, either—like ye, Dick, ye born deevil,' looking at me. 'But I misdoot sair ye'll die wi' your boots on. There's a smack o' Johnnie Armstrong in the glint o' yer e'e. Ye'll be to dree yer weird, there's nae help for't.'

'What's all that lingo, Mr. M'Intyre!' called out Jim, all good-natured again. 'Is it French or Queensland blacks' yabber? Blest if I understand a word of it. But I didn't want to be nasty, only I am regular shook on this old moke, I believe, and he's as square as Mr. Falkland's dogcart horse.'

'Maybe ye bocht him fair eneugh. I'll no deny you. I saw the receipt mysel'. But where did yon lang-leggit, long-lockit, Fish River moss-trooping callant win haud o' him? Answer me that, Jeems.'

'That says nothing,' answered Jim. 'I'm not supposed to trace back every horse in the country and find out all the people that owned him since he was a foal. He's mine now, and mine he'll be till I get a better one.'

'A contuma-acious and stiff-necked generation,' said the old man, walking off and shaking his head. 'And yet he's a fine laddie; a gra-and laddie wad he be with good guidance. It's the Lord's doing, nae doot, and we daurna fault it; it's wondrous in our een.'

That was the way old Mac always talked. Droll lingo, wasn't it?

CHAPTER IX

WELL, away we went to this township. Bundah was the name of it; not that there was anything to do or see when we got there. It was the regular up-country village, with a public-house, a store, a pound, and a blacksmith's shop. However, a public-house is not such a bad place—at any rate it's better than nothing when a fellow's young and red-hot for anything like a bit of fun, or even a change. Some people can work away day after day, and year after year, like a bullock in a team or a horse in a chaff-cutting machine. It's all the better for them if they can, though I suppose they never enjoy themselves except in a cold-blooded sort of way. But there's other men that can't do that sort of thing, and it's no use talking. They must have life and liberty and a free range. There's some birds, and animals too, that either pine in a cage or kill themselves, and I suppose it's the same way with some men. They can't stand the cage of what's called honest labour, which means working for some one else for twenty or thirty years, never having a day to yourself, or doing anything you like, and saving up a trifle for your old age when you can't enjoy it. I don't wonder youngsters break traces and gallop off like a colt out of a team.

Besides, sometimes there's a good-looking girl even at a bush public, the daughter or the barmaid, and it's odd, now, what a difference that makes. There's a few glasses of grog going, a little noisy, rattling talk, a few smiles and a saucy answer or two from the girl, a look at the last newspaper, or a bit of the town news from the landlord; he's always time to read. Hang him—I mean confound him—for he's generally a sly old spider who sucks us fellows pretty dry, and then don't care what becomes of us. Well, it don't amount to much, but it's life—the only taste of it that chaps like us are likely to get. And people may talk as much as they like; boys, and men too, will like it, and take to it, and hanker after it, as long as the world lasts. There's danger in it, and misery, and death often enough comes of it, but what of that? If a man wants a swim on the sea-shore he won't stand all day on the beach because he may be drowned or snapped up by a shark, or knocked against a rock, or tired out and drawn under by the surf. No, if he's a man he'll jump in and enjoy himself all the more because the waves are high and the waters deep. So it was very good fun to us, simple as it might sound to some people. It was pleasant to be bowling along over the firm green turf, along the plain, through the forest, gully,

and over the creek. Our horses were fresh, and we had a scurry or
two, of course; but there wasn't one that could hold a candle to
Jim's brown horse. He was a long-striding, smooth goer, but he got
over the ground in wonderful style. He could jump, too, for Jim
put him over a big log fence or two, and he sailed over them like a
forester buck over the head of a fallen wattle.

Well, we'd had our lark at the Bundah Royal Hotel, and were
coming home to tea at the station, all in good spirits, but sober
enough, when, just as we were crossing one of the roads that came
through the run—over the 'Pretty Plain,' as they called it—we heard
a horse coming along best pace. When we looked who should it be
but Miss Falkland, the owner's only daughter.

She was an only child, and the very apple of her father's eye, you
may be sure. The shearers mostly knew her by sight, because she
had taken a fancy to come down with her father a couple of times
to see the shed when we were all in full work.

A shed's not exactly the best place for a young lady to come into.
Shearers are rough in their language now and then. But every
man liked and respected Mr. Falkland, so we all put ourselves on
our best behaviour, and the two or three flash fellows who had no
sense or decent feeling were warned that if they broke out at all they
would get something to remember it by.

But when we saw that beautiful, delicate-looking creature stepping
down the boards between the two rows of shearers, most of them
stripped to their jerseys and working like steam-engines, looking
curiously and pitifully at the tired men and the patient sheep, with
her great, soft, dark eyes and fair white face like a lily, we began to
think we'd heard of angels from heaven, but never seen one before.

Just as she came opposite Jim, who was trying to shear sheep and
sheep with the 'ringer' of the shed, who was next on our right, the
wether he was holding kicked, and knocking the shears out of his
hand, sent them point down against his wrist. One of the points
went right in, and though it didn't cut the sinews, as luck would
have it, the point stuck out at the other side; out spurted the blood,
and Jim was just going to let out when he looked up and saw Miss
Falkland looking at him, with her beautiful eyes so full of pity and
surprise that he could have had his hand chopped off, so he told
me afterwards, rather than vex her for a moment. So he shut up
his mouth and ground his teeth together, for it was no joke in the
way of pain, and the blood began to run like a blind creek after a
thunderstorm.

'Oh! poor fellow. What a dreadful cut! Look, papa!' she cried
out. 'Hadn't something better be bound round it? How it bleeds!
Does it pain much?'

'Not a bit, miss!' said Jim, standing up like a schoolboy going to
say his lesson. 'That is, it doesn't matter if it don't stop my shearing.'

'Tar!' sings out my next-door neighbour. 'Here, boy; tar wanted for No. 36. That'll put it all right, Jim; it's only a scratch.'

'You mind your shearing, my man,' said Mr. Falkland quietly. 'I don't know whether Mr. M'Intyre will quite approve of that last sheep of yours. This is rather a serious wound. The best thing is to bind it up at once.'

Before any one could say another word Miss Falkland had whipped out her soft fine cambric handkerchief and torn it in two.

'Hold up your hand,' she said. 'Now, papa, lend me yours.' With the last she cleared the wound of the flowing blood, and then neatly and skilfully bound up the wrist firmly with the strips of cambric. This she further protected by her father's handkerchief, which she helped herself to and finally stopped the blood with.

Jim kept looking at her small white hands all the time she was doing it. Neither of us had ever seen such before—the dainty skin, the pink nails, the glittering rings.

'There,' she said, 'I don't think you ought to shear any more to-day; it might bring on inflammation. I'll send to know how it gets on to-morrow.'

'No, miss; my grateful thanks, miss,' said Jim, opening his eyes and looking as if he'd like to drop down on his knees and pray to her. 'I shall never forget your goodness, Miss Falkland, if I live till I'm a hundred.' Then Jim bent his head a bit—I don't suppose he ever made a bow in his life before—and then drew himself up as straight as a soldier, and Miss Falkland made a kind of bow and smile to us all and passed out.

Jim did shear all the same that afternoon, though the tally wasn't any great things. 'I can't go and lie down in a bunk in the men's hut,' he said; 'I must chance it,' and he did. Next day it was worse and very painful, but Jim stuck to the shears, though he used to turn white with the pain at times, and I thought he'd faint. However, it gradually got better, and except a scar, Jim's hand was as good as ever.

Jim sent back Mr. Falkland's handkerchief after getting the cook to wash it and iron it out with a bit of a broken axletree; but the strips of white handkerchief—one had C. F. in the corner—he put away in his swag, and made some foolish excuse when I laughed at him about it.

She sent down a boy from the house next day to ask how Jim's hand was, and the day after that, but she never came to the shed any more. So we didn't see her again.

So it was this young lady that we saw coming tearing down the back road, as they called it, that led over the Pretty Plain. A good way behind we saw Mr. Falkland, but he had as much chance of coming up with her as a cattle dog of catching a 'brush flyer.'

The stable boy, Billy Donnellan, had told us (of course, like all those sort of youngsters, he was fond of getting among the men and listening to them talk) all about Miss Falkland's new mare.

She was a great beauty and thoroughbred. The stud groom had bought her out of a travelling mob from New England when she was dog-poor and hardly able to drag herself along. Everybody thought she was going to be the best lady's horse in the district; but though she was as quiet as a lamb at first she had begun to show a nasty temper lately, and to get very touchy. 'I don't care about chestnuts myself,' says Master Billy, smoking a short pipe as if he was thirty; 'they've a deal of temper, and she's got too much white in her eye for my money. I'm afeard she'll do some mischief afore we've done with her; and Miss Falkland's that game as she won't have nothing done to her. I'd ride the tail off her but what I'd bring her to, if I had my way.'

So this was the brute that had got away with Miss Falkland the day we were coming back from Bundah. Some horses, and a good many men and women, are all pretty right as long as they're well kept under and starved a bit at odd times. But give them an easy life and four feeds of corn a day, and they're troublesome brutes, and mischievous too.

It seems this mare came of a strain that had turned out more devils and killed more grooms and breakers than any other in the country. She was a Troubadour, it seems; there never was a Troubadour yet that wouldn't buck and bolt, and smash himself and his rider, if he got a fright, or his temper was roused. Men and women, horses and dogs, are very much alike. I know which can talk best. As to the rest, I don't know whether there's so much for us to be proud of.

It seems that this cranky wretch of a mare had been sideling and fidgeting when Mr. Falkland and his daughter started for their ride; but had gone pretty fairly—Miss Falkland, like my sister Aileen, could ride anything in reason—when suddenly a dead limb dropped off a tree close to the side of the road.

I believe she made one wild plunge, and set to; she propped and reared, but Miss Falkland sat her splendidly and got her head up. When she saw she could do nothing that way, she stretched out her head and went off as hard as she could lay legs to the ground.

She had one of those mouths that are not so bad when horses are going easy, but get quite callous when they are over-eager and excited. Anyhow, it was like trying to stop a mail-coach going down Mount Victoria with the brake off.

So what we saw was the wretch of a mare coming along as if the devil was after her, and heading straight across the plain at its narrowest part; it wasn't more than half-a-mile wide there, in fact, it was more like a flat than a plain. The people about Boree didn't see much open country, so they made a lot out of what they had.

The mare, like some women when they get their monkey up, was clean out of her senses, and I don't believe anything could have held her under a hide rope with a turn round a stockyard post. This was what she wanted, and if it had broken her infernal neck so much the better.

Miss Falkland was sitting straight and square, with her hands down, leaning a bit back, and doing her level best to stop the brute. Her hat was off and her hair had fallen down and hung down her back—plenty of it there was, too. The mare's neck was stretched straight out; her mouth was like a deal board, I expect, by that time.

We didn't sit staring at her all the time, you bet. We could see the boy ever so far off. We gathered up our reins and went after her, not in a hurry, but just collecting ourselves a bit to see what would be the best way to wheel the brute and stop her.

Jim's horse was far and away the fastest, and he let out to head the mare off from a creek that was just in front and at the end of the plain.

'By George!' said one of the men—a young fellow who lived near the place—'the mare's turning off her course, and she's heading straight for the Trooper's Downfall, where the policeman was killed. If she goes over that, they'll be smashed up like a matchbox, horse and rider.'

'What's that?' I said, closing up alongside of him. We were all doing our best, and were just in the line to back up Jim, who looked as if he was overhauling the mare fast.

'Why, it's a bluff a hundred feet deep—a straight drop—and rocks at the bottom. She's making as straight as a bee-line for it now, blast her!'

'And Jim don't know it,' I said; 'he's closing up to her, but he doesn't calculate to do it for a quarter of a mile more; he's letting her take it out of herself.'

'He'll never catch her in time,' said the young chap. 'My God! it's an awful thing, isn't it? and a fine young lady like her—so kind to us chaps as she was.'

'I'll see if I can make Jim hear,' I said, for though I looked cool I was as nearly mad as I could be to think of such a girl being lost before our eyes. 'No, I can't do that, but I'll *telegraph*.'

CHAPTER   X

Now Jim and I had had many a long talk together about what we should do in case we wanted to signal to each other very pressing. We thought the time might come some day when we might be near enough to sign, but not to speak. So we hit upon one or two things a little out of the common.

The first idea was, in case of one wanting to give the other the office that he was to look out his very brightest for danger, and not to trust to what appeared to be the state of affairs, the sign was to hold up your hat or cap straight over your head. If the danger threatened on the left, to shift to that side. If it was very pressing and on the jump, as it were, quite unexpected, and as bad as bad could be, the signalman was to get up on the saddle with his knees and turn half round.

We could do this easy enough and a lot of circus tricks besides. How had we learned them? Why, in the long days we had spent in the saddle tailing the milkers and searching after lost horses for many a night.

As luck would have it Jim looked round to see how we were getting on, and up went my cap. I could see him turn his head and keep watching me when I put on the whole box and dice of the telegraph business. He 'dropped,' I could see. He took up the brown horse, and made such a rush to collar the mare that showed he intended to see for himself what the danger was. The cross-grained jade! She was a well-bred wretch, and be hanged to her! Went as if she wanted to win the Derby and gave Jim all he knew to challenge her. We could see a line of timber just ahead of her, and that Jim was riding for his life.

'By——! they'll both be over it,' said the young shearer. 'They can't stop themselves at that pace, and they must be close up now.'

'He's neck and neck,' I said. 'Stick to her, Jim, old man!'

We were all close together now. Several of the men knew the place, and the word had been passed round.

No one spoke for a few seconds. We saw the two horses rush up at top speed to the very edge of the timber.

'By Jove! they're over. No! he's reaching for her rein. It's no use. Now—now! She's saved! Oh, my God! they're both right. By the Lord, well done! Hurrah! One cheer more for Jim Marston!'

It was all right. We saw Jim suddenly reach over as the horses were going stride and stride; saw him lift Miss Falkland from her saddle as if she had been a child and place her before him; saw the brown horse prop, and swing round on his haunches in a way that showed he had not been called the crack 'cutting out' horse on a big cattle run for nothing. We saw Jim jump to the ground and lift the young lady down. We saw only one horse.

Three minutes after Mr. Falkland overtook us, and we rode up together. His face was white, and his dry lips couldn't find words at first. But he managed to say to Jim, when we got up—

'You have saved my child's life, James Marston, and if I forget the service may God in that hour forget me. You are a noble fellow. You must allow me to show my gratitude in some way.'

'You needn't thank me so out and out as all that, Mr. Falkland,' said Jim, standing up very straight and looking at the father first, and then at Miss Falkland, who was pale and trembling, not altogether from fear, but excitement, and trying to choke back the sobs that would come out now and then. 'I'd risk life and limb any day before Miss Falkland's finger should be scratched, let alone see her killed before my eyes. I wonder if there's anything left of the mare, poor thing; not that she don't deserve it all, and more.'

Here we all walked forward to the deep creek bank. A yard or two farther and the brown horse and his burden must have gone over the terrible drop, as straight as a plumb-line, on to the awful rocks below. We could see where the brown had torn up the turf as he struck all four hoofs deep into it at once. Indeed, he had been newly shod, a freak of Jim's about a bet with a travelling blacksmith. Then the other tracks, the long score on the brink—over the brink—where the frightened, maddened animal had made an attempt to alter her speed, all in vain, and had plunged over the bank and the hundred feet of fall.

We peered over, and saw a bright-coloured mass among the rocks below—very still. Just at the time one of the ration-carriers came by with a spring cart. Mr. Falkland lifted his daughter in and took the reins, leaving his horse to be ridden home by the ration-carrier. As for us we rode back to the shearers' hut, not quite so fast as we came, with Jim in the middle. He did not seem inclined to talk much.

'It's lucky I turned round when I did, Dick,' he said at last, 'and saw you making the "danger-look-out-sharp" signal. I couldn't think what the dickens it was. I was so cocksure of catching the mare in half-a-mile farther that I couldn't help wondering what it was all about. Anyhow, I knew we agreed it was never to be worked for nothing, so thought the best thing I could do was to call in the mare, and see if I could find out anything then. When I got alongside, I could see that Miss Falkland's face was that white that something must be up. It weren't the mare she was afraid of. She was coming back to her. It took something to frighten her, I knew. So it must be something I did not know, or didn't see.

'"What is it, Miss Falkland?" I said.

'"Oh!" she cried out, "don't you know? Another fifty yards and we'll be over the downfall where the trooper was killed. Oh, my poor father!"

'"Don't be afraid," I said. "We'll not go over if I can help it."

'So I reached over and got hold of the reins. I pulled and jerked. She said her hands were cramped, and no wonder. Pulling double for a four-mile heat is no joke, even if a man's in training. Fancy a woman, a young girl, having to sit still and drag a runaway horse all the time. I couldn't stop the brute; she was boring like a wild bull. So just as we came pretty close I lifted Miss Falkland off the saddle and yelled at old Brownie as if I had been on a cattle camp, swinging round to the near side at the same time. Round he came like one o'clock. I could see the mare make one prop to stop herself, and then go flying right through the air, till I heard a beastly "thud" at the bottom.

'Miss Falkland didn't faint, though she turned white and then red, and trembled like a leaf when I lifted her down, and looked up at me with a sweet smile, and said—

'"Jim, you have paid me for binding up your wrist, haven't you? You have saved me from a horrible death, and I shall think of you as a brave and noble fellow all the days of my life."

'What could I say?' said Jim. 'I stared at her like a fool. "I'd have gone over the bank with you, Miss Falkland," I said, "if I could not have saved you."

'"Well, I'm afraid some of my admirers would have stopped short of that, James," she said. She did indeed. And then Mr. Falkland and all of you came up.'

'I say, Jim,' said one of the young fellows, 'your fortune's made. Mr. Falkland 'll stand a farm, you may be sure, for this little fakement.'

'And I say, Jack,' says old Jim, very quiet like, 'I've told you all the yarn, and if there's any chaff about it after this the cove will have to see whether he's best man or me; so don't make any mistake now.'

There was no more chaff. They weren't afraid. There were two or three of them pretty smart with their hands, and not likely to take much from anybody. But Jim was a heavy weight and could hit like a horse kicking; so they thought it wasn't good enough, and left him alone.

Next day Mr. Falkland came down and wanted to give Jim a cheque for a hundred; but he wouldn't hear of so much as a note. Then he said he'd give him a billet on the run—make him under-overseer; after a bit buy a farm for him and stock it. No! Jim wouldn't touch nothing or take a billet on the place. He wouldn't leave his family, he said. And as for taking money or anything else

for saving Miss Falkland's life, it was ridiculous to think of it.
There wasn't a man of the lot in the shed, down to the tarboy, that
wouldn't have done the same, or tried to. All that was in it was
that his horse was the fastest.

'It's not a bad thing for a poor man to have a fast horse now and
then, is it, Mr. Falkland?' he said, looking up and smiling, just
like a boy. He was very shy, was poor Jim.

'I don't grudge a poor man a good horse or anything else he likes
to have or enjoy. You know that, all of you. It's the fear I have
of the effect of the dishonest way that horses of value are come by,
and the net of roguery that often entangles fine young fellows like
you and your brother; that's what I fear,' said Mr. Falkland, looking
at the pair of us so kind and pitiful like.

I looked him in the face, though I felt I could not say he was
wrong. I felt, too, just then, as if I could have given all the world
to be afraid of no man's opinion.

What a thing it is to be perfectly honest and straight—to be able
to look the whole world in the face!

But if more gentlemen were like Mr. Falkland I do really believe
no one would rob them for very shame's sake. When shearing
was over we were all paid up—shearers, washers, knock-about men,
cooks, and extra shepherds. Every soul about the place except Mr.
M'Intyre and Mr. Falkland seemed to have got a cheque and a
walking-ticket at the same time. Away they went, like a lot of
boys out of school; and half of 'em didn't show as much sense either.
As for me and Jim we had no particular wish to go home before
Christmas. So as there's always contracts to be let about a big run
like Banda, we took a contract for some bush work, and went at it.
Mr. M'Intyre looked quite surprised. But Mr. Falkland praised us
up, and was proud we were going to turn over a new leaf.

Nobody could say at that time we didn't work. Fencing, dam-
making, horse-breaking, stock-riding, from making hay to building
a shed, all bush work came easy enough to us, Jim in particular; he
took a pleasure in it, and was never happier than when he'd had a
real tearing day's work and was settling himself after his tea to a
good steady smoke. A great smoker he'd come to be. He never
was much for drinking except now and again, and then he could
knock it off as easy as any man I ever seen. Poor old Jim! He was
born good and intended to be so, like mother. Like her, his luck
was dead out in being mixed up with a lot like ours.

One day we were out at the back making some lambing yards.
We were about twenty miles from the head station and had about
finished the job. We were going in the next day. We had been
camping in an old shepherd's hut and had been pretty jolly all by
ourselves. There was first-rate feed for our horses, as the grass was
being saved for the lambing season. Jim was in fine spirits, and as

we had plenty of good rations and first-rate tobacco we made ourselves pretty comfortable.

'What a jolly thing it is to have nothing on your mind!' Jim
used to say. 'I hadn't once, and what a fine time it was! Now I'm
always waking up with a start and expecting to see a policeman or
that infernal half-caste. He's never far off when there's villainy on.
Some fine day he'll sell us all, I really do believe.'

'If he don't somebody else will; but why do you pitch upon him?
You don't like him somehow; I don't see that he's worse than any
other. Besides, we haven't done anything much to have a reward put
on us.'

'No! that's to come,' answered Jim, very dismally for him. 'I don't
see what else is to come of it. Hist! isn't that a horse's step coming
this way? Yes, and a man on him, too.'

It was a bright night, though only the stars were out; but the
weather was that clear that you could see ever so well and hear
ever so far also. Jim had a blackfellow's hearing; his eyes were like
a hawk's; he could see in about any light, and read tracks like a
printed book.

I could hear nothing at first; then I heard a slight noise a good
way off, and a stick breaking every now and then.

'Talk of the devil!' growled Jim, 'and here he comes. I believe
that's Master Warrigal, infernal scoundrel that he is. Of course he's
got a message from our respectable old dad or Starlight, asking us
to put our heads in a noose for them again.'

'How do you know?'

'I know it's that ambling horse he used to ride,' says Jim. 'I can
make out his sideling kind of way of using his legs. All amblers
do that.'

'You're right,' I said, after listening for a minute. 'I can hear
the regular pace, different from a horse's walk.'

'How does he know we're here, I wonder?' says Jim.

'Some of the telegraphs piped us, I suppose,' I answered. 'I begin
to wish they forgot us altogether.'

'No such luck,' says Jim. 'Let's keep dark and see what this
black snake of a Warrigal will be up to. I don't expect he'll ride
straight up to the door.'

He was right. The horse hoofs stopped just inside a thick bit of
scrub, just outside the open ground on which the hut stood. After
a few seconds we heard the cry of the mopoke. It's not a cheerful
sound at the dead of night, and now, for some reason or other, it
affected Jim and me in much the same manner. I remembered
the last time I had heard the bird at home, just before we started
over for Terrible Hollow, and it seemed unlucky. Perhaps we
were both a little nervous; we hadn't drunk anything but tea for
weeks. We drank it awfully black and strong, and a great lot of it.
Anyhow, as we heard the quick light tread of the horse pacing in

his two-feet-on-one-side way over the sandy, thin-grassed soil, every moment coming nearer and nearer, and this queer dismal-voiced bird hooting its hoarse deep notes out of the dark tree that swished and sighed-like in front of the sand-hill, a queer feeling came over both of us that something unlucky was on the boards for us. We felt quite relieved when the horse's footsteps stopped. After a minute or so we could see a dark form creeping towards the hut.

CHAPTER XI

WARRIGAL left his horse at the edge of the timber, for fear he might want him in a hurry, I suppose. He was pretty 'fly,' and never threw away a chance as long as he was sober. He could drink a bit, like the rest of us, now and then—not often—but when he did it made a regular devil of him—that is, it brought the devil out that lives low down in most people's hearts. He was a worse one than usual, Jim said. He saw him once in one of his break-outs, and heard him boast of something he'd done. Jim never liked him afterwards. For the matter of that he hated Jim and me too. The only living things he cared about were Starlight and the three-cornered weed he rode, that had been a 'brumbee,' and wouldn't let any one touch him, much less ride him, but himself. How he used to snort if a stranger came near him! He could kick the eye out of a mosquito, and bite too, if he got the chance.

As for Warrigal, Starlight used to knock him down like a log if he didn't please him, but he never offered to turn upon him. He seemed to like it, and looked regular put out once when Starlight hurt his knuckles against his hard skull.

Us he didn't like, as I said before—why, I don't know—nor we him. Likes and dislikes are curious things. People hardly know the rights of them. But if you take a regular strong down upon a man or woman when you first see 'em it's ten to one that you'll find some day as you've good reason for it. We couldn't say what grounds we had for hating the sight of Warrigal neither, for he was as good a tracker as ever followed man or beasts. He could read all the signs of the bush like a printed book. He could ride any horse in the world, and find his way, day or night, to any place he'd ever once been to in his life.

Sometimes we should have been hard pushed when we were making across country at night only for him. Hour after hour he'd ride ahead through scrub or forest, up hill or down dale, with that brute of a horse of his—he called him 'Bilbah'—ambling away, till our horses, except Rainbow, used to shake the lives out of us jogging. I believe he did it on purpose.

He was a fine shot, and could catch fish and game in all sorts of ways that came in handy when we had to keep dark. He had pluck enough, and could fight a pretty sharp battle with his fists if he wasn't overweighted. There were white men that didn't at all find him a good thing if they went to bully him. He tried it on with

Jim once, but he knocked the seven senses out of him inside of three rounds, and that satisfied him. He pretended to make up, but I was always expecting him to play us some dog's trick yet. Anyway, so far he was all right, and as long as Starlight and us were mixed up together, he couldn't hurt one without the other. He came gliding up to the old hut in the dull light by bits of moves, just as if he'd been a bush that had changed its place. We pretended to be asleep near the fire.

He peeped in through a chink. He could see us by the firelight, and didn't suppose we were watching him.

'Hullo, Warrigal!' sung out Jim suddenly, 'What's up now? Some devil's work, I suppose, or you wouldn't be in it. Why don't you knock at a gentleman's door when you come a-visiting?'

'Wasn't sure it was you,' he answered, showing his teeth; 'it don't do to get sold. Might been troopers, for all I know.'

'Pity we wasn't,' said Jim; 'I'd have the hobbles on you by this time, and you'd have got "fitted" to rights. I wish I'd gone into the police sometimes. It isn't a bad game for a chap that can ride and track, and likes a bit of rough-and-tumble now and then.'

'If I'd been a police tracker I'd have had as good a chance of nailing you, Jim Marston,' spoke up Warrigal. 'Perhaps I will some day. Mr. Garton wanted me bad once, and said they'd never go agin me for old times. But that says nothin'. Starlight's out at the back and the old man, too. They want you to go to them—sharp.'

'What for?'

'Dunno. I was to tell you, and show the camp; and now gimme some grub, for I've had nothing since sunrise but the leg of a 'possum.'

'All right,' said Jim, putting the billy on; 'here's some damper and mutton to go on with while the tea warms.'

'Wait till I hobble out Bilbah; he's as hungry as I am, and thirsty too, my word.'

'Take some out of the barrel; we shan't want it to-morrow,' said Jim.

Hungry as Warrigal was—and when he began to eat I thought he never would stop—he went and looked after his horse first, and got him a couple of buckets of water out of the cask they used to send us out every week. There was no surface water near the hut. Then he hobbled him out of a bit of old sheep-yard, and came in.

The more I know of men the more I see what curious lumps of good and bad they're made up of. People that won't stick at anything in some ways will be that soft and good-feeling in others—ten times more so than your regular good people. Any one that thinks all mankind's divided into good, bad, and middlin', and that they can draft 'em like a lot of cattle—some to one yard, some to another—don't know much. There's a mob in most towns though, I think, that wants boilin' down bad. Some day they'll do it, maybe;

they'll have to when all the good country's stocked up. After Warrigal had his supper he went out again to see his horse, and then coiled himself up before the fire and wouldn't hardly say another word.

'How far was it to where Starlight was?'

'Long way. Took me all day to come.'

'Had he been there long?'

'Yes; had a camp there.'

'Anybody else with him?'

'Three more men from this side.'

'Did the old man say we were to come at once?'

'Yes, or leave it alone—which you liked.'

Then he shut his eyes, and his mouth too, and was soon as fast asleep as if he never intended to wake under a week.

'What shall we do, Jim?' I said; 'go or not?'

'If you leave it to me,' says Jim, 'I say, don't go. It's only some other cross cattle or horse racket. We're bound to be nobbled some day. Why not cut it now, and stick to the square thing? We couldn't do better than we're doing now. It's rather slow, but we'll have a good cheque by Christmas.'

'I'm half a mind to tell Warrigal to go back and say we're not on,' I said. 'Lots of other chaps would join without making any bones about it.'

'Hoo—hoo—hoo—hoo,' sounded once more the night-bird from the black tree outside.

'D—— the bird! I believe he's the devil in shape of a mopoke! And yet I don't like Starlight to think we're afraid. He and the old man might be in a fix and want help. Suppose we toss up?'

'All right,' says Jim, speaking rather slowly.

You couldn't tell from his face or voice how he felt about it; but I believe now—more than that, he let on once to me—that he was awfully cut up about my changing, and thought we were just in for a spell of straightforward work, and would stash the other thing for good and all.

We put the fire together. It burnt up bright for a bit. I pulled out a shilling.

'If it's head we go, Jim; if it's women, we stay here.'

I sent up the coin; we both bent over near the fire to look at it. The head was uppermost.

'Hoo—hoo—hoo—hoo,' came the night-bird's harsh croak.

There was a heavyish stake on that throw, if we'd only known. Only ruin—only death. Four men's lives lost, and three women made miserable for life.

Jim and I looked at one another. He smiled and opened the door.

'It's all the fault of that cursed owl, I believe,' he said; 'I'll have his life if he waits till it's daylight. We must be off early and get up our horses. I know what a long day for Warrigal and that ambling three-cornered devil of his means—seventy or eighty miles, if it's a yard.'

We slept sound enough till daybreak, and *could sleep* then, whatever was on the card. As for Jim, he slept like a baby always once he turned in. When I woke I got up at once. It was half dark; there was a little light in the east. But Warrigal had been out before me, and was leading his horse up to the hut with the hobbles in his hand.

Our horses were not far off; one of them had a bell on. Jim had his old brown, and I had a chestnut that I thought nearly as good. We weren't likely to have anything to ride that wasn't middlin' fast and plucky. Them that overhauled us would have to ride for it. We saddled up and took our blankets and what few things we couldn't do without. The rest stopped in the hut for any one that came after us. We left our wages, too, and never asked for 'em from that day to this. A trifle like that didn't matter after what we were going in for. More's the pity.

As we moved off my horse propped once or twice, and Warrigal looked at us in a queer side sort of way and showed his teeth a bit—smile nor laugh it wasn't, only a way he had when he thought he knew more than we did.

'My word! your horse's been where the feed's good. We're goin' a good way to-day. I wonder if they'll be as flash as they are now.'

'They'll carry us wherever that three-cornered mule of yours will shuffle to to-night,' said Jim. 'Never you mind about them. You ride straight, and don't get up to any monkey tricks, or, by George, I'll straighten you, so as you'll know better next time.'

'You know a lot, Jim Marston,' said the half-caste, looking at him with his long dark sleepy eyes which I always thought were like a half-roused snake's. 'Never mind, you'll know more one or these days. We'd better push on.'

He went off at a hand-gallop, and then pulled back into a long darting kind of canter, which Bilbah thought was quite the thing for a journey—anyhow, he never seemed to think of stopping it—went on mile after mile as if he was not going to pull up this side of sundown. A wiry brute, always in condition, was this said Bilbah, and just at this time as hard as nails. Our horses had been doing nothing lately, and being on good young feed had, of course, got fat, and were rather soft.

After four or five miles they began to blow. We couldn't well pull up; the ground was hard in places and bad for tracking. If we went on at the pace we should cook our horses. As soon as we got into a bit of open I raced up to him.

'Now, look here, Warrigal,' I said, 'you know why you're doing this, and so do I. Our horses are not up to galloping fifty or sixty miles on end just off a spell and with no work for months. If ycu don't pull up and go our pace I'll knock you off your horse.

'Oh! you're riled!' he said, looking as impudent as he dared, but slackening all the same. 'Pulled up before if I knowed your horses were getting baked. Thought they were up to anything, same as you and Jim.'

'So they are. You'll find that one of these days. If there's work ahead you ought to have sense enough not to knock smoke out of fresh horses before we begin.'

'All right. Plenty of work to do, my word. And Starlight said, "Tell 'em to be here to-day if they can." I know he's afraid of some one follerin' up our tracks, as it is.'

'That's all right, Warrigal; but you ride steady all the same, and don't be tearing away through thick timber, like a mallee scrubber that's got into the open and sees the devil behind him until he can get cover again. We shall be there to-night if it's not a hundred miles, and that's time enough.'

We did drop in for a long day, and no mistake. We only pulled up for a short halt in the middle, and Warrigal's cast-iron pony was off again, as if he was bound right away for the other side of the continent. However, though we were not going slow either, but kept up a reasonable fast pace, it must have been past midnight when we rode into Starlight's camp; very glad Jim and I were to see the fire—not a big one either. We had been taking it pretty easy, you see, for a month or two, and were not quite so ready for an eighty-mile ride as if we had been in something like training. The horses had had enough of it, too, though neither of them would give in, not if we'd ridden 'em twenty mile farther. As for Warrigal's Bilbah he was near as fresh as when he started, and kept tossin' his head an' amblin' and pacin' away as if he was walkin' for a wager round a ring in a show-yard.

As we rode up we could see a gunyah made out of boughs, and a longish wing of dogleg fence, made light but well put together. As soon as we got near enough a dog ran out and looked as if he was going to worry us; didn't bark either, but turned round and waited for us to get off.

'It's old Crib,' said Jim, with a big laugh; 'blest if it ain't. Father's somewhere handy. They're going to take up a back block and do the thing regular: Marston, Starlight, and Company—that's the fakement. They want us out to make dams or put up a woolshed or something. I don't see why they shouldn't, as well as Crossman and Fakesley. It's six of one and half-a-dozen of the other, as far as being on the square goes. Depend upon it, dad's turned over a new leaf.'

'Do you fellows want anything to eat?' said a voice that I knew to be Starlight's. 'If you do there's tea near the fire, and some grub in that flour bag. Help yourselves and hobble out your horses. We'll settle matters a bit in the morning. Your respected parent's abed in his own camp, and it's just as well not to wake him, unless you want his blessing ere you sleep.'

We went with Starlight to his gunyah. A path led through a clump of pines, so thick that a man might ride round it and never dream there was anything but more pines inside. A clear place had been made in the sandhill, and a snug crib enough rigged with saplings and a few sheets of bark. It was neat and tidy, like everything he had to do with. 'I was at sea when I was young,' he once said to Jim, when he was a bit 'on,' 'and a man learns to be neat there.' There was a big chimney outside, and a lot of leaves and rushes out of a swamp which he had made Warrigal gather.

'Put your blankets down there, boys, and turn in. You'll see how the land lies in the morning.' We didn't want asking twice, Jim's eyes were nigh shut as it was. The sun was up when we woke.

Outside the first thing we saw was father and Starlight talking. Both of these seemed a bit cranky. 'It's a d—— shame,' we heard Starlight say, as he turned and walked off. 'We could have done it well enough by ourselves.'

'I know what I'm about,' says father; 'it's all or none. What's the use of crying after being in it up to our neck?'

'Some day you'll think different,' says Starlight, looking back at him.

I often remembered it afterwards.

'Well, lads,' says father, looking straight at us, 'I wasn't sure as you'd come. Starlight has been barneying with me about sending for you. But we've got a big thing on now, and I thought you'd like to be in it.'

'We have come,' says I, pretty short. 'Now we're here what's the play called, and when does the curtain rise? We're on.' I was riled, vexed at Starlight talking as if we were children, and thought I'd show as we were men, like a young fool as I was.

'All right,' says father, and he sat down on a log, and began to tell us how there was any quantity of cattle running at the back where they were camped—a good lot strayed and mixed up, from the last dry season, and had never been mustered for years. The stockmen hardly ever came out till the autumn musters. One of the chaps that was in it knew all this side and had told them. They were going to muster for a month or so, and drive the mob right through to Adelaide. Store cattle were dear then, and we could get them off easy there and come back by sea. No one was to know we were not regular overlanders; and when we'd got the notes in our pockets it would be a hard matter to trace the cattle or prove that we were the men that sold 'em.

'How many head do you expect to get?' says Jim.

'A thousand or twelve hundred; half of 'em fat, and two-thirds of them young cattle.'

'By George! that's something like a haul; but you can't muster such a lot as that without a yard.'

'I know that,' says father. 'We're putting up a yard on a little plain about a mile from here. When they find it, it'll be an old nest, and the birds flown.'

'Well, if that ain't the cheekiest thing I ever heard tell of,' says I laughingly. 'To put up a yard at the back of a man's run, and muster his cattle for him! I never heard the like before, nor any one else. But suppose the cove or his men come across it?'

'‘Tain't no ways likely,' says father. 'They're the sleepiest lot of chaps in this frontage I ever saw. It's hardly worth while "touching"' them. There's no fun in it. It's like shooting pheasants when they ain't preserved. There's no risk, and when there's no risk there's no pleasure. Anyway that's my notion.'

'Talking about risks, why didn't you work that Marquis of Lorne racket better? We saw in the papers that the troopers hunted you so close you had to kill him in the ranges.'

Father looked over at us and then began to laugh—not long, and he broke off short. Laughing wasn't much in his line.

'Killed him, did we? And a horse worth nigh on to two thousand pounds. You ought to have known your old father better than that. We did kill *a* chestnut horse, one we picked out a purpose; white legs, white knee, short under lip, everything quite regular. We even fed him for a week on prairie grass, just like the Marquis had been eating. Bless you, we knew how to work all that. We deceived Windhall his own self, and he thinks he's pretty smart. No! the Marquis is all safe—you know where.'

I opened my eyes and stared at father.

'You've some call to crow if you can work things like that. How you ever got him away beats me; but not more than how you managed to keep him hid with a ring of troopers all round you from every side of the district.'

'We had friends,' father said. 'Me and Warrigal done all the travelling by night. No one but him could have gone afoot, I believe, much less led a blood horse through the beastly scrub and ranges he showed us. But the devil himself could not beat him and that little brute Bilbah in rough country.'

'I believe you,' I said, thinking of our ride yesterday. 'It's quite bad enough to follow him on level ground. But don't you think our tracks will be easy to follow with a thousand head of cattle before us? Any fool could do that.'

'It ain't that as I'm looking at,' said father; 'of course an old woman could do it, and knit stockings all the time; but our dart is to be off and have a month's start before anybody knows they are off the run. They won't think of mustering before fat cattle takes a bit of a turn. That won't be for a couple of months yet. Then they may catch us if they can.'

We had a long talk with Starlight, and what he said came to much the same. One stockman they had 'squared,' and he was to stand in. They had got two or three flash chaps to help muster and drive, who were to swear they thought we were dealers, and had bought cattle all right. One or two more were to meet us farther on. If we could get the cattle together and clear off before anything was suspected the rest was easy. The yard was nearly up, and Jim and I wired in and soon finished it. It didn't want very grand work putting into it as long as it would last our time. So we put it up roughly, but pretty strong, with pine saplings. The drawing in was the worst, for we had to 'hump' the most of them ourselves. Jim couldn't help bursting out laughing from time to time.

'It does seem such a jolly cheeky thing,' he said. 'Driving off a mob of cattle on the quiet I've known happen once or twice; but I'm dashed if ever I heard tell of putting up duffing improvements of a superior class on a cove's run and clearing off with a thousand drafted cattle, all quiet and regular, and him pottering about his home-station and never "dropping" to it no more than if he was in Sydney.'

'People ought to look after their stock closer than they do,' I said. 'It is their fault almost as much as ours. But they are too lazy to look after their own work, and too miserable to pay a good man to do it for them. They just get a half-and-half sort of fellow that'll take low wages and make it up with duffing, and of course he's not likely to look very sharp after the back country.'

'You're not far away,' says Jim; 'but don't you think they'd have to look precious sharp and get up very early in the morning to be level with chaps like father and Starlight, let alone Warrigal, who's as good by night as day? Then there's you and me. Don't try and make us out better than we are, Dick; we're all d—— scoundrels, that's the truth of it, and honest men haven't a chance with us, except in the long-run—except in the long-run. That's where they'll have us, Dick Martson.'

'That's quite a long speech for you, Jim,' I said; 'but it don't matter much that I know of whose fault it is that we're in this duffing racket. It seems to be our fate, as the chap says in the book. We'll have a jolly spree in Adelaide if this journey comes out right. And now let's finish this evening off. To-morrow they're going to yard the first mob.'

After that we didn't talk much except about the work. Starlight and Warrigal were out every day and all day. The three new hands were some chaps who formed part of a gang that did most of the horse-stealing in that neighbourhood, though they never showed up. The way they managed it was this: They picked up any good-looking nag or second-class racehorse that they fell across, and took them to a certain place. There they met another lot of fellows, who took the horses from them and cleared out to another colony; at the same time they left the horses they had brought. So each lot travelled different ways, and were sold in places where they were quite strange and no one was likely to claim them.

After a man had had a year or two at this kind of work, he was good, or rather bad, for anything. These young chaps, like us, had done pretty well at these games, and one of them, falling in with Starlight, had proposed to him to put up a couple of hundred head of cattle on Outer Back Momberah, as the run was called; then father and he had seen that a thousand were as easy to get as a hundred. Of course there was a risky feeling, but it wasn't such bad fun while it lasted. We were out all day running in the cattle. The horses were in good wind and condition now; we had plenty of rations—flour, tea, and sugar. There was no cart, but some good pack-horses, just the same as if we were a regular station party on our own run. Father had worked all that before we came. We had the best of fresh beef and veal too—you may be sure of that —there was no stint in that line; and at night we were always sure of a yarn from Starlight—that is, if he was in a good humour. Sometimes he wasn't, and then nobody dared speak to him, not even father.

He was an astonishing man, certainly. Jim and I used to wonder, by the hour, what he'd been in the old country. He'd been all over the world—in the Islands and New Zealand; in America, and among Malays and other strange people that we'd hardly ever heard of. Such stories as he'd tell us, too, about slaves and wild chiefs that he'd lived with and gone out to fight with against their enemy. 'People think a great deal of a dead man now and then in this innocent country,' he said once when the grog was uppermost; 'why, I've seen fifty men killed before breakfast, and in cold blood, too, chopped up alive, or next thing to it; and a drove of slaves—men, women, and children—as big nearly as our mob, handed over to a slave-dealer, and driven off in chains just as you'd start a lot of station cattle. They didn't like it, going off their run either, poor devils. The women would try and run back after their pickaninnies when they dropped, just like that heifer when Warrigal knocked her calf on the head to-day.' What a man he was! This was something like life, Jim and I thought. When we'd sold the cattle, if we got 'em down to Adelaide all right, we'd take a voyage to some foreign country, perhaps, and see sights too. What a paltry thing working for a pound a week seemed when a rise like this was to be made!

Well, the long and short of it is that we mustered the cattle quite comfortably, nobody coming anext or anigh us any more than if we'd taken the thing by contract. You wouldn't have thought there was anybody nearer than Bathurst. Everything seemed to be in our favour. So it was, just at the start. We drafted out all the worst and weediest of the cattle, besides all the old cows, and when we counted the mob out we had nearly eleven hundred first-rate store cattle; lots of fine young bullocks and heifers, more than half fat—altogether a prime well-bred mob that no squatter or dealer could fault in any way if the price was right. We could afford to sell them for a shade under market price for cash. Ready money, of course, we were bound to have.

Just as we were starting there was a fine roan bull came running up with a small mob.

'Cut him out, and beat him back,' says father; 'we don't want to be bothered with the likes of him.'

'Why, I'm dashed if that ain't Hood's imported bull,' says Billy the Boy, a Monaro native that we had with us. 'I know him well. How's he come to get back? Why, the cove gave two hundred and fifty notes for him afore he left England, I've heard 'em say.'

'Bring him along,' said Starlight, who came up just then. 'In for a penny, in for a pound. They'll never think of looking for him on the Coorong, and we'll be there before they miss any cattle worth talking about.'

So we took 'Fifteenth Duke of Cambridge' along with us; a red roan he was, with a little white about the flank. He wasn't more than four year old. He'd been brought out from England as a yearling. How he'd worked his way out to this back part of the run, where a bull of his quality ain't often seen, nobody could say. But he was a lively, active beast, and he'd got into fine hard fettle with living on saltbush, dry grass, and scrub for the last few months, so he could travel as well as the others. I took particular notice of him, from his little waxy horns to his straight locks and long square quarters. And so I'd need to—but that came after. He had only a little bit of a private brand on the shoulder. That was easily faked, and would come out quite different.

CHAPTER XII

WE didn't go straight ahead along any main track to the Lower
Murray and Adelaide exactly. That would have been a little too
open and barefaced. No; we divided the mob into three, and settled
where to meet in about a fortnight. Three men to each mob. Father
and Warrigal took one lot; they had the dog, old Crib, to help them.
He was worth about two men and a boy. Starlight, Jim, and I had
another; and the three stranger chaps another. We'd had a couple
of knockabouts to help with the cooking and stockyard work. They
were paid by the job. They were to stay at the camp for a week,
to burn the gunyahs, knock down the yard, and blind the track as
much as they could.

Some of the cattle we'd left behind they drove back and forward
across the track every day for a week. If rain came they were to
drop it, and make their way into the frontage by another road. If
they heard about the job being blown or the police set on our track,
they were to wire to one of the border townships we had to pass.
Weren't we afraid of their selling us? No, not much; they were well
paid, and had often given father and Starlight information before,
though they took care never to show out in the cattle or horse-stealing way themselves. As long as chaps in our line have money to
spend, they can always get good information, and other things too.
It is when the money runs short that the danger comes in. I don't
know whether cattle-duffing was ever done in New South Wales
before on such a large scale, or whether it will ever be done again.
Perhaps not. These wire fences stop a deal of cross-work; but it
was done then, you take my word for it—a man's word as hasn't
that long to live that it's worth while to lie—and it all came out right;
that is as far as our getting safe over, selling the cattle, and having
the money in our pockets.

We kept on working by all sorts of outside tracks on the main
line of road—a good deal by night, too—for the first two or three
hundred miles. After we crossed the Adelaide border we followed
the Darling down to the Murray. We thought we were all right,
and got bolder. Starlight had changed his clothes, and was dressed
like a swell—away on a roughish trip, but still like a swell.

'They were his cattle; he had brought them from one of his
stations on the Narran. He was going to take up country in the
Northern Territory. He expected a friend out from England with a
lot more capital.'

Jim and I used to hear him talking like this to some of the squatters whose runs we passed through, as grave as you please. They used to ask him to stay all night, but he always said 'he didn't like to leave his men. He made it a practice on the road.' When we got within a fortnight's drive of Adelaide, he rode in and lived at one of the best hotels. He gave out that he expected a lot of cattle to arrive, and got a friend that he'd met in the billiard-room (and couldn't he play surprisin'?) to introduce him to one of the leading stock agents there. So he had it all cut and dry, when one day Warrigal and I rode in, and the boy handed him a letter, touching his hat respectfully, as he had been learned to do, before a lot of young squatters and other swells that he was going out to a picnic with.

'My confounded cattle come at last,' he says. 'Excuse me for mentioning business. I began to hope they'd never come; 'pon my soul I did. The time passes so deuced pleasantly here. Well, they'll all be at the yards to-morrow. You fellows had all better come and see them sold. There'll be a little lunch, and perhaps some fizz. You go to the stock agents, Runnimall and Co.; here's their address, Jack,' he says to me, looking me straight in the eyes. 'They'll send a man to pilot you to the yards; and now off with you, and don't let me see your face till to-morrow.'

How he carried it off! He cantered away with the rest of the party, as if he hadn't a thought in the world except about pleasure and honest business. Nobody couldn't have told that he wasn't just like them other young gentlemen with only their stock and station to think about, and a little run at the races now and then. And what a risk he was running every minute of his life, he and all the rest of us. I wasn't sorry to be out of the town again. There were lots of police, too. Suppose one of them was to say, 'Richard Marston, I arrest you for——' It hardly mattered what. I felt as if I should have tumbled down with sheer fright and cowardliness. It's a queer thing you feel like that off and on. Other times a man has as much pluck in him as if his life was worth fighting for—which it isn't.

The agent knew all about us (or thought he did), and sent a chap to show Mr. Carisforth's cattle (Charles Carisforth, Esq., of Sturton, Yorkshire and Banda, Waroona, and Ebor Downs, New South Wales; that was the name he went by) to the way to the yards. We were to draft them all next morning into separate pens—cows and bullocks, steers and heifers, and so on. He expected to sell them all to a lot of farmers and small settlers that had taken up a new district lately and were very short of stock.

'You couldn't have come into a better market, young fellow,' says the agent's man to me. 'Our boss he's advertised 'em that well as there'll be smart bidding between the farmers and some of the squatters. Good store cattle's been scarce, and these is in such rattling condition. That's what'll sell 'em. Your master seems a regular free-handed sort of chap. He's the jolliest squatter there's been in town these years, I hear folk say. Puts 'em in mind of Hawdon and Evelyn Sturt in the old overlander days.'

Next day we were at the yards early, you bet. We wanted to have time to draft them into pens of twenty to fifty each, so that the farmers and small settlers might have a chance to buy. Besides, it was the last day of our work. Driving all day and watching half the night is pretty stiffish work, good weather and bad, when you've got to keep it up for months at a time, and we'd been three months and a week on the road.

The other chaps were wild for a spree. Jim and I had made up our minds to be careful; still, we had a lot to see in a big town like Adelaide; for we'd never been to Sydney even in our lives, and we'd never seen the sea. That was something to look at for the first time, wasn't it?

Well, we got the cattle drafted to rights, every sort and size and age by itself, as near as could be. That's the way to draft stock, whether they're cattle, sheep, or horses; then every man can buy what he likes best, and isn't obliged to lump up one sort with another. We had time to have a bit of dinner. None of us had touched a mouthful since before daylight. Then we began to see the buyers come.

There'd been a big tent rigged, as big as a small woolshed, too. It came out in a cart, and then another cart came with a couple of waiters, and they laid out a long table of boards on trestles with a real first-class feed on it, such as we'd never seen in our lives before. Fowls and turkeys and tongues and rounds of beef, beer and wine in bottles with gilt labels on. Such a set-out it was. Father began to growl a bit. 'If he's going to feed the whole country this way, he'll spend half the stuff before we get it, let alone drawing a down on the whole thing.' But Jim and me could see how Starlight had been working the thing to rights while he was swelling it in the town among the big bugs. We told him the cattle would fetch that much more money on account of the lunch and the blowing the auctioneer was able to do. These would pay for the feed and the rest of the fal-lals ten times over. 'When he gets in with men like his old pals he loses his head, I believe,' father says, 'and fancies he's what he used to be. He'll get "fitted" quite simple some day if he doesn't keep a better look-out.'

That might be, but it wasn't to come about this time. Starlight came riding out by and by, dressed up like a real gentleman, and lookin' so different that Jim and I hardly dared speak to him—on a splendid horse too (not Rainbow, he'd been left behind; he was always left within a hundred miles of the Hollow, and he could do it in one day if he was wanted to), and a lot of fine dressed chaps with him—young squatters and officers, and what not. I shouldn't have been surprised if he'd had the Governor out with him. They told us afterwards he did dine at Government House reg'lar, and was made quite free and welcome there.

Well, he jumps down and shakes hands with us before them all. 'Well, Jack! Well, Bill!' and so on, calls us his good faithful fellows, and how well we'd brought the cattle over; nods to father, who didn't seem able to take it all in; says he'll back us against any stockmen in Australia; has up Warrigal and shows him off to the company. 'Most intelligent lad.' Warrigal grinned and showed his white teeth. It was as good as a play.

Then everybody goes to lunch—swells and selectors, Germans and Paddies, natives and immigrants, a good many of them, too, and there was eating and drinking and speechifying till all was blue. By-and-by the auctioneer looks at his watch. He'd had a pretty good tuck-in himself, and they must get to business.

Father opened his eyes at the price the first pen brought, all prime young bullocks, half fat most of them. Then they all went off like wildfire; the big men and the little men bidding, quite jealous, sometimes one getting the lot, sometimes another. One chap made a remark about there being such a lot of different brands; but Starlight said they'd come from a sort of depôt station of his, and were the odds and ends of all the mobs of store cattle that he'd purchased the last four years. That satisfied 'em, particularly as he said it in a careless, fierce way which he could put on, as if it was like a man's —— impudence to ask him anything. It made the people laugh; I could see that.

By-and-by we comes to the imported bull. He was in a pen by himself, looking first-rate. His brand had been faked, and the hair had grown pretty well. It would have took a sharp hand to know him again.

'Well, gentlemen,' says the auctioneer, 'here is the imported bull "Duke of Brunswick." It ain't often an animal of his quality comes in with a mob of store cattle; but I am informed by Mr. Carisforth that he left orders for the whole of the cattle to be cleared off the run, and this valuable animal was brought away in mistake. He was to return by sea; but as he happens to be here to-day, why, sooner than disappoint any intending buyer, Mr. Carisforth has given me instructions to put him up, and if he realises anything near his value he will be sold.'

'Yes!' drawls Starlight, as if a dozen imported bulls, more or less, made no odds to him, 'put him up, by all means, Mr. Runnimall. Expectin' rather large shipment of Bates's "Duchess" tribe next month. Rather prefer them on the whole. The "Duke" here is full of Booth blood, so he may just as well go with the others. I shall never get what he cost, though; I know that. He's been a most expensive animal to me.'

Many a true word spoken in jest. He had good call to know him, as well as the rest of us, for a most expensive animal, before all was said and done. What he cost us all round it would be hard indeed to cipher up.

Anyhow, there was a great laugh at Starlight's easy way of taking it. First one and then another of the squatters that was going in for breeding began to bid, thinking he'd go cheap, until they got warm, and the bull went up to a price that we never dreamed he'd fetch. Everything seemed to turn out lucky that day. One would have thought they'd never seen an imported bull before. The young squatters got running one another, as I said before, and he went up to £270! Then the auctioneer squared off the accounts as sharp as he could; an' it took him all his time, what with the German and the small farmers, who took their time about it, paying in greasy notes and silver and copper, out of canvas bags, and the squatters, who were too busy chaffing and talking among themselves to pay at all. It was dark before everything was settled up, and all the lots of cattle delivered. Starlight told the auctioneer he'd see him at his office, in a deuced high and mighty kind of way, and rode off with his new friend.

All of us went back to our camp. Our work was over, but we had to settle up among ourselves and divide shares. I could hardly believe my eyes when I saw the cattle all sold and gone, and nothing left at the camp but the horses and the swags.

When we got there that night it was late enough. After tea father and I and Jim had a long yarn, settling over what we should do and wondering whether we were going to get clean away with our share of the money after all.

'By George!' says Jim, 'it's a big touch, and no mistake. To think of our getting over all right, and selling out so easy, just as if they was our own cattle. Won't there be a jolly row when it's all out, and the Momberah people miss their cattle?' (more than half 'em was theirs). 'And when they muster they can't be off seein' they're some hundreds short.'

'That's what's botherin' me,' says father. 'I wish Starlight hadn't been so thundering flash with it all. It'll draw more notice on us, and every one'll be gassin' about his big sale, and all that, till people's set on to ask where the cattle come from, and what not.'

'I don't see as it makes any difference,' I said. 'Somebody was bound to buy 'em, and we'd have had to give the brands and receipts just the same. Only if we'd sold to any one that thought there was a cross look about it, we'd have had to take half money, that's all. They've fetched a rattling price, through Starlight's working the oracle with those swells, and no mistake.'

'Yes, but that ain't all of it,' says the old man, filling his pipe. 'We've got to look at what comes after. I never liked that imported bull being took. They'll rake all the colonies to get hold of him again, partic'ler as he sold for near three hundred pound.'

'We must take our share of the risk along with the money,' said Jim. 'We shall have our whack of that according to what they fetched to-day. It'll be a short life and a merry one, though, dad, if we go on big licks like this. What'll we tackle next—a bank or Government House?'

'Nothing at all for a good spell, if you've any sense,' growled father. 'It'll give us all we know to keep dark when this thing gets into the papers, and the police in three colonies are all in full cry like a pack of beagles. The thing is, what'll be our best dart now?'

'I'll go back overland,' says he. 'Starlight's going to take Warrigal with him, and they'll be off to the islands for a turn. If he knows what's best for him, he'll never come back. These other chaps say they'll separate and sell their horses when they get over to the Murray low down, and work their way up by degrees. Which way are you boys going?'

'Jim and I to Melbourne by next steamer,' I said. 'May as well see a bit of life now we're in it. We'll come back overland when we're tired of strange faces.'

'All right,' says father, 'they won't know where I'm lyin' by for a bit, I'll go bail, and the sooner you clear out of Adelaide the better. News like ours don't take long to travel, and you might be nabbed very simple. One of ye write a line to your mother and tell her where you're off to, or she'll be frettin' herself and the gal too—frettin' over what can't be helped. But I suppose it's the natur' o' some women.'

We done our settling-up next day. All the sale money was paid over to Starlight. He cashed the cheques and drew the lot in notes and gold—such a bundle of 'em there was. He brought them out to us at the camp, and then we 'whacked' the lot. There were eight of us that had to share and share alike. How much do you think we had to divide? Why, not a penny under four thousands pounds. It had to be divided among the eight of us. That came to five hundred a man. A lot of money to carry about, that was the worst of it.

Next day there was a regular split and squander. We didn't wait long after daylight, you bet. Father was off and well on his way before the stars were out of the sky. He took Warrigal's horse, Bilbah, back with him; he and Starlight was going off to the islands together, and couldn't take horses with them. But he was real sorry to part with the cross-grained varmint; I thought he was going to blubber when he saw father leading him off. Bilbah wouldn't go neither at first; pulled back, and snorted and went on as if he'd never seen only one man afore in his life. Father got vexed at last and makes a sign to old Crib; he fetches him such a 'heeler' as gave him something else to think of for a few miles. He didn't hang back much after that.

The three other chaps went their own road. They kept very dark all through. I know their names well enough, but there's no use in bringing them up now.

Jim and I cuts off into the town, thinking we was due for a little fun. We'd never been in a big town before, and it was something new to us. Adelaide ain't as grand quite as Melbourne or Sydney, but there's something quiet and homelike about it to my thinking—great wide streets, planted with trees; lots of steady-going German farmers, with their vineyards and orchards and droll little waggons. The women work as hard as the men, harder perhaps, and get brown and scorched up in no time—not that they've got much good looks to lose; leastways none we ever saw.

We could always tell the German farmers' places along the road from one of our people by looking outside the door. If it was an Englishman or an Australian, you'd see where they'd throwed out the teapot leavings; if it was a German, you wouldn't see nothing. They drink their own sour wine, if their vines are old enough to make any, or else hop beer, but they won't lay out their money in the tea chest or sugar bag; no fear, or the grog either, and not far wrong. Then the sea! I can see poor old Jim's face now the day we went down to the port and he seen it for the first time.

'So we've got to the big waterhole at last,' he said. 'Don't it make a man feel queer and small to think of its going away right from here where we stand to the other side of the world? It's a long way across.'

'Jim,' says I, 'and to think we've lived all our lives up to this time and never set eyes on it before. Don't it seem as if one was shut up in the bush, or tied to a gum tree, so as one can never have a chance to see anything? I wonder we stayed in it so long.'

'It's not a bad place, though it is rather slow and wired in some-times,' says Jim. 'We might be sorry we ever left it yet. When does the steamer go to Melbourne?'

'The day after to-morrow.'

'I'll be glad to be clear off; won't you?'

We went to the theatre that night, and amused ourselves pretty well next day and till the time came for our boat to start for Melbourne. We had altered ourselves a bit, had our hair cut and our beards trimmed by the hairdresser. We bought fresh clothes, and what with this, and the feeling of being in a new place and having more money in our pockets than we'd ever dreamed about before, we looked so transmogrified when we saw ourselves in the glass that we hardly knew ourselves. We had to change our names, too, for the first time in our lives; and it went harder against the grain than you'd think, for all we were a couple of cattle-duffers, with a warrant apiece sure to be after us before the year was out.

'It sounds ugly,' says Jim, after we had given our names as John Simmons and Henry Smith at the hotel where we put up at till the steamer was ready to start. 'I never thought that Jim Marston was to come to this—to be afraid to tell a fat, greasy-looking fellow like that innkeeper what his real name was. Seems such a pitiful mean lie, don't it, Dick?'

'It isn't so bad as being called No. 14, No. 221, as they sing out for the fellows in Berrima Gaol. How would you like that, Jim?'

'I'd blow my brains out first,' cried out Jim, 'or let some other fellow do it for me. It wouldn't matter which.'

It was very pleasant, those two or three days in Adelaide, if they'd only lasted. We used to stroll about the lighted streets till all hours, watching the people and the shops and everything that makes a large city different from the country. The different sorts of people, the carts and carriages, buggies and drays, pony-carriages and spring-carts, all jumbled up together; even the fruit and flowers and oysters and fish under the gas-lights seemed strange and wonderful to us. We felt as if we would have given all the world to have got mother and Aileen down to see it all. Then Jim gave a groan.

'Only to think,' says he, 'that we might have had all this fun some day, and bought and paid for it honest. Now it isn't paid for. It's out of some other man's pocket. There's a curse on it; it will have to be paid in blood or prison time before all's done. I could shoot myself for being such a cursed fool.'

'Too late to think of that,' I said; 'we'll have some fun in Melbourne for a bit, anyhow. For what comes after we must "chance it," as we've done before, more than once or twice, either.'

. . . .

Next day our steamer was to sail. We got Starlight to come down with us and show us how to take our passage. We'd never done it before, and felt awkward at it. He'd made up his mind to go to New Zealand, and after that to Honolulu, perhaps to America.

'I'm not sure that I'll ever come back, boys,' he said, 'and if I were you I don't think I would either. If you get over to San Francisco you'd find the Pacific Slope a very pleasant country to live in. The people and the place would suit you all to pieces. At any rate I'd stay away for a few years and wait till all this blows over.'

I wasn't sorry when the steamer cleared the port, and got out of sight of land. There we were—where we'd never been before—in blue water. There was a stiff breeze, and in half-an-hour we shouldn't have turned our heads if we'd seen Hood and the rest of 'em come riding after us on seahorses, with warrants as big as the mainsail. Jim made sure he was going to die straight off, and the pair of us wished we'd never seen Outer Back Momberah, nor Hood's cattle, nor Starlight, nor Warrigal. We almost made up our minds to keep straight and square to the last day of our lives. However, the wind died down a bit next day, and we both felt a lot better—better in body and worse in mind—as often happens. Before we got to Melbourne we could eat and drink, smoke and gamble, and were quite ourselves again. We'd laid it out to have a reg'lar good month of it in town, takin' it easy, and stopping nice and quiet at a good hotel, havin' some reasonable pleasure. Why shouldn't we see a little life? We'd got the cash, and we'd earned that pretty hard. It's the hardest earned money of all, that's got on the cross, if fellows only knew, but they never do till it's too late.

When we got tired of doing nothing, and being in a strange place, we'd get across the border, above Albury somewhere, and work on the mountain runs till shearing came round again; and we could earn a fairish bit of money. Then we'd go home for Christmas after it was all over, and see mother and Aileen again. How glad and frightened they'd be to see us. It wouldn't be safe altogether, but go we would.

CHAPTER XIII

WE got to Melbourne all right, and though it's a different sort of a place from Sydney, it's a jolly enough town for a couple of young chaps with money in their pockets. Most towns are, for the matter of that. We took it easy, and didn't go on the spree or do anything foolish. No, we weren't altogether so green as that. We looked out for a quiet place to lodge, near the sea—St. Kilda they call it, in front of the beach—and we went about and saw all the sights, and for a time managed to keep down the thought that perhaps sooner or later we'd be caught, and have to stand our trial for this last affair of ours, and maybe one or two others. It wasn't a nice thing to think of; and now and then it used to make both of us take an extra drop of grog by way of driving the thoughts of it out of our heads. That's the worst of not being straight and square. A man's almost driven to drink when he can't keep from thinking of all sorts of miserable things day and night. We used to go to the horse-yards now and then, and the cattle-yards, too. It was like old times to see the fat cattle and sheep penned up at Flemington, and the butchers riding out on their spicy nags or driving trotters. But their cattle-yards was twice as good as ours, and me and Jim used often to wonder why the Sydney people hadn't managed to have something like them all these years, instead of the miserable cockatoo things at Homebush that we'd often heard the drovers and squatters grumble about.

However, one day, as we was sitting on the rails, talking away quite comfortable, we heard one butcher say to another, 'My word, this is a smart bit of cattle-duffing—a thousand head, too!' 'What's that?' says the other man. 'Why, haven't you heard of it?' says the first one, and he pulls a paper out of his pocket, with this in big letters: 'Great Cattle Robbery.—A thousand head of Mr. Hood's cattle were driven off and sold in Adelaide. Warrants are out for the suspected parties, who are supposed to have left the colony.' Here was a bit of news! We felt as if we could hardly help falling off the rails; but we didn't show it, of course, and sat there for half-an-hour, talking to the buyers and sellers and cracking jokes like the others. But we got away home as soon as we could, and then we began to settle what we should do.

Warrants were out, of course, for Starlight, and us, too. He was known, and so were we. Our descriptions were sure to be ready to send out all over the country. Warrigal they mightn't have noticed. It was common enough to have a black boy or a half-caste with a lot

of travelling cattle. Father had not shown up much. He had an old
pea-jacket on, and they mightn't have dropped down to him or the
three other chaps that were in it with us; they were just like any
other road hands. But about there being warrants out, with descriptions, in all the colonies, for a man to be identified, but generally
known as Starlight, and for Richard and James Marston, we were
as certain as that we were in St. Kilda, in a nice quiet little inn, over-
looking the beach; and what a murder it was to have to leave it at all.

Leave the place we had to do at once. It wouldn't do to be strollin'
about Melbourne with the chance of every policeman we met taking
a look at us to see if we tallied with a full description they had at
the office: 'Richard and James Marston are twenty-five and twenty-
two, respectively; both tall and strongly built; having the appearance
of bushmen. Richard Marston has a scar on left temple. James
Marston has lost a front tooth,' and so on. When we came to think
of it, they couldn't be off knowing us, if they took it into their heads
to bail us up any day. They had our height and make. We couldn't
help looking like bushmen—like men that had been in the open air all
their lives, and that had a look as if saddle and bridle rein were more
in our way than the spade and plough-handle. We couldn't wash
the tan off our skins; faces, necks, arms, all showed pretty well that
we'd come from where the sun was hot, and that we'd had our share
of it. They had my scar, got in a row, and Jim's front tooth, knocked
out by a fall from a horse when he was a boy; there was nothing for
it but to cut and run.

'It was time for us to go, my boys,' as the song the Yankee sailor
sung us one night runs, and then, which way to go? Every ship was
watched that close a strange rat couldn't get a passage, and, besides,
we had that feeling we didn't like to clear away altogether out of the
old country; there was mother and Aileen still in it, and every man,
woman, and child that we'd known ever since we were born. A
chap feels that, even if he ain't much good other ways. We couldn't
stand the thought of clearin' out for America, as Starlight advised us.
It was like death to us, so we thought we'd chance it somewhere in
Australia for a bit longer.

Now where we put up a good many drovers from Gippsland used
to stay, as they brought in cattle from there. The cattle had to be
brought over Swanston Street Bridge and right through the town after
twelve o'clock at night. We'd once or twice, when we'd been out
late, stopped to look at them, and watched the big heavy bullocks and
fat cows staring and starting and slipping all among the lamps and
pavements, with the street all so strange and quiet, and laughed at
the notion of some of the shopkeepers waking up and seeing a couple
of hundred wild cattle, with three or four men behind 'em, shoul-
dering and horning one another, then rushing past their doors at a
hard trot, or breaking into a gallop for a bit.

Some of these chaps, seeing we was cattle-men and knew most things in that line, used to open out about where they'd come from, and what a grand place Gippsland was—splendid grass country, rivers that run all the year round, great fattening country; and snowy mountains at the back, keeping everything cool in the summer. Some of the mountain country, like Omeo, that they talked a lot of, seemed about one of the most out-of-the-way places in the world. More than that, you could get back to old New South Wales by way of the Snowy River, and then on to Monaro. After that we knew where we were.

Going away was easy enough, in a manner of speaking; but we'd been a month in Melbourne, and when you mind that we were not bad-looking chaps, fairishly dressed, and with our pockets full of money, it was only what might be looked for if we had made another friend or two besides Mrs. Morrison, the landlady of our inn, and Gippsland drovers. When we had time to turn round a bit in Melbourne, of course we began to make a few friends. Wherever a man goes, unless he keeps himself that close that he won't talk to any one or let any one talk to him, he's sure to find some one he likes to be with better than another. If he's old and done with most of his fancies except smokin' and drinkin' it's a man. If he's young and got his life before him it's a woman. So Jim and I hadn't been a week in Melbourne before we fell across of couple of—well, friends—that we were hard set to leave. It was a way of mine to walk down to the beach every evening and have a look at the boats in the bay and the fishermen, if there were any—anything that might be going on. Sometimes a big steamer would be coming in, churning the water under her paddles and tearing up the bay like a hundred bunyips. The first screw-boat Jim and I saw we couldn't make out for the life of us what she moved by. We thought all steamers had paddles. Then the sailing-boats, flying before the breeze like seagulls, and the waves, if it was a rough day, rolling and beating and thundering on the beach. I generally stayed till the stars came out before I went back to the hotel. Everything was so strange and new to a man who'd seen so little else except green trees that I was never tired of watching, and wondering, and thinking what a little bit of a shabby world chaps like us lived in that never seen anything but a slab hut, maybe, all the year round, and a bush public on high days and holidays.

Sometimes I used to feel as if we hadn't done such a bad stroke in cutting loose from all this. But then the horrible feeling would come back of never being safe, even for a day, of being dragged off and put in the dock, and maybe shut up for years and years. Sometimes I used to throw myself down upon the sand and curse the day when I ever did anything that I had any call to be ashamed of and put myself in the power of everything bad and evil in all my life through.

Well, one day I was strolling along, thinking about these things, and wondering whether there was any other country where a man could go and feel himself safe from being hounded down for the rest of his life, when I saw a woman walking on the beach ahead of me. I came up with her before long, and as I passed her she turned her head and I saw she was one of two girls that we had seen in the landlady's parlour one afternoon. The landlady was a good, decent Scotch woman, and had taken a fancy to both of us (particularly to Jim—as usual). She thought—she was that simple—that we were up-country squatters from some far-back place, or overseers. Something in the sheep or cattle line everybody could see that we were. There was no hiding that. But we didn't talk about ourselves overmuch, for very good reasons. The less people say the more others will wonder and guess about you. So we began to be looked upon as bosses of some sort, and to be treated with a lot of respect that we hadn't been used to much before. So we began to talk a bit—natural enough—this girl and I. She was a good-looking girl, with a wonderful fresh clear skin, full of life and spirits, and pretty well taught. She and her sister had not been a long time in the country; their father was dead, and they had to live by keeping a very small shop and by dress-making. They were some kind of cousins of the landlady and the same name, so they used to come and see her of evenings and Sundays. Her name was Kate Morrison and her sister's was Jeanie. This and a lot more she told me before we got back to the hotel, where she said she was going to stay that night and keep Mrs. Morrison company.

After this we began to be a deal better acquainted. It all came easy enough. The landlady thought she was doing the girls a good turn by putting them in the way of a couple of hard-working well-to-do fellows like us; and as Jim and the younger one, Jeanie, seemed to take a fancy to each other, Mrs. Morrison used to make up boating parties, and we soon got to know each other well enough to be joked about falling in love and all the rest of it.

After a bit we got quite into the way of calling for Kate and Jeanie after their day's work was done, and taking them out for a walk. I don't know that I cared so much for Kate in those days anyhow, but by degrees we got to think that we were what people call in love with each other. It went deeper with her than me, I think. It mostly does with women. I never really cared for any woman in the world except Gracey Storefield, but she was far away, and I didn't see much likelihood of my being able to live in that part of the world, much less to settle down and marry there. So, though we'd broken a six-pence together and I had my half, I looked upon her as ever so much beyond me and out of my reach, and didn't see any harm in amusing myself with any woman that I might happen to fall across.

So, partly from idleness, partly from liking, and partly seeing that the girl had made up her mind to throw in her lot with me for good and all, I just took it as it came; but it meant a deal more than that, if I could have foreseen the end.

I hadn't seen a great many women, and had made up my mind that, except a few bad ones, they was mostly of one sort—good to lead, not hard to drive, and, above all, easy to see through and understand.

I often wonder what there was about this Kate Morrison to make her so different from other women; but she was born unlike them, I expect. Anyway, I never met another woman like her. She wasn't out-and-out handsome, but there was something very taking about her. Her figure was pretty near as good as a woman's could be; her step was light and active; her feet and hands were small, and she took a pride in showing them. I never thought she had any temper different from other women; but if I'd noticed her eyes, surely I'd have seen it there. There was something very strange and out of the way about them. They hardly seemed so bright when you looked at them first; but by degrees, if she got roused and set up about anything, they'd begin to burn with a steady sort of glitter that got fiercer and brighter till you'd think they'd burn everything they looked at. The light in them didn't go out again in a hurry, either. It seemed as if those wonderful eyes would keep on shining, whether their owner wished it or not.

I didn't find out all about her nature at once—trust a woman for that. Vain and fond of pleasure I could see she was; and from having been always poor, in a worrying, miserable, ill-contented way, she had got to be hungry for money and jewels and fine clothes; just like a person that's been starved and shivering with cold longs for a fire and a full meal and a warm bed. Some people like these things when they can get them; but others never seem to think about anything else, and would sell their souls or do anything in the whole world to get what their hearts are set on. When men are like this they're dangerous, but they hardly hurt anybody, only themselves. When women are born with hearts of this sort it's a bad look-out for everybody they come near. Kate Morrison could see that I had money. She thought I was rich, and she made up her mind to attract me, and go shares in my property, whatever it might be. She won over her younger sister, Jeanie, to her plans, and our acquaintance was part of a regular put-up scheme. Jeanie was a soft, good-tempered, good-hearted girl, with beautiful fair hair, blue eyes, and the prettiest mouth in the world. She was as good as she was pretty, and would have worked away without grumbling in that dismal little shop from that day to this, if she'd been let alone. She was only just turned seventeen. She soon got to like Jim a deal too well for her own good, and used to listen to his talk about the country across the border, and such simple yarns as he could tell her, poor old Jim! until she said she'd go and live with him under a salt-bush if he'd come back and marry her after Christmas. And of course he did promise.

He didn't see any harm in that. He intended to come back if he could, and so did I for that matter. Well, the long and short of it was that we were both regularly engaged and had made all kinds of plans to be married at Christmas and go over to Tasmania or New Zealand, when this terrible blow fell upon us like a shell. I did see one explode at a review in Melbourne—and, my word! what a scatteration it made.

Well, we had to let Kate and Jeanie know the best way we could that our business required us to leave Melbourne at once, and that we shouldn't be back till after Christmas, if then.

It was terrible hard work to make out any kind of a story that would do. Kate questioned and cross-questioned me about the particular kind of business that called us away like a lawyer (I've seen plenty of that since) until at last I was obliged to get a bit cross and refuse to answer any more questions.

Jeanie took it easier, and was that down-hearted and miserable at parting with Jim that she hadn't the heart to ask any questions of anyone, and Jim looked about as dismal as she did. They sat with their hands in each other's till it was nearly twelve o'clock, when the old mother came and carried the girls off to bed. We had to start at daylight next morning; but we made up our minds to leave them a hundred pounds apiece to keep for us until we came back, and promised if we were alive to be at St. Kilda next January, which they had to be contented with.

Jeanie did not want to take the money; but Jim said he'd very likely lose it, and so persuaded her.

We were miserable and low-spirited enough ourselves at the idea of going away all in a hurry. We had come to like Melbourne, and had bit by bit cheated ourselves into thinking that we might live comfortably and settle down in Victoria, out of reach of our enemies, and perhaps live and die unsuspected.

From this dream we were roused up by the confounded advertisement. Detectives and constables would be seen to be pretty thick in all the colonies, and we could not reasonably expect not to be taken some time or other, most likely before another week.

We thought it over and over again, in every way. The more we thought over it the more dangerous it seemed to stop in Melbourne. There was only one thing for it, that was to go straight out of the country. The Gippsland men were the only bushmen we knew at all well, and perhaps that door might shut soon.

So we paid our bill. They thought us a pair of quiet, respectable chaps at that hotel, and never would believe otherwise. People may say what they like, but it's a great thing to have some friends that can say of you—

'Well, I never knew no harm of him; a better-tempered chap couldn't be; and all the time we knowed him he was that particular about his bills and money matters that a banker couldn't have been more regular. He may have had his faults, but we never seen 'em. I believe a deal that was said of him wasn't true, and nothing won't ever make me believe it.'

These kind of people will stand up for you all the days of your life, and stick to you till the very last moment, no matter what you turn out to be. Well, there's something pleasant in it; and it makes you think human nature ain't quite such a low and paltry thing as some people tries to make out. Anyhow, when we went away our good little landlady and her sister was that sorry to lose us, as you'd have thought they was our blood relations. As for Jim, everyone in the house was fit to cry when he went off, from the dogs and cats upwards. Jim never was in no house where everybody didn't seem to take naturally to him. Poor old Jim!

We bought a couple of horses, and rode away down to Sale with these chaps that had sold their cattle in Melbourne and was going home. It rained all the way, and it was the worst road by chalks we'd ever seen in our lives; but the soil was wonderful, and the grass was something to talk about; we'd hardly ever seen anything like it. A few thousand acres there would keep more stock than half the country we'd been used to.

We didn't stay more than a day or so in Sale. Every morning at breakfast someone was sure to turn up the paper and begin jabbering about the same old infernal business, Hood's cattle, and what a lot were taken, and whether they'll catch Starlight, and the other men, and so on.

We heard of a job at Omeo while we were in Sale, which we thought would just about suit us. All the cattle on a run there were to be mustered and delivered to a firm of stock agents that had bought them; they wanted people to do it by contract at so much a head. Anybody who took it must have money enough to buy stock horses. The price per head was pretty fair, what would pay well, and we made up our minds to go in for it.

So we made a bargain; bought two more horses each, and started away for Omeo. It was near 200 miles from where we were. We got up there all right, and found a great rich country with a big lake, I don't know how many feet above the sea. The cattle were as wild as hares, but the country was pretty good to ride over. We were able to keep our horses in good condition in the paddocks, and when we had mustered the whole lot we found we had a handsome cheque to get.

It was a little bit strange buckling to after the easy life we'd led for the last few months; but after a day or two we found ourselves as good men as ever, and could spin over the limestone boulders and through the thick mountain timber as well as ever we did. A man soon gets right again in the fresh air of the bush; and as it used to snow there every now and then the air was pretty fresh, you bet, particularly in the mornings and evenings.

After we'd settled up we made up our minds to get as far as Monaro, and wait there for a month or two. After that we might go in for the shearing till Christmas, and then whatever happened we would both make a strike back for home, and have one happy week, at any rate, with mother and Aileen.

We tried as well as we could to keep away from the large towns and the regular mail coach road. We worked on runs where the snow came down every now and then in such a way as to make us think that we might be snowed up alive some fine morning. It was very slow and tedious work, but the newspapers seldom came there, and we were not worried day after day with telegrams about our Adelaide stroke, and descriptions of Starlight's own look and way of speaking. We got into the old way of working hard all day and sleeping well at night. We could eat and drink well; the corned beef and the damper were good, and Jim, like when we were at the back of Boree when Warrigal came, wished that we could stick to this kind of thing always, and never have any fret or crooked dealings again as long as we lived.

But it couldn't be done. We had to leave and go shearing when the spring came on. We did go, and went from one big station to the other when the spring was regularly on and shearers were scarce. By-and-by the weather gets warmer, and we had cut our last shed before the first week in December.

Then we couldn't stand it any longer.

'I don't care,' says Jim, 'if there's a policeman standing at every corner of the street, I must make a start for home. They may catch us, but our chance is a pretty good one; and I'd just as soon be lagged outright as have to hide and keep dark and moulder away life in some of these God-forsaken spots.'

So we made up to start for home and chance it. We worked our way by degrees up the Snowy River, by Buchan and Galantapee, and gradually made towards Balooka and Buckley's Crossing. On the way we crossed some of the roughest country we had ever seen or ridden over.

'My word, Dick,' said Jim one day, as we were walking along and leading our horses, 'we could find a place here if we were hard pushed near as good for hiding in as the Hollow. Look at that bit of tableland that runs up towards Black Mountain, any man that could find a track up to it might live there for a year and all the police of the country be after him.'

'What would he get to eat if he was there?'

'That long chap we stayed with a Wargulmerang told us that there were wild cattle on all those tablelands. Often they get snowed up in winter and die, making a circle in the snow. Then fish in all the creeks, besides the old Snowy, and there are places on the south side of him that people didn't see once in five years. I believe I shall make a camp for myself on the way, and live in it till they've forgot all about these cursed cattle. Rot their hides, I wish we'd never have set eyes on one of them.'

'So do I; but like many things in the world it's too late—too late. Jim!'

CHAPTER XIV

ONE blazing hot day in the Christmas week Jim and I rode up the 'gap' that led from the Southern road towards Rocky Creek and the little flat near the water where our hut stood. The horses were tired, for we'd ridden a long way, and not very slow either, to get to the old place. How small and queer the old homestead looked, and everything about it after all we had seen. The trees in the garden were in full leaf, and we could see that it was not let go to waste. Mother was sitting in the verandah sewing, pretty near the same as we went away, and a girl was walking slowly up from the creek carrying a bucket of water. It was Aileen. We knew her at once. She was always as straight as a rush, and held her head high, as she used to do; but she walked very slow, and looked as if she was dull and weary of everything. All of a sudden Jim jumped off, dropped his horse's bridle on the ground, and started to run towards her. She didn't see him till he was pretty close; then she looked up astonished-like, and put her bucket down. She gave a sudden cry and rushed over to him; the next minute she was in his arms, sobbing as if her heart would break.

I came along quiet. I knew she'd be glad to see me—but, bless you, she and mother cared more for Jim's little finger than for my whole body. Some people have a way of gettin' the biggest share of nearly everybody's liking that comes next or anigh 'em. I don't know how it's done, or what works it. But so it is; and Jim could always count on every man, woman, and child, wherever he lived, wearing his colours and backing him right out, through thick and thin.

When I came up Aileen was saying—

'Oh, Jim, my dear old Jim! now I'll die happy; mother and I were only talking of you to-day, and wondering whether we should see you at Christmas—and now you have come. Oh, Dick! and you, too. But we shall be frightened every time we hear a horse's tread or dog's bark.'

'Well, we're here now, Aileen, and that's something. I had a great notion of clearing out for San Francisco and turning Yankee. What would you have done then?'

We walked up to the house, leading our horses, Jim and Aileen hand in hand. Mother looked up and gave a scream; she nearly fell down; when we got in her face was as white as a sheet.

'Mother of Mercy! I vowed to you for this,' she said; 'sure she hears our prayers. I wanted to see ye both before I died, and I didn't think you'd come. I was afraid ye'd be dreadin' the police, and maybe stay away for good and all. The Lord be thanked for all His mercies!'

We went in and enjoyed our tea. We had had nothing to eat that day since breakfast; but better than all was Aileen's pleasant, clever tongue, though she said it was getting stiff for want of exercise. She wanted to know all about our travels, and was never tired of listening to Jim's stories of the wonders we had seen in the great cities and the strange places we had been to.

'Oh! how happy you must have been!' she would say, 'while we have been pining and wearying here, all through last spring and summer, and then winter again—cold and miserable it was last year; and now Christmas has come again. Don't go away again for a good while, or mother and I'll die straight out.'

Well, what could we say? Tell her we'd never go away at all if we could help it—only she must be a good girl and make the best of things, for mother's sake? When had she seen father last?

'Oh! he was away a good while once; that time you and Jim were at Mr. Falkland's back country. You must have had a long job then; no wonder you've got such good clothes and look so smartened up like. He comes every now and then, just like he used. We never know what's become of him.'

'When was he here last?'

'Oh! about a month ago. He said he might be here about Christmas; but he wasn't sure. And so you saved Miss Falkland from being killed off her horse, Jim? Tell me all about it, like a good boy, and what sort of a looking young lady is she?'

'All right,' said Jim. 'I'll unload the story bag before we get through; there's a lot in there yet; but I want to look at you and hear you talk just now. How's George Storefield?'

'Oh! he's just the same good, kind, steady-going fellow he always was,' says she. 'I don't know what we should do without him when you're away. He comes and helps with the cows now and then. Two of the horses got into Bargo pound, and he went and released them for us. Then a storm blew off best part of the roof and the barn, and the bit of wheat would have been spoiled only for him. He's the best friend we have.'

'You'd better make sure of him for good and all,' I said. 'I suppose he's pretty well-to-do now with that new farm he bought the other day.'

'Oh! you saw that,' she said. 'Yes; he bought out the Cumberers. They never did any good with Honeysuckle Flat, though the land was so good. He's going to lay it all down in lucerne, he says.'

'And then he'll smarten up the cottage, and sister Aileen'll go over, and live in it,' says Jim; 'and a better thing she couldn't do.'

'I don't know,' she said. 'Poor George, I wish I was fonder of him. There never was a better man, I believe; but I cannot leave mother yet, so it's no use talking.' Then she got up and went in.

'That's the way of the world,' says Jim. 'George worships the ground she treads on, and she can't make herself care two straws about him. Perhaps she will in time. She'll have the best home and the best chap in the whole district if she does.'

'There's a deal of "if" in this world,' I said; 'and "if" we're "copped" on account of that last job, I'd like to think she and mother had some one to look after them, good weather and bad.'

'We might have done that, and not killed ourselves with work either,' said Jim, rather sulkily for him; and he lit his pipe and walked off into the bush without saying another word.

I thought, too, how we might have been ten times, twenty times, as happy if we'd only kept on steady ding-dong work, like George Storefield, having patience and seeing ourselves get better off—even a little—year by year. What had he come to? And what lay before us? And though we were that fond of poor mother and Aileen that we would have done anything in the world for them—that is, we would have given our lives for them any day—yet we had left them—father, Jim, and I—to lead this miserable, lonesome life, looked down upon by a lot of people not half good enough to tie their shoes, and obliged to a neighbour for help in every little distress.

Jim and I thought we'd chance a few days at home, no matter what risk we ran; but still we knew that if warrants were out the old home would be well watched, and that it was the first place the police would come to. So we made up our minds not to sleep at home, but to go away every night to an old deserted shepherd's hut, a couple of miles up the gully, that we used to play in when we were boys. It had been strongly built at first; time was not much matter then, and there were no wages to speak of, so that it was a good shelter. The weather was that hot, too, it was just as pleasant sleeping under a tree as anywhere else. So we didn't show at home more than one at a time, and took care to be ready for a bolt at any time, day or night, when the police might show themselves. Our place was middling clear all round now, and it was hard for any one on horseback to get near it without warning; and if we could once reach the gully we knew we could run faster than any man could ride.

One night, latish, just as we were walking off to our hut there was a scratching at the door; when we opened it there was old Crib! He ran up to both of us and smelt round our legs for a minute to satisfy himself; then jumped up once to each of us as if he thought he ought to do the civil thing, wagged his stump of a tail, and laid himself down. He was tired, and had come a long way. We could see that, and that he was footsore, too. We knew that father wasn't so very far off, and would soon be in. If there'd been anybody strange there Crib would have run back fast enough; then father 'd have dropped there was something up and not shown. No fear of the dog not knowing who was right and who wasn't. He could tell every sort of a man a mile off, I believe. He knew the very walk of the police troopers' horses, and would growl, father said, if he heard their hoofs rattle on the stones of the road.

About a quarter of an hour after father walks in, quiet as usual. Nothing never made no difference to him, except he thought it was worth while. He was middlin' glad to see us, and behaved kind enough to mother, so the poor soul looked quite happy for her. It was little enough of that she had for her share. By-and-by father walks outside with us, and we had a long private talk.

It was a brightish kind of starlight night. As we walked down to the creek I thought how often Jim and I had come out on just such a night 'possum hunting, and came home so tired that we were hardly able to pull our boots off. Then we had nothing to think about when we woke in the morning but to get in the cows; and didn't we enjoy the fresh butter and the damper and bacon and eggs at breakfast time! It seems to me the older people get the more miserable they get in this world. If they don't make misery for themselves other people do it for 'em; or just when everything's going straight, and they're doing their duty first-rate and all that, some accident happens 'em just as if they was the worst people in the world. I can't make it out at all.

'Well, boys,' says dad, 'you've been lucky so far; suppose you had a pretty good spree in Melbourne? You seen the game was up by the papers, didn't you? But why didn't you stay where you were?'

'Why, of course, that brought us away,' says Jim; 'we didn't want to be fetched back in irons, and thought there was more show for it in the bush here.'

'But even if they'd grabbed Starlight,' says the old man, 'you'd no call to be afeard. Not much chance of his peaching, if it had been a hanging matter.'

'You don't mean to say there ain't warrants against us and the rest of the lot?' I said.

'There's never a warrant out agin any one but Starlight,' said the old man. 'I've had the papers read to me regular, and I rode over to Bargo and saw the reward of £200 (a chap alongside of me read it) as is offered for a man generally known as Starlight, supposed to have left the country; but not a word about you two and me, or the boy, or them other coves.'

'So we might as well have stayed where we were, Jim.' Jim gave a kind of a groan. 'Still, when you look at it, isn't it queer,' I went on, 'that they should only spot Starlight and leave us out? It looks as if they was keepin' dark for fear of frightening us out of the country, but watching all the same.'

'It's this way I worked it,' says father, rubbing his tobacco in his hands the old way, and bringing out his pipe: 'they couldn't be off marking down Starlight along of his carryin' on so. Of course he drawed notice to himself all roads. But the rest of us only come in with the mob, and soon as they was sold stashed the camp and cleared out different ways. Them three fellers is in Queensland long ago, and nobody was to know them from any other road hands. I was back with the old mare and Bilbah in mighty short time. I rode 'em night and day, turn about, and they can both travel. You kept pretty quiet, as luck had it, and was off to Melbourne quick. I don't really believe they dropped to any of us, bar Starlight; and if they don't nab him we might get shut of it altogether. I've known worse things as never turned up in this world, and never will now.' Here the old man showed his teeth as if he were going to laugh, but thought better of it.

'Anyhow, we'd made it up to come home at Christmas,' says Jim; 'but it's all one. It would have saved us a deal of trouble in our minds all the same if we'd known there was no warrants out after us two. I wonder if they'll nail Starlight.'

'They can't be well off it,' said father. 'He's gone off his head, and stopped in some swell town in New Zealand—Canterbury, I think it's called—livin' tiptop among a lot of young English swells, instead of makin' off for the Islands, as he laid out to do.'

'How do you know he's there?' I said.

'I know, and that's enough,' snarls father. 'I hear a lot in many ways about things and people that no one guesses on, and I know this—that he's pretty well marked down by old Stillbrook the detective as went down there a month ago.'

'But didn't you warn him?'

'Yes, of course, as soon as I heard tell; but it's too late, I'm thinking. He has the devil's luck as well as his own, but I always used to tell him it would fail him yet.'

'I believe you're the smartest man of the crowd, dad,' says Jim, laying his hand on father's shoulder. He could pretty nigh get round the old chap once in a way, could Jim, surly as he was. 'What do you think we'd better do? What's our best dart?'

Father shook off his hand, but not roughly, and his voice wasn't so hard when he said—

'Why, stop at home quiet, of course, and sleep in your beds at night. Don't go planting in the gully, or some one 'll think you're wanted, and let on to the police. Ride about the country till I give you the office. Never fear but I'll have word quick enough. Go about and see the neighbours round just as usual.'

Jim and I was quite stunned by this bit of news; no doubt we was pretty sorry as ever we left Melbourne, but there was nothing for it now but to follow it out. After all, we were at home, and it was pleasant to think we wouldn't be hunted for a bit and might ride about the old place and enjoy ourselves a bit. Aileen was as happy as the day was long, and poor mother used to lay her head on Jim's neck and cry for joy to have him with her. Even father used to sit in the front, under the quinces, and smoke his pipe, with old Crib at his feet, most as if he thought he was happy. I wonder if he ever looked back to the days when he was farmin' boy and hadn't took to poaching? He must have been a smart, handy kind of lad, and what a different look his face must have had then!

We had our own horses in pretty good trim, so we foraged up Aileen's mare, and made it up to ride over to George Storefield's, and gave him a look-up. He'd been away when we came, and now we heard he was home.

'George has been doing well all this time, of course,' I said. 'I expect he'll turn squatter some day and be made a magistrate.'

'Like enough,' says Jim. 'More than one we could pick began lower down than him, and sits on the Bench and gives coves like us a turn when we're brought up before 'em. Fancy old George sayin', "Is anything known, constable, of this prisoner's anter-seedents?" as I heard old Higgler say one day at Bargo.'

'Why do you make fun of these things, Jim dear?' says Aileen, looking so solemn and mournful like. 'Oughtn't a steady worker to rise in life, and isn't it sad to see cleverer men and better workers— if they liked—kept down by their own fault?'

'Why wasn't your roan mare born black or chestnut?' says Jim, laughing, and pretending to touch her up. 'Come along, and let's see if she can trot as well as she used to do?'

'Poor Lowan,' says she, patting the mare's smooth neck (she was a wonderful neat, well-bred, dark roan, with black points—one of dad's, perhaps, that he'd brought her home one time he was in special good humour about something. Where she was bred or how, nobody ever knew); 'she was born pretty and good. How little trouble her life gives her. It's a pity we can't all say as much, or have as little on our minds.'

'Who's fault's that?' says Jim. 'The dingo must live as well as the collie or the sheep either. One's been made just the same as the other. I've often watched a dingo turn round twice, and then pitch himself down in the long grass like as if he was dead. He's not a bad sort, old dingo, and has a good time of it as long as it lasts.'

'Yes, till he's trapped or shot or poisoned some day, which he always is,' said Aileen bitterly. 'I wonder any man should be content with a wicked life and a shameful death.' And she struck Lowan with a switch, and spun down the slope of the hill between the trees like a forester-doe with the hunter-hound behind her.

When we came up with her she was all right again, and tried to smile. Whatever put her out for the time she always worked things by kindness, and would lead us straight if she could. Driven, she knew we couldn't be; and I believe she did us about ten times as much good that way as if she had scolded and raged, or even sneered at us.

When we rode up to Mr. Storefield's farm we were quite agreeable

and pleasant again, Jim makin' believe his horse could walk fastest,
and saying that her mare's pace was only a double shuffle of an amble
like Bilbah's, and she declaring that the mare's was a true walk—
and so it was. The mare could do pretty well everything but talk,
and all her paces were first-class.

Old Mrs. Storefield was pottering about in the garden with a big
sun-bonnet on. She was a great woman for flowers.

'Come along in, Aileen, my dear,' she said. 'Gracey's in the dairy;
she'll be out directly. George only came home yesterday. Who be
these you've got with ye? Why, Dick!' she says, lookin' again with
her sharp, old, grey eyes, 'it's you, boy, is it? Well, you've changed
a deal, too; and Jim, too. Is he as full of mischief as ever? Well,
God bless you, boys, I wish you well! I wish you well. Come in out
of the sun, Aileen; and one of you take the horses up to the stable.
You'll find George there somewhere.'

Aileen had jumped down by this time, and had thrown her rein
to Jim, so we rode up to the stable, and a very good one it was, not
long put up, that we could see. How the place had changed, and
how different it was from ours! We remembered the time when their
hut wasn't a patch on ours, when old Isaac Storefield, that had been
gardener at Mulgoa to some of the big gentlemen in the old days,
had saved a bit of money and taken up a farm; but bit by bit their
place had been getting better and bigger every year, while ours had
stood still and now was going back.

CHAPTER XV

GEORGE STOREFIELD'S place, for the old man was dead and all the place belonged to him and Gracey, quite stunned Jim and me. We'd been away more than a year, and he'd pulled down the old fences and put up new ones—first-rate work it was too; he was always a dead hand at splitting. Then there was a big hay-shed, chock-full of good sweet hay and wheat sheaves, and, last of all, the new stable, with six stalls and a loft above, and racks, all built of ironbark slabs, as solid and reg'lar as a church, Jim said.

They'd a good six-roomed cottage and a new garden fence ever so long. There were more fruit trees in the garden and a lot of good draught horses standing about, that looked well, but as if they'd come off a journey.

The stable door opens, and out comes old George as hearty as ever, but looking full of business.

'Glad to see you, boys,' he says; 'what a time you've been away! Been away myself these three months with a lot of teams carrying. I've taken greatly to the business lately. I'm just settling up with my drivers, but put the horses in, there's chaff and corn in the mangers, and I'll be down in a few minutes. It's well on to dinner-time, I see.'

We took the bridles off and tied up the horses—there was any amount of feed for them—and strolled down to the cottage again.

'Wonder whether Gracey's as nice as she used to be,' says Jim. 'Next to Aileen I used to think she wasn't to be beat. When I was a little chap I believed you and she must be married for certain. And old George and Aileen. I never laid out any one for myself, I remember.'

'The first two don't look like coming off,' I said. 'You're the likeliest man to marry and settle if Jeanie sticks to you.'

'She'd better go down to the pier and drown herself comfortably,' said Jim. 'If she knew what was before us all, perhaps she would. Poor little Jeanie! We'd no right to drag other people into our troubles. I believe we're getting worse and worse. The sooner we're shot or locked up the better.'

'You won't think so when it comes, old man,' I said. 'Don't bother your head—it ain't the best part of you—about things that can't be helped. We're not the only horses that can't be kept on the course —with a good turn of speed, too.'

'"They want shooting like the dingoes," as Aileen said. They're never no good, except to ruin those that back 'em and disgrace their owners and the stable they come out of. That's our sort, all to pieces. Well, we'd better come in. Gracey 'll think we're afraid to face her.'

When we went away last Grace Storefield was a little over seventeen, so now she was nineteen all out, and a fine girl she'd grown. Though I never used to think her a beauty, now I almost began to think she must be. She wasn't tall, and Aileen looked slight alongside of her; but she was wonderful fair and fresh coloured for an Australian girl, with a lot of soft brown hair and a pair of clear blue eyes that always looked kindly and honestly into everybody's face. Every look of her seemed to wish to do you good and make you think that nothing that wasn't square and right and honest and true could live in the same place with her.

She held out both hands to me and said—

'Well, Dick, so you're back again. You must have been to the end of the world, and Jim, too. I'm very glad to see you both.'

She looked into my face with that pleased look that put me in mind of her when she was a little child and used to come toddling up to me, staring and smiling all over her face the moment she saw me. Now she was a grown woman, and a sweet-looking one, too. I couldn't lift her up and kiss her as I used to do, but I felt as if I should like to do it all the same. She was the only creature in the whole world, I think, that liked me better than Jim. I'd been trying to drive all thoughts of her out of my heart, seeing the tangle I'd got into in more ways than one; but now the old feeling which had been a part of me ever since I'd grown up came rushing back stronger than ever. I was surprised at myself, and looked queer, I daresay.

Then Aileen laughed, and Jim comes to the rescue and says—

'Dick doesn't remember you, Gracey. You've grown such a swell, too. You can't be the little girl we used to carry on our backs.'

'Dick remembers very well,' she says, and her very voice was ever so much fuller and softer, 'don't you, Dick?' and she looked into my face as innocent as a child. 'I don't think he could pull me out of the water and carry me up to the cottage now.'

'You tumble in and we'll try,' says Jim; 'first man to keep you for good—eh, Gracey? It's fine hot weather, and Aileen shall see fair play.'

'You're just as saucy as ever, Jim,' says she, blushing and smiling. 'I see George coming, so I must go and fetch in dinner. Aileen's going to help me instead of mother. You must tell us all about your travels when we sit down.'

When George came in he began to talk to make up for lost time, and told us where he had been—a long way out in some new back country, just taken up with sheep. He had got a first-rate paying price for his carriage out, and had brought back and delivered a full load of wool.

'I intend to do it every year for a bit,' he said. 'I can breed and feed a good stamp of draught horse here. I pay drivers for three waggons and drive the fourth myself. It pays first-rate so far, and we had very fair feed all the way there and back.'

'Suppose you get a dry season,' I said, 'how will that be?'

'We shall have to carry forage, of course; but then carriage will be higher, and it will come to the same thing. I don't like being so long away from home; but it pays first-rate, and I think I see a way to its paying better still.'

'So you've ridden over to show them the way, Aileen,' he said, as the girls came in; 'very good of you it was. I was afraid you'd forgotten the way.'

'I never forget the way to a friend's place, George,' she said, 'and you've been our best friend while these naughty boys have left mother and me so long by ourselves. But you've been away yourself.'

'Only four months,' he said; 'and after a few more trips I shan't want to go away any more.'

'That will be a good day for all of us,' she said. 'You know, Gracey, we can't do without George, can we? I felt quite deserted, I can tell you.'

'He wouldn't have gone away at all if you'd held up your little finger, you know that, you hard-hearted girl,' said Grace, trying to frown. 'It's all your fault.'

'Oh! I couldn't interfere with Mr. Storefield's business,' said Aileen, looking very grave. 'What kind of a country was it you were out in?'

'Not a bad place for sheep and cattle and blacks,' said poor George, looking rather glum; 'and not a bad country to make money or do anything but live in, but that hot and dry and full of flies and mosquitoes that I'd sooner live on a pound a week down here than take a good station as a present there. That is, if I was contented,' he went on to say, with a sort of a groan.

There never was a greater mistake in the world, I believe, than for a man to let a woman know how much he cares for her. It's right enough if she's made up her mind to take him, no odds what happens. But if there's any half-and-half feeling in her mind about him, and she's uncertain and doubtful whether she likes him well enough, all this down-on-your-knees business works against you, more than your worst enemy could do. I didn't know so much about it then. I've found it out since, worse luck. And I really believe if George had had the savey to crack himself up a little, and say he'd met a nice girl or two in the back country and hid his hand, Aileen would have made it up with him that very Christmas, and been a happy woman all her life.

When old Mrs. Storefield came in she put us through our facings pretty brisk—where we'd been, what we'd done? What took us to Melbourne,—how we liked it? What kind of people they were? and so on. We had to tell her a good lot, part of it truth, of course, but pretty mixed. It made rather a good yarn, and I could see Grace was listening with her heart as well as her ears. Jim said generally we met some very nice people in Melbourne named Jackson, and they were very kind to us.

'Were there any daughters in the family, Jim?' asked Grace.

'Oh! yes, three.'

'Were they good-looking?'

'No, rather homely, particularly the youngest.'

'What did they do?'

'Oh! their mother kept a boarding-house. We stayed there.'

I don't think I ever knew Jim do so much lying before; but after he'd begun he had to stick to it. He told me afterwards he nearly broke down about the three daughters; but was rather proud of making the youngest the ugliest.

'I can see Gracey's as fond of you as ever she was, Dick,' says he; 'that's why she made me tell all those crammers. It's an awful pity we can't all square it, and get spliced this Christmas. Aileen would take George if she wasn't a fool, as most women are. I'd like to bring Jeanie up here, and join George in the carrying business. It's going to be a big thing, I can see. You might marry Gracey, and look after both places while we were away.'

'And how about Kate?'

'The devil take her! and then he'd have a bargain. I wish you'd never dropped across her, and that she wasn't Jeanie's sister,' blurts out Jim. 'She'll bring bad luck among us before she's done, I feel, as sure as we're standing here.'

'It's all a toss up—married or lagged, bush-work or road-work (in irons), free or bond. We can't tell how it will be with us this day year.'

'I've half a mind to shoot myself,' says Jim, 'and end it all. I would, too, only for mother and Aileen. What's the use of life that isn't life, but fear and misery, from one day's end to another, and we only just grown up? It's d—d hard that a chap's brains don't grow along with his legs and arms.'

We didn't ride home till quite the evening. Grace would have us stay for tea; it was a pretty hot day, so there was no use riding in the sun. George saddled his horse, and he and Grace rode part of the way home with us. He'd got regular sunburnt like us, and, as he could ride a bit, like most natives, he looked better outside of a horse than on his own legs, being rather thick-set and shortish; but his heart was in the right place, like his sister's, and his head was screwed on right, too. I think more of old George now than I ever did before, and wish I'd had the sense to value his independent straight-ahead nature, and the track it led him, as he deserved.

Jim and I rode in front, with Gracey between us. She had on a neat habit and a better hat and gloves than Aileen, but nothing could ever give her the seat and hand and light, easy, graceful way with her in the saddle that our girl had. All the same she could ride and drive too, and as we rode side by side in the twilight, talking about the places I'd been to, and she wanting to know everything (Jim drew off a bit when the road got narrow), I felt what a fool I'd been to let things slide, and would have given my right hand to have been able to put them as they were three short years before.

At last we got to the Gap; it was the shortest halt from their home. George shook hands with Aileen, and turned back.

'We'll come and see you next——' he said.

'Christmas Eve!' said Aileen.

'Christmas Eve let it be,' says George.

'All right,' I said, holding Grace's hand for a bit. And so we parted—for how long, do you think?

CHAPTER XVI

WHEN we got home it was pretty late, and the air was beginning to cool after the hot day. There was a low moon, and everything showed out clear, so that you could see the smallest branches of the trees on Nulla Mountain, where it stood like a dark cloud-bank against the western sky. There wasn't the smallest breeze. The air was that still and quiet you could have heard anything stir in the grass, or almost a 'possum digging his claws into the smooth bark of the white gum trees. The curlews set up a cry from time to time; but they didn't sound so queer and shrill as they mostly do at night. I don't know how it was, but everything seemed quiet and pleasant and homelike, as if a chap might live a hundred years, if it was all like this, and keep growing better and happier every day. I remember all this so particular because it was the only time I'd felt like it for years, and I never had the same feeling afterwards —nor likely to.

'Oh! what a happy day I've had,' Aileen said, on a sudden. Jim and I and her had been riding a long spell without speaking. 'I don't know when I've enjoyed myself so much; I've got quite out of the way of being happy lately, and hardly know the taste of it. How lovely it would be if you and Jim could always stay at home like this, and we could do our work happy and comfortable together, without separating, and all this deadly fear of something terrible happening, that's never out of my mind. Oh! Dick, won't you promise me to stop quiet and work steady at home, if you—if you and Jim haven't anything brought against you?'

She bent forward and looked into my face as she said this. I could see her eyes shine, and every word she said seemed to come straight from her heart. How sad and pitiful she looked, and we felt for a moment just as we did when we were boys, and she used to come and persuade us to go on with our work and not grieve mother, and run the risk of a licking from father when he came home.

Her mare, Lowan, was close alongside of my horse, stepping along at her fast, tearing walk, throwing up her head and snorting every now and then, but Aileen sat in her saddle better than some people can sit in a chair; she held the rein and whip together and kept her hand on mine till I spoke.

'We'll do all we can, Aileen dear, for you and poor mother, won't we, Jim?' I felt soft and down-hearted then, if ever I did. 'But it's too late—too late! You'll see us now and then; but we can't stop at home quiet, nor work about here all the time as we used to do. That day's gone. Jim knows it as well as me. There's no help for it now. We'll have to do like the rest—enjoy ourselves a bit while we can, and stand up to our fight when the trouble comes.'

She took her hand away, and rode on with her rein loose and her head down. I could see the tears falling down her face, but after a bit she put herself to rights, and we rode quietly up to the door. Mother was working away in her chair, and father walking up and down before the door smoking.

When we were letting go the horses, father comes up and says—

'I've got a bit of news for you, boys; Starlight's been took, and the darkie with him.'

'Where?' I said. Somehow I felt struck all of a heap by hearing this. I'd got out of the way of thinking they'd drop on him. As for Jim, he heard it straight enough, but he went on whistling and patting the mare's neck, teasing her like, because she was so uneasy to get her head-stall off and run after the others.

'Why, in New Zealand, to be sure. The blamed fool stuck there all this time, just because he found himself comfortably situated among people as he liked. I wonder how he'll fancy Berrima after it all? Sarves him well right.'

'But how did you come to hear about it?' We knew father couldn't read nor write.

'I have a chap as is paid to read the papers reg'lar, and to put me on when there's anything in 'em as I want to know. He's been over here to-day and give me the office. Here's the paper he left.'

Father pulls out a crumpled-up, dirty-lookin' bit of newspaper. It wasn't much to look at; but there was enough to keep us in readin', and thinkin', too, for a good while, as soon as we made it out. In pretty big letters, too.

IMPORTANT CAPTURE BY DETECTIVE STILLBROOK, OF THE NEW SOUTH WALES POLICE.

That was atop of the page, then comes this:—

Our readers may remember the description given in this journal, some months since, of a cattle robbery on the largest scale, when upwards of a thousand head were stolen from one of Mr. Hood's stations, driven to Adelaide, and then sold, by a party of men whose names have not as yet transpired. It is satisfactory to find that the leader of the gang, who is well known to the police by the assumed name of 'Starlight,' with a half-caste lad recognised as an accomplice, has been arrested by this active officer. It appears that, from information received, Detective Stillbrook went to New Zealand, and, after several months' patient search, took his passage in the boat which left that colony, in order to meet the mail steamer, outward bound, for San Francisco. As the passengers were landing he arrested a gentlemanlike and well-dressed personage, who, with his servant, was about to proceed to Menzies' Hotel. Considerable surprise was manifested by the other passengers, with whom the prisoner had become universally popular. He indignantly denied all knowledge of the charge; but we have reason to believe that there will be no difficulty as to identification. A large sum of money in gold and notes was found upon him. Other arrests are likely to follow.

This looked bad; for a bit we didn't know what to think. While Jim and I was makin' it all out, with the help of a bit of candle we smuggled out—we dursn't take it inside—father was smokin' his pipe —in the old fashion—and saying nothing. When we'd done he put up his pipe in his pouch and begins to talk.

'It's come just as I said, and knowed it would, through Starlight's cussed flashness and carryin's on in fine company. If he'd cleared out and made for the Islands, as I warned him to do, and he settled to, or as good, afore he left us that day at the camp, he'd been safe in some o' them 'Merikin places he was always gassin' about, and all this wouldn't 'a happened.'

'He couldn't help that,' says Jim; 'he thought they'd never know him from any other swell in Canterbury or wherever he was. He's been took in like many another man. What I look at is this: he won't squeak. How are they to find out that we had any hand in it?'

'That's what I'm dubersome about,' says father, lightin' his pipe again. 'Nobody down there got much of a look at me, and I let my beard grow on the road and shaved clean soon's I got back, same as I always do. Now the thing is, does any one know that you boys was in the fakement?'

'Nobody's likely to know but him and Warrigal. The knock-abouts and those other three chaps won't come it on us for their own sakes. We may as well stop here till Christmas is over and then make down to the Barwon, or somewhere thereabouts. We could take a long job at droving till the derry's off a bit.'

'If you'll be said by me,' the old man growls out, 'you'll make tracks for the Hollow afore daylight and keep dark till we hear how the play goes. I know Starlight's as close as a spring-lock; but that chap Warrigal don't cotton to either of you, and he's likely to give you away if he's pinched himself—that's my notion of him.'

'Starlight 'll keep him from doing that,' Jim says; 'the boy 'll do nothing his master don't agree to, and he'd break his neck if he found him out in any dog's trick like that.'

'Starlight and he ain't in the same cell, you take your oath. I don't trust no man except him. I'll be off now, and if you'll take a fool's advice, though he is your father, you'll go too; we can be there by daylight.'

Jim and I looked at each other.

'We promised to stay Chris'mas with mother and Aileen,' says he, 'and if all the devils in hell tried to stop us, I wouldn't break my word. But we'll come to the Hollow on Boxing Day, won't we, Dick?'

'All right! It's only two or three days. The day after to-morrow's Chris'mas Eve. We'll chance that, as it's gone so far.'

'Take your own way,' growls father. 'Fetch me my saddle. The old mare's close by the yard.'

Jim fetches the saddle and bridle, and Crib comes after him, out of the verandah, where he had been lying. Bless you! he knew something was up. Just like a Christian he was, and nothing ever happened that dad was in as he wasn't down to.

'May as well stop till morning, dad,' says Jim, as we walked up to the yard.

'Not another minute,' says the old man, and he whips the bridle out of Jim's hand and walks over to the old mare. She lifts up her head from the dry grass and stands as steady as a rock.

'Good-bye,' he says, and he shook hands with both of us; 'if I don't see you again I'll send you word if I hear anything fresh.'

In another minute we heard the old mare's hoofs proceeding away among the rocks up the gully, and gradually getting fainter in the distance.

Then we went in. Mother and Aileen had been in bed an hour ago, and all the better for them. Next morning we told mother and Aileen that father had gone. They didn't say much. They were used to his ways. They never expected him till they saw him, and had got out of the fashion of asking why he did this or that. He had reasons of his own, which he never told them, for going or coming, and they'd left off troubling their heads about it. Mother was always in dread while he was there, and they were far easier in their minds when he was away off the place.

As for us, we had made up our minds to enjoy ourselves while we could, and we had come to this way of thinking, that most likely nothing was known of our being in the cattle affair that Starlight and the boy had been arrested for. We knew nothing would drag it out of Starlight about his pals in this or any other job. Now they'd got him, it would content them for a bit, and maybe take off their attention from us and the others that were in it.

There were two days to Christmas. Next day George and his sister would be over, and we all looked forward to that for a good reminder of old times. We were going to have a merry Christmas at home for once in a way. After that we would clear out and get away to some of the far out stations, where chaps like ourselves always made to when they wanted to keep dark. We might have the luck of other men that we had known of, and never be traced till the whole thing had died out and been half-forgotten. Though we didn't say much to each other we had pretty well made up our minds to go straight from this out. We might take up a bit of back country, and put stock on it with some of the money we had left. Lots of men had begun that way that had things against them as bad as us, and had kept steady, and worked through in course of time. Why shouldn't we as well as others? We wanted to see what the papers said of us, so we rode over to a little post town we knew of and got a copy of the *Evening Times*. There it all was in full:—

CATTLE-LIFTING EXTRAORDINARY.

We have heard from time to time of cattle being stolen in lots of reasonable size, say, from ten to one hundred, or even as high as two hundred head at the outside. But we never expected to have to record the erecting of a substantial stockyard and the carrying off and disposing of a whole herd, estimated at a thousand or eleven hundred head, chiefly the property of one proprietor. Yet this has been done in New South Wales, and done, we regret to say, cleverly and successfully. It has just transpired, beyond all possibility of mistake, that Mr. Hood's Outer Back Momberah run has suffered to that extent in the past winter. The stolen herd was driven to Adelaide, and there sold openly. The money was received by the robbers, who were permitted to decamp at their leisure.

When we mention the name of the notorious 'Starlight,' no one will be surprised that the deed was planned, carried out, and executed with con-summate address and completeness. It seems matter of regret that we cannot persuade this illustrious depredator to take the command of our police force, that body of life-assurers and property-protectors which has proved so singularly ineffective as a preventive service in the present case. On the well-known proverbial principle we might hope for the best results under Mr. Starlight's intelligent supervision. We must not withhold our approval as to one item of success which the force has scored. Starlight himself and a half-caste henchman have been cleverly captured by Detective Stillbrook, just as the former, who has been ruffling it among the 'aristocratic' settlers in Christchurch, was about to sail for Honolulu. The names of his other accomplices, six in number, it is said, have not as yet transpired.

This last part gave us confidence, but all the same we kept everything ready for a bolt in case of need. We got up our horses every evening and kept them in the yard all night. The feed was good by the creek now—a little dried up, but plenty of bite, and better for horses that had been ridden far and fast than if it was green. We had enough of last year's hay to give them a feed at night, and that was all they wanted. They were two pretty good ones and not slow either. We took care of that when we bought them. Nobody ever saw us on bad ones since we were boys, and we had broken them in to stand and be caught day or night, and to let us jump on and off at a moment's notice.

All that day, being awful hot and close, we stayed in the house and yarned away with mother and Aileen till they thought—poor souls—that we had turned over a new leaf and were going to stay at home and be good boys for the future. When a man sees how little it takes to make women happy—them that's good and never thinks of anything but doing their best for everybody belonging to 'em—it's wonderful how men ever make up their minds to go wrong and bring all that loves them to shame and grief. When they've got nobody but themselves to think of it don't so much matter as I know of; but to keep on breaking the hearts of those as never did you anything but good, and wouldn't if they lived for a hundred years, is cowardly and unmanly any way you look at it. And yet we'd done very little else ourselves these years and years.

We all sat up till nigh on to midnight with our hands in one another's—Jim down at mother's feet; Aileen and I close beside them on the old seat in the verandah that father made such a time ago. At last mother gets up, and they both started for bed. Aileen seemed as if she couldn't tear herself away. Twice she came back, then she kissed us both, and the tears came into her eyes. 'I feel too happy,' she said; 'I never thought I should feel like this again. God bless you both, and keep us all from harm.' 'Amen,' said mother from the next room. We turned out early, and had a bathe in the creek before we went up to the yard to let out the horses. There wasn't a cloud in the sky; it was safe to be a roasting hot day, but it was cool then. The little waterhole where we learned to swim when we were boys was deep on one side and had a rocky ledge to jump off. The birds just began to give out a note or two; the sun was rising clear and bright, and we could see the dark top of Nulla Mountain getting a sort of rose colour against the sky.

'George and Gracey'll be over soon after breakfast,' I said; 'we must have everything look ship-shape as well as we can before they turn up.'

'The horses may as well go down to the flat,' Jim says; 'we can catch them easy enough in time to ride back part of the way with them. I'll run up Lowan, and give her a bit of hay in the calf-pen.'

We went over to the yard, and Jim let down the rails and walked in. I stopped outside. Jim had his horse by the mane, and was patting his neck as mine came out, when three police troopers rose up from behind the bushes, and covering us with their rifles called out, 'Stand, in the Queen's name!'

Jim made one spring on to his horse's back, drove his heels into his flank, and was out through the gate and half-way down the hill before you could wink.

Just as Jim cleared the gate a tall man rose up close behind me and took a cool pot at him with a revolver. I saw Jim's hat fly off, and another bullet grazed his horse's hip. I saw the hair fly, and the horse made a plunge that would have unseated most men with no saddle between their legs. But Jim sat close and steady and only threw up his arm and gave a shout as the old horse tore down the hill a few miles an hour faster.

'D—n those cartridges,' said the tall trooper; 'they always put too much powder in them for close shooting. Now, Dick Marston!' he went on, putting his revolver to my head, 'I'd rather not blow your brains out before your people, but if you don't put up your hands, by —— I'll shoot you where you stand.' I had been staring after Jim all the time; I believe I had never thought of myself till he was safe away.

'Get your horses, you d—d fools,' he shouts out to the men, 'and

see if you can follow up that madman. He's most likely knocked
off against a tree by this time.'

There was nothing else for it but to do it and be handcuffed. As
the steel locks snapped I saw mother standing below wringing her
hands, and Aileen trying to get her into the house.

'Better come down and get your coat on, Dick,' said the senior
constable. 'We want to search the place, too. By Jove! we shall
get pepper from Sir Ferdinand when we go in. I thought we had
you both as safe as chickens in a coop. Who would have thought
of Jim givin' us the slip, on a barebacked horse, without so much as
a halter? I'm devilish sorry for your family; but if nothing less than
a thousand head of cattle will satisfy people, they must expect trouble
to come of it.'

'What are you talking about?' I said. 'You've got the wrong story
and the wrong men.'

'All right; we'll see about that. I don't know whether you want
any breakfast, but I should like a cup of tea. It's deuced slow work
watching all night, though it isn't cold. We've got to be in Bargo
barracks to-night, so there's no time to lose.'

It was all over now—the worst *had* come. What fools we had been
not to take the old man's advice, and clear out when he did. He
was safe in the Hollow, and would chuckle to himself—and be
sorry, too—when he heard of my being taken, and perhaps Jim.
The odds were he might be smashed against a tree, perhaps killed,
at the pace he was going on a horse he could not guide:

They searched the house, but the money they didn't get. Jim
and I had taken care of that, in case of accidents. Mother sat rocking herself backwards and forwards, every now and then crying out
in a pitiful way, like the women in her country do, I've heard
tell, when some one of their people is dead; 'keening,' I think they
call it. Well, Jim and I were as good as dead. If the troopers
had shot the pair of us there and then, same as bushmen told us
the black police did their prisoners when they gave 'em any trouble,
it would have been better for everybody. However, people don't
die all at once when they go to the bad, and take to stealing or
drinking, or any of the devil's favourite traps. Pity they don't, and
have done with it once and for all.

I know I thought so when I was forced to stand there with my
hands chained together for the first time in my life (though I'd
worked for it, I know that); and to see Aileen walking about laying
the cloth for breakfast like a dead woman, and know what was in
her mind.

The troopers were civil enough, and Goring, the senior constable,
tried to comfort them as much as he could. He knew it was no
fault of theirs; and though he said he meant to have Jim if mortal
men and horses could do it he thought he had a fair chance of
getting away. 'He's sure to be caught in the long-run, though,' he

went on to say. 'There's a warrant out for him, and a description in every *Police Gazette* in the colonies. My advice to him would be to come back and give himself up. It's not a hanging matter, and as it's the first time you've been fitted, Dick, the judge, as like as not, will let you off with a light sentence.'

So they talked away until they had finished their breakfast. I couldn't touch a mouthful for the life of me, and as soon as it was all over they ran up my horse and put the saddle on. But I wasn't to ride him. No fear! Goring put me on an old screw of a troop horse, with one leg like a gate-post. I was helped up and my legs tied under his belly. Then one of the men took the bridle and led me away. Goring rode in front and the other men behind.

As we rose the hill above the place I looked back and saw mother drop down on the ground in a kind of fit, while Aileen bent over her and seemed to be loosening her dress. Just at that moment George Storefield and his sister rode up to the door. George jumped off and rushed over to Aileen and mother. I knew Gracey had seen me, for she sat on her horse as if she had been turned to stone, and let her reins drop on his neck. Strange things have happened to me since, but I shall never forget that to the last day of my miserable life.

CHAPTER XVII

I WASN'T in the humour for talking, but sometimes anything's better than one's own thoughts. Goring threw in a word from time to time. He'd only lately come into our district, and was sure to be promoted, everybody said. Like Starlight himself, he'd seen better days at home in England; but when he got pinched he'd taken the right turn and not the wrong one, which makes all the difference. He was earning his bread honest, anyway, and he was a chap as liked the fun and dash of a mounted policeman's life. As for the risk—and there is some danger, more than people thinks, now and then—he liked that the best of it. He was put out at losing Jim; but he believed he couldn't escape, and told me so in a friendly way. 'He's inside a circle and he can't get away, you mark my words,' he said, two or three times. 'We have every police-station warned by wire, within a hundred miles of here, three days ago. There's not a man in the colony sharper looked after than Master Jim is this minute.'

'Then you only heard about us three days ago?' I said.

'That's as it may be,' he answered, biting his lip. 'Anyhow, there isn't a shepherd's hut within miles that he can get to without our knowing it. The country's rough, but there's word gone for a black tracker to go down. You'll see him in Bargo before the week's out.'

I had a good guess where Jim would make for, and he knew enough to hide his tracks for the last few miles if there was a whole tribe of trackers after him.

That night we rode into Bargo. A long day too we'd had—we were all tired enough when we got in. I was locked up, of course, and as soon as we were in the cell Goring said, 'Listen to me,' and put on his official face—devilish stern and hard-looking he was then, in spite of all the talking and nonsense we'd had coming along.

'Richard Marston, I charge you with unlawfully taking, stealing, and carrying away, in company with others, one thousand head of mixed cattle, more or less, the property of one Walter Hood, of Outer Back, Momberah, in or about the month of June last.'

'All right; why don't you make it a few more while you're about it?'

'That'll do,' he said, nodding his head, 'you decline to say anything. Well, I can't exactly wish you a merry Christmas—fancy this being

Christmas Eve, by Jove!—but you'll be cool enough this deuced hot weather till the sessions in February, which is more than some of us can say. Good-night.' He went out and locked the door. I sat down on my blanket on the floor and hid my head in my hands. I wonder it didn't burst with what I felt then. Strange that I shouldn't have felt half as bad when the judge, the other day, sentenced me to be a dead man in a couple of months. But I was young then.

Christmas Day! Christmas Day! So this is how I was to spend it after all, I thought, as I woke up at dawn, and saw the grey light just beginning to get through the bars of the window of the cell.

Here was I locked up, caged, ironed, disgraced, a felon and an outcast for the rest of my life. Jim, flying for his life, hiding from every honest man, every policeman in the country looking after him, and authorised to catch him or shoot him down like a sheep-killing dog. Father living in the Hollow, like a black-fellow in a cave, afraid to spend the blessed Christmas with his wife and daughter, like the poorest man in the land could do if he was only honest. Mother half dead with grief, and Aileen ashamed to speak to the man that loved and respected her from her childhood. Gracey Storefield not daring to think of me or say my name, after seeing me carried off a prisoner before her eyes. Here was a load of misery and disgrace heaped up together, to be borne by the whole family, now and for the time to come—by the innocent as well as the guilty. And for what? Because we had been too idle and careless to work regularly and save our money, though well able to do it, like honest men. Because, little by little, we had let bad, dishonest ways and flash manners grow upon us, all running up an account that had to be paid some day.

And now the day of reckoning had come—sharp and sudden with a vengeance! Well, what call had we to look for anything else? We had been working for it; now we had got it, and had to bear it. Not for want of warning, neither. What had mother and Aileen been saying ever since we could remember? Warning upon warning. Now the end had come just as they said. Of course I knew in a general way that I couldn't be punished or be done anything to right off. I knew law enough for that. The next thing would be that I should have to be brought up before the magistrates and committed for trial as soon as they could get any evidence.

After breakfast, flour and water or hominy, I forget which, the warder told me that there wasn't much chance of my being brought up before Christmas was over. The police magistrate was away on a month's leave, and the other magistrates would not be likely to attend before the end of the week, anyway. So I must make myself comfortable where I was. Comfortable!

'Had they caught Jim?'

'Well, not that he'd heard of; but Goring said it was impossible for him to get away. At twelve he'd bring me some dinner.'

I was pretty certain they wouldn't catch Jim, in spite of Goring being so cocksure about it. If he wasn't knocked off the first mile or so, he'd find ways of stopping or steadying his horse, and facing him up to where we had gone to join father at the tableland of the Nulla Mountain. Once he got near there he could let go his horse. They'd be following his track, while he made the best of his way on foot to the path that led to the Hollow. If he had five miles' start of them there, as was most likely, all the blacks in the country would never track where he got to. He and father could live there for a month or so, and take it easy until they could slip out and do a bit of father's old trade. That was about what I expected Jim to do, and as it turned out I was as nearly right as could be. They ran his track for ten miles. Then they followed his horse-tracks till late the second day, and found that the horse had slued round and was making for home again with nobody on him. Jim was nowhere to be seen, and they'd lost all that time, never expecting that he was going to dismount and leave the horse to go his own way.

They searched Nulla Mountain from top to bottom; but some of the smartest men of the old Mounted Police and the best of the stockmen in the old days—men not easy to beat—had tried the same country many years before, and never found the path to the Hollow. So it wasn't likely any one else would. They had to come back and own that they were beat, which put Goring in a rage and made the inspector, Sir Ferdinand Morringer, blow them all up for a lot of duffers and old women. Altogether they had a bad time of it, not that it made any difference to me.

After the holidays a magistrate was fished up somehow, and I was brought before him and the apprehending constable's evidence taken. Then I was remanded to the Bench at Nomah, where Mr. Hood and some of the other witnesses were to appear. So away we started for another journey. Goring and a trooper went with me, and all sorts of care was taken that I didn't give them the slip on the road. Goring used to put one of my handcuffs on his own wrist at night, so there wasn't much chance of moving without waking him. I had an old horse to ride that couldn't go much faster than I could run, for fear of accident. It was even betting that he'd fall and kill me on the road. If I'd had a laugh in me, I should have had a joke against the Police Department for not keeping safer horses for their prisoners to ride. They keep them till they haven't a leg to stand upon, and long after they can't go a hundred yards without trying to walk on their heads they're thought good enough to carry packs and prisoners.

'Some day,' Goring said, 'one of those old screws will be the death of a prisoner before he's committed for trial, and then there'll be a row over it, I suppose.'

We hadn't a bad journey of it on the whole. The troopers were civil enough, and gave me a glass of grog now and then when they had one themselves. They'd done their duty in catching me, and that was all they thought about. What came afterwards wasn't their look-out. I've no call to have any bad feeling against the police, and I don't think most men of my sort have. They've got their work to do, like other people, and as long as they do what they're paid for, and don't go out of their way to harass men for spite, we don't bear them any malice. If one's hit in fair fight it's the fortune of war. What our side don't like is men going in for police duty that's not in their line. That's interfering, according to our notions, and if they fall into a trap or are met with when they don't expect it they get it pretty hot. They've only themselves to thank for it.

Goring, I could see by his ways, had been a swell, something like Starlight. A good many young fellows that don't drop into fortunes when they come out here take to the police in Australia, and very good men they make. They like the half-soldiering kind of life, and if they stick steady at their work, and show pluck and gumption, they mostly get promoted. Goring was a real smart, dashing chap, a good rider for an Englishman; that is, he could set most horses, and hold his own with us natives anywhere but through scrub and mountain country. No man can ride there, I don't care who he is, the same as we can, unless he's been at it all his life. There we have the pull—not that it is so much after all. But give a native a good horse and thick country, and he'll lose any man living that's tackled the work after he's grown up.

By-and-by we got to Nomah, a regular hot hole of a place, with a log lock-up. I was stuck in, of course, and had leg-irons put on for fear I should get out, as another fellow had done a few weeks back. Starlight and Warrigal hadn't reached yet; they had farther to come. The trial couldn't come till the Quarter Sessions. January, and February too, passed over, and all this time I was mewed up in a bit of a place enough to stifle a man in the burning weather we had.

I heard afterwards that they wanted to bring some of the cattle over, so as Mr. Hood could swear to 'em being his property. But he said he could only swear to its being his brand; that he most likely had never set eyes on them in his life, and couldn't swear on his own knowledge that they hadn't been sold, like lots of others, by his manager. So this looked like a hitch, as juries won't bring a man in guilty of cattle-stealing unless there's clear swearing that the animals he sold were the property of the prosecutor, and known by him to be such.

Mr. Hood had to go all the way to Adelaide himself, and they told me we might likely have got out of it all, only for the imported bull. When he saw him he said he could swear to him point blank, brand or no brand. He'd no brand on him, of course, when he left England; but Hood happened to be in Sydney when he came out, and at the station when he came up. He was stabled for the first six months, so he used to go and look him over every day, and tell visitors what a pot of money he'd cost, till he knew every hair in his tail, as the saying is. As soon as he seen him in Adelaide he said he could swear to him as positive as he could to his favourite riding horse. So he was brought over in a steamer from Adelaide, and then drove all the way up to Nomah. I wished he'd broken his neck before we ever saw him.

Next thing I saw was Starlight being brought in, handcuffed, between two troopers, and looking as if he'd ridden a long way. He was just as easy-going and devil-may-care as ever. He said to one of the troopers—

'Here we are at last, and I'm deuced glad of it. It's perfectly monstrous you fellows haven't better horses. You ought to make me remount agent, and I'd show you the sort of horses that ought to be bought for police service. Let me have a glass of beer, that's a good fellow, before I'm locked up. I suppose there's no tap worth speaking of inside.'

The constable laughed, and had one brought to him.

'It will be some time before you get another, captain. Here's a long one for you; make the most of it.'

Where, in the devil's name, is that Warrigal? I thought to myself. Has he given them the slip? He had, as it turned out. He had slipped the handcuffs over his slight wrists and small hands, bided his time, and then dashed into a scrub. There he was at home. They rode and rode, but Warrigal was gone like a rock wallaby. It was a good while before he was as near the gaol again.

All this time I'd been wondering how it was they came to drop on our names so pat, and to find out that Jim and I had a share in the Momberah cattle racket. All they could have known was that we left the back of Boree at a certain day; and that was nothing, seeing that for all they knew we might have gone away to new country or anywhere. The more I looked at it the more I felt sure that some one had given to the police information about us—somebody who was in it and knew all about everything. It wasn't Starlight. We could have depended our life on him. It might have been one of the other chaps, but I couldn't think of any one, except Warrigal. He would do anything in the world to spite me and Jim, I knew; but then he couldn't hurt us without drawing the net tighter round Starlight. Sooner than hurt a hair of his head he'd have put his hand into the fire and kept it there. I knew that from things I'd seen him do.

Starlight and I hadn't much chance of a talk, but we managed to get news from each other, a bit at a time; that can always be managed. We were to be defended, and a lawyer fetched all the way from Sydney to fight our case for us. The money was there. Father managed the other part of it through people he had that did every kind of work for him; so when the judge came up we should have a show for it.

The weary, long summer days—every one of them about twenty hours long—came to an end somehow or other. It was so hot and close and I was that miserable I had two minds to knock my brains out and finish the whole thing. I couldn't settle to read, as I did afterwards. I was always wishing and wondering when I'd hear some news from home, and none ever came. Nomah was a bit of a place where hardly anybody did anything but idle and drink, and spend money when they had it. When they had none they went away. There wasn't even a place to take exercise in, and the leg-irons I wore night and day began to eat into my flesh. I wasn't used to them in those days. I could feel them in my heart, too. Last of all I got ill, and for a while was so weak and low they thought I was going to get out of the trial altogether.

At last we heard that the judge and all his lot were on the road, and would be up in a few days. We were almost as glad when the news came as if we were sure of being let off. One day they did come, and all the little town was turned upside down. The judge stopped at one hotel (they told us); the lawyers at another. Then the witnesses in ours and other cases came in from all parts, and made a great difference, especially to the publicans. The jurors were summoned, and had to come, unless they had a fancy for being fined. Most of this I heard from the constables; they seemed to think it was the only thing that made any difference in their lives. Last of all I heard that Mr. Hood had come, and the imported bull, and some other witnesses.

There were some small cases first, and then we were brought out, Starlight and I, and put in the dock. The court was crammed and crowded; every soul within a hundred miles seemed to have come in; there never was so many people in the little courthouse before. Starlight was quietly dressed, and looked as if he was there by mistake. Anybody would have thought so, the way he lounged and stared about, as if he thought there was something very curious and hard to understand about the whole thing. I was so weak and ill that I couldn't stand up, and after a while the judge told me to sit down, and Starlight too. Starlight made a most polite bow, and thanked his Honour, as he called him. Then the jury were called up, and our lawyer began his work. He stood alongside of Starlight, and whispered something to him, after which Starlight stood up, and about every second man called out 'Challenge'; then that juror had to go down. It took a good while to get our jury all together. Our lawyer seemed very particular about the sort of jury he was satisfied with; and when they did manage to get twelve at last they were not the best-looking men in the court by a very long way.

The trial had to go on, and then the Crown Prosecutor made a speech, in which he talked about the dishonesty which was creeping unchecked over the land, and the atrocious villainy of criminals who took a thousand head of cattle in one lot, and made out the country was sure to go to destruction if we were not convicted. He said that unfortunately they were not in a position to bring many of the cattle back that had been taken to another colony; but one remarkable animal was as good for purposes of evidence as a hundred. Such an animal he would produce, and he would not trespass on the patience of the jurors and gentlemen in attendance any longer, but call his first witness.

John Dawson, sworn: Was head stockman and cattle manager at Momberah; knew the back country, and in a general way the cattle running there; was not out much in the winter; the ground was boggy, and the cattle were hardly ever mustered till spring; when he did go, with some other stock-riders, he saw at once that a large number of the Momberah cattle, branded HOD and other brands, were missing; went to Adelaide a few months later; saw a large number of cattle of the HOD brand, which he was told had been sold by the prisoner now before the court, and known as Starlight, and others, to certain farmers; he could swear that the cattle he saw bore Mr. Hood's brand; could not swear that he recognised them as having been at Momberah in his charge; believed so, but could not swear it; he had seen a short-horn bull outside of the court this morning; he last saw the said bull at the station of Messrs. Fordham Brothers, near Adelaide; they made a communication to him concerning the bull; he would and could swear to the identity of the animal with the Fifteenth Duke of Cambridge, an imported short-horn bull, the property of Mr. Hood; had seen him before that at Momberah; knew that Mr. Hood had bought said bull in Sydney, and was at Momberah when he was sent up; could not possibly be mistaken; when he saw the bull at Momberah, nine months since, he had a small brand like H on the shoulder; Mr. Hood put it on in witness's presence; it was a horse-brand, now it resembled J-E; the brand had been 'faked' or cleverly altered; witness could see the original brand quite plain underneath; as far as he knew Mr. Hood never sold or gave any one authority to take the animal; he had missed him some months since, and always believed he had strayed; knew the bull to be a valuable animal, worth several hundred pounds.

We had one bit of luck in having to be tried in an out-of-the-way place like Nomah. It was a regular outside bush township, and though the distance oughtn't to have much to say to people's honesty, you'll mostly find that these far-out, back-of-beyond places have got men and women to match 'em.

Except the squatters and overseers, the other people's mostly a shady lot. Some's run away from places that were too hot to hold 'em. The women ain't the men's wives that they live with, but somebody else's—who's well rid of 'em too if all was known. There's most likely a bit of horse and cattle stealing done on the quiet, and the publicans and storekeepers know who are their best customers, the square people or the cross ones. It ain't so easy to get a regular up-and-down straight-ahead jury in a place of this sort. So Starlight and I knew that our chance was a lot better than if we'd been tried at Bargo or Dutton Forest, or any steady-going places of that sort.

If we'd made up our minds from the first that we were to get into it it wouldn't have been so bad; we'd have known we had to bear it. Now we might get out of it, and what a thing it would be to feel free again, and walk about in the sun without any one having the right to stop you. Almost, that is—there were other things against us; but there wasn't so much of a chance of their turning up. This was the great stake. If we won we were as good as made. I felt ready to swear I'd go home and never touch a shilling that didn't come honest again. If we lost it seemed as if everything was so much the worse, and blacker than it looked at first, just for this bit of hope and comfort.

After the bull had been sworn to by Mr. Hood and another witness, they brought up some more evidence, as they called it, about the other cattle we had sold in Adelaide. They had fetched some of the farmers up that had been at the sale. They swore straight enough to having bought cattle with certain brands from Starlight. They didn't know, of course, at the time whose they were, but they could describe the brands fast enough. There was one fellow that couldn't read nor write, but he remembered all the brands, about a dozen, in the pen of steers he bought, and described them one by one. One brand, he said, was like a long-handled shovel. It turned out to be ⌐D. TD—Tom Dawson's, of Mungeree. About a hundred of his were in the mob. They had drawn back for Mungeree, as was nearly all frontage and cold in the winter. He was the worst witness for us of the lot, very near. He'd noticed everything and forgot nothing.

'Do you recognise either of the prisoners in the dock?' he was asked.

'Yes; both of 'em,' says he. I wish I could have got at him. 'I see the swell chap first—him as made out he was the owner, and gammoned all the Adelaide gentlemen so neat. There was a half-caste chap with him as followed him about everywhere; then there was another man as didn't talk much, but seemed, by letting down sliprails and what not, to be in it. I heard this Starlight, as he calls hisself now, say to him, "You have everything ready to break camp by ten o'clock, and I'll be there to-morrow and square up." I thought he meant to pay their wages. I never dropped but what they was his men—his hired servants—as he was going to pay off or send back.'

'Will you swear,' our lawyer says, 'that the younger prisoner is the man you saw at Adelaide with the cattle?'

'Yes; I'll swear. I looked at him pretty sharp, and nothing ain't likely to make me forget him. He's the man, and that I'll swear to.'

'Were there not other people there with the cattle?'

'Yes; there was an oldish, very quiet, but determined-like man—he had a stunnin' dorg with him—and a young man something like this gentleman—I mean the prisoner. I didn't see the other young man nor the half-caste in court.'

'That's all very well,' says our lawyer, very fierce; 'but will you swear, sir, that the prisoner Marston took any charge or ownership of the cattle?'

'No, I can't,' says the chap. 'I see him a drafting 'em in the morning, and he seemed to know all the brands, and so on; but he done no more than I've seen hired servants do over and over again.'

The other witnesses had done, when some one called out, 'Herbert Falkland,' and Mr. Falkland steps into the court. He walks in quiet and a little proud; he couldn't help feeling it, but he didn't show it in his ways and talk, as little as any man I ever saw.

He's asked by the Crown Prosecutor if he's seen the bull outside of the court this day.

'Yes; he has seen him.'

'Has he ever seen him before?'

'Never, to his knowledge.'

'He doesn't, then, know the name of his former owner?'

'Has heard generally that he belonged to Mr. Hood, of Momberah; but does not know it of his own knowledge.'

'Has he ever seen, or does he know either of the prisoners?'

'Knows the younger prisoner, who has been in the habit of working for him in various ways.'

'When was prisoner Marston working for him last?'

'He, with his brother James, who rendered his family a service he shall never forget, was working for him, after last shearing, for some months.'

'Where were they working?'

'At an out-station at the back of the run.'

'When did they leave?'

'About April or May last.'

'Was it known to you in what direction they proceeded after leaving your service?'

'I have no personal knowledge; I should think it improper to quote hearsay.'

'Had they been settled up with for their former work?'

'No, there was a balance due to them.'

'To what amount?'

'About twenty pounds each was owing.'

'Did you not think it curious that ordinary labourers should leave so large a sum in your hands?'

'It struck me as unusual, but I did not attach much weight to the circumstance. I thought they would come back and ask me for it before the next shearing. I am heartily sorry that they did not do so, and regret still more deeply that two young men worthy of a better fate should have been arraigned on such a charge.'

'One moment, Mr. Falkland,' says our counsel, as they call them, and a first-rate counsellor ours was. If we'd been as innocent as two schoolgirls he couldn't have done more for us. 'Did the prisoner Marston work well and conduct himself properly while in your employ?'

'No man better,' says Mr. Falkland, looking over to me with that pitying kind of look in his eyes as made me feel what a fool and rogue I'd been ten times worse than anything else. 'No man better; he and his brother were in many respects, according to my overseer's report, the most hard-working and best-conducted labourers in the establishment.'

CHAPTER XVIII

MR. RUNNIMALL, the auctioneer, swore that the older prisoner placed certain cattle in his hands, to arrive, for sale in the usual way, stating that his name was Mr. Charles Carisforth, and that he had several stations in other colonies. Had no reason for doubting him. Prisoner was then very well dressed, was gentlemanly in his manners, and came to his office with a young gentleman of property whom he knew well. The cattle were sold in the usual way for rather high prices, as the market was good. The proceeds in cash were paid over to the prisoner, whom he now knew by the name of Starlight. He accounted for there being an unusual number of brands by saying publicly at the sale that the station had been used as a depôt for other runs of his, and the remainder lots of store cattle kept there.

He had seen a short-horn bull outside of the court this day branded 'J-E' on the shoulder. He identified him as one of the cattle placed in his hands for sale by the prisoner Starlight. He sold and delivered him according to instructions. He subsequently handed over the proceeds to the said prisoner. He included the purchase money in a cheque given for the bull and other cattle sold on that day. He could swear positively to the bull; he was a remarkable animal. He had not the slightest doubt as to his identity.

'Had he seen the prisoner Marston when the cattle were sold, now alleged to belong to Mr. Hood?'

'Yes; he was confident that prisoner was with some other men whom he (witness) did not particularly remark. He helped to draft the cattle, and to put them in pens on the morning of the sale.'

'Was he prepared to swear that prisoner Marston was not a hired servant of prisoner Starlight?'

'No; he could not swear. He had no way of knowing what the relations were between the two. They were both in the robbery; he could see that.'

'How could you see that?' said our lawyer. 'Have you never seen a paid stockman do all that you saw prisoner Marston do?'

'Well, I have; but somehow I fancy this man was different.'

'We have nothing to do with your fancies, sir,' says our man, mighty hot, as he turns upon him; 'you are here to give evidence as to facts, not as to what you fancy. Have you any other grounds for connecting prisoner Marston with the robbery in question?'

'No. he had not.'

'You can go down, sir, and I only wish you may live to experience some of the feelings which fill the breasts of persons who are unjustly convicted.'

.   .   .   .   .   .

This about ended the trial. There was quite enough proved for a moderate dose of transportation. A quiet, oldish-looking man got up now and came forward to the witness-box. I didn't know who he was; but Starlight nodded to him quite pleasant. He had a short, close-trimmed beard, and was one of those nothing-particular-looking old chaps. I'm blessed if I could have told what he was. He might have been a merchant, or a squatter, or a head clerk, or a wine merchant, or a broker, or lived in the town, or lived in the country; any of half-a-dozen trades would suit him. The only thing that was out of the common was his eyes. They had a sort of curious way of looking at you, as if he wondered whether you was speaking true, and yet seein' nothing and tellin' nothing. He regular took in Starlight (he told me afterwards) by always talking about the China Seas; he'd been there, it seems; he'd been every-where; he'd last come from America; he didn't say he'd gone there to collar a clerk that had run off with two or three thousand pounds, and to be ready to meet him as he stepped ashore.

Anyhow he'd watched Starlight in Canterbury when he was riding and flashing about, and had put such a lot of things together that he took a passage in the same boat with him to Melbourne. Why didn't he arrest him in New Zealand? Because he wasn't sure of his man. It was from something Starlight let out on board ship. He told me himself afterwards that he made sure of his being the man he wanted; so he steps into the witness-box, very quiet and respectable-looking, with his white waistcoat and silk coat—it was hot enough to fry beef-steaks on the roof of the courthouse that day —and looks about him. The Crown Prosecutor begins with him as civil as you please.

'My name is Stephen Stillbrook. I am a sergeant detective of police in the service of the Government of New South Wales. From information received, I proceeded to Canterbury, in New Zealand, about the month of September last. I saw there the older prisoner, who was living at a first-class hotel in Christchurch. He was moving in good society, and was apparently possessed of ample means. He frequently gave expensive entertainments, which were attended by the leading inhabitants and high officials of the place. I myself obtained an introduction to him, and partook of his hos-pitality on several occasions. I attempted to draw him out in con-versation about New South Wales; but he was cautious, and gave me to understand that he had been engaged in large squatting transactions in another colony. From his general bearing and from the character of his associates, I came to the belief that he was not the individual named in the warrant, and determined to return to

Sydney. I was informed that he had taken his passage to Melbourne in a mail steamer. From something which I one day heard his half-caste servant say, who, being intoxicated, was speaking carelessly, I determined to accompany them to Melbourne. My suspicions were confirmed on the voyage. As we went ashore at the pier at Sandridge I accosted him. I said, "I arrest you on suspicion of having stolen a herd of cattle, the property of Walter Hood, of Momberah.' Prisoner was very cool and polite, just as any other gentleman would be, and asked me if I did not think I'd made a most ridiculous mistake. The other passengers began to laugh, as if it was the best joke in the world. Starlight never moved a muscle. I've seen a good many cool hands in my time, but I never met any one like him. I had given notice to one of the Melbourne police as he came aboard, and he arrested the half-caste, known as Warrigal. I produced a warrant, the one now before the court, which is signed by a magistrate of the territory of New South Wales.'

The witnessing part was all over. It took the best part of the day, and there we were all the time standing up in the dock, with the court crammed with people staring at us. I don't say that it felt as bad as it might have done nigh home. Most of the Nomah people looked upon fellows stealing cattle or horses, in small lots or big, just like most people look at boys stealing fruit out of an orchard, or as they used to talk of smugglers on the English coast, as I've heard father tell of. Any man might take a turn at that sort of thing, now and then, and not be such a bad chap after all. It was the duty of the police to catch him. If they caught him, well and good, it was so much the worse for him; if they didn't, that was their look-out. It wasn't anybody else's business anyhow. And a man that wasn't caught, or that got turned up at his trial, was about as good as the general run of people; and there was no reason for any one to look shy at him.

After the witnesses had said all they knew our lawyer got up and made a stunning speech. He made us out such first-rate chaps that it looked as if we ought to get off flying. He blew up the squatters in a general way for taking all the country, and not giving the poor man a chance—for neglecting their immense herds of cattle and suffering them to roam all over the country, putting temptation in the way of poor people, and causing confusion and recklessness of all kinds. Some of these cattle are never seen from the time they are branded till they are mustered, every two or three years apparently. They stray away hundreds of miles—probably a thousand—who is to know? Possibly they are sold. It was admitted by the prosecutor that he had sold 10,000 head of cattle during the last six years, and none had been rebranded to his knowledge. What means had he of knowing whether these cattle that so much was said about had not been legally sold before? It was a most monstrous thing that men like his clients—men who were an honour to the land they lived in—should be dragged up to the very centre of the continent upon a paltry charge like this—a charge which rested upon the flimsiest evidence it had ever been his good fortune to demolish.

With regard to the so-called imported bull, the case against his clients was apparently stronger, but he placed no reliance upon the statements of the witnesses, who averred that they knew him so thoroughly that they could not be deceived in him. He distrusted their evidence and believed the jury would distrust it too. The brand was as different as possible from the brand seen to have been on the beast originally. One short-horn was very like another. He would not undertake to swear positively in any such case, and he implored the jury, as men of the world, as men of experience in all transactions relating to stock (here some of the people in the court grinned), to dismiss from their minds everything of the nature of prejudice, and looking solely at the miserable, incomplete, unsatisfactory nature of the evidence, to acquit the prisoners.

It sounded all very pleasant after everything before had been so rough on our feelings, and the jury looked as if they'd more than half made up their minds to let us off.

Then the judge put on his glasses and began to go all over the evidence, very grave and steady like; and read bits out of the notes which he'd taken very careful all the time. Judges don't have such an easy time of it as some people thinks they have. I've often wondered as they take so much trouble, and works away so patient trying to find out the rights and wrongs of things for people that they never saw before, and won't see again. However, they try to do their best, all as I've ever seen, and they generally get somewhere near the right and justice of things. So the judge began and read— went over the evidence bit by bit, and laid it all out before the jury, so as they couldn't but see it where it told against us, and, again, where it was a bit in our favour.

As for the main body of the cattle, he made out that there was strong grounds for thinking as we'd taken and sold them at Adelaide, and had the money too. The making of a stockyard at the back of Momberah was not the thing honest men would do. But neither of us prisoners had been seen there. There was no identification of the actual cattle, branded 'HOD,' alleged to have been stolen, nor could Mr. Hood swear positively that they were his cattle, had never been sold, and were a portion of his herd. It was in the nature of these cases that identification of live stock, roaming over the immense solitudes of the interior, should be difficult, occasionally impossible. Yet he trusted that the jury would give full weight to all the circumstances which went to show a continuous possession of the animals alleged to be stolen. The persons of both prisoners had been positively sworn to by several witnesses as having been seen at the sale of the cattle referred to. They were both remarkable-looking men, and such as if once seen would be retained in the memory of the beholder.

But the most important piece of evidence (here the judge stopped and took a pinch of snuff) was that afforded by the short-horn bull, 'Fifteenth Duke of Cambridge'—he had been informed that was his name. That animal, in the first place, was sworn to most positively by Mr. Hood, and claimed as his property. Other credible witnesses testified also to his identity, and corroborated the evidence of Mr. Hood in all respects; the ownership and identity of the animal are thus established beyond all doubt.

Then there was the auctioneer, Mr. Runnimall, who swore that this animal had been, with other cattle, placed in his hands for sale by the older prisoner. The bull is accordingly sold publicly by him, and in the prisoner's presence. He subsequently receives from the witness the price, about £270, for which the bull was sold. The younger prisoner was there at the same time, and witnessed the sale of the bull and other cattle, giving such assistance as would lead to the conclusion that he was concerned in the transaction.

He did not wish to reflect upon this or any other jury, but he could not help recalling the fact that a jury in that town once committed the unpardonable fault, the crime, he had almost said, of refusing to find a prisoner guilty against whom well-confirmed evidence had been brought. It had been his advice to the Minister for Justice, so glaring was the miscarriage of justice to which he referred, that the whole of the jurymen who had sat upon that trial should be struck off the roll. This was accordingly done.

He, the judge, was perfectly convinced in his own mind that no impropriety of this sort was likely to be committed by the intelligent, respectable jury whom he saw before him; but it was his duty to warn them that, in his opinion, they could not bring in any verdict but 'Guilty' if they respected their oaths. He should leave the case confidently in their hands, again impressing upon them that they could only find one verdict if they believed the evidence.

． ． ． ． ．

The jury all went out. Then another case was called on, and a fresh jury sworn in for to try it. We sat in the dock. The judge told Starlight he might sit down, and we waited till they came back. I really believe that waiting is the worst part of the whole thing, the bitterest part of the punishment. I've seen men when they were being tried for their lives—haven't I done it, and gone through it myself?—waiting there an hour—two hours, half through the night, not knowing whether they was to be brought in guilty or not. What a hell they must have gone through in that time—doubt and dread, hope and fear, wretchedness and despair, over and over and over again. No wonder some of 'em can't stand it, but keeps twitching and shifting and getting paler and turning faint when the jury comes back, and they think they see one thing or the other written in their faces. I've seen a strong man drop down like a dead body when the judge opened his mouth to pass sentence on him. I've seen 'em faint, too, when the foreman of the jury said 'Not guilty.' One chap, he was an innocent up-country fellow, in for his first bit of duffing, like we was once, he covered his face with his hands when he found he was let off, and cried like a child. All sorts and kinds of different ways men takes it. I was in court once when the judge asked a man who'd just been found guilty if he'd anything to say why he shouldn't pass sentence of death upon him. He'd killed a woman, cut her throat, and a regular right down cruel murder it was (only men'll kill women and one another, too, for some causes, as long as the world lasts); and he just leaned over the dock rails, as if he'd been going to get three months, and said, cool and quiet, 'No, your Honour; not as I know of.' He'd made up his mind to it from the first, you see, and that makes all the difference. He knew he hadn't the ghost of a chance to get out of it, and when his time came he faced it. I remember seeing his worst enemy come into the court, and sit and look at him then just to see how he took it, but he didn't make the least sign. That man couldn't have told whether he seen him or not.

Starlight and I wasn't likely to break down—not much—whatever the jury did or the judge said. All the same, after an hour had passed, and we still waiting there, it began to be a sickening kind of feeling. The day had been all taken up with the evidence and the rest of the trial; all long, dragging hours of a hot summer's day. The sun had been blazing away all day on the iron roof of the court-house and the red dust of the streets, that lay inches deep for a mile all round the town. The flies buzzed all over the courthouse, and round and round, while the lawyers talked and wrangled with each other; and still the trial went on. Witness after witness was called, and cross-examined and bullied, and confused and contradicted till he was afraid to say what he knew or what he didn't know. I began to think it must be some kind of performance that would go on for ever and never stop, and the day and it never could end.

At last the sun came shining level with the lower window, and we knew it was getting late. After a while the twilight began to get dimmer and greyer. There isn't much out there when the sun goes down. Then the judge ordered the lamps to be lighted.

Just at that time the bailiff came forward.

'Your Honour, the jury has agreed.' I felt my teeth shut hard; but I made no move or sign. I looked over at Starlight. He yawned. He did, as I'm alive.

'I wish to heaven they'd make more haste,' he said quietly; 'his Honour and we are both being done out of our dinners.'

I said nothing. I was looking at the foreman's face. I thought I
knew the word he was going to say, and that word was 'Guilty.'
Sure enough I didn't hear anything more for a bit. I don't mind
owning that. Most men feel that way the first time. There was a
sound like rushing waters in my ears, and the courthouse and the
people all swam before my eyes.

The first I heard was Starlight's voice again, just as cool and
leisurely as ever. I never heard any difference in it, and I've known
him speak in a lot of different situations. If you shut your eyes
you couldn't tell from the tone of his voice whether he was fighting
for his life or asking you to hand him the salt. When he said the
hardest and fiercest thing—and he could be hard and fierce—he didn't
raise his voice; he only seemed to speak more distinct like. His eyes
were worse than his voice at such times. There weren't many men
that liked to look back at him, much less say anything.

Now he said, 'That means five years at Berrima, Dick, if not seven.
It's cooler than these infernal logs, that's one comfort.'

I said nothing. I couldn't joke. My throat was dry, and I felt
hot and cold by turns. I thought of the old hut by the creek, and
could see mother sitting rocking herself, and crying out loud, and
Aileen with a set, dull look on her face as if she'd never speak or
smile again. I thought of the days, months, years that were to pass
under lock and key, with irons and shame and solitude all for
company. I wondered if the place where they shut up mad people
was like a gaol, and why we were not sent there instead.

I heard part of what the judge said, but not all—bits here and
there. The jury had brought in a most righteous verdict; just what
he should have expected from the effect of the evidence upon an
intelligent, well-principled Nomah jury. (We heard afterwards
that they were six to six, and then agreed to toss up how the verdict
was to go.) 'The crime of cattle and horse stealing had assumed
gigantic proportions. Sheep, as yet, appeared to be safe; but then
there were not very many within a few hundred miles of Nomah.
It appeared to him that the prisoner known as Starlight, though from
old police records his real name appeared to be——'

Here he drew himself up and faced the judge in defiance. Then
like lightning he seemed to change, and said—

'Your Honour, I submit that it can answer no good purpose to
disclose my alleged name. There are others—I do not speak for
myself.'

The judge stopped a bit; then hesitated. Starlight bowed. 'I do
not—a—know whether there is any necessity to make public a name
which many years since was not better known than honoured. I
say the—a—prisoner known as Starlight has, from the evidence, taken
the principal part in this nefarious transaction. It is not the first
offence, as I observe from a paper I hold in my hand. The younger

prisoner, Marston, has very properly been found guilty of criminal complicity with the same offence. It may be that he has been concerned in other offences against the law, but of that we have no proof before this court. He has not been previously convicted. I do not offer advice to the elder criminal; his own heart and conscience, the promptings of which I assume to be dulled, not obliterated, I feel convinced, have said more to him in the way of warning, condemnation, and remorse than could the most impressive rebuke, the most solemn exhortation from a judicial bench. But to the younger man, to him whose vigorous frame has but lately attained the full development of early manhood, I feel compelled to appeal with all the weight which age and experience may lend. I adjure him to accept the warning which the sentence I am about to pass will convey to him, to endure his confinement with submission and repentance, and to lead during his remaining years, which may be long and comparatively peaceful, the free and necessarily happy life of an honest man. The prisoner Starlight is sentenced to seven years' imprisonment; the prisoner Richard Marston to five years' imprisonment; both in Berrima Gaol.'

I heard the door of the dock unclose with a snap. We were taken out; I hardly knew how. I walked like a man in his sleep. 'Five years, Berrima Gaol! Berrima Gaol!' kept ringing in my ears.

The day was done, the stars were out, as we moved across from the courthouse to the lock-up. The air was fresh and cool. The sun had gone down; so had the sun of our lives, never to rise again.

Morning came. Why did it ever come again? I thought. What did we want but night?—black as our hearts—dark as our fate—dismal as the death which likely would come quick as a living tomb, and the sooner the better. Mind you, I only felt this way the first time. All men do, I suppose, that haven't been born in gaols and workhouses. Afterwards they take a more everyday view of things.

'You're young and soft, Dick,' Starlight said to me as we were rumbling along in the coach next day, with hand and leg-irons on, and a trooper opposite to us. 'Why don't I feel like it? My good fellow, I have felt it all before. But if you sear your flesh or your horse's with a red-hot iron you'll find the flesh hard and callous ever after. My heart was seared once—ay, twice—and deeply, too. I have no heart now, or if I ever feel at all it's for a horse. I wonder how old Rainbow gets on.'

'You were sorry father let us come in the first time,' I said. 'How do you account for that, if you've no heart?'

'Really! Well, listen, Richard. Did I? If you guillotine a man—cut off his head, as they do in France, with an axe that falls like the monkey of a pile-driver—the limbs quiver and stretch, and move almost naturally for a good while afterwards. I've seen the performance more than once. So I suppose the internal arrangements immediately surrounding my heart must have performed some

CHAPTER XIX

It took us a week's travelling or more to get to Berrima. Sometimes we were all night in the coach as well as all day. There were other passengers in the coach with us. Two or three bushmen, a station overseer with his wife and daughter, a Chinaman, and a lunatic that had come from Nomah, too. I think it's rough on the public to pack madmen and convicts in irons in the same coach with them. But it saves the Government a good deal of money, and the people don't seem to care. They stand it, anyhow.

We would have made a bolt of it if we'd had a chance, but we never had, night nor day, not half a one. The police were civil, but they never left us, and slept by us at night. That is, one watched while the other slept. We began to sleep soundly ourselves and to have a better appetite. Going through the fresh air had something to do with it, I daresay. And then there was no anxiety. We had played for a big stake and lost. Now we had to pay and make the best of it. It was the tenth day (there were no railways then to shorten the journey) when we drove up to the big gate and looked at the high walls and dark, heavy lines of Berrima Gaol, the largest, the most severe, the most dreaded of all the prisons in New South Wales. It had leaked out the day before, somehow, that the famous Starlight and the other prisoner in the great Momberah cattle robbery were to be brought in this particular day. There was a fair-sized crowd gathered as we were helped down from the coach. At the side of the crowd was a small mob of blacks with their dogs, spears, 'possum rugs and all complete. They and their gins and pickaninnies appeared to take great notice of the whole thing. One tallish gin, darker than the others, and with her hair tucked under an old bonnet, wrapped her 'possum cloak closely round her shoulders and pushed up close to us. She looked hard at Starlight, who appeared not to see her. As she drew back some one staggered against her; an angry scowl passed over her face, so savage and bitter that I felt quite astonished. I should have been astonished, I mean, if I had not been able, by that very change, to know again the restless eyes and grim set mouth of Warrigal.

It was only a look, and he was gone. The lock creaked, the great iron door swung back, and we were swallowed up in a tomb—a stone vault where men are none the less buried because they have separate cells. They do not live, though they appear to be alive; they move, and sometimes speak, and appear to hear words. Some have to be sent away and buried outside. They have been dead a long time, but have not seemed to want putting in the ground. That makes no change in them—not much, I mean. If they sleep it's all right; if they don't sleep anything must be happiness after the life they have escaped. 'Happy are the dead' is written on all prison walls.

What I suffered in that first time no tongue can tell. I can't bear now to think of it and put it down. The solitary part of it was enough to drive any man mad that had been used to a free life. Day after day, night after night, the same and the same and the same over again.

Then the dark cells. I got into them for a bit. I wasn't always as cool as I might be—more times that mad with myself that I could have smashed my own skull against the wall, let alone any one else's. There was one of the warders I took a dislike to from the first, and he to me, I don't doubt. I thought he was rough and surly. He thought I wanted to have my own way, and he made it up to take it out of me, and run me every way he could. We had a goodish spell of fighting over it, but he gave in at last. Not but what I'd had a lot to bear, and took a deal of punishment before he jacked up. I needn't have had it. It was all my own obstinacy and a sort of dogged feeling that made me feel I couldn't give in. I believe it done me good, though. I do really think I should have gone mad else, thinking of the dreadful long months and years that lay before me without a chance of getting out.

Sometimes I'd take a low fit and refuse my food, and very near give up living altogether. The least bit more, and I'd have died outright. One day there was a party of ladies and gentlemen came to be shown over the gaol. There was a lot of us passing into the exercise yard. I happened to look up for a minute, and saw one of the ladies looking steadily at us, and oh! what a pitying look there was in her face. In a moment I saw it was Miss Falkland, and, by the change that came into her face, that she knew me again, altered as I was. I wondered how she could have known me. I was a different-looking chap from when she had seen me last. With a beastly yellow-grey suit of prison clothes, his face scraped smooth every day, like a fresh-killed pig, and the look of a free man gone out of his face for ever—how any woman, gentle or simple, ever can know a man in gaol beats me. Whether or no, she knew me. I suppose she saw the likeness to Jim, and she told him, true enough, she'd never forget him nor what he'd done for her.

I just looked at her, and turned my head away. I felt as if I'd make a fool of myself if I didn't. All the depth down that I'd fallen since I was shearing there at Boree rushed into my mind at once. I nearly fell down, I know. I was very weak and low then; I'd only just come out of the doctor's hands.

I was passing along with the rest of the mob. I heard her voice quite clear and firm, but soft and sweet, too. How sweet it sounded to me then!

'I wish to speak a few words to the third prisoner in the line—the tall one. Can I do so, Captain Wharton?'

'Oh! certainly, Miss Falkland,' said the old gentleman, who had brought them all in to look at the wonderful neat garden, and the baths, and the hospital, and the unnatural washed-up, swept-up barracks that make the cleanest gaol feel worse than the roughest hut. He was the visiting magistrate, and took a deal of interest in the place, and believed he knew all the prisoners like a book. 'Oh! certainly, my dear young lady. Is Richard Marston an acquaintance of yours?'

'He and his brother worked for my father at Boree,' she said, quite stately. 'His brother saved my life.'

I was called back by the warder. Miss Falkland stepped out before them all, and shook hands with me. Yes, *she shook hands with me,* and the tears came into her eyes as she did so.

If anything could have given a man's heart a turn the right way that would have done it. I felt again as if some one cared for me in the world, as if I had a soul worth saving. And people may talk as they like, but when a man has the notion that everybody has given him up as a bad job, and has dropped troubling themselves about him, he gets worse and worse, and meets the devil half-way.

She said—

'Richard Marston, I cannot tell how grieved I am to see you here. Both papa and I were so sorry to hear all about those Momberah cattle.'

I stammered out something or other, I hardly knew what.

She looked at me again with her great beautiful eyes like a wondering child.

'Is your brother here, too?'

'No, Miss Falkland,' I said. 'They've never caught Jim yet, and, what's more, I don't think they will. He jumped on a barebacked horse without saddle or bridle, and got clear.'

She looked as if she was going to smile, but she didn't. I saw her eyes sparkle, though, and she said softly—

'Poor Jim! so he got away; I am glad of that. What a wonderful rider he was! But I suppose he will be caught some day. Oh, I do so wish I could say anything that would make you repent of what you have done, and try to do better by and by. Papa says you have a long life before you most likely, and might do so much with it yet. You will try, for my sake; won't you now?'

'I'll do what I can, miss,' I said; 'and if I ever see Jim again I'll tell him of your kindness.'

'Thank you, and good-bye,' she said, and she held out her hand again and took mine. I walked away, but I couldn't help holding my head higher, and feeling a different man, somehow.

I ain't much of a religious chap, wasn't then, and I am farther off it now than ever, but I've heard a power of the Bible and all that read in my time; and when the parson read out next Sunday about Jesus Christ dying for men, and wanting to have their souls saved, I felt as if I could have a show of understanding it better than I ever did before. If I'd been a Catholic, like Aileen and mother, I should have settled what the Virgin Mary was like when she was alive, and never said a prayer to her without thinking of Miss Falkland.

While I was dying one week and getting over it another, and going through all the misery every fellow has in his first year of gaol, Starlight was just his old self all the time. He took it quite easy, never gave any one trouble, and there wasn't a soul in the place that wouldn't have done anything for him. The visiting magistrate thought his a most interesting case, and believed in his heart that he had been the means of turning him from the error of his ways—he and the chaplain between them, anyhow. He even helped him to be allowed to be kept a little separate from the other prisoners (lest they should contaminate him!), and in lots of ways made his life a bit easier to him.

It was reported about that it was not the first time that he had been in gaol. That he'd 'done time,' as they call it, in another colony. He might or he might not. He never said. And he wasn't the man, with all his soft ways, you'd like to ask about such a thing.

By the look of it you wouldn't think he cared about it a bit. He took it very easy, read half his time, and had no sign about him that he wasn't perfectly satisfied. He intended when he got out to lead a new life, the chaplain said, and be the means of keeping other men right and straight.

One day we had a chance of a word together. He got the soft side of the chaplain, who thought he wanted to convert me and take me out of my sulky and obstinate state of mind. He took good care that we were not overheard or watched, and then said rather loud, for fear of accidents—

'Well, Richard, how are you feeling? I am happy to say that I have been led to think seriously of my former evil ways, and I have made up my mind, besides, to use every effort in my power to clear out of this infernal collection of tombstones when the moon gets dark again, about the end of this month.'

'How have you taken to become religious?' I said. 'Are you quite sure that what you say can be depended upon? And when did you get the good news?'

'I have had many doubts in my mind for a long time,' he said, 'and have watched and prayed long, and listened for the word that was to come; and the end of it is that I have at length heard the news that makes the soul rejoice, even for the heathen, the boy Warrigal, who will be waiting outside these walls with fresh horses. I must now leave you, my dear Richard,' he said; 'and I hope my words will

have made an impression on you. When I have more to communi-
cate for your good I will ask leave to return.'

After I heard this news I began to live again. Was there a chance
of our getting out of this terrible tomb into the free air and sunshine
once more? However it was to be managed I could not make out.
I trusted mostly to Starlight, who seemed to know everything, and to
be quite easy about the way it would all turn out.'

All that I could get out of him afterwards was that on a certain
night a man would be waiting with two horses outside of the gaol
wall; and that if we had the luck to get out safe, and he thought we
should, we would be on their backs in three minutes, and all the
police in New South Wales wouldn't catch us once we got five
minutes' start.

This was all very well if it came out right; but there was an
awful lot to be done before we were even near it. The more I began
to think over it the worse it looked; sometimes I quite lost heart, and
believed we should never have half a chance of carrying out our
plan.

We knew from the other prisoners that men had tried from time to
time to get away. Three had been caught. One had been shot dead
—he was lucky—another had fallen off the wall and broke his leg.
Two had got clear off, and had never been heard of since.

We were all locked up in our cells every evening, and at five
o'clock, too. We didn't get out till six in the morning; a long, long
time. Cold enough in the bitter winter weather, that had then
come in, and a long, weary, wretched time to wait and watch for
daylight.

Well, first of all, we had to get the cell door open. That was the
easiest part of the lot. There's always men in a big gaol that all
kinds of keys and locks are like large print to. They can make most
locks fly open like magic; what's more, they're willing to do it for anybody else, or show them how. It keeps their hand in; they have a
pleasure in spiting those above them whenever they can do it.

The getting out of the cell was easy enough, but there was a lot
of danger after you had got out. A passage to cross, where the
warder, with his rifle, walked up and down every half-hour all night;
then a big courtyard; then another smaller door in the wall; then the
outer yard for those prisoners who are allowed to work at stone-
cutting or out-of-door trades.

After all this there was the great outer wall to climb up and drop
down from on the other side.

We managed to pick our night well. A French convict, who liked
that sort of thing, gave me the means of undoing the cell door. It
was three o'clock in the morning, when in winter most people are
sleepy that haven't much on their minds. The warder that came
down the passage wasn't likely to be asleep, but he might have
made it up in his mind that all was right, and not taken as much

notice as usual. This was what we trusted to. Besides, we had got
a few five-pound notes smuggled in to us, and though I wouldn't
say that we were able to bribe any of the gaolers, we didn't do ourselves any harm in one or two little ways by throwing a few
sovereigns about.

I did just as I was told by the Frenchman, and I opened the cell
door as easy as a wooden latch. I had to shut it again for fear the
warder would see it and begin to search and sound the alarm at
once. Just as I'd done this he came down the passage. I had only
time to crouch down in the shadow when he passed me. That was
right; now he would not be back for half-an-hour.

I crawled and scrambled, and crept along like a snake until little
by little I got to the gate through the last wall but one. The lock
here was not so easy as the cell door, and took me more time. While
I stood there I was in a regular tremble with fright, thinking some one
might come up, and all my chance would be gone. After a bit the
lock gave way, and I found myself in the outer yard. I went over to
the wall and crept along it till I came to one of the angles. There
I was to meet Starlight. He was not there, and he was to bring some
spikes to climb the wall with, and a rope, with two or three other
things.

I waited and waited for half-an-hour, which seemed a month.
What was I to do if he didn't come? I could not climb the thirty-
foot wall by myself. One had to be cautious, too, for there were
towers at short distances along the wall; in every one of these a
warder, armed with a rifle, which he was sure to empty at anyone
that looked like gaol-breaking. I began to think he had made a mistake in the night. Then, that he had been discovered and caught
the moment he tried to get out of the cell. I was sure to be caught
if he was prevented from coming; and shutting up would be harder
to bear than ever.

Then I heard a man's step coming up softly; I knew it was Starlight. I knew his step, and thought I would always tell it from a
thousand other men's; it was so light and firm, so quick and free.
Even in a prison it was different from other men's; and I remembered everything he had ever said about walking and running, both
of which he was wonderfully good at.

He was just as cool as ever. 'All right, Dick; take these spikes.'
He had half-a-dozen stout bits of iron; how ever he got them I know
no more than the dead, but there they were, and a light strong coil
of rope as well. I knew what the spikes were for, of course; to drive
into the wall between the stones and climb up by. With the rope
we were to drop ourselves over the wall the other side. It was thirty
feet high—no fool of a drop. More than one man had been picked
up disabled at the bottom of it. He had a short stout piece of iron
that did to hammer the spikes in; and that had to be done very soft
and quiet, you may be sure.

It took a long time. I thought the night would be over and the daylight come before it was all done; it was so slow. I could hear the tick-tack of his iron every time he knocked one of the spikes in. Of course he went higher every time. They were just far enough apart for a man to get his foot on from one to another. As he went up he had one end of the coil of the rope round his wrist. When he got to the top he was to draw it up to fasten to the top spike, and lower himself down by it to the ground on the other side. At last I felt him pull hard on the rope. I held it, and put my foot on the first spike. I don't know that I should have found it so very easy in the dark to get up by the spikes—it was almost black-fellows' work, when they put their big toe into a notch cut in the smooth stem of a gum tree that runs a hundred feet without a branch, and climb up the outside of it—but Jim and I had often practised this sort of climbing when we were boys, and were both pretty good at it. As for Starlight, he had been to sea when he was young, and could climb like a cat.

When I got to the top I could just see his head above the wall. The rope was fastened well to the top spike, which was driven almost to the head into the wall. Directly he saw me, he began to lower himself down the rope, and was out of sight in a minute. I wasn't long after him, you may be sure. In my hurry I let the rope slip through my hands so fast they were sore for a week afterwards. But I didn't feel it then. I should hardly have felt it if I had cut them in two, for as my feet touched the ground in the darkness I heard the stamp of a horse's hoof and the jingle of a bit—not much of a sound, but it went through my heart like a knife, along with the thought that I was a free man once more; that is, free in a manner of speaking. I knew we couldn't be taken then, bar accidents, and I felt ready to ride through a regiment of soldiers.

As I stood up a man caught my hand and gave it a squeeze as if he'd have crushed my fingers in. I knew it was Jim. Of course, I'd expected him to be there, but wasn't sure if he'd be able to work it. We didn't speak, but started to walk over to where two horses were standing, with a man holding 'em. It was pretty dark, but I could see Rainbow's star—just in his forehead it was—the only white he had about him. Of course it was Warrigal that was holding them.

'We must double-bank my horse,' whispers Jim, 'for a mile or two, till we're clear of the place; we didn't want to bring a lot of horses about.'

He jumped up, and I mounted behind him. Starlight was on Rainbow in a second. The half-caste disappeared, he was going to keep dark for a few days and send us the news. Jim's horse went off as if he had only ten stone on his back instead of pretty nigh five-and-twenty. And we were free! Lord God! to think that men can be such fools as ever to do anything of their own free will and guiding that puts their liberty in danger when there's such a world

CHAPTER XX

WHAT a different feel from prison air the fresh night breeze had as we swept along a lonely outside track! The stars were out, though the sky was cloudy now and then, and the big forest trees looked strange in the broken light. It was so long since I'd seen any. I felt as if I was going to a new world. None of us spoke for a bit. Jim pulled up at a small hut by the roadside; it looked like a farm, but there was not much show of crops or anything about the place. There was a tumble-down old barn, with a strong door to it, and a padlock; it seemed the only building that there was any care taken about. A man opened now the door of the hut and looked out.

'Look sharp,' says Jim. 'Is the horse all right and fit?'

'Fit enough to go for the Hawkesbury Guineas. I was up and fed him three hours ago. He's——'

'Bring him out, and be hanged to you,' says Jim; 'we've no time for chat.'

The man went straight to the barn, and after a minute or two brought out a horse—the same I'd ridden from Gippsland, saddled and bridled, and ready to jump out of his skin. Jim leaned forward and put something into his hand, which pleased him, for he held my rein and stirrup, and then said—

'Good luck and a long reign to you,' as we rode away.

All this time Starlight had sat on his horse in the shade of a tree a good bit away. When we started he rode alongside of us. We were soon in a pretty fair hand-gallop, and we kept it up. All our horses were good, and we bowled along as if we were going to ride for a week without stopping.

What a ride it was! It was a grand night, anyway I thought so. I blessed the stars, I know. Mile after mile, and still the horses seemed to go all the fresher the farther they went. I felt I could ride on that way for ever. As the horses pulled and snorted and snatched at their bridles I felt as happy as ever I did in my life. Mile after mile it was all the same; we could hear Rainbow snorting from time to time and see his star move as he tossed up his head. We had many a night ride after together, but that was the best. We had laid it out to make for a place we knew not so far from home. We dursn't go there straight, of course, but nigh enough to make a dart to it whenever we had word that the coast was clear.

We knew directly we were missed, the whole countryside would be turned out looking for us, and that every trooper within a hundred miles would be hoping for promotion in case he was lucky enough to drop on either of the Marstons or the notorious Starlight. His name had been pretty well in every one's mouth before, and would be a little more before they were done with him.

It was too far to ride to the Hollow in a day, but Jim had got a place ready for us to keep dark in for a bit, in case we got clear off. There's never any great trouble in us chaps finding a home for a week or two, and somebody to help us on our way as long as we've the notes to chuck about. All the worse in the long-run. We rode hardish (some people would have called it a hand-gallop) most of the way; up hill and down, across the rocky creeks, through thick timber. More than one river we had to swim. It was mountain water, and Starlight cursed and swore, and said he would catch his death of cold. Then we all laughed; it was the first time we'd done that since we were out. My heart was too full to talk, much less laugh, with the thought of being out of that cursed prison and on my own horse again, with the free bush breeze filling my breast, and the free forest I'd lived in all my life once more around me. I felt like a king, and as for what might come afterwards I had no more thought than a schoolboy has of his next year's lessons at the beginning of his holidays. It might come now. As I took the old horse by the head and raced him down the mountain side, I felt I was living again and might call myself a man once more.

The sun was just rising, the morning was misty and drizzling; the long sour-grass, the branches of the scrubby trees, everything we touched and saw was dripping with the night dew, as we rode up a 'gap' between two stiffish hills. We had been riding all night from track to track, sometimes steering by guesswork. Jim seemed to know the country in a general way, and he told us father and he had been about there a good deal lately, cattle-dealing and so on. For the last hour or so we had been on a pretty fair beaten road, though there wasn't much traffic on it. It was one of the old mail tracks once, but new coach lines had knocked away all the traffic. Some of the old inns had been good big houses, well kept and looked after then. Now lots of them were empty, with broken windows and everything in ruins; others were just good enough to let to people who would live in them, and make a living by cultivating a bit and selling grog on the sly. Where we pulled up was one of those places, and the people were just what you might expect.

First of all there was the man of the house, Jonathan Barnes, a tall, slouching, flash-looking native; he'd been a little in the horse-racing line, a little in the prize-fighting line—enough to have his nose broken, and was fond of talking about 'pugs' as he'd known intimate —a little in the farming and carrying line, a little in every line that meant a good deal of gassing, drinking, and idling, and mighty little hard work. He'd a decent, industrious little wife, about forty times too good for him, and the girls, Bella and Maddie, worked well, or else he'd have been walking about the country with a swag on his back. They kept him and the house, too, like many another man, and he took all the credit of it, and ordered them about as if he'd been the best and straightest man in the land. If he made a few pounds now and then he'd drop it on a horse-race before he'd had it a week. They were glad enough to see us, anyhow, and made us comfortable, after a fashion. Jim had brought fresh clothes, and both of us had stopped on the road and rigged ourselves out, so that we didn't look so queer as men just out of the jug mostly do, with their close-shaved faces, cropped heads, and prison clothes. Starlight had brought a false moustache with him, which he stuck on, so that he looked as much like a swell as ever. Warrigal had handed him a small parcel, which he brought with him, just as we started; and, with a ring on his finger, some notes and gold in his pocket, he ate his breakfast, and chatted away with the girls as if he'd only ridden out for a day to have a look at the country.

Our horses were put in the stable and well looked to, you may be sure. The man that straps a cross cove's horse don't go short of a half-crown—two or three of them, maybe. We made a first-rate breakfast of it; what with the cold and the wet and not being used to riding lately, we were pretty hungry, and tired too. We intended to camp there that day, and be off again as soon as it was dark.

Of course we ran a bit of a risk, but not as bad as we should by riding in broad daylight. The hills on the south were wild and rangy enough, but there were all sorts of people about on their business in the daytime; and of course any of them would know with one look that three men, all on well-bred horses, riding right across country and not stopping to speak or make free with anyone, were likely to be 'on the cross'—all the more if the police were making particular inquiries about them. We were all armed, too, now. Jim had seen to that. If we were caught, we intended to have a flutter for it. We were not going back to Berrima if we knew it.

So we turned in, and slept as if we were never going to wake again. We'd had a glass of grog or two, nothing to hurt, though; and the food and one thing and another made us sleep like tops. Jim was to keep a good look-out, and we didn't take off our clothes. Our horses were kept saddled, too, with the bridles on their heads, and only the bits out of their mouths— we could have managed without the bits at a pinch—everything ready to be out of the house in one minute, and in saddle and off full-split the next. We were learned that trick pretty well before things came to an end.

Besides that, Jonathan kept a good look-out, too, for strangers of the wrong sort. It wasn't a bad place in that way. There was a long stony track coming down to the house, and you could see a horseman or a carriage of any kind nearly a mile off. Then, in the old times, the timber had been cleared pretty nigh all round the place, so there was no chance of any one sneaking up unknown to people.

There couldn't have been a better harbour for our sort, and many a
jolly spree we had there afterwards. Many a queer sight that old
table in the little parlour saw years after, and the notes and gold and
watches and rings and things I've seen the girls handling would have
stunned you. But that was all to come.

Well, about an hour before dark Jim wakes us up, and we both
felt as right as the bank. It took a good deal to knock either of us
out of time in those days. I looked round for a bit and then burst
out laughing.

'What's that about, Dick?' says Jim, rather serious.

'Blest if I didn't think I was in the thundering old cell again,' I
said. 'I could have sworn I heard the bolt snap as your foot sounded
in the room.'

'Well, I hope we shan't, any of us, be shopped again for a while,'
says he, rather slow like. 'It's bad work, I'm afraid, and worse to
come; but we're in it up to our neck and must see it out. We'll
have another feed and be off at sundown. We've the devil's own ride
before daylight.'

'Anybody called?' says Starlight, sauntering in, washed and
dressed and comfortable-looking. 'You told them we were not at
home, Jim, I hope.'

Jim smiled in spite of himself, though he wasn't in a very gay
humour. Poor old Jim was looking ahead a bit, I expect, and didn't
see anything much to be proud of.

We had a scrumptious feed that night, beefsteaks and eggs, fresh
butter and milk, things we hadn't smelt for months. Then the girls
waited on us; a good-looking pair they was, too, full of larks and fun
of all kinds, and not very particular what sort of jokes they laughed
at. They knew well enough, of course, where we'd come from, and
what we laid by all day and travelled at night for; they thought none
the worse of us for that, not they. They'd been bred up where they'd
heard all kinds of rough talk ever since they was little kiddies, and
you couldn't well put them out.

They were a bit afraid of Starlight at first, though, because they
seen at once that he was a swell. Jim they knew a little of; he and
father had called there a good deal the last season, and had done a
little in the stock line through Jonathan Barnes. They could see I
was something in the same line as Jim. So I suppose they had
made it up to have a bit of fun with us that evening before we
started. They came down into the parlour where our tea was, dressed
out in their best and looking very grand, as I thought, particularly as
we hadn't seen the sight of so much as a woman's bonnet and shawl
for months and months.

'Well, Mr Marston,' says the eldest girl, Bella, to Jim, 'we didn't
expect you'd travel this way with friends so soon. Why didn't you
tell us, and we'd have had everything comfortable?'

'Wasn't sure about it,' says Jim, 'and when you ain't it's safest to hold your tongue. There's a good many things we all do that don't want talking about.'

'I feel certain, Jim,' says Starlight, with his soft voice and pleasant smile, which no woman as I ever saw could fight against long, 'that any man's secret would be safe with Miss Bella. I would trust her with my life freely—not that it's worth a great deal.'

'Oh! Captain,' says poor Bella, and she began to blush quite innocent like, 'you needn't fear; there ain't a girl from Shoalhaven to Albury that would let on which way you were heading, if they were to offer her all the money in the country.'

'Not even a diamond necklace and earrings? Think of a lovely pendant, a cross all brilliants, and a brooch to match, my dear girl.'

'I wouldn't "come it," unless I could get that lovely horse of yours,' says the youngest one, Maddie; 'but I'd do anything in the world to have him. He's the greatest darling I ever saw. Wouldn't he look stunning with a side-saddle? I've a great mind to "duff" him myself one of these days.'

'You shall have a ride on Rainbow next time we come,' says Starlight. 'I've sworn never to give him away or sell him, that is as long as I'm alive; but I'll tell you what I'll do—I'll leave him to you in my will.'

'How do you mean?' says she, quite excited like.

'Why, if I drop one of these fine days—and it's on the cards any time—you shall have Rainbow; but, mind now, you're to promise me' —here he looked very grave—'that you'll neither sell him, nor lend him, nor give him away as long as you live.'

'Oh! you don't mean it,' says the girl, jumping up and clapping her hands; 'I'd sooner have him than anything I ever saw in the world. Oh! I'll take such care of him. I'll feed him and rub him over myself; only I forgot, I'm not to have him before you're dead. It's rather rough on you, isn't it?'

'Not a bit,' says Starlight; 'we must all go when our time comes. If anything happens to me soon he'll be young enough to carry you for years yet. And you'll win all the ladies' hackney prizes at the shows.'

'Oh! I couldn't take him.'

'But you must now. I've promised him to you, and though I am a—well—an indifferent character, I never go back on my word.'

'Haven't you anything to give me, Captain?' says Bella; 'you're in such a generous mind.'

'I must bring you something,' says he, 'next time we call. What shall it be? Now's the time to ask. I'm like the fellow in the *Arabian Nights*, the slave of the ring—your ring.' Here he took the girl's hand, and pretending to look at a ring she wore took it up and kissed it. It wasn't a very ugly one neither. 'What will you have, Bella?'

'I'd like a watch and chain,' she said, pretending to look a little offended. 'I suppose I may as well ask for a good thing at once.'

Starlight pulled out a pocket-book, and, quite solemn and regular, made a note of it.

'It's yours,' he said, 'within a month. If I cannot conveniently call and present it in person, I'll send it by a sure hand, as they used to say; and now, Jim, boot and saddle.'

The horses were out by this time; the groom was walking Rainbow up and down; he'd put a regular French-polish on his coat, and the old horse was arching his neck and chawing his bit as if he thought he was going to start for the Bargo Town Plate. Jonathan himself was holding our two horses, but looking at him.

'My word!' he said, 'that's a real picture of a horse; he's too good for a—well—these roads; he ought to be in Sydney carrying some swell about and never knowing what a day's hardship feels like. Isn't he a regular out-and-outer to look at? And they tell me his looks is about the worst of him. Well—here's luck!' Starlight had called for drinks all round before we started. 'Here's luck to roads and coaches, and them as lives by 'em. They'll miss the old coaching system some day —mark my word. I don't hold with these railways they're talkin' about—all steam and hurry-scurry; it starves the country.'

'Quite right, Jonathan,' says Starlight, throwing his leg over Rainbow, and chucking the old groom a sovereign. 'The times have never been half as good as in the old coaching days, before we ever smelt a funnel in New South Wales. But there's a coach or two left yet, isn't there? and sometimes they're worth attending to.'

He bowed and smiled to the girls, and Rainbow sailed off with his beautiful easy, springy stride. He always put me in mind of the deer I once saw at Mulgoa, near Penrith; I'd never seen any before. My word! how one of them sailed over a farmer's wheat paddock fence. He'd been in there all night, and when he saw us coming he just up and made for the fence, and flew it like a bird. I never saw any horse have the same action, only Rainbow. You couldn't tire him, and he was just the same the end of the day as the beginning. If he hadn't fallen into Starlight's hands as a colt he'd have been a second-class racehorse, and wore out his life among touts and ringmen. He was better where he was. Off we went; what a ride we had that night! Just as well we'd fed and rested before we started, else we should never have held out. All that night long we had to go, and keep going. A deal of the road was rough—near the Shoalhaven country, across awful deep gullies with a regular climb-up the other side, like the side of a house. Through dismal ironbark forests that looked as black by night as if all the tree-trunks were cast-iron and the leaves gun-metal. The night wasn't as dark as it might have been, but now and again there was a storm, and the whole sky turned as black as a wolf's throat, as father used to say. We got a few knocks and scrapes against the trees, but, partly through the horses being pretty clever in their kind of way, and having sharpish eyesight of our own, we pulled through. It's no use talking, sometimes I thought Jim must lose his way. Starlight told us he'd made up his mind that we were going round and round, and would fetch up about where we'd started from, and find the Moss Vale police waiting there for us.

'All right, Captain,' says Jim; 'don't you flurry yourself. I've been along this track pretty often this last few months, and I can steer by the stars. Look at the Southern Cross there; you keep him somewhere on the right shoulder, and you'll pull up not so very far off that black range above old Rocky Flat.'

'You're not going to be so mad as to call at your own place, Jim, are you?' says he. 'Goring's sure to have a greyhound or two ready to slip in case the hare makes for her old form.'

'Trust old dad for that,' says Jim; 'he knows Dick and you are on the grass again. He'll meet us before we get to the place and have fresh horses. I'll bet he's got a chap or two that he can trust to smell out the traps if they are close handy the old spot. They'll be mighty clever if they get on the blind side of father.'

'Well, we must chance it, I suppose,' I said; 'but we were sold once, and I've not much fancy for going back again.'

'They're all looking for you the other way this blessed minute I'll go bail,' says Jim. 'Most of the coves that bolt from Berrima takes down the southern road to get across the border into Port Phillip as soon as they can work it. They always fancy they are safer there.'

'So they are in some ways; I wouldn't mind if we were back there again,' I said. 'There's worse places than Melbourne; but once we get to the Hollow, and that'll be some time to-day, we may take it easy and spell for a week or two. How they'll wonder what the deuce has become of us.'

The night was long, and that cold that Jim's beard was froze as stiff as a board; but I sat on my horse, I declare to heaven, and never felt anything but pleasure and comfort to think I was loose again. You've seen a dog that's been chained up. Well, when he's let loose, don't he go chevying and racing about over everything and into everything that's next or anigh him? He'll jump into water or over a fence, and turn aside for nothing. He's mad with joy and the feeling of being off the chain; he can't hardly keep from barking till he's hoarse, and rushing through and over everything till he's winded and done up. Then he lies down with his tongue out and considers it all over.

Well, a man's just like that when he's been on the chain. He mayn't jump about so much, though I've seen foreign fellows do that when their collar was unbuckled; but he feels the very same things in his heart as that dog does, you take my word for it.

So, as I said, though I was sitting on a horse all that long cold winter's night through, and had to mind my eye a bit for the road and the rocks and the hanging branches, I felt my heart swell that much and my courage rise that I didn't care whether the night was going to turn into a snowstorm like we'd been in Kiandra way, or whether we'd have a dozen rivers to swim, like the head-waters of the M'Alister, in Gippsland, as nearly drowned the pair of us. There I sat in my saddle like a man in a dream, lettin' my horse follow Jim's up hill and down dale, and half the time lettin' go his head and givin' him his own road. Everything, too, I seemed to notice and to be pleased with somehow. Sometimes it was a rock wallaby out on the feed that we'd come close on before we saw one another, and it would jump away almost under the horse's neck, taking two or three awful long springs and lighting square and level among the rocks after a drop-leap of a dozen feet, like a cat jumping out of a window. But the cat's got four legs to balance on and the kangaroo only two. How they manage it and measure the distance so well, God only knows. Then an old 'possum would sing out, a black-furred flying squirrel—pongos, the blacks call 'em—would come sailing down from the top of an ironbark tree, with all his stern sails spread, as the sailors say, and into the branches of another, looking as big as an eagle-hawk. And then we'd come round the corner of a little creek flat and be into the middle of a mob of wild horses that had come down from the mountain to feed at night. How they'd scurry off through the scrub and up the range, where it was like the side of a house, and that full of slate-bars all upon edge that you could smell the hoofs of the brumbies as the sharp stones rasped and tore and struck sparks out of them like you do the parings in a blacksmith's shop.

Then, just as I thought daybreak was near, a great mopoke flits close over our heads without any rustling or noise, like the ghost of a bird, and begins to hoot in a big, bare, hollow tree just ahead of us. Hoo-hoo! hoo-hoo! The last time I heard it, it made me shiver a bit. Now I didn't care. I was a desperate man that had done bad things, and was likely to do worse. But I was free of the forest again, and had a good horse under me; so I laughed at the bird and rode on.

CHAPTER XXI

DAYLIGHT broke when we were close up to the Black Range, safe enough, a little off the line but nothing to signify. Then we hit off the track that led over the Gap and down into a little flat on a creek that ran the same way as ours did.

Jim had managed for father and Warrigal to meet us somewhere near here with fresh horses. There was an old shepherd's hut that stood by itself almost covered with marshmallows and nettles. As we came down the steep track a dog came up snuffing and searching about the grass and stones as if he'd lost something. It was Crib.

'Now we're getting home, Jim,' says Starlight. 'It's quite a treat to see the old scamp again. Well, old man,' he said to the dog, 'how's all getting on at the Hollow?' The dog came right up to Rainbow and rubbed against his fetlock, and jumped up two or three times to see if he could touch his rider. He was almost going to bark, he seemed that glad to see him and us.

Dad was sitting on a log by that hut smoking, just the same as he was before he left us last time. He was holding two fresh horses, and we were not sorry to see them. Horses are horses, and there wasn't much left in our two. We must have ridden a good eighty miles that night, and it was as bad as a hundred by daylight.

Father came a step towards us as we jumped off. By George, I was that stiff with the long ride and the cold that I nearly fell down. He'd got a bit of a fire, so we lit our pipes and had a comfortable smoke.

'Well, Dick, you're back agin, I see,' he says, pretty pleasant for him. 'Glad to see you, Captain, once more. It's been lonesome work —nobody but me and Jim and Warrigal, that's like a bear with a sore head half his time. I'd a mind to roll into him once or twice, and I should, too, only for his being your property like.'

'Thank you, Ben, I'll knock his head off myself as soon as we get settled a bit. Warrigal's not a bad boy, but a good deal like a Rocky Mountain mule; he's no good unless he's knocked down about once a month or so, only he doesn't like any one but me to do it.'

'You'll see him about a mile on,' says father. 'He told me he'd be behind the big rock where the tree grows—on the left of the road. He said he'd get you a fresh horse, so as he could take Rainbow back to the Hollow the long way round.'

Sure enough after we'd just got well on the road again Warrigal comes quietly out from behind a big granite boulder and shows himself. He was riding Bilbah, and leading a well-bred, good-looking chestnut. He was one of the young ones out of the Hollow. He'd broken him and got him quiet. I remembered when I was there first spotting him as a yearling. I knew the blaze down his face and his three white legs.

Warrigal jumps off Bilbah and throws down the bridle. Then he leads the chestnut up to where Starlight was standing smoking, and throws himself down at his feet, bursting out crying like a child. He was just like a dog that had found his master again. He kept looking up at Starlight just like a dog does, and smiling and going on just as if he never expected to see such a good thing again as long as he lived.

'Well, Warrigal,' says Starlight, very careless like, 'so you've brought me a horse, I see. You've been a very good boy. Take Rainbow round the long way into the Hollow. Look after him, whatever you do, or I'll murder you. Not that he's done, or anything near it; but had enough for one ride, poor old man. Off with you!' He changed the saddle, and Warrigal hopped on to Bilbah, and led off Rainbow, who tossed his head and trotted away as if he'd lots to spare, and hadn't had twelve hours under saddle; best part without a halt or a bait. I've seen a few good 'uns in my time, but I never saw the horse that was a patch on Rainbow, take him all round.

We pushed on again, then, for ten miles, and somewhere about eight o'clock we pulled up at home—at home. Aileen knew we were coming, and ran out to meet us. She threw her arms round me, and kissed and cried over me for ever so long before she took any notice of Starlight, who'd got down and was looking another way. 'Oh! my boy, my boy,' she said, 'I never thought to see you again for years. How thin you've got and pale, and strange looking. You're not like your old self at all. But you're in the bush again now, by God's blessing. We must hide you better next time. I declare I begin to feel quite wicked, and as if I could fight the police myself.'

'Well spoken, Miss Marston,' said Starlight, just lifting his hat and making a bit of a bow like, just as if she was a real lady; but he was the same to all women. He treated them all alike with the same respect of manner as if they were duchesses; young or old, gentle or simple—it made no odds to him. 'We must have your assistance if we're to do any good. Though whether it wouldn't be more prudent on your part to cut us all dead, beginning with your father, I shouldn't like to say.'

Aileen looked at him, surprised and angry like for a second. Then she says—

'Captain Starlight, it's too late now; but words can never tell how I hate and despise the whole thing. My love for Dick got the better of my reason for a bit, but I could—— Why, how pale you look!'

He was growing pale, and no mistake. He had been ill for a bit before he left Berrima, though he wouldn't give in, and the ride was rather too much for him, I suppose. Anyhow, down he tumbles in a dead faint. Aileen rushed over and lifted up his head. I got some water and dabbed it over him. After a bit he came to. He raises himself on his elbows and looks at Aileen. Then he smiles quietly and says—

'I'm quite ashamed of myself. I'm growing as delicate as a young lady. I hope I haven't given you much trouble.'

When he got up and walked to the verandah he quite staggered, showing he was that weak as he could hardly walk without help.

'I shall be all right,' he said, 'after a week's riding again.'

'And where are you going when you leave this place?' she asked. 'Surely you and my brothers never can live in New South Wales after all that has passed.'

'We must try, at all events, Miss Marston,' Starlight answered, raising up his head and looking proud. 'You will hear something of us before long.'

We made out that there was no great chance of our being run into at the old place. Father went on first with Crib. He was sure to give warning in some way, best known to father himself, if there was any one about that wasn't the right sort. So we went up and went in.

Mother was inside. I thought it was queer that she didn't come outside. She was always quick enough about that when we came home before, day or night. When I went in I could see, when she got up from her chair, that she was weak, and looked as if she'd been ill. She looked ever so much older, and her hair was a lot greyer than it used to be.

She held out her arms and clung round my neck as if I'd been raised from the dead. So I was in a kind of a way. But she didn't say much, or ask what I was going to do next. Poor soul! she knew it couldn't be much good anyway; and that if we were hunted before, we'd be worse hunted now. Those that hadn't heard of our little game with the Momberah cattle would hear of our getting out of Berrima Gaol, which wasn't done every day.

We hadn't a deal of time to spare, because we meant to start off for the Hollow that afternoon, and get there some time in the night, even if it was late. Jim and dad knew the way in almost blindfold. Once we got there we could sleep for a week if we liked, and take it easy all roads. So father told mother and Aileen straight that we'd come for a good comfortable meal and a rest, and we must be off again.

'O! father, can't Dick and Jim stop for a day?' cries out Aileen. 'It does seem so hard when we haven't seen Dick for such a while; and he shut up, too, all the time.'

'D'ye want to have us all took the same as last time?' growls father. 'Women's never contented as I can see. For two pins I wouldn't have brought them this way at all. I don't want to be making roads from this old crib to the Hollow, only I thought you'd like one look at Dick.'

'We must do what's best, of course,' said poor Aileen; 'but it's hard—very hard on us. It's mother I'm thinking of, you know. If you knew how she always wakes up in the night, and calls for Dick, and cries when she wakes up, you'd try to comfort her a bit more, father.'

'Comfort her!' says dad; 'why, what can I do? Don't I tell you if we stay about here we're shopped as safe as anything ever was? Will that comfort her, or you either? We're safe to-day because I've got telegraphs on the outside that the police can't pass without ringing the bell—in a way of speaking. But you see to-morrow there'll be more than one lot here, and I want to be clean away before they come.'

'You know best,' says Aileen; 'but suppose they come here to-morrow morning at daylight, as they did last time, and bring a black tracker with them, won't he be able to follow up your track when you go away to-night?'

'No, he won't; for this reason, we shall all ride different ways as soon as we leave here. A good while before we get near the place where we all meet we shall find Warrigal on the look-out. He can take the Captain in by another track, and there'll be only Jim and I and the old dog, the only three persons that'll go in the near way.'

'And when shall we see—see—any of you again?'

'Somewheres about a month, I suppose, if we've luck. There's a deal belongs to that. You'd better go and see what there is for us to eat. We've a long way and a rough way to go before we get to the Hollow.'

Aileen was off at this, and then she set to work and laid a clean tablecloth in the sitting-room and set us down our meal—breakfast, or whatever it was. It wasn't so bad—corned beef, first-rate potatoes, fresh damper, milk, butter, eggs. Tea, of course, it's the great drink in the bush; and although some doctors say it's no good, what would bushmen do without it?

We had no intention of stopping the whole night, though we were tempted to do so—to have one night's rest in the old place where we used to sleep so sound before. It was no good thinking of anything of that kind, any how, for a good while to come. What we'd got to do was to look out sharp and not be caught simple again like we was both last time.

After we had our tea we sat outside the verandah, and tried to make the best of it. Jim stayed inside with mother for a good while; she didn't leave her chair much now, and sat knitting by the hour together. There was a great change come over her lately. She didn't seem to be afraid of our getting caught as she used to be, nor half as glad or sorry about anything. It seemed like as if she'd made up her mind that everything was as bad as it could be, and past mending. So it was; she was right enough there. The only one who was in real good heart and spirits was Starlight. He'd come round again, and talked and rattled away, and made Aileen and Jim and me laugh, in spite of everything. He said we had all fine times before us now for a year or two, any way. That was a good long time. After that anything might happen. What it would be he neither knew nor cared. Life was made up of short bits; sometimes it was hard luck; sometimes everything went jolly and well. We'd got our liberty again, our horses, and a place to go to, where all the police in the country would never find us. He was going in for a short life and a merry one. He, for one, was tired of small adventures, and he was determined to make the name of Starlight a little more famous before very long. If Dick and Jim would take his advice—the advice of a desperate, ill-fated outcast, but still staunch to his friends—they would clear out, and leave him to sink or swim alone, or with such associates as he might pick up, whose destination would be no great matter whatever befell them. They could go into hiding for a while—make for Queensland and then go into the Northern Territory. There was new country enough there to hide all the fellows that were 'wanted' in New South Wales.

'But why don't you take your own advice?' said Aileen, looking over at Starlight as he sat there quite careless and comfortable-looking, as if he'd no call to trouble his head about anything. 'Isn't your life worth mending or saving? Why keep on this reckless miserable career which you yourself expect to end ill?'

'If you ask me, Miss Marston,' he said, 'whether my life—what is left of it—is worth saving, I must distinctly answer that it is not. It is like the last coin or two in the gambler's purse, not worth troubling one's head about. It must be flung on the board with the rest. It might land a reasonable stake. But as to economising and arranging details that would surely be the greatest folly of all.'

I heard Aileen sigh to herself. She said nothing for a while; and then old Crib began to growl.. He got up and walked along the track that led up the hill. Father stood up, too, and listened. We all did except Starlight, who appeared to think it was too much trouble, and never moved or seemed to notice.

Presently the dog came walking slowly back, and coiled himself up again close to Starlight, as if he had made up his mind it didn't matter. We could hear a horse coming along at a pretty good bat over the hard, rocky, gravelly road. We could tell it was a single horse, and more than that, a bare-footed one, coming at a hand-gallop up hill and down dale in a careless kind of manner. This wasn't likely to be a police trooper. One man wouldn't come by himself to a place like ours at night; and no trooper, if he did come, would clatter along a hard track, making row enough to be heard more than a mile off on a quiet night.

'It's all right,' says father. 'The old dog knowed him; it's Billy the Boy. There's something up.'

Just as he spoke we saw a horseman come in sight; and he rattled down the stony track as hard as he could lick. He pulled up just opposite the house, close by where we were standing. It was a boy about fifteen, dressed in a ragged pair of moleskin trousers, a good deal too large for him, but kept straight by a leather strap round the waist. An old cabbage-tree hat and a blue serge shirt made up the rest of his rig. Boots he had on, but they didn't seem to be fellows, and one rusty spur. His hair was like a hay-coloured mop, half hanging over his eyes, which looked sharp enough to see through a gum tree and out at the other side.

He jumped down and stood before us, while his horse's flanks heaved up and down like a pair of bellows.

"Well, what's up?" says father.

'My word, governor, you was all in great luck as I come home last night, after bein' away with them cattle to pound. Bobby, he don't know a p'leeceman from a wood-an'-water joey; he'd never have dropped they was comin' here unless they'd pasted up a notice on the door.'

'How did you find out, Billy?' says father, 'and when'll they be here?'

'Fust thing in the morning,' says the young wit, grinning all over his face. 'Won't they be jolly well sold when they rides up and plants by the yard, same as they did last time, when they took Dick.'

'Which ones was they?' asks father, fillin' his pipe quite business-like, just as if he'd got days to spare.

'Them two fellers from Bargo; one of 'em's a new chum—got his hair cut short, just like Dick's. My word, I thought he'd been waggin' it from some a' them Gov'ment institoosh'ns. I did raly, Dick, old man.'

'You're precious free and easy, my young friend,' says Starlight, walking over. 'I rather like you. You have a keen sense of humour, evidently; but can't you say how you found out that the men were her Majesty's police officers in pursuit of us?'

'You're Cap'n Starlight, I suppose,' says the youngster, looking straight and square at him, and not a bit put out. 'Well, I've been pretty quick coming; thirty mile inside of three hours, I'll be bound. I heard them talking about you. It was Starlight this and Starlight that all the time I was going in and out of the room, pretending to look for something, and mother scolding me.'

'Had they their uniform on?' I asked.

'No fear. They thought we didn't tumble, I expect; but I seen their horses hung up outside, both shod all round; bits and irons bright. Stabled horses, too, I could swear. Then the youngest chap —his with the old felt hat—walked like this.'

Here he squared his shoulders, put his hands by his side, and marched up and down, looking for all the world like one of them chaps that played at soldiering in Bargo.

'There's no hiding the military air, you think, Billy?' said Starlight. 'That fellow was a recruit, and had been drilled lately.'

'I d'no. Mother got 'em to stay, and began to talk quite innocent-like of the bad characters there was in the country. Ha! ha! It was as good as a play. Then they began to talk almost right out about Sergeant Goring having been away on a wrong scent, and how wild he was, and how he would be after Starlight's mob to-morrow morning at daylight, and some p'leece was to meet him near Rocky Flat. They didn't say they was the p'leece; that was about four o'clock, and getting dark.'

'How did you get the horse?' says Jim. 'He's not one of yours, is he?'

'Not he,' says the boy; 'I wish I had him or the likes of him. He belongs to old Driver. I was just workin' it how I'd get out and catch our old moke without these chaps being fly as I was going to talligrarph, when mother says to me—

'"Have you fetched in the black cow?"

'We ain't got no black cow, but I knowed what she meant. I says—

'"No, I couldn't find her."

'"You catch old Johnny Smoker and look for her till you do find her, if it's ten o'clock to-night," says mother, very fierce. "Your father'll give you a fine larrupin' if he comes home and there's that cow lost."

'So off I goes and mans old Johnny, and clears out straight for here. When I came to Driver's I runs his horses up into a yard nigh the angle of his outside paddock and collars this little 'oss, and lets old Johnny go in hobbles. My word, this cove can scratch!'

'So it seems,' says Starlight; 'here's a sovereign for you, youngster. Keep your ears and eyes open; you'll always find that good information brings a good price. I'd advise you to keep away from Mr Marston, sen., and people of his sort, and stick to your work, if I thought there was the least earthly chance of your doing so; but I see plainly that you're not cut out for the industrious, steady-going line.'

'Not if I know it,' said the boy, 'I want to see life before I die. I'm not going to keep on milling and slaving day after day all the year round. I'll cut it next year as sure as a gun. I say, won't you let me ride a bit of the way with ye?'

'Not a yard,' says father, who was pretty cranky by this time; 'you go home again and put that horse where you got him. We don't want old Driver tracking and swearing after us because you ride his horses; and keep off the road as you go back.'

Billy the Boy nodded his head, and, jumping into his saddle, rode off again at much about the same pace he'd come at. He was a regular reckless young devil, as bold as a two-year-old colt in a brand-ing-yard, that's ready to jump at anything and knock his brains out against a stockyard post, just because he's never known any real regular hurt or danger, and can't ¬realise it. He was terrible cruel to horses, and would ruin a horse in less time than any man or boy I ever seen. I always thought from the first that he'd come to a bad end. Howsoever, he was a wonderful chap to track and ride; none could beat him at that; he was nearly as good as Warrigal in the bush. He was as cunning as a pet dingo, and would look as stupid before any one he didn't know, or thought was too respectable, as if he was half an idiot. But no one ever stirred within twenty or thirty miles of where he lived without our hearing about it. Father fished him out, having paid him pretty well for some small service, and ever after that he said he could sleep in peace.

We had the horses up, ready saddled and fed, by sundown, and as soon as the moon rose we made a start of it. I had time for a bit of a talk with Aileen about the Storefields, though I couldn't bring my-self to say their names at first. I was right in thinking that Gracey had seen me led away a prisoner by the police. She came into the hut afterwards with Aileen, as soon as mother was better, and the two girls sat down beside one another and cried their eyes out, Aileen said.

George Storefield had been very good, and told Aileen that, what-ever happened us or the old man, it would make no difference to him or to his feelings towards her. She thanked him, but said she could never consent to let him disgrace himself by marrying into a family like ours. He had come over every now and then, and had seen they wanted for nothing when father and Jim were away; but she always felt her heart growing colder towards him and his prosperity while we were so low down in every way. As for Gracey, she (Aileen) believed that she was in love with me in a quiet, steady way of her own, without showing it much, but that she would be true to me, if I asked her, to the end of the world, and she was sure that she could never marry any one else as long as I lived. She was that sort of girl. So didn't I think I ought to do everything I could to get a better character, and try and be good enough for such a girl? She knew girls pretty well. She didn't think there was such another girl in the whole colony, and so on.

And when we went away where were we going to hide? I could not say about particular distances, but I told her generally that we'd keep out of harm's way, and be careful not to be caught. We might see her and mother now and then, and by bush-telegraphs and other people we could trust should be able to send news about ourselves.

'What's the Captain going to do?' she said suddenly. 'He doesn't look able to bear up against hardship like the rest of you. What beautiful small hands he has, and his eyes are like sleeping fires.'

'Oh, he's a good deal stronger than he looks,' I said; 'he's the smartest of the lot of us, except it is dad, and I've heard the old man say he must knock under to him. But don't you bother your head about him; he's quite able to take care of himself, and the less a girl like you thinks about a man like him the better for her.'

'Oh, nonsense,' she said, at the same time looking down in a half-confused sort of way. 'I'm not likely to think about him or any one else just now; but it seems such a dreadful thing to think a man like him, so clever and daring, and so handsome and gentle in his ways, should be obliged to lead such a life, hunted from place to place like—like——'

'Like a bush-ranger, Ailie,' I said, 'for that'll be the long and short of it. You may as well know it now, we're going to "turn out."'

'You don't say that, Dick,' she said. 'Oh! surely you will never be so mad. Do you want to kill mother and me right out? If you do, why not take a knife or an axe and do it at once? Her you've been killing all along. As for me, I feel so miserable and degraded and despairing at times that but for her I could go and drown myself in the creek when I think of what the family is coming to.'

'What's the use of going on like that, Aileen?' I said, roughly. 'If we're caught now, whatever we do, great or small, we're safe for years and years in gaol. Mayn't we as well be hung for a sheep as a lamb? What odds can it make? We'll only have bolder work than duffing cattle and faking horse-brands like a lot of miserable crawlers that are not game for anything more sporting.'

'I hear, I hear,' says sister, sitting down and putting her head in her hands. 'Surely the devil has power for a season to possess himself of the souls of men, and do with them what he will. I know how obstinate you are, Dick. Pray God you may not have poor Jim's blood to answer for as well as your own before all is done. Good-bye. I can't say God bless you, knowing what I do; but may He turn your heart from all wicked ways, and keep you from worse and deadlier evil than you have committed! Good-night. Why, oh why, didn't we all die when we were little children!'

CHAPTER XXII

I BROUGHT it out sudden-like to Aileen before I could stop myself, but it was all true. How we were to make the first start we couldn't agree; but we were bound to make another big touch, and this time the police would be after us for something worth while. Anyhow, we could take it easy at the Hollow for a bit, and settle all the ins and outs without hurrying ourselves.

Our dart now was to get to the Hollow that night some time, and not to leave much of a track either. Nobody had found out the place yet, and wasn't going to if we knew. It was too useful a hiding-place to give away without trouble, and we swore to take all sorts of good care to keep it secret, if it was to be done by the art of man.

We went up Nulla Mountain the same way as we remembered doing when Jim and I rode to meet father that time he had the lot of weaners. We kept wide and didn't follow on after one another so as to make a marked trail. It was a long, dark, dreary ride. We had to look sharp so as not to get dragged off by a breast-high bough in the thick country. There was no fetching a doctor if anyone was hurt. Father rode ahead. He knew the ins and outs of the road better than any of us, though Jim, who had lived most of his time in the Hollow after he got away from the police, was getting to know it pretty well. We were obliged to go slow mostly—for a good deal of the track lay along the bed of a creek, full of boulders and rocks, that we had to cross over so many times in a mile. The sharp-edged rocks, too, overhung low enough to knock your brains out if you didn't mind.

It was far into the night when we got to the old yard. There it stood, just as I recollect seeing it the time Jim and I and father branded the weaners. It had only been used once or twice since. It was patched up a bit in places, but nobody seemed to have gone next or nigh it for a long time. The grass had grown up round the sliprails; it was as strange and forsaken-looking as if it belonged to a deserted station.

As we rode up a man comes out from an angle of the fence and gives a whistle. We knew, almost without looking, that it was Warrigal. He'd come there to meet Starlight and take him round some other way. Every track and short cut there was in the mountains was as easy to him as the road to George Storefield's was to us. Nulla Mountain was full of curious gullies and caves and places that the devil himself could hardly have run a man to ground in, unless he'd lived near it all his life as Warrigal had. He wasn't very free in showing them to us, but he'd have made a bridge of his own body any time to let Starlight go safe. So when they rode away together we knew he was safe whoever might be after us, and that we should see him in the Hollow some time next day.

We went on for a mile or two farther; then we got off, and turned our horses loose. The rest of the way we had to do on foot. My horse and Jim's had got regularly broke into Rocky Flat, and we knew that they'd go home as sure as possible, not quite straight, but keeping somewhere in the right direction. As for father, he always used to keep a horse or two, trained to go home when he'd done with him. The pony he rode to-night would just trot off, and never put his nose to the ground almost till he got wind of home.

We humped our saddles and swags ourselves; a stiffish load, too, but the night was cool, and we did our best. It was no use growling. It had to be done, and the sooner the better. It seemed a long time—following father step by step—before we came to the place where I thought the cattle were going to be driven over the precipice. Here we pulled up for a bit and had a smoke. It was a queer time and a queer look-out.

Three o'clock in the morning—the stars in the sky, and it so clear that we could see Nulla Mountain rising up against it, a big black lump, without sign of tree or rock; underneath the valley, one sea of mist, and we just agoing to drop into it on the other side of the Hollow, the clear hill we called the Sugar-loaf. Everything seemed dead, silent, and solitary, and a rummier start than all, here were we —three desperate men, driven to make ourselves a home in this lonesome, God-forsaken place! I wasn't very fanciful by that time, but if the devil had risen up to make a fourth amongst us I shouldn't have been surprised. The place, the time, and the men seemed regularly cut out for him and his mob.

We smoked our pipes out, and said nothing to each other, good or bad. Then father makes a start, and we follow him; took a goodish while, but we got down all right, and headed for the cave. When we got there our troubles were over for a while. Jim struck a match and had a fire going in no time; there was plenty of dry wood, of course. Then father rolls a keg out of a hole in the wall; first-rate dark brandy it was, and we felt a sight better for a good stiff nip all round. When a man's cold and tired, and hungry, and down on his luck as well, a good caulker of grog don't do him no harm to speak of. It strings him up and puts him straight. If he's anything of a man he can stand it, and feel all the better for it; but it's a precious sight too easy a lesson to learn, and there's them that can't stop, once they begin, till they've smothered what brains God Almighty put inside their skulls, just as if they was to bore a hole and put gunpowder in. No! they wouldn't stop if they were sure of going to heaven straight, or to hell next minute if they put the last glass to their lips. I've heard men say it, and knew they meant it. Not the worst sort of men, either.

We were none of us like that. Not then, anyhow. We could take or leave it, and though dad could do with his share when it was going, he always knew what he was about, and could put the peg in any time. So we had one strongish tot while the tea was boiling. There was a bag of ship biscuit; we fried some hung beef, and made a jolly good supper. We were that tired we didn't care to talk much, so we made up the first last thing and rolled ourselves in our blankets; I didn't wake till the sun had been up an hour or more.

I woke first; Jim was fast asleep, but dad had been up a goodish while and got things ready for breakfast. It was a fine, clear morning; everything looked beautiful, 'specially to me that had been locked up away from this sort of thing so long. The grass was thick and green round the cave, and right up to the big sandstone slabs of the floor, looking as if it had never been eat down very close. No more it had. It would never have paid to have overstocked the Hollow. What cattle and horses they kept there had a fine time of it, and were always in grand condition.

Opposite where we were the valley was narrow. I could see the standstone precipices that walled us in, a sort of yellowish, white colour, all lighted up with the rays of the morning sun, looking like gold towers against the heavy green forest timber at the foot of them. Birds were calling and whistling, and there was a little spring that fell drip, drip over a rough rock basin all covered with ferns. A little mob of horses had fed pretty close up to the camp, and would walk up to look curious-like, and then trot off with their heads and tails up. It was a pretty enough sight that met my eyes on waking. It made me feel a sort of false happiness for a time, to think we had such a place to camp in on the quiet, and call our own, in a manner of speaking.

Jim soon woke up and stretched himself. Then father began, quite cheerful like—

'Well, boys, what d'ye think of the Hollow again? It's not a bad earth for the old dog-fox and his cubs when the hounds have run him close. They can't dig him out here, or smoke him out either. We've no call to do anything but rest ourselves for a week or two anyhow; then we must settle on something and buckle to it more business-like. We've been too helter-skelter lately, Jim and I. We was beginning to run risks, got nearly dropped on more nor once.'

There's no mistake, it's a grand thing to wake up and know you've got nothing to do for a bit but to take it easy and enjoy yourself. No matter how light your work may be, if it's regular and has to be done every day, the harness'll gall somewhere; you get tired in time and sick of the whole thing.

Jim and I knew well that, bar accidents, we were as safe in the Hollow as we used to be in our beds when we were boys. We'd searched it through and through last time, till we'd come to believe that only three or four people, and those sometimes not for years at a time, had ever been inside of it. There were no tracks of more.

We could see how the first gang levied; they were different. Every now and then they had a big drink—'a made carouse,' as the books says—when they must have done wild, strange things, something like the Spanish Main buccaneers we'd read about. They'd brought captives with them, too. We saw graves, half-a-dozen together, in one place. *They* didn't belong to the band.

We had a quiet, comfortable meal, and a smoke afterwards. Then Jim and I took a long walk through the Hollow, so as to tell one another what was in our minds, which we hadn't a chance to do before. Before we'd gone far Jim pulls a letter out of his pocket and gives it to me.

'It was no use sending it to you, old man, while you was in the jug,' he says; 'it was quite bad enough without this, so I thought I'd keep it till we were settled a bit like. Now we're going to set up in business on our own account you'd best look over your mail.'

I knew the writing well, though I hadn't seen it lately. It was from her—from Kate Morrison that was. It began—not the way most women write, like *her*, though—

So this is the end of your high and mighty doings, Richard Marston, passing yourself and Jim off as squatters. I don't blame him—[no, of course not, nobody ever blamed Jim, or would, I suppose, if he'd burned down Government House and stuck up his Excellency as he was coming out of church]—but when I saw in the papers that you had been arrested for cattle stealing I knew for the first time how completely Jeanie and I had been duped.

I won't pretend that I didn't think of the money you were said to have, and how pleasant it would be to spend some of it after the miserable, scrambling, skimping life we had lately been used to. But I loved you, Dick Marston, for *yourself*, with a deep and passionate love which you will never know now, which you would scorn and treat lightly, perhaps, if you did know. You may yet find out what you have lost, if ever you get out of that frightful gaol.

I was not such a silly fool as to pine and fret over our romance so cruelly disturbed, though Jeanie was; it nearly broke her heart. No, Richard, my nature is not of that make. I generally get even with people who wrong me. I send you a photo, giving a fair idea of myself and my *husband*, Mr. Mullockson. I accepted his offer soon after I saw your adventures, and those of your friend Starlight, in every newspaper in the colonies. I did not hold myself bound to live single for your sake, so did what most women do, though they pretend to act from other motives, I disposed of myself to the best advantage.

Mr. Mullockson has plenty of money, which is *nearly* everything in this world, so that I am comfortable and well off, as far as that goes. If I am not happy that is your fault—your fault, I say, because I am not able to tear your false image and false self from my thoughts. Whatever happens to me in the future you may consider yourself to blame for. I should have been a happy and fairly good woman, as far as women go, if you had been true, or rather if everything about you had not been utterly false and despicable.

You think it fortunate after reading this, I daresay, that we are separated for ever, *but we may meet again*, Richard Marston. *Then* you may have reason to curse the day, as I do most heartily, when you first set eyes on

KATE MULLOCKSON.

Not a pleasant letter, by no manner of means. I was glad I didn't get it while I was eating my heart out under the stifling low roof of the cell at Nomah, or when I was bearing my load at Berrima. A few pounds more when the weight was all I could bear and live would have crushed the heart out of me. I didn't want anything to cross me when I was looking at mother and Aileen and thinking how, between us, we'd done everything our worst enemy could have wished us to do. But here, when there was plenty of time to think over old days and plan for the future, I could bear the savage, spiteful sound of the whole letter and laugh at the way she had got out of her troubles by taking up with a rough old fellow whose cheque-book was the only decent thing about him. I wasn't sorry to be rid of her either. Since I'd seen Gracey Storefield again every other woman seemed disagreeable to me. I tore up the letter and threw it away, hoping I had done for ever with a woman that no man living would ever have been the better for.

'Glad you take it so quiet,' Jim says, after holding his tongue longer than he did mostly. 'She's a bad, cold-hearted jade, though she is Jeanie's sister. If I thought my girl was like her, she'd never have another thought from me, but she isn't, and never was. The worse luck I've had the closer she's stuck to me, like a little brick as she is. I'd give all I ever had in the world if I could go to her and say, "Here I am, Jim Marston, without a penny in the world, but I can look every man in the face, and we'll work our way along the road of life cheerful and loving together." But I *can't* say it, Dick, that's the devil of it, and it makes me so wild sometimes that I could knock my brains out against the first ironbark tree I come across.'

I didn't say anything, but I took hold of Jim's hand and shook it. We looked in each other's eyes for a minute; there was no call to say anything. We always understood one another, Jim and I.

As we were safe to stop in the Hollow for long spells at a time we took a good look over it, as far as we could do on foot. We found a rum sort of place at the end of a long gully that went easterly from the main flat. In one way you'd think the whole valley had been an arm of the sea some time or other. It was a bit like Sydney Harbour in shape, with one principal valley and no end of small cover and gullies running off from it, and winding about in all directions. Even the sandstone walls, by which the whole affair, great and small, was hemmed in, were just like the cliff about South Head; there were lines, too, on the face of them, Jim and I made out, just like where the waves had washed marks and levels on the sea-rock. We didn't trouble ourselves much about that part of it. Whatever might have been there once, it grew stunning fine grass now, and there was beautiful clear, fresh water in all the creeks that ran through it.

Well, we rambled up the long, crooked gully that I was talking about till about half-way up it got that narrow that it seemed stopped by a big rock that had tumbled down from the top and blocked the path. It was pretty well grown over with wild raspberries and climbers.

'No use going farther,' says Jim; 'there's nothing to see.'

'I don't know that. Been a track here some time. Let's get round and see.'

When we got round the rock the track was plain again; it had been well worn once, though neither foot nor hoof much had been along it for many a year. It takes a good while to wear out a track in a dry country.

The gully widened out bit by bit, till at last we came to a little round, green flat, right under the rock walls which rose up a couple of thousand feet above it on two sides. On the flat was an old hut —very old it seemed to be, but not in bad trim for all that. The roof was of shingles, split, thick, and wedge shaped; the walls of heavy ironbark slabs, and there was a stone chimney.

Outside had been a garden; a few rose trees were standing yet, ragged and stunted. The wallabies had trimmed them pretty well, but we knew what they were. Been a corn-patch, too—the marks where it had been hoed up were there, same as they used to do in old times when there were more hoes than ploughs and more convicts than horses and working bullocks in the country.

'Well, this is a rum start,' says Jim, as we sat down on a log outside that looked as if it had been used for a seat before. 'Who the deuce ever built this gunyah and lived in it by himself for years and years? You can see it was no two or three months' time he done here. There's the spring coming out of the rock he dipped his water from. The track's reg'lar worn smooth over the stones leading to it. There was a fence round this garden, some of the rails lying there rotten enough, but it takes time for sound hard wood to rot. He'd a stool and table too, not bad ones either, this Robinson Crusoe cove. No end of manavilins either. I wonder whether he come here before them first—Government men—chaps we heard of. Likely he did, and died here too. He might have chummed in with them, of course, or he might not. Perhaps Starlight knows something about him, or Warrigal. We'll ask them.

We fossicked about for a while to see if the man who lived so long by himself in this lonely place had left anything behind him to help us make out what sort he was. We didn't find much. There was writing on the walls here and there, and things cut on the fireplace posts. Jim couldn't make head or tail of them, nor me either.

'The old cove may have left something worth having behind him,' he said, after staring at the cold hearth ever so long. 'Men like him often leave gold pieces and jewels and things behind them, locked up in brass-bound boxes; leastways the story-books say so.

I've half a mind to root up the old hearth-stone; it's a thundering heavy one, ain't it? I wonder how he got it here all by himself.'

'It *is* pretty heavy,' I said. 'For all we know he may have had help to bring it in. We've no time now to see into it; we'd better make tracks and see if Starlight has made back. We shall have to shape after a bit, and we may as well see how he stands affected.'

'He'll be back safe enough. There's no pull in being outside now with all the world chevying after you and only half rations of food and sleep.'

Jim was right. As we got up to the cave we saw Starlight talking to the old man and Warrigal letting go the horse. They'd taken their time to come in, but Warrigal knew some hole or other where they'd hid before very likely, so they could take it easier than we did the night we left Rocky Creek.

'Well, boys!' says Starlight, coming forward quite heartily, 'glad to see you again; been taking a walk and engaging yourself this fine weather? Rather nice country residence of ours, isn't it? Wonder how long we shall remain in possession! What a charm there is in home! No place like home, is there, governor?'

Dad didn't smile, he very seldom did that, but I always thought he never looked so glum at Starlight as he did at most people.

'The place is well enough,' he growled, 'if we don't smother it all by letting our tracks be followed up. We've been dashed lucky so far, but it'll take us all we know to come in and out, if we've any roadwork on hand, and no one the wiser.'

'It can be managed well enough,' says Starlight. 'Is that dinner ever going to be ready? Jim, make the tea, there's a good fellow; I'm absolutely starving. The main thing is never to be seen together except on great occasions. Two men, or three at the outside, can stick up any coach or travellers that are worth while. We can get home one by one without half the risk there would be if we were all together. Hand me the corned beef, if you please, Dick. We must hold a council of war by-and-by.'

We were smoking our pipes and lying about on the dry floor of the cave, with the sun coming in just enough to make it pleasant, when I started the ball.

'We may as well have it out now what lay we're going upon and whether we're all agreed in our minds *to turn out,* and do the thing in the regular good, old-fashioned Sydney-side style. It's risky, of course, and we're sure to have a smart brush or two; but I'm not going to be jugged again, not if I know it, and I don't see but what bush-ranging—yes, *bush-ranging,* it's no use saying one thing and meaning another—ain't as safe a game, let alone the profits of it, as mooching about cattle-duffing and being lagged in the long-run all the same.'

CHAPTER XXIII

'BECAUSE it's too late,' growled father; 'too late by years. It's sink or swim with all of us. If we work together we may make ten thousand pounds or more in the next four or five years, enough to clear out with altogether if we've luck. If any of us goes snivelling in now and giving himself up, they'd know there's something crooked with the lot of us, and they'll run us down somehow. I'll see 'em all in the pit of h—l before I give in, and if Jim does, he opens the door and sells the pass on us. You can both do what you like.' And here the old man walked bang away and left us.

'No use, Dick,' says Jim. 'If he won't it's no use my giving in. I can't stand being thought a coward. Besides, if you were nabbed afterwards people might say it was through me. I'd sooner be killed and buried a dozen times over than that. It's no use talking —it isn't to be—we had better make up our minds once for all, and then let the matter drop.'

Poor old Jim. He had gone into it innocent from the very first. He was regular led in because he didn't like to desert his own flesh and blood, even if it was wrong. Bit by bit he had gone on, not liking or caring for the thing one bit, but following the lead of others, till he reached his present pitch. How many men, and women too, there are in the world who seem born to follow the lead of others for good or evil! They get drawn in somehow, and end by paying the same penalty as those that meant nothing else from the start.

The finish of the whole thing was this: that we made up our minds to turn out in the bush-ranging line. It might seem foolish enough to outsiders, but when you come to think of it we couldn't better ourselves much. We could do no worse than we had done, nor run any greater risk to speak of. We were 'long sentence men' as it was, sure of years and years in prison; and, besides, we were certain of something extra for breaking gaol. Jim and Warrigal were 'wanted,' and might be arrested by any chance trooper who could recollect their description in the *Police Gazette*. Father might be arrested on suspicion and remanded again and again until they could get some evidence against him for lots of things that he'd been in besides the Momberah cattle. When it was all boiled down it came to this: that we could make more money in one night by sticking up a coach or a bank than in any other way in a year. That when we had done it, we were no worse off than we were now, as far as being outlaws, and there was a chance—not a very grand one, but still a chance—that we might find a way to clear out of New South Wales altogether.

So we settled it at that. We had plenty of good horses—what with the young ones coming on, that Warrigal could break, and what we had already. There was no fear of running short of horse-flesh. Firearms we had enough for a dozen men. They were easy enough to come by. We knew that by every mail-coach that travelled on the Southern or Western line there was always a pretty fair sprinkling of notes sent in the letters, besides what the passengers might carry with them, watches, rings, and other valuables. It wasn't the habit of people to carry arms, and if they did, there isn't one in ten that uses 'em. It's all very well to talk over a dinner-table, but any one who's been stuck up himself knows that there's not much chance of doing much in the resisting line.

Suppose you're in a coach, or riding along a road. Well, you're expected and waited for, and the road party knows the very moment you'll turn up. They see you a'coming. You don't see them till it's too late. There's a log or something across the road, if it's a coach, or else the driver's walking his horses up a steepish hill. Just at the worst pinch or at a turn, some one sings out 'Bail up.' The coachman sees a strange man in front, or close alongside of him, with a revolver pointed straight at him. He naturally don't like to be shot, and he pulls up. There's another man covering the passengers in the body of the coach, and he says if any man stirs or lifts a finger he'll give him no second chance. Just behind, on the other side, there's another man—perhaps two. Well, what's any one, if he's ever so game, to do? If he tries to draw a weapon, or move ever so little, he's rapped at that second. He can only shoot one man, even if his aim is good, which it's not likely to be. What is more, the other passengers don't thank him—quite the contrary—for drawing the fire on them. I have known men take away a fellow's revolver lest he should get them all into trouble. That was a queer start, wasn't it? Actually preventing a man from resisting. They were quite right, though; he could only have done mischief and made it harder for himself and every one else. If the passengers were armed, and all steady and game to stand a flutter, something might be done, but you don't get a coach-load like that very often. So it's found better in a general way to give up what they have quietly and make no fuss about it. I've known cases where a single bush-ranger was rushed by a couple of determined men, but that was because the chap was careless, and they were very active and smart. He let them stand too near him. They had him, simple enough, and he was hanged for his carelessness; but when there's three or four men, all armed and steady, it's no use trying the rush dodge with them.

Of course there were other things to think about: what we were to do with the trinkets and bank-notes and things when we got them—how to pass them, and so on. There was no great bother about that. Besides Jonathan Barnes and chaps of his sort, dad knew a few 'fences' that had worked for him before. Of course we had to suffer a bit in value. These sort of men make you pay through the nose for everything they do for you. But we could stand that out of our profits, and we could stick to whatever was easy to pass and some of the smaller things that were light to carry about. Men that make £300 or £400 of a night can afford to pay for accommodation.

The big houses in the bush, too. Nothing's easier than to stick up one of them—lots of valuable things, besides money, often kept there, and it's ten to one against any one being on the look-out when the boys come. A man hears they're in the neighbourhood, and keeps a watch for a week or two. But he can't be always waiting at home all day long with double-barrelled guns, and all his young fellows and the overseer that ought to be at their work among their cattle or sheep on the run idling their time away. No, he soon gets sick of that, and either sends his family away to town till the danger's past, or he 'chances it,' as people do about a good many things in the country. Then some fine day, about eleven or twelve o'clock, or just before tea, or before they've gone to bed, the dogs bark, and three or four chaps seem to have got into the place without anybody noticing 'em, the master of the house finds all the revolvers looking his way, and the thing's done. The house is cleared out of everything valuable, though nobody's harmed or frightened—in a general way, that is—a couple of the best horses are taken out of the stable, and the next morning there's another flaring article in the local paper. A good many men tried all they knew to be prepared and have a show for it; but there was only one that managed to come out right.

We didn't mean to turn out all in a minute. We'd had a rough time of it lately, and we wanted to wait and take it easy in the Hollow and close about for a month or so before we began business.

Starlight and I wanted to let our beards grow. People without any hair on their faces are hardly ever seen in the country now, except they've been in gaol lately, and of course we should have been marked men.

We saw no reason why we shouldn't take it easy. Starlight was none too strong, though he wouldn't own it; he wouldn't have fainted as he did if he had. He wanted good keep and rest for a month, and so did I. Now that it was all over I felt different from what I used to do, only half the man I once was. If we stayed in the Hollow for a month the police might think we'd gone straight out of the country and slack off a bit. Anyhow, as long as they didn't hit the trail off to the entrance, we couldn't be in a safer place, and though there didn't seem much to do we thought we'd manage to hang it out somehow. One day we were riding all together in the afternoon, when we happened to come near the gully where Jim and I had gone up and seen the Hermit's Hut, as we had christened it. Often we had talked about it since; wondered about the man who had lived in it, and what his life had been.

This time we'd had all the horses in and were doing a bit of colt-breaking. Warrigal and Jim were both on young horses that had only been ridden once before, and we had come out to give them a hand.

'Do you know anything about that hut in the gully?' I asked Starlight.

'Oh, yes, all there is to know about it; and that's not much. Warrigal told me that, while the first gang that discovered this desirable country residence were in possession, a stranger accidentally found out the way in. At first they were for putting him to death, but on his explaining that he only wanted a solitary home and should neither trouble nor betray them, they agreed to let him stay. He was "a big one gentleman," Warrigal said; but he built the hut himself, with occasional help from the men. He was liberal with his gold, of which he had a small store, while it lasted. He lived here many years, and was buried under a big peach tree that he had planted himself.'

'A queer start, to come and live and die here; and about the strangest place to pick for a home I ever saw.'

'There's a good many strange people in the colony, Dick, my boy,' says Starlight, 'and the longer you live the more you'll find of them. Some day, when we've got quiet horses, we'll come up and have a regular overhauling of the spot. It's years since I've been there.'

'Suppose he turned out some big swell from the old country? Dad says there used to be a fellow in the old days, in the colony. He might have left papers and things behind him that might turn to good account.'

'Whatever he did leave was hidden away. Warrigal says he was a little chap when he died, but he says he remembers men making a great coroboree over him when he died, and they could find nothing. They always thought he had money, and he showed them one or two small lumps of gold, and what he said was gold-dust washed out from the creek bed.'

As we had no call to work now, we went in for a bit of sport every day. Lord! how long it seemed since Jim and I had put the guns on our shoulders and walked out in the beautiful fresh part of the morning to have a day's shooting. It made us feel like boys again. When I said so the tears came into Jim's eyes and he turned his head away. Father came one day; he and old Crib were a stunning pair for pot shooting, and he was a dead game shot, though we could be at him with the rifle and revolver.

There was a pretty fair show of game too. The lowan (Mallee

hen, they're mostly called) and talegalla (brush turkey) were thick
enough in some of the scrubby corners. Warrigal used to get the
lowan eggs—beautiful pink, thin-shelled ones they are, first-rate to
eat, and one of 'em a man's breakfast. Then there were pigeons,
wild ducks, quail, snipe now and then, besides wallaby and other
kangaroos. There was no fear of starving, even if we hadn't a tidy
herd of cattle to come upon.

The fishing wasn't bad either. The creeks ran towards the north-
west watershed and were full of codfish, bream, and perch. Even
the Jewfish wasn't bad with their skins off. They all tasted pretty
good, I tell you, after a quick broil, let alone the fun of catching
them. Warrigal used to make nets out of cooramin bark, and put
little weirs across the shallow places, so as we could go in and
drive the fish in. Many a fine cod we took that way. He knew
all the blacks' ways as well as a good many of ours. The worst of
him was that, except in hunting, fishing, and riding, he'd picked up
the wrong end of the habits of both sides. Father used to set
snares for the brush kangaroo and the bandicoots, like he'd been
used to do for the hares in the old country. We could always
manage to have some kind of game hanging up. It kept us amused
too.

But I don't know whatever we should have done, that month we
stayed there, at the first—we were never so long idle again—without
the horses. We used to muster them twice a week, run 'em up
into the big receiving yard, and have a regular good look over 'em till
we knew every one of 'em like a book.

Some of 'em was worth looking at, my word! 'D'ye see that big
upstanding three-year-old dark bay filly, with a crooked streak down
her face,' Starlight would say, 'and no brand but your father's on?
Do you know her name? That's young Termagant, a daughter
of Mr. Rouncival's racing mare of the same name that was stolen
a week before she was born, and her dam was never seen alive
again. Pity to kill a mare like that, wasn't it? Her sire was Repeater,
the horse that ran the two three-mile heats with Mackworth, in grand
time, too.' Then, again, 'That chestnut colt with the white legs
would be worth five hundred all out if we could sell him with his
right name and breeding, instead of having to do without a pedigree.
We shall be lucky if we get a hundred clear for him. The black
filly with the star—yes, she's thoroughbred too, and couldn't have
been bought for money. Only a month old and unbranded, of
course, when your father and Warrigal managed to bone the old
mare. Mr. Gibson offered £50 reward, or £100 on conviction.
Wasn't he wild! That big bay horse, Warrior, was in training for
a steeplechase when I took him out of Mr. King's stable. I rode
him 120 miles before twelve next day. Those two browns are Mr.
White's famous buggy horses. He thought no man could get the
better of him. But your old father was too clever. I believe he could

shake the devil's own four-in-hand—(coal black, with manes and
tails touching the ground, and eyes of fire, some German fellow
says they are)—and the Prince of Darkness never be the wiser. The
pull of it is that once they're in here they're never heard of again
till it's time to shift them to another colony, or clear them out and
let the buyer take his chance.

'You've some plums here,' I said. 'Even the cattle look pretty
well bred.'

'Always go for pedigree stock, "Fifteenth Duke" notwithstanding.
They take no more keep than rough ones, and they're always saleable.
That red short-horn heifer belongs to the Butterfly Red Rose tribe;
she was carried thirty miles in front of a man's saddle the day she
was calved. We suckled her on an old brindle cow; she doesn't
look the worse for it. Isn't she a beauty? We ought to go in for
an annual sale here. How do you think it would pay?'

All this was pleasant enough, but it couldn't last for ever. After
the first week's rest, which was real pleasure and enjoyment, we
began to find the life too dull and dozy. We'd had quite enough
of a quiet life, and began to long for a bit of work and danger again.
Chaps that have got something on their minds can't stand idleness;
it plays the bear with them. I've always found they get thinking
and thinking till they get a low fit like, and then if there's any grog
handy they try to screw themselves up with that. It gives them a
lift for a time, but afterwards they have to pay for it over and over
again. That's where the drinking habit comes in—they can't help it—
they must drink. If you'll take the trouble to watch men (and
women, too) that have been 'in trouble' you'll find that nineteen out
of every twenty drink like fishes when they get the chance. It ain't
the love of the liquor, as teetotalers and those kind of goody people
always are ramming down your throat—it's the love of nothing. But
it's the fear of their own thoughts—the dreadful misery—the anxiety
about what's to come, that's always hanging like a black cloud over
their heads. That's what they can't stand; and liquor, for a bit, mind
you—say a few hours or so—takes all that kind of feeling clean away.
Of course it returns, harder than before, but that says nothing. It
can be driven away. All the heavy-heartedness which a man feels,
but never puts into words, flies away with the first or second glass of
grog. If a man was suffering pains of any kind, or was being stretched
on the rack (I never knew what a rack was till I'd time for reading in
gaol, except a horse-rack), or was being flogged, and a glass of anything he could swallow would make him think he was on a feather
bed enjoying a pleasant doze, wouldn't he swig it off, do you think?
And suppose there are times when a man feels as if hell couldn't
be much worse than what he's feeling all the long day through—and
I tell you there are—I, who have often stood it hour after hour—
won't he drink then? And why shouldn't he?

We began to find that towards the end of the day we all of us found the way to father's brandy keg—that by nightfall the whole lot of us had quite as much as we could stagger under. I don't say we regularly went in for drinking; but we began to want it by twelve o'clock every day, and to keep things going after that till bedtime. In the morning we felt nervous and miserable; on the whole we weren't very gay till the sun was over the foreyard.

Anyhow, we made it up to clear out and have the first go-in for a touch on the southern line the next week as ever was. Father was as eager for it as anybody. He couldn't content himself with this sort of Robinson Crusoe life any longer, and said he must have a run and a bit of work of some sort or he'd go mad. This was on the Saturday night. Well, on Sunday we sent Warrigal out to meet one of our telegraphs at a place about twenty miles off, and to bring us any infomation he could pick up and a newspaper. He came back about sundown that evening, and told us that the police had been all over the country after us, and that Government had offered £200 reward for our apprehension—mine and Starlight's—with £50 each for Warrigal and Jim. They had an idea we'd all shipped for America. He sent us a newspaper. There was some news; that is, news worth talking about. Here was what was printed in large letters on the outside:—

WONDERFUL DISCOVERY OF GOLD AT THE TURON

We have much pleasure in informing our numerous constituents that gold, similar in character and value to that of San Francisco, has been discovered on the Turon River by those energetic and experienced practical miners, Messrs. Hargraves and party. The method of cradling is the same, the appliances required are simple and inexpensive, and the proportional yield of gold highly reassuring. It is impossible to forecast the results of this most momentous discovery. It will revolutionise the new world. It will liberate the old. It will precipitate Australia into a nation.

Meanwhile, numberless inconveniences, even privations, will arise—to be endured unflinchingly—to be borne in silence. But courage, England, we have hitherto achieved victory.

This news about the gold breaking out in such a place as the Turon made a great difference in our notions. We hardly knew what to think at first. The whole country seemed upside down. Warrigal used to sneak out from time to time, and come back open-mouthed, bringing us all sorts of news. Everybody, he said, was coming up from Sydney. There would be nobody left there but the Governor. What a queer start—the Governor sitting lonely in a silent Government House, in the middle of a deserted city! We found out that it was true after we'd made one or two short rides out ourselves. Afterwards the police had a deal too much to do to think of us. We didn't run half the chance of being dropped on to that we used to do. The whole country was full of absconders and deserters, servants, shepherds, shopmen, soldiers, and sailors—all running away from their work, and making in a blind sort of way for the diggings, like a lot of caterpillars on the march.

We had more than half a notion about going there ourselves, but we turned it over in our minds, and thought it wouldn't do. We should be sure to be spotted anywhere in New South Wales. All the police stations had our descriptions posted up, with a reward in big letters on the door. Even if we were pretty lucky at the start we should always be expecting them to drop on us. As it was, we should have twenty times the chance among the coaches, that were sure to be loaded full up with men that all carried cash, more or less; you couldn't travel then in the country without it. We had twice the pull now, because so many strangers, that couldn't possibly be known to the police, were straggling over all the roads. There was no end of bustle and rush in every line of work and labour. Money was that plentiful that everybody seemed to be full of it. Gold began to be sent down in big lots, by the Escort, as it was called—sometimes ten thousand ounces at a time. That was money if you liked—forty thousand pounds!—enough to make one's mouth water—to make one think dad's prophecy about the ten thousand pounds wasn't so far out after all.

Just at the start most people had a kind of notion that the gold would only last a short time, and that things would be worse than before. But it lasted a deal longer than any of us expected. It was 1850 that I'm talking about. It's getting on for 1860 now, and there seems more of it about than ever there was.

Most of our lives we'd been used to the southern road, and we kept to it still. It wasn't right in the line of the gold diggings, but it wasn't so far off. It was a queer start when the news got round about to the other colonies, after that to England, and I suppose all the other old world places, but they must have come by ship-loads, the road was that full of new chums—we could tell 'em easy by their dress, their fresh faces, their way of talk, their thick sticks, and new guns and pistols. Some of them you'd see dragging a hand-cart with another chap, and they having all their goods, tools, and clothes on it. Then there'd be a dozen men, with a horse and cart, and all their swags in it. If the horse jibbed at all, or stuck in the deep ruts—and wasn't it a wet season?—they'd give a shout and a rush, and tear out cart and horse and everything else. They told us that there were rows of ships in Sydney Harbour without a soul to take care of them; that the soldiers were running away to the diggings just as much as the sailors; clergymen and doctors, old hands and new chums, merchants and lawyers. They all seemed as if they couldn't keep away from the diggings that first year for their lives.

All stock went up double and treble what they were before. Cattle and sheep we didn't mind about. We could do without them now. But the horse market rose wonderfully, and that made a deal of odds to us, you may be sure.

It was this way. Every man that had a few pounds wanted a horse to ride or drive; every miner wanted a wash-dirt cart and a horse to draw it. The farmer wanted working horses, for wasn't hay sixty or seventy pounds a ton, and corn what you liked to ask for it? Every kind of harness horse was worth forty, fifty, a hundred pounds apiece, and only to ask it; some of 'em weedy and bad enough. Heaven knows. So between the horse trade and the road trade we could see a fortune sticking out, ready for us to catch hold of whenever we were ready to collar.

CHAPTER XXIV

OUR first try-on in the coach line was with the Goulburn mail. We knew the road pretty well, and picked out a place where they had to go slow and couldn't get off the road on either side. There's always places like that in a coach road near the coast, if you look sharp and lay it out beforehand. This wasn't on the track to the diggings, but we meant to leave that alone till we got our hand in a bit. There was a lot of money flying about the country in a general way where there was no sign of gold. All the storekeepers began to get up fresh goods, and to send money in notes and cheques to pay for them. The price of stock kept dealers and fat cattle buyers moving, who had their pockets full of notes as often as not.

Just as you got nearly through Bargo Brush on the old road there was a stiffish hill that the coach passengers mostly walked up, to save the horses—fenced in, too, with a nearly new three-rail fence, all ironbark, and not the sort of thing that you could ride or drive over handy. We thought this would be as good a place as we could pick, so we laid out the whole thing as careful as we could beforehand.

The three of us started out from the Hollow as soon as we could see in the morning; a Friday it was, I remember it pretty well—good reason I had, too. Father and Warrigal went up the night before with the horses we were to ride. They camped about twenty miles on the line we were going, at a place where there was good feed and water, but well out of the way and on a lonely road. There had been an old sheep station there and a hut, but the old man had been murdered by the hut-keeper for some money he had saved, and a story got up that it was haunted by his ghost. It was known as the 'Murdering Hut,' and no shepherd would ever live there after, so it was deserted. We weren't afraid of shepherds alive or dead, so it came in handy for us, as there was water and feed in an old lambing paddock. Besides, the road to it was nearly all a lot of rock and scrub from the Hollow, that made it an unlikely place to be tracked from.

Our dodge was to take three quiet horses from the Hollow and ride them there, first thing; then pick up our own three—Rainbow and two other out-and-outers—and ride bang across the southern road. When things were over we were to start straight back to the Hollow. We reckoned to be safe there before the police had time to know which way we'd made.

It all fitted in first-rate. We cracked on for the Hollow in the morning early, and found dad and Warrigal all ready for us. The horses were in great buckle, and carried us over to Bargo easy enough before dark. We camped about a mile away from the road, in as thick a place as we could find, where we made ourselves as snug as things would allow. We had brought some grub with us and a bottle of grog, half of which we finished before we started out to spend the evening. We hobbled the horses out and let them have an hour's picking. They were likely to want all they could get before they saw the Hollow again.

It was near twelve o'clock when we mounted. Starlight said—
'By Jove, boys, it's a pity we didn't belong to a troop of irregular horse instead of this rotten colonial Dick Turpin business, that one can't help being ashamed of. They would have been delighted to have recruited the three of us, as we ride, and our horses are worth best part of ten thousand rupees. What a tent-pegger Rainbow would have made, eh, old boy?' he said, patting the horse's neck. 'But Fate won't have it, and it's no use whining.'

The coach was to pass half-an-hour after midnight. An awful long time to wait, it seemed. We finished the bottle of brandy, I know. I thought they never would come, when all of a sudden we saw the lamp.

Up the hill they came slow enough. About half-way up they stopped, and most of the passengers got out and walked up after her. As they came closer to us we could hear them laughing and talking and skylarking, like a lot of boys. They didn't think who was listening. 'You won't be so jolly in a minute or two,' I thinks to myself.

They were near the top when Starlight sings out, 'Stand! Bail up!' and the three of us, all masked, showed ourselves. You never saw a man look so scared as the passenger on the box-seat, a stout, jolly commercial, who'd been giving the coachman Havana cigars, and yarning and nipping with him at every house they passed. Bill Webster, the driver, pulls up all standing when he sees what was in Starlight's hand, and holds the reins so loose for a minute I thought they'd drop out of his hands. I went up to the coach. There was no one inside—only an old woman and a young one. They seemed struck all of a heap, and couldn't hardly speak for fright.

The best of the joke was that the passengers started running up full split to warm themselves, and came bump against the coach before they found out what was up. One of them had just opened out for a bit of blowing. 'Billy, old man,' he says, 'I'll report you to the Company if you crawl along this way,' when he catches sight of me and Starlight, standing still and silent, with our revolvers pointing his way. By George! I could hardly help laughing. His jaw dropped, and he couldn't get a word out. His throat seemed quite dry.

'Now, gentlemen,' says Starlight, quite cool and cheerful-like, 'you understand her Majesty's mail is stuck up, to use a vulgar expression, and there's no use resisting. I must ask you to stand in a row there by the fence, and hand out all the loose cash, watches or rings you may have about you. Don't move; don't I say, sir, or I must fire.' (This was to a fidgety, nervous man who couldn't keep quiet.) 'Now, Number One, fetch down the mail bags; Number Two, close up here.'

Here Jim walked up, revolver in hand, and Starlight begins at the first man, very stern—

'Hand out your cash; keep back nothing, if you value your life.'

You never saw a man in such a funk. He was a store-keeper, we found afterwards. He nearly dropped on his knees. Then he handed Starlight a bundle of notes, a gold watch, and took a handsome diamond ring from his finger. This Starlight put into his pocket. He handed the notes and watch to Jim, who had a leather bag ready for them. The man sank down on the ground; he had fainted.

He was left to pick himself up. No. 2 was told to shell out. They all had something. Some had sovereigns, some had notes and small cheques, which are as good in a country place. The squatters draw too many to know the numbers of half that are out, so there's no great chance of their being stopped. There were eighteen male passengers, besides the chap on the box-seat. We made him come down. By the time we'd got through them all it was best part of an hour.

I pulled the mail bags through the fence and put them under a tree. Then Starlight went to the coach where the two women were. He took off his hat and bowed.

'Unpleasant necessity, madam, most painful to my feelings altogether, I assure you. I must really ask you—ah—is the young lady your daughter, madam?'

'Not at all,' says the oldest, stout, middle-aged woman; 'I never set eyes on her before.'

'Indeed, madam,' says Starlight, bowing again; 'excuse my curiosity, I am desolated, I assure you, but may I trouble you for your watches and purses?'

'As you're a gentleman,' said the fat lady, 'I fully expected you'd have let us off. I'm Mrs. Buxter, of Bobbrawobbra.'

'Indeed! I have no words to express my regret,' says Starlight; 'but, my dear lady, hard necessity compels me. Thanks, very much,' he said to the young girl.

She handed over a small old Geneva watch and a little purse. The plump lady had a gold watch with a chain and purse to match.

'Is that all?' says he, trying to speak stern.

'It's my very all,' says the girl, 'five pounds. Mother gave me her watch, and I shall have no money to take me to Bowning, where I am going to a situation.'

Her lips shook and trembled and the tears came into her eyes.

Starlight carefully handed Mrs. Buxter's watch and purse to Jim. I saw him turn round and open the other purse, and he put something in, if I didn't mistake. Then he looked in again.

'I'm afraid I'm rather impertinent,' says he, 'but your face, Miss—ah —Elmsdale, thanks—reminds me of some one in another world—the one I once lived in. Allow me to enjoy the souvenir and to return your effects. No thanks; that smile is ample payment. Ladies, I wish you a pleasant journey.'

He bowed. Mrs. Buxter did not smile, but looked cross enough at the young lady, who, poor thing, seemed pretty full up and inclined to cry at the surprise.

'Now then, all aboard,' sings out Starlight; 'get in, gentlemen, our business matters are concluded for the night. Better luck next time. William, you had better drive on. Send back from the next stage, and you will find the mail bags under that tree. They shall not be injured more than can be helped. Good-night!'

The driver gathered up his reins and shouted to his team, that was pretty fresh after their spell, and went off like a shot. We sat down by the roadside with one of the coach lamps that we had boned and went through all the letters, putting them back after we'd opened them, and popping all notes, cheques, and bills into Jim's leather sack. We did not waste more time over our letter-sorting than we could help, you bet; but we were pretty well paid for it— better than the post-office clerks are, by all accounts. We left all the mail bags in a heap under the tree, as Starlight had told the driver; and then, mounting our horses, rode as hard as we could lick to where dad and Warrigal were camped.

When we overhauled the leather sack into which Jim had stowed all the notes and cheques we found that we'd done better than we expected, though we could see from the first it wasn't going to be a bad night's work. We had £370 in notes and gold, a biggish bag of silver, a lot of cheques—some of which would be sure to be paid— seven gold watches and a lot of silver ones, some pretty good. Mrs. Buxter's watch was a real beauty, with a stunning chain. Starlight said he should like to keep it himself, and then I knew Bella Barnes was in for a present. Starlight was one of those chaps that never forgot any kind of promise he'd once made. Once he said a thing it would be done as sure as death—if he was alive to do it; and many a time I've known him take the greatest lot of trouble, no matter how pushed he might be, to carry out something which another man would have never troubled his head about.

We got safe to the Murdering Hut, and a precious hard ride it was, and tried our horses well, for, mind you, they'd been under saddle best part of twenty-four hours when we got back, and had done a good deal over a hundred miles. We made a short halt while the tea was boiling, then we all separated for fear a black tracker might have been loosed on our trail, and knowing well what blood-hounds they are sometimes.

Warrigal and Starlight went off together as usual; they were pretty safe to be out of harm's way. Father made off on a line of his own. We took the two horses we'd ridden out of the Hollow, and made for that place the shortest way we knew. We could afford to hit out—horse-flesh was cheap to us—but not to go slow. Time was more than money to us now—it was blood, or next thing to it.

'I'll go anywhere you like,' says Jim, stretching himself. 'It makes no odds to me now where we go. What do you think of it, dad?'

'I think you've no call to leave here for another month, anyhow; but as I suppose some folks'll play the fool some road or other you may as well go there as anywhere else. If you must go you'd better take some of these young horses with you and sell them while prices keep up.'

'Capital idea,' says Starlight; 'I was wondering how we'd get those colts off. You've the best head amongst us, governor. We'll start out to-day and muster the horses, and we can take Warrigal with us as far as Jonathan Barnes's place.'

We didn't lose time once we'd made up our minds to anything. So that night all the horses were in and drafted ready—twenty-five upstanding colts, well bred, and in good condition. We expected they'd fetch a lot of money. They were all quiet, too, and well broken in by Warrigal, who used to get so much a head extra for this sort of work, and liked it. He could do more with a horse than any man I ever saw. They never seemed to play up with him as young horses do with other people. Jim and I could ride 'em easy enough when they was tackled, but for handling and catching and getting round them we couldn't hold a candle to Warrigal.

The next thing was to settle how to work it when we got to the diggings. We knew the auctioneers there and everywhere else would sell a lot of likely stock and ask no questions; but there had been such a lot of horse-stealing since the diggings broke out that a law had been passed on purpose to check it. In this way: If any auctioneer sold a stolen horse and the owner claimed it before six months the auctioneer was held liable. He had to return the horse and stand for the loss. But they found a way to make themselves right. Men generally do if a law's over sharp; they get round it somehow or other. So the auctioneers made it up among themselves to charge ten per cent. on the price of all horses that they sold, and make the buyer pay it. For every ten horses they sold they could afford to return one. The proof of an animal being stolen didn't turn up above once in fifty or a hundred times, so they could well afford the expense when it did.

It wasn't an easy thing to drive horses out of the Hollow, 'specially those that had been bred or reared there. But they were up to all that kind of thing, dad and Starlight. First there was a yard at the lower end of the gully that led up where we'd first seen Starlight come down, and a line of fence across the mountain walls on both sides, so that stock once in there couldn't turn back. Then they picked out a couple or three old mares that had been years and years in the Hollow, and been used to be taken up this track and knew their way back again. One they led up; dad went first with her, and another followed; then the colts took the track after them, as stock will. In half-an-hour we had them all up at the top, on the table-land, and ready to be driven anywhere. The first day we meant to get most of the way to Jonathan Barnes's place, and to stop there and have a bit of a spell the second. We should want to spell the horses and make 'em up a bit, as it was a longish drive over rough country to get there. Besides, we wanted all the information we could get about the diggings and other matters, and we knew Jonathan was just that open-mouthed, blatherskitin' sort of chap that would talk to everybody he saw, and hear mostly all that was going on.

A long, hard day was that first one. The colts tried to make back every now and then, or something would start them, and they'd make a regular stampede for four or five miles as hard as they could lay leg to ground. It wasn't easy to live with 'em across broken country, well-bred 'uns like them, as fast as racehorses for a short distance; but there were as good behind 'em, and Warrigal was pretty nearly always near the lead, doubling and twisting and wheeling 'em the first bit of open ground there was. He was A1 through timber, and no mistake. We got to a place father knew, where there was a yard, a little before dark; but we took care to watch them all night for fear of accidents. It wouldn't do to let 'em out of our sight about there. We should never have set eyes on 'em again, and we knew a trick worth two of that.

Next day, pretty early, we got to Barnes's, where we thought we should be welcome. It was all right. The old man laughed all over his face when he saw us, and the girls couldn't do enough for us when they heard we'd had scarce a morsel to eat or drink that day.

'Why, you're looking first-rate, Captain!' says Bella. 'Dick, I hardly knowed ye—the mountain air seems to agree with you. Maddie and I thought you was never going to look in no more. Thought you'd clean forgot us—didn't we, Mad? Why, Dick, what a grand beard you've grown! I never thought you was so handsome before!'

'I promised you a trifling present when I was here last, didn't I, Bella?' says Starlight. 'There.' He handed her a small parcel, carefully tied up. 'It will serve to remind you of a friend.'

'Oh, what a lovely, splendid duck of a watch!' says the girl, tearing open the parcel. 'And what a love of a chain! and lots of charms, too. Where, in all the world, did you get this? I suppose you didn't buy it in George Street.'

'It *was* bought in George Street,' says he; 'and here's the receipt;

you needn't be afraid of wearing it to church or anywhere else.
Here's Mr. Flavelle's name, all straight and square. It's quite new, as
you can see.'

Jim and I stared. Dad was outside, seeing the horses fed, with
Warrigal. We made sure at first it was Mrs. Buxter's watch and
chain; but he knew better than to give the girl anything that she
could be brought into trouble for wearing, if it was identified on her;
so he'd sent the cash down to Sydney, and got the watch sent up to
him by one of father's pals. It was as right as the bank, and nobody
could touch it or her either. That was Starlight all over; he never
seemed to care much for himself. As to anything he told a woman,
she'd no call to trouble herself about whether it would be done or
not.

'It'll be my turn next,' says Maddie. 'I can't afford to wait till—
till—the Captain leaves me that beauty horse of his. It's too long.
I might be married before that, and my old man cut up rough. Jim
Marston, what are you going to give me? I haven't got any earrings worth looking at, except these gold hoops that everybody
knows.'

'All right,' says Jim. 'I'll give you and Bell a pair each, if you're
good girls, when we sell the horses, unless we're nailed at the Turon.
What sort of a shop is it? Are they getting much gold?'

'Digging it out like potatoes,' says Bella; 'so a young chap told us
that come this way last week. My word! didn't he go on about the
coach being stuck up. Mad and I nearly choked ourselves laughing.
We made him tell it over twice. He said a friend of his was in it—in
the coach, that is—and we could have told him friends of ours was in
it, too, couldn't we?'

'And what did he think of it all?'

'Oh, he was a new chum; hadn't been a year out. Not a bad cut
of a young feller. He was awful shook on Mad; but she wouldn't
look at him. He said if it was in England the whole countryside
would rise up and hunt such scoundrels down like mad dogs; but in a
colony like this people didn't seem to know right from wrong.'

'Did he, indeed?' says Starlight. 'Ingenuous youth! When he
lives a little longer he'll find that people in England, and, indeed,
everywhere else, are very much like they are here. They'll wink
at a little robbery, or take a hand themselves if it's made worth their
while. And what became of your English friend?"

'Oh! he said he was going on to Port Phillip. There's a big diggings broke out there, too, he says; and he has some friends there,
and he thinks he'll like that side better.'

'I think we'd better cut the Sydney "side," too,' says Starlight.
'What do you say, Maddie? We'll be able to mix up with these new
chum Englishmen and Americans that are coming here in swarms,
and puzzle Sergeant Goring and his troopers more than ever.'

'Oh! come, now! that would be mean,' says Maddie. 'I wouldn't be drove away from my own part of the country, if I was a man, by anybody. I'd stay and fight it out. Goring was here the other day, and tried to pick out something from father and us about the lot of you.'

'Ha!' says Starlight, his face growing dark, and different-looking about the eyes from what I'd ever seen him, 'did he? He'd better beware. He may follow up my trail once too often. And what did you tell him?'

'We told him a lot of things,' says the girl; 'but I am afeared they was none of 'em true. He didn't get much out of us, nor wouldn't if he was to come once a week.'

'I expect not,' says Jim; 'you girls are smart enough. There's no man in the police or out of it that'll take much change out of you. I'm most afraid of your father, though, letting the cat out of the bag; he's such an old duffer to blow.'

'He was nearly telling the sergeant he'd seen a better horse lately here than his famous chestnut Marlborough, only Bella trod on his toe, and told him the cows was in the wheat. Of course Goring would have dropped it was Rainbow, or some well-bred horse you chaps have been shaking lately.'

'You're a regular pearl of discretion, my dear,' says Starlight, 'and it's a pity, like some other folks, you haven't a better field for the exercise of your talents. However, that's very often the way in this world, as you'll perhaps find out when you're old and ugly, and the knowledge can't do you any good. Tell us all you heard about the coach accident.'

'My word! it was the greatest lark out,' says Maddie. She'd twice the fun in her the other had, and was that good-tempered nothing seemed to put her out. 'Everybody as come here seemed to have nothing else to talk about. Those that was going to the diggings, too, took it much easier than those that was coming away.'

'How was that?'

'Well, the chaps that come away mostly have some gold. They showed us some pretty fair lumps and nuggets, I can tell you. They seemed awfully gallied about being stuck up and robbed of it, and they'd heard yarns of men being tied to trees in the bush and left there to die.'

'Tell them for me, my fair Madeline, that Starlight and Company don't deal with single diggers; ours is a wholesale business—eh, Dick? We leave the retail robbery to meaner villains.'

We had the horses that quiet by this time that we could drive them the rest of the way to the Turon by ourselves. We didn't want to be too big a mob at Barnes's house. Any one might come in accidental, and it might get spread about. So after supper Warrigal was sent back; we didn't want his help any more, and he might draw attention. The way we were to take in the horses, and sell them, was all put up.

Jim and I were to drive them the rest of the way across the ranges to the Turon. Barnes was to put us on a track he knew that would take us in all right, and yet keep away from the regular highway. Starlight was to stay another day at Barnes's, keeping very quiet, and making believe, if any one came, to be a gentleman from Port Phillip that wasn't very well. He'd come in and see the horses sold, but gammon to be a stranger, and never set eyes on us before.

'My word!' said Barnes, who just came in at the time, 'you've made talk enough for all the countryside with that mail coach racket of yours. Every man, woman, and child that looks in here's sure to say, "Did you hear about the Goulburn mail being stuck up?" "Well, I did hear something," I says, and out it all comes. They wonder first whether the bush-rangers will be caught; where they're gone to that the police can't get 'em; how it was that one of 'em was so kind to the young lady as to give her new watch back, and whether Captain Starlight was as handsome as people say, and if Mrs. Buxter will ever get her watch back with the big reward the Government offered. More than that, whether they'll stick up more coaches or fly the country.'

'I'd like to have been there and see how Bill Webster looked,' says Maddie. 'He was here one day since, and kept gassin' about it all as if he wouldn't let none of you do only what he liked. I didn't think he was that game, and told him so. He said I'd better take a seat some day and see how I liked it. I asked him wasn't they all very good-looking chaps, and he said Starlight was genteel-lookin', but there was one great, big, rough-lookin' feller—that was you, Jim—as was ugly enough to turn a cask of beer sour.'

'I'll give him a hammerin' for that yet,' grumbles old Jim. 'My word, he was that shaky and blue-lookin' he didn't know whether I was white or black.'

We had a great spree that night in a quiet way, and got all the fun as was to be had under the circumstances. Barnes came out with some pretty good wine which Starlight shouted for all round. The old woman cooked us a stunning good dinner, which we made the girls sit down to and some cousins of theirs that lived close by. We were merry enough before the evening was out. Bella Barnes played the piano middling, and Maddie could sing first-rate, and all of them could dance. The last thing I recollect was Starlight showing Maddie what he called a minuet step, and Jonathan and the old woman sitting on the sofa as grave as owls.

Anyhow, we all enjoyed ourselves. It was a grand change after being so long alone. The girls romped and laughed and pretended to be offended every now and then, but we had a regular good lark of it, and didn't feel any the worse at daylight next morning.

Jim and I were away before sunrise, and after we'd once got on the road that Jonathan showed us we got on well enough. We were dressed just like common bushmen. There were plenty on the road just then bringing cattle and horses to the diggings. It was well known that high prices were going there and that everybody paid in cash. No credit was given, of course.

We had on blue serge shirts, moleskin trousers, and roughish leather gaiters that came up to the knee, with ponchos strapped on in front; inside them was a spare shirt or two; we had oldish felt hats, as if we'd come a good way. Our saddles and bridles were rusty-looking and worn; the horses were the only things that were a little too good, and might bring the police to suspect us. We had to think of a yarn about them. We looked just the same as a hundred other long-legged six-foot natives with our beards and hair pretty wild—neither better nor worse.

As soon as Starlight came on to the Turon he was to rig himself out as a regular swell, and gammon he'd just come out from England to look at the goldfields. He could do that part wonderfully well. We would have backed him to take in the devil himself, if he saw him, let alone goldfields police, if Sergeant Goring wasn't about.

The second day Jim and I were driving quietly and easy on the road, the colts trotting along as steady as old stock horses, and feeding a bit every now and then. We knew we were getting near the Turon, so many tracks came in from all parts, and all went one way. All of a sudden we heard a low rumbling, roaring noise, something like the tide coming in on the seashore.

'I say, Jim, old man, we haven't made any mistake—crossed over the main range and got back to the coast, have we?'

'Not likely,' he said; 'but what the deuce is that row? I can't reckon it up for the life of me.'

I studied and studied. On it went grinding and rattling like all the round pebbles in the world rolling on a beach with a tidy surf on. I tumbled at last.

'Remember that thing with the two rockers we saw at the Hermit's Hut in the Hollow?' I said to Jim. 'We couldn't make out what it was. I know now; it was a gold cradle, and there's hundreds and thousands rocking there at the Turon. That's what's the matter.'

'We're going to see some life, it strikes me,' says he. 'We'll know it all directly. But the first thing we've got to do is to shut these young 'uns up safe in the sale-yard. Then we can knock round this town in comfort.'

We went outside of a rocky point, and sure enough here was the first Australian gold-diggings in full blast. What a sight it was, to be sure! Jim and I sat in our saddles while the horses went to work on the green grass of the flat, and stared as if we'd seen a bit of another world. So it was another world to us, straight away from the sad-voiced solitudes of the bush.

Barring Sydney or Melbourne, we'd never seen so many men in a crowd before; and how different they looked from the crawling people of a town! A green-banked rapid river ran before us, through a deep narrow valley. The bright green flats looked so strange with the yellow water rippling and rushing between them. Upon that small flat, and by the bank, and in the river itself, nearly 20,000 men were at work, harder and more silently than any crowd we'd ever seen before. Most of 'em were digging, winding up greenhide buckets filled with gravel from shafts, which were sunk so thickly all over the place that you could not pass between without jostling some one. Others were driving carts heavily laden with the same stuff towards the river, in which hundreds of men were standing up to their waists washing the gold out of tin pans, iron buckets, and every kind of vessel or utensil. By far the greater number of miners used things like child's cradles, rocking them to and fro while a constant stream of yellow water passed through. Very little talk went on; every man looked feverishly anxious to get the greatest quantity of work done by sundown.

Foot police and mounted troopers passed through the crowd every now and then, but there was apparently no use or no need for them; that time was to come. Now and then some one would come walking up, carrying a knapsack, not a swag, and showing by his round, rosy face that he hadn't seen a summer's sun in Australia. We saw a trooper riding towards us, and knowing it was best to take the bull by the horns, I pushed over to him, and asked if he could direct us to where Mr. Stevenson's, the auctioneer's, yard was.

'Whose horses are these?' he said, looking at the brands. 'B.M., isn't it?'

'Bernard Muldoon, Lower Macquarie,' I answered. 'There's a friend of his, a new chum, in charge; he'll be here to-morrow.'

'Go on down Main Street [the first street in a diggings is always called Main Street] as you're going,' he said carelessly, giving us all a parting look through, 'and take the first lane to the right. It takes you to the yard. It's sale-day to-morrow; you're in luck.'

It was rather sharp work getting the colts through men, women, and children, carts, cradles, shafts, and tin dishes; but they were a trifle tired and tender-footed, so in less than twenty minutes they were all inside of a high yard, where they could scarcely see over the cap, with a row of loose boxes and stalls behind. We put 'em into Joe Stevenson's hands to sell—that was what every one called the auctioneer—and walked down the long street.

My word, we were stunned, and no mistake about it. There was nothing to see but a rocky river and a flat, deep down between hills like we'd seen scores and scores of times all our lives and thought nothing of, and here they were digging gold out of it in all directions, just like potatoes, as Maddie Barnes said. Some of the lumps we saw —nuggets they called 'em—was near as big as new potatoes, without a word of a lie in it. I couldn't hardly believe it; but I saw them passing the little washleather bags of gold dust and lumps of dirty yellow gravel, but heavier, from one to the other just as if they were nothing—nearly £4 an ounce they said it was all worth, or a trifle under. It licked me to think it had been hid away all the time, and not even the blacks found it out. I believe our blacks are the stupidest, laziest beggars in the whole world. That old man who lived and died in the Hollow, though—*he* must have known about it; and the queer-looking thing with the rockers we saw near his hut, that was the first cradle ever was made in Australia.

The big man of the goldfield seemed to be the Commissioner. We saw him come riding down the street with a couple of troopers after his heels, looking as if all the place, and the gold, too, belonged to him. He had to settle all the rows and disputes that came up over the gold, and the boundaries of the claims, as they called the twenty-foot paddocks they all washed in, and a nice time he must have had of it! However, he was pretty smart and quick about it. The diggers used to crowd round and kick up a bit of a row sometimes when two lots of men were fighting for the same claim and gold coming up close by; but what he said was law, and no mistake. When he gave it out they had to take it and be content. Then he used to ride away and not trouble his head any more about it; and after a bit of barneying it all seemed to come right. Men liked to be talked to straight, and no shilly-shally.

What I didn't like so much was the hunting about of the poor devils that had not got what they called a licence—a printed thing giving 'em leave for to dig gold on the Crown lands. This used to cost a pound or thirty shillings a month—I forget rightly which—and, of course, some of the chaps hadn't the money to get it with—spent what they had, been unlucky, or run away from somewhere, and come up as bare of everything to get it out of the ground.

You'd see the troopers asking everybody for their licences, and those that hadn't them would be marched up to the police camp and chained to a big log, sometimes for days and days. The Government hadn't time to get up a lock-up, with cells and all the rest of it, so they had to do the chain business. Some of these men had seen better days, and felt it; the other diggers didn't like it either, and growled a good deal among themselves. We could see it would make bad blood some day; but there was such a lot of gold being got just then that people didn't bother their heads about anything more than they could help—plenty of gold, plenty of money, people bringing up more things every day from the towns for the use of the diggers. You could get pretty near anything you wanted by paying for it. Hard work from daylight to dark, with every now and then a big find to sweeten it, when a man could see as much money lying at his foot, or in his hand, as a year's work—no, nor five—hadn't made for him before. No wonder people were not in a hurry to call out for change in a place like the Turon in the year 1850!

The first night put the stuns on us. Long rows of tents, with big roaring log fires in front hot enough to roast you if you went too near;

mobs of men talking, singing, chaffing, dealing—all as jolly as a lot of schoolboys. There was grog, too, going, as there is everywhere. No publics were allowed at first, so, of course, it was sold on the sly.

It's no use trying to make men do without grog, or the means of getting it; it never works. I don't hold with every shanty being licensed and its being under a man's nose all day long; but if he has the money to pay for it, and wants to have an extra glass of grog or two with his friends, or because he has other reasons, he ought to be able to get it without hardships being put in his way.

The Government was afraid of there being tremendous fights and riots at the diggings, because there was all sorts of people there, English and French, Spaniards and Italians, natives and Americans, Greeks and Germans, Swedes and negroes, every sort and kind of man from every country in the world seemed to come after a bit. But they needn't have been frightened at the diggers. As far as we saw they were the sensiblest lot of working men we ever laid eyes on; not at all inclined to make a row for nothing—quite the other way. But the shutting off of public-houses led to sly grog tents, where they made the digger pay a pound a bottle for his grog, and didn't keep it very good either.

When the police found a sly grog tent they made short work of it, I will say. Jim and I were close by, and saw them at the fun. Somebody had informed on the man, or they had some other reason; so they rode down, about a dozen troopers, with the Commissioner at their head. He went in and found two casks of brandy and one of rum, besides a lot of bottled stuff. They didn't want that for their own use, he believed.

First he had the heads knocked in of the hogsheads; then all the bottled wine and spirits were unpacked and stowed in a cart, while the straw was put back in the tent. Then the men and women were ordered to come outside, and a trooper set fire to the straw. In five minutes the tent and everything in it was a mass of flame.

There was a big crowd gathered round outside! They began to groan when the trooper lit the straw, but they did nothing, and went quietly home after a bit. We had the horses to see after next day. Just before the sale began, at twelve o'clock, and a goodish crowd had turned up, Starlight rides quietly up, the finest picture of a new chum you ever set eyes on. Jim and I could hardly keep from bursting out laughing.

He had brought up a quiet cobby sort of stock horse from the Hollow, plain enough, but a wonder to go, particularly over broken country. Of course, it didn't do to bring Rainbow out for such work as this. For a wonder, he had a short tail. Well, he'd squared this cob's tail and hogged his mane so that he looked like another animal. He was pretty fat, too.

He was dressed up to the nines himself, and if we didn't expect him we wouldn't have known him from a crow. First of all, he had a thick rough suit of tweed clothing on, all the same colour, with a round fell hat. He had a brand new saddle and bridle, that hadn't got the yellow rubbed off them yet. He had an English hunting whip in his hand, and brown hogskin gloves. He had tan leather gaiters that buttoned up to his knees. He'd shaved his beard all but his moustache and a pair of short whiskers.

He had an eyeglass in his eye, which he let drop every now and then, putting it up when he wanted to look at anybody.

When he rode up to the yard everybody stared at him, and one or two of the diggers laughed and began to call out 'Joe.' Jim and I thought how sold some of them would have been if he turned on them and they'd found out who it was. However, he pushed up to the auctioneer, without looking out right or left, and drawled—

'May I—er—ask if you are Mr.—er—Joseph Stevenson?'

'I'm Joe Stevenson,' says the auctioneer. 'What can I do for you?'

'Oh!—a—here is a letter from my friend, Mr. Bernard Muldoon, of the Lower Macquarie—er—requesting you to sell these horses faw him; and—er—hand over the pwoceeds to—er—me—Mr. Augustus Gwanby—aw!"

Stevenson read the letter, nodded his head, said, 'All right; I'll attend to it,' and went on with the sale.

It didn't take long to sell our colts. There were some draught stock to come afterwards, and Joe had a day's work before him. But ours sold well. There had not been anything like this for size, quality, and condition. The Commissioner sent down and bought one. The Inspector of Police was there, and bought one recommended by Starlight. They fetched high prices, from fifty to eighty-five guineas, and they came to a fairish figure the lot.

When the last horse was sold, Starlight says, 'I feel personally obliged to you, Mr.—aw—Stevenson—faw the highly satisfactory manner in which you have conducted the sale, and I shall inform my friend, Mr. Muldoon, of the way you have sold his stock.'

'Much obliged, sir,' says Joe, touching his hat. 'Come inside and I'll give you the cheque.'

'Quite unnecessary now,' says Starlight; 'but as I'm acting for a friend, it may be as well.'

We saw him pocket the cheque, and ride slowly over to the bank, which was half-tent, half-bark hut.

We didn't think it safe to stay on the Turon an hour longer than we were forced to do. We had seen the diggings, and got a good notion of what the whole thing was like; sold the horses and got the money, that was the principal thing. Nothing for it now but to get back to the Hollow. Something would be sure to be said about the horses being sold, and when it came out that they were not Muldoon's there would be a great flare-up. Still they could not prove that the horses were stolen. There wasn't a wrong brand or a faked one in the lot. And no one could swear to a single head of them, though the whole lot were come by on the cross, and father could have told who owned every one among them. That was curious, wasn't it?

We put in a night at Jonathan Barnes's on our way back. Maddie got the earrings, and Bella the making of a new riding habit, which she had been wanting and talking about for a good while. Starlight dressed up, and did the new chum young Englishman, eyeglass and all, over again, and repeated the conversation he had with the Inspector of Police about his friend Mr. Muldoon's illness, and the colts he recommended. It was grand, and the girls laughed till they cried again. Well, those were merry days; we *did* have a bit of fun sometimes, and if the devil was dogging us he kept a good way out of sight. It's his way at the start when fellows take the downward track.

.   .   .   .

We got back safe enough, and father opened his eyes when he saw the roll of notes Starlight counted over as the price of the colts. 'Horse-breeding's our best game,' says the old man, 'if they're going to pay such prices as this. I've half a mind to start and take a lot over to Port Phillip.'

CHAPTER XXV

OUR next chance came through father. He was the intelligence man, and had all the news sent to him—roundabout it might be, but it always came, and was generally true; and the old man never troubled anybody twice that he couldn't believe in, great things or small. Well, word was passed about a branch bank at a place called Ballabri, where a goodish bit of gold was sent to wait the monthly escort. There was only the manager and one clerk there now, the other cove having gone away on sick leave. Towards the end of the month the bank gold was heaviest and the most notes in the safe. The smartest way would be to go into the bank just before shutting-up time—three o'clock, about—and hand a cheque over the counter. While the clerk was looking at it, out with a revolver and cover him. The rest was easy enough. A couple more walked in after, and while one jumped over the counter and bailed up the manager the other shut the door. Nothing strange about that. The door was always shut at three o'clock sharp. Nobody in town would drop to what might be going on inside till the whole thing was over, and the swag ready to be popped into a light trap and cleared off with.

That was the idea. We had plenty of time to think it over and settle it all, bit by bit, beforehand.

So one morning we started early and took the job in hand. Every little thing was looked through and talked over a week before. Father got Mr. White's buggy-horses ready and took Warrigal with him to a place where a man met him with a light four-wheeled Yankee trap and harness. Dad was dressed up to look like a back-country squatter. Lots of 'em were quite as rough-looking as he was, though they drive as good horses as any gentleman in the land. Warrigal was togged out something like a groom, with a bit of the station-hand about him. Their saddles and bridles they kept with 'em in the trap; they didn't know when they might want them. They had on their revolvers underneath their coats. We were to go round by another road and meet at the township.

Well, everything turned out first-rate. When we got to Ballabri there was father walking his horses up and down. They wanted cooling, my word. They'd come pretty smart all the way, but they were middlin' soft, being in great grass condition and not having done any work to speak of for a goodish while, and being a bit above themselves in a manner of speaking. We couldn't help laughing to see how solemn and respectable dad looked.

'My word,' said Jim, 'if he ain't the dead image of old Mr. Carter, of Brahway, where we shore three years back. Just such another hard-faced, cranky-looking old chap, ain't he, Dick? I'm that proud of him I'd do anything he asked me now, blest if I wouldn't!'

'Your father's a remarkable man,' says Starlight, quite serious; 'must have made his way in life if he hadn't shown such a dislike to anything on the square. If he'd started a public-house and a pound about the time he turned his mind to cattle-duffing as one of the fine arts, he'd have had a bank account by this time that would have kept him as honest as a judge. But it's the old story. I say, where are the police quarters? It's only manners to give them a call.'

We rode over to the barracks. They weren't much. A four-roomed cottage, a log lock-up with two cells, a four-stalled stable, and a horse-yard. Ballabri was a small township with a few big stations, a good many farms about it, and rather more public-houses than any other sort of buildings in it. A writing chap said once, 'A large, well-filled graveyard, a small church mostly locked up, six public-houses, gave the principal features of Ballabri township. The remaining ones appear to be sand, bones, and broken bottles, with a sprinkling of inebriates and blackfellows.' With all that there was a lot of business done there in a year by the stores and inns, particularly since the diggings. Whatever becomes of the money made in such places? Where does it all go to? Nobody troubles their heads about that.

A goodish lot of the first people was huddled away in the grave-yard under the sand ridges. Many an old shepherd had hobbled into the Travellers' Rest with a big cheque for a fortnight's spree, and had stopped behind in the graveyard, too, for company. It was always a wonderful place for steadying lushingtons, was Ballabri.

Anyhow we rode over to the barracks because we knew the senior constable was away. We'd got up a sham horse-stealing case the day before, through some chaps there that we knew. This drawed him off about fifty mile. The constable left behind was a youngish chap, and we intended to have a bit of fun with him. So we went up to the garden-gate and called out for the officer in charge of police quite grand.

'Here I am,' says he, coming out, buttoning up his uniform coat. 'Is anything the matter?'

'Oh! not much,' says I; 'but there's a man sick at the Sportsman's Arms. He's down with the typhus fever or something. He's a mate of ours, and we've come from Mr. Grant's station. He wants a doctor fetched.'

'Wait a minute till I get my revolver,' says he, buttoning up his waistcoat. He was just fresh from the depôt; plucky enough, but not up to half the ways of the bush.

'You'll do very well as you are,' says Starlight, bringing out his pretty sharp, and pointing it full at his head. You stay there till I give you leave.'

He stood there quite stunned, while Jim and I jumped off and muzzled him. He hadn't a chance, of course, with one of us on each side, and Starlight threatening to shoot him if he raised a finger.

'Let's put him in the logs,' says Jim. 'My word! just for a lark; turn for turn. Fair play, young fellow. You're being "run in" yourself now. Don't make a row, and no one'll hurt you.'

The keys were hanging up inside, so we pushed him into the farthest cell and locked both doors. There were no windows, and the lock-up, like most bush ones, was built of heavy logs, just roughly squared, with the ceiling the same sort, so there wasn't much chance of his making himself heard. If any noise did come out the town people would only think it was a drunken man, and take no notice.

We lost no time then, and Starlight rode up to the bank first. It was about ten minutes to three o'clock. Jim and I popped our horses into the police stables, and put on a couple of their waterproof capes. The day was a little showery. Most of the people we heard afterwards took us for troopers from some other station on the track of bush-rangers, and not in regular uniform. It wasn't a bad joke, though, and the police got well chaffed about it.

We dodged down very careless like to the bank, and went in a minute or two after Starlight. He was waiting patiently with the cheque in his hand till some old woman got her money. She counted it, shillings, pence, and all, and then went out. The next moment Starlight pushed his cheque over. The clerk looks at it for a moment, and quick-like says, 'How will you have it?'

'This way,' Starlight answered, pointing his revolver at his head, 'and don't you stir or I'll shoot you before you can raise your hand.'

The manager's room was a small den at one side. They don't allow much room in country banks unless they make up their mind to go in for a regular swell building. I jumped round and took charge of the young man. Jim shut and locked the front door while Starlight knocked at the manager's room. He came out in a hurry, expecting to see one of the bank customers. When he saw Starlight's revolver, his face changed quick enough, but he made a rush to his drawer where he kept his revolver, and tried to make a fight of it, only we were too quick for him. Starlight put the muzzle of his pistol to his forehead and swore he'd blow out his brains there and then if he didn't stop quiet. We had to use the same words over and over again. Jim used to grin sometimes. They generally did the business, though, so of course he was quite helpless. We hadn't to threaten him to find the key of the safe, because it was unlocked and the key in it. He was just locking up his gold and the day's cash as we came in.

We tied him and the young fellow fast, legs and arms, and laid them down on the floor while we went through the place. There was a good lot of gold in the safe, all weighed and labelled ready for the escort, which called there once a month. Bundles of notes, too; bags of sovereigns, silver, and copper. The last we didn't take. But all the rest we bundled up or put into handy boxes and bags we found there. Father had come up by this time as close as he could to the back-yard. We carried everything out and put them into his express waggon; he shoved a rug over them and drove off, quite easy and comfortable. We locked the back door of the bank and chucked away the key, first telling the manager not to make a row for ten minutes or we might have to come back again. He was a plucky fellow, and we hadn't been rough with him. He had sense enough to see that he was overmatched, and not to fight when it was no good. I've known bankers to make a regular good fight of it, and sometimes come off best when their places were stuck up; but not when they were bested from the very start, like this one. No man could have had a show, if he was two or three men in one, at the Ballabri money-shop. We walked slap down to the hotel—then it was near the bank—and called for drinks. There weren't many people in the streets at that time in the afternoon, and the few that did notice us didn't think we were any one in particular. Since the diggings broke out all sorts of travellers a little out of the common were wandering all about the country—speculators in mines, strangers, new chums of all kinds; even the cattle-drovers and stockmen, having their pockets full of money, began to put on more side and dress in a flash way. The bush people didn't take half the notice of strangers they would have done a couple of years before.

So we had our drinks, and shouted for the landlord and the people in the bar; walked up to the police station, took out our horses, and rode quickly off, while father was nearly five miles away on a cross-road, making Mr. White's trotters do their best time, and with seven or eight thousand pounds' worth of gold and cash under the driving seat. That, I often think, was about the smartest trick we ever did. It makes me laugh when I remember how savage the senior constable was when he came home, found his sub in a cell, the manager and his clerk just untied, the bank robbed of nearly everything, and us gone hours ago, with about as much chance of catching us as a mob of wild cattle that got out of the yard the night before.

Just about dark father made the place where the man met him with the trap before. Fresh horses was put in and the man drove slap away another road. He and Warrigal mounted the two brown horses and took the stuff in saddlebags, which they'd brought with 'em. They were back at the Hollow by daylight, and we got there about an hour afterwards. We only rode sharp for the first twenty miles or so, and took it easier afterwards.

If sticking up the Goulburn mail made a noise in the country, you may depend the Ballabri bank robbery made ten times as much. Every little newspaper and all the big ones, from one end of the colony to the other, were full of it. The robbery of a bank in broad daylight, almost in the middle of the day, close to a police station, and with people going up and down the streets, seemed too out-and-out cheeky to be believed. What was the country coming to? 'It was the fault of the gold that unsettled young fellows' minds,' some said, 'and took them away from honest industry.' Our minds had been unsettled long before the gold, worse luck. Some shouted for more police protection; some for vigilance committees; all bush-rangers and horse-thieves to be strung up to the next tree. The whole countryside was in an uproar, except the people at the diggings, who had most of them been in other places, and knew that, compared with them, Australia was one of the safest countries any man could live or travel in. A good deal of fun was made out of our locking up the constable in his own cell. I believe he got blown up, too, and nearly dismissed by his inspector for not having his revolver on him and ready for use. But young men that were any good were hard to get for the police just then, and his fault was passed over. It's a great wonder to me more banks were not robbed when you think of it. A couple of young fellows are sent to a country place; there's no decent buildings, or anything reasonable for them to live in, and they're expected to take care of four or five thousand pounds and a lot of gold, as if it was so many bags of potatoes. If there's police, they're half their time away. The young fellows can't be all their time in the house, and two or three determined men, whether they're bush-rangers or not, that like to black their faces, and walk in at any time that they're not expected, can sack the whole thing, and no trouble to them. I call it putting temptation in people's way, and some of the blame ought to go on the right shoulders. As I said before, the little affair made a great stir, and all the police in the country were round Ballabri for a bit, tracking and tracking till all hours, night and day; but they couldn't find out what had become of the wheel-marks, nor where our horse tracks led to. The man that owned the express waggon drove it into a scrubby bit of country and left it there; he knew too much to take it home. Then he brought away the wheels one by one on horseback, and carted the body in a long time after with a load of wool, just before a heavy rain set in and washed out every track as clean as a whistle.

Nothing in that year could keep people's thoughts long away from the diggings, which was just as well for us. Everything but the gold was forgotten after a week. If the harbour had dried up or Sydney town been buried by an earthquake, nobody would have bothered themselves about such trifles so long as the gold kept turning up hand over hand the way it did. There seemed no end to it. New diggings jumped up every day, and now another big rush broke out in Port Phillip that sent every one wilder than ever.

Starlight and us two often used to have a quiet talk about Melbourne. We all liked that side of the country; there seemed an easier chance of getting straight away from there than any part of New South Wales, where so many people knew us and everybody was on the look-out.

All kinds of things passed through our minds, but the notion we liked best was taking one of the gold ships bodily and sailing her away to a foreign port, where her name could be changed, and she never heard of again, if all went well. That would be a big touch and no mistake. Starlight, who had been at sea, and was always ready for anything out of the way and uncommon, the more dangerous the better, thought it might be done without any great risk or bother.

'A ship in harbour,' he said, 'is something like the Ballabri bank. No one expects anything to happen in harbour, consequently there's no watch kept or any look-out that's worth much. Any sudden dash with a few good men and she'd be off and out to sea before any one could say "knife."'

Father didn't like this kind of talk. He was quite satisfied where we were. We were safe there, he said; and, as long as we kept our heads, no one need ever be the wiser how it was we always seemed to go through the ground and no one could follow us up. What did we fret after? Hadn't we everything we wanted in the world—plenty of good grub, the best of liquor, and the pick of the country-side for horses, besides living among our own friends and in the country we were born in, and that had the best right to keep us. If we once got among strangers and in another colony we should be 'given away' by some one or other, and be sure to come to grief in the long-run.

Well, we couldn't go and cut out this ship all at once, but Jim and I didn't leave go of the notion, and we had many a yarn with Starlight about it when we were by ourselves.

What made us more set upon clearing out of the country was that we were getting a good bit of money together, and of course we hadn't much chance of spending it. Every place where we'd been seen was that well watched there was no getting nigh it, and every now and then a strong mob of police, ordered down by tele-graph, would muster at some particular spot where they thought there was a chance of surrounding us. However, that dodge wouldn't work. They couldn't surround the Hollow. It was too big, and the gullies between the rocks too deep. You could see across a place sometimes that you had to ride miles round to get over. Besides, no one knew there was such a place, leastways that we were there, any more than if we had been in New Zealand.

CHAPTER XXVI

AFTER the Ballabri affair we had to keep close for weeks and weeks. The whole place seemed to be alive with police. We heard of them being on Nulla Mountain and close enough to the Hollow now and then. But Warrigal and father had places among the rocks where they could sit up and see everything for miles round. Dad had taken care to get a good glass, too, and he could sweep the country round about almost down to Rocky Flat. Warrigal's eyes were sharp enough without a glass, and he often used to tell us he seen things—men, cattle, and horses—that we couldn't make out a bit in the world. We amused ourselves for a while the best way we could by horse-breaking, shooting, and what not; but we began to get awful tired of it, and ready for anything, no matter what, that would make some sort of change.

One day father told us a bit of news that made a stir in the camp, and nearly would have Jim and me clear out altogether if we'd had any place to go to. For some time past, it seems, dad had been grumbling about being left to himself so much, and, except this last fakement, not having anything to do with the road work. 'It's all devilish fine for you and your brother and the Captain there to go flashin' about the country and sporting your figure on horseback, while I'm left alone to do the housekeepin' in the Hollow. I'm not going to be wood-and-water Joey, I can tell ye, not for you nor no other men. So I've made it right with a couple of chaps as I've know'd these years past, and we can do a touch now and then, as well as you grand gentlemen, on the "high toby," as they call it where I came from.'

'I didn't think you were such an old fool, Ben,' said Starlight; 'but keeping this place here a dead secret is our sheet-anchor. Lose that, and we'll be run into in a week. If you let it out to any fellow you come across, you will soon know all about it.'

'I've known Dan Moran and Pat Burke nigh as long as I've known you, for the matter of that,' says father. 'They're safe enough, and they're not to come here or know where I hang out neither. We've other places to meet, and what we do'll be clean done, I'll go bail.'

'It doesn't matter two straws to me, as I've told you many a time,' said Starlight, lighting a cigar (he always kept a good supply of them). 'But you see if Dick and Jim, now, don't suffer for it before long.'

'It was I as told you about the place, wasn't it?' growls father; 'don't you suppose I know how to put a man right? I look to have my turn at steering this here ship, or else the crew better go ashore for good.'

Father had begun to drink harder now than he used; that was partly the reason. And when he'd got his liquor aboard he was that savage and obstinate there was no doing anything with him. We couldn't well part. We couldn't afford to do without each other. So we had to patch it up the best way we could, and let him have his own way. But we none of us liked the new-fangled way, and made sure bad would come of it.

We all knew the two men, and didn't half like them. They were the head men of a gang that mostly went in for horse-stealing, and only did a bit of regular bush-ranging when they was sure of getting clear off. They'd never shown out the fighting way yet, though they were ready enough for it if it couldn't be helped.

Moran was a dark, thin, wiry-looking native chap, with a big beard, and a nasty beady black eye like a snake's. He was a wonderful man outside of a horse, and as active as a cat, besides being a deal stronger than any one would have taken him to be. He had a drawling way of talking, and was one of those fellows that liked a bit of cruelty when he had the chance. I believe he'd rather shoot any one than not, and when he was worked up he was more like a devil than a man. Pat Burke was a broad-shouldered, fair-complexioned fellow, most like an Englishman, though he was a native too. He'd had a small station once, and might have done well (I was going to say) if he'd had sense enough to go straight. What rot it all is! Couldn't we all have done well, if the devils of idleness and easy-earned money and false pride had let us alone?

Father said his bargain with these chaps was that he should send down to them when anything was up that more men was wanted for, and they was always to meet him at a certain place. He said they'd be satisfied with a share of whatever the amount was, and that they'd never want to be shown the Hollow or to come anigh it. They had homes and places of their own, and didn't want to be known more than could be helped. Besides this, if anything turned up that was real first chop, they could always find two or three more young fellows that would stand a flutter, and disappear when the job was done. This was worth thinking over, he said, because there weren't quite enough of us for some things, and we could keep these other chaps employed at outside work.

There was something in this, of course, and dad was generally near the mark, there or thereabouts, so we let things drift. One thing was that these chaps could often lay their hands upon a goodish lot of horses or cattle; and if they delivered them to any two of us twenty miles from the Hollow, they could be popped in there, and neither they or any one else the wiser. You see, father didn't mind taking a hand in the bush-ranging racket, but his heart was with the cattle and horse-duffing that he'd been used to so long, and he couldn't quite give it up. It's my belief he'd have sooner made a ten-pound note by an unbranded colt or a mob of fat cattle than five times as much in any other way. Every man to his taste, they say.

Well, between this new fad of the old man's and our having a notion that we had better keep quiet for a spell and let things settle down a bit, we had a long steady talk, and the end of it was that we made up our minds to go and put in a month or two at the diggings.

We took a horse apiece that weren't much account, so we could either sell them or lose them, it did not make much odds which, and made a start for Jonathan Barnes's place. We got word from him every now and then, and knew that the police had never found out that we had been there, going or coming. Jonathan was a blowing, blatherskiting fool; but his very foolishness in that way made them think he knew nothing at all. He had just sense enough not to talk about us, and they never thought about asking him. So we thought we'd have a bit of fun there before we settled down for work at the Turon. We took old saddles and bridles, and had a middling-sized swag in front, just as if we'd come a long way. We dressed pretty rough, too; we had longish hair and beards, and (except Starlight) might have been easy taken for down-the-river stockmen or drovers.

When we got to Barnes's place he and the old woman seemed ever so glad to see us. Bella and Maddie rushed out, making a great row, and chattering both at a time.

'Why, we thought you were lost, or shot, or something,' Bella says. 'You might have sent us a letter, or a message, only I suppose you didn't think it worth while.'

'What a bad state the country's getting in,' says Maddie. 'Think of them bush-rangers sticking up the bank at Ballabri, and locking up the constable in his own cell. Ha! ha! The police magistrate was here to-night. You should have heard Bella talking so nice and proper to him about it.'

'Yes, and you said they'd all be caught and hanged,' said Bella; 'that it was settin' such a bad example to the young men of the colony. My word! it was as good as a play. Mad was so full of her fun, and when the P.M. said they'd be sure to be caught in the long-run, Maddie said they'd have to import some thoroughbred police to catch 'em, for our Sydney-side ones didn't seem to have pace enough. This made the old gentleman stare, and he looked at Maddie as if she was out of her mind. Didn't he, Mad?'

'I do think it's disgraceful of Goring and his lot not to have run them in before,' says Starlight, 'but it wouldn't do for us to interfere.'

'Ah! but Sir Ferdinand Morringer's come up now,' says Maddie. 'He'll begin to knock saucepans out of all the boys between here and

Weddin' Mountain. He was here, too, and asked us a lot of questions about people who were "wanted" in these parts.'

'He fell in love with Maddie, too,' says Bella, 'and gave her one of the charms off his watch chain—such a pretty one, too. He's going to catch Starlight's mob, as he calls them. Maddie says she'll send him word if ever she knows of their being about.'

'Well done, Maddie!' says Jim; 'so you may, just an hour or two after we've started. There won't be much likelihood of his over-hauling us then. He won't be the first man that's been fooled by a woman, will he?'

'Or the last, Jim,' says Bella. 'What do you say, Captain? It seems to me we're doing all the talking, and you're doing all the listening. That isn't fair, you know. We like to hear ourselves talk, but fair play is bonny play. Suppose you tell us what you've been about all this time. I think tea's ready.'

We had our innings in the talking line; Jim and Maddie made noise enough for half-a-dozen. Starlight let himself be talked to. and didn't say much himself; but I could see even he, that had seen a lot of high life in his time, was pleased enough with the nonsense of a couple of good-looking girls like these—regular bush-bred fillies as they were—after being shut up in the Hollow for a month or two.

Before we'd done a couple of travellers rode up. Jonathan's place was getting a deal more custom now—it lay near about the straight line for the Turon, and came to be known as a pretty comfortable shop. Jonathan came in with them, and gave us a wink as much as to say, 'It's all right.'

'These gentlemen's just come up from Sydney,' he said; 'not long from England, and wants to see the diggings. I told 'em you might be going that way, and could show 'em the road.'

'Very happy,' says Starlight. 'I am from Port Phillip last myself, and think of going back to Honolulu after I've made the round of the colonies. My good friends and travelling companions are on their way for the Darling. We can all travel together.'

'What a fortunate thing we came here, Clifford, eh?' says one young fellow, putting up his eyeglass. 'You wanted to push on. Now we shall have company, and not lose our way in this beastly "bush," as they call it.'

'Well, it does look like luck,' says the other man. 'I was beginning to think the confounded place was getting farther off every day. Can you show us our rooms, if you please? I suppose we couldn't have a bath?'

'Oh yes, you can,' said Maddie; 'there's a creek at the bottom of the garden, only there's snakes now and then at night. I'll get you towels.'

'In that case I think I shall prefer to wait till the morning,' says the tall man. 'It will be something to look forward to.'

We were afraid the strangers would have spoiled our fun for the evening, but they didn't; we made out afterwards that the tall one was a lord. They were just like anybody else, and when we got the piano to work after tea they made themselves pleasant enough, and Starlight sang a song or two—he could sing, and no mistake, when he liked—and then one of them played a waltz, and the girls danced together, and Starlight had some champagne in, said it was his birthday, and he'd just thought of it, and they got quite friendly and jolly before we turned in.

Next day we made a start, promising the girls a nugget each for a ring out of the first gold we got, and they promised to write to us and tell us if they heard any news. They knew what to say, and we shouldn't be caught simple if they could help it. Jim took care, though, to keep well off the road, and take all the short cuts he knew. We weren't quite safe till we was in the thick of the mining crowd. That's the best place for a man, or woman either, to hide that wants to drop out of sight and never be seen again. Many a time I've known a man, called Jack or Tom among the diggers, and never thought of as anything else, working like them, drinking and taking his pleasure and dressing like them, till he made his pile or died, or something, and then it turned out he was the Honourable Mr. So-and-So, Captain This, or Major That; perhaps the Reverend Somebody—though that didn't happen often.

We were all the more contented, though, when we heard the row of the cradles and the clang and bang of the stampers in the quartz-crushing batteries again, and saw the big crowd moving up and down like a hill of ants, the same as when we'd left Turon last. As soon as we got into the main street we parted. Jim and I touched our hats and said good-bye to Starlight and the other two, who went away to the crack hotel. We went and made a camp down by the creek, so that we might turn to and peg out a claim, or buy out a couple of shares, first thing in the morning.

Except the Hollow, it was the safest place in the whole country just now, as we could hear that every week fresh people were pouring in from all the other colonies, and every part of the world. The police on the diggings had their own work pretty well cut out for them, what with old hands from Van Dieman's Land, Californians—and, you may bet, roughs and rascals from every place under the sun. Besides, we wanted to see for ourselves how the thing was done, and pick up a few wrinkles that might come in handy afterwards. Our dodge was to take a few notes with us, and buy into a claim—one here, one there—not to keep together for fear of consequences. If we worked and kept steady at it, in a place where there were thousands of strangers of all kinds, it would take the devil himself to pick us out of such a queer, bubbling, noisy, mixed-up pot of hell-broth.

Things couldn't have dropped in more lucky for us than they

did. In this way. Starlight was asked by the two swells to join
them, because they wanted to do a bit of digging, just for the
fun of it; and he made out he'd just come from Melbourne, and
hadn't been six months longer in the country than they had. Of
course he was sunburnt a bit. He got that in India, he said. My
word! they played just into his hand, and he did the new-chum
swell all to pieces, and so natural that no one could have picked him
out from them. He dressed like them, talked like them, and never
let slip a word except about shooting in England, hunting in
America and India, besides gammoning to be as green about all
Australian ways as if he'd never seen a gum tree before. They took
up a claim, and bought a tent. Then they got a wages-man to
help them, and all four used to work like niggers. The crowd
christened them 'The Three Honourables,' and used to have great
fun watching them working away in their jerseys, and handling
their picks and shovels like men. Starlight used to drawl just like
the other two, and asked questions about the colony; and walk about
with them on Sundays and holidays in fashionable cut clothes. He'd
brought money, too, and paid his share of the expenses, and something over. It was a great sight to see at night, and people said
like nothing else in the world just then. Every one turned out for
an hour or two at night, and then was the time to see the Turon in its
glory. Big, sunburnt men, with beards, and red silk sashes round
their waists, with a sheath-knife and revolvers mostly stuck in
them, and broad-leaved felt hats on. There were Californians, then
foreigners of all sorts—Frenchmen, Italians, Germans, Spaniards,
Greeks, Negroes, Indians, Chinamen. They were a droll, strange,
fierce-looking crowd. There weren't many women at first, but they
came pretty thick after a bit. A couple of theatres were open, a
circus, hotels with lots of plate-glass windows and splendid bars, all
lighted up, and the front of them, anyhow, as handsome at first sight
as Sydney or Melbourne. Drapers and grocers, ironmongers, general
stores, butchers and bakers, all kept open until midnight, and every
place was lighted up as clear as day. It was like a fairy-story place,
Jim said; he was as pleased as a child with the glitter and show and
strangeness of it all. Nobody was poor, everybody was well dressed,
and had money to spend, from the children upwards. Liquor seemed
running from morning to night, as if there were creeks of it; all the
same there was very little drunkenness and quarrelling. The police
kept good order, and the miners were their own police mostly, and
didn't seem to want keeping right. We always expected the miners
to be a disorderly, rough set of people—it was quite the other way.
Only we had got into a world where everybody had everything
they wanted, or else had the money to pay for it. How different
it seemed from the hard, grinding, poverty-stricken life we had been
brought up to, and all the settlers we knew when we were young!
People had to work hard for every pound they made then, and,

if they hadn't the ready cash, obliged to do without, even if it was bread to eat. Many a time we'd had no tea and sugar when we were little, because father hadn't the money to pay for it. That was when he stayed at home and worked for what he got. Well, it was honest money, at any rate—pity he hadn't kept that way.

Now all this was changed. It wasn't like the same country. Everybody dressed well, lived high, and the money never ran short, nor was likely to as long as the gold kept spreading, and was found in 10, 20, 50 pound nuggets every week or two. We had a good claim, and began to think about six months' work would give us enough to clear right away with. We let our hair grow long, and made friends with some Americans, so we began to talk a little like them, just for fun, and most people took us for Yankees. We didn't mind that. Anything was better than being taken for what we were. And if we could get clear off to San Francisco there were lots of grand new towns springing up near the Rocky Mountains, where a man could live his life out peaceably, and never be heard of again.

As for Starlight, he'd laid it out with his two noble friends to go back to Sydney in two or three months, and run down to Honolulu in one of the trading vessels. They could get over to the Pacific slope, or else have a year among the Islands, and go anywhere they pleased. They had got that fond of Haughton, as he called himself —Frank Haughton—that nothing would have persuaded them to part company. And wasn't he a man to be fond of?—always ready for anything, always good-tempered except when people wouldn't let him, ready to work or fight or suffer hardship, if it came to that, just as cheerful as he went to his dinner—never thinking or talking much about himself, but always there when he was wanted. You couldn't have made a more out-and-out, all-round man to live and die with; and yet, wasn't it a murder, that there should be that against him, when it came out, that spoiled the whole lot? We used to meet now and then, but never noticed one another except by a bit of a nod or a wink, in public. One day Jim and I were busy puddling some dirt, and we saw Sergeant Goring ride by with another trooper. He looked at us, but we were splashed with yellow mud, and had handkerchiefs tied over our heads. I don't think mother would have known us. He just glanced over at us and took no notice. If he didn't know us there was no fear of any one else being that sharp to do it. So we began to take it easy, and to lose our fear of being dropped on at any time. Ours was a middling good claim, too; two men's ground; and we were lucky from the start. Jim took to the pick and shovel work from the first, and was as happy as a man could be.

After our day's work we used to take a stroll through the lighted streets at night. What a place it had grown to be, and how different it was from being by ourselves at the Hollow. The gold was coming

THIS meeting with Kate Morrison put the stuns upon me and Jim, and no mistake. We never expected to see her up at the Turon, and it all depended which way the fit took her now whether it would be a fit place for us to live in any longer. Up to this time we had done capital well. We had been planted as close as if we had been at the Hollow. We'd had lots of work, and company, and luck. It began to look as if our luck would be dead out. Anyhow, we were at the mercy of a tiger-cat of a woman who might let loose her temper at any time and lay the police on to us, without thinking twice about it. We didn't think she knew Starlight was there, but she was knowing enough for anything. She could put two and two together, and wait and watch, too. It gave me a fit of the shivers every time I thought of it. This was the last place I ever expected to see her at. However, you never can tell what'll turn up in this world. She might have got over her tantrums.

Of course we went over to the Prospectors' Arms that night, as the new hotel was called, and found quite a warm welcome. Mrs. Mullockson had turned into quite a fashionable lady since the Melbourne days; dressed very grand, and talked and chaffed with the commissioner, the police inspectors, and goldfield officers from the camp as if she'd been brought up to it. People lived fast in those goldfield days; it don't take long to pick up that sort of learning.

The Prospectors' Arms became quite the go, and all the swell miners and quartz reefers began to meet there as a matter of course. There was Dandy Green, the Lincolnshire man from Beevor, that used to wear no end of boots and spend pounds and pounds in blacking. He used to turn out with everything clean on every morning, fit to go to a ball, as he walked on to the brace. There was Ballersdorf, the old Prussian soldier, that had fought against Boney, and owned half-a-dozen crushing machines and a sixth share in the Great Wattle Flat Company; Dan Robinson, the man that picked up the 70 pound nugget; Sam Dawson, of White Hills, and Peter Paul, the Canadian, with a lot of others, all known men, went there regular. Some of them didn't mind spending fifty or a hundred pounds in a night if the fit took them. The house began to do a tremendous trade, and no mistake.

Old Mullockson was a quiet, red-faced old chap, who seemed to do all Kate told him, and never bothered himself about the business, except when he had to buy fresh supplies in the wine and spirit line.

There he was first chop. You couldn't lick him for quality. And so the place got a name.

But where was Jeanie all this time? That was what Jim put me up to ask the first night we came. 'Oh! Jeanie, poor girl, she was stopping with her aunt in Melbourne.' But Kate had written to her, and she was coming up in a few weeks. This put Jim in great heart. What with the regular work and the doing well in the gold line, and Jeanie coming up, poor old Jim looked that happy that he was a different man. No wonder the police didn't know him. He had grown out of his old looks and ways; and though they rubbed shoulders with us every day, no one had eyes sharp enough to see that James Henderson and his brother Dick—mates with the best men on the field—were escaped prisoners, and had a big reward on them besides.

Nobody knew it, and that was pretty nigh as good as if it wasn't true. So we held on, and made money hand over fist. We used to go up to the hotel whenever we'd an evening to spare, but that wasn't often. We intended to keep our money this time, and no publican was to be any the better for our hard work.

As for Kate, I couldn't make her out. Most times she'd be that pleasant and jolly no one could help liking her. She had a way of talking to me and telling me everything that happened, because I was an old friend she said—that pretty nigh knocked me over, I tell you. Other times she was that savage and violent no one would go near her. She didn't care who it was—servants or customers, they all gave her a wide berth when she was in her tantrums. As for old Mullockson, he used to take a drive to Sawpit Gully or Ten-Mile as soon as ever he saw what o'clock it was—and glad to clear out, too. She never dropped on to me, somehow. Perhaps she thought she'd get as good as she gave; I wasn't over good to lead, and couldn't be drove at the best of times. No! not by no woman that ever stepped.

One evening Starlight and his two swell friends comes in, quite accidental like. They sat down at a small table by themselves and ordered a couple of bottles of foreign wine. There was plenty of that if you liked to pay a guinea a bottle. I remember when common brandy was that price at first, and I've seen it fetched out of a doctor's tent as medicine. It paid him better than his salts and rhubarb. That was before the hotels opened, and while all the grog was sold on the sly. They marched in, dressed up as if they'd been at George Street, though everybody knew one of 'em had been at the windlass all day with the wages man, and the other two below, working up to their knees in water; for they'd come on a drift in their claim, and were puddling back. However, that says nothing; we were all in good clothes and fancy shirts and ties. Miners don't go about in their working suits. The two Honourables walked over to the bar first of all, and said a word or two to Kate, who was all smiles and as pleasant as you please. It was one of her good days. Starlight put up his eyeglass and stared round as if we were all a lot of queer animals out of a caravan. Then he sat down and took up the *Turon Star*. Kate hardly looked at him, she was so taken up with his two friends, and, woman-like, bent on drawing them on, knowing them to be big swells in their own country. We never looked his way, except on the sly, and no one could have thought we'd ever slept under one tree together, or seen the things we had.

When the waiter was opening their wine one of the camp officers comes in that they had letters to. So they asked him to join them, and Starlight sends for another bottle of Moselle—something like that, he called it.

'The last time I drank wine as good as this,' says Starlight, 'was at the Caffy Troy, something or other, in Paris. I wouldn't mind being there again, with the Variety Theatre to follow. Would you, Clifford?'

'Well, I don't know,' says the other swell. 'I find this amazing good fun for a bit. I never was in such grand condition since I left Oxford. This eight-hours' shift business is just the right thing for training. I feel fit to go for a man's life. Just feel this, Despard,' and he holds out his arm to the camp swell. 'There's muscle for you!'

'Plenty of muscle,' said Mr. Despard, looking round. He was a swell that didn't work, and wouldn't work, and thought it fine to treat the diggers like dogs. Most of the commissioners and magistrates were gentlemen and acted as such; but there were a few young fools like this one, and they did the Government a deal of harm with the diggers more than they knew. 'Plenty of muscle,' says he, 'but devilish little society.'

'I don't agree with you,' says the other Honourable. 'It's the most amusing and in a way instructive place for a man who wants to know his fellow-creatures I was ever in. I never pass a day without meeting some fresh variety of the human race, man or woman; and their experiences are well worth knowing, I can tell you. Not that they're in a hurry to impart them; for that there's more natural, unaffected good manners on a digging than in any society I ever mingled in I shall never doubt. But when they see you don't want to patronise, and are content to be a simple man among men, there's nothing they won't do for you or tell you.'

'Oh, d—n one's fellow-creatures; present company excepted,' says Mr. Despard, filling his glass, 'and the man that grew this "tipple." They're useful to me now and then and one has to put up with this crowd; but I never could take much interest in them.'

'All the worse for you, Despard,' says Clifford. 'You're wasting your chances—golden opportunities in every sense of the word. You'll never see such a spectacle as this, perhaps, again as long as you live. It's a fancy dress ball with real characters.'

'Dashed bad characters, if we only knew,' says Despard, yawning. 'What do you say, Haughton?' looking at Starlight, who was playing with his glass and not listening much by the look of him.

'I say, let's go into the little parlour and have a game of picquet, unless you'll take some more wine. No? Then we'll move. Bad characters, you were saying? Well, you camp fellows ought to be able to give an opinion.'

They sauntered through the big room, which was just then crowded with a curious company, as Clifford said. I suppose there was every kind of man and miner under the sun. Not many women, but what there was not a little out of the way in looks and manners. We kept on working away all the time. It helped to stop us from thinking, and every week we had a bigger deposit-receipt in the bank where we used to sell our gold. People may say what they like, but there's nothing like a nest egg; seeing it grow bigger keeps many a fellow straight, and he gets to like adding to it, and feels the pull of being careful with his money, which a poor man that never has anything worth saving doesn't. Poor men are the most extravagant, I've always found. They spend all they have, which middling kind of people just above them don't. They screw and pinch to bring up their children, and what not; and dress shabby and go without a lot which the working man never thinks of stinting himself in. But there's the parson here to do that kind of thing. I'm not the proper sort of cove to preach. I'd better leave it to him. So we didn't spend our money foolish, like most part of the diggers that had a bit of luck; but we had to do a fair thing. We got through a lot of money every week, I expect. Talking of foolish things, I saw one man that had his horse shod with gold, regular pure gold shoes. The blacksmith made 'em—good solid ones, and all regular. He rode into the main street one holiday, and no end of people stopped him and lifted up his horse's feet to see. They weighed 7 oz. 4 dwt. each. Rainbow ought to have been shod that way. If ever a horse deserved it he did. But Starlight didn't go in for that kind of thing. Now and then some of the old colonial hands, when they were regularly 'on the burst,' would empty a dozen of champagne into a bucket or light their pipes with a ten-pound note. But these were not everyday larks, and were laughed at by the diggers themselves as much as anybody.

But of course some allowance had to be made for men not making much above wages when they came suddenly on a biggish stone, and sticking the pick into it found it to be a gigantic nugget worth a small fortune. Most men would go a bit mad over a stroke of luck like that, and they did happen now and then. There was the Boennair nugget, dug at Louisa Creek by an Irishman, that weighed 364 oz. 11 dwt. It was sold in Sydney for £1156. There was the King of Meroo nugget, weighing 157 oz.; and another one that only scaled 71 oz. seemed hardly worth picking up after the others,

only £250 worth or so. But there was a bigger one yet on the grass
if we'd only known, and many a digger, and shepherd too, had sat
down on it and lit his pipe, thinking it no better than other lumps
of blind white quartz that lay piled up all along the crown of the
ride.

Mostly after we'd done our day's work and turned out clean and
comfortable after supper, smoking our pipes, we walked up the
street for an hour or two. Jim and I used to laugh a bit in a queer
way over the change it was from our old bush life at Rocky Flat
when we were boys, before we had any thoughts beyond doing our
regular day's work and milking the cows and chopping wood enough
to last mother all day. The little creek, that sounded so clear in
the still night when we woke up, rippling and gurgling over the
stones, the silent, dark forest all round on every side; and on moonlight nights the moon shining over Nulla Mountain, dark and overhanging all the valley, as if it had been sailing in the clear sky
over it ever since the beginning of the world. We didn't smoke
then, and we used to sit in the verandah, and Aileen would talk to
us till it was time to go to bed.

Even when we went into Bargo, or some of the other country
towns, they did not seem so much brighter. Sleepy-looking, steady-
going places they all were, with people crawling about them like a
lot of old working bullocks. Just about as sensible, many of 'em.
What a change all this was! Main Street at the Turon! Just as
bright as day at twelve o'clock at night. Crowds walking up and
down, bars lighted up, theatres going on, dance-houses in full swing,
billiard-tables where you could hear the balls clicking away till
daylight; miners walking down to their night shifts, others turning
out after sleeping all the afternoon, quite fresh and lively; half-a-
dozen troopers clanking down the street, back from escort duty.
Everybody just as fresh at midnight as at breakfast time—more so,
perhaps. It was a new world.

One thing's certain; Jim and I would never have had the chance
of seeing as many different kinds of people in a hundred years if it
hadn't been for the gold. No wonder some of the young fellows
kicked over the traces for a change—a change from sheep, cattle, and
horses, ploughing and reaping, shearing and bullock-driving; the
same old thing every day; the same chaps to talk to about the same
things. It does seem a dead-and-live kind of life after all we've seen
and done since. However, we'd a deal better have kept to the
bulldog's motter, 'Hang on,' and stick to it, even if it was a shade
slow and stupid. We'd have come out right in the end, as all coves
do that hold fast to the right thing and stick to the straight course,
fair weather or foul. I can see that now, and many things else.

But to see the big room at the Prospectors' Arms at night—the
hall, they called it—was a sight worth talking about—as Jim and I
walked up and down, or sat at one of the small tables smoking

our pipes, with good liquor before us. It was like a fairy-tale come true to chaps like us, though we had seen a little life in Sydney and Melbourne.

What made it so different from any other place we'd ever seen or thought of before was the strange mixture of every kind and sort of man and woman; to hear them all jabbering away together in different languages, or trying to speak English, used to knock us altogether. The American diggers that we took up with had met a lot of foreigners in California and other places. They could speak a little Spanish and French, and got on with them. But Jim and I could only stare and stand open-mouthed when a Spanish-American chap would come up with his red sash and his big sheath-knife, while they'd yabber away quite comfortable.

It made us feel like children, and we began to think what a fine thing it would be to clear out by Honolulu, and so on to San Francisco, as Starlight was always talking about. It would make men of us, at any rate, and give us something to think about in the days to come.

If we could clear out what a heaven it would be! I could send over for Gracey to come to me. I knew she'd do that, if I was only once across the sea, ready and willing to lead a new life, and with something honest-earned and hard-worked-for to buy a farm with. Nobody need know. Nobody would even inquire in the far West where we'd come from or what we'd done. We should live close handy to one another—Jim and Jeanie, Gracey and I—and when dad went under, mother and Aileen could come out to us; and there would still be a little happiness left us, for all that was come and gone. Ah! if things would only work out that way.

Well, more unlikely things happen every day. And still the big room gets fuller. There's a band strikes up in the next room and the dancing begins. This is a ball night. Kate has started that game. She's a great hand at dancing herself, and she manages to get a few girls to come up; wherever they come from nobody knows, for there's none to be seen in the day-time. But they turn out wonderfully well dressed, and some of them mighty good-looking; and the young swells from the camp come down, and the diggers that have been lucky and begin to fancy themselves. And there's no end of fun and flirting and nonsense, such as there always is when men and women get together in a place where they're not obliged to be over-particular. Not that there was any rowdiness or bad behaviour allowed. A goldfield is the wrong shop for that. Any one that didn't behave himself would have pretty soon found himself on his head in the street, and lucky if he came out of it with whole bones.

I once tried to count the different breeds and languages of the men in the big room one night. I stopped at thirty. There were Germans, Swedes, Danes, Norwegians, Russians, Italians, Greeks,

Jews, Spaniards, Frenchmen, Maltese, Mexicans, Negroes, Indians, Chinamen, New Zealanders, English, Irish, Scotch, Welsh, Australians, Americans, Canadians, Creoles, gentle and simple, farmers and labourers, squatters and shepherds, lawyers and doctors. They were all alike for a bit, all pretty rich; none poor, or likely to be; all workers and comrades; nobody wearing much better clothes or trying to make out he was higher than anybody else. Everybody was free with his money. If a fellow was sick or out of luck, or his family was down with fever, the notes came freely—as many as were wanted, and more when that was done. There was no room for small faults and vices; everything and everybody was worked on a high scale. It was a grand time—better than ever was in our country before or since. Jim and I always said we felt better men while the flash time lasted, and hadn't a thought of harm or evil about us. We worked hard enough, too, as I said before; but we had good call to do so. Every week when we washed up we found ourselves a lot forrarder, and could see if it held on like this for a few months more we should have made our 'pile,' as the diggers called it, and be able to get clear off without much bother.

Because it wasn't now as it was in the old times, when Government could afford to keep watch upon every vessel, big and little, that left the harbour. Now there was no end of trouble in getting sailors to man the ships, and we could have worked our passage easy enough; they'd have taken us and welcome, though we'd never handled a rope in our lives before. Besides that, there were hundreds of strangers starting for Europe and America by every vessel that left. Men who had come out to the colony expecting to pick up gold in the streets, and had gone home disgusted; lucky men, too, like ourselves, who had sworn to start for home the very moment they had made a fair thing. How were any police in the world to keep the run of a few men that had been in trouble before among such a mixed-up mob?

Now and then we managed to get a talk with Starlight on the sly. He used to meet us at a safe place by night, and talk it all over. He and his mates were doing well, and expected to be ready for a start in a few months, when we might meet in Melbourne and clear out together. He believed it would be easy, and said that our greatest danger of being recognised was now over—that we had altered so much by living and working among the diggers that we could pass for diggers anywhere.

'Why, we were all dining at the Commissioner's yesterday,' he said, 'when who should walk in but our old friend Goring. He's been made inspector now; and, of course, he's a great swell and a general favourite. The Commissioner knew his family at home, and makes no end of fuss about him. He left for the Southern district, I am glad to say. I felt queer, I must say; but, of course, I didn't show it. We were formally introduced. He caught me with that sudden glance of his—devilish sharp eyes, he has—and looks me full in the face.

'"I don't remember your name, Mr. Haughton," said he; "but your face seems familiar to me somehow. I can't think where I've met you before."

'"Must have been at the Melbourne Club," says I, pulling my moustache. "Met a heap of Sydney people there."

'"Perhaps so," says he. "I used to go and lunch there a good deal. I had a month's leave last month, just after I got my step. Curious it seems, too," says he; "I can't get over it."

'"Fill your glass and pass the claret," says the Commissioner. "Faces are very puzzling things met in a different state of existence. I don't suppose Haughton's wanted, eh, Goring?"

'This was held to be a capital joke, and I laughed too in a way that would have made my fortune on the stage. Goring laughed too, and seemed to fear he'd wounded my feelings, for he was most polite all the rest of the evening.'

'Well, if *he* didn't smoke you,' says Jim, 'we're right till the Day of Judgment. There's no one else there that's half a ghost of a chance to swear to us.'

'Except,' says I——

'Oh! Kate?' says Jim; 'never mind her. Jeanie's coming up to be married to me next month, and Kate's getting so fond of you again that there's no fear of her letting the cat out.'

'That's the very reason. I never cared two straws about her, and now I hate the sight of her. She's a revengeful devil, and if she takes it into her head she'll turn on us some fine day as sure as we're alive.'

'Don't you believe it,' says Jim; 'women are not so bad as all that.' ('Are they not?' says Starlight.) 'I'll go bail we'll be snug and safe here till Christmas, and then we'll give out, say we're going to Melbourne for a spree, and clear straight out.'

CHAPTER XXVIII

As everything looked so fair-weather-like, Jim and Jeanie made it up to be married as soon after she came up as he could get a house ready. She came up to Sydney, first by sea and after that to the diggings by the coach. She was always a quiet, hard-working, good little soul, awful timid, and prudent in everything but in taking a fancy to Jim. But that's neither here nor there. Women will take fancies as long as the world lasts, and if they happen to fancy the wrong people the more obstinate they hold on to 'em. Jeanie was one of the prettiest girls I ever set eyes on in her way, very fair and clear coloured, with big, soft blue eyes, and hair like a cloud of spun silk. Nothing like her was ever seen on the field when she came up, so all the diggers said.

When they began to write to one another after we came to the Turon, Jim told her straight out that, though we were doing well now, it mightn't last. He thought she was a great fool to leave Melbourne when she was safe and comfortable, and come to a wild place, in a way like the Turon. Of course he was ready and willing to marry her; but, speaking all for her own good, he advised her not. She'd better give him up and set her mind on somebody else. Girls that was anyway good-looking and kept themselves proper or decent were very scarce in Melbourne and Sydney now, considering the number of men that were making fortunes and were anxious to get a wife and settle down. A girl like her could marry anybody—most likely some one above her own rank in life. Of course she wouldn't have no one but Jim, and if he was ready to marry her, and could get a little cottage, she was ready too. She would always be his own Jeanie, and was willing to run any kind of risk so as to be with him and near him, and so on.

Starlight and I both tried to keep Jim from it all we knew. It would make things twice as bad for him if he had to turn out again, and there was no knowing the moment when we might have to make a bolt for it; and where could Jeanie go then?

But Jim had got one of his obstinate fits. He said we were regularly mixed up with the diggers now. He never intended to follow any other life, and wouldn't go back to the Hollow or take part in any fresh cross work, no matter how good it might be. Poor old Jim! I really believe he'd made up his mind to go straight from the very hour he was buckled to Jeanie; and if he'd only had common luck he'd have been as square and right as George Storefield to this very hour.

I was near forgetting about old George. My word! he was getting on faster than we were, though he hadn't a golden hole. He was gold-finding in a different way, and no mistake. One day we saw a stoutish man drive up Main Street to the camp, with a well groomed horse, in a dogcart, and a servant with him; and who was this but old George? He didn't twig us. He drove close alongside of Jim, who was coming back from the creek, where he'd been puddling, with two shovels and a pick over his shoulder, and a pair of old yellow trousers on, and him splashed up to the eyes. George didn't know him a bit. But we knew him and laughed to ourselves to see the big swell he had grown into. He stopped at the camp and left his dogcart outside with his man. Next thing we saw was the Commissioner walking about outside the camp with him, and talking to him just as if he was a regular intimate friend.

The Commissioner, that was so proud that he wouldn't look at a digger or shake hands with him, not if he was a young marquis, as long as he was a digger. 'No!' he used to say, 'I have to keep my authority over these thousands and tens of thousands of people, some of them very wild and lawless, principally by moral influence, though, of course, I have the Government to fall back upon. To do that I must keep up my position, and over-familiarity would be the destruction of it.' When we saw him shaking hands with old George and inviting him to lunch we asked one of the miners next to our claim if he knew what that man's name and occupation was there.

'Oh!' he says, 'I thought everybody knew him. That's Storefield, the great contractor. He has all the contracts for horse-feed for the camps and police stations; nearly every one between here and Kiandra. He's took 'em lucky this year, and he's making money hand over fist.'

Well done, steady old George! No wonder he could afford to drive a good horse and a swell dogcart. He was getting up in the world. We were a bit more astonished when we heard the Commissioner say—

'I am just about to open court, Mr. Storefield. Would you mind taking a few cases with me this morning?'

We went into the courthouse just for a lark. There was old George sitting on the bench as grave as a judge, and a rattling good magistrate he made too. He disagreed from the Commissioner once or twice, and showed him where he was right, too, not in the law but in the facts of the case, where George's knowing working men and their ways gave him the pull. He wasn't over sharp and hard either, like some men directly they're raised up a bit, just to show their power. But just seemed to do a fair thing, neither too much one way or the other. George stayed and had lunch at the camp with the Commissioner when the court was adjourned, and

he drove away afterwards with his upstanding eighty-guinea horse—
horses was horses in those days—just as good a gentleman to look at
as anybody. Of course we knew there was a difference, and he'd
never get over a few things he'd missed when he was young, in the
way of education. But he was liked and respected for all that, and
made welcome everywhere. He was a man as didn't push himself
one bit. There didn't seem anything but his money and his good-
natured honest face, and now and then a bit of a clumsy joke, to
make him a place. But when the swells make up their minds to
take a man in among themselves they're not half as particular as
commoner people; they do a thing well when they're about it.

So George was hail-fellow-well-met with all the swells at the camp,
and the bankers and big storekeepers, and the doctors and lawyers
and clergymen, all the nobs there were at the Turon; and when
the Governor himself and his lady came up on a visit to see what
the place was like, why George was taken up and introduced as if
he'd been a regular blessed curiosity in the way of contractors, and
his Excellency hadn't set eyes on one before.

'My word! Dick,' says Jim, 'it's a murder he and Aileen didn't
cotton to one another in the old days. She'd have been just the girl
to have fancied all this sort of swell racket, with a silk gown and
dressed up a bit. There isn't a woman here that's a patch on her
for looks, is there now, except Jeanie, and she's different in her ways.'

I didn't believe there was. I began to think it over in my own
mind, and wonder how it came about that she'd missed all her
chances of rising in life, and if ever a woman was born for it she
was. .I couldn't help seeing whose fault it was that she'd been kept
back and was now obliged to work hard, and almost ashamed to show
herself at Bargo and the other small towns; not that the people
were ever shy of speaking to her, but she thought they might be,
and wouldn't give them a chance. In about a month up comes
Jeanie Morrison from Melbourne, looking just the same as the very
first evening we met Kate and her on the St. Kilda beach. Just as
quiet and shy and modest-looking—only a bit sadder, and not quite
so ready to smile as she'd been in the old days. She looked as if
she'd had a grief to hide and fight down since then. A girl's first
sorrow when something happened to her love! They never look
quite the same afterwards. I've seen a good many, and if it was
real right down love, they were never the same in looks or feelings
afterwards. They might 'get over it,' as people call it; but that's a
sort of healing over a wound. It don't always cure it, and the wound
often breaks out again and bleeds afresh.

Jeanie didn't look so bad, and she was that glad to see Jim again
and to find him respected as a hard-working, well-to-do miner that
she forgot most of her disappointments and forgave him his share
of any deceit that had been practised upon her and her sister.
Women are like that. They'll always make excuses for men they're

fond of and blame anybody else that can be blamed or that's within reach. She thought Starlight and me had the most to do with it—perhaps we had; but Jim could have cut loose from us any time before the Momberah cattle racket much easier than he could now. I heard her say once that she thought other people were much more to blame than poor James—people who ought to have known better, and so on. By the time she had got to the end of her little explanation Jim was completely whitewashed of course. It had always happened to him, and I suppose always would. He was a man born to be helped and looked out for by every one he came near.

Seeing how good-looking Jeanie was thought, and how all the swells kept crowding round to get a look at her, if she was near the bar, Kate wanted to have a ball and show her off a bit. But she wouldn't have it. She right down refused and close upon quarrelled with Kate about it. She didn't take to the glare and noise and excitement of Turon at all. She was frightened at the strange-looking men that filled the streets by day and the hall at the Prospectors' by night. The women she couldn't abide. Anyhow she wouldn't have nothing to say to them. All she wanted—and she kept at Jim day after day till she made him carry it out—was for him to build or buy a cottage, she didn't care how small, where they could go and live quietly together. She would cook his meals and mend his clothes, and they would come into town on Saturday nights only and be as happy as kings and queens. She didn't come up to dance or flirt, she said, in a place like Turon, and if Jim didn't get a home for her she'd go back to her dressmaking at St. Kilda. This woke up Jim, so he bought out a miner who lived a bit out of the town. He had made money and wanted to sell his improvements and clear out for Sydney. It was a small four-roomed weatherboard cottage, with a bark roof, but very neatly put on. There was a little creek in front, and a small flower garden, with rose trees growing up the verandah posts. Most miners, when they're doing well, make a garden. They take a pride in having a neat cottage and everything about it shipshape. The ground, of course, didn't belong to him, but he held it by his miner's right. The title was good enough, and he had a right to sell his goodwill and improvements.

Jim gave him his price and took everything, even to the bits of furniture. They weren't much, but a place looks awful bare without them. The dog, and the cock and hens he bought too. He got some real nice things in Turon—tables, chairs, sofas, beds, and so on; and had the place lined and papered inside, quite swell. Then he told Jeanie the house was ready, and the next week they were married. They were married in the church—that is, the iron building that did duty for one. It had all been carted up from Melbourne—framework, roof, seats, and all—and put together at Turon. It didn't look so bad after it was painted, though it was awful hot in summer.

Here they were married, all square and regular, by the Scotch clergyman. He was the first minister of any kind that came up to the diggings, and the men had all come to like him for his straightforward, earnest way of preaching. Not that we went often, but a good few of us diggers went every now and then just to show our respect for him; and so Jim said he'd be married by Mr. Mackenzie and no one else. Jeanie was a Presbyterian, so it suited her all to pieces.

Well, the church was chock-full. There never was such a congregation before. Lots of people had come to know Jim on the diggings, and more had heard of him as a straightgoing, good-looking digger, who was free with his money and pretty lucky. As for Jeanie, there was a report that she was the prettiest girl in Melbourne, and something of that sort, and so they all tried to get a look at her. Certainly, though there had been a good many marriages since we had come to the Turon, the church had never held a handsomer couple. Jeanie was quietly dressed in plain white silk. She had on a veil; no ornaments of any kind or sorts. It was a warmish day, and there was a sort of peach-blossom colour on her cheeks that looked as delicate as if a breath of air would blow it away. When she came in and saw the crowd of bronze bearded faces and hundreds of strange eyes bent on her, she turned quite pale. Then the flush came back on her face, and her eyes looked as bright as some of the sapphires we used to pick up now and then out of the river-bed. Her hair was twisted up in a knot behind; but even that didn't hide the lovely colour nor what a lot there was of it. As she came in with her slight figure and modest sweet face that turned up to Jim's like a child's, there was a sort of hum in the church that sounded very like breaking into a cheer.

Jim certainly was a big upstanding chap, strong built but active with it, and as fine a figure of a man as you'd see on the Turon or any other place. He stood about six feet and an inch, and was as straight as a rush. There was no stiffness about him either. He was broad-shouldered and light flanked, quick on his pins, and as good a man—all round—with his hands as you could pick out of the regular prize ring. He was as strong as a bullock, and just as good a man at the end of a day as at the start. With the work we'd had for the last five or six months we were all in top condition, as hard as a board and fit to work at any pace for twenty-four hours on end. He had an open, merry, laughing face, had Jim, with straight features and darkish hair and eyes. Nobody could ever keep angry with Jim. He was one of those kind of men that could fight to some purpose now and then, but that most people found it very hard to keep bad friends with.

Besides the miners, there were lots of other people in church who had heard of the wedding and come to see us. I saw Starlight and the two Honourables, dressed up as usual, besides the Commissioner and the camp officers; and more than that, the new Inspector of Police, who'd only arrived the day before. Sir Ferdinand Morringer, even he was there, dividing the people's attention with the bride. Besides that, who should I see but Bella and Maddie Barnes and old Jonathan. They'd ridden into the Turon, for they'd got their riding habits on, and Bella had the watch and chain Starlight had given her. I saw her look over to where he and the other two were, but she didn't know him again a bit in the world. He was sitting there looking as if he was bored and tired with the whole thing—hadn't seen a soul in the church before, and didn't want to see 'em again.

I saw Maddie Barnes looking with all her eyes at Jim, while her face grew paler. She hadn't much colour at the best of times, but she was a fine-grown, lissom, good-looking girl for all that, and as full of fun and games as she could stick. Her eyes seemed to get bigger and darker as she looked, and when the parson began to read the service she turned away her head. I always thought she was rather soft on Jim, and now I saw it plain enough. He was one of those rattling, jolly kind of fellows that can't help being friendly with every girl he meets, and very seldom cares much for any one in particular. He had been backward and forward a good deal with father before we got clear of Berrima, and that's how poor Maddie had come to take the fancy so strong and set her heart upon him.

It must be hard lines for a woman to stand by, in a church or anywhere else, and see the man she loves given away, for good and all, buckled hard and fast to another woman. Nobody took much notice of poor Maddie, but I watched her pretty close, and saw the tears come into her eyes, though she let 'em run down her face before she'd pull out her handkerchief. Then she put up her veil and held up her head with a bit of a toss, and I saw her pride had helped her to bear it. I don't suppose anybody else saw her, and if they did they'd only think she was cryin' for company—as women often do at weddings and all kinds of things. But I knew better. She wouldn't peach, poor thing! Still, I saw that more than one or two knew who we were and all about us that day.

We'd only just heard that the new Inspector of Police had come on to the field; so of course everybody began to talk about him and wanted to have a look at him. Next to the Commissioner and the P.M., the Inspector of Police is the biggest man in a country town or on a goldfield. He has a tremendous lot of power, and, inside of the law, can do pretty much what he pleases. He can arrest a man on suspicion and keep him in gaol for a month or two. He can have him remanded from time to time for further evidence, and make it pretty hot for him generally. He can let him out when he proves innocent, and nobody can do anything. All he has to say is: 'There was a mistake in the man's identity'; or, 'Not sufficient proof.' Anything of that sort. He can walk up to any man he likes (or dislikes) and tell him to hold up his hands for the handcuffs, and shoot him if he resists. He has servants to wait on him, and orderly troopers to ride behind him; a handsome uniform like a cavalry officer; and if he's a smart, soldierly, good-looking fellow, as he very often is, he's run after a good deal and can hold his head as high as he pleases. There's a bit of risk sometimes in apprehending desperate—ahem!—bad characters, and with bush-rangers and people of that sort, but nothing more than any young fellow of spirit would like mixed up with his work. Very often they're men of good family in the old country that have found nothing to do in this, and have taken to the police. When it was known that this Ferdinand Morringer was a real baronet and had been an officer in the Guards, you may guess how the flood of goldfields talk rose and flowed and foamed all round him. It was Sir Ferdinand this and Sir Ferdinand that wherever you went. He was going to lodge at the Royal. No, of course he was going to stay at the camp! He was married and had three children. Not a bit of it; he was a bachelor, and he was going to be married to Miss Ingersoll, the daughter of the bank manager of the Bank of New Holland. They'd met abroad. He was a stall, fine-looking man. Not at all, only middle-sized; hadn't old Major Trenck, the superintendent of police, when he came to enlist and said he had been in the Guards, growled out, 'Too short for the Guards!'

'But I was not a private,' replied Sir Ferdinand.

'Well, anyhow there's a something about him. Nobody can deny he looks like a gentleman; my word, he'll put some of these Weddin' Mountain chaps thro' their facin's, you'll see,' says one miner.

'Not he,' says another; 'not if he was ten baronites in one; all the same, he's a manly-looking chap and shows blood.'

This was the sort of talk we used to hear all round us—from the miners, from the storekeepers, from the mixed mob at the Prospectors' Arms, in the big room at night, and generally all about. We said nothing, and took care to keep quiet, and do and say nothing to be took hold of. All the same, we were glad to see Sir Ferdinand. We'd heard of him before from Goring and the other troopers; but he'd been on duty in another district, and hadn't come in our way.

One evening we were all sitting smoking and yarning in the big room of the hotel, and Jim, for a wonder—we'd been washing up—when we saw one of the camp gentlemen come in, and a strange officer of police with him. A sort of whisper ran through the room, and everybody made up their minds it was Sir Ferdinand. Jim and I both looked at him.

'Wa-al!' said one of our Yankee friends, 'what 'yur twistin' your necks at like a flock of geese in a corn patch? How d'ye fix it that a lord's better'n any other man?'

'He's a bit different, somehow,' I says. 'We're not goin' to kneel down or knuckle under to him, but he don't look like any one else in this room, does he?'

'He's no slouch, and he looks yer square and full in the eye,' like

CHAPTER XXIX

JIM and his wife moved over to the cottage in Specimen Gully; the miners went back to their work, and there was no more talk or bother about the matter. Something always happened every day at the Turon which wiped the last thing clean out of people's mind. Either it was a big nugget, or a new reef, or a tent robbery, a gold-buyer stuck up and robbed in the Iron-barks, a horse-stealing match, a fight at a dance-house, or a big law case. Accidents and offences happened every day, and any of them was enough to take up the whole attention of every digger on the field till something else turned up.

Not that we troubled our heads over much about things of this sort. We had set our minds to go on until our claims were worked out, or close up; then to sell out, and with the lot we'd already banked to get down to Melbourne and clear out. Should we ever be able to manage that? It seemed getting nearer, nearer, like a star that a man fixes his eyes on as he rides through a lonely bit of forest at night. We had all got our eyes fixed on it, Lord knows, and were working double tides, doing our very best to make up a pile worth while leaving the country with. As for Jim, he and his little wife seemed that happy that he grudged every minute he spent away from her. He worked as well as ever—better, indeed, for he never took his mind from his piece of work, whatever it was, for a second. But the very minute his shift was over Jim was away along the road to Specimen Gully, like a cow going back to find her calf. He hardly stopped to light his pipe now, and we'd only seen him once up at town, and that was on a Saturday night with Jeanie on his arm.

Well, the weeks passed over, and at long last we got on as far in the year as the first week in December. We'd given out that we might go somewhere to spend our Christmas. We were known to be pretty well in, and to have worked steady all these months since the early part of the year. We had paid our way all the time, and could leave at a minute's notice without asking any man's leave.

If we were digging up gold like potatoes we weren't the only ones. No, not by a lot. There never was a richer patch of alluvial, I believe, in any of the fields, and the quantity that was sent down in one year was a caution. Wasn't the cash scattered about then? Talk of money, it was like the dirt under your feet—in one way, certainly—as the dirt was more often than not full of gold.

We could see things getting worse on the field after a bit. We didn't set up to be any great shakes ourselves, Jim and I; but we didn't want the field to be overrun by a set of scoundrels that were the very scum of the earth, let alone the other colonies. We were afraid they'd go in for some big foolish row, and we should get dragged in for it. That was exactly what we didn't want.

With the overflowing of the gold, as it were, came such a town and such a people to fill it, as no part of Australia had ever seen before. When it got known by newspapers, and letters from the miners themselves to their friends at home what an enormous yield of gold was being dug out of the ground in such a simple fashion, all the world seemed to be moving over. At that time nobody could tell a lie hardly about the tremendous quantity that was being got and sent away every week. This was easy to know, because the escort returns were printed in all the newspapers every week; so everybody could see for themselves what pounds and hundred-weights and tons —yes, tons of gold—were being got by men who often, as like as not, hadn't to dig above twenty or thirty feet for it, and had never handled a pick or a shovel in their lives before they came to the Turon.

There were plenty of good men at the diggings. I will say this for the regular miners, that a more manly, straightgoing lot of fellows no man ever lived among. I wish we'd never known any worse. We were not what might be called highly respectable people ourselves—still, men like us are only half-and-half bad, like a good many more in this world. They're partly tempted into doing wrong by opportunity, and kept back by circumstances from getting into the straight track afterwards. But on every goldfield there's scores and scores of men that always hurry off there like crows and eagles to a carcass to see what they can rend and tear and fatten upon. They ain't very particular whether it's the living or the dead, so as they can gorge their fill. There was a good many of this lot at the Turon, and though the diggers gave them a wide berth, and helped to run them down when they'd committed any crime, they couldn't be kept out of sight and society altogether.

We used to go up sometimes to see the gold escort start. It was one of the regular sights of the field, and the miners that were off shift and people that hadn't much to do generally turned up on escort day. The gold was taken down to Sydney once a week in a strong express waggon—something like a Yankee coach, with leather springs and a high driving seat; so that four horses could be harnessed. One of the police sergeants generally drove, a trooper fully armed with rifle and revolver on the box beside him. In the back seat two more troopers with their Sniders ready for action; two rode a hundred yards ahead, and another couple about the same distance behind.

We always noticed that a good many of the sort of men that never seemed to do any digging and yet always had good clothes and money to spend used to hang about when the escort was starting. People in the crowd 'most always knew whether it was a 'big' escort or a 'light' one. It generally leaked out how many ounces had been sent by this bank and how much by that; how much had come from the camp, for the diggers who did not choose to sell to the banks were allowed to deposit their gold with an officer at the camp, where it was carefully weighed, and a receipt given to them stating the numbers of ounces, pennyweights and grains. Then it was forwarded by the escort, deducting a small percentage for the carriage and safe keeping. Government did not take all the risk upon itself. The miner must run his chance if he did not sell. But the chance was thought good enough; the other thing was hardly worth talking about. Who was to be game to stick up the Government escort, with eight police troopers, all well armed and ready to make a fight to the death before they gave up the treasure committed to their charge. The police couldn't catch all the horse-stealers and bush-rangers in a country that contained so many millions of acres of waste land; but no one doubted that they would a first-rate fight, on their own ground as it were, and before they'd let anything be taken away from them that had been counted out, box by box, and given into their charge.

We had as little notion of trying anything of the sort ourselves than as we had of breaking into the Treasury in Sydney by night. But those who knew used to say that if the miners had known the past history of some of the men that used to stand up and look on, well dressed or in regular digger rig, as the gold boxes were being brought out and counted into the escort drag, they would have made a bodyguard to go with it themselves when they had gold on board, or have worried the Government into sending twenty troopers in charge instead of six or eight.

One day, as Jim and I happened to be at the camp just as the escort was starting, the only time we'd been there for a month, we saw Warrigal and Moran standing about. They didn't see us; we were among a lot of other diggers, so were were able to take them out of winding a bit.

They were there for no good, we agreed. Warrigal's sharp eyes noted everything about the whole turn-out—the sergeant's face that drove, the way the gold boxes were counted out and put in a kind of fixed locker underneath the middle of the coach. He saw where the troopers sat before and behind, and I'll be bound came away with a wonderful good general idea of how the escort travelled, and of a good many things more about it that nobody guessed at. As for Moran, we could see him fix his eyes upon the sergeant who was driving, and look at him as if he could look right through him. He never took his eyes off him the whole time, but glared at him like a maniac; if some of his people hadn't given him a shove as they passed he would soon have attracted people's attention. But the crowd was too busy looking at the well-conditioned prancing horses and the

neatly got up troopers of the escort drag to waste their thoughts upon
a common bushman, however he might stare. When he turned away
to leave he ground out a red-hot curse betwixt his teeth. It made us
think that Warrigal's coming about with him on this line counted
for no good.

They slipped through the crowd again, and, though they were
pretty close, they never saw us. Warrigal would have known us
however we might have been altered, but somehow he never turned
his head our way. He was like a child, so taken up with all the
things he saw that his great-grandfather might have jumped up from
the Fish River Caves, or wherever he takes his rest, and Warrigal
would never have wondered at him.

'That's a queer start!' says Jim, as we walked on our homeward
path. 'I wonder what those two crawling, dingo-looking beggars were
here for? Never no good. I say, did you see that fellow Moran
look at the sergeant as if he'd eat him? What eyes he has, for all the
world like a black snake! Do you think he's got any particular down
on him?'

'Not more than on all police. I suppose he'd rub them out, every
mother's son, if he could. He and Warrigal can't stick up the escort
by themselves.'

We managed to get a letter from home from time to time now we'd
settled, as it were, at the Turon. Of course they had to be sent in the
name of Henderson, but we called for them at the post-office, and
got them all right. It was a treat to read Aileen's letters now. They
were so jolly and hopeful-like besides what they used to be. Now
that we'd been so long, it seemed years, at the diggings, and were
working hard, doing well, and getting quite settled, as she said, she
believed that all would go right, and that we should be able really to
carry out our plans of getting clear away to some country where we
could live safe and quiet lives. Women are mostly like that. They
first of all believe all that they're afraid of will happen. Then, as
soon as they see things brighten up a bit, they're as sure as fate
everything's bound to go right. They don't seem to have any kind of
feeling between. They hate making up their minds, most of 'em
as I've known, and jump from being ready to drown themselves one
moment to being likely to go mad with joy another. Anyhow you
take 'em, they're better than men, though. I'll never go back on
that.

So Aileen used to send me and Jim long letters now, telling us that
things were better at home, and that she really thought mother was
cheerfuller and stronger in health than she'd been ever since—well,
ever since—that had happened. She thought her prayers had been
heard, and that we were going to be forgiven for our sins and allowed, by God's mercy, to lead a new life. She quite believed in our
leaving the country, although her heart would be nearly broken

by the thought that she might never see us again, and a lot more of the same sort.

Poor mother! she had a hard time of it if ever any one ever had in this world, and none of it her own fault as I could see. Some people gets punished in this world for the sins other people commit. I can see that fast enough. Whether they get it made up to 'em afterwards, of course I can't say. They ought to, anyhow, if it can be made up to 'em. Some things that are suffered in this world can't be paid for, I don't care how they fix it.

More than once, too, there was a line or two on a scrap of paper slipped in Aileen's letters from Gracey Storefield. She wasn't half as good with the pen as Aileen, but a few words from the woman you love goes a long way, no matter what sort of a fist she writes. Gracey made shift to tell me she was so proud to hear I was doing well; that Aileen's eyes had been twice as bright lately; that mother looked better than she'd seen her this years; and if I could get away to any other country she'd meet me in Melbourne, and would be, as she'd always been, 'your own Gracey'—that's the way it was signed.

When I read this I felt a different man. I stood up and took an oath—solemn, mind you, and I intended to keep it—that if I got clear away I'd pay her for her love and true heart with my life, what was left of it, and I'd never do another crooked thing as long as I lived. Then I began to count the days to Christmas.

I wasn't married like Jim, and it not being very lively in the tent at night, Arizona Bill and I mostly used to stroll up to the Prospectors' Arms. We'd got used to sitting at the little table, drinking our beer or what not, smoking our pipes and listening to all the fun that was going on. Not that we always sat in the big hall. There was a snug little parlour beside the bar that we found more comfortable, and Kate used to run in herself when business was slack enough to leave the barmaid; then she'd sit down and have a good solid yarn with us.

She made a regular old friend of me, and, as she was a handsome woman, always well dressed, with lots to say and plenty of admirers, I wasn't above being singled out and made much of. It was partly policy, of course. She knew our secret, and it wouldn't have done to have let her let it out or be bad friends, so that we should be always going in dread of it. So Jim and I were always mighty civil to her, and I really thought she'd improved a lot lately and turned out a much nicer woman than I thought she could be.

We used to talk away about old times, regular confidential, and though she'd great spirits generally, she used to change quite sudden sometimes and say she was a miserable woman, and wished she hadn't been in such a hurry and married as she had. Then she'd crack up Jeanie, and say how true and constant she'd been, and how she was rewarded for it by marrying the only man she ever loved. She used to blame her temper; she'd always had it, she said, and couldn't get rid of it; but she really believed, if things had turned out different, she'd have been a different woman, and any man she really loved would never have had no call to complain. Of course I knew what all this meant, but thought I could steer clear of coming to grief over it.

That was where I made the mistake. But I didn't think so then, or how much hung upon careless words and looks.

Well, somehow or other she wormed it out of me that we were off somewhere at Christmas. Then she never rested till she'd found out that we were going to Melbourne. After that she seemed as if she'd changed right away into somebody else. She was that fair and soft-speaking and humble-minded that Jeanie couldn't have been more gentle in her ways; and she used to look at me from time to time as if her heart was breaking. I didn't believe that, for I didn't think she'd any heart to break.

One night, after we'd left about twelve o'clock, just as the house shut up, Arizona Bill says to me—

'Say, pard, have yer fixed it up to take that young woman along when you pull up stakes?'

'No,' I said; 'isn't she a married woman? and, besides, I haven't such a fancy for her as all that comes to.'

'Ye heven't?' he said, speaking very low, as he always did, and taking the cigar out of his mouth—Bill always smoked cigars when he could get them, and not very cheap ones either; 'well, then, I surmise you're lettin' her think quite contrary, and there's bound to be a muss if you don't hide your tracks and strike a trail she can't foller on.'

'I begin to think I've been two ends of a dashed fool; but what's a man to do?'

'See here, now,' he said; 'you hev two cl'ar weeks afore ye. You slack off and go slow; that'll let her see you didn't sorter cotton to her more'n's in the regulations.'

'And have a row with her?'

'Sartin,' says Bill, 'and hev the shootin' over right away. It's a plaguey sight safer than letting her carry it in her mind, and then laying for yer some day when ye heven't nary thought of Injuns in your head. That's the very time a woman like her's bound to close on yer and lift yer ha'r if she can.'

'Why, how do you know what she's likely to do?'

'I've been smokin', pard, while you hev been talkin', sorter careless like. I've had my eyes open and seen Injun sign mor'n once or twice either. I've hunted with her tribe afore, I guess, and old Bill ain't forgot all the totems and the war paint.'

After this Bill fresh lit his cigar, and wouldn't say any more. But I could see what he was driving at, and I settled to try all I knew to keep everything right and square till the time came for us to make our dart.

I managed to have a quiet talk with Starlight. He thought that by taking care, being very friendly, but not too much so, we might get clean off, without Kate or any one else being much the wiser.

Next week everything seemed to go on wheels—smooth and fast, no hitches anywhere. Jim reckoned the best of our claim would be worked out by the 20th of the month, and we'd as good as agreed to sell our shares to Arizona Bill and his mate, who were ready, as Bill said, 'to plank down considerable dollars' for what remained of it. If they got nothing worth while, it was the fortune of war, which a digger never growls at, no matter how hard hit he may be. If they did well, they were such up and down good fellows, and such real friends to us, that we should have grudged them nothing.

As for Jeanie, she was almost out of her mind with eagerness to get back to Melbourne and away from the diggings. She was afraid of many of the people she saw, and didn't like others. She was terrified all the time Jim was away from her, but she would not hear of living at the Prospectors' Arms with her sister.

'I know where that sort of things leads to,' she said; 'let us have our own home, however rough.'

Kate went out to Specimen Gully to see her sister pretty often, and they sat and talked and laughed, just as they did in old times, Jeanie said. She was a simple little thing, and her heart was as pure as quartz crystal. I do really believe she was no match for Kate in any way. So the days went on. I didn't dare stay away from the Prospectors' Arms, for fear she'd think I wanted to break with her altogether, and yet I was never altogether comfortable in her company. It wasn't her fault, for she laid herself out to get round us all, even old Arizona Bill, who used to sit solemnly smoking, looking like an Indian chief or a graven image, until at last his brick-coloured, grizzled old face would break up all of a sudden, and he'd laugh like a youngster. As the days drew nigh Christmas I could see a restless expression in her face that I never saw before. Her eyes began to shine in a strange way, and sometimes she'd break off short in her talk and run out of the room. Then she'd pretend to wish we were gone, and that she'd never seen us again. I could hardly tell what to make of her, and many a time I wished we were on blue water and clear away from all chance of delay and drawback.

CHAPTER XXX

We made up our minds to start by Saturday's coach. It left at night and travelled nigh a hundred miles by the same hour next morning. It's more convenient for getting away than the morning. A chap has time for doing all kinds of things just as he would like; besides, a quieter time to slope than just after breakfast. The Turon daily mail was well horsed and well driven. Nightwork though it was, and the roads dangerous in places, the five big double-reflector lamps, one high up over the top of the coach in the middle with two pair more at the side, made everything plain. We Cornstalks never thought of more than the regular pair of lamps, pretty low down, too, before the Yankee came and showed us what cross-country coaching was. We never knew before. My word, they taught us a trick or two. All about riding came natural, but a heap of dodges about harness we never so much as heard of till they came to the country with the gold rush.

We'd made all our bits of preparations, and thought nothing stood in the way of a start next evening. This was Friday. Jim hadn't sold his bits of traps, because he didn't want it to be known he wasn't coming back. He left word with a friend he could trust, though, to have 'em all auctioned and the goodwill of his cottage, and to send the money after him. My share and his in the claim went to Arizona Bill and his mate. We had no call to be ashamed of the money that stood to our credit in the bank. That we intended to draw out, and take with us in an order or a draft, or something, to Melbourne. Jeanie had her boxes packed, and was so wild with looking forward to seeing St. Kilda beach again that she could hardly sleep or eat as the time drew near.

Friday night came; everything had been settled. It was the last night we should either of us spend at the Turon for many a day—perhaps never. I walked up and down the streets, smoking, and thinking it all over. The idea of bed was ridiculous. How wonderful it all seemed! After what we had gone through and the state we were in less than a year ago, to think that we were within so little of being clear away and safe for ever in another country, with as much as would keep us comfortable for life. I could see Gracey, Aileen, and Jeanie, all so peaceful and loving together, with poor old mother, who had lost her old trick of listening and trembling whenever she heard a strange step or the tread of a horse. What a glorious state of things it would be! A deal of it was owing to the gold. This wonderful gold! But for it we shouldn't have had such a chance in a hundred years. I was that restless I couldn't settle, when I thought, all of a sudden, as I walked up and down, that I had promised to go and say good-bye to Kate Mullockson, at the Prospectors' Arms, the night before we started. I thought for a moment whether it would be safer to let it alone. I had a strange, unwilling kind of feeling about going there again; but at last, half not knowing what else to do, and half not caring to make an enemy of Kate, if I could help it, I walked up.

It was latish. She was standing near the bar, talking to half-a-dozen people at once, as usual; but I saw she noticed me at once. She quickly drew off a bit from them all; said it was near shutting-up time, and, after a while, passed through the bar into the little parlour where I was sitting down. It was just midnight. The night was half over before I thought of coming in. So when she came in and seated herself near me on the sofa I heard the clock strike twelve, and most of the men who were walking about the hall began to clear out.

Somehow, when you've been living at a place for a goodish while, and done well there, and has friends as has stuck by you, as we had at the Turon, you feel sorry to leave it. What you've done you're sure of, no matter how it mayn't suit you in some ways, nor how much better you expect to be off where you are going to. You had that and had the good of it. What the coming time may bring you can't reckon on. All kinds of cross luck and accidents may happen. What's the use of money to a man if he smashes his hip and has to walk with a crutch all his days? I've seen a miner with a thousand a month coming in, but he'd been crushed pretty near to death with a fall of earth, and about half of him was dead. What's a good dinner to a man that his doctor only allows him one slice of meat, a bit of bread, and some toast and water? I've seen chaps like them, and I'd sooner a deal be the poorest splitter, slogging away with a heavy maul, and able, mind you, to swing it like a man, than one of those broken-down screws. We'd had a good time there, Jim and I. We always had a kind spot in our hearts for Turon and the diggings afterwards. Hard work, high pay, good friends that would stick to a man back and edge, and a safe country to lie in plant in as ever was seen. We was both middlin' sorry, in a manner of speaking, to clear out. Not as Jim said much about it on account of Jeanie; but he thought it all the same.

Well, of course, Kate and I got talkin' and talkin', first about the diggings, and then about other things, till we got to old times in Melbourne, and she began to look miserable and miserabler whenever she spoke about marrying the old man, and wished she'd drownded herself first. She made me take a whisky—a stiffish one that she mixed herself—for a parting glass, and I felt it took a bit of effect upon me. I'd been having my whack during the day. I wasn't no ways drunk; but I must have been touched more or less, because I felt myself to be so sober.

'You're going at last, Dick,' says she; 'and I suppose we shan't meet again in a hurry. It was something to have a look at you now and then. It reminded me of the happy old times at St. Kilda.'

'Oh, come, Kate,' I said, 'it isn't quite so bad as all that. Besides, we'll be back again in February, as like as not. We're not going for ever.'

'Are you telling me the truth, Richard Marston?' says she, standing up and fixing her eyes full on me—fine eyes they were, too, in their way; 'or are you trying another deceit, to throw me off the scent and get rid of me? Why should you ever want to see my face after you leave?'

'A friendly face is always pleasant. Anyhow, Kate, yours is, though you did play me a sharpish trick once, and didn't stick to me like some women might have done.'

'Tell me this,' she said, leaning forward, and putting one hand on my shoulder, while she seemed to look through the very soul of me —her face grew deadly pale, and her lips trembled, as I'd seen them do once before when she was regular beyond herself—'will you take me with you when you go for good and all? I'm ready to follow you round the world. Don't be afraid of my temper. No woman that ever lived ever did more for the man she loved than I'll do for you. If Jeanie's good to Jim—and you know she is—I'll be twice the woman to you, or I'll die for it. Don't speak!' she went on; 'I know I threw you over once. I was mad with rage and shame. You know I had cause, hadn't I, Dick? You know I had. To spite you, I threw away my own life then; now it's a misery and a torment to me every day I live. I can bear it no longer, I tell you. It's killing me—killing me day by day. Only say the word, and I'll join you in Melbourne within a week—to be yours, and yours only, as long as I live.'

I didn't think there was that much of the loving nature about her. She used to vex me by being hard and uncertain when we were courting. I knew then she cared about me, and I hadn't a thought about any other woman. Now when I didn't ask her to bother herself about me, and only to let me alone and go her own way, she must turn the tables on me, and want to ruin the pair of us slap over again.

She'd thrown her arms round my neck and was sobbing on my shoulder when she finished. I took her over to the sofa and made her sit down by the side of me.

'Kate,' I said, 'this won't do. There's neither rhyme nor reason about it. I'm as fond of you as ever I was, but you must know well enough if you make a bolt of it now there'll be no end of a bobbery, and everybody's thoughts will be turned our way. We'll be clean bowled—the lot of us. Jim and I will be jugged. You and Jeanie will be left to the mercy of the world, worse off by a precious sight than ever you were in your lives. Now, if you look at it, what's the good of spoiling the whole jimbang for a fancy notion about me? You and I are safe to be first-rate friends always, but it will be the ruin of both of us if we're fools enough to want to be more. You're living here like a regular queen. You've got a good husband, that's proud of you and gives you everything you can think of. You took him yourself, and you're bound to stick to him. Besides, think of poor Jeanie and Jim. You'll spoil all their happiness; and, more than all—don't make any mistake—you know what Jeanie thinks of a woman who leaves her husband for another man.'

If you let a woman have a regular good cry and talk herself out, you can mostly bring her round in the end. So after a bit Kate grew more reasonable. That bit about Jeanie fetched her, too. She knew her own sister would turn against her—not harsh like, but she'd never be the same to her again as long as she lived.

The lamp had been put out in the big hall. There was only one in this parlour, and it wasn't over bright. I talked away, and last of all she came round to my way of thinking; at any rate not to want to clear off from the old man now, but to wait till I came back, or till I wrote to her.

'You are right, Dick,' she said at last, 'and you show your sense in talking the way you have; though, if you loved as I do, you could not do it. But, once more, there's no other woman that you're fonder of than me? It isn't that that makes you so good? Dick Marston good!' and here she laughed bitterly. 'If I thought that I should go mad.'

What was I to do? I could not tell her that I loved Gracey Storefield ten times as much as I'd ever cheated myself into thinking I cared about her. So I swore that I cared more for her than any woman in the whole world, and always had done so.

This steadied her. We parted good friends, and she promised to keep quiet and try and make the best of things. She turned up the lamp to show me the way out, though the outer door of the hall was left open night and day. It was a way we had at the Turon; no one troubled themselves to be particular about such trifles as furniture and so on. There was very little small robbery there; it was not worth while. All petty stealers were most severely punished into the bargain.

As I stood up to say good-bye a small note dropped out of my breast-pocket. It had shifted somehow. Kate always had an eye like a hawk. With one spring she pounced upon it, and before I could interfere opened and read it! It was Gracey Storefield's. She stood for one moment and glared in my face. I thought she had gone mad. Then she threw the bit of paper down and trampled upon it, over and over again.

'So, Dick Marston,' she cried out hoarsely, her very voice changed, 'you have tricked me a second time! Your own Gracey! your own Gracey! and this, by the date, at the very time you were letting me persuade myself, like a fool, like an idiot that I was, that you still care for me! You have put the cap to your villainy now. And, as God made me, you shall have cause—good cause—to fear the woman you have once betrayed and twice scorned. Look to yourself.'

She gazed at me for a moment with a face from which every trace of expression had vanished, except that of the most devilish fury and spite—the face of an evil spirit more than of a woman; and then she walked slowly away. I couldn't help pitying her, though I cursed my own folly, as I had done a thousand times, that I had ever turned my head or spoken a word to her when first she crossed my path. I got into the street somehow; I hardly knew what to think or to do. That danger was close at our heels I didn't doubt for a moment. Everything seemed changed in a minute. What was going to happen? Was I the same Dick Marston that had been strolling up Main Street a couple of hours ago? All but off by the to-morrow evening's coach, and with all the world before me, a good round sum in the bank; best part of a year's hard, honest work it was the price of, too.

Then all kinds of thoughts came into my head. Would Kate, when her burst of rage was over, go in for revenge in cold blood? She could hardly strike me without at the same time hurting Jeanie through Jim. Should I trust her- Would she come right, kiss, and make friends, and call herself a madwoman—a reckless fool—as she'd often done before? No; she was in bitter earnest this time. It did not pay to be slack in making off. Once we had been caught napping, and once was enough.

The first thing to do was to warn Jim—poor old Jim, snoring away, most like, and dreaming of taking the box-seat for himself and Jeanie at the agent's next morning. It seemed cruel to wake him, but it would have been crueller not to do so.

I walked up the narrow track that led up to the little gully with the moon shining down upon the white quartz rock. The pathway wound through a 'blow' of it. I threw a pebble at the door and waited till Jim came out.

'Who's there? Oh! it's you, old man, is it? It's rather late for a call; but if you've come to spend the evening I'll get up, and we'll have a smoke, anyhow.'

'You dress yourself, Jim,' I said, 'as quick as you can. Put on your hat and come with me; there's something up.'

'My God!' says Jim, 'what is it? I'm a rank coward now I've got Jeanie. Don't go and tell me we've got to cut and run again.'

'Something like it,' I said. 'If it hasn't come to that yet, it's not far off.'

We walked up the gully together. Jim lit his pipe while I told him shortly what had happened to me with Kate.

'May the devil fly away with her!' said Jim savagely, 'for a bad-minded, bad-hearted jade; and then he'd wish he'd left her where she was. She'd be no chop-down there even. I think sometimes she can't be Jeanie's sister at all. They must have changed her, and mothered the wrong child on the old woman. My word! but it's no laughing matter. What's to be done?'

'There's no going away by the coach to-morrow, I'm afraid. She's just the woman to tear straight up the camp and let it all out before her temper cooled. It would take a week to do that. The sergeant or Sir Ferdinand knows all about it now. They'll lose no time, you may be certain.'

'And must I leave without saying good-night to Jeanie?' says Jim. 'No, by ——! If I have half-a-dozen bullets through·me, I'll go back and hold her in my arms once more before I'm hunted off and through the country like a wild dog once more. If that infernal Kate has given us away, by George, I could go and kill her with my own hand! The cruel, murdering, selfish brute, I believe she'd poison her mother for a ten-pound note!'

'No use swearing at Kate, Jim,' I said; 'that won't mend matters. It's not the first time by a thousand that I've wished I'd never set eyes on her; but if I'd never seen her that day on St. Kilda beach you'd never known Jeanie. So there's evens as well as odds. The thing is, what are we to do now?'

'Dashed if I know. I feel stupid about tackling the bush again; and what can I do with Jeanie? I wish I was dead. I've half a mind to go and shoot that brute of a woman and then myself. But then, poor Jeanie! poor little Jeanie! I can't stand it, Dick; I shall go mad!'

I thought Jim was going to break out crying just as he used when he was a boy. His heart was a big soft one; and though he could face anything in the way of work or fighting that a man dare do, and do two men's share very like, yet his tears, mother said, laid very near his eyes, and till he was a grown man they used to pump up on all sorts of occasions.

'Come, be a man, Jim,' I said, 'we've got to look the thing in the face; there's no two ways about it. I shall go to Arizona Bill's claim and see what he says. Anyhow, I'll leave word with him what to do when we're gone. I'd advise you not to try to see Jeanie; but if you will you must, I suppose. Good-bye, old man. I shall make my way over to Jonathan's, borrow a horse from him, and make tracks for the Hollow as soon as I can. You'd better leave Jeanie here and do the same.'

Jim groaned, but said nothing. He wrung my hands till the bones seemed to crack, and walked away without a word. We knew it was a chance whether we should meet again.

I walked on pretty quick till I came to the flat where Arizona Bill and his mates had their sluicing claim. There were six of them altogether, tall wiry men all of them; they'd mostly been hunters and trappers in the Rocky Mountains before the gold was struck at Suttor's Mill, in the Sacramento Valley. They had been digging in '49 in California, but had come over when they heard from an old

mate of a placer diggings at Turon, richer than anything they had
ever tried in America.

This camp was half a mile from ours, and there was a bit of broken
ground between, so that I thought I was safe in having a word with
them before I cleared for Barnes's place, though I took care not to go
near our own camp hut. I walked over, and was making straight for
the smallest hut, when a rough voice hailed me.

'Hello! stranger, ye came darned near going to h—l with your boots
on. What did yer want agin that thar cabin?'

I saw then that in my hurry I had gone stumbling against a small
hut where they generally put their gold when the party had been
washing up and had more than was safe to start from camp with. In
this they always put a grizzled old hunter, about whom the yarn was
that he never went to sleep, and could shoot anything a mile off. It
was thought a very unlikely thing that any gold he watched would
ever go crooked. Most people considered him a deal safer caretaker
than the escort.

'Oh! it's you, is it?' drawled Sacramento Joe. 'Why, what's doin'
at yer old camp?'

'What about?' said I.

'Wal, Bill and I seen three or four half-baked vigilantes that call
themselves police; they was a setting round the hut and looked as if
they was awaiting for somebody.'

'Tell Bill I want him, Joe,' I said.

'Can't leave guard nohow,' says the true grit old hunter, pointing to
his revolver, and dodging up and down with his lame leg, a crooked
arm, and a seam in his face like a terrible wound there some time or
other. 'I darsn't leave guard. You'll find him in that centre tent,
with the red flag on it.'

I lifted the canvas flap of the door and went in. Bill raised himself
in the bed and looked at me quite coolly.

'I was to your location a while since,' he said. 'Met some friends
of yours there, too. I didn't cotton to 'em muchly. Something has
eventuated. Is that so?'

'Yes. I want your help.' I told him shortly all I could tell him
in the time.

.   .   .   .   .   .

He listened quietly, and made no remark for a time.

'So you hev bin a road agent. You and Jim, that darned innocent
old cuss, robbing mails and cattle ranches. It is a real scoop up for
me, you bet. I'd heern of bush-ranging in Australia, but I never
reckoned on their bein' men like you and Jim. So the muchacha
went back on yer—snakes alive! I kinder expected it. I reckon
you're bound to git.'

'Yes, Bill, sharp's the word. I want you to draw my money and
Jim's out of the bank; it's all in my name. There's the deposit receipt.
I'll back it over to you. You give Jeanie what she wants, and send

the rest when I tell you. Will you do that for me, Bill? I've always been on the square with you and your mates.'

'You hev, boy, that I'll not deny, and I'll corral the dollars for you. It's an all-fired muss that men like you and Jim should have a black mark agin your record. A spry hunter Jim would have made. I'd laid out to have had him to Arizona yet—and you're a going to dust out right away, you say?'

'I'm off now. Jim's waited too long, I expect. One other thing; let Mr. Haughton, across the creek, have this before daylight.'

'What, the Honourable!!! Lawful heart! Wal, I hope ye may strike a better trail yet. Yer young, you and Jim, poor old Jim. Hold on. Hev ye nary shootin' iron?'

'No time,' I said. 'I haven't been to the camp.'

'Go slow, then. Wait here; you'll want suthin', may be, on the peraira. If you do, boy; Jim made good shootin' with this, ye mind. Take it and welcome; it'll mind ye of old Arizona Bill.'

He handed me a beautifully finished little repeating rifle, hardly heavier than a navy revolver, and a small bag of cartridges.

'Thar, that'll be company for ye, in case ye hev to draw a bead on the—any one—just temp'ry like. Our horses is hobbled in Bates's clearing. Take my old sorrel if ye can catch him.' He stopped for a second and put his hand in a listening fashion. His hunter's ear was quicker than mine. 'Thar's a war party on the trail, I reckon. It's a roughish crossing at Slatey Bar,' and he pointed towards the river, which we could plainly hear rushing over a rocky bed. We shook hands, and as I turned down the steep river bank I saw him walk slowly into his tent and close the canvas after him.

The line he pointed to was the one I fixed in my own mind to take long before our talk was over. The Turon, always steep-banked, rocky in places, ran here under an awful high bluff of slate rock. The rushing water in its narrow channel had worn away the rock a good deal, and left ledges or bars under which a deal of gold had been found. Easy enough to cross here on a kind of natural ford. We had many a time walked over on Sundays and holidays for a little kangaroo-shooting now and then. It was here Jim one day, when we were all together for a ramble, surprised the Americans by his shooting with the little Ballard rifle.

As I crossed there was just moon enough to show the deep pools and the hurrying, tearing waters of the wild river, foaming betwixt the big boulders and jags of rock which the bar was strewed with. In front the bank rose 300 feet like the roof of a house, with great overhanging crags of slate rock, and a narrow track in and out between. If I had light enough to find this and get to the top—the country was terribly rough for a few miles, with the darkness coming on—I should be pretty well out of reach by daylight.

I had just struck the track when I heard voices and a horse's tramp on the other side of the river. They seemed not to be sure whether

I'd crossed or not, and were tracking up and down on each side of the bar. I breasted the hill track faster than I had done for many a day, and when I got to the top stopped to listen, but could hear nothing. The moon had dropped suddenly; the forest was as black as pitch. You couldn't see your hand before you.

I knew that I was safe now, if a hundred men were at my heels, till daybreak at any rate. I had the two sides of the gullly to guide me. I could manage to make to the farm where the sorrel was at grass with a lot of other diggers' horses. If I could get a saddle and catch the old horse I could put many a mile between me and them before sundown. I stood still when I reached the top of the bluff, partly to get breath and partly to take a last look at old Turon.

Below lay the goldfield clearly marked out by hundreds of camp-fires that were still red and showed bright in the darkened sky. The course of the river was marked by them, in and out, as most of the shallow diggings had followed the river flats. Far back the fires glowed against the black forest, and just before the moon fell I could catch the shine of the water in the deeper reaches of the river.

It was the very picture of what I'd read about an army in camp—lines of tents and a crowd of men all spread out over a bit of land hardly big enough for a flock of sheep. Now and then a dog would bark—now a revolver would go off. It was never quiet on Turon diggings, day or night.

Well, there they all were, tents and diggers, claims and wind-lasses, pumps and water-wheels. I had been happy enough there, God knows; and perhaps I was looking at it all for the last time. As I turned and made down the hill into the black forest that spread below me like the sea, I felt as if I was leaving everything that was any good in life behind with the Turon lights, and being hunted once more, in spite of myself, into a desert of darkness and despair.

CHAPTER XXXI

I GOT to Bates's paddocks about daylight, and went straight up to the hut where the man lived that looked after it. Most of the diggers that cared about their horses paid for their grass in farmers' and squatters' paddocks, though the price was pretty high. Old Bates, who had a bit of a good grassed flat, made a pretty fair thing out of it by taking in horses at half-a-crown a week apiece. As luck would have it, the man in charge knew me; he'd seen me out with the Yankees one day, and saw I was a friend with them, and when I said I'd come for Bill's sorrel he thought it likely enough, and got out the saddle and bridle. I tipped him well, and went off, telling him I was going to Wattle Flat to look at a quartz-crushing plant that was for sale. I accounted for coming up so early by saying I'd lost my road, and that I wanted to get to Wattle Flat sharp, as another chap wished to buy the plant. I cut across the range, kept the sun on my right hand, and pushed on for Jonathan's. I got there early, and it's well I did. I rode the sorrel hard, but I knew he was pretty tough, and I was able to pay for him if I killed him. I trusted to leaving him at Jonathan's, and getting a fresh horse there. What with the walk over the bluff and the forest, having no sleep the night before, and the bother and trouble of it all, I was pretty well used up. I was real glad to see Jonathan's paddock fence and the old house we'd thought so little of lately. It's wonderful how soon people rise grand notions and begin to get too big for their boots.

'Hello, Dick, what's up?' says Jonathan. 'No swag, 'lastic-side boots, flyaway tie, new rifle, old horse; looks a bit fishy, don't it!'

'I can't stop barneying,' I said. 'Have you a decent horse to give me? The game's up. I must ride night and day till I get home. Heard anything?'

'No; but Billy the Boy's just rode up. I hear him a-talkin' to the gals. He knows if anybody does. I'll take the old moke and put him in the paddock. I can let you have a stunner.'

'All right; I'll go in and have some breakfast. It's as much as I dare stop at all now.'

'Why, Dick Marston, is that you? No, it can't be,' said both girls together. 'Why, you look like a ghost. He doesn't; he looks as if he'd been at a ball all night. Plenty of partners, Dick?'

'Never mind, Dick,' says Maddie; 'go and make yourself comfortable in that room, and I'll have breakfast for you while you'd let a cow out of the bail. We don't forget our friends.'

'If all our friends were as true as you, Maddie,' I said, rather down-like, 'I shouldn't be here to-day.'

'Oh! that's it, is it?' says she; 'we're only indebted to somebody's laying the traps on—a woman of course—for your honour's company. Never mind, old man, I won't hit you when you're down. But, I say, you go and have a yarn with Billy the Boy—he's in the kitchen. I believe the young imp knows something, but he won't let on to Bell and I.'

While the steaks were frying—and they smelt very good, bad as I felt—I called out Master Billy and had a talk with him. I handed him a note to begin with. It was money well spent, and, you mark my words, a shilling spent in grog often buys a man twenty times the worth of it in information, let alone a pound.

Billy had grown a squarish-set, middle-sized chap; his hair wasn't so long, and his clothes were better; his eye was as bright and bold-looking. As he stood tapping one of his boots with his whip, he looked for all the world like a bull-terrier.

'My colonial oath, Dick, you're quite the gentleman—free with your money just the same as ever. You takes after the old governor; he always paid well if you told him the truth. I remember him giving me a hidin' when I was a kiddy for saying something I wasn't sure of. My word! I was that sore for a week after I couldn't button my shirt. But ain't it a pity about Jim?'

'Oh, that's it. What about Jim?'

'Why, the p'leece grabbed him, of course. You fellers don't think you're going on for ever and ever, keepin' the country in a state of terrorism, as the papers say. No, Dick, it's wrong and wicked and sinful. You'll have to knock under and give us young uns a chance.'

Here the impudent young rascal looked in my face as bold as brass and burst out laughing. He certainly was the cheekiest young scoundrel I ever came across. But in his own line you couldn't lick him.

'Jim's took,' he said, and he looked curiously over at me. 'I see the p'leece a-takin' him across the country to Bargo early this morning. There was poor old Jim a-lookin' as if he was goin' to be hanged, with a chap leading the screw he was on, and Jim's long legs tied underneath. I was gatherin' cattle, I was. I drew some up just for a stall, and had a good look.'

'How many men were with him?'

'Only two; and they're to pass through Bargo Brush about sundown to-night, or a bit earlier. I asked one of the men the road; said I'd lost myself, and would be late home. Ha! ha! ha!'

And how the young villain laughed till the tears came into his eyes, while he danced about like a blackfellow.

'See here, Billy,' I said, 'here's another pound for you, and there'll be a fiver after if you stick well to me to-day. I won't let Jim be walked off to Berrima without a flutter to save him. It'll be the death of him. He's not like me, and he's got a young wife besides.'

'More fool he, Dick. What does a cross cove want with a wife? He can't never expect to do any good with a wife follerin' of him about. I'm agin marrying, leastways as long as a chap's sound on his pins. But I'll stick to you, Dick, and, what's more, I can take you a short cut to the brush, and we can wait in a gully and see the traps come up. You have a snack and lie down for a bit. I seen you were done when you came up. I'll have the horses ready saddled up.'

'How about the police? Suppose they come this way.'

'Not they. They split and took across towards the Mountain Hut, where you all camped with the horses. I didn't see 'em; but I cut their tracks. Five shod horses. They might be here to-morrow.'

A bush telegraph ain't a bad thing. They're not all as good as Billy the Boy. But the worst of 'em, like a bad sheep dog, is a deal better than none.

A bush telegraph, you see, is mostly worked about the neighbourhood he was born in. He's not much good anywhere else. He's like a blackfellow outside of his own 'tauri.' He's at sea. But within twenty or thirty miles of where he was born and bred he knows every track, every range, every hill, every creek, as well as all the short cuts and by-roads. He can bring you miles shorter than any one that only follows the road. He can mostly track like a blackfellow, and tell you whether the cattle or horses which he sees the tracks of are belonging to his country or are strangers. He can get you a fresh horse on a pinch, night or day, for he knows everybody's paddocks and yards, as well as the number, looks, pace, and pluck of everybody's riding horses—of many of which he has 'taken a turn' out of— that is, ridden them hard and far, and returned them during the night. Of course he can be fined—even imprisoned for this—when he is caught in the act. Herein lies the difficulty. I felt like another man after a wash, a nip, and a real good meal, with the two girls sitting close by, and chattering away as usual.

'Do you know,' says Bella, 'it half serves you right. Not that that Port Phillip woman was right to peach. She ought to have had her tongue torn out first, let alone go open-mouthed at it. But mightn't you have come down here from the Turon on Sundays and holidays now and then, and had a yarn with us all?'

'Of course we ought, and we deserved to be kicked—the lot of us; but there were good reasons why we didn't like to. We were regularly boxed up with the diggers, nobody knew who we were, or where we came from, and only for this Jezebel never would have known. If we'd come here they'd have all dropped that we were old friends, and then they'd have known all about us."

'Well, I'm glad you've lost your characters,' says Maddie. 'You won't have to be so particular now, and you can come as often as Sir Ferdinand will let you. Good-bye. Billy's waving his hat.'

It wasn't long before I was in the saddle and off again. I'd made a bit of a bargain with Jonathan, who sold me a pair of riding boots, butcher's, and a big tweed poncho. The boots were easier to take a long rough ride in than trousers, and I wanted the poncho to keep the Ballard rifle under. It wouldn't do to have it in your hand all the time.

As we rode along I settled upon the way I'd try and set poor Jim free. Bad off as I was myself I couldn't bear to see him chained up, and knew that he was going for years and years to a place more wicked and miserable than he'd ever heard of.

After riding twenty miles the sun was getting low, when Billy pointed to a trail which came broad ways across the road, and which then followed it.

'Here they are—p'leece, and no mistake. Here's their horses' tracks right enough. Here's the prisoner's horse, see how he stumbled? and this road they're bound to go till they cross the Stony point, and get into Bargo Brush, near a creek.'

We had plenty of time by crossing a range and running blind creek down to be near the place where the troopers must pass as they crossed the main creek. We tied up the horses a hundred yards' distance behind us in the forest, and I made ready to rescue Jim, if it could be managed anyhow.

How was it to be done? I could depend on the rifle carrying true at short ranges; but I didn't like the notion of firing at a man behind his back, like. I hardly knew what to do, when all of a sudden two policemen showed up at the end of the track nearest the creek.

One man was a bit in front—riding a fine horse, too. The next one had a led horse, on which rode poor old Jim, looking as if he was going to be hanged that day, as Billy said, though I knew well he wasn't thinking about himself. I don't believe Jim ever looked miserable for so long since he was born. Whatever happened to him before, he'd have a cry or a fight, and it would be over. But now his poor old face looked that wretched and miserable, as if he'd never smile again as long as he lived. He didn't seem to care where they took him; and when the old horse stumbled and close upon fell down he didn't take notice.

When I saw that, my mind was made up. I couldn't let them take him away to his death. I could see he wouldn't live a month. He'd go fretting his life about Jeanie, and after the free life he'd always led he'd fall sick like the blacks when they're shut up, and die without any reason but because a wild bird won't live in a cage.

So I took aim and waited till they were just crossing the creek into the forest. The leading man was just riding up the bank, and the one that led Jim's horse was on the bit of a sand bed that the water had brought down. He was the least bit ahead of Jim, when I pulled trigger, and sent a ball into him, just under the collar-bone. I fired high on purpose. He drops off his saddle like a dead man. The next minute Billy the Boy raises the most awful corroboree of screams and howls, enough for a whole gang of bush-rangers, if they went in for that sort of thing. He emptied four chambers of his revolver at the leading trooper right away, and I fired at his horse. The constable never doubted—the attack was so sudden and savage like—but there was a party of men hid in the brush. Billy's shots had whistled round him, and mine had nearly dropped his horse, so he thought it no shame to make a bolt and leave his mate, as seemed very bad hit, in our hands.

His horse's hand-gallop growed fainter and fainter in the distance, and then we unbound poor Jim set his feet at liberty and managed to dispose of the handcuffs. Jim's face began to look more cheerful, but he was down in the mouth again when he saw the wounded man. He began at once to do all he could for him. We stopped a short distance behind the brush, which had already helped us well.

Jim propped up the poor chap, whose life-blood was flowing red through the bullet-hole, and made him as comfortable as he could. 'I must take your horse, mate,' he says; 'but you know it's only the fortune of war. A man must look after himself. Some one'll come along the road soon.' He mounted the trooper's horse, and we slipped through the trees—it was getting dark now—till we came to our horses. Then we all rode off together. We took Billy the Boy with us until he put us on to a road that led us into the country that we knew. We could make our own way from there, and so we sent off our scout, telling him to ride to the nearest township and say he'd seen a trooper lying badly wounded by the Bargo Brush roadside. The sooner he was seen to, the better chance he'd have.

Jim brightened up considerably after this. He told me how he'd gone back to say good-bye to Jeanie—how the poor girl went into fits, and he couldn't leave her. By the time she got better the cottage was surrounded by police; there was no use being shot down without a chance, so he gave himself up.

'My word, Dick,' he said, 'I wished for a bare-backed horse, and a deep gully, then; but it wasn't to be. There was no horse handy, and I'd only have been carried into my own place a dead man and frightened the life out of poor Jeanie as well.'

'You're worth a dozen dead men yet, Jim,' I said. 'Keep up your pecker, old man. We'll get across to the Hollow some time within the next twenty-four hours, and there we'll be safe anyhow. They can't touch Jeanie, you know; and you're not short of what cash she'll want to keep her till this blows over a bit.'

'And what am I to do all the time?' he says so pitiful like. 'We're that fond of one another, Dick, that I couldn't hardly bear her out of my sight, and now I'll be months and months and months without a look at her pretty face, where I've never seen anything yet but love and kindness. Too good for me she always was; and what have I brought her to? My God! Dick, I wish you'd shot me instead of the constable, poor devil!'

'Well, you wasn't very far apart,' I says, chaffing like. 'If that old horse they put you on had bobbed forward level with him you'd have got plugged instead. But it's no use giving in, Jim. We must stand up to our fight now, or throw up the sponge. There's no two ways about it.'

We rattled on then without speaking, and never cried crack till we got to Nulla Mountain, where we knew we were pretty safe not to be followed up. We took it easier then, and stopped to eat a bit of bread and meat the girls had put up for me at Jonathan's. I'd never thought of it before. When I took the parcel out of the pocket of my poncho I thought it felt deuced heavy, and there, sure enough, was one of those shilling flasks of brandy they sell for chaps to go on the road with.

Brandy ain't a good thing at all times and seasons, and I've seen more than one man, or a dozen either, that might just as well have sawed away at their throats with a blunt knife as put the first glass to their lips. But we was both hungry, thirsty, tired, miserable, and pretty well done and beaten, though we hadn't had time to think about it. That drop of brandy seemed as if it had saved our lives. I never forgot it, nor poor Maddie Barnes for thinking of it for me. And I did live to do her a good turn back—much as there's been said again me, and true enough, too.

It was a long way into the night, and not far from daylight, either, when we stumbled up to the cave—dead beat, horses and men both. We'd two minds to camp on the mountain, but we might have been followed up, hard as we'd ridden, and we didn't like to throw a chance away. We didn't want the old man to laugh at us, and we didn't want to do any more time in Berrima—not now, any-how. We'd been living too gay and free a life to begin with the jug all over again.

So we thought we'd make one job of it, and get right through, if we had to sleep for a week after it. It would be slow enough, but anything was better than what we'd gone through lately.

After we'd got down the mountain and on the flat land of the valley it rested our feet a bit, that was pretty nigh cut to pieces with the rocks. Our horses were that done we dursn't ride 'em for hours before. As we came close, out walks old Crib, and smells at us. He knew us in a minute, and jumped up and began to try and lick Jim's hand: the old story. He just gave one sort of sniff at me, as much as to say, 'Oh! it's you, is it?' Then he actually gave a kind of half-bark. I don't believe he'd barked for years, such a queer noise it was. Any-how, it woke up dad, and he came out pretty sharp with a revolver in his hand. As soon as he saw the old dog walking alongside of us he knew it was right, and begins to feel for his pipe. First thing father always did as soon as any work or fighting or talking was over was to get out his pipe and light it. He didn't seem the same man without it.

'So you've found your way back again, have ye?' he says. 'Why, I thought you was all on your way to Californy by this time. Ain't this Christmas week? Why, I was expecting to come over to Ameriky myself one of these days, when all the derry was over——Why, what's up with the boy?'

Jim was standing by, sayin' nothing, while I was taking off the saddles and bridles and letting the horses go, when all of a sudden he gives a lurch forward, and if the old man hadn't laid hold of him in his strong arms and propped him up he'd have gone down face foremost like a girl in a dead faint.

'What's up with him, Dick?' says father, rather quick, almost as if he was fond of him, and had some natural feeling—sometimes I raly think he had—'been any shooting?'

'Yes; not at him, though. Tell you all about it in the morning. He's eaten nothing, and we've been travelling best part of twenty-four hours right off the reel.'

'Hold him up while I fetch out the pannikin. There's plenty of grub inside. He'll be all right after a sleep.'

A drop of rum and water brought him to, and after that we made ourselves a cup of tea and turned in. The sun was pretty high when I woke. When I looked out there was the old man sitting on the log by the fire, smoking. What was a deal more curious, I saw the half-caste, Warrigal, coming up from the flat, leading a horse and carrying a pair of hobbles. Something made me look over to a particular corner where Starlight always slept when he was at the Hollow, Sure enough there was the figure of a man rolled up in a cloak. I knew by the way his boots and things were thrown about that it could be no other than Starlight.

CHAPTER XXXII

I'D settled in my mind that it couldn't be any one else, when he sat up, yawned, and looked round as if he had not been away from the old place a week.

'Ha! Richard, here we are again! "Feeds the boar in the old frank?" The governor told me you and Jim had made back. Dreadful bore, isn't it? Just when we'd all rubbed off the rust of our bush life and were getting civilised. I feel very seriously ill-treated, I assure you. I have a great mind to apply to the Government for compensation. That's the worst of these new inspectors, they are so infernally zealous.'

'You were too many for them, it seems. I half thought you might have been nailed. How the deuce did you get the office in time?'

'The faithful Warrigal, as usual, gave me timely warning, and brought a horse, of course. He will appear on the Judgment Day leading Rainbow, I firmly believe. Why he should be so confoundedly anxious about my welfare I can't make out—I can't, really. It's his peculiar form of mania, I suppose. We all suffer from some madness or other.'

'How the blazes did he know the police were laid on to the lot of us?' I said.

'I didn't know myself that your Kate had come the double on you. I might have known she would, though. Well, it seems Warrigal took it into his semi-barbaric head to ride into Turon and loaf about, partly to see me, and partly about another matter that your father laid him on about. He was standing about near the Prospectors' Arms, late on Friday night, doing nothing and seeing everything, as usual, when he noticed Mrs. Mullockson run out of the house like a Bedlamite. "My word, that missis big one coolah!" was his expression, and made straight for the camp. Now Warrigal had seen you come out just before. He doesn't like you and Jim over much—bad taste, I tell him, on his part—but I suppose he looks upon you as belonging to the family. So he stalked the fair and furious Kate.'

'That was how it was, then?'

'Yes, much in that way. I must say, Dick, that if you are so extremely fond of—well—studying the female character, you should carry on the pursuit more discreetly. Just see what this miscalculation has cost your friends!'

'Confound her! She's a heartless wretch, and I hope she'll die in a ditch.'

'Exactly. Well, she knocked, and a constable opened the outer door.

'"I want to see Sir Ferdinand," she says.

'"He's in bed and can't be disturbed," says the bobby. "Any message I can deliver?"

'"I have important information," says she. "Rouse him up, or you'll be sorry for it."

'"Won't it do to-morrow morning?" says he.

'"No, it won't," says she, stamping her foot. "Do what I tell you, and don't stand there like a fool."

'She waited a bit. Then, Warrigal says, out came Sir Ferdinand, very polite. "What can I do for you," says he, "Mrs. Mullockson?"

'"Should you like to know where the Marstons are, Sir Ferdinand," says she, "Dick and Jim?"

'"Know? Would I not?" says he. "No end of warrants out for them; since that Ballabri Bank robbery they seem to have disappeared under ground. And that fellow Starlight, too! Most remarkable man of his day. I'd give my eyes to put the bracelets upon him."

'She whispered something into his ear.

'"Guard, turn out," he roars out first; then, dropping his voice, says out, "My dear Mrs. Mullockson" (you should hear Warrigal imitate him), "you have made my fortune—officially, I mean, of course. I shall never forget your kindness. Thanks, a thousand times."

'"Don't thank me," she says, and she burst out crying, and goes slowly back to the hotel.

'Warrigal had heard quite enough. He rips over to Daly's mob, borrows a horse, saddle, and bridle, and leads him straight down to our camp. He roused me up about one o'clock, and I could hardly make explanations to my mates. Such stunning good fellows they were, too! I wonder whether I shall ever associate with gentlemen again? The chances are against it.

'I had all kinds of trouble to tell them I was going away with Warrigal, and yet not to tell too much.

'"What the dickens," says Clifford, "can you want, going away with this familiar of yours at this hour of the night? You're like the fellow in Scott's novel (*Anne of Geierstein*) that I was reading over again yesterday—the mysterious stranger that's called for at midnight by the Avenger of Blood, departs with him and is never seen more."

'"In case you never see me afterwards," I said, "we'd better say good-bye. We've been good mates and true friends, haven't we?"

'"Never better," he said. "I don't know what we shall do without you. But, of course, you're not going very far?"

'"Good-bye, in case," I said. "Anyhow, I'll write you a line," and as I shook hands with them—two regular trumps, if ever there were any in the world—I had a kind of notion I'd never see them again. Hardly think I shall, either. Sir Ferdinand surrounded the hut about an hour later, and made them come out one by one—both of them and the wages man. I daresay they were surprised.

'"Where's the fourth man, Clifford?" says Sir Ferdinand. "Just ask him to come out, will you?"

'"What, Frank Haughton?" says he.

'I heard most of this from that young devil, Billy the Boy. He saw Sir Ferdinand ride up, so he hid close by, just for the fun of hearing how he got on. He'd seen Warrigal and me ride away.

'"Frank Devil!" bangs out Sir Ferdinand, who's begun to get his monkey up. "How should I know his infernal purser's name? No man, it seems to me, has his right name on this confounded goldfield. I mean Starlight—Starlight the cattle stealer, the mail robber, the bush-ranger, whose name is notorious over the three colonies and New Zealand to boot—your intimate friend and partner for the last nine months!"

'"You perfectly amaze me," says Clifford. "But can't you be mistaken? Is your information to be depended upon?"

'"Mine came from a jealous woman," says Sir Ferdinand. "They may generally be depended upon for a straight tip. But we're losing time. When did he leave the claim, and which way did he go?"

'"I have no idea which way he went," says Clifford. "He did not say, but he left about an hour since."

'"On foot or on horseback?"

'"On horseback."

'"Any one with him?"

'"Yes, another horseman."

'"What was he like?"

'"Slight, dark man, youngish, good-looking."

'"Warrigal the half-caste! By George! warrants out for him also," says Sir Ferdinand. "On a good horse, of course, with an hour's start. We may give up the idea of catching him this time. Follow him up as a matter of form. Good-bye, Clifford. You'll hear news of your friend before long, or I'm much mistaken."

'"Stop, Sir Ferdinand, you must pardon me; but I don't exactly understand your tone. The man that we knew by the name of Frank Haughton may be, as you say, an escaped criminal. All I know is that he lived with us since we came here, and that no fellow could have behaved more truly like a man and a gentleman. As far as we are concerned, I have a material guarantee that he has been scrupulously honest. Do you mean to hint for one moment that we were aware of his previous history, or in any way mixed up with his acts?"

'"If I do, what then?" says Sir Ferdinand, laughing.

'"The affair is in no way ludicrous," says Clifford, very stiff and dignified. "I hold myself to have received an insult, and must ask you to refer me to a friend."

'"Do you know that I could arrest you and Hastings now and lock you up on suspicion of being concerned with him in the Ballabri

Bank robbery?" says Sir Ferdinand in a stern voice. "Don't look so indignant. I only say I could. I am not going to do so, of course. As to fighting you, my dear fellow, I am perfectly at your service at all times and seasons whenever I resign my appointment as Inspector of Police for the colony of New South Wales. The Civil Service regulations do not permit of duelling at present, and I found it so deuced hard to work up to the billet that I am not going to imperil my continuance therein. After all, I had no intention of hurting your feelings, and apologise if I did. As for that rascal Starlight, he would deceive the very devil himself."

'And so Sir Ferdinand rode off.'

'How did you come; by Jonathan's?'

'We called nowhere. Warrigal, as usual, made a short cut of his own across the bush—scrubs, gullies, mountains, all manner of desert paths. We made the Hollow yesterday afternoon, and went to sleep in a nook known to us of old. We dropped in to breakfast here at daylight, and I felt sleepy enough for another snooze.'

'We're all here again, it seems,' I said, sour enough. 'I suppose we'll have to go on the old lay; they won't let us alone when we're doing fair work and behaving ourselves like men. They must take the consequences, d—n them!'

'Ha! very true,' says Starlight in his dreamy kind of way. 'Most true, Richard. Society should make a truce occasionally, or proclaim an amnesty with offenders of our stamp. It would pay better than driving us to desperation. How is Jim? He's worse off than either of us, poor fellow.'

'Jim's very bad. He can't get over being away from Jeanie. I never saw him so down in the mouth this years.'

'Poor old Jim, he's a deal too good for the place. Sad mistake this getting married. People should either keep straight or have no relatives to bear the brunt of their villainies. "But soft," as they say in the play, "where am I?" I thought I was a virtuous miner again. Here we are at this devil-discovered, demon-haunted old Hollow again—first cousin to the pit of Acheron. There's no help for it, Dick. We must play our parts gallantly, as demons of this lower world, or get hissed off the stage.'

. . . . .

We didn't do much for a few days, you may be sure. There was nothing to do, for one thing; and we hadn't made up our mind what our line was to be. One thing was certain: there would be more row made about us than ever. We should have all the police in the country worried and barked at by the press, the people, the Government, and their superior officers till they got something to show about us. Living at the diggings under the nose of the police, without their having the least suspicion who we were, was bad enough; but the rescue of Jim and the shooting of a policeman in charge of him was more serious—the worst thing that had happened yet.

There would be the devil to pay if they couldn't find a track of us. No doubt money would be spent like water in bribing any one who might give information about us. Every one would be tried that we had ever been known to be friendly with. A special body of men could be told off to make a dart to any spot they might get wind of near where we had been last seen.

We had long talks and barneys over the whole thing—sometimes by ourselves with Starlight, sometimes with father. A long time it was before we settled upon any regular put-up bit of work to do.

Sooner or later we began to see the secret of the Hollow would be found out. There was no great chance in the old times with only a few shepherds and stock riders wandering through the bush, once in a way straggling over the country. But now the whole colony swarmed with miners, who were always prospecting, as they called it—that is, looking out for fresh patches of gold. Now, small parties of these men—bold, hardy, experienced chaps—would take a pick and shovel, a bucket, and a tin dish, with a few weeks' rations, and scour the whole countryside. They would try every creek, gully, hillside, and river-bed. If they found the colour of gold, the least trace of it in a dish of wash-dirt, they would at once settle down themselves. If it went rich the news would soon spread, and a thousand men might be gathered in one spot—the bank of a small creek, the side of a steep range—within a fortnight, with ten thousand more sure to follow within a month.

That might happen at any time on one of the spurs of Nulla Mountain; and the finding out of the track down to the Hollow by some one of the dozens of rambling, shooting, fishing diggers would be as certain to happen as the sun to rise.

Well, the country had changed, and we were bound to change with it. We couldn't stop boxed up in the Hollow day after day, and month after month, shooting and horse-breaking, doing nothing and earning nothing.

If we went outside there were ten times more men looking out for us than ever, ten times more chance of our being tracked or run down than ever. That we knew from the newspapers. How did we see them? Oh, the old way. We sent out our scout, Warrigal, and he got our letters and papers, too, from a 'sure hand,' as Starlight said the old people in the English wars used to say.

The papers were something to see. First he brought us in a hand-bill that was posted in Bargo, like this:—

FIVE HUNDRED POUNDS REWARD

The above reward will be paid to any one giving information as to the whereabouts of Richard Marston, James Marston, and a man whose name is unknown, but who can be identified chiefly by the appellation of Starlight.

'Pleasing way of drawing attention to a gentleman's private residence,' says Starlight, smiling first and looking rather grim afterwards. 'Never mind, boys, they'll increase that reward yet, by Jove! It will have to be a thousand apiece if they don't look a little sharper.'

We laughed, and dad growled out—

'Don't seem to have the pluck, any on ye, to tackle a big touch again. I expect they'll send a summons for us next, and get old Bill Barkis, the bailiff at Bargo, to serve it.'

'Come, come, governor,' says Starlight, 'none of that. We've got quite enough devil in us yet, without your stirring him up. You must give us time, you know. Let's see what this paper says. *Turon Star!* What a godsend to it!

'BUSH-RANGERS!
'STARLIGHT AND THE MARSTONS AGAIN

'The announcement will strike our readers, if not with the most profound astonishment, certainly with considerable surprise, that these celebrated desperadoes, for whose apprehension such large sums have been offered, for whom the police in all the colonies have made such unremitting search, should have been discovered in our midst. Yet such is the case. On this very morning, from information received, our respected and efficient Inspector of Police, Sir Ferdinand Morringer, proceeded soon after midnight to the camp of Messrs. Clifford and Hastings. He had every reason to believe that he would have had no difficulty in arresting the famous Starlight, who, under the cognomen of the Honourable Frank Haughton, has been for months a partner in this claim. The shareholders were popularly known as "the three Honourables," it being rumoured that both Mr. Clifford and Mr. Hastings were entitled to that prefix, if not to a more exalted one.

'With characteristic celerity, however, the famous outlaw had shortly before quitted the place, having received warning and been provided with a fast horse by his singular retainer, Warrigal, a half-caste native of the colony, who is said to be devotedly attached to him, and who has been seen from time to time on the Turon.

'Of the Marston brothers, the elder one, Richard, would seem to have been similarly apprised, but James Marston was arrested in his cottage in Specimen Gully. Having been lately married, he was apparently unwilling to leave his home, and lingered too long for prudence.

'While rejoicing, as must all good citizens, at the discovery of evil-doers and the capture of one member of a band of notorious criminals, we must state in fairness and candour that their conduct has been, while on the field as miners, free from reproach in every way. For James Marston, who was married but a short while since to a Melbourne young lady of high personal attractions and the most winning amiability, great sympathy has been expressed by all classes.'

So much for the *Star*. Everybody is sorry for you, old man,' he says to Jim. 'I shouldn't wonder if they'd make you a beak if you'd stayed there long enough. I'm afraid Dick's dropping the policeman won't add to our popularity, though.'

'He's all right,' I said. 'Hurrah! look here. I'm glad I didn't finish the poor beggar. Listen to this from the *Turon Banner*:—

'BUSH-RANGING REVIVED

'The good old days have apparently not passed away for ever, when mail robberies and hand-to-hand conflicts with armed robbers were matters of weekly occurrence. The comparative lull observable in such exciting occurrences of late has been proved to be but the ominous hush of the elements that precedes the tempest. Within the last few days the mining community has been startled by the discovery of the notorious gang of bush-rangers, Starlight and the Marstons, domiciled in the very heart of the diggings, attired as ordinary miners, and—for their own purposes possibly—leading the laborious lives proper to the avocation. They have been fairly successful, and as miners, it is said, have shown themselves to be manly and fair-dealing men. We are not among those who care to judge their fellow-men harshly. It may be that they had resolved to forsake the criminal practices which had rendered them so unhappily celebrated. James Marston had recently married a young person of most respectable family and prepossessing appearance. As far as may be inferred from this step and his subsequent conduct, he had cut loose from his former habitues. He, with his brother, Richard Marston, worked an adjoining claim to the Arizona Sluicing Company, with the respected shareholders of which they were on terms of intimacy. The well-known Starlight, as Mr. Frank Haughton, became partner and tent-mate with the Hon. Mr. Clifford and Mr. Hastings, an aristocratic society in which the manners and bearing of this extraordinary man permitted him to mingle without suspicion of detection.

'Suddenly information was furnished to the police respecting all three men. We are not at present aware of the source from which the clue was obtained. Suffice it to say that Sir Ferdinand Morringer promptly arranged for the simultaneous action of three parties of police with the hope of capturing all three outlaws. But in two cases the birds were flown. Starlight's *âme damnée*, a half-caste named Warrigal, had been observed on the field the day before. By him he was doubtless furnished with a warning, and the horse upon which he left his abode shortly before the arrival of Sir Ferdinand. The elder Marston had also eluded the police. But James Marston, hindered possibly by domestic ties, was captured at his cottage at Specimen Gully. For him sympathy has been universally expressed. He is regarded rather as a victim than as an active agent in the many criminal offences chargeable to the account of Starlight's gang.

'Since writing the above we have been informed that trooper Walsh, who, with another constable, was escorting James Marston to Bargo Gaol, has been brought in badly wounded. The other trooper reports that he was shot down and the party attacked by persons concealed in the thick timber near Wild Horse Creek, at the edge of Bargo Brush. In the confusion that ensued the prisoner escaped. It was at first thought that Walsh was fatally injured, but our latest report gives good hope of his recovery.

'We shall be agreeably surprised if this be the end and not the commencement of a series of darker tragedies.'

CHAPTER XXXIII

A MONTH'S loafing in the Hollow. Nothing doing and nothing to think of except what was miserable enough, God knows. Then things began to shape themselves, in a manner of speaking. We didn't talk much together; but each man could see plain enough what the others were thinking of. Dad growled out a word now and then, and Warrigal would look at us from time to time with a flash in his hawk's eyes that we'd seen once or twice before and knew the meaning of. As for Jim, we were bound to do something or other, if it was only to keep him from going melancholy mad. I never seen any man changed more from what he used to be than Jim did. He that was the most careless, happy-go-lucky chap that ever stepped, always in a good temper and full of his larks. At the end of the hottest day in summer on the plains, with no water handy, or the middle of the coldest winter night in an ironbark forest, and we sitting on our horses waiting for daylight, with the rain pouring down our backs, not game to light a fire, and our hands that cold we could hardly hold the reins, it was all one to Jim. Always jolly, always ready to make little of it all. Always ready to laugh or chaff or go on with monkey tricks like a boy. Now it was all the other way with him. He'd sit grizzling and smoking by himself all day long. No getting a word out of him. The only time he seemed to brighten up was once when he got a letter from Jeanie. He took it away into the bush and stayed hours and hours.

From never thinking about anything or caring what came uppermost, he seemed to have changed all on the other tack and do nothing but think. I'd seen a chap in Berrima something like him for a month or two; one day he manned the barber's razor and cut his throat. I began to be afraid Jim would go off his head and blow his brains out with his own revolver. Starlight himself got to be cranky and restless-like, too. One night he broke out as we were standing smoking under a tree, a mile or so from the cave—

'By all the devils, Dick, I can't stand this sort of thing much longer. We shall go mad or drink ourselves to death'— (we'd all been pretty well 'on' the night before)—'if we stick here till we're trapped or smoked out like a 'guana out of a tree spout. We must make a rise somehow, and try for blue water again. I've been fighting against the notion the whole time we've been here, but the devil and your old dad (who's a near relative, I believe) have been too strong for us. Of course, you know what it's bound to be?'

'I suppose so. I know when dad was away last week he saw that beggar and some of his mates. They'd partly made it up a while back, but didn't fancy doing it altogether by themselves. They've been waiting on the chance of our standing in and your taking command.'

'Of course, the old story,' he says, throwing his cigar away, and giving a half laugh—such a laugh it was, too. 'Captain Starlight again, I suppose. The paltry vanity of leadership, and of being in the front of my fellow-men, has been the ruin of me ever since I could recollect. If my people had let me go into the army, as I begged and prayed of them to do, it might have been all the other way. I recollect that day and hour when my old governor refused my boyish petition, laughed at me—sneered at me. I took the wrong road then. I swear to you, Dick, I never had thought of evil till that cursed day which made me reckless and indifferent to everything. And this is the end—a wasted life, a felon's doom! Quite melodramatic, isn't it, Richard? Well, we'll play out the last act with spirit. "Enter first robber," and so on. Good-night.'

He walked away. I never heard him say so much about himself before. It set me thinking of what luck and chance there seemed to be in this world. How men were not let do what they knew was best for 'em—often and often—but something seemed to drive 'em farther and farther along the wrong road, like a lot of stray wild cattle that wants to make back to their own run, and a dog here, a fence the other way. A man on foot or a flock of sheep always keeps frightening 'em farther and farther from the old beat till they get back into a bit of back country or mallee scrub and stop there for good. Cattle and horses and men and women are awful like one another in their ways, and the more you watch 'em the more it strikes you.

Another day or two idling and card-playing, another headache after too much grog at night, brought us to a regular go in about business, and then we fixed it for good.

We were to stick up the next monthly gold escort. That was all. We knew it would be a heavy one and trusted to our luck to get clear off with the gold, and then take a ship for Honolulu or San Francisco. A desperate chance; but we were desperate men. We had tried to work hard and honest. We had done so for best part of a year. No one could say we had taken the value of a halfpenny from any man. And yet we were not let stay right when we asked for nothing but to be let alone and live out the rest of our lives like men.

They wouldn't have us that way, and now they must take us across the grain, and see what they would gain by that. So it happened we went out one day with Warrigal to show us the way, and after riding for hours and hours, we came to a thick scrub. We rode through it till we came to an old cattle track. We followed that till we came to a tumble-down slab hut with a stockyard beside it. The yard had been mended, and the rails were up. Seven or eight horses were inside, all in good condition. As many men were sitting or standing about smoking outside the old hut.

When we rode up they all came forward and we had it out. We knew who was coming, and were ready for 'em. There was Moran, of course, quiet and savage-looking, just as like a black snake as ever, twisting about with his deadly, glittering eyes, wanting to bite some one. There was Daly and Burke, Wall and Hulbert, and two or three more—I won't say who they were now—and if you please who should come out of the hut last but Master Billy the Boy, as impudent as you like, with a pipe in his mouth, and a revolver in his belt, trying to copy Moran and Daly. I felt sorry when I see him, and thought what he'd gradually come to bit by bit, and where he'd most likely end, all along of the first money he had from father for telegraphing. But after all I've a notion that men and women grow up as they are intended to from the beginning. All the same as a tree from seed. You may twist it this road or that, make it a bit bigger or smaller according to the soil or the way it's pruned and cut down when it's young, but you won't alter the nature of that tree or the fruit that it bears. You won't turn a five-corner into a quince, or a geebung into an orange, twist and twine, and dig and water as you like. So whichever way Billy the Boy had been broken and named he'd have bolted and run off the course. Take a pet dingo now. He might look very tame, and follow them that feed him, and stand the chain; but as soon as anything passed close that he could kill, he'd have his teeth into it and be lapping its blood before you could say 'knife,' and the older he got the worse he'd be.

'Well, Dick,' says this young limb of Satan, 'so you've took to the Queen's highway agin, as the chap says in the play. I thought you and Jim was a-going to jine the Methodies or the Sons of Temperance at Turon, you both got to look so thunderin' square on it. Poor old Jim looks dreadful down in the mouth, don't he, though?'

'It would be all the better for you if you'd joined some other body, you young scamp,' I said. 'Who told you to come here? I've half a mind to belt you home again to your mother;' and I walked towards him.

'No, you won't, Dick Marston; don't you make any mistake,' says the young bull-pup, looking nasty. 'I'm as good a man as you, with this little tool.' Here he pulled out his revolver. 'I've as much right to turn out as you have. What odds is it to you what I do?'

I looked rather foolish at this, and Moran and Burke began to laugh.

'You'd better set up a night-school, Dick,' says Burke, 'and get Billy and some of the other flash kiddies to come. They might turn over a new leaf in time.'

'If you'll stand up, or Moran there, that's grinning behind you, I'll make some of ye laugh on the wrong side,' I said.

'Come on,' drawls Moran, taking off his coat, and walking up; 'I'd like to have a smack at you before you go into the Church.'

We should have been at it hammer and tongs—we both hated one another like poison—only the others interfered, and Billy said we ought to be ashamed of ourselves for quarrelling like schoolboys. We were nice sort of chaps to stick up a gold escort. That made a laugh, and we knocked off.

Well, it looked as if no one wanted to speak. Then Hulbert, a very quiet chap, says, 'I believe Ben Marston's the oldest man here; let's hear what he's got to say.'

Father gets up at once, and looks steady at the rest of 'em, takes his pipe out of his mouth, and shakes the baccy out. Then he says—

'All on ye knows without my telling what we've come here about, and what there's hangin' to it. It's good enough if it's done to rights; but, make no mistake, boys, it's a battle as must be fought game, and right back to the ropes, or not at all. If there's a bird here that won't stand the steel he'd better be put in a bag and took home again.'

'Never mind about the steel, daddy,' says one of the new men. 'We're all good for a flutter when the wager's good. What'll it be worth a man, and where are we going to divide? We know your mob's got some crib up in the mountains that no one knows about. We don't want the swag took there and planted. It mightn't be found easy.'

'Did ever a one of ye heer tell o' me actin' crooked?' says father. 'Look here, Bill, I'm not as young as I was, but you stand up to me for three rounds and I'll take some of the cheek out of yer.'

Bill laughed.

'No fear, daddy, I'd sooner face Dick or Jim. But I only want what's fair between man and man. It's a big touch, you know, and we can't take it to the bank to divide, like diggers, or summons yer either.'

'What's the good of growlin' and snappin'?' says Burke. 'We're all goin' in regular, I suppose, share and share alike?' The men nodded. 'Well, there's only one way to make things shipshape, and that's to have a captain. We'll pick one of ourselves, and whatever he says we'll bind ourselves to do—life or death. Is that it, boys?'

'Yes, yes; that's the only way,' came from all hands.

'Now, the next thing to work is who we're to make captain of. There's one here as we can all depend on, who knows more about road-work than all the rest of us put together. You know who I mean; but I don't want ye to choose him or any man because I tell you. I propose Starlight for captain if he'll take it, and them that don't believe me let 'em find a better man if they can.'

'I vote for Dan Moran,' says another man, a youngish, farmer-looking chap. 'He's a bushman, like ourselves, and not a half-bred swell, that's just as likely to clear out when we want him most as do anything else.'

'You go back to the Springs and feed them pigs, Johnny,' says father, walking towards the young chap. 'That's about what *you're* bred for; nobody'll take you for a swell, quarter-bred, or anything else. Howsoever, let's draw lots for it. Every man put his fancy down on a bit of paper, and put 'em into my old hat here.'

This was done after a bit, and the end of it was ten votes for Starlight and two or three for Moran, who looked savage and sulkier than ever.

When this was over Starlight walked over from where he was standing, near me and Jim, and faced the crowd. He drew himself up a bit, and looked round as haughty as he used to do when he walked up the big room at the Prospectors' Arms in Turon—as if all the rest of us was dirt under his feet.

'Well, my lads,' he said, 'you've done me the great honour to elect me to be your captain. I'm willing to act, or I shouldn't be here. If you're fools enough to risk your lives and liberties for a thousand ounces of gold a man, I'm fool enough to show you the way.'

'Hurrah!' said half-a-dozen of them, flinging up their hats. 'We're on, Captain. Starlight for ever! You ride ahead and we'll back up.'

'That will do,' he says, holding up his hand as if to stop a lot of dogs barking; 'but listen to me.' Here he spoke a few words in that other voice of his that always sounded to me and Jim as if it was a different man talking, or the devil in his likeness. 'Now mind this before we go: you don't quite know me; you will by-and-by, perhaps. When I take command of this gang, for this bit of work or any other, my word's law—do you hear? And if any man disputes it or disobeys my orders, by ———, I'll shoot him like a dog.'

As he stood there looking down on the lot of 'em, as if he was their king, with his eyes burning up at last with that slow fire that lay at the bottom of 'em, and only showed out sometimes, I couldn't help thinking of a pirate crew that I'd read of when I was a boy, and the way the pirate captain ruled 'em.

CHAPTER XXXIV

WE were desperate fidgety and anxious till the day came. While we were getting ready two or three things went wrong, of course. Jim got a letter from Jeanie, all the way from Melbourne, where she'd gone. It seems she'd got her money from the bank—Jim's share of the gold—all right. She was a saving, careful little woman, and she told him she'd enough to keep them both well for four or five years, anyhow. What she wanted him to do was to promise that he'd never be mixed up in any more dishonest work, and to come away down to her at once.

'It was the easiest thing in the world,' she said, 'to get away from Melbourne to England or America. Ships were going every day, and glad to take any man that was strong and willing to work his passage for nothing; they'd pay him besides.'

She'd met one or two friends down there as would do anything to help her and him. If he would only get down to Melbourne all would yet be well; but she begged and prayed him, if he loved her, and for the sake of the life she hoped to live with him yet, to come away from his companions and take his own Jeanie's advice, and try and do nothing wrong for the future.

If Jim had got his letter before we made up matters, just at the last, he'd have chucked up the sponge and cleared out for good and all. He as good as said so; but he was one of them kind of men that once he'd made a start never turned back. There'd been some chaff, to make things worse, between Moran and Daly and some of the other fellows about being game and what not, specially after what father said at the hut, so he wouldn't draw out of it now.

I could see it fretted him worse than anything since we came back, but he filled himself up with the idea that we'd be sure to get the gold all right, and clear out different ways to the coast, and then we'd have something worth while leaving off with. Another thing, we'd been all used to having what money we wanted lately, and we none of us fancied living like poor men again in America or anywhere else. We hadn't had hardly a scrap from Aileen since we'd come back this last time. It wasn't much odds. She was regular broken-hearted; you could see it in every line.

'She had been foolish enough to hope for better things,' she said; 'now she expected nothing more in this world, and was contented to wear out her miserable life the best way she could. If it wasn't that her religion told her it was wrong, and that mother depended on her, she'd drown herself in the creek before the door. She couldn't think why some people were brought into this miserable world at all. Our family had been marked out to evil, and the same fate would follow us to the end. She was sorry for Jim, and believed if he had been let take his own road that he would have been happy and prosperous to-day. It was a pity he could not have got away safely to Melbourne with his wife before that wicked woman, who deserved to be burnt alive, ruined everything. Even now we might all escape, the country seemed in so much confusion with all the strangers and bad people' (bad people—well, every one thinks their own crow the blackest) 'that the goldfields had brought into it, that it wouldn't be hard to get away in a ship somehow. If nothing else bad turned up perhaps it might come to pass yet.'

This was the only writing we'd had from poor Aileen. It began all misery and bitterness, but got a little better at the end. If she and Gracey could have got hold of Kate Morrison there wouldn't have been much left of her in a quarter of an hour, I could see that.

Inside was a little bit of paper with one line, 'For my sake,' that was all. I knew the writing; there was no more. I could see what Gracey meant, and wished over and over again that I had the chance of going straight, as I'd wished a thousand times before, but it was too late, too late! When the coach is running down hill and the brake's off, it's no use trying to turn. We had all our plan laid out and settled to the smallest thing. We were to meet near Eugowra Rocks a good hour or two before the escort passed, so as to have everything ready. I remember the day as well as if it was yesterday. We were all in great buckle and very fit, certainly. I don't think I ever felt better in my life. There must be something out-and-out spiriting in a real battle when a bit of a scrimmage like this sent our blood boiling through our veins; made us feel as if we weren't plain Dick and Jim Marston, but regular grand fellows, in a manner of speaking. What fools men are when they're young—and sometimes after that itself—to be sure.

We started at daylight, and only stopped once on the road for a bite for ourselves and to water the horses, so that we were in good time. We brought a little corn with us, just to give the horses something; they'd be tied up for hours and hours when we got to the place pitched on. They were all there before us; they hadn't as good horses by a long chalk as we had, and two of their packers were poor enough. Jim and I were riding ahead with Starlight a little on the right of us. When the fellows saw Rainbow they all came crowding round him as if he'd been a show.

'By George!' says Burke, 'that's a horse worth calling a horse, Captain. I often heard tell of him, but never set eyes on him before. I've two minds to shake him and leave you my horse and a share of the gold to boot. I never saw his equal in my life, and I've seen some plums too.'

'Honour among—well—bush-rangers, eh, Burke?' says Starlight cheerily. 'He's the right sort, isn't he? We shall want good goers to-night. Are we all here now? We'd better get to business.'

Yes, they were all there, a lot of well-built, upstanding chaps, young and strong, and fit to do anything that a man could do in the way of work or play. It was a shame to see them there (and us too, for the matter of that), but there was no get away now. There will be fools and rogues to the end of the world, I expect. Even Moran looked a bit brighter than he did last time. He was one of those chaps that a bit of real danger smartens up. As for Burke, Daly, and Hulbert, they were like a lot of schoolboys, so full of their fun and larks.

Starlight just spoke a word to them all; he didn't talk much, but looked hard and stern about the face, as a captain ought to do. He rode up to the gap and saw where the trees had been cut down to block up the road. It would be hard work getting the coach through there now—for a bit to come.

After that our horses and the two packers were left behind with Warrigal and father, close enough for hearing, but well out of the way for seeing; it was behind a thick belt of timber. They tied up some to trees and short-hobbled others, keeping them all so as to be ready at a moment's notice. Our men hid themselves behind rocks and stumps on the high side of the road so as they could see well, and had all the shadow on their side. Wall and Hulbert and their lot had their mob of horses, packers, and all planted away, and two young fellows belonging to their crowd minding them.

We'd been ready a good bit when a cove comes tearing up full bat. We were watching to see how he shaped, and whether he looked likely to lay on the police, when I saw it was Billy the Boy.

'Now I call this something like,' says he, pulling up short; 'army in readiness, the enemy not far off. My word, it is a fine thing to turn out, ain't it, Dick? Do you chaps feel shaky at all? Ain't yer gallied the least little bit? They're a-comin'!'

'How long will they be?' Starlight said. 'Just remember that you're not skylarking at a pound-yard, my boy.'

'All right, Captain,' he answered, quiet enough. 'I started on ahead the moment I saw 'em leave the camp. They're safe to be here in ten minutes now. You can see 'em when they come into the flat. I'll clear out to the back for a bit. I want 'em to think I come up permiskus-like when it's over.' So the young rascal galloped away till the trees hid him, and in a quarter of an hour more we saw the leaders of the four-horse drag that carried the escort gold turn round on the forest road and show out into the flat.

It gave me a queer feeling just at first. We hadn't been used to firing on the Queen's servants, not in cold blood, anyhow, but it was them or us for it now. There was no time to think about it. They came along at a steady trot up the hill. We knew the Turon sergeant of police that drove, a tall man with a big black beard down to his chest. He had been in an English dragoon regiment, and could handle the ribbons above a bit. He had a trooper alongside him on the box with his rifle between his knees. Two more were in the body of the drag. They had put their rifles down and were talking and laughing, not expecting anything sudden. Two more of the mounted men rode in front, but not far. The couple behind were a good way off. All of a sudden the men in front came on the trees lying across the road. They pulled up short, and one of them jumped down and looked to see if anything could be done to move them. The other man held his horse. The coach drove up close, so that they were bunched up pretty well together.

'Who the devil has been doing that?' sung out the sergeant. 'Just as if the road isn't bad enough without these infernal lazy scoundrels of bullock-drivers cutting down trees to make us go round. It's a beastly track here at the best of times.'

'I believe them trees have been fallen on purpose,' says the trooper that was down. 'There's been men, and horses too, about here to-day, by the tracks. They're up to no good!'

'Fire!'

The order was given in Starlight's clear, bold voice. Just like a horn it sounded. You might have heard it twice as far off. A dozen shots followed the next second, making as much row as fifty because of the way the sound echoed among the rocks.

I never saw a bigger surprise in my life, and wasn't likely to do, as this was my first regular battle. We had plenty of time to take aim, and just at first it looked as if the whole blessed lot of the police was killed and wounded.

The sergeant threw up his arms and fell off the box like a log, just under the horses' feet. One of the troopers on ahead dropped, he that was holding the horses, and both horses started off at full gallop. The two men in the body of the drag were both hit—one badly. So when the two troopers came up full gallop from the back they found us cutting the traces of the team, that was all plunging like mad, and letting the horses go.

We opened fire on them directly they showed themselves; of course they couldn't do much in the face of a dozen men, all well armed and behind good cover. They kept it up for a bit till one of their horses was hit, and then made tracks for Turon to report that the escort had been stuck up by twenty or thirty men at Eugowra Rocks—the others had come up with the pack-horses by this time, along with Master Billy the Boy firing his revolver and shouting enough for half-a-dozen; so we looked a big crowd—that all the men were shot dead, wounded, or taken prisoners, and that a strong force had better be despatched at once to recapture the gold.

A good deal of this was true, though not all. The only man killed was the sergeant. He was shot clean through the heart, and never stirred again. Of the five other men, three were badly wounded and two slightly. We attended to them as well as we could, and tied the others so that they would not be able to give any bother for an hour or two at any rate.

Then the trouble began about dividing the gold. We opened the sort of locker there was in the centre of the coach and took out the square boxes of gold. They held canvas bags, all labelled and weighed to the grain, of about 1000 oz. each. There were fourteen boxes in all. Not a bad haul.

Some of the others couldn't read or write, and they wouldn't trust us, so they brought their friend with them, who was an educated man sure enough. We were a bit stunned to see him, holding the sort of position he did at the Turon. But there he was, and he did his work well enough. He brought a pair of scales with him and weighed the lot, and portioned it all out amongst us just the same as Mr. Scott, the banker, used to do for us at the Turon when we brought in our month's washing-up. We had 5000 oz. Starlight had an extra share on account of being captain, and the rest had somewhere about 8000 oz. or 9000 oz. among them. It wasn't so bad.

Dad wasn't long before he had our lot safely packed and on his two pack-horses. Warrigal and he cleared out at a trot, and went out of sight in a jiffy. It was every man for himself now. We waited a bit to help them with their swag; it was awful heavy. We told them that their pack-horses would never carry it if there was anything of a close run for it.

'Suppose you think you've got the only good horse in the country, Dick Marston,' says Daly. 'We'll find a horse to run anything you've got, barrin' Rainbow. I've got a little roan horse here as shall run ever a horse ye own, for three mile, for a hundred notes, with twelve stone up. What do you think of that, now?'

'Don't take your shirt off, Patsey,' I said. 'I know the roan's as good as ever was foaled' (so he was; the police got him after Patsey was done for, and kept him till he died of old age), 'but he's in no condition. I'm talking of the pack-horses; they're not up to much, as you'll find out.'

We didn't want to rush off at once, for fear the other fellows might say something afterwards if anything happened cross. So we saw them make a fair start for a spot on Weddin' Mountain, where they thought they were right. We didn't think we could be caught once we made tracks in earnest. After a couple or three hours' riding we should be pretty safe, and daylight would see us at the Hollow.

We stopped, besides, to do what we could for the wounded men. They were none of them regularly done for, except the sergeant. One man was shot through the lungs, and was breathing out blood every now and then. We gave them some brandy and water, and covered them all up and left them as comfortable as we could.

Besides that, we sent Billy the Boy, who couldn't be recognised, to the camp to have a doctor sent as soon as possible. Then we cleared and started off, not the way we had to go, but so as we could turn into it.

We couldn't ride very slow after such a turn as that, so we made the pace pretty hot for the first twenty miles or so. By Jove! it was a great ride; the forest was middling open, and we went three parts speed when we could see before us. The horses seemed to go as if they knew there was something up. I can see Rainbow now, swinging along with that beautiful bounding style of going he had, snorting now and then and sending out his legs as if one hundred miles, more or less, was nothing. His head up, his eye shining like a star, his nostrils open, and every now and then, if anything got up, he'd give a snort as if he'd just come up out of the bush. They'd had a longish day and a fast ride before they got to Eugowra, just enough to eat to keep them from starving, with a drink of water. Now they were going the same style back, and they'd never had the saddles off their backs. All the night through we rode before we got to the top of Nulla Mountain; very glad to see it we were then. We took it easy for a few miles now and again, then we'd push on again. We felt awful sleepy at times; we'd been up and at it since the morning before; long before daylight, too. The strangeness and the chance of being followed kept us up, else I believe we'd have dropped off our horses' backs, regular dead beat.

We lost ground now and then through Warrigal not being there to guide us, but Jim took the lead and he wasn't far out; besides, the horses knew which way to steer for their grass at the Hollow. They wouldn't let us go much off the line if it was ever so dark. We gave 'em their heads mostly. The sun was just rising as we rode across the last tableland. We got off and stumbled along, horses and men, down the track to the Hollow. Dad and Warrigal hadn't come back; of course they couldn't stand the pace we did. They'd have to camp for a bit, but they both knew of plants and hiding holes, where all the police in the colony couldn't find them. We knew they'd turn up some time next day. So we let go our horses, and after a bit of supper laid down and slept till well on in the afternoon.

When I looked round I saw the dog sleeping at Jim's feet, old Crib. He never left father very far, so of course the old man must be home, or pretty close up. I was that dead beat and tired out that I turned over and went to sleep for another couple of hours. When I next woke up I was right and felt rested, so I put on my things, had a good wash, and went out to speak to father. He was sitting by the fire outside smoking, just as if he'd never been away.

CHAPTER XXXV

'We done that job to rights if we never done another, eh, lad?' says father, reaching out for a coal to put in his pipe.

'Seems like it,' I said. 'There'll be a deuce of a bobbery about it. We shan't be able to move for a bit, let alone clear out.'

'We'll show 'em a trick or two yet,' says dad. I could see he'd had a tot, early as it was. 'I wonder how them chaps got on? But we'll hear soon.'

'How shall we hear anything? Nobody'll be mad enough to show out of here for a bit.'

'I could get word here,' says father, 'if there was a police barrack on the top of Nulla Mountain. I've done it afore, and I can do it again.'

'Well, I hope it won't be long, for I'm pretty full up of this staying-at-home business in the Hollow. It's well enough for a bit, but it's awful slow when you've too much of it.'

'It wouldn't be very slow if we was all grabbed and tried for our lives, Mr. Dick Marston. Would ye like that better for a change?' says the old man, showing his teeth like a dog that's making up his mind to have ye and don't see where he's to get first bite. 'You leave the thing to them as knows more than you do, or you'll find yourself took in, and that precious sharp.'

'You'll find your pals, Burke and Moran, and their lot will have their turn first,' I said, and with that I walked off, for I saw the old man had been drinking a bit after his night's work, and that always started his temper the wrong way. There was no doing anything with him then, as I knew by long experience. I was going to ask him where he'd put the gold, but thought it best to leave that for some other time.

By and by, when we all turned out and had some breakfast, we took a bit of a walk by ourselves and talked it over. We could hardly think it was all done and over.

'The gold escort stuck up. Fourteen thousand ounces of gold taken. Sergeant Hawkins shot dead. The robbers safe off with their booty.'

This is the sort of thing that we were sure to see in all the papers. It would make a row and no mistake. It was the first time such a thing had been thought of, much less carried out 'to rights,' as father said, 'in any of the colonies.' We had the five thousand ounces of gold, sure enough, too. That was something; whether we should be let enjoy it, or what chance we had of getting right away out of the country, was quite another matter. We were all sorry for Sergeant Hawkins, and would have been better pleased if he'd been only wounded like the others. But these sorts of things couldn't be helped. It was the fortune of war; his luck this time, ours next. We knew what we had to expect. Nothing would make much difference. 'As well be hung for a sheep as a lamb.' We were up to our necks in it now, and must fight our way out the best way we could.

Bar any man betraying the secret of the Hollow, we might be safe for years to come, as long as we were not shot or taken in fair fight. And who was to let out the secret? No one but ourselves had the least notion of the track or where it led to, or of such a place as the Hollow being in the colony. Only us five were in possession of the secret. We never let any of these other men come near, much less to it. We took good care never to meet them within twenty miles of it. Father was a man that, even when he was drunk, never let out what he didn't want other people to know. Jim and I and Starlight were not likely to blab, and Warrigal would have had his throat cut sooner than let on about anything that might be against Starlight, or that he told him not to do.

We had good reason, then, to think ourselves safe as long as we had such a place to make for whenever we were in danger or had done a stroke. We had enough in gold and cash to keep us comfortable in any other country—provided we could only get there. That was the rub. When we'd got a glass or two in our heads we thought it was easy enough to get across country, or to make away one by one at shearing time, disguised as swagsmen, to the coast. But when we thought it over carefully in the mornings, particularly when we were a bit nervous after the grog had died out of us, it seemed a rather blue look-out.

There was the whole countryside pretty thick with police stations, where every man, from the sergeant to the last-joined recruit, knew the height, size, colour of hair, and so on of every one of us. If a suspicious-looking man was seen or heard of within miles the telegraph wires could be set to work. He could be met, stopped, searched, and overhauled. What chance would any of us have then?

'Don't flatter yourselves, my boy?' Starlight said, when we'd got the length of thinking how it was to be done, 'that there's any little bit of a chance, for a year or two at any rate, of getting away. Not a kangaroo rat could hop across from one scrub to another if there was the least suspicion upon him without being blocked or run into. Jim, old man, I'm sorry for you, but my belief is we're quartered here for a year or two certain, and the sooner we make up our minds to it the better.'

Here poor old Jim groaned. 'Don't you think,' he said, quite timid-like, 'that about shearing-time a man might take his chance, leading an old horse with a swag on, as if he wanted to get shearing in some of the big down-the-river sheds?'

'Not a bit of it,' says Starlight. 'You're such a good-looking, up-standing chap that you're safe to be pulled up and made answer for yourself before you'd get fifty miles. If you rode a good horse they'd think you were too smart-looking for a regular shearer, and nail you at once.'

'But I'd take an old screw with a big leg,' pleaded Jim. 'Haven't I often seen a cove walking and leading one just to carry his blankets and things?'

'Then they'd know a chap like you, full of work and a native to boot, ought to have a better turn-out—if it wasn't a stall. So they'd have you for that.'

'But there's Isaac Lawson and Campbelltown. You've seen them. Isaac's an inch taller than me, and the same cut and make. Why shouldn't they stop them when they're going shearing? They're square enough, and always was. And Campbelltown's a good deal like Dick, beard and all.'

'Well, I'll bet you a new meerschaum that both men are arrested on suspicion before shearing. Of course they'll let them go again; but, you mark my words, they'll be stopped, as well as dozens of others. That will show how close the search will be.'

'I don't care,' says Jim, in his old, obstinate way, which he never put on except very seldom. 'I'll go in a month or two—police or no police. I'll make for Melbourne if there was an army of soldiers between me and Jeanie.'

We had to settle where the gold was to be hid. After a lot of talk we agreed to keep one bag in a hole in the side of the wall of the cave, and bury the others in the place where we'd found old Mr. Devereux's box. His treasure had laid many a year safe and sound without anybody touching it, and we thought ours might do the same. Besides, to find it they must get into the Hollow first. So we packed it out bag by bag, and made an ironbark coffin for it, and buried it away there, and put some couch-grass turfs on it. We knew they'd soon grow up, and nobody could tell that it hadn't always been covered up the same as the rest of the old garden.

It felt pretty hard lines to think we shouldn't be able to get away from this lonely place after the life we'd led the last year; but Starlight wasn't often wrong, and we came to the same way of thinking ourselves when we looked at it all round, steady and quiet like.

We'd been a week or ten days all by ourselves, horse-breaking, fishing, and shooting a bit, thinking how strange it was that we should have more than £20,000 in gold and money and not be able to do anything with it, when dad, sudden like, said he'd go out himself and get some of the newspapers, and perhaps a letter or two if any came.

Starlight laughed at him a bit for being foolhardy, and said we should hear of his being caught and committed for trial. 'Why, they'll know the dog,' says he, 'and make him give evidence in court. I've known that done before now. Inspector Merlin nailed a chap through his dog.'

Father grinned. 'I know'd that case—a sheep-stealing one. They wanted to make out Brummy was the man as owned the dorg—a remarkable dorg he was, too, and had been seen driving the sheep.'

'Well, what did the dog do? Identify the prisoner, didn't he?'

'Well, the dashed fool of a coolie did. Jumps up as soon as he was brought into court, and whines and scratches at the dock rails and barks, and goes on tremenjus, trying to get at Brummy.'

'How did his master like it?'

'Oh! Brummy? He looked as black as the ace of spades. He'd have made it hot for that dorg if he could ha' got at him. But I suppose he forgave him when he came out.'

'Why should he?'

'Because the jury fetched him in guilty without leaving the box, and the judge give him seven years. You wouldn't find this old varmint a-doin' no such foolishness as that.'

Here he looks at Crib, as was lyin' down a good way off, and not letting on to know anything. He saw father's old mare brought up, though, and saddled, and knowed quite well what that meant. He never rode her unless he was going out of the Hollow.

'I believe that dog could stick up a man himself as well as some fellows we know,' says Starlight, 'and he'd do it, too, if your father gave him the word.'

. . . . .

While we were taking it easy, and except for the loneliness of it as safe as if we had been out of the country altogether, Moran and the other fellows hadn't quite such a good time of it. They were hunted from pillar to post by the police, who were mad to do something to meet the chaff that was always being cast up to them of having a lot of bush-rangers robbing and shooting all over the country and not being able to take them. There were some out-of-the way places enough in the Weddin' Mountains, but none like the Hollow, where they could lie quiet and untroubled for weeks together, if they wanted. Besides, they had lost their gold by their own foolishness in not having better pack-horses, and hadn't much to carry on with, and it's not a life that can be worked on the cheap, I can tell you, as we often found out. Money comes easy in our line, but it goes faster still, and a man must never be short of a pound or two to chuck about if he wants to keep his information fresh, and to have people working for him night and day with a will.

So they had some every-day sort of work cut out to keep themselves going, and it took them all their time to get from one part of the country where they were known to some other place where they weren't expected. Having out-and-out good hacks, and being all of them chaps that had been born in the bush and knew it like a book, it was wonderful how they managed to rob people at one place one day, and then be at some place a hundred miles off the next. Ever so many times they came off, and they'd call one another Starlight and Marston, and so on, till the people got regularly dumbfoundered, and couldn't tell which of the gang it was that seemed to be all over the country, and in two places at the same time. We used to laugh ourselves sometimes, when we'd hear tell that all the travellers passing Big Hill on a certain day were 'stuck up by Wall's gang and robbed.' Every man Jack that came along for hours was made to stand behind a clump of trees with two of the gang guarding them, so as the others couldn't see them as they came up. They all had to deliver up what they'd got about 'em, and no one was allowed to stir till sundown, for fear they should send word to the police. Then the gang went off, telling them to stay where they were for an hour or else they'd come back and shoot them.

This would be on the western road, perhaps. Next day a station on the southern road, a hundred and twenty miles off, would be robbed by the same lot. Money and valuables taken away, and three or four of the best horses. Their own they'd leave behind in such a state that any one could see how far and fast they'd been ridden.

They often got stood to, when they were hard up for a mount, and it was this way. The squatters weren't alike, by any manner of means, in their way of dealing with them. Many of them had lots of fine riding-horses in their paddocks. These would be yarded some fine night, the best taken and ridden hard, perhaps returned next morning, perhaps in a day or two.

It was pretty well known who had used them, but nothing was said; the best policy, some think, is to hold a candle to the devil, especially when the devil's camped close handy to your paddock, and might any time sack your house, burn down your woolshed and stacks, or even shoot at your worshipful self if he didn't like the way you treated him and his imps.

These careful, respectable people didn't show themselves too forward either in giving help or information to the police. Not by no means. They never encouraged them to stay when they came about the place, and weren't that over liberal in feeding their horses, or giving them a hand in any way, that they'd come again in a hurry. If they were asked about the bush-rangers, or when they'd been last seen, they were very careful, and said as little as possible.

No one wonders at people like the Barnes's, or little farmers, or the very small sort of settlers, people with one flock of sheep or a few cows, doing this sort of thing; they have a lot to lose and nothing to get if they gain ill-will. But regular country gentlemen, with big properties, lots of money, and all the rest of it, they're there to show a good example to the countryside, whether it paid for the time or whether it didn't; and all us sort of chaps, on the cross or not, like them all the better for it.

When I say all of us, I don't mean Moran. A sulky, black-hearted, revengeful brute he always was—I don't think he'd any manly feeling about him. He was a half-bred gipsy, they told us that knew where he was reared, and Starlight said gipsy blood was a queer cross, for devilry and hardness it couldn't be beat; he didn't wonder a bit at Moran's being the scoundrel he was.

No doubt he 'had it in' for more than one of the people who helped the police to chevy Wall and his lot about. From what I know of him I was sure he'd do some mischief one of these days, and make all the country ten times as hot against us as they were now. He had no mercy about him. He'd rather shoot a man any day than not; and he'd burn a house down just for the pleasure of seeing how the owner looked when it was lighted.

Starlight used to say he despised men that tried to save themselves cowardly-like more than he could say, and thought them worse than the bush-rangers themselves. Some of them were big people, too.

But other country gentlemen, like Mr. Falkland, were quite of a different pattern. If they all acted like him I don't think we should any of us have reigned as long as we did. They helped and encouraged the police in every possible way. They sent them information whenever they had received any worth while. They lent them horses freely when their own were tired out and beaten. More than that, when bush-rangers were supposed to be in the neighbourhood they went out with them themselves, lying out and watching through the long cold nights, and taking their chance of a shot as well as those that were paid for it.

Now there was a Mr. Whitman that had never let go a chance from the start of running their trail with the police, and had more than once given them all they knew to get away. He was a native of the country, like themselves, first-class horseman and tracker, a hardy, game sort of a chap that thought nothing of being twenty-four hours in the saddle, or sitting under a fence watching for the whole of a frosty night.

Well, he was pretty close to Moran once, who had been out by himself; that close he ran him he made him drop his rifle and ride for his life. Moran never forgave him for this, and one day when they had all been drinking pretty heavy he managed to persuade Wall, Hulbert, Burke, and Daly to come with him and stick up Whitman's house.

'I sent word to him I'd pay him out one of these fine days,' he drawled out, 'and he'll find that Dan Moran can keep his word.'

He picked a time when he knew Whitman was away at another station. I always thought Moran was not so game as he gave himself out to be. And I think if he'd had Whitman's steady eyes looking at him, and seeing a pistol in his hand, he wouldn't have shot as straight as he generally did when he was practising at a gum tree.

Anyhow, they laid it out all right, as they thought, to take the place unawares. They'd been drinking at a flash kind of inn no great way off, and when they rode up to the house it seems they were all of 'em three sheets in the wind, and fit for any kind of villainy that came uppermost. As for Moran, he was a devil unchained. I know what he was. The people in the house that day trembled and shook when they heard the dogs bark and saw five strange horsemen ride through the back gate into the yard.

They'd have trembled a deal more if they'd known what was coming.

CHAPTER XXXVI

WHEN we found that by making darts and playing hide and seek with the police in this way we could ride about the country more comfortable like, we took matters easier. Once or twice we tried it on by night, and had a bit of a lark at Jonathan's, which was a change after having to keep dark so long. We'd rode up there after dark one night, and made ourselves pretty snug for the evening, when Bella Barnes asked us if we'd dropped across Moran and his mob that day.

'No,' says I. 'Didn't know they were about this part. Why, weren't they at Monckton's the day before yesterday?'

'Ah! but they came back last night, passed the house to-day going towards Mr. Whitman's, at Darjallook. I don't know, but I expect they're going to play up a bit there, because of his following them up that time the police nearly got Moran.'

'What makes you think that? They're only going for what they can get; perhaps the riding-horses and any loose cash that's knocking about.'

'Billy the Boy was here for a bit,' says Maddie. 'I don't like that young brat, he'll turn out bad, you take my word for it; but he said Moran knew Mr. Whitman was away at the Castlereagh station, and was going to make it a warning to them all.'

'Well, it's too bad,' said Bella; 'there's no one there but Mrs. Whitman and the young ladies. It's real cowardly, I call it, to frighten a parcel of women. But that Moran's a brute and hasn't the feelings of a man about him.'

'We must ride over, boys,' says Starlight, yawning and stretching himself. 'I was looking forward to a pleasant evening here, but it seems to me we ought to have a say in this matter. Whitman's gone a trifle fast, and been hard on us; but he's a gentleman, and goes straight for what he considers his duty. I don't blame him. If these fellows are half-drunk they'll burn the place down I shouldn't wonder, and play hell's delight.'

'And Miss Falkland's up there too, staying with the young ladies,' says Maddie. 'Why, Jim, what's up with you? I thought you wasn't taking notice.'

'Come along, Dick,' says Jim, quite hoarse-like, making one jump to the door. 'Dash it, man, what's the use of us wasting time jawing here? By——, if there's a hair of her head touched I'll break Moran's neck, and shoot the lot of them down like crows.'

'Good-bye, girls,' I said; 'there's no time to lose.'

Starlight made a bow, polite to the last, and passed out. Jim was on his horse as we got to the stable door. Warrigal fetched Starlight's, and in half a minute Jim and he were off together along the road full split, and I had as much as I could do to catch them up within the next mile. It wasn't twenty miles to Whitman's place, Darjallook, but the road was good, and we did it in an hour and twenty minutes, or thereabouts. I know Starlight lit a match and looked at his watch when we got near the front gate.

We could see nothing particular about the house. The lights shone out of the windows, and we heard the piano going.

'Seems all right,' says Starlight. 'Wonder if they came, after all? They'll think we want to stick the place up if we ride up to the hall door. Get off and look out tracks, Warrigal.'

Warrigal dismounted, lit a couple of matches, and put his head down close to the soft turf, as if he was going to smell it.

'Where track?' says Starlight.

'There!' says Warrigal, pointing to something we couldn't see if we'd looked for a month. 'Bin gone that way. That one track Moran's horse. I know him; turn foot in likit cow. Four more track follow up.'

'Why, they're in the house now, the infernal scoundrels,' says Starlight. 'You stay here with the horses, Warrigal; we'll walk up. If you hear shooting, tie them to the fence and run in.'

We walked up very quiet to the house—we'd all been there before, and knew where the front parlour was—over the lawn and two flower-beds, and then up to the big bow-window. The others stood under an old white cedar tree that shadowed all round. I looked in, and, by George! my face burned, cold as it was. There was Moran lying back in an arm-chair, with a glass of grog in his hand, takin' it easy and makin' himself quite at home. Burke and Daly were sitting in two chairs near the table, looking a long way from comfortable; but they had a couple of bottles of brandy on the table and glasses, and were filling up. So was Moran. They'd had quite as much as was good for them. The eldest Miss Whitman was sitting at the piano, playing away tune after tune, while her eyes were wandering about and her lips trembling, and every now and then she'd flush up all over her face; then she'd turn as white as a sheet, and look as if she'd fall off the stool. The youngest daughter was on her knees by her, on the other side, with her head in her lap. Every now and then I could hear a sob come from her, but stifled-like, as if she tried to choke it back as much as she could.

Burke and Daly had their pistols on the table, among the bottles— though what they wanted 'em there for I couldn't see—and Moran had stuck his on the back of the piano. That showed me he was close up drunk, for he was a man as never hardly let go of his revolver.

Mrs. Whitman was sitting crouched up in a chair behind her daughter, with a stony face, looking as if the end of the world was come. I hardly knew her again. She was a very kind woman, too; many a glass of grog she'd given me at shearing time, and medicine too, once I was sick there with influenza.

But Miss Falkland; I couldn't keep my eyes off her. She was sitting on the sofa against the wall, quite upright, with her hands before her, and her eyes looking half proudly, half miserable, round the room. You couldn't hardly tell she was frightened except by a kind of twitching of her neck and shoulders.

Presently Moran, who was more than half-boozed as it was, and kept on drinking, calls out to Miss Whitman to sing a song.

'Come, Miss Polly,' says he, 'you can sing away fast enough for your dashed old father and some o' them swells from Bathurst. By George, you must tune your pipe a bit this time for Dan Moran.'

The poor girl said she couldn't sing just then, but she'd play as much as he liked.

'Yer'd better sing now,' he drawls out, 'unless ye want me to come and make you. I know you girls wants coaxing sometimes.'

Poor Miss Mary breaks out at once into some kind of a song— the pitifullest music ever you listened to. Only I wanted to wait a bit, so as to come in right once for all, I'd have gone at him, hammer and tongs, that very minute.

All this time Burke and Daly were goin' in steady at the brandy, finished one bottle and tackled another. They began to get noisy and talked a lot, and sung a kind of a chorus to Miss Mary's song.

After the song was over, Moran swore he'd have another one. She'd never sing for him any more, he said, unless she took a fancy to him, and went back to the Weddin' Mountains with them.

'It ain't a bad name for a mountain, is it, miss?' says he, grinning. Then, fixing his black snake's eyes on her, he poured out about half a tumbler of brandy and drank it off.

'By gum!' he says, 'I must have a dance; blest if I don't! First chop music—good room this—three gals and the missus—course we must. I'm regular shook on the polka. You play us a good 'un, Polly, or whatever yer name is. Dan Moran's goin' to enjoy himself this night if he never sees another. Come on, Burke. Patsey, stand up, yer blamed fool. Here goes for my partner.'

'Come, Moran,' says Burke. 'none of your larks; we're very jolly, and the young ladies ain't on for a hop; are ye, miss?' and he looked over at the youngest Miss Whitman, who stared at him for a moment, and then hid her face in her hands.

'Are you a-goin' to play as I told yer?' says Moran. 'D'ye think yer know when yer well off?'

The tone of voice he said this in and the look seemed to frighten the poor girl so that she started an old-style polka there and then, which made him bang his heels on the floor and spin round as if

he'd been at a dance-house. As soon as he'd done two or·three
turns he walks over to the sofa and sits down close to Miss Falkland,
and put his arm round her waist.

'Come, Fanny Falkland,' says he, 'or whatever they call yer; you're
so dashed proud yer won't speak to a bush cove at all. You can·go
home by·'n-by, and tell your father that you had a twirl-round with
Dan Moran, and helped to make the evening pass pleasant at Darjallook afore it was burned.'

Anything like the disgust, misery, and rage mixed up that came
into Miss Falkland's face all in a moment and together-like, I never
saw. She made no sound, but her face grew paler and paler; she
turned white to the lips, as trembled and worked in spite of her.
She struggled fierce and wild for nigh a solid minute to clear herself
from him, while her beautiful eyes moved about like I've seen a
wild animal's caught in a trap. Then, when she felt her strength
wasn't no account against his, she gave one piercing, terrible scream,
so long and unnatural-like in the tone of it that it curdled my very
blood.

I lifted up the window-sash quick, and jumped in; but before I
made two steps Jim sprang past me, and raised his pistol.

'Drop her!' he shouts to Moran; 'you hound! Leave go Miss Falkland, or by the living God I'll blow your head off, Dan Moran, before
you can lift your hand! How dare you touch her, you cowardly
dog!'

Moran was that stunned at seeing us show up so sudden that he
was a good bit took off his guard, cool card as he was in a general way.
Besides, he'd left his revolver on the piano close by the arm-chair,
where his grog was. Burke and Daly were no better off. They
found Starlight and Warrigal covering them with their pistols, so
that they'd have been shot down before they could so much as
reach for their tools.

But Jim couldn't wait; and just as Moran was rising on his feet,
feeling for the revolver that wasn't in his belt (and that I never
heard of his being without but that once), he jumps at him like a wallaroo, and, catching him by the collar and waist-belt, lifts him clean
off his feet as if he'd been a child, and brings him agen the corner
of the wall with all his full strength. I thought his brains was
knocked out, dashed if I didn't. I heard Moran's head sound against
the stone wall with a dull sort of thud; and on the floor he drops
like a dead man—never made a kick. By George! we all thought he
had killed him.

'Stash that, now,' says Burke; 'don't touch him again, Jim Marston.
He's got as much as'll do him for a bit; and I don't say it don't serve
him right. I don't hold with being rough to women. It ain't·manly,
and we've got wives and kids of our own.'

'Then why the devil didn't you stop it?' says Starlight. 'You
deserve the same sauce, you·and Daly, for sitting·there like a couple

of children, and letting that ruffian torment these helpless ladies. If you fellows go on sticking up on your own account, and I hear a whisper of your behaving yourselves like brutes, I'll turn policeman myself for the pleasure of running you in. Now, mind that, you and Daly too. Where's Wall and Hulbert?'

'They went to yard the horses.'

'That's fair game, and all in the day's work. I don't care what you take or whom you shoot for that matter, as long as it's all in fair fight; but I'll have none of this sort of work if I'm to be captain, and you're all sworn to obey me, mind that. I'll have to shoot a man yet, I see, as I've done before now, before I can get attended to. That brute's coming to. Lift him up, and clear out of this place as soon as you can. I'll wait behind.'

They blundered out, taking Moran with them, who seemed quite stupid like, and staggered as he walked. He wasn't himself for a week after, and longer too, and threatened a bit, but he soon saw he'd no show, as all the fellows, even to his own mates, told him he deserved all he got.

Old Jim stood up by the fireplace after that, never stirring nor speaking, with his eyes fixed on Miss Falkland, who had got back her colour, and though she panted a bit and looked raised like, she wasn't much different from what we'd seen her before at the old place. The two Misses Whitman, poor girls, were standing up with their arms round one another's necks, and the tears running down their faces like rain. Mrs. Whitman was lying back in her chair with her hands over her face, cryin' to herself quiet and easy, and wringing her hands.

Then Starlight moved forward and bowed to the ladies as if he was just coming into a ballroom, like I saw him once at a swell ball they gave for the hospital at Turon.

'Permit me to apologise, Mrs. Whitman, and to you, my dear young ladies, for the rudeness of one of my men, whom I unhappily was not able to restrain. I have had the pleasure of meeting Mr. Whitman, and I hope you will express my regret that I was not in time to save you from the great annoyance to which you have been subjected.'

'Oh! I shall be grateful all my life to you, and so, I'm sure, will Mr. Whitman, when he returns; and, oh! Sir Ferdinand, if you and these two good young men, who, I suppose, are policemen in plain clothes, had not come in, goodness only knows what would have become of us.'

'I am afraid you are labouring under some mistake, my dear madam. I have not the honour to be Sir Ferdinand Morringer or any other baronet at present; but I assure you I feel the compliment intensely. I am sure my good friends here, James and Richard Marston, do equally.'

Here the Misses Whitman, in spite of all their terror and anxiety,

were so tickled by the idea of their mother mistaking Starlight and
the Marstons for Sir Ferdinand and his troopers that they began to
laugh, not but what they were sober enough in another minute.

Miss Falkland got up then and walked forward, looking just the
way her father used to do. She spoke to Starlight first.

'I have never seen you before, but I have often heard of you,
Captain Starlight, if you will allow me to address you by that title.
Believe me when I say that by your conduct to-night you have won
our deepest gratitude—more than that, our respect and regard. Whatever may be your future career, whatever the fate that your wild
life may end in, always believe there are those who will think of
you, pray for you, rejoice in your escapes, and sorrow sincerely for
your doom. I can answer for myself, and I am sure for my cousins
also.'

Here the Misses Whitman said:—

'Yes, indeed, we will—to our life's end.'

Then she turned to Jim, who still stood there looking at her with
his big grey eyes, that had got ever so much darker lately.

'You, poor old Jim,' she said, and she took hold of his brown
hand and held it in her own, 'I am more sorry than I can tell to
hear all I have done about you and Dick too. This is the second
time you have saved me, and I am not the girl to forget it, if I could
only show my gratitude. Is there any way?'

'There's Jeanie,' just them two words he said.

'Your wife? Oh yes, I heard about her,' looking at him so kind
and gentle-like. 'I saw it all in the papers. She's in Melbourne,
isn't she? What is her address?'

'Esplanade Hotel, St. Kilda,' says Jim, taking a small bit of a
letter out of his pocket.

'Very well, Jim, I have a friend who lives near it. She will find
her out, and do all for her that can be done. But why don't you—
why don't all of you contrive to get away somehow from this hateful
life, and not bring ruin and destruction on the heads of all who
love you? Say you will try for their sake—for my sake.'

'It's too late, Miss Falkland,' I said. 'We're all thankful to you
for the way you've spoken. Jim and I would be proud to shed our
blood for you any time, or Mr. Falkland either. We'll do what we
can, but we'll have to fight it out to the end now, and take our
chance of the bullet coming before the rope. Good-night, Miss Falkland, and good luck to you always.'

She shook hands heartily with me and Jim, but when she came
to Starlight he raised her hand quite respectful like and just touched
it with his lips. Then he bowed low to them all and walked slowly
out.

When we got to the public-house, which wasn't far off, we found
that Moran and the other two had stayed there a bit till Wall and
Hulbert came; then they had a drink all round and rode away.

The publican said Moran was in an awful temper, and he was afraid he'd have shot somebody before the others got him started and clear of the place.

'It's a mercy you went over, Captain,' says he; 'there'd have been the devil to pay else. He swore he'd burn the place down before he went from here.'

'He'll get caught one of these fine days,' says Starlight. 'There's more risk at one station than half-a-dozen road scrimmages, and that he'll find, clever as he thinks himself.'

'Where's Mr. Whitman, Jack?' says I to the landlord (he wasn't a bad sort, old Jack Jones). 'What made him leave his place to the mercy of the world, in a manner of speaking?'

'Well, it was this way. He heard that all the shepherds at the lower station had cut it to the diggings, ye see; so he thought he'd make a dart up to the Castlereagh and rig'late the place a bit. He'll be back afore morning.'

'How d'ye know that?'

'Well, he's ridin' that famous roan pony o' his, and he always comes back from the station in one day, though he takes two to go; eighty-five miles every yard of it. It's a big day, but that pony's a rum 'un, and can jump his own height easy. He'll be welcome home to-night.'

'I daresay he will, and no wonder. The missus must ha' been awful frightened, and the young ladies, too. Good-night, Jack'; and we rattled off.

It wasn't so very late after all when we got back to Jonathan's; so, as the horses wanted a bit of a rest and a feed, we roused up the girls and had supper. A very jolly one it was, my word.

They were full of curiosity, you bet, to know how we got on when they heard Moran was there and the others. So bit by bit they picked it out of us. When they heard it all, Maddie got up and threw her arms round Jim's neck.

'I may kiss you now you're married,' she says, 'and I know there's only one woman in the world for you; but you deserve one from every woman in the country for smashing that wretch Moran. It's a pity you didn't break his neck. Never mind, old man; Miss Falkland won't forget you for that, you take my word. I'm proud of you, that I am.'

Jim just sat there and let her talk to him. He smiled in a serious kind of way when she ran over to him first; but, instead of a good-looking girl, it might have been his grandmother for all he seemed to care.

'You're a regular old image, Jim,' says she. 'I hope none of my other friends'll get married if it knocks all the go out of them, same as it has from you. However, you can stand up for a friend, can't you? You wouldn't see me trod upon; d'ye think you would, now? I'd stand up for you, I know, if you was bested anywhere.'

'My dear Maddie,' says Starlight, 'James is in that particular stage of infatuation when a man only sees one woman in the whole world. I envy him, I assure you. When your day comes you will understand much of what puzzles you at present.'

'I suppose so,' said Maddie, going back to her seat with a wondering, queer kind of look. 'But it must be dreadful dull being shut in for weeks and weeks in one place, perhaps, and with only one man.'

'I have heard it asserted,' he says, 'that a slight flavour of monotony occasionally assails the honeymoon. Variety is the salt of life, I begin to think. Some of these fine days, Maddie, we'll both get married and compare notes.'

'You'll have to look out, then,' says Bella. 'All the girls about here are getting snapped up quick. There's such a lot of young bankers, Government officers, and swells of all sorts about the diggings now, not to reckon the golden-hole men, that we girls have double the pull we had before the gold. Why, there was my old schoolmate, Clara Mason, was married last week to such a fine young chap, a surveyor. She'd only known him six weeks.'

'Well, I'll come and dance at your wedding if you'll send me an invite,' says Starlight.

'Will you, though?' she said. 'Wouldn't it be fun? Unless Sir Ferdinand was there. He's a great friend of mine, you know.'

'I'll come if his Satanic Majesty himself was present (he occasionally does attend a wedding, I've heard), and bring you a present, too, Bella; mind, it's a bargain.'

'There's my hand on it,' says she. 'I wonder how you'll manage it, but I'll leave that to you. It mightn't be so long, either. And now it's time for us all to go to bed. Jim's asleep, I believe, this half-hour.'

CHAPTER XXXVII

This bit a of barney, of course, made bad blood betwixt us and Moran's mob, so for a spell Starlight and father thought it handier for us to go our own road and let them go theirs. We never could agree with chaps like them, and that was the long and short of it. They were a deal too rough and ready for Starlight; and as for Jim and me, though we were none too good, we couldn't do some of the things these coves was up to, nor stand by and see 'em done, which was more. This time we made up our mind to go back to the Hollow and drop out of notice altogether for a bit, and take a rest like.

We hadn't heard anything of Aileen and the old mother for weeks and weeks, so we fixed it that we should sneak over to Rocky Flat, one at a time, and see how things were going, and hearten 'em up a bit. When we did get to the Hollow, instead of being able to take it easy, as we expected, we found things had gone wrong as far as the devil could send 'em that way if he tried his best. It seems father had taken a restless fit himself, and after we were gone had crossed Nulla Mountain to some place above Rocky Flat, to where he could see what went on with a strong glass.

Before I go further I might as well tell you that, along with the whacking big reward that was offered for all of us, a good many coves as fancied themselves a bit had turned amateur policemen, and had all kinds of plans and dodges for catching us dead or alive. Now, men that take to the bush like us don't mind the regular paid force much, or bear them any malice. It's their duty to catch us or shoot us if we bolt, and ours to take all sorts of good care that they shan't do either if we can help it.

Well, as I was sayin', we don't have it in for the regulars in the police; it's all fair pulling, 'pull devil, pull baker,' some one has to get the worst of it. Now it's us, now it's them, that gets took or rubbed out, and no more about it.

But what us cross coves can't stand and are mostly sure to turn nasty on is the notion of fellows going into the man-hunting trade, with us for game, either for the fun of it or for the reward. That reward means the money paid for our blood. *We don't like it.* It may seem curious, but we don't; and them as take up the line as a game to make money or fun out of, when they've no call to, find out their mistake, sometimes when it's a deal too late.

Now we'd heard that a party of four men—some of them had been

gaol warders and some hadn't—had made it up to follow us up and
get us one way or the other if it was to be done. They weren't in
the police, but they thought they knew quite as much as the police
did; and, besides, the reward, £5000, if they got our lot and any one
of the others, was no foolish money.

Well, nothing would knock it out of these chaps' heads but that
we were safe to be grabbed in the long-run trying to make into the
old home. This was what made them gammon to be surveyors
when they first came, as we heard about, and go measuring and tape-
lining about, when there wasn't a child over eight years old on
the whole creek that couldn't have told with half an eye they wasn't
nothing of the sort.

Well, as bad luck would have it, just as father was getting down
towards the place he meets Moran and Daly, who were making
over to the Fish River on a cattle-duffing lay of their own. They
were pretty hard up; and Moran after his rough and tumble with
Jim, in which he had come off second best, was ready for anything
—anything that was bad, that is.

After he'd had a long yarn with them about cattle and horses and
what not, he offered them a ten-pound note each if they'd do what
he told them. Dad always carried money about with him; he said
it came in handy. If the police didn't take him, they wouldn't get
it; and if they did take him, why, nothing would matter much and
it might go with the rest. It came in handy enough this time, anyhow, though it helped what had been far better left undone.

I remember what a blinded rage father got into when he first
had Aileen's letter, and heard that these men were camped close
to the old house, poking about there all day long, and worrying
and frightening poor Aileen and mother.

Well, it seems on this particular day they'd been into the little
township, and I suppose got an extra glass of grog. Anyhow, when
they came back they began to be more venturesome than they
generally were. One chap came into the house and began talking
to Aileen, and after a bit mother goes into her bedroom, and Aileen
comes out into the verandah and begins to wash some clothes in a
tub, plashing the water pretty well about and making it a bit uncomfortable for any one to come near her.

What must this fool do but begin to talk about what white arms
she'd got—not that they were like that much; she'd done too much
hard work lately to have her arms, or hands either, look very grand;
and at last he began to be saucy, telling her as no Marston girl
ought to think so much of herself, considerin' who and what she
was. Well, the end of it was father heard a scream, and he looked
out from where he was hidden and saw Aileen running down the
garden and the fellow after her. He jumps out, and fires his revolver
slapbang at the chap; it didn't hit him, but it went that close that
he stopped dead and turned round to see who it was.

'Ben Marston, by all that's lucky, boys!' says he, as two of the other chaps came running down at the shot. 'We've got the ould sarpint out of his hole at last.' With that they all fires at father as quick as they could draw; and Aileen gives one scream and starts running along the track up the hill that leads to George Storefield's place.

Father drops; one of the bullets had hit him, but not so bad as he couldn't run, so he ups again and starts running along the gully, with the whole four of them shouting and swearin' after him, making sure they got him to rights this time.

'Two hundred a man, boys,' the big fellow in the lead says; 'and maybe we'll take tay with the rest of 'em now.'

They didn't know the man they were after, or they'd have just as soon have gone to 'take tea,' as they called it, with a tiger.

Father put on one of his old poacher dodges that he had borrowed from the lapwing in his own country, that he used to tell us about when we were boys (our wild duck'll do just the same), and made himself out a deal worse than he was. Father could run a bit, too; he'd been fast for a mile when he was young, and though he was old now he never carried no flesh to signify, and was as hard as nails. So what with knowing the ground, and they being flat-country men, he kept just out of pistol-shot, and yet showed enough to keep 'em filled up with the notion that they'd run him down after a bit.

They fired a shot every now and then, thinking a chance one might wing him, but this only let Moran and Daly see that some one was after dad, and that the hunt was coming their way.

They held steady where they had been told to stop, and looked out for the men they'd been warned of by father. As he got near this place he kept lettin' 'em git a bit nearer and nearer to him, so as they'd follow him up just where he wanted. It gave them more chance of hitting him, but he didn't care about that, now his blood was up—not he. All he wanted was to get them. Dad was the coolest old cove, when shooting was going on, ever I see. You'd think he minded bullets no more than bottle-corks.

Well, he goes stumbling and dragging himself like up the gully, and they, cocksure of getting him, closing up and shooting quicker and quicker, when just as he jumps down the Black Gully steps a bullet did hit him in the shoulder under the right arm, and staggers him in good earnest. He'd just time to cut down the bank and turn to the left along the creek channel, throwing himself down on his face among the bushes, when the whole four of 'em jumps down the bank after him.

'Stand!' says Moran, and they looked up and saw him and Daly covering them with their revolvers. Before they'd time to draw, two of 'em rolls over as dead as door-nails.

The other two were dumbfoundered and knocked all of a heap

by suddenly finding themselves face to face with the very men they'd been hunting after for weeks and weeks. They held up their pistols, but they didn't seem to have much notion of using them—particularly when they found father had rounded on 'em too, and was standing a bit away on the side looking very ugly and with his revolver held straight at 'em.

'Give in! Put down your irons,' says Moran, 'or by ——, we'll drop ye where ye stand.'

'Come on,' says one, and I think he intended to make a fight for it.

He'd 'a been better off if he had. It couldn't have been worse for him; but the other one didn't see a chance, and so he says—

'Give in, what's the good? There's three to two.'

'All right,' says the other chap, the big one; and they put down their pistols.

It was curious now as these two were both men that father and Moran had a down on. They'd better have fought it out as long as they could stand up. There's no good got by givin' in that I ever seen. Men as does so always drop in for it worse in the end.

First thing, then, they tied 'em with their hands behind 'em, and let 'em stand up near their mates that were down—dead enough, both of them, one shot through the heart and one through the head.

Then Moran sits down and has a smoke, and looks over at 'em.

'You don't remember me, Mr. Hagan?' says he, in his drawling way.

'No,' says the poor chap; 'I don't think I do.'

'But I remember you devilish well,' says Moran; 'and so you'll find afore we leave this.' Then he took another smoke. 'Weren't you warder in Berrima Gaol, says he, 'about seven year ago? Ah! now we're coming to it. You don't remember getting Daniel Moran —a prisoner serving a long sentence there—seven days' solitary on bread and water for what you called disobedience of orders and insolence?'

'Yes, I do remember now. I'd forgotten your face. I was only doing my duty, and I hope you won't bear any malice.'

'It was a little thing to you, maybe,' says Moran; 'but if you'd had to do seven long days and long cold nights in that devil's den, you'd 'a thought more about it. But you will now. My turn's come.'

'I didn't do it to you more than to the rest. I had to keep order in the gaol, and devilish hard work it was.'

'You're a liar,' says Moran, striking him across the face with his clenched hand. 'You had a down on me because I wouldn't knuckle down to you like some of them, and so you dropped it on to me every turn you could get. I was a youngster then, and might have grown into a man if I'd been let. But fellows like you are enough to turn any man into a devil if they've got him in their power.'

'Well, I'm in your power now,' says he. 'Let's see how you'll shape.'

'I don't like ye any the worse for being cheeky,' says Moran, 'and standing up to me, but it's too late. The last punishment I got, when I was kept in irons night and day for a month because I'd tried to get out, I swore I'd have your life if ever I came across ye.'

'You'll never shoot me in cold blood,' says the poor devil, beginning to look blue about the lips.

'I don't know what old Ben's going to do with the man he found chevying his daughter,' says Moran, looking at him with his deadly black-snake eyes, 'but I'm a-goin' to shoot you as soon as I've smoked out this pipe, so don't you make any mistake.'

'I don't mind a shot or two,' says Daly, 'but I'm dashed if I can stand by and see men killed in cold blood. You coves have your own reasons, I suppose, but I shall hook it over to the Fish River. You know where to find me.' And he walked away to where the horses were and rode off.

.   .   .   .   .   .

We got fresh horses and rode over quick to Rocky Flat. We took Warrigal with us, and followed our old track across Nulla Mountain till we got within a couple of miles of the place. Warrigal picked up the old mare's tracks, so we knew father had made over that way, and there was no call for us to lose time running his trail any longer. Better go straight on to the house and find out what had happened there. We sent Warrigal on ahead, and waited with our horses in our hands till he come back to us.

In about an hour he comes tearing back, with his eyes staring out of his head.

'I bin see old missis,' he says. 'She yabber that one make-believe constable bin there. Gammon-like it surveyor, and bimeby old man Ben gon' alonga hut, and that one pleeceman fire at him and all about, and him break back alonga gully.'

'Any of 'em come back?' says Jim.

'Bale! me see um tent-dog tied up. Cake alonga fireplace, all burn to pieces. No come home last night. I b'lieve shot 'em old man longa gully.'

'Come along, boys,' says Starlight, jumping into his saddle. 'The old man might have been hit. We must run the tracks and see what's come of the governor. Four to one's big odds.'

We skirted the hut and kept out wide till Warrigal cut the tracks, which he did easy enough. We couldn't see a blessed thing. Warrigal rode along with his head down, reading every tuft of grass, every little stone turned up, every foot of sand, like a book.

'Your old fader run likit Black Gully. Two fellow track here— bullet longa this one tree.' Here he pointed to a scratch on the side of a box tree, in which the rough bark had been shivered.

'Bimeby two fellow more come; 'nother one bullet; 'nother one here, too. This one blood drop longa white leaf.'

Here he picked up a dried gum leaf, which had on the upper side a dark red spot, slightly irregular.

We had it all now. We came to a place where two horses had been tied to a tree. They had been stamping and pawing, as if they had been there a goodish while and had time to get pretty sick of it.

'That near side one Moran's horse, pigeon-toes; me know 'em,' says Warrigal. 'Off side one Daly's roan horse, new shoes on. You see um hair, rub himself longa tree.'

'What the blazes were they doing hereabouts?' says Starlight. 'This begins to look complicated. Whatever the row was, Daly and he were in it. There's no one rich enough to rob hereabouts, is there? I don't like the look of it. Ride on, boys.'

We said nothing to each other, but rode along as fast as Warrigal could follow the line. The sky, which was bright enough when we started, clouded over, and in less than ten minutes the wind rose and rain began to pour down in buckets, with no end of thunder and lightning. Then it got that cold we could hardly sit on our horses for trembling. The sky grew blacker and blacker. The wind began to whistle and cry till I could almost swear I heard some one singing out for help. Nulla Mountain was as black as your hat, and a kind of curious feeling crept over me, I hardly knew why, as if something was going to happen; I didn't know what.

I fully expected to find father dead; and, though he wasn't altogether a good father to us, we both felt bad at the notion of his lyin' there cold and stiff. I began to think of him as he used to be when we were boys, and when he wasn't so out and out hard—and had a kind word for poor mother and a kiss for little Aileen.

But if he were shot or taken, why hadn't these other men come back? We had just ridden by their tents, and they looked as if they'd just been left for a bit by men who were coming back at night. The dog was howling and looked hungry. Their blankets were all thrown about. Anyhow, there was a kettle on the fire, which was gone out, and, more than that, there was the damper that Warrigal had seen lying in the ashes all burnt to a cinder.

Everything looked as if they'd gone off in a hurry, and never come back at night or since. One of their horses was tied with a tether rope close to the tent poles, and he'd been walking round and trampling down the grass, as if he'd been there all night. We couldn't make it out.

We rode on, hardly looking at one another, but following Warrigal, who rattled on now, hardly looking at the ground at all, like a dog with a burning scent. All of a sudden he pulls up, and points to a dip into a cross gully, like an old river, which we all knew.

'You see 'um crow? I b'leeve longa Black Gully.'

Sure enough, just above the drop down, where we used to gallop our ponies in old times and laugh to see 'em throw up their tails, there was half-a-dozen crows and a couple of eagle-hawks high up in the sky, wheeling and circling over the same place.

'By George! they've got the old man,' says Jim. 'Come on, Dick. I never thought poor old dad would be run down like this.'

'Or he's got them!' says Starlight, curling his lip in a way he had. 'I don't believe your old governor's dead till I see him. The devil himself couldn't grab him on his own ground.'

CHAPTER XXXVIII

WE all pulled up at the side of the gully or dry creek, whatever it was, and jumped off our horses, leaving Warrigal to look after them, and ran down the rocky sides of it.

'Great God!' Starlight cries out; 'what's that?' and he pointed to a small sloping bit of grass just underneath the bank. 'Who are they? Can they be asleep?'

They were asleep never to wake. As we stood side by side by the dead men, for there were four of them, we shook so, Jim and I, that we leaned against one another for support. We had never seen a sight before that like it. I never want to do so again.

There they lay, four dead men. We didn't know them ourselves, but guessed they were Hagan and his lot. How else did they come there? and how could dad have shot them all by himself, and laid them out there? Were Daly and Moran with him? This looked like Moran's damnable work.

We looked and looked. I rubbed my eyes. Could it be real? The sky was dark, and the daylight going fast. The mountain hung over us black and dreadful-looking. The wind whimpered up and down the hillside with a sort of cry in it. Everything was dark and dismal and almost unnatural-looking.

All four men were lying on their backs side by side, with their eyes staring up to the sky—staring—staring! When we got close beside them we could see they had all been shot—one man through the head, the rest through the body. The two nearest to me had had their hands tied; the bit of rope was lying by one and his wrist was chafed.

One had been so close to the man that shot him that the powder had burnt his shirt. It wasn't for anything they had either, for every man's notes (and one had four fives and some ones) were pinned to them outside of their pockets, as if to show every one that those who killed them wanted their blood and not their money.

'This is a terrible affair, boys,' said Starlight; and his voice sounded strange and hoarse. 'I never thought we should be mixed up with a deed like this. I see how it was done. They have been led into a trap. Your father has made 'em think they could catch him; and had Daly and Moran waiting for them—one on each side of this hole here. Warrigal'—for he had tied up his horse and crept up—'how many bin here?'

Warrigal held up three fingers.

'That one ran down here—one after one. I see 'em boot. Moran stand here. Patsey Daly lie down behind that ole log. All about boot-nail mark. Old man Ben he stand here. Dog bite'm this one.'

Here he stooped and touched a dead man's ankle. Sure enough there was the mark of Crib's teeth, with the front one missing, that had been kicked down his throat by a wild mare.

'Two fellow tumble down fust-like; then two fellow bimeby. One—two—three fellow track go along a flat that way. Then that one get two horses and ridem likit Fish River. Penty blood tumble down here.'

This was the ciphering up of the whole thing. It was clear enough now. Moran and Daly had waited for them here, and had shot down the two first men. Of the others, it was hard to say whether they died in fair fight or had been taken prisoners and shot afterwards. Either way, it was bad enough. What a noise it would make! The idea of four men, well known to the Government, and engaged in hunting down outlaws, on whose head a price was set, to be deliberately shot—murdered in cold blood, as there was some ground for thinking to be the case. What would be the end of it all?

We had done things that were bad enough, but a deliberate, cold-blooded, shameful piece of bloodshed like this had never been heard of in New South Wales before.

There was nothing more to be done. We couldn't stay any longer looking at the dead men; it was no use burying them, even if we'd had the time. We hadn't done it, though we should be sure to be mixed up with it somehow.

'We must be moving, lads,' said Starlight. 'As soon as this gets wind there'll be another rush out this way, and every policeman and newspaper reporter in the country will be up at Black Gully. When they're found everybody will see that they've been killed for vengeance and not for plunder. But the sooner they're found the better.'

'Best send word to Billy the Boy,' I said; 'he'll manage to lay them on without hurting himself.'

'All right. Warrigal knows a way of communicating with him; I'll send him off at once. And now the sooner we're at the Hollow the better for everybody.'

We rode all night. Anything was better than stopping still with such thoughts as we were likely to have for companions. About daylight we got to the Hollow. Not far from the cave we found father's old mare with the saddle on and the reins trailing on the ground. There was a lot of blood on the saddle too, and the reins were smeared all about with it; red they were to the buckles; so was her mane.

We knew then something was wrong, and that the old man was hard hit, or he'd never have let her go loose like that. When we got to the cave the dog came out to meet us, and then walked back whining in a queer way towards the log at the mouth, where we used to sit in the evenings.

There was father, sure enough, lying on his face in a pool of blood, and to all appearances as dead as the men we'd just left.

We lifted him up, and Starlight looked close and careful at him by the light of the dawn, that was just showing up over the tree tops to the east.

'He's not dead; I can feel his heart beat,' he said. 'Carry him in, boys, and we'll soon see what's the matter with him.'

We took his waistcoat and shirt off—a coat he never wore unless it was raining. Hard work we had to do it, they was so stuck to his skin when the blood had dried.

'By gum! he's been hit bad enough,' says Jim. 'Look here, and here; poor old dad!'

'There's not much "poor" about it, Jim,' says Starlight. 'Men that play at bowls must expect to get rubbers. They've come off second best in this row, and I wish it had been different, for several reasons.'

Dad was hit right through the top of the left shoulder. The ball had gone through the muscle and lodged somewhere. We couldn't see anything of it. Another bullet had gone right through him, as far as we could make out, under the breast on the right-hand side.

'That looks like a good-bye shot,' says Starlight; 'see how the blood comes welling out still; but it hasn't touched the lungs. There's no blood on his lips, and his breathing is all right. What's this? Only through the muscle of the right arm. That's nothing; and this graze on the ribs, a mere scratch. Dash more water in his face, Jim. He's coming to.'

After a few minutes he did come to, sure enough, and looked round when he found himself in bed.

'Where am I?' says he.

'You're at home,' I said, 'in the Hollow.'

'Dashed if I ever thought I'd get here,' he says. 'I was that bad I nearly tumbled off the old mare miles away. She must have carried me in while I was unsensible. I don't remember nothing after we began to get down the track into the Hollow. Where is she?'

'Oh! we found her near the cave, with the saddle and bridle on.'

'That's all right. Bring me a taste of grog, will ye; I'm a'most dead with thirst. Where did I come from last, I wonder? Oh, I seem to know now. Settling accounts with that —— dog that insulted my gal. Moran got square with t'other. That'll learn 'em to leave old Ben Marston alone when he's not meddling with them.'

'Never mind talking about that now,' I said. 'You had a near shave of it, and it will take you all your time to pull through now.'

'I wasn't hit bad till just as I was going to drop down into Black

Gully,' he said. 'I stood one minute, and that cursed wretch Hagan had a steady shot at me. I had one at him afterwards, though, with his hands tied, too.'

'God forgive you!' says Jim, 'for shooting men in cold blood. I couldn't do it for all the gold in Turon, nor for no other reason. It'll bring us bad luck, too; see if it don't.'

'You're too soft, Jim,' says the old man. 'You ain't a bad chap; but any young fellow of ten years old can buy and sell you. Where's that brandy and water?'

'Here it is,' says Jim; 'and then you lie down and take a sleep. You'll have to be quiet and obey orders now—that is if a few more years' life's any good to you.'

The brandy and water fetched him to pretty well, but after that he began to talk, and we couldn't stop him. Towards night he got worse and worse and his head got hotter, and he kept on with all kinds of nonsense, screeching out that he was going to be hung and they were waiting to take him away, but if he could get the old mare he'd be all right; besides a lot of mixed-up things about cattle and horses that we didn't know the right of.

Starlight said he was delirious, and that if he hadn't some one to nurse him he'd die as sure as fate. We couldn't be always staying with him, and didn't understand what was to be done much. We didn't like to let him lie there and die, so at long last we made up our minds to see if we could get Aileen over to nurse him for a few weeks.

Well, we scribbled a bit of a letter and sent Warrigal off with it. Wasn't it dangerous for him? Not a bit of it. He could go anywhere all over the whole country, and no trooper of them all could manage to put the bracelets on him. The way he'd work it would be to leave his horse a good way the other side of George Storefield's, and to make up as a regular blackfellow. He could do that first-rate, and talk their lingo, too, just like one of themselves. Gin or blackfellow, it was all the same to Warrigal. He could make himself as black as soot, and go barefooted with a blanket or a 'possum rug round him and beg for siccapence, and nobody'd ever bowl him out. He took us in once at the diggings; Jim chucked him a shilling, and told him to go away and not come bothering near us.

So away Warrigal went, and we knew he'd get through somehow. He was one of those chaps that always does what they're told, and never comes back and says they can't do it, or they've lost their horse, or can't find the way, or they'd changed their mind, or something.

No; once he'd started there was no fear of him not scoring somehow or other. Whatever Starlight told him to do, day or night, foul weather or fair, afoot or on horseback, that thing was done if Warrigal was alive to do it.

What we'd written to Aileen was telling her that father was that bad we hardly thought he'd pull through, and that if she wanted to save his life she must come to the Hollow and nurse him.

How to get her over was not the easiest thing in the world, but she could ride away on her old pony without anybody thinking but she was going to fetch up the cows, and then cut straight up the gully to the old yard in the scrub on Nulla Mountain. One of us would meet her there with a fresh horse and bring her safe into the Hollow. If all went well she would be there in the afternoon on a certain day; anyhow, we'd be there to meet her, come or no come.

She wouldn't fail us, we were dead sure. She had suffered a lot by him and us, too; but, like most women, the very moment anything happened to any of us, even to dad, everything flew out of her head, except that we were sick or sorry and wanted her help. Help, of course; wasn't she willing to give that, and her rest and comfort, health, even life itself, to wear herself out, hand and foot, for any one of her own family?

So poor Aileen made her way up all alone to the old scrub stock-yard. Jim and I had ridden up to it pretty early (he wouldn't stop behind) with a nice, well-bred little horse that had shone a bit at country races for her to ride on. We waited there a goodish while, we lying down and our horses hung up not far off for fear we might be 'jumped' by the police at any time.

At last we sees the old pony's head coming bobbing along through the scrub along the worn-out cattle track, grown up as it was, and sure enough there was Aileen on him, with her grey riding skirt and an old felt hat on. She'd nothing with her; she was afraid to bring a ha'porth of clothes or anything for fear they should any of 'em tumble that she was going a long way, and, perhaps, follow her up. So she had to hand that over to Warrigal, and trust to him to bring it on some way or other. We saw her before she saw us, and Jim gave a whistle just as he used to do when he was coming home late at night. She knew it at once, and a smile for a minute came over her pale face; such a sad sort of one it was, too, as if she was wondering at herself that she could feel that pleased at anything.

Whatever thoughts was in her mind, she roused up the old pony, and came towards us quick as soon as she catches sight of us. In two seconds Jim had lifted her down in his strong arms, and was holding her off the ground and hugging her as if she'd been a child. How the tears ran down her cheeks, though all the time she was kissing him with her arms round his neck; and me, too, when I came up, just as if we were boys and girls again.

After a bit she wiped her eyes, and said—

'How's father?'

'Very bad,' I said; 'off his head, and raving. It'll be a close thing with him. Here's your horse now, and a good one, too. We must let the old pony go; he'll make home fast enough.'

She patted his neck and we turned him loose. He slued round and went away steady, picking a bit as he went. He'd be home next day easy enough, and nobody the wiser where he'd been to.

We'd brought a bit to eat and a glass of wine for the girl in case she was faint, but she wouldn't take anything but a crust of bread and a drink of water. There was a spring that ran all the year round near the cattle-yard; and off went we, old Lieutenant holding up his head and showing himself off. He didn't get such a rider on his back every day.

'What a dear horse,' she said, as she pulled him together a bit like and settled herself fair and square in the saddle. 'Oh, how I could enjoy all this if—if——— O my God! shall we ever know a moment's peace and happiness in this world again? Are we always to be sunk in wretchedness and misery as long as we live?'

We didn't lose much time after that, you be sure. Up and down, thick and open, rough or smooth, we made the pace good, and Aileen gave us all we knew to keep ahead of her. We had a good light when we got to the drop down into the Hollow. The sun was just setting, and if we'd had time or thought to give to the looks of things, no doubt it was a grand sight.

All the Hollow was lighted up, and looked like a green sea with islands of trees in it. The rock towers on the other side of the range were shining and glittering like as if they were made of crystallised quartz or diamonds—red and white. There was a sort of mist creeping up the valley at the lower end under the mountain that began to soften the fire colours, and mix them up like. Even the mountain, that mostly looked black and dreary, frowning at our ways, was of purple and gold, with pale shadows of green and grey.

Aileen pulled up as we did, and jumped off our horses.

'So this is the Hollow,' she said, half talking to herself, 'that I've heard and thought so much about. What a lovely, lovely place! Surely it ought to have a different effect on the people that lived there.'

'Better come off, Ailie, and lead your horse down here,' says Jim, 'unless you want to ride down, like Starlight did, the first time we saw him.'

'Starlight! is he here?' she said, in a surprised sort of way. 'I never thought of that.'

'Of course he is; where else should he be? Why don't you lead on, Dick?'

'Won't you get off? It's not altogether safe,' I said, 'though Lieutenant's all right on his old pins.'

'Safe!' she said, with a bitter sort of laugh. 'What does it matter if a Marston girl does break her neck, or her heart either?'

She never said another word, but sat upright with a set face on her, as the old horse picked his way down after ours, and except when he put his foot on a rolling stone, never made a slip or a stumble all the way down, though it was like going down the side of a house.

When we got to the valley we put on a spurt to the cave, and found Warrigal sitting on the log in front of us. He'd got home first, of course, and there was Aileen's bundle, a biggish one too, alongside of him. We could hear father raving and screaming out inside dreadful. Starlight wasn't nigh hand anywhere. He had walked off when Warrigal came home, and left him to watch the old man.

'He been like that all the time, Warrigal?'

'No! Captain say big one sleep. Him give him medicine like; then wake up and go on likit that. I believe him bad along a cobra.'

Aileen had jumped off her horse and gone in to the old man the moment we came up and she heard his voice.

All that long night we could hear him talking to himself, groaning, cursing, shouting, arguing. It was wonderful how a man who talked so little as father could have had so many thoughts in his mind. But then they all are boxed up together in every man's heart. At a time like this they come racing and tumbling out like a flock of sheep out of a yard when the hurdle's down. What a dashed queer thing human nature is when you come to think of it. That a man should be able to keep his tongue quiet, and shut the door on all the sounds and images and wishes that goes racing about inside of his mind like wild horses in a paddock!

One day he'll be smiling and sensible, looking so honest all the time. Next day a knock on the head or a little vein goes crack in the brain (as the doctor told me); then the rails are down, and everything comes out with a rush into the light of day—right and wrong, foul and fair, station brands and clear-skins, it don't make no difference.

Father was always one of the closest men that ever lived. ·He never told us much about his old life at home or after he came out here. Now he was letting drop things here and there that helped us to a few secrets he'd never told to no man. They made poor Aileen a bit more miserable than she'd been before, if that was possible; but it didn't matter much to us. We were pretty tired ourselves that night, and so we got Aileen all she wanted, and left her alone with him.

While we were away to meet her some one had taken the trouble to put up a bit of a partition, separating that part of the cave from the other; it was built up of stone—there was plenty about—and not so roughly done either. It made Aileen feel a lot more comfortable. Of course there was only one man who could have done it; and that was Starlight.

CHAPTER XXXIX

TOWARDS morning father went into a heavy sleep; he didn't wake till the afternoon. Poor Aileen was able to get a doze and change her dress. After breakfast, while we were having a bit of a chat, in walks Starlight. He bowed to Aileen quite respectful, as he always did to a woman, and then shook hands with her.

'Welcome to the Hollow, Miss Marston,' he said. 'I can't say how charmed I am in one sense, though I regret the necessity which brought you here.'

'I'm glad to come, and only for poor father's being so bad I could delight in the life here.'

'How do you find your father?'

'He is asleep now, and perhaps the rest will do him good.'

'He may awake free from fever,' says Starlight. 'I took the risk of giving him an opiate before you came, and I think the result has been favourable.'

'Oh! I hope he will be better when he wakes,' says Aileen, 'and that I shall not have to watch through another dreadful night of raving. I can hardly bear it.'

'You must make your brothers take their share; it's not fair to you.'

'Thank you; but I feel as if I couldn't leave him to anybody but myself. He seems so weak now; a little neglect might kill him.'

'Pardon me, Miss Marston; you overrate the danger. Depend upon it, your respected parent will be quite a different man in a week, though it may be a month or more before he is fully recovered. You don't know what a constitution he has.'

'You have given me fresh hope,' she said. 'I feel quite cheered up —that is' (and she sighed) 'if I could be cheerful again about anything.'

Here she walked into the cave and sat down by father to watch till he awoke, and we all went out about our daily work, whatever it was —nothing very wonderful, I daresay, but it kept us from thinking.

Starlight was right. As luck would have it, father woke up a deal better than when he laid down. The fever had gone away, his head was right again, and he began to ask for something to eat—leastways to drink, first. But Aileen wouldn't give him any of that, and very little to eat. Starlight had told her what to do in case he wanted what wasn't good for him, and as she was pretty middling obstinate, like himself, she took her own ways.

After this he began to get right; it wasn't easy to kill old dad. He seemed to be put together with wire and whipcord; not made of flesh and blood like other men. I don't wonder old England's done so much and gone so far with her soldiers and sailors if they was bred like him. It's my notion if they was caught young, kept well under command, and led by men they respected, a regiment or a man-of-war's crew like him would knock smoke out of any other thousand men the world could put up. More's the pity there ain't some better way of keeping 'em straight than there is.

He was weak for a bit—very weak; he'd lost a deal of blood; and, try how he would, he couldn't stand up long at a time, and had to give in and lie down in spite of himself. It fretted him a deal, of course; he'd never been on his back before, and he couldn't put up with it. Then his temper began to show again, and Aileen had a deal to bear and put up with.

We'd got a few books, and there was the papers, of course, so she used to read to him by the hour together. He was very fond of hearing about things, and, like a good many men that can't read and write, he was clever enough in his own way. When she'd done all the newspapers—they were old ones (we took care not to get any fresh ones, for fear she'd see about Hagan and the others)—she used to read about battles and sea-fights to him; he cared about them more than anything, and one night, after her reading to him about the battle of Trafalgar, he turned round to her and says, 'I ought to have been in that packet, Ailie, my girl. I was near going for a sailor once, on board a man-o'-war, too. I tried twice to get away to sea, that was before I'd snared my first hare, and something stopped me both times. Once I was fetched back and flogged, and pretty nigh starved. I never did no good afterwards. But it's came acrost me many and many a time that I'd been a different sort o' chap if I'd had my will then. I was allays fond o' work, and there couldn't be too much fightin' for me; so a man-o'-war in those days would have been just the thing to straighten me. That was the best chance I ever had. Well, I don't say as I haven't had others—plenty in this country, and good ones too; but it was too late—I'd got set. When a man's young, that's the time he can be turned right way or wrong. It's none so easy afterwards.'

He went to sleep then, and Aileen said that was the only time he ever spoke to her in that way. We never heard him talk like that, nor nobody else, I expect.

If we could have got some things out of our heads, that was the pleasantest time ever we spent in the Hollow. After father could be left by himself for a few hours we got out the horses, and used to take Aileen out for long rides all over the place, from one end to the other. It did her good, and we went to every hole and corner in it. She was never tired of looking at the great rock towers, as we used to call 'em, where the sandstone walls hung over, just like the pic-

tures of castles, till, Starlight said, in the evenings you could fancy
you saw flags waving and sentinels walking up and down on them.

One afternoon we went out to the place where the old hermit had
lived and died. We walked over his old garden, and talked about
the box we'd dug up, and all the rest of it. Starlight came with us,
and he persuaded Aileen to ride Rainbow that day, and, my word,
they made a splendid pair.

She'd dressed herself up that afternoon just a little bit more than
common, poor thing, and put a bit of pink ribbon on and trimmed up
her hat, and looked as if she began to see a little more interest in
things. It didn't take much to make her look nice, particularly on
horseback. Her habit fitted her out and out, and she had the sort of
figure that, when a girl can ride well, and you see her swaying,
graceful and easy-like, to every motion of a spirited horse, makes you
think her handsomer than any woman can look on the ground. We
rode pretty fast always, and it brought a bit of colour to her face.
The old horse got pulling and prancing a bit, though he was that
fine-tempered he'd carry a child almost, and Jim and I thought we
hadn't seen her look like herself before this for years past.

It was a beautiful warm evening, though summer was over, and
we were getting into the cold nights and sharp mornings again, just
before the regular winter weather. There was going to be a change,
and there were a few clouds coming up from the north-west; but for
all that it had been quite like a spring day. The turf on all the flats in
the Hollow was splendid and sound. The grass had never been cut
up with too heavy stocking (which ruins half the country, I believe),
and there was a good thick undergrowth underneath. We had two
or three little creeks to cross, and they were pretty full, except at the
crossing places, and rippled over the stones and sparkled in the sun
like the brooks we'd heard tell of in the old country. Everything was
so quiet, and bright and happy-looking, that we could hardly fancy
we were the men we were; and that all this wild work had been going
on outside of the valley that looked so peaceful and innocent.

There was Starlight riding alongside of Aileen on his second-best
horse, and he was no commoner either (though he didn't come up to
Rainbow, nor no other horse I ever saw), talking away in his pleasant,
easy-going way. You'd think he hadn't got a thing to trouble him in
the world. She, for a wonder, was smiling, and seemed to be enjoying herself for once in a way, with the old horse arching his neck,
and spinning along under her as light as a greyhound, and as smooth
as oil. It was something like a pleasant ride. I never forgot that
evening, and I never shall.

We rode up to the ruined hut of the solitary man who had lived
there so long, and watched the sun go down so often behind the
rock towers from his seat under that big peach tree.

'What a wonderful thing to think of!' Aileen says, as she slipped
down off her side-saddle.

We dismounted, too, and hung up our horses.

'Only to think that he was living here before we were born, or father came to Rocky Flat. Oh! if we could have come here when we were little how we should have enjoyed it! It would have seemed fairyland to us.'

'It always astonishes me,' said Starlight, 'how. any human being can consent to live, year after year, the same life in the same place. I should go mad half-a-dozen times over. Change and adventure are the very breath of my nostrils.'

'He had the memory of his dead wife to keep him,' said Aileen. 'Her spirit soothed the restless heart that would have wandered far into the wilds again.'

'It may be so,' said Starlight dreamily. 'I have known no such influences. An outlaw I, by forest laws, almost since the days of my boyhood, I shall be so till the day of my death,' he added.

'If I were a man I should go everywhere,' said Aileen, her eyes sparkling and her face regular lighted up. 'I have never been anywhere or seen anything, hardly so much as a church, a soldier, a shop-window, or the sea, begging his pardon for putting him last. But oh! what a splendid thing to be rich; no, not that altogether, but to be able to go wherever you liked, and have enough not to be troubled about money.'

'To be free, and have a mind at ease; it doesn't seem so much,' said Starlight, talking almost to himself; 'and yet how we fools and madmen shut ourselves out of it for ever, for ever, sometimes by a single act of folly, hardly crime. That comes after.'

'The sun is going down behind the great rock tower,' Aileen says, as if she hadn't heard him. Perhaps she didn't. When people have a lot on their minds they're half their time thinking their own thoughts. 'How all the lovely colours are fading away. Life seems so much like that—a little brightness, then grey twilight, night and darkness so soon after.'

'Now and then there's a star; you must admit that, Miss Marston,' says he, cheerful and pleasant again; he was never down for long at a time. 'And there's that much-abused luminary, the moon; you'll see her before we get home. We're her sworn votaries and worshippers, you know.'

We had to ride a bit to get home with any kind of light, for we didn't want father to be growling or kicking up a row with Warrigal that we left to look after him. But a few miles didn't matter much on such a road, and with horses in such buckle as ours.

The stars came out after a while, and the sky was that clear, without a cloud in it, that it was a better light to ride by than the moon throws. Jim and I sometimes rode on one side and sometimes the other; but there was old Rainbow always in the lead, playing with his bit and arching his neck, and going with Aileen's light weight on him as if he could go on all night at the same pace and think nothing of it; and I believe he could.

When we got home dad was grumpy, and wondered what we wanted riding the horses about when there was nothing to do and nothing to see. But Warrigal had made him a pot of tea, and he was able to smoke now; so he wasn't so bad after all. We made ourselves pretty comfortable—Aileen said she'd got a good appetite, for a wonder—and we sat chatting round the fire and talking away quite like old days till the moon was pretty high.

Father didn't get well all at once. He went back twice because he would try to do too much, and wouldn't be said by Starlight or Aileen either when he took a thing into his head; then he'd have to be nursed and looked after day and night again just the same as ever. So it took near a month before he was regularly on his pins again, and going about as he did before he was hit. His right arm was a bit stiff, too; it used to pain and make him swear awful now and again. Anyhow, Aileen made us that comfortable and happy while she was there, we didn't care how long he took getting well.

Those were out and out the pleasantest days we ever spent in the Hollow—the best time almost Jim and I had had since we were boys. Nearly every day we rode out in the afternoon, and there wasn't a hole or corner, a spring or a creek inside the walls of the old Hollow that we didn't show Aileen. She was that sort of girl she took an interest in everything; she began to know all the horses and cattle as well as we did ourselves. Rainbow was regular given up to her, and the old horse after a bit knew her as well as his master. I never seen a decent horse that didn't like to have a woman on his back; that is, if she was young and lissom and could ride a bit. They seem to know, in a sort of way. I've seen horses that were no chop for a man to ride, and that wouldn't be particular about bucking you off if the least thing started them, but went as quiet as mice with a girl on their backs.

So Aileen used to make Rainbow walk and amble his best, so that all the rest of us, when she did it for fun, had to jog. Then she'd jump him over logs or the little trickling deep creeks that ran down to the main water; or she'd pretend to have a race and go off full gallop, riding him at his best for a quarter of a mile; then he'd pull up as easy as if he'd never gone out of a walk.

'How strange all this is,' she said one day; 'I feel as if I were living on an island. It's quite like playing at "Robinson Crusoe," only there's no sea. We don't seem to be able to get out all the same. It's a happy, peaceful life, too. Why can't we keep on for ever like this, and shut out the wicked, sorrowful world altogether?'

'Quite of your opinion, Miss Marston; why should we ever change?' says Starlight, who was sitting down with the rest of us by the side of our biggest river. We had been fishing all the afternoon and done well. 'Let us go home no more; I am quite contented. But what about poor Jim? He looks sadder every day.'

'He is fretting for his wife, poor fellow, and I don't wonder. You are one of those natures that never change, Jim; and if you don't get away soon, or see some chance of rejoining her, you will die. How you are to do it I don't know.'

'I am bound to make a try next month,' says Jim. 'If I don't do something towards it I shall go mad.'

'You could not do a wiser thing,' says Starlight, 'in one way, or more foolish thing in another. Meantime, why should we not make the best of the pleasant surroundings with which Nature provides us here—green turf, sparkling water, good sport, and how bright a day! Could we be more favoured by Fortune, slippery dame that she is? It is an Australian Decameron without the naughty stories.'

'Do you know, sometimes I really think I am enjoying myself,' said Aileen, half to herself, 'and then I feel that it must be a dream. Such dreadful things are waiting for me—for us all.' Then she shuddered and trembled.

She did not know the most dreadful thing of all yet. We had carefully kept it from her. We chanced its not reaching her ears until after she had got home safe and had time to grieve over it all by herself.

We had a kind of feeling somehow that us four might never meet again in the same way, or be able to enjoy one another's company for a month, without fear of interruption, again, as long as we lived.

So we all made up our minds, in spite of the shadow of evil that would crawl up now and then, to enjoy each other's company while it lasted, and make the best of it.

Starlight for all that seemed altered like, and every now and then he'd go off with Warrigal and stay away from daylight to dark. When he did come he'd sit for hours with his hands before him and never say a word to any one. I saw Aileen watch him when he looked like that, not that she ever said anything, but pretented to take it as a matter of course.

Other times he'd be just as much the other way. He'd read to her, and he had a good many books, poetry, and all kinds of things stowed away in the part of the cave he called his own. And he'd talk about other countries that he'd been in, and the strange people he'd seen, by the hour together, while she would sit listening and looking at him, hardly saying a thing, and regular bound up in his words. And he could talk once he was set agoing. I never saw a man that could come up to him.

Aileen wasn't one of those sort of girls that took a fancy to any good-looking sort of fellow that came across her. Quite the other way. She seemed to think so little about it that Jim and I always used to say she'd be an old maid, and never marry at all. And she used to say she didn't think she ever would. She never seemed to trouble her head about the thing at all, but I always knew that if ever she did set her fancy upon a man, and take a liking to him, it would not be for a year or two, but for ever. Though she'd mother's good heart and softness about her, she'd a dash of dad's obstinacy in her blood, and once she made up her mind about anything she wasn't easy turned.

Jim and I could see clear enough that she was taking to Starlight; but then so many women had done that, had fallen in love with him and had to fall out again—as far as we could see. He used to treat them all alike—very kind and respectful, but like a lot of children. What was the use of a wife to him? 'No,' he said, once or twice, 'I can bear my fate, because my blood does not run in the veins of a living soul in Australia. If it were otherwise I could not bear my reflections. As it is, the revolver has more than once nearly been asked to do me last service.'

Though both Aileen and he seemed to like each other, Jim and I never thought there was anything in it, and let them talk and ride and walk together just as they pleased. Aileen always had a good word for Starlight, and seemed to pity him so for having to lead such a life, and because he said he had no hope of ever getting free from it. Then, of course, there was a mystery about him. Nobody knew who he'd been, or almost where he had come from—next to nothing about him had ever come out. He was an Englishman—that was certain—but he must have come young to the colony. No one could look at him for a moment and see his pale, proud face, his dark eyes—half-scornful, half-gloomy, except when he was set up a bit (and then you didn't like to look at them at all)—without seeing that he was a gentleman to the tips of his delicate-looking fingers, no matter what he'd done, or where he'd been.

He was rather over the middle size; because he was slight made, he always looked rather tall than not. He was tremendous strong, too, though he didn't look that, and as active as a cat, though he moved as if walking was too much trouble altogether, and running not to be thought of.

We didn't expect it would do either of 'em much good. How could it, even if they did fall in love with one another and make it up to get married? But they were both able to take care of themselves, and it was no use interfering with 'em either. They weren't that sort.

Starlight had plenty of money, besides his share of the gold. If we could ever get away from this confounded rock-walled prison, good as it was in some ways; and if he and Aileen and the rest of us could make a clean dart of it and get to America, we could live there free and happy yet, in spite of all that had come and gone.

Aileen wasn't like to leave poor old mother as long as she wanted her, so it couldn't come off for a year or two at earliest, and many things were sure to happen in the meanwhile. So we let all the talking and walking and riding out in the evening go on as much as they pleased, and never said anything or seemed to take any notice at all about it.

All this time mother was at George Storefield's. When Aileen ran over that time, he said it wasn't fit for them to live at Rocky Flat by themselves. So he went over that very day—like a good fellow, as he was—and brought over the old woman, and made them both stay at his house, safe and comfortable. When Aileen said she had to go away to nurse dad he said he would take care of mother till she came back, and so she'd been there all the time. She knew Mrs. Storefield (George's mother) well in the old times; so they used to sit by the kitchen fire when they wanted to be extra comfortable, and knit stockings and talk over the good old times to their hearts' content.

If it hadn't been for old Mrs. Storefield I don't expect mother would have contented herself there—the cottage was not so grand, Aileen told us, and Gracey had to dress a bit now. George had kept on making more money in every way he tried it, and of course he began, bit by bit, to live according to his means.

He'd bought cattle-stations on the Lachlan just when the gold broke out first, and everybody thought station property was never going to be worth nothing again. Now, since cattle had risen and meat and all to such a price, he was making money hand over fist. More than that, as I said before, he'd been made a magistrate, and all the swells began to take notice of him—not altogether because he'd made money either; what I call the real swells, as far as I see, won't do that. If they don't care for a man—no matter how much money he's made—they hold shy of him. But if he's a straight-going good sort of fellow, that has his head screwed on the right way, and don't push himself forward too much, they'll meet him half-way, and a very good thing, too.

We could see George was going upwards and out of our lot, beginning to mix with different people and get different notions—not but what he was always kind and friendly in his way to Aileen and mother, and would have been to us if he'd ever seen us. But all his new friends were different kind of people, and after a bit, Aileen said, we'd only be remembered as people he'd known when he was young, and soon, when the old lady died, we'd be asked into the kitchen and not into the parlour. Aileen used to laugh when she talked like this, and say she'd come and see George when he'd married a lady, and what fun it would be to remind Gracey of the time they threshed the oats out together at Rocky Flat. But still, laugh and all, I could see, though she talked that way, it made her feel wretched all the while, because she couldn't help thinking that we ought to have done just as well as George, and might have been nigh-hand as far forward if we'd kept straight. If we'd only kept straight! Ah, there was where the whole mistake lay.

It often seems to me as if men and women ought to have two lives —an old one and a new one—one to repent of the other; the first one to show men what they ought to keep clear of in the second. When you think how foolish-like and childish man or woman commits their first fault, not so bad in itself, but enough often to shut them out from nearly all their chances of good in this world, it does seem hardish that one life should end all under the sun. Of course, there's the other, and we don't know what's coming, but there's so many different notions about that a chap like me gets puzzled, and looks on it as out of his line altogether.

We weren't sorry to have a little excuse to stop quiet at home for this month. We couldn't have done no good by mooching about, and ten to one, while the chase was so hot after all that were supposed to have had a hand in rubbing out Hagan and his lot, we should have been dropped upon. The whole country was alive with scouting parties, as well as the regulars. You'd have thought the end of the world was come. Father couldn't have done a better thing for himself and all of us than get hit as he did. It kept him and us out of harm's way, and put them off the scent, while they hunted Moran and Burke and the rest of their lot for their lives. They could hardly get a bit of damper out of a shepherd's hut without it being known to the police, and many a time they got off by the skin of their teeth.

CHAPTER XL

At last father got well, and said he didn't see what good Aileen could do stopping any longer in the Hollow, unless she meant to follow up bush-ranging for a living. She'd better go back and stay along with her mother. If George Storefield liked to have 'em there, well and good; things looked as if it wasn't safe now for a man's wife and daughter, and if he'd got into trouble, to live peaceable and quiet in their own house. He didn't think they need be afraid of any one interfering with them for the future, though. Here dad looked so dark that Aileen began to think he was going to be ill again. We'd all start and go a bit of the way with her next day—to the old stockyard or a bit farther; she could ride from there, and take the horse back with her and keep him if she liked.

'You've been a good gal to me,' he says to her; 'you always was one; and your mother's been a good woman and a good wife; tell her I said so. I'd no call to have done the things I have, or left home because it wasn't tidy and clean and a welcome always when I came back. It's been rough on her, and on you too, my gal; and if it'll do her any good, tell her I'm dashed sorry. You can take this trifle of money. You needn't boggle at it; it's honest got and earned, long before this other racket. Now you can go. Kiss your old dad; like as not you won't see him again.'

We'd got the horses in. I lifted her up on to the saddle, and she rode out. Her horse was all on the square, so there was no harm in her taking him back with her, and off we went. Dad didn't go after all. We took it easy out to the old stockyard. We meant to camp there for half-an-hour, and then to send her on, with Warrigal to keep with her and show her the way home.

'We didn't want to make the time too short. What a lovely day it was! The mountain sides were clogged up with mist for an hour after we started; still, any one that knew the climate would have said it was going to be a fine day. There wasn't a breath of air; everything was that still that not a leaf on any of the trees so much as stirred.

When we came to the pass out of the valley, we none of us got off; it was better going up than coming down, and it would have tired Aileen out at the start to walk up. So the horses had to do their climbing. It didn't matter much to them. We were all used to it, horses and riders. Jim and I went first, then Warrigal, then Aileen and Starlight. After we got up to the top we all stopped and halted a bit to look round.

Just then, as if he'd waited for us, the sun came out from behind the mountain; the mists lifted and rolled away as if they had been grey curtains. Everything showed clear out like a playhouse, the same Jim and I used to see in Melbourne. From where we stood you could see everything, the green valley flats with the big old trees in clumps, some of 'em just the same as they'd been planted. The two little river-like silver threads winding away among the trees, and far on the opposite side the tall grey rock towers shining among the forest edges of the high green wall. Somehow the sun wasn't risen enough to light up the mountain. It looked as black and dismal as if it was nightfall coming on.

'Good-bye, old Hollow!' Aileen called out, waving her hand. 'Everything looks bright and beautiful except the mountain. How gloomy it appears, as if it held some dreadful secret—doesn't it? Ah! what a pleasant time it has been for me. Am I the same Aileen Marston that went in there a few weeks since? And now I suppose there will be more misery and anxiety waiting for all of us when I get back. Well, come what will, I have had a little happiness on this earth. In heaven there must be rest.'

We all rode on, but none of us seemed to care to say much. Every step we went seemed to be taking us away from the place where we'd all been so happy together. The next change was sure to be for the worse. What it would be, or when it would come, we none of us could tell.

Starlight and Aileen rode together most of the way, and talked a good deal, we could see. Before we got to the stockyard she rode over to Jim and cheered him up as much as she could about Jeanie. She said she'd write to her, and tell her all about him, and how happy we'd all been together lately; and tell her that Jim would find some way to get down to her this spring, if he could manage it any road.

'If I'm above ground, tell her I'll be with her,' says poor old Jim, 'before Christmas. If she don't see me then I'll be dead, and she may put on black and make sure she's a widow.'

'Oh, come, you mustn't talk like that, Jim, and look to the bright side a bit. There's a good chance yet, now the country's so full of diggers and foreigners. You try your luck, and you'll see your wife yet.'

Then she came to me, and talked away just like old times.

'You're the eldest, Dick,' she said, 'and so it's proper for me to say what I'm going to say.' Then she told me all that was in her heart about Starlight. He and she had made it up that if he could get away to a foreign country she would join him there, and take mother with her. There was to be no marrying or love-making unless they could carry out that plan. Then she told me that she had always had the same sort of feeling towards him. 'When I saw him first I thought I had never seen a man before—never one that I could care for or think of marrying. And now he has told me that he loves me —loves me, a poor ignorant girl that I am; and I will wait for him all my life, and follow him all round the world. I feel as if I could die for him, or wear out my life in trying to make him happy. And yet, and yet,' she said, and all her face grew sad, and put on the old look that I knew so well, so hopeless, so full of quiet bearing of pain, 'I have a kind of feeling at my heart that it will never be. Something will happen to me or to him. We are all doomed to sorrow and misfortune, and nothing can save us from our fate.'

'Aileen, dear,' I said, 'you are old enough to know what's best for yourself. I didn't think Starlight was on for marrying any woman, but he's far and away the best man we've ever known, so you can please yourself. But you know what the chances are. If he gets clear off, or any of us, after what's been done, you're right. But it's a hundred to one against it.'

'I'll take the odds,' says she, holding up her head. 'I'm willing to put my life and happiness, what little there's left of it, on the wager. Things can't well be worse.'

'I don't know,' I said. 'I ought to tell you—I must tell you something before we part, though I'd a deal rather not. But you'll bear it better now than in a surprise.'

'Not more blood, more wickedness,' she said, in a half-whisper, and then she looks up stern and angry-like. 'When is this list of horrible things to stop?'

'It was none of our doing. Moran and Daly were in it, and——'

'And none of you? Swear that,' she said, so quick and pitiful-like. 'None of us,' I said again; 'nor yet Warrigal.'

'Then who did it? Tell me all. I'm not a child. I will know.'

'You remember the man that was rude to you at Rocky Flat, and father and he fired at one another?'

'Of course I do, cowardly wretch that he was. Then Moran was waiting for them up the gully? I wondered that they did not come back next day.'

'They never came back,' I said.

'Why, you don't mean to tell me that they are all dead, all four? —those strong men! Oh, surely not, Dick?' and she caught hold of my arm, and looked up into my face.

'Yes, Aileen, all. We came after and followed up dad, when we got home; it's a wonder he did it by himself. But we saw them all four lying stretched out.'

She put down her head and never spoke more till we parted.

.   .   .   .   .   .

We turned back, miserable enough all of us, God knows. After having Aileen to make the place bright and pleasant and cheer us all up, losing her was just as if all the little pleasure we had in our lives was dropped out of them—like the sun going out of the sky, and the wind rising; like the moon clouding over, and a fog burying up every thing—dark and damp, the same as we'd had it many a time cattle-driving by night. We hardly spoke a word to one another all the way home, and no wonder.

Next day we all sat about, looking more down on our luck, dad said, than any day since we'd 'turned out.' Then Starlight told him about him and Aileen, how they'd made it up to be married some day or other. Not yet, of course; but if he could get away by Melbourne to some of these places—the islands on the Pacific coast, where vessels were always sailing for—he didn't see why his luck shouldn't change. 'I have always thought your daughter,' he says to father, 'one of the grandest women I ever met, in any degree, gentle or simple. She has had the imprudence to care for me; so, unless you have some well-grounded objection—and I don't say you haven't, mind you, I should if I were in your place—you may as well say you're contented, and wish us luck!'

Father was a long time before he said anything. He sat there, looking very sullen and set-like, while Starlight lit a cigar and walked quietly up and down a few paces off.

Dad answers at last. 'I don't say but what other lads would have suited better if they'd come off, but most things goes contrary in this world. The only thing as I'm doubtful of, Captain, is your luck. If that's bad, all the trying and crying won't set it right. And it's great odds as you'll be caught or shot afore the year's out. For that matter, every one of us is working for Government on the same road. But the gal's a good gal, and if she's set her fancy on you I won't block her. You're a pair of dashed fools, that's all, botherin' your heads with the like at a time like this, when you boys are all more likely to have a rope round your necks than any gal's arms, good or bad. Have your own way. You always managed to get it, somehow or other, ever since I knowed ye.'

After this father lit his pipe and went into the cave.

By and by he comes out again and catches the old mare.

'I ain't been out of this blessed hole,' he says, 'for a month of Sundays. I'm dead tired of seeing nothin' and doin' nothin'. I'll crawl over to old Davy's for our letters and papers. We ain't heard nothing for a year, seems to me.'

Dad was strong enough to get about in the saddle again, and we weren't sorry to get shut of him for a bit. He was that cranky at times there was no living with him. As for ourselves, we were regular wild for some sort of get away for a bit of a change; so we hadn't talked it over very long before we made up our minds to take a run over to Jonathan Barnes's and have a bit of fun, just to take the taste out of our mouths of Aileen's going away.

We had to dress ourselves very quiet and get fresh horses—nags that had nothing particular about them to make people look, at the same time with a bit of go in them in case we were pushed at any time.

No sooner said than done. We went to work and got everything ready, and by three o'clock we were off—all three of us, and never in better heart in our lives—for a bit of fun or devilment; it didn't matter which came first.

When we got to Jonathan's it was latish, but that didn't matter to us or to the girls neither; they were always ready for a bit of fun, night or day. However, just at first they pretended to be rather high and mighty about this business of Hagan's.

'Oh! it's you, is it?' says Bella, after we walked in. I don't know as it's safe for us to be knowing such dangerous characters. There's a new law against harbouring, father says. He's pretty frightened, I can tell you, and for two pins we'd be told to shut the door in your faces.'

'You can do that if you like now,' says I; 'we shan't want telling twice, I daresay. But what makes you so stiff to-night?'

'Why, Hagan's business, of course,' says Maddie; 'four men killed in cold blood. Only I know you couldn't and wouldn't be in it I'd not know any of ye from a crow. There now.'

'Quite right, most beauteous Madeline,' says Starlight! 'it was a very dreadful affair, though I believe there was some reason for old Ben being angry. Of course, you know we weren't within miles of the place when it was done. You remember the night we were here last?'

'Of course we do, Captain, quite well. Weren't you going to dance at Bella's wedding and all? You'll have to do that sooner than we expected though.'

'Glad to hear it, but listen to me, my dear; I want you to know the truth. We rode straight back to the—to where we lived—and, of course, found the old man gone away from the place. We tracked him right enough, but came up when it was all over. Daly and Moran were the chief actors in that tragedy.'

'Oh, we said it was Moran's work from the first, didn't we, Bell? It's just the line he's cut out for. I always think he ought to have a bowl and dagger. He looks like the villain on the stage.'

'On or off the stage he can support the principal part in that line most naturally,' says Starlight; 'but I prophesy he will be cut off in the midst of his glorious career. He's beastly cunning, but he'll be trapped yet.'

'It's a pity Jim can't stay a few days with us,' says Maddie; 'I believe we'd find a way of passing him on to Victoria. I've known more than one or two, or half-a-dozen either, that has been put through the same way.'

'For God's sake, Mad; lay me on!' says poor Jim, 'and I'll go on my knees to you.'

'Oh, I daresay,' says Maddie, looking saucy, 'but I like a man to be fond of some woman in a proper way, even if it isn't me; so I'll do what I can to help you to your wife and pickaninny.'

'We must get you into the police force, Maddie,' says Starlight, 'or make you a sort of inspector, unattached, if you're so clever at managing these little affairs. But what's the idea?'

'Well,' says she, settling herself in a chair, spreading out her dress, and looking very knowing, 'there's an old gentleman being driven all the way overland in a sort of light Yankee trap, and the young fellow that's driving has to find horses and feed 'em and get so much for the trip.'

'Who is it?' says I.

'Oh! you know him,' says Maddie, looking down, 'he's a great friend of mine, a steady-going, good-conducted chap, and he's a little —you understand—well, shook on me. I could persuade him a bit, that is——'

'I don't doubt that at all,' says I.

'Oh! you know him a little. He says he saw you at the Turon; he was working with some Americans. His name's Joe Moreton.'

'I remember him well enough; he used to wear a moustache and a chin beard, and talk Yankee. Only for that he was a good deal like Jim; we always said so.'

'Do you see anything now, Dick, you that's so sharp?' says Maddie.

'Bless my soul,' says Starlight, 'of course, it is as clear as your beautiful eyes. Jim is to shave his beard, talk like a Yankee, and go in Joe Moreton's place. I see it all. Maddie persuading Joe to consent to the exchange of duties.'

'But what will his employer say?'

'Oh! he's as bad as bad can be with the sandy blight,' says Maddie, 'wears green goggles, poor old gentleman. He'll never know nothing, and he'll be able to swear up for Jim if the police pull him anywhere this side of the Murray.'

We'd told Maddie that money needn't stand in the way, so she was to promise Joe the full sum that he was to get for his contract would be paid to him in cash that night—Jim to pay his own expenses as he went, the same as he was to do himself. Of course she could get the money from old Jonathan. A word from us then was worth a deal more than that'd come to. Money wasn't the worst thing we had to care about.

They would have to change clothes, and he'd tell Jim about the horses, the stages, and how to answer the old cove, and what to do to humour him as they went along. If he'd had his full eyesight he might have noticed some difference, but as it was, it was as much as the poor old chap, she believed, could see there was a driver at all. His eyes was bound up mostly; he had a big shade over 'em, and was half the night swabbing and poulticing, and putting lotion into 'em. He'd got sandy blight that bad it would take months to get right. Once you get a touch like that it's a terror, I can tell you. I've had it that bad myself I had to be led about.

After a lot of talking, that Jim was to try his luck as the Rev. Mr. Watson's coachman, he was mad to get away somehow, and such another chance might never turn up in a month of Sundays. He would have plenty of time to shave his beard and make himself look as like as ever he could to Joe Moreton. Maddie said she'd see after that, and it would be as good as a play. Lucky for old Jim we'd all taken a fancy at the Turon, for once in a way, to talk like Arizona Bill and his mates, just for the fun of the thing. There were so many Americans there at first, and they were such swells, with their silk sashes, bowie knives, and broad-leafed 'full-share' hats, that lots of the young native fellows took a pride in copying them, and could walk and talk and guess and calculate wonderful well considering. Besides, most of the natives have a sort of slow, sleepy way of talking, so it partly came natural to this chap, Joe Moreton, and Jim. There couldn't be a better chance, so we thought we'd stay a day and give Jim a send off all square and regular. It wasn't no ways too safe, but we wanted a bit of a jollification and we thought we'd chance it.

That night we had a regular good ball. The girls got some of the young fellows from round about to come over, and a couple or two other girls, and we had no end of fun. There was plenty of champagne, and even Jim picked up a bit; and what with being grateful to Maddie for giving him this lift, and better in spirits on the chance of seeing Jeanie again, he was more like his own self. Maddie said he looked so handsome she had half a mind to throw over Joe Moreton after all.

Joe came rather latish, and the old gentleman had a cup of tea and went to bed at once, leaving word for Joe that he wanted to start almost before daylight, or as soon as he could see to drive, so as to get half-way on their stage before the sun was hot.

After Joe had seen to his horses and put the trap away he came into the house and had a glass or two, and wired in with the rest of us like a good 'un. After a bit we see Maddie corner him off and have a long talk, very serious too. After that they went for a walk in the garden and was away a good while. When she came back she looked over at Jim and nodded, as much as to say, 'It's all right,' and I saw poor old Jim's face brighten up as if a light had passed over it.

By and by she came over and told us all about it. She'd had a hard matter to manage it, for Joe was a square sort of fellow, that had a place of his own, and at first didn't like the notion of being mixed up with our crowd at all. But he was regular shook on Maddie, and she went at him as only a woman can, and I dare say, though she didn't tell us, made it part of the bargain, if she was to marry him, to help Jim in this particular way. He was to be well paid for this journey by old Mr. Watson, and he wanted a bit of money before harvest or he wouldn't have taken the job at all.

The end of it was that Jim and Joe sat up ever so late, pretty well on to daylight, smoking and yarning, and Joe practising Jim in all the things he was to do and say, giving him a kind of chart of the stages, and telling him the sort of answers he was to give to the old chap. It was just before daylight when they knocked off, and then Joes goes and peels off his duds and hands 'em over to Jim, rough great-coat and all—up to his chin and down to his toes.

Joe takes Jim's togs. They fitted him all to pieces, and Jim hands him over his horse, saddle, revolver, and spurs, and tells him the old horse is a real plum, and he hopes he'll be good to him. Then Jim shakes hands with us all round. Blessed if the girls wasn't up too, and had some coffee smoking hot for us. 'We can sleep when you're all gone,' says Maddie, 'and perhaps we shan't see old Jim any more' (this was said when Joe was out of the room), 'so here's good luck; and when you've got your wife and child again don't forget Maddie Barnes.' Then she shook hands with him, and made a quick bolt to her own room. Queer things women are, my word.

When old Jim drove round to the front with the pair of horses, setting up square with his big coat and Joe's 'full-share' hat on him, we all bursted out laughing. He'd first of all gone to the old gentleman's room and sung out, 'All aboard, sir, time's up,' just to liven him up a bit. Joe kept away down at the stable.

Well, presently out comes the old chap, with a veil on and his green goggles, winkin' and blinkin' as if he couldn't see a door from a window. He drinks off a cup of coffee and takes a munch of bread and butter, makes a kind of bow to Bella, and shuffles into his carriage. Jim touches up the horses and away they go. We rose a bit of a cheer. Maddie waved her handkerchief out of the window. Jim looked round and raised his whip. That was the last sight any of us had of him for many a day. Poor old Jim!

CHAPTER XLI

We hadn't been long at home, just enough to get tired of doing nothing, when we got a letter from Bella Barnes, telling us that she was going to get married the day after the Turon races, and reminding Starlight that he had promised to come to her wedding. If he didn't think it was too risky, she hoped he'd come. There was going to be a race ball, and it was sure to be good fun. It would be a good wind-up, and Maddie was coming out a great swell. Sir Ferdinand would be there, but there'd be such a crowd anybody would pass muster, and so on.

'Yours sincerely,
'Isabella Barnes.

'P.S.—There was a big handicap, with 500 added; hadn't we a good horse enough?'

'Well done, Bella!' says Starlight. 'I vote we go, Dick. I never went to a hop with a price on my head before. A thousand pounds too! Quite a new sensation. It settles the question. And we'll enter Rainbow for the handicap. He ought to be good enough for anything they're likely to have.'

'Captain Starlight's Rainbow, 9 st. 8 lb.,' I said, 'with Dick Marston to lead him up to the judge's box. How will that wash? And what are the police going to be about all the time? Bella's gone out of her senses about her marriage and thinks we are too.'

'You're a good fellow, Richard, and staunch, but you're like your father—you haven't any imagination. I see half-a-dozen ways of doing the whole thing. Besides, our honour's concerned. I never made a promise yet, for good or for evil, that I didn't carry out, and some have cost me dearly enough, God knows. Fancy running our horses and going to the ball under the noses of the police—the idea is delicious!'

'I daresay you're about tired of your life,' I said. 'I'm pretty sure I am; but why we should ride straight into the lion's mouth, to please a silly girl, I can't see. I haven't over much sense, I know, or I shouldn't be here; but I'm not such a dashed fool as all that comes to.'

'My mind is made up, Richard—I have decided irrevocably. Of course, you needn't come, if you see objections; but I'll bet you my Dean and Adams revolver and the Navy Colt against your repeating rifle that I do all I've said, and clear out safe.'

'Done!' I said. 'I've no doubt you'll try; but you might as well try

to pull down the walls of Berrima Gaol with a hay-rake. You'll make
Sir Ferdinand's fortune, that's all. He always said he'd die happy
if he could only bag you and the Marstons. He'll be made Inspector-
General of Police.'

Starlight smiled in his queer, quiet way.

'If he doesn't rise to the top of the tree until he takes me—alive, I
mean—he'll die a sub-inspector. But we'd better sleep on it. This
is an enterprise of great pith and moment, and requires no end of
thought. We must get your sister to come over. That will crown
all.'

'Good-night,' I said, rather hasty. 'We'd better turn the Hollow
into Tarban Creek, and advertise for boarders.'

Next morning I expected he'd think better of it—we'd had a glass
or two of grog; but no, he was more set on it than ever, and full of
dodges to work it to rights. He certainly was wonderful clever in all
sorts of ways when there was any devilment to be carried out. Half
as much in the straight way would have made a man of him. But
that's the way of the world all over. He ain't the only one.

As for father, he was like me, and looked on the notion as rank
foolishness. He swore straight on end for about twenty minutes, and
then said he expected Starlight would have his own way as usual;
but he'd play at that game once too often. He supposed he'd be left
in the Hollow all by himself, with Warrigal and the dog for company.

'Warrigal goes with me—might want him,' says Starlight. 'You're
losing your nerve, governor. Perhaps you'd like to go to the ball
too?'

Father gave a sort of growl, and lit his pipe and wouldn't say no
more. Starlight and I regular talked it out, and, after I'd heard all
he had to say, it didn't look quite so impossible as it did at first. We
were to work apart. He was to get in with some of the betting men
or sporting people that always came to country races, and I was to
find out some of our old digger mates and box up with them.
Warrigal would shift for himself and look after the horses, and have
them ready in case we had to clear at short notice.

'And who was to enter Rainbow and look after him?'

'Couldn't we get old Jacob Benton; he's the best trainer I've seen
since I left home? Billy the Boy told us the other day he was out
of a job, and was groom at Jonathan's; had been sacked for getting
drunk, and so on. He'll be all the more likely to keep sober for a
month.'

'The very man,' I said. 'He can ride the weight, and train too.
But we can't have him here, surely!'

'No; but I can send the horse to him at Jonathan's, and he can
get him fit there as well as anywhere. There's nearly a month yet;
he's pretty hard, and he's been regularly exercise lately.'

Jack Benton was a wizened, dried-up old Yorkshireman. He'd

been head man in a good racing stable, but drink had been the ruin of him—lost him his place, and sent him out here. He could be trusted to go right through with a job like ours, for all that. Like many men that drink hard, he was as sober as a judge between one burst and another. And once he took over a horse in training he touched nothing but water till the race was run and the horse back in his box. Then he most times went in an awful perisher—took a month to it, and was never sober day or night the whole time. When he'd spent all his money he'd crawl out of the township and get away into the country more dead than alive, and take the first job that offered. But he was fonder of training a good horse than anything else in the world; and if he'd got a regular flyer, and was treated liberal, he'd hardly allow himself sleep or time to eat his meals till he'd got him near the mark. He could ride, too, and was an out-and-out judge of pace.

When we'd regular chalked it out about entering Rainbow for the Grand Turon Handicap, we sent Warrigal over to Billy the Boy, and got him to look up old Jacob. He agreed to take the old horse, the week before the races, and give him a last bit of French-polish if we'd keep him in steady work till then. From what he was told of the horse he expected he would carry any weight he was handicapped for and pull it off easy. He was to enter him in his own name, the proper time before the races. If he won he was to have ten per cent. on winnings; if he lost, a ten-pound note would do him. He could ride the weight with some lead in his saddle, and he'd never wet his lips with grog till the race was over.

So that part of the work was chalked out. The real risky business was to come. I never expected we should get through all straight. But the more I hung back the more shook on it Starlight seemed to be. He was like a boy home from school sometimes—mad for any kind of fun with a spice of devilment in it.

About a week before the races we all cleared out, leaving father at home, and pretty sulky too. Warrigal led Rainbow; he was to take him to Jonathan Barnes's, and meet old Jacob there. He was to keep him until it was time to go to Turon. We didn't show there ourselves this time; we were afraid of drawing suspicion on the place.

We rode right into Turon, taking care to be well after dark. A real pleasure it was to see the old place again. The crooked streets, the lighted-up shops, the crowd of jolly diggers walking about smoking, or crowding round the public-house bars, the row of the stampers in the quartz-crushing machines going night and day. It all reminded me of the pleasant year Jim and I had spent here. I wished we'd never had to leave it. We parted just outside the township for fear of accidents. I went to a little place I knew, where I put up my horse—could be quiet there, and asked no questions. Starlight, as usual, went to the best hotel, where he ordered everybody about and was as big a swell as ever. He had been out in the north-west coun-try, and was going to Sydney to close for a couple of stations that had been offered to him.

That night he went to the barber, had his hair cut and his beard shaved, only leaving his moustache and a bit of whisker like a ribbon. He put on a suit of tweed, all one colour, and ordered a lot more clothes, which he paid for, and were to be left at the hotel till he re-turned from Sydney.

Next day he starts for Sydney; what he was going to do there he didn't say, and I didn't ask him. He'd be back the day before the races, and in good time for all the fun, and Bella's wedding into the bargain. I managed to find out that night that Kate Mullockson had left Turon. She and her husband had sold their place and gone to another diggings just opened. I was glad enough of this, for I knew that her eyes were sharp enough to spy me out whatever disguise I had on; and even if she didn't I should always have expected to find her eyes fixed upon me. I breathed freer after I heard this bit of news.

The gold was better even than when we were there. A lot of men who were poor enough when we were there had made fortunes. The field never looked better, and the hard-driving, well-paid, jolly mining life was going on just the same as ever, every one making money fast—spending it faster—and no one troubling themselves about anything except how much the washdirt went to the load, and whether the sinking was through the false bottom or not.

When I first came I had a notion of mating in with some diggers, but when I saw how quiet everybody took it, and what thousands of strangers there were all over the place, I gave myself out for a speculator in mining shares from Melbourne. So I shaved off most of my beard, had my hair cut short, and put on a tall hat. I thought that would shift any sort of likeness there might be to my old self, and, though it was beastly uncomfortable, I stuck to it all the time.

I walked about among the stables and had a good look at all the horses that were in training. Two or three good ones, as usual, and a lot of duffers. If Rainbow wasn't beat on his condition, he had pace and weight-carrying for the best of them. I hardly thought he could lose it, or a bigger stake in better company. I was that fond of the horse I thought he was good enough for an English Derby.

Well, I kept dark, you be sure, and mooned about, buying a share at a low price now and then just to let 'em see I had money and meant something. My name was Mr. Bromford, and I lived at Peter-sham, near Sydney.

The day before the races there was a lot of excitement in the town. Strangers kept pouring in from everywhere round about, and all the hotels were crammed full. Just as I was wondering whether Star-light was going to turn up till next day I saw a four-in-hand drag rattle down the street to the principal inn, and a crowd gather round it as three gentlemen got out and went into the inn.

'You'll see after all our luggage, will you, ostler?' says one of them to the groom, 'and whatever you do don't forget my umbrella!'

Some of the diggers laughed.

'Know those coves?' I said to a man that stopped at the same house as I did.

'Don't you know? Them's the two Mr. Dawsons, of Wideview, great sporting men, natives, and ever so rich. They've some horses to run to-morrow. That's a new chum from England that's come up with 'em.'

I hardly knew him at first. His own mother wouldn't, I believe. He'd altered himself that wonderful as I could hardly even now think it was Starlight; and yet he wasn't a bit like the young Englishman he gammoned to be last year, or the Hon. Frank Haughton either. He had an eyeglass this time, and was a swell from top to toe. How and when he'd picked up with the Mr. Dawsons I couldn't tell; but he'd got a knack of making people like him—especially when they didn't know him. Not that it was worse when they did. It wasn't for that. He was always the same. The whitest man I ever knew, or ever shall—that I say and stick to—but of course people can't be expected to associate with men that have 'done time.' Well, next day was the races. I never saw such a turn-out in the colony before. Every digger on the field had dropped work for the day; all the farmers, and squatters, and country people had come in for miles round on all sides. The Commissioner and all the police were out in full uniform, and from the first moment the hotels were opened in the morning till breakfast time all the bars were full, and the streets crowded with miners and strangers and people that seemed to have come from the ends of the earth. When I saw the mob there was I didn't see so much to be jerran about, as it was fifty to one in favour of any one that was wanted, in the middle of such a muster of queer cattle as was going on at Turon that day.

About eleven o'clock every one went out to the course. It wasn't more than a mile from town. The first race wasn't to be run till twelve; but long before that time the road was covered with horsemen, traps of every kind and sort, every horse and mare in the whole district.

Most of the miners went in four-horse coaches and 'buses that were plying all day long from the town and back; very few walked. The country people mostly drove in springcarts, or rode on horseback. Any young fellows that had a good horse liked to show him off, of course; the girls in habits of their own make, perhaps, and now and then a top hat, though they looked very well too. They could ride, some of them, above a bit, and it made me think of the old days when Jim and I and Aileen used to ride into Bargo races together, and how proud we were of her, even when she was a little thing, and we used to groom up the old pony till we nearly scrubbed the hide off him.

It was no use thinking of that kind of thing, and I began to wonder how Starlight was getting on with his friends, when I saw the Dawsons' drag come up the straight, with four upstanding, ripping bay horses in top condition, and well matched. There was Starlight on the box seat, alongside of Jack Dawson, the eldest brother, who could handle the ribbons in style, and was a man every inch of him, only a bit too fast; didn't care about anything but horses and dogs, and lived every day of his life. The other brother was standing up behind, leaning over and talking to Starlight, who was 'in great form,' as he used to say himself, and looked as if he'd just come out of a bandbox.

He had on a silk coat buttoned round him, a white top hat with a blue silk veil. His eyeglass was stuck in his eye all the time, and he had kid gloves on that fitted his hands like wax. I really couldn't hardly take my oath he was the same man, and no wonder nobody else couldn't. I was wondering why Sir Ferdinand wasn't swelling about, bowing to all the ladies, and making that thoroughbred of his dance and arch his neck, when I heard some one say that he'd got news that Moran and the rest of 'em had stuck up a place about forty miles off, towards Forbes, and Sir Ferdinand had sworn at his luck for having to miss the races; but started off just as he was, and taken all the troopers but two with him.

'Who brought the news?'

'Oh! a youngster called William Jones—said he lived out there. A black boy, came with him that couldn't hardly speak English; he went with 'em to show the way.'

'Well, but how did they know it was true?' says I. 'It might have been only a stall.'

'Oh, the young fellow brought a letter from the overseer, saying they might hold out for a few hours, if the police came along quick.'

'It's a good thing they started at once,' says I. 'Them boys are very useful sometimes, and blackfellows too.'

I went off then, and had a laugh to myself. I was pretty middling certain it was Billy the Boy and Warrigal. Starlight had wrote the note before we started, only I didn't think they'd be game to deliver it themselves.

Now the police was away, all but a couple of young fellows—I went and had a look to make sure—that didn't know any of us by sight, I thought we might enjoy ourselves for once in a way without watching every one that came nigh us. And we did enjoy ourselves. I did, I know; though you'd think, as we carried our lives in our hands, in a manner of speaking, the fun couldn't have been much. But it's a queer world! Men like us, that don't know what's to happen to them from one day to another, if they can only see their way for a week ahead, often have more real pleasure in the bit of time they have to themselves than many a man has in a year that has no call to care about time or money or be afraid of anybody.

As for Starlight, if he'd been going to be hung next week it would have been all one to him. He'd have put off thinking about it until about an hour before, and then would have made all his arrangements and done the whole business quietly and respectably, without humbug, but without any flashness either. You couldn't put him wrong, or make him do or say anything that was out of place.

However, this time nobody was going to be hung or took or anything else. We'd as good as got a free pardon for the time being, now the police was away; no one else would have meddled with us if we'd had our names printed on our hats. So we made the most of it, I expect. Starlight carried on all sorts of high ropes. He was introduced to all the nobs, and I saw him in the grandstand and the saddling paddock, taking the odds in tens and fifties from the ringmen —he'd brought a stiffish roll of notes with him—and backing the Dawson stable right out.

It turned out afterwards that he'd met them at an inn on the mountains, and helped them to doctor one of their leaders that had been griped. So they took a fancy to him, and, being free-hearted sort of fellows, asked him to keep them company in the drag, and let one of the grooms ride his horse. Once he started he kept them alive, you may be sure, and by the time they got to Turon they were ready to go round the world with him, and swore they'd never met such a man in their lives—very likely they hadn't either. He was introduced to the judge and the stewards and the Commissioner and the police magistrate, and as much fuss made over him as if he was the Governor's son. It was as good as a play. I got up as near as I dared once or twice, and I couldn't hardly keep from bursting out laughing when I saw how grave he talked and drawled and put up his eyeglass, and every now and then made 'em all laugh, or said something reminded him of India, where he'd last come from.

Well, that was a regular fizzer of a spree, if we never had another. The racing was very fair, and, as luck would have it, the Dawson horses won all the big money, and, as they started at longish odds, they must have made a pot of money, and Starlight too, as he'd gone in for a docker for their stable. This made them better friends than ever, and it was Dawson here and Lascelles there all over the course.

Well, the day went over at last, and all of them that liked a little fun and dancing better than heavy drinking made it up to go to the race ball. It was a subscription affair—guinea tickets, just to keep out the regular roughs, and the proceeds to go to the Turon Jockey Club Fund. All the swells had to go, of course, and, though they knew it would be a crush and pretty mixed, as I heard Starlight say, the room was large, the band was good, and they expected to get a fair share of dancing after an hour or so.

Starlight and the Dawsons dined at the camp, and were made a good deal of—their health drunk and what not—and Starlight told us afterwards he returned thanks for the strangers and visitors; said he'd been told Australia was a rough place, but he never expected to find so much genuine kindness and hospitality and, he might add, so much refinement and gentlemanly feeling. Speaking for himself, he had never expected, considering his being a total stranger, to be welcomed so cordially and entertained so handsomely, more particularly at the mess of her Majesty's goldfields officials, whose attention on this occasion they might be assured he would never forget. He would repeat, the events of this particular day would never be effaced from his memory. (Tremendous cheering.)

After dinner, and when the champagne had gone round pretty reasonable, the Commissioner proposed they should all adjourn to the ball, when, if Mr. Lascelles cared about dancing, he ventured to think a partner or two could be found for him. So they all got up and went away down to the hall of the Mechanics' Institute—a tremendous big room that had been built to use as a theatre, and to give lectures and concerts in. These sort of things are very popular at diggings. Miners like to be amused, and have plenty of money to spend when times are good. There was hardly a week passed without some kind of show being on when we went there.

I walked down quietly an hour or so before most of the people, so as to be in the way to see if Aileen came. We'd asked her to come on the chance of meeting us there, but we hadn't got any word, and didn't know whether she could manage it nor whether George would bring her. I had a sort of half-and-half notion that perhaps Gracey might come, but I didn't like to think of it for fear of being disappointed, and tried to make believe I didn't expect her.

I gave in my ticket and walked in about eight o'clock, and sat down pretty close to the door so that I could see the people as they came in. I didn't feel much up to dancing myself, but I'd have ridden a thousand miles to have had the chance of seeing those two girls that night.

I waited and waited while one after another came in, till the big hall was pretty near filled, and at nine o'clock or so the music struck up, and the first dance began. That left the seats pretty bare, and between listening to the music and looking at the people, and thinking I was back again at the old claim and passing half-an-hour at a dance-house, I didn't mind the door so much till I heard somebody give a sort of sigh not very far off, and I looked towards the door and saw two women sitting between me and it.

They were Aileen and Gracey sure enough. My head almost turned round, and I felt my heart beat—beat in a way it never did when the bullets were singing and whistling all about. It was the suddenness of it, I expect. I looked at them for a bit. They didn't see me, and were just looking about them as I did. They were dressed very quiet, but Gracey had a little more ornament on her, and a necklace or something round her neck. Aileen was very pale, but her beautiful dark hair was dressed up a bit with one rosebud in it, and her eyes looked bigger and brighter than they used to do. She looked sad enough, but every now and then Gracey said something that made her smile a bit, and then I thought she was the handsomest girl in the room. Gracey had just the same steady, serious, kind face as ever; she'd hardly changed a bit, and seemed pleased, just like a child at the play, with all that was going on round about.

There was hardly anybody near the corner where they were, so I got up and went over. They both looked at me for a minute as if they'd never seen me before, and then Aileen turned as pale as death, and Gracey got altogether as red, and both held out their hands. I sat down by the side of Aileen, and we all began to talk. Not much at first, and very quiet, for fear notice might be taken, but I managed to let them know that the police had all been called off in another direction, and that we should be most likely safe till to-morrow or next day.

'Oh, dear!' says Gracey, 'wasn't it awfully rash of you to come here and run all this risk just to come to Bella Barnes's wedding? I believe I ought to be jealous of that girl.'

'All Starlight's fault,' I said; 'but anyhow, it's through him we've had this meeting here. I was dead against coming all the time, and I never expected things to turn out so lucky as they have done.'

'Will he be here to-night?' Aileen says, very soft and timid like. 'I almost wished I'd stayed away, but Gracey here would come. Young Cyrus Williams brought us. He wanted to show his wife the races and take her to the ball. There they are, dancing together. George is away at the races.'

'You will see Starlight about ten or eleven o'clock, I expect,' I said. 'He's dining with the Commissioner and the camp officers. They'll all come together, most likely.'

'Dining at the camp!' says Aileen, looking regularly perished. 'You don't mean to say they've taken him?'

'I mean what I say. He's here with the Mr. Dawsons, of Wideview, and has been hand-and-glove with all the swells. I hardly think you'll know him. It's as much as I did.'

Poor Aileen gave another sigh.

'Do you think he'll know me?' she says. 'Oh! what a foolish girl I was to think for a moment that he could care about a girl like me. Oh! I wish I had never come.'

'Nonsense,' says Gracey, who looked a deal brighter on it. 'Why, if he's the man you say he is, this will only bring him out a bit. What do you think, Di—' I mean Mr. Jones?'

'That's right, Miss Storefield,' says I. 'Keep to the company manners to-night. We don't know who may be listening; but I'm not much afraid of being bowled out this particular night. Somehow I feel ready to chance everything for an hour's happiness like this.'

Gracey said nothing, but looked down, and Aileen kept turning towards the door as if she half hoped and was half afraid of seeing him come in. By and by we heard someone say, 'Here comes the Commissioner; all the camp will be here now,' and there was a bit of a move to look at them as they came in.

CHAPTER XLII

A GOOD many gentlemen and ladies that lived in the town and in the diggings, or near it, had come before this and had been dancing away and enjoying themselves, though the room was pretty full of diggers and all sorts of people. But as everybody was quiet and well behaved, it didn't make much odds who was there.

But, of course, the Commissioner was the great man of the whole place, and the principal visitors, like the Mr. Dawsons and some others, were bound to come along with him. Then there were the other Government officers, the bankers and surveyors, lawyers and doctors, and so on. All of them took care to come a little late with their wives and families so as to be in the room at the same time as the swell lot.

Bella Barnes was going to marry a surveyor, a wildish young fellow, but a good one to work as ever was. She was going to chance his coming straight afterwards. He was a likely man to rise in his office, and she thought she'd find a way to keep him out of debt and drinking and gambling too.

Well, in comes the Commissioner and his friends, very grand indeed, all dressed like swells always do in the evening, I believe, black all over, white tie, shining boots, white kid gloves, flower in their buttonhole, all regular. People may laugh, but they did look different from the others—showed more blood like. I don't care what they say, there is such a thing.

Close by the Commissioner, laughing and talking, was the two Mr. Dawsons; and—I saw Aileen give a start—who should come next, cheek by jowl with the police magistrate, whom he'd been making laugh with something he'd said as they came in, but Starlight himself, looking like a regular prince—their pictures anyhow—and togged out to the nines like all the rest of 'em. Aileen kept looking at him as he lounged up the ballroom, and I thought she'd fall down in a faint or bring herself to people's notice by the wild, earnest, sad way she looked at him. However he'd got his clothes and the rest of it that fitted him like as if they'd been grown for him, I couldn't think. But of course he'd made all that right when he went to Sydney, and had 'em sent up with his luggage in Mr. Dawson's drag.

Though he didn't seem to notice anything, I saw that he knew us. He looked round for a moment, and smiled at Aileen.

'That's a pretty girl,' he said to one of the young fellows; 'evidently from the country. I must get introduced to her.'

'Oh, we'll introduce you,' says the other man. 'They're not half bad fun, these bush girls, some of them.'

Well, a new dance was struck up by the band just after they'd got up to the top of the room, and we saw Starlight taken up and introduced to a grand lady, the wife of the head banker. The Commissioner and some of the other big wigs danced in the same quadrille. We all moved a bit higher to get a good look at him. His make-up was wonderful. We could hardly believe our eyes. His hair was a deal shorter than he ever wore it (except in one place), and he'd shaved nearly all but his moustache. That was dark brown and heavy. You couldn't see his mouth except when he smiled, and then his teeth were as white as Warrigal's nearly and as regular. There was a softness, too, about his eyes when he was in a good temper and enjoying himself that I hardly ever saw in a man's face. I could see Aileen watching him when he talked to this lady and that, and sometimes she looked as if she didn't enjoy it.

He was only waiting his chance, though, for after he'd had a dance or two we saw him go up to one of the stewards. They had big rosettes on, and presently they walked round to us, and the steward asked the favour of Aileen's name, and then begged, by virtue of his office, to present Lieutenant Lascelles, a gentleman lately from India, who had expressed a wish to be introduced to her. Such a bow Starlight made, too. We could hardly help staring. Poor Aileen hardly knew whether to laugh or to cry when he sat down beside her and asked for the pleasure of a dance.

She wouldn't do that. She only came there to see him, she said, and me; but he persuaded her to walk round the room, and then they slipped into one of the supper-rooms, where they were able to talk without being disturbed, and say what they had in their hearts. I got Gracey to take a turn with me, and we were able to have our little say. She was, like Aileen, miserable enough and afraid to think of our ever having the chance of getting married and living happy like other people, but she told me she would wait and remain faithful to me—if it was to her life's end—and that as soon as I could get away from the country and promise her to leave our wild lives behind she was ready to join us and follow me all over the world. Over and over again she tried to persuade me to get away like Jim, and said how happy he was now, and how much better it was than stopping where we were and running terrible risks every day and every hour. It was the old story over again; but I felt better for it, and really meant to try and cut loose from all this cross work. We hadn't too much time. Aileen was fetched back to her seat, and then Starlight went off to his friends at the other end of the room, and was chaffed for flirting with a regular currency lass by one of the Dawsons.

'I admire his taste,' says the Commissioner. 'I really think she's the prettiest girl in the room if she was well dressed and had a little more animation. I wonder who she is? What's her name, Lascelles? I suppose you know all about her by this time.'

'Her name is Martin, or Marston, or some such name,' answered Starlight, quite cool and pleasant. 'Deuced nice, sensible girl, painfully quiet, though. Wouldn't dance, though, at all, and talked very little.'

'By jove! I know who she is,' says one of the young chaps. 'That's Aileen Marston, sister to Dick and Jim. No wonder she isn't over lively. Why, she has two brothers bush-rangers, regular out-and-outers. There's a thousand on each of their heads.'

'Good gad!' says Starlight; 'you don't say so! Poor girl! What a most extraordinary country! You meet with surpwises every day, don't you?'

'It's a pity Sir Ferdinand isn't here,' said the Commissioner. 'I believe she's an acquaintance of his. I've always heard she was a splendid girl, though, poor thing, frets to death about her family. I think you seem to have cheered her up, though, Lascelles. She doesn't look half so miserable as she did an hour ago.'

'Naturally, my dear fellow,' says Starlight, pulling his moustache; 'even in this savage country—beg your pardon—one's old form seems to be appreciated. Pardon me, I must regain my partner; I am engaged for this dance.'

'You seem disposed to make the most of your opportunities,' says the Commissioner. 'Dawson, you'll have to look after your friend. Who's the enslaver now?'

'I didn't quite catch her name,' says Starlight, lazily; 'but it's that tall girl near the pillar, with the pale face and dark eyes.'

'You're not a bad judge for a new chum,' says one of the goldfield subs. 'Why, that's Maddie Barnes. I think she's the pick of all the down-the-river girls, and the best dancer here, out-and-out. Her sister's to be married to-morrow, and we're all going to see her turned off.'

'Really, now?' says Starlight, putting up his eyeglass. 'I begin to think I must write a book. I'm falling upon adventures hourly. Oh, the "Morgen-blatter." What a treat! Can she valse, do you think?'

'You try her,' says the young fellow. 'She's a regular stunner.'

It was a fine, large room, and the band, mostly Germans, struck up some outlandish queer sort of tune that I'd never heard anything like before; whatever it was it seemed to suit most of the dancing people, for the floor was pretty soon full up, and everybody twisting round and round as if they were never going to stop. But, to my mind, there was not a couple there that was a patch on Maddie and Starlight. He seemed to move round twice as light and easy as any one else; he looked somehow different from all the others. As for Maddie, wherever she picked it up, she went like a bird, with a free, springy sort of sliding step, and all in time to the music, anybody could see. After a bit some of the people sat down, and I could hear them passing their remarks and admiring both of 'em till the music stopped. I couldn't make out whether Aileen altogether liked it or not; anyhow she didn't say anything.

About an hour afterwards the camp party left the room, and took Starlight with them. Some one said there was a little loo and hazard at the Commissioner's rooms. Cyrus Williams was not in a hurry to go home, or his young wife either, so I stayed and walked about with the two girls, and we had ever so much talk together, and enjoyed ourselves for once in a quiet way. A good crowd was sure to be at Bella Barnes's wedding next day. It was fixed for two o'clock, so as not to interfere with the races. The big handicap was to be run at three, so we should be able to be at the church when Bella was turned off, and see Rainbow go for the great race of the day afterwards. When that was run we intended to clear. It would be time for us to go then. Things were middling straight, but it mightn't last.

Next day was the great excitement of the meeting. The 'big money' was all in the handicap, and there was a big field, with two or three cracks up from Sydney, and a very good local horse that all the diggers were sweet on. It was an open race, and every man that had a note or a fiver laid it out on one horse or another.

Rainbow had been entered in proper time and all regular by old Jacob, under the name of Darkie, which suited in all ways. He was a dark horse, sure enough; dark in colour, and dark enough as to his performances—nobody knew much about them. We weren't going to enter him in his right name, of course.

Old Jacob was a queer old fellow in all his ways and notions, so we couldn't stable him in any of the stables in Turon, for fear of his being 'got at,' or something. So when I wanted to see him the day before, the old fellow grinned, and took me away about a mile from the course; and there was old Rainbow, snug enough—in a tent, above all places!—but as fine as a star, and as fit as ever a horse was brought to the post.

'What's the fun of having him under canvas?' I said. 'Who ever heard of a horse being trained in a tent before?—not but what he looks first-chop.'

'I've seen horses trained in more ways than one,' says he, 'and I can wind 'em up, in the stable and out of it, as mighty few in this country can—that is, when I put the muzzle on. There's a deal in knowing the way horses is brought up. Now this here's an excitable hoss in a crowd.'

'Is he?' I said. 'Why he's as cool and steady as an old trooper when——'

'When powder's burning and bullets is flying,' says the old chap, grinning again; 'but this here's a different crowd. When he's got a training saddle and seven or eight stone up, and there's two or three hundred horses rattling about this side on him and that, it brings out the old racehorse feeling that's in his blood, and never had a chance to show itself afore.'

'I see, and so you want to keep him quiet till the last minute?'

'That's just it,' says he; 'I've got the time to a second'—here he pulls out a big old turnip of a silver watch—'and I'll have him up just ready to be weighed out last. I never was late in my life.'

'All right,' I said, 'but don't draw it too fine. Have you got your weight all right?'

'Right to a hounce,' says he; 'nine stun four they've put on him, and him an untried horse. I told 'em it was weighting him out of the race, but they laughed at me. Never you mind, though, he can carry weight and stay too. My ten per cent.'s as safe as the bank. He'll put the stuns on all them nobs, too, that think a race-horse must always come out of one of their training stables.'

'Well, good-bye, old man,' says I, 'and good luck. One of us will come and lead you into the weighing yard, if you pull it off, and chance the odds, if Sir Ferdinand himself was at the gate.'

'All right,' says he, 'I'll look out for you,' and off he goes. I went back and told Aileen and Gracey, and we settled that they were to drive out to the course with Cyrus Williams and his wife. I rode, thinking myself safer on horseback, for fear of accidents. Starlight, of course, went in the Dawsons' drag, and was going to enjoy himself to the last minute. He had his horse ready at a moment's notice, and Warrigal was not far off to give warning, or to bring up his horse if we had to ride for it.

Well, the first part of the day went well enough, and then about half-past one we all went down to the church. The young fellow that was to marry Bella Barnes was known on the field and well liked by the miners, so a good many of them made it up to go and see the wedding. They'd heard of Bella and Maddie, and wanted to see what they looked like.

The church was on the side of the town next the racecourse, so they hadn't far to go. By and by, as the crowd moved that way, Starlight says to the Commissioner—

'Where are all these good folks making for?'

'Why, the fact is there's to be a wedding,' he says, 'and it excites a good deal of attention, as the young people are well known on the field and popular. Bella Barnes and her sister are very fine girls in their way. Suppose we go and look on too! There won't be anything now before the big race.'

'By Jove! a first-rate ideah,' says Starlight. 'I should like to see an Australian wedding above all things.'

'This will be the real thing, then,' says Mr. Jack Dawson. 'Let's drive up to our hotel, put up the horses, have a devil and a glass of champagne, and we can be back easy in time for the race.' So away they went. Cyrus drove the girls and his wife in his dogcart, so we were there all ready to see the bride come up.

It looked a regular grand affair, my word. The church was that crammed there was hardly a place to sit or stand in. Every woman, young and old, in the countryside was there, besides hundreds of diggers who sat patiently waiting, as if some wonderful show were going to take place. Aileen and Gracey had come in early and got a pew next to the top almost. I stood outside. There was hardly a chance for any one else to get in.

By and by up comes old Jonathan, driving a respectable-looking carriage, with his wife and Bella and Maddie all in white silk and satin, and looking splendid. Out he gets, and takes Bella to walk up the middle of the church. When he went in with Bella, Maddie had one look in, and it seemed so crammed full of people that she looked frightened and drew back. Just then up comes the Mr. Dawsons and Starlight, with the Commissioner and a few more.

Directly he sees Maddie draw back, Starlight takes the whole thing in, and walked forward.

'My dear young lady,' says he, 'will you permit me to escort you up the aisle? The bride appears to have preceded you.'

He offered her his arm, and, if you'll believe me, the girl didn't know him a bit in the world, and stared at him like a perfect stranger.

'It's all right, Miss Maddie,' says the Commissioner. He had a way of knowing all the girls, as far as a laugh or a bit of chaff went, especially if they were good-looking. 'Mr. Lascelles is an English gentleman, newly arrived, and a friend of mine. He's anxious to learn Australian ways.'

She took his arm then and walked on, never looking at him, but quite shy-like, till he whispered a word in her ear which brought more colour into her face than any one had seen there before for a year.

'My word, Lascelles knows how to talk to 'em,' says Jack Dawson. 'He's given that girl a whip that makes her brighten up. What a chap he is; you can't lick him.'

'Pretty fair all round, I should say,' says the other brother, Bill. 'Hullo! are we to go on the platform with the parson and the rest of 'em?'

The reason was that as we went up the church all together, all in a heap, with the Barneses and the bride, they thought we must be related to 'em; and the church, being choke-full, they shunted us on to the place inside the rails, where we found ourselves drafted into the small yard with the bridegroom, the bride, the parson, and all that mob.

There wasn't much time to spare, what with the racing and the general bustle of the day. The miners gave a sort of buzz of admiration as Bella and Maddie and the others came up the aisle. They looked very well, there's no manner of doubt. They were both tallish girls, slight, but well put together, and had straight features and big bright eyes, with plenty of fun and meaning in 'em. All they wanted was a little more colour like, and between the hurry for time and Bella getting married, a day's work that don't come often in any one's life, and having about a thousand people to look at 'em, both the girls were flushed up a good deal. It set them off first-rate. I never saw either of them look so handsome before. Old Barnes had come down well for once, and they were dressed in real good style—hadn't overdone it neither.

When the tying-up fakement was over everything went off first-rate. The bridegroom was a hardy-looking, upstanding young chap that looked as if work was no trouble to him. Next to a squatter I think a Government surveyor's the best billet going. He can change about from one end of the district to another. He has a good part of his time the regular free bush life, with his camp and his men, and the harder he works the more money he makes. Then when he comes back to town he can enjoy himself and no mistake. He is not tied to regular hours like other men in the service, and can go and come when he likes pretty well. Old Barnes would be able to give Bella and her sister a tidy bit of money some day, and if they took care they'd be comfortable enough off after a few years. He might have looked higher, but Bella would make any man she took to a slashing good wife, and so she did him. So the parson buckles them to, and the last words were said. Starlight steps forward and says, 'I believe it's the custom in all circles to salute the bride, which I now do,' and he gave Bella a kiss before every one in the most high and mighty and respectful manner, just as if he was a prince of the blood. At the same time he says, 'I wish her every happiness and good fortune in her married life, and I beg of her to accept this trifling gift as a souvenir of the happy occasion.' Then he pulls off a ring from his little finger and slips it on hers. The sun glittered on it for a moment. We could see the stones shine. It was a diamond ring, every one could see. Then the Commissioner steps forward and begs to be permitted the same privilege, which made Bella laugh and blush a bit. Directly after Mr. Chanewood, who had stood quiet enough alongside of his wife, tucked her arm inside of his and walked away down the church, as if he thought this kind of thing was well enough in its way, but couldn't be allowed to last all day.

When they got into the carriage and drove off the whole church was cleared, and they got such a cheer as you might have heard at Tambaroora. The parson was the only living soul left near the building in five minutes. Everybody was in such a hurry to get back to the course and see the big race of the meeting.

Starlight slipped away in the crowd from his two friends, and managed to get a quiet few minutes with me and Gracey and Aileen; she was scolding him between jest and earnest for the kissing business, and said she thought he was going to leave off these sort of attentions to other girls.

'Not that she knew you at first, a bit in the world,' Aileen said. 'I watched her face pretty close, and I'm sure she thought you were some grand gentleman, a friend of the Commissioner's and the Mr. Dawsons.'

'My dearest girl,' said he, 'it was a promise I made months since that I should attend Bella's wedding, and I never break my word, as I hope you will find. These girls have been good friends and true to us in our need. We all owe them much. I don't suppose we shall cross each other's path again.'

There wasn't much more time. We both had to move off. He had just time to catch his drag, and I had to get my horse. The Dawsons bullied him a bit for keeping them waiting, and swore he had stayed behind to flirt with some of the girls in the church after the wedding was over.

'You're not to be trusted when there's temptation going,' Jack Dawson said. 'Saw you talking to that Marston girl. If you don't mind you'll have your head knocked off. They're a rum lot to deal with, I can tell you.'

'I must take care of myself,' he said, laughing. 'I have done so in other lands, and I suppose yours is no exception.'

'This is a dashed queer country in some ways, and with deuced strange people in it, too, as you'll find by the time you've had your colonial experience,' says Bill Dawson; 'but there goes the saddling-bell!'

The course had 20,000 people on it now if there was one. About a dozen horses stood stripped for the race, and the betting men were yelling out the odds as we got close enough to the stand to hear them. We had a good look at the lot. Three or four good-looking ones among them, and one or two flyers that had got in light as usual. Rainbow was nowhere about. Darkie was on the card, but no one seemed to know where he was or anything about him. We expected he'd start at 20 to 1, but somehow it leaked out that he was entered by old Jacob Benton, and that acted as a damper on the layers of the odds. 'Old Jake's generally there or thereabouts. If he's a duffer, it's the first one he's brought to the post. Why don't the old varmint show up?'

This was what I heard about and round, and we began to get uneasy ourselves, for fear that something might have happened to him or the horse. About 8 or 9 to 1 was all we could get, and that we took over and over again.

As the horses came up the straight, one after the other, having their pipe-openers, you'd have thought no race had been run that week, to see the interest all the people took in it. My word, Australia is a horsey country, and no mistake. With the exception of Arabia, perhaps, as they tell us about, I can't think as there's a country on the face of the earth where the people's fonder of horses. From the time they're able to walk, boys and girls, they're able to ride, and ride well. See the girls jump on bare-backed, with nothing but a gunny-bag under 'em, and ride over logs and stones, through scrub and forest, down gullies, or along the side of a mountain. And a horse race, don't they love it? Wouldn't they give their souls almost—and they do often enough—for a real flyer, a thoroughbred, able to run away from everything in a country race. The horse is a fatal animal to us natives, and many a man's ruin starts from a bit of horse-flesh not honestly come by.

But our racing ain't going forward, and the day's passing fast. As I said, everybody was looking at the horses—coming along with the rush of the thoroughbred when he's 'on his top' for condition; his coat like satin, and his legs like iron. There were lots of the bush girls on horseback, and among them I soon picked out Maddie Barnes. She was dressed in a handsome habit and hat. How she'd had time to put them on since the wedding I couldn't make out, but women manage to dress faster sometimes than others. She'd wasted no time anyhow.

She was mounted on a fine, tall, upstanding chestnut, and Joe Moreton was riding alongside of her on a good-looking bay, togged out very superior also. Maddie was in one of her larking humours, and gave Joe quite enough to do to keep time with her.

'I don't see my horse here yet,' she says to Joe, loud enough for me to hear; but she knew enough not to talk to me or pretend to know me. 'I want to back him for a fiver. I hope that old Jacob hasn't gone wrong.'

'What do you call your horse?' says Joe. 'I didn't know your father had one in this race.'

'No fear,' says Maddie; 'only this horse was exercised for a bit near our place. He's a regular beauty, and there isn't a horse in this lot fit to see the way he goes.'

'Who does he belong to?' says Joe.

'That's a secret at present,' says she; 'but you'll know some day, when you're a bit older, if you behave yourself. He's Mr. Jacob Benton's Darkie now, and you bet on him to the coat on your back.'

'I'll see what I think of him first,' says Joe, who didn't fancy having a horse rammed down his throat like that.

'If you don't like him you don't like me,' says Maddie. 'So mind that, Joe Moreton.'

Just as she spoke there was a stir in the crowd, and old Jacob came along across the course leading a horse with a sheet on, just as easy-going as if he'd a day to spare. One of the stewards rode up to him, and asked him what he meant by being so late.

The old chap pulls out his watch. 'You'll stick to your advertised time, won't you? I've time to weigh, time to pull off this here sheet and my overcoat, time to mount, and a minute to spare. I never was late in my life, governor.'

Most of the riding mob was down with the racehorses, a distance or so from the stand, where they was to start, the course being over two miles. So the weighing yard and stand was pretty well empty, which was just what old Jacob expected.

The old man walks over to the scales and has himself weighed all regular, declaring a pound overweight for fear of accidents. He gets down as quiet and easy as possible to the starting point, and just in time to walk up steadily with the other horses, when down goes the starter's flag, and 'Off' was the word. Starlight and the Dawsons were down there waiting for him. As they went away one of the ringmen says, 'Ten to one against Darkie. I lay Darkie.' 'Done,' says Starlight; 'will you do it in tens?' 'All right,' says the 'book.' 'I'll take you,' says both the Dawsons, and he entered their names.

They'd taken all they could get the night before at the hotel; and as no one knew anything about Darkie, and he had top weight, he hadn't many backers.

CHAPTER XLIII

Mr. Dawson drove pretty near the stand then, and they all stood up in the drag. I went back to Aileen and Gracey Storefield. We were close by the winning post when they came past; they had to go another time round.

The Sydney horses were first and second, the diggers' favourite third; but old Rainbow, lying well up, was coming through the ruck hard held and looking full of running. They passed close by us. What a sight it is to see a dozen blood horses in top condition come past you like a flash of lightning! How their hoofs thunder on the level turf! How the jockeys' silk jackets rustle in the wind they make! How muscles and sinew strain as they pretty near fly through the air! No wonder us young fellows, and the girls, too, feel it's worth a year of their lives to go to a good race. Yes, and will to the world's end. 'O you darling Rainbow!' I heard Aileen say. 'Are you going to win this race and triumph over all these grand horses? What a sight it will be! I didn't think I could have cared for a race so much.'

It didn't seem hardly any time before they were half-way round again, and the struggle was on, in good downright earnest. One of the Sydney horses began to shake his tail. The other still kept the lead. Then the Turon favourite—a real game pebble of a little horse—began to show up.

'Hotspur, Hotspur! No. Bronzewing has it—Bronzewing. It's Bronzewing's race. Turon for ever!' the crowd kept yelling.

'Oh! look at Rainbow!' says Aileen. And just then, at the turn, old Jacob sat down on him. The old horse challenged Bronzewing, passed him, and collared Hotspur. 'Darkie! Darkie!' shouts everybody. 'No! Hotspur—Darkie's coming—Darkie—Darkie! I tell yer Darkie.' And as old Jacob made one last effort, and landed him a winner by a clear head, there was a roar went up from the whole crowd that might have been heard at Nulla Mountain.

Starlight jumps off the drag and leads the old horse into the weighing yard. The steward says 'Dismount.' No fear of old Jacob getting down before he heard that. He takes his saddle in his lap and gets into the scales. 'Weight,' says the clerk. Then the old fellow mounts and rides past the judge's box. 'I declare Mr. Benton's horse Darkie to be the winner of the Turon Grand Handicap, Bronzewing second horse, Hotspur third,' says he.

Well, there was great cheering and hollering, though none knew exactly whose horse he was or anything about him; but an Australian crowd always likes to see the best horse win—and they like fair play—so Darkie was cheered over and over again, and old Jacob too.

Aileen stroked and petted him and patted his neck and rubbed his nose, and you'd raly thought the old horse knew her, he seemed so gentle-like. Then the Commissioner came down and said Mrs. Hautley, the police magistrate's wife, and some other ladies wanted to see the horse that had won the race. So he was taken over there and admired and stroked till old Jacob got quite crusty.

'It's an odd thing, Dawson,' says the Commissioner, 'nobody here knows this horse; where he was bred, or anything about him. Such a grand animal as he is, too! I wish Morringer could have seen him; he's always raving about horses. How savage he'll be to have missed all the fun!'

'He's a horse you don't see every day,' says Bill Dawson. 'I'll give a couple of hundred for him right off.'

'Not for sale at present,' says old Jacob, looking like a cast-iron image. 'I'll send ye word when he is.'

'All right,' says Mr. Dawson. 'What a shoulder, what legs, what loins he has! Ah! well, he'll be weighted out now, and you will be glad to sell him soon.'

'Our heads won't ache then,' says Jacob, as he turns round and rides away.

'Very neat animal, shows form,' drawls Starlight. 'Worth three hundred in the shires for a hunter; if he can jump, perhaps more; but depends on his manners—must have manners in the hunting-field, Dawson, you know.'

'Manners or not,' says Bill Dawson, 'it's my opinion he could have won that race in a canter. I must find out more about him and buy him if I can.'

'I'll go you halves if you like,' says Starlight. 'I weally believe him to be a good animal.'

Just then up rides Warrigal. He looks at the old horse as if he had never seen him before, nor us neither. He rides close by the heads of Mr. Dawson's team, and as he does so his hat falls off, by mistake, of course. He jumps off and picks it up, and rides slowly down towards the tent.

It was the signal to clear. Something was up.

I rode back to town with Aileen and Gracey; said good-bye—a hard matter it was, too—and sloped off to where my horse was, and was out of sight of Turon in twenty minutes.

Starlight hails a cabby (he told me this afterwards) and gets him to drive him over to the inn where he was staying, telling the Dawsons he'd have the wine put in ice for the dinner, that he wanted to send off a letter to Sydney by the post, and he'd be back on the course in an hour, in good time for the last race.

In about half-an-hour back comes the same cabman and puts a note into Bill Dawson's hand. He looks at it, stares, swears a bit, and then crumples it up and puts it into his pocket.

Just as it was getting dark, and the last race just run, back comes

Sir Ferdinand and all the police. They'd ridden hard, as their horses showed, and Sir Ferdinand (they say) didn't look half as good-natured as he generally did.

'You've lost a great meeting, Morringer,' says the Commissioner. 'Great pity you had to be off just when you did. But that's just like these infernal scoundrels of bush-rangers. They always play up at the most inconvenient time. How did you get on with them?'

'Get on with them?' roars Sir Ferdinand, almost making a hole in his manners—he was that tired out and done he could hardly sit on his horse—'why, we've been sold as clean as a whistle. I believe some of the brutes have been here all the time.'

'That's impossible,' says the Commissioner. 'There's been no one here that the police are not acquainted with; not that I suppose Jackson and Murphy know many of the cross boys.'

'No strange men nor horses, no disguises?' says Sir Ferdinand. Here he brings out a crumpled bit of paper, written on—

If sur firdnand makes haist back heel be in time to see Starlite's Raneboe win the handy capp.   BILLY THE BOY.

'I firmly believe that young scoundrel, who will be hanged yet, strung us on after Moran ever so far down south, just to leave the coast clear for the Marstons, and then sent me this, too late to be of any use.'

'Quite likely. But the Marstons couldn't be here, let alone Starlight, unless—by Jove! but that's impossible. Impossible! Whew! Here, Jack Dawson, where's your Indian friend?'

'Gone back to the inn. Couldn't stand the course after the handicap. You're to dine with us, Commissioner; you too, Scott; kept a place, Sir Ferdinand, for you on the chance.'

'One moment, pardon me. Who's your friend?'

'Name Lascelles. Just from home—came by India. Splendid fellow! Backed Darkie for the handicap—we did too—won a pot of money.'

'What sort of a horse is this Darkie?'

'Very grand animal. Old fellow had him in a tent, about a mile down the creek; dark bay, star in forehead. Haven't seen such a horse for years. Like the old Emigrant lot.'

Sir Ferdinand beckoned to a senior constable.

'There's a tent down there near the creek, I think you said, Dawson. Bring up the racehorse you find there, and any one in charge.'

'And now I think I'll drive in with you, Dawson' (dismounting, and handing his horse to a trooper). 'I suppose a decent dinner will pick me up, though I feel just as much inclined to hang myself as do anything else at present. I should like to meet this travelled friend of yours; strangers are most agreeable.'

Sir Ferdinand was right in thinking it was hardly worth while going through the form of seeing whether we had waited for him. Lieutenant Lascelles, on leave from his regiment in India, had taken French leave. When inquiry was made at the hotel, where dinner had been ordered by Mr. Dawson and covers laid for a dozen, he had just stepped out. No one seemed to know exactly where to find him. The hotel people thought he was with the Mr. Dawsons, and they thought he was at the hotel. When they surrounded the tent, and then rushed it, all that it contained was the body of old Jacob Benton, lying dead drunk on the floor. A horse-rug was over him, his racing saddle under his head, and his pockets stuffed with five-pound notes. He had won his race and got his money, so he was not bound in honour to keep sober a minute longer.

Rainbow was gone, and there was nothing to be got out of him as to who had taken him or which way he had gone. Nobody seemed to have 'dropped' to me. I might have stayed at Turon longer if I'd liked. But it wasn't good enough by a long way.

We rode away straight home, and didn't lose time on the road, you bet. Not out-and-out fast, either; there was no need for that. We had a clear two hours' start of the police, and their horses were pretty well knocked up by the pace they'd come home at, so they weren't likely to overhaul us easy.

It was a grand night, and, though we didn't feel up to much in the way of talking, it wasn't bad in its way. Starlight rode Rainbow, of course; and the old horse sailed away as if a hundred miles or a thousand made no odds to him.

Warrigal led the way in front. He always went as straight as a line, just the same as if he'd had a compass in his forehead. We never had any bother about the road when he led the way.

'There's nothing like adventure,' says Starlight, at last. 'As some one says, who would have thought we should have come out so well? Fortune favours the brave, in a general way, there's no doubt. By George! what a comfort it was to feel one's self a gentleman again and to associate with one's equals. Ha! ha! how savage Sir Ferdinand is by this time, and the Commissioner! As for the Dawsons, they'll make a joke of it. Fancy me dining at the camp! It's about the best practical joke I ever carried out, and I've been in a good many.'

'The luckiest turn we've ever had,' says I. 'I never expected to see Gracey and Aileen there, much less to go to a ball with them and no one to say no. It beats the world.'

'It makes it all the rougher going back, that's the worst of it,' says he. 'Good God! what fools, idiots, raving lunatics we've all been! Why, but for our own infernal folly, should we be forced to shun our fellow-men, and hide from the light like beasts of prey? What are we better? Better?—nay, a hundred times worse. Some day I shall shoot myself, I know I shall. What a muff Sir Ferdinand must be; he's missed me twice already.'

Here he rode on, and never opened his mouth again till we began to rise the slope at the foot of Nulla Mountain. When the dark fit was on him it was no use talking to him. He'd either not seem to hear you, or else he'd say something which made you sorry for opening your mouth at all. It gave us all we could do to keep along with him. He never seemed to look where he was going, and rode as if he had a spare neck at any rate. When we got near the pass to the mountain, I called out to him that he'd better pull up and get off. Do you think he'd stop or make a sign he heard me? Not a bit of it. He just started the old horse down when he came to the path in the cliff as if it was the easiest road in the world. He kept staring straight before him while the horse put down his feet, as if it was regular good fun treading up rugged, sharp rocks and rolling stones, and turf wasn't worth going over. It seemed to me as if he wanted to kill himself for some reason or other. It would have been easy enough with some horses, but you could have ridden Rainbow down the roof of a house and jumped him into the front balcony, I firmly believe. You couldn't throw him down; if he'd dropped into a well he'd have gone in straight and landed on his legs.

Dad was glad enough to see us; he was almost civil, and when he heard that Rainbow had won the 'big money' he laughed till I thought he'd do himself mischief, not being used to it. He made us tell him over again about Starlight and I going to the ball, and our seeing Aileen and Gracey there; and when he came to the part where Starlight made the bride a present of a diamond ring I thought he never would have done chuckling to himself. Even old Crib looked at me as if he didn't use to think me much of a fellow, but after this racket had changed his mind.

'Won't there be a jolly row in the papers when they get all these different characters played by one chap, and that man the Captain?' says he. 'I knew he was clever enough for anything; but this beats all. I don't believe now, Captain, you'll ever be took.'

'Not alive!' says Starlight, rather grim and gloomy-looking; then he walks off by himself.

We stabled Rainbow, of course, for a week or two after this— being in training, it wouldn't do to turn him out straight at once. Hardy as he was, no horse could stand that altogether; so we kept him under shelter in a roughish kind of a loose box we had knocked up, and fed him on bush hay. We had a small stack of that in case we wanted to keep a horse in—which we did sometimes. In the daytime he was loose in the yard. After a bit, when he was used to the weather, he was turned out again with his old mob, and was never a hair the worse of it. We took it easy ourselves, and sent out Warrigal for the letters and papers. We expected to knock a good bit of fun out of them when they came.

Sure enough, there was the deuce and all to pay when the big

Sydney papers got hold of it, as well as the little *Turon Star* and the *Banner*.

Was it true that the police had again been hoodwinked, justice derided, and the law set at defiance by a gang of ruffians who would have been run down in a fortnight had the police force been equal to the task entrusted to them? Was the moral sentiment of the country population so perverted, so obliterated, that robbers and murderers could find safe harbourage, trustworthy friends, and secret intelligence? Could they openly show themselves in places of public resort, mingle in amusements, and frequent the company of unblemished and distinguished citizens; and yet more, after this flagrant insult to the Government of the land, to every sacred principle of law and order, they could disappear at will, apparently invisible and invulnerable to the officers of the peace and the guardians of the public safety? It was incredible, it was monstrous, degrading, nay, intolerable, and a remedy would have to be found either in the reorganisation of an inefficient police force or in the resignation of an incapable Ministry.

'Good for the *Sydney Monitor*,' says Starlight; 'that reporter knows how to double-shot his guns, and winds up with a broadside. Let us see what the *Star* says. I had a bet with the editor, and paid it, as it happened. Perhaps he'll temper justice with mercy. Now for a start:—

'That we have had strong casts from time to time and exciting performances at our local theatres, no one will deny; but perhaps the inhabitants of Turon never witnessed a more enthralling melodrama than was played during the first two days of our race meeting before a crowded and critical audience, and never, we can state from a somewhat extended experience of matters dramatic, did they gaze on a more finished actor than the gentleman who performed the leading part. Celebrated personages have ere now graced our provincial boards. On the occasion of the burning of the Theatre-Royal in Sydney, we were favoured with the presence in our midst of artists who rarely, if ever before, had quitted the metropolitan stage. But our *jeune premier* in one sense has eclipsed every darling of the tragic or the comic muse.
'Where is there a member of the profession who could have sustained his part with faultless ease and self-possession, being the whole time aware of the fact that he smiled and conversed, danced and diced, dined and slept (ye gods! did he sleep?), with a price upon his head—with the terrible doom of dishonour and inevitable death hanging over him, consequent upon a detection which might occur at any moment?
'Yet was there a stranger guest among us who did all this and more with unblenching brow, unruffled self-possession, unequalled courtesy, who, if discovered, would have been arrested and consigned to a lock-up, only to be exchanged for the gloom and the manacles of the condemned cell. He, indeed, after taking a prominent part in all the humours of the vast social gathering by which the Turon miners celebrated their annual games, disappeared with the almost magical mystery which has already marked his proceedings.
'Whom could we possibly allude to but the celebrated, the illustrious, we grieve to be compelled to add, the notorious Starlight, the hero of a hundred legends, the Australian Claude Duval?
'Yes, almost incredible as it may seem to our readers and persons at a distance imperfectly acquainted with exceptional phases of colonial life, the robber chief (and, for all we know, more than one of his aides-de-camp) was among us, foremost among the betting men, the observed of all observers in the grand stand, where, with those popular country gentlemen, the Messrs.

Dawson, he cheered the winners in the two great races, both of which, with demoniac luck, he had backed heavily.

'We narrate as a plain, unvarnished truth that this accomplished and semi-historical personage raced a horse of his own, which turns out now to have been the famous Rainbow, an animal of such marvellous speed, courage, and endurance that as many legends are current about him as of Dick Turpin's well-known steed. He attended the marriage, in St. Matthew's Church, of Miss Isabel Barnes, the daughter of our respected neighbour, Mr. Jonathan Barnes, when he presented the bride with a costly and beautiful diamond ring, completing the round of his vagaries by dining on invitation with the Commissioner at the camp mess, and, with that high official, honouring our race ball with his presence, and sunning himself in the smiles of our fairest maidens.

'We are afraid that we shall have exhausted the fund of human credulity, and added a fresh and original chapter to those tales of mystery and imagination of which the late Edgar Allan Poe was so masterly a delineator.

'More familiarly rendered, it seems that the fascinating Captain Starlight— "as mild a mannered man" (like Lambre) "as ever scuttled a ship or cut a throat," presented himself opportunely at one of the mountain hostelries, to the notice of our good-hearted squires of Wideview, Messrs. William and John Dawson. One of their wheelers lay at the point of death—a horse of great value—when the agreeable stranger suggested a remedy which effected a sudden cure.

'With all their generous instincts stirred, the Messrs. Dawson invited the gentleman to take a seat in their well-appointed drag. He introduced himself as Mr. Lascelles, holding a commission in an Indian regiment of Irregular Horse, and now on leave, travelling chiefly for health.

'Just sufficiently sunburned, perfect in manner, full of information, humorous and original in conversation, and with all the *prestige* of the unknown, small wonder that "The Captain" was regarded as a prize, socially considered, and introduced right and left. Ha! ha! What a most excellent jest, albeit rather keen, as far as Sir Ferdinand is concerned! We shall never, never cease to recall the humorous side of the whole affair. Why, we ourselves, our august editorial self, actually had a bet in the stand with the audacious pretender, and won it, too. Did he pay up? Of course he did. A "pony," to wit, and on the nail. He does nothing by halves, *notre capitaine*. We have been less promptly reimbursed, indeed, not paid at all, by gentlemen boasting a fairer record. How graciously he smiled and bowed as, with his primrose kid gloves, he disengaged the two tenners and a five-pound note from his well-filled receptacle.

'The last time we had seen him was in the dock at Nomah, being tried in the great cattle case, that *cause célèbre*. To do him justice, he was quite as cool and unconcerned there, and looked as if he was doing the amateur casual business without ulterior liabilities.

'Adieu! fare thee well, Starlight, bold Rover of the Waste; we feel inclined to echo the lament of the ancient Lord Douglas—

> "'Tis pity of him, too," he cried;
> "Bold can he speak, and fairly ride;
> I warrant him a warrior tried."

It is in the interests of justice, doubtless, that thou be hunted down, and expiate by death-doom the crimes which thou and thy myrmidons have committed against society in the sight of God and man. But we cannot, for the life of us, take a keen interest in thy capture. We owe thee much, Starlight; many a slashing leader, many a spicy paragraph, many a stately reflection on contemporary morals hast thou furnished us with. Shall we haste to the slaughter of the rarest bird—golden ovaried? We trow not. Get thee to the wilderness, and repent thee of thy sins. Why should we judge thee? Thou hast, if such dubious donation may avail, an editor's blessing. Depart, and "stick up" no more.'

'Well done, the *Turon Star!*' says Starlight, after he read it all out. 'I call that very fair. There's a flavour of good feeling underneath much of that nonsense, as well as of porter and oysters. It does a fellow a deal more good than slanging him to believe that he's human after all, and that men think so.'

'Do you reckon that chap was sober when he wrote that?' says father. 'Blest if I can make head or tail of it. Half what them fellows put down is regular rot. Why couldn't he have cut it a bit shorter, too?'

CHAPTER XLIV

'THE *Banner* comes next,' says Starlight, tearing it open. 'We shall have something short and sweet after the *Star*. How's this?

'STARLIGHT AGAIN.

'This mercurial brigand, it would appear, has paid Turon another visit, but, with the exception of what may be considered the legalised robbery of the betting ring, has not levied contributions. Rather the other way, indeed. A hasty note for Mr. Dawson, whom he had tricked into temporary association by adopting one of the disguises he can so wonderfully assume, requested that gentleman to receive the Handicap Stakes, won by his horse, Darkie, *alias* Rainbow, and to hand them over to the treasurer of the Turon Hospital, which was accordingly done.

'Sir Ferdinand and the police had been decoyed away previously nearly 100 miles by false intelligence as to Moran and his gang. Our town and treasure were thus left undefended for forty-eight hours, while a daring criminal and his associates mingled unsuspected with all classes. We have always regarded the present system—facetiously called police protection—as a farce. This latter fiasco will probably confirm the idea with the public at large. We, unlike a contemporary, have no morbid sympathy with crime—embroidered or otherwise; our wishes, as loyal subjects, are confined to a short shrift and a high gallows for all who dare to obstruct the Queen's highway.'

'That's easy to understand, barrin' a word here and there,' says father, taking his pipe out of his mouth and laying it down; 'that's the way they used to talk to us in the old days. Dashed if I don't think it's the best way after all. You know where you are. The rest's flummery. All on us as takes to the cross does it with our eyes open, and deserves all we gets.'

'I'm afraid you're right, governor; but why didn't these moral ideas occur to you, for instance, and others earlier in life?

'Why?' says father, getting up and glaring with his eyes, 'because I was a blind, ignorant dog when I was young, as had never been taught nothing, and knowed nothing, not so much as him there' (pointing to Crib), 'for he knows what his business is, and I didn't. I was thrashed and starved, locked up in a gaol, chained and flogged after that, and half the time for doing what I didn't know was wrong, and couldn't know more than one of them four-year-old colts out there that knocks his head agin the yard when he's roped, and falls backards and breaks his neck if he ain't watched. Whose business was it to have learned me better? That I can't rightly say, but it seemed it was the business of the Government people to gaol me, and iron me, and flog me. Was that justice? Any man's sense'll tell him it wasn't. It's been them and me for it since I got my liberty, and if I had had a dozen lives they'd all have gone the same road!'

We none of us felt in the humour to say much after that. Father had got into one of his tantrums, and when he did he was fit to be tied; only I'd not have took the contract for something. Whatever it was that had happened to him in the old times when he was a Government man he didn't talk about. Only every now and then he'd let out just as he did now, as if nothing could ever set him straight again, or keep him from fighting against them, as he called the swells and the Government, and everybody almost that was straight-going and honest. He'd been at it a good many years, one way and another, and any one that knew him didn't think it likely he'd change.

The next dust we got into was all along of a Mr. Knightley, who lived a good way down to the south, and it was one of the worst things we ever were mixed up in. After the Turon races and all that shine, somehow or other we found that things had been made hotter for us than ever since we first turned out. Go where we would, we found the police always quick on our trail, and we had two or three very close shaves of it. It looked as if our luck was dead out, and we began to think our chance of getting across the border to Queensland, and clear out of the colony that way, looked worse every day.

Dad kept foraging about to get information, and we sent Warrigal and Billy the Boy all over the country to find out how it was things were turning out so contrary.

Sir Ferdinand was always on the move, but we knew he couldn't do it all himself unless he got the office from some one who knew the ropes better than he did.

Last of all we dropped on to it.

There was one of the Goldfields Commissioners, a Mr. Knightley, a very keen, cool hand; he was a great sporting man, and a dead shot, like Mr. Hamilton. Well, this gentleman took it into his head to put on extra steam and try and run us down. He'd lost some gold by us in the escort robbery, and not forgotten it; so it seems he'd been trying his best to fit us ever since. Just at first he wasn't able for much, but later on he managed to get information about us and our beat, whenever we left the Hollow, and he put two and two together, and very nearly dropped on us, as I said before, two or three times. We heard, too, that he should say he'd never rest till he had Starlight and the Marstons, and that if he could get picked police he'd bring us in within a month, dead or alive.

We didn't care much about blowing of this sort in a general way; but one of dad's telegraphs sent word in that Mr. Knightley had a couple of thousand pounds' worth of gold from a new diggings lodged at his private residence for a few days till he could get the escort to call for it; that there was only him and a German doctor, a great scholar he was, named Schiller, in the house.

Moran and Daly knew about this, and they were dead on for sticking up the place and getting hold of the gold. Besides that, we felt savage about his trying to run us in. Of course, it was his duty and that of all magistrates and commissioners in a general way. But he wasn't an officer of police, and we thought he was going outside of his line. So when all came to all, we made up our minds to learn him a lesson to stick to his own work; besides, a thousand ounces of gold was no foolish touch, and we could kill two birds with one stone. Moran, Daly, and Joe Wall were to be in it besides. We didn't like working with them. Starlight and I were dead against it. But we knew they'd tackle it by themselves if we backed out. So we agreed to make one thing of it. We were to meet at a place about ten miles off and ride over there together.

Just about ten o'clock we closed in on the place, and left Billy the Boy and Warrigal with the horses, while we sneaked up. We couldn't get near, though, without his knowing it, for he always had a lot of sporting dogs—pointers, retrievers, kangaroo dogs, no end. They kicked up a deuce of a row, and barked and howled enough to raise the dead, before we got within a quarter of a mile from the house.

Of course he was on his guard then, and before long the bullets began to fly pretty thick among us, and we had to take cover to return fire and keep as dark as we could. No doubt this Dr. Schiller loaded the guns and handed them to him, else he couldn't have made such play as he did.

We blazed away, too, and as there was no stable at the back we surrounded the house and tried hard to find an opening. Devil a chance there seemed to be; none of us dared show. So sure as we did we could hear one of those Winchester rifle bullets sing through the air, almost on the top of us. We all had a close shave more than once for being too fast.

For more than half the night he kept cannonading away, and we didn't seem able to get any nearer the place. At last we drew lots which should try and get up close to the place, so as to make a rush while we poured in our broadside and open a door to let us in.

The lot fell upon Patsey Daly. 'Good-bye, all,' he said. 'I'm dashed if I don't think Knightley will bag me. I don't half like charging him, and that's God's truth. Anyhow, I'll try for that barrel there; and if I get behind it I can fire from short range and make him come out.'

He made a rush, half on his hands and knees, and managed to get behind this barrel, where he was safe from being hit as long as he kept well behind it. Then he peppered away, right and left.

On the left of the verandah there was a door stood partly open, and after a bit a man in a light overcoat and a white hat, like Mr. Knightley always wore, showed himself for a second. Daly raps away at this, and the man staggers and falls. Patsey shows himself for a moment from behind the cask, thinking to make a rush forward; that minute Mr. Knightley, who was watching him from a window (the other was only an image), lets drive at him, cool and steady, and poor

Patsey drops like a cock, and never raised his head again. He was shot through the body. He lingered a bit; but in less than an hour he was a dead man.

We began to think at last that we had got in for a hot thing, and that we should have to drop it like Moran's mob at Kadombla. However, Starlight was one of those men that won't be beat, and he kept getting more and more determined to score. He crept away to the back of the building, where he could see to fire at a top window close by where the doctor and Mr. Knightley had been potting at us.

He had the repeating rifle he'd won from me; he never let it go afterwards, and he could make wonderful shooting with it. He kept it going so lively that they began to be hard pressed inside, and had to fire away twice as much ammunition as they otherwise would. It always beat me how they contrived to defend so many points at once. We tried back and front, doors and windows. Twenty times we tried a rush, but they were always ready—so it seemed—and their fire was too hot for us to stand up to, unless we wanted to lose every second man.

The shooting was very close. Nearly every one of us had a scratch —Starlight rather the worse, as he was more in the front and showed himself more. His left arm was bleeding pretty free, but he tied a handkerchief over it and went on as if nothing had happened, only I could see that his face had that set look he only got now and then, and his eyes began to show out a fierce light.

At last we began to see that the return fire was slacking off, while ours was as brisk as ever.

'Hurrah!' says Starlight. 'I believe they'll give in soon. If they had any cartridges they would have had every man of us in that last rush. Let's try another dodge. Here goes for a battering-ram, Dick!'

He pointed to a long, heavy sapling which had been fetched in for a sleeper or something of that sort. We picked it up, and, taking a run back, brought it with all its weight against the front door. In it went like a sheet of bark; we almost fell as we ran forward and found ourselves in a big, dark hall. It seemed very queer and strange, everything was so silent and quiet.

We half expected another volley. But nothing came. We could only stand and wait. The others had gone round the side of the house.

'Get to a corner, Dick; they're always the safest places. We must mind it isn't an ambush. What the devil's the matter? Are they going to suicide, like the people in the round tower of Jhansi?'

'There are no women here,' I said. 'There's no saying what Mr. Knightley might do if his wife had been here.'

'Thank God, she's away at Bathurst,' said Starlight. 'I hate seeing women put out. Besides, everybody bows down to Mrs. Knightley. She's as good as she's handsome, I believe, and that's saying a great deal.'

Just then Moran and Wall managed to find their way into the other side of the house, and they came tearing into the hall like a pair of colts. They looked rather queer when they saw us three and no one else.

'What in thunder's up?' says Moran. 'Are they all gone to bed, and left us the spare rooms? Poor Patsey won't want one, anyhow?'

'Better make some search upstairs,' says Starlight. 'Who'll go first? You make a start, Moran; you like fighting people.'

'Couldn't think of going before the Captain,' says Moran, with a grin. 'I'll follow where you lead.'

'All right!' says Starlight; 'here goes,' and he started to walk up-stairs, when all of a sudden he stopped and looked up as if something had surprised him above a bit. Then he stepped back and waited. I noticed he took off his hat and leaned against the wall.

It was an old-fashioned house for that part of the world, built a good many years ago by a rich settler, who was once the owner of all that side of the country. The staircase was all stone, ornamented every way it could be. Three or four people could walk abreast easy enough.

Just about half-way up was a broad landing, and on this, all of a sudden, appeared four people, inclined by their ways to come down to where we were, while we were all wondering, for a reason you'll see afterwards.

It was Mr. Knightley who took the lady's arm—it was his wife, and she had been there all the time, firing at us as like as not, or at any rate helping. The others followed, and they all walked quite solemn and steady-like down the stairs together.

It was a strange sight. There we were standing and leaning about the dark hall, staring and wondering, and these people walking down to meet us like ghosts, without speaking or anything else.

Mr. Knightley was a tall, handsome man, with a grand black beard that came down to his chest. He walked like a lord, and had that kind of manner with him that comes to people that have always been used to be waited on and have everything found for them in this world. As for his wife, she was given in to be the handsomest woman in the whole countryside—tall and graceful, with a beautiful smile, and soft fair hair. Everybody liked and respected her, gentle and simple—everybody had a good word for her. You couldn't have got any one to say different for a hundred pounds. There are some people, here and there, like this among the gentlefolk, and, say what you like, it does more to make coves like us look a little closer at things and keep away from what's wrong and bad than all the par-sons' talk twice over. Mrs. Knightley was the only woman that ever put me in mind of Miss Falkland, and I can't say more than that.

So, as I said before, it was quite a picture to see them walk slowly and proudly down and sweep into the hall as if they'd been marching into a ballroom. We had both seen them at the ball at the Turon, and everybody agreed they were the handsomest couple there.

Now they were entering their own hall in a different way. But you couldn't have told much of what they felt by their faces. He was a proud man, and felt bitterly enough that he had to surrender to a gang of men that he hated and despised, that he'd boasted he could run down and capture in a month. Now the tables were turned. He and his beautiful wife were in our power, and, to make matters worse, one of our band lay dead, beside the inner wall, killed by his hand.

What was to be his doom? And who could say how such a play might end?

I looked at our men. As they stepped on to the floor of the hall and looked round Mrs. Knightley smiled. She looked to me like an angel from heaven that had come by chance into the other place and hadn't found out her mistake. I saw Starlight start as he looked at her. He was still leaning against the wall, and there was a soft, sorrowful look in his eyes, like I remember noticing once before while he was talking to Aileen about his early days, a thing he never did but once. Part of her hair had straggled down, and hung in a sort of ringlet by her face. It was pale, but clear and bright-looking, and there was a thin streak of blood across her forehead that showed as she came underneath the lamp-light from the landing above.

I looked over at Moran. He and Wall sat in a corner, looking as grim and savage as possible, while his deadly black eyes had a kind of gloomy fire in them that made him look like a wild beast in a cage.

Mr. Knightley was a man that always had the first word in everything, and generally the best of an argument—putting down anybody who differed from him in a quiet, superior sort of way.

He began now. 'Well, my men, I have come down to surrender, and I'm sorry to be obliged to do so. But we have fired our last cartridge—the doctor thought we had a thousand left—in which case, I may as well tell you, you'd never have had this pleasure. Captain Starlight, I surrender my sword—or should do so if I had one. We trust to receive honourable treatment at your hands.'

'I'm sure the Captain will never permit any harm to come to me,' says Mrs. Knightley, with a look in her eyes that, in spite of herself, said a deal more than words. 'Why, I danced vis-à-vis to him in a quadrille at the Turon ball.'

'I shall never forget the honour,' says Starlight, walking forward and bowing low. 'Permit me to offer you a chair, madam; you look faint.'

As he did so she sank down in it, and really looked as if she would faint away. It wouldn't have been much wonder if she had after what she'd gone through that night.

Then Mr. Knightley began again. He wanted to know how we

So Mr. Knightley stood up and faced them all like a man. He was one of those chaps that makes up their mind pretty quick about the sort of people they've got to deal with, and if there's anything to be said or done lets 'em have it 'straight from the shoulder.' As he stood there—straight and square—with his head thrown back, and his eyes —very bright and sharp they were—looking every man's face over as if he was reading a notice and had no time to spare, you couldn't have told, from his look, or voice, or manner, whether he was afraid that things would go wrong, or whether he was dead sure they'd go right. Some men are like that. Others you can tell every thought that's passing through their minds just as if it was printed in big letters on their breasts, like a handbill: '£200 reward,' and so on.

Well, Mr. Knightley wasn't one of that sort, though I saw him keep his eye a trifle longer on Moran than the rest of 'em.

'Now then, boys,' he says, 'we've had our flutter out. I've done my best, and you've done yours. I've bagged one of your lot, and you've done your best to pot me. See here,' and he lifts up the collar of his coat and shows a hole through it, touches his head on the side, and brings away a red mark; and takes out his watch with the case all battered in by a revolver bullet. 'You can't say I hadn't cause to show fight,' and he points to his wife. 'Where's the man among you that wouldn't have done the same? An Englishman's house is his castle. What am I to expect?'

He looked over at Starlight, but he didn't take no notice, and made no sign. I saw Mrs. Knightley look over at him, too. It was the first time I ever seen him look hard when there was a woman in the case, and such a one! But he kept his face set and stern-like.

Then Moran breaks in—

'Expect, be blowed! What the —— do you expect now we've got yer to rights; are we going to let you off after knocking over Daly? No dashed fear, mister, we'll serve you the same way as you served him, as soon as we've had some grub and another glass or two of your grog. You've got some fairish stuff here.'

'Why, Moran,' says Mr. Knightley, still making believe to joke— and, by George! if he could laugh then, he could sing a song with a bullet through him—'you're getting bad-tempered since you used to be horse-breaking for Mr. Lowe. Don't you remember that chestnut Sir Henry colt that no one else could ride, and I backed you not to get thrown, and won a fiver? But I'm a man of the world and know how to play a losing game at billiards as well as most men. Look here, now! Daly's dead. We can't bring him to life again, can we? If you shoot me, you'll be nothing to the good, and have every spare man in the three colonies at your heels. This is a game of brag, though the stakes are high. I'll play a card. Listen. You shall have a hundred fivers—£500 in notes—by to-morrow at four o'clock, if you'll let Mrs. Knightley and the doctor ride to Bathurst for the money. What do you say?'

'D—n you and your money, too,' growled Moran. 'We'll have your blood, and nothing else. D'yer hear that? You're a dead man now; if you're not buried by this time to-morrow, it won't be because you're not as ready for it as Patsey is.'

I saw Mrs. Knightley turn round and clasp her hands; her face grew as white as death, but she said nothing, only looked over at Starlight, and her eyes grew bigger and bigger, while her mouth trembled just the least bit.

'You're off your head, Moran,' says Mr. Knightley, pulling out a cigar and lighting it. 'But I suppose you're the chief man, and all the rest must do as you tell them.'

'Suppose we talk it over,' says Starlight, very quiet, but I knew by the first word that he spoke something was coming. 'Daly dropped, and it can't be helped. Accidents will happen. If you play at bowls you must take rubbers. It has been a fair fight; no one can say otherwise. Let us put it to the vote. I propose that Mr. Knightley's offer be accepted. Not that I intend to take a shilling of the money.'

'Nor me either,' says I. 'So you three chaps will have it to share between you. I don't see that we can do better. A fight's a fight, and if Patsey got his gruel it might have happened to Mr. Knightley himself. As for shooting in cold blood, I'm not on, and so I tell you.'

'I suppose you think you and Starlight's going to boss the lot of us, because you've been doing it fine at the Turon races along with a lot of blasted swells as 'ud scrag us if they had the chance, and we're to take so much a head for our dashed lives, because we're only working chaps. Not if Dan Moran knows it. What we want is satisfaction—blood for blood—and we're a-goin' to have it, eh, mates?'

Wall and Hulbert hadn't said anything before this. They were not bad chaps underneath, but Moran was such a devil when he was raised that they didn't like to cross him. Besides, they had a down on Mr. Knightley, and wanted to sheet it home to him somehow. They had got to the brandy, too, and it didn't make matters any better, you take my word for it.

Starlight didn't speak for a minute or two. I couldn't think what he was at. If Jim had been there we should have been right, three to three. Now we were two to three. I knew Starlight had a good card to play, and was ready to play it, but he was waiting on the deal.

Mr. Knightley must have had some sort of notion of the hand; he was wonderful quick at picking up the points of the game.

He said nothing, and looked as cool as you please, smoking his cigar as if he had nothing on his mind and wanted a rest. The lady sat quite still and pale, but her beautiful eyes kept wandering round from one to another, like some pretty creature caught in a trap. Dr. Schiller found it hard lines on him to keep quiet all this time—he couldn't hold it in no longer.

'Good heafens!' he says, 'are you men, and will not say nodings when you haf such an ovver as dis? Subbose you shood us all, what then? Will not the whole coundry rice and hund you down like mat docks?'

'That won't make it any better for you, mate,' says Moran, with a grin. 'When you and he's lying under that old tree outside, it'll make no odds to yer whether our rope's a long or a short 'un.'

'Quite right, Moran,' says Mr. Knightley. 'Doctor, he has you there.'

Starlight moved a step or two over towards him, as if he was uncertain in his mind. Then he says to Wall and Hulbert—

'See here, men; you've heard what Moran says, and what I think. Which are you going to do? To help in a brutal, cowardly murder, and never be able to look a man in the face again, or to take this money to-morrow?—a hundred and seventy each in notes, mind, and get away quietly—or are you going to be led by Moran, and told what you are to do like children?'

'Oh come, Dan, let's take the stuff,' says Wall. 'I think it's good enough. What's the use of being contrary? I think the Captain's right. He knows a dashed sight more than us.'

'He be hanged!' says Moran, with eyes glaring and the whole of his face working like a man in a fit. 'He's no Captain of mine, and never was. I'll never stir from here till I have payment in blood for Daly's life. We may as well be hung for a sheep as a lamb. I've sworn to have that man's life to-night, and have it I will.'

'You'll have ours first, you bloodthirsty, murdering dog,' says Starlight; and, as he spoke, he slipped his revolver into Mr. Knightley's hand, who covered Moran that moment. I drew mine, too, and had Wall under aim. Starlight's repeating rifle was up like lightning.

Mrs. Knightley covered her eyes, the old woman screamed, and the doctor sat down on a chair and puffed away at his meerschaum pipe.

'We're three to three, now,' says Starlight; 'you've only to move a finger and you're a dead man. Wall and Hulbert can have a hand in it if they haven't had shooting enough for one evening. Do your worst, you black-hearted brute! I've two minds to take you and run you in myself, if it's only to give you a lesson in manners.'

Moran's face grew as black as an ironbark tree after a bush fire. He raised his revolver, and in one second we should have been in the middle of a desperate hand-to-hand fight; and God knows how it might have ended hadn't Hulbert struck up his arm, and spoke out like a man.

'It's no use, Dan, we won't stand it. You're a dashed fool and want to spoil everything for a bit of temper. We'll take the notes and let Mrs. Knightley and the doctor clear out for Bathurst if you'll say honour bright that you'll be at the Black Stump by to-morrow evening at five, and won't give the police the office.'

Moran, slow and sulkily, put down his hand and glared round like a dingo with the dogs round him—as if he didn't know which to snap at first. Then he looked at Mr. Knightley with a look of hellish rage and spite that ten devils couldn't have improved upon, and, throwing himself down on a chair, drank off half a tumbler of brandy.

'Settle it amongst yourselves, and be —— to you,' he said. 'You're all agin me now; but, by ——, I'll be square with some of ye yet.'

It was all over now. Mr. Knightley took a match out of the silver match-box at his watch-chain, and lit another cigar. I saw the tears trickling through Mrs. Knightley's fingers. Then she turned away her head, and after a minute or two was as calm and quiet as ever.

'You know your way about the place, Wall,' says Mr. Knightley, as if he was in his own house, just the same as usual; 'run up the horses, there's a good fellow; they're in the little horse paddock. Mrs. Knightley's is a grey, and the doctor's is a mouse-coloured mare with a short tail; you can't mistake them. The sooner they're off the sooner you'll handle the cash.'

Wall looked rather amused, but went out, and we heard him rattle off to go round the paddock. The doctor went upstairs, and buckled on a long-necked pair of old-fashioned spurs, and Mrs. Knightley walked away like a woman in a dream to her own room, and soon afterwards returned in her riding-habit and hat.

I foraged about and found the side-saddle and bridle in the harness-room. Everything was in tip-top order there—glass sides for keeping the dust off the four-in-hand harness and all that kind of thing. All the bits and stirrup-irons like silver. There wasn't much time lost in saddling-up, you bet!

We watched pretty close lest Moran should take a new fancy into his head, but he stuck to the brandy bottle, and very soon put himself from fighting or anything else. I wasn't sorry to see it. I was well aware he was as treacherous as a dingo, and could sham dead or anything else to gain his ends and throw people off their guards.

Well, the horses were brought out, and when Mr. Knightley lifted his wife up on to her saddle on the high-crested grey thoroughbred with a dash of Arab blood from an old Satellite strain, I guess he was never better pleased with anything in the world. They looked in each other's eyes for a minute, and then the old horse started off along the road to Bathurst with his fast, springy walk. Starlight took off his hat and bowed low in the most respectful way. Mrs.

Knightley turned in her saddle and tried to say something, but the words wouldn't come—she could only wave her hand—and then her head went down nearly to her saddle. The doctor scrambled on to his horse's back, and trotted off after her. The grey moved off, shaking his head, at a beautiful, easy, springy canter. We raised a cheer, and they swept round a corner of the road and out of sight.

'You'll find these rather good, Captain,' says Mr. Knightley, handing Starlight his cigar-case. 'There's a box upstairs in my dressing-room. If you'll allow me I'll order in dinner. There ought to be something decent if my old cook hasn't been frightened out of his life, but I think he has seen too much to be put out of his way by a little shooting.'

'Now I think of it,' says Starlight, 'I do really feel disposed for refreshment. I say, Wall, see if you can't get that ferocious friend of yours into a room where he can sleep off his liquor. I really must apologise for his bad manners; but you see how the case stands.'

'Perfectly, my dear fellow,' says Mr. Knightley. 'Don't mention it. I shall always feel personally indebted to you for far more than I can express. But let that pass for the present. What shall we do to pass the evening? You play picquet and hazard, of course?'

'Do I not,' says Starlight, his eyes lighting up in a way I didn't remember. 'It's many a day since I've met with any one near my old form.'

'Then suppose we have a game or two,' says Mr. Knightley, 'after dinner or supper, whichever we choose to call it. I have cards; they luckily came up the other day. In the meantime you will find the claret very fair, and this cold wild turkey—I shot a brace last Thursday—is not to be despised.'

We had a rattling good feed, and no mistake, whatever it was. The turkey was a grand bird, and weighed 21 lb., he told us. The cook had sent in some hot potatoes, and chaps like us that had been riding, walking, and fighting for twenty hours right on end had just the sort of appetite that a bird of that kind deserved. He was as fat as butter, too. They feed on dandelion seeds at that time of the year. It gives 'em a sort of gamy flavour such as no other bird, wild or tame, has. To my liking the wild turkey beats the black duck even. He's the best game bird that flies in the bush.

Mr. Knightley, too, now his wife was safe on her way to Bathurst, and things seemed going well, was full of fun, and kept us all going. He helped everybody twice over, and wouldn't hear of any one keeping the bottle standing. The night was close rather, and we were all that thirsty it went down like mother's milk. Wall and Hulbert got pleasant enough and joined in, now that Moran was out of the way. He was snoring in a back room, and, like a man in the dead-house of a bush shanty, not likely to wake before sunrise. Mr. Knightley told us some out-and-out good yarns, and Hulbert and Wall swore that if they'd known he was such a good sort they'd never have thought of sticking up the place. He said he had been quite mistaken about them, and that another time he should know better than to volunteer for work that was not part of his duty. By that time the claret had gone round pretty often; and without being screwed we'd all had our tongues loosened a bit.

After that we lit our pipes, and we three began to play all-fours and euchre, sometimes one pair, sometimes another. As for Mr. Knightley and Starlight, they got out a curious filigree sort of a little card-table and began to play some outlandish game that I didn't know, and to look very serious over it.

They had notes for counters, and I could see, as I looked over every now and then, that each man was doing all he knew to best the other. Sometimes one had the show; sometimes the other. We got tired and had another smoke and turned in. The beds were snug and comfortable. Mr. Knightley showed us where to go, and we wanted a good night's rest bad enough.

Just before I turned in I went up to the table. They looked as keen at it as if they'd just begun, and I heard Starlight say, 'I owe you a hundred now. I'll play you double or quits.' So I left them to it. I could see they were not on for bed just then. Both men were cool enough, but I could see that Starlight (and I'd never known him touch a card before) was one of those men that would never rise from the table as long as he had a shilling left, and would stake everything he had in the world upon the turn of a card.

We all slept sound, but most of us were up at sunrise. It doesn't do for chaps in our line to be caught napping, and the police might have got wind where we were at work. We had our horses to look to, and to give a look round in a general way to see if things were right.

Starlight and Mr. Knightley didn't turn out, they took it easy, perhaps they'd been up later than us; anyhow, they didn't show till breakfast, when they both made pretty fair time over the eatables.

My word! it was a breakfast, though we'd got a bit tired waiting for it. The old cook had hashed up the turkey; it was stunning, almost better than the day before. Then bacon and eggs, grilled steak, fresh bread and butter, coffee and tea, water-cresses. Really, I thought we never should stop. It was lucky the police didn't come, or we shouldn't have done much in the fighting line, or the runaway either. As it turned out, Sir Ferdinand wasn't so very far off the line, but he took another road. He never had any luck somehow in following us up, though he had some first-rate chances. Moran was off his feed, and wouldn't come in. He took a nip and walked down to the creek. We were all glad enough to get shut of him.

After breakfast and a turn round the stables, blest if Starlight and Mr. Knightley didn't have out the cards again, and at it they went as fresh and keen as ever. We didn't know what in the world to do with ourselves till it was time to start to ride out to the Black Stump, where we were to meet the doctor and collar the £500. They didn't waste a minute of their time, till about half-past twelve Starlight puts down his cards very gently, and says he—

'I'm afraid we have no more time to spare. I've enjoyed the play more than I have done anything for years. I leave you £100 now in notes, and you must take my I O U for the balance. What bank shall I pay it into?'

'The Australian,' says Mr. Knightley. 'At your convenience, of course.'

'Within a month,' says Starlight, bowing. 'And now a glass of wine and a biscuit, it's time to be off.'

We had something as good, nearer the mark than that, and Moran sat down, too, and played a good knife and fork. He'd come to, after his booze, and was ready for any fresh villainy, as usual. He didn't let on to be nasty, but he looked sulky enough, and I saw his eye fixed on Mr. Knightley and Starlight now and then as if he'd have given a good deal to have had them where they hadn't so many at their backs.

CHAPTER XLVI

WE ate well and drank better still at the lunch, although we had such a regular tuck-out at breakfast time. Mr. Knightley wouldn't hear of any of us shirking our liquor, and by the time we'd done all hands were pretty well on. Moran himself began to look pleasant, or as good a sample of it as I'd ever seen in him. Mr. Knightley could get round the devil himself, I believe. I never saw his equals at that business; and this particular time he was in great feather, seeing that he was likely to get out of an ugly business all right. He was as sure of the £500 in notes being there at the appointed hour as he was of the sun setting that particular evening.

'I think it's a fair thing,' says Starlight at last, looking at his watch. Mr. Knightley wasn't the first to speak, no fear. 'Take us all our time to get to the Black Stump. We shall have to ride, too.' Moran and Wall got up and fetched their horses. Mr. Knightley's was led up by one of his men. He was a big handsome roan, in top condition, and the man was riding a black horse with a tan muzzle that looked a trifle better, if anything. Mr. Knightley turned out in boots and breeches, with a gold fox's head on his scarf, swell hunting fashion, as they do it at home, Starlight said.

When Starlight's horse came up he was as lame as a tree, couldn't put his foot to the ground; got a kick or a strain, or trod on a glass bottle or something. Anyhow he had only three legs that he could rise a move out of. Starlight looked rather glum. He wasn't his second best or his third best, either. All the same, a horse is a horse, and I never saw the man yet that a lame horse didn't put out a bit.

'Confound it,' says he, 'what a nuisance! It's just the way with these infernal half-bred brutes; they always let me down at the wrong time.'

'Look here, old fellow,' says Mr. Knightley, 'leave him behind and take this black horse the boy's on; he's one of the finest hacks you ever crossed. I refused sixty guineas for him the other day from Morringer.'

'Thanks, very much,' says Starlight, brightening up a bit; 'but I hardly like to deprive you of him. Won't you want him yourself?'

'Oh, I can manage without him,' says Mr. Knightley. 'I'll let you have him for fifty and allow you ten pounds for your screw. You can add it on to your I O U, and pay it in with the other.'

We all laughed at this, and Moran said if he was dealing with Mr. Knightley he'd get him a pound or two cheaper. But Starlight said, very serious-like, that the arrangement would suit him very well. So he had his saddle shifted, and the groom led back the bay and turned him loose in the paddock.

We mounted then, and it looked as if we were all matched for a race to the Black Stump. Moran had a good horse, and when he set him going in the first bit of thick timber we came to, it took a man, I tell you, to keep him in sight. Starlight made the black horse hit out in a way that must have been a trifle strange to him unless he'd been in training lately. As for Mr. Knightley, he took it easy and sailed away on one side with Joe Wall and me. He played it out cool to the last, and wasn't going to hurry himself for anybody.

Half-an-hour before sundown we rode up to the Black Stump. It was a rum-looking spot, but everybody knew it for miles round. There was nothing like it anywhere handy. It was within a reasonable distance of Bathurst, and not so far from a place we could make to, where there was good shelter and hiding, too, if we were pushed.

There were two or three roads led up to it, and crossed there—one from Bathurst, one to Turon, and another straight into the forest country, which led range by range to Nulla Mountain. We could see on a good way ahead, and, though there was no one at the tree when we came, a single horseman was riding along the road for Bathurst. We all drew rein round the stump. It had been a tremendous big old ironbark tree—nobody knew how old, but it had had its top blown off in a thunderstorm, and the carriers had lighted so many fires against the roots of it that it had been killed at last, and the sides were as black as a steamer's funnel. After a bit we could make out the doctor's short-tailed, mousy mare and him powdering along at a sort of hand gallop.

When he came up close, he took off his hat and made a bow. 'Chentlemen of the roat, I salude you,' he says. 'You haf kebt your bromise to the letter, and you will fint that Albert von Schiller has kept his. Hauptman!' says he to Starlight, 'I delifer to you the ransom of dies wothy chentleman and his most excellend and hoch-besahltes laty, who has much recovered from her fadigues, and I demant his freetom.'

'Well done, most trust-repaying and not-ever-to-be-entirely-forgotten herald,' says Starlight. 'I hand over to these worthy free companions the frank-geld; isn't that the term?—and when they have counted it (for they won't take your word or mine), the Graf here—most high-born and high-beseeming, but uncommonly-near-ending his glorious career magnate—will be restored to you. Very pleasant company we've found him. I should like to have my revenge at picquet, that's all.'

While this was going on Starlight had collared the bundle of notes from the doctor, and chucked it over quite careless-like to Moran. 'There it is for you,' says he. 'You can divide it between you. Dick and I stand out this time; and you can't say you've done badly.'

Moran didn't say anything, but he and Wall got off their horses and sat down on their heels—native fashion. Then they turned to, counting out the notes one by one. They were all fivers—so it took some time—as they neither of 'em weren't very smart at figures, and after they'd got out twenty or thirty they'd get boxed, like a new hand counting sheep, and have to begin all over again. It must have been aggravating to Mr. Knightley, and he was waiting to be let go, in a manner of speaking. He never showed it, but kept smoking and yarning with Starlight, pointing out how grand the sun was just a-setting on the Bulga Mountains—just for all the world as if he'd given a picnic, and was making himself pleasant to the people that stayed longest.

At long last they'd got to the end of the conning, and divided the notes. Moran tied his up in a bunch, and rolled 'em in his poncho; but Wall crammed his into his pocket and made 'em all stick out like a boy that's been stealing apples. When they mounted their horses, Mr. Knightley shook hands with me and Starlight. Then he turns round to Moran and Wall—'We're parting good friends after all's said and done,' he says. 'Just as well matters have been settled this way. Come, now, in cool blood, ain't you rather glad, Moran?'

'Dashed if I know,' growls he. 'All I know is, you're deuced well out of it; your luck mayn't be so good another time.'

'Nor yours either, my friend,' says Mr. Knightley, drawing up his bridle-rein. 'I had only a snap-shot at you when that bullet went through your poncho, or you'd be lying alongside of Daly. However, I needn't waste my breath talking to that brute,' he says to Starlight. 'I know well all I owe to you and Dick Marston here. Some day I may repay it.'

'You mean what I owe you,' says Starlight, turning it off with a laugh. 'Never fear, you'll find that paid to your credit in the bank. We have agents in all sorts of places. Good-bye, and a safe ride home. My respectful compliments to Mrs. Knightley. Perhaps you'd better follow the doctor now.' The old gentleman had got tired waiting, and ridden on slow and easy.

Two or three weeks after, Starlight and I were taking a ride towards the Bogan Road, not that we was on for anything particular, but just having a turn round for want of something else to do, when we saw a big mob of cattle coming along, with three or four stock-riders behind 'em. Then we met a loaded dray and team in front, that had rations and swags and a tent. The driver asked us if we knew a good place to camp. He was a talking sort of chap, and we yarned away with him for a bit. He told us how the boss was behind in a dogcart and tandem, with two led horses besides. The cattle were going to take up a new run he'd bought on the Lower Bogan, an out-and-out wild place; but he'd got the country cheap, and thought it would pay in the end. He was going ahead after a stage or two, but just now he was camping with them.

'My word, he's well in, is the cove,' says the horse-driver; 'he's got half-a-dozen stations besides this one. He'll be one of the richest men in Australia yet.'

After we saw the cattle (about a thousand head) we thought it would be a middling day's work to 'stick up' the cove and put him through. Going to form a new station, he'd very like have cash about, as he'd have to pay for a lot of things on the nail just at first. If he was such a swell, too, he'd have a gold watch and perhaps a few more trifles. Anyhow, he was good for the day's expenses, and we thought we'd try it on.

So we passed the cattle and rode quietly along the road till we saw his dogcart coming; then we stopped inside a yarran scrub, just as he came by—a square-built man he seemed to be, muffled up in a big rough coat. It was a cool morning. We rode up sharpish, and showed our revolvers, singing out to him to 'bail up.' He pulled up quick and stared at us. So we did at him. Then the three of us burst out laughing—regular roared again.

Who should it be but old George Storefield.

'Well, this is a prime joke,' says he. 'I knew you were out somewhere on this road; but I never thought I should live to be stuck up by you, Dick Marston.'

I looked foolish. It was rather a stunner when you come to think of it.

'I beg a thousand pardons,' says Starlight. 'Ridiculous mistake. Want of something to occupy our time. "For Satan finds some mischief still," etc. Isn't that the way the hymn runs? Wonderfully true, isn't it? You'll accept our apologies, Mr. Storefield, I trust. Poor Dick here will never get over it.'

'How was I to know? Why, George, old man, we thought it was the Governor turned squatter, or old Billy Wentworth himself. Your trade pays better than ours, let alone being on the square. Well, shake hands; we'll be off. You won't tell the girls, there's a good fellow, will you?'

'I can't promise,' says old George; 'it's too good a joke.' Here he laughed a good one. 'It isn't often a man gets stuck up by his friends like this. Tell you what; come and have some lunch, and we'll talk it over.'

His man rode up then with the spare horse. Luckily, he was a good way behind, as fellows will keep when they're following a trap, so that they can't be any good when they're wanted. In this case it was just as well. He hadn't seen anything.

'Hobble the horses out and put on their nose-bags, Williams,' says he, 'and then get out the lunch. Put the things under that tree.'

They took out the horses, and the chap got out a basket with cold beef and bread and half a tongue and a bottle of good whisky and water-bag.

We sat down on the grass, and as we'd been riding since sunrise

We did pretty well in the feed line, and had a regular good bit of fun.
I never thought old George had so much go in him; but good times
had made him twice the man he used to be.

After a bit he sends the groom down to the Cowall to water the
horses, and, says he—

'Captain, you'd better come and manage Willaroon down there,
with Dick for stockman. There's a fortune in it, and it's a good way
off yet. Nobody would think of looking for you there. You're a
new chum, just out from home, you know. Plenty of spare country.
I'll send you some cattle to start you on a new run after a bit.'

'If we could throw our past behind us, I'd do it, and thank God on
my knees,' says Starlight. 'It would make me almost a happy man
again. But why think of that or any other honest life in this colony
now? We've debarred ourselves from it now and for ever. Our
only hope is in another land—America—if we can get away. We
shan't be long here now; we're both sick of this accursed work.'

'The sooner the better,' says George, taking his hand and giving it
a hearty grip. 'And, look here, you work your way quietly down to
Willaroon. That's my place, and I'll give you a line across to the
Queensland border. From there you can get over to Townsville, and
it's easy to sail from there to the islands or any port out of reach of
harm from here.'

'We'll tackle it next month if we're alive,' says I. So we parted.

Not long after this we get a letter from Jim. He'd heard all
about the way to do it from a man he'd met in Melbourne that had
worked his way down overland from the North. He said once you
were there, or near there, there was little or no chance of being interfered with. Jeanie was always in a fright every day Jim went away
lest he might be taken and not let come back. So she was always
keeping him up to the mark, making him inquire here and look out
there until he got a bit of information which told him what he
wanted.

This man that worked in the store with him was a fast sort of
card, who had been mate of a brig cruising all about and back to
Sydney with sandalwood, beche-de-mer, and what they call island
trade.

Well, the captain of the craft, who was part owner, had settled in
his mind that he'd trade regular with San Francisco now, and touch
at Honolulu going and coming. He was to be back at Gladstone in
about three months, and then start for California straight away.

This was the very thing, just made to suit us all to pieces. If we
could make out to one of the Queensland northern ports it would be
easy enough to ship under different names. Once in America, we'd
be in a new world, and there'd be nothing to stop us from leading a
new life.

CHAPTER XLVII

When we got the notion into our heads, we set to work to carry it out. We didn't want to leave Aileen and mother behind. So it was settled that I was to go over and see them, and try and persuade them to go down to Melbourne and stop with Jeanie after Jim had started.

Then, if we all got safe over to San Francisco, Jeanie and they could come over by the first ship that sailed. There was no down upon them, so they could do anything they liked. The main thing was to get Jim off safe and me and Starlight. After that the rest might come along when they pleased. As for dad, he was to take his own road; to go and stay as he chose. It wasn't much use trying to make him do anything else. But he was more like to stop at the old Hollow than anywhere else. It wouldn't have seemed home to him anywhere else, even where he was born, I believe.

The first thing of all was to go to the old place and see mother and Aileen. They were both back at the old cottage, and were a bit more comfortable now. George Storefield had married a lady—a real lady, as Aileen said—and, though she was a nice, good-tempered young woman as ever was, Aileen, of course, wouldn't stay there any longer. She thought home was the best place after all.

We took a couple of days figuring it out at the Hollow. Starlight had a map, and we plotted it out, and marked all the stages which could be safely made—went over all the back tracks and cross-country lines; some we had travelled before, and others of which we knew pretty well from hearsay.

After we'd got all this cut and dry, I started away one beautiful sunshiny morning to ride over to Rocky Flat. I remember the day as well as yesterday, because I took notice of it at the time, and had better cause to remember it before all was over. Everything looked so lovely as I began to clear the foot hills of Nulla Mountain. The birds seemed to chirp and whistle gayer than they ever did before. The dewdrops on the grass and all the twigs and shoots of the trees looked as if it was covered with diamonds and rubies as the sun began to shine and melt some of them. My horse stepped along limber and free. 'O Lord,' I says to myself out aloud, 'what a happy cove I might be if I could start fresh—knowing what I know—and not having all these things against me!'

When I got on to the tableland above Rocky Flat I took a good look at the whole place. Everything was as quiet and peaceful as if nothing had ever happened within miles of it—as if I hadn't had

Goring's handcuffs on me—as if Jim hadn't had the bullets whistling round him, and risked his life on an unbridled horse—as if the four dead men had not lain staring up to the sky in the gully up yonder for days before they were found and buried.

But now it looked as if only two or three people had ever been there from the beginning of the world. The wild ducks swam and splashed in the little waterhole above the house. Two or three of the cows were walking down to the creek, as quiet and peaceable as you please. There was some poultry at the back, and the little garden was done up that nicely as it hadn't been for many a day.

After I'd pretty well settled in my own mind that there was no one anext or anigh the old place, I drew up by degrees, bit by bit, and sneaked across the creek. I was just making for the barn when I saw two horsemen pop up sudden round the back of the house and ride towards the front gate. I saw with half an eye they were Sir Ferdinand Morringer and a trooper.

Lucky for me they were looking up the gully instead of my way, and, though my heart nearly stood still, I rode as hard as I could lick for the gate of the barn, which was betwixt me and them. They never looked round. They were too much taken up with watching the spot where Hagan and his lot were found. I had just time to chevy straight into the barn and pull off my saddle and bridle and hide under the hay when they shifted full towards where I'd been and then hung up their horses. The trooper tied his to a dead branch of a tree, and then went moving about. I was mortally afraid of his stumbling against something and spoiling the whole affair.

It seems Sir Ferdinand had never given up the notion of our turning up at Rocky Flat some day or other; so he used to take a turn himself that way every now and again on the chance, and a very good chance it nearly turned out to be. Besides this, it seems since he'd heard of her being at the ball at Turon he'd taken a great fancy to Aileen, and used to talk to her as much as she'd let him, when she was at George Storefield's and any other place where he met her. He wouldn't have had much chance of saying the second word, only he was a good-natured, amusing sort, and always as respectful to her as if she'd been a lady. Besides, Aileen had a kind of fancy that it might make things no worse for us if she was civil to him. Any way, she thought, as women will do, that she might get something out of him perhaps once in a way that would be of use to us. I don't believe as it would make a scrap of difference one way or the other. And, like people who try to be too clever, she was pretty near being caught in her own trap this time. Not that I blame the poor thing, she did all for the best, and would have given the eyes out of her head, I believe, to have done us real good, and seen us clear of all our troubles.

Well, she brings a chair out on the verandah, and Sir Ferdinand he sat down on a bench there for half-an-hour, talking away and laughing, just as gentlemen will to pretty girls, no matter who they are. And I could see Aileen look up and laugh now and then, pleased like. She couldn't help it. And there was I stuck in the confounded barn among the straw all the time looking out through one of the cracks and wondering if he was ever going to clear out. Sometimes I thought the trooper, who was getting tired of dodging about doing nothing, couldn't be of seeing my horse's tracks leading slap into the barn door. But he was thinking of something else, or else wasn't much in the tracking line. Some men would see a whole army of fresh tracks, as plain as print, right under their noses and wouldn't drop down to anything.

However, last of all I saw him unhitch his horse and take the bridle on his arm, and then Aileen put on her hat and walked up to the top of the ridge along the stony track with him. Then I saw him mount and start off at a rattling good bat along the road to Turon and the trooper after him. I felt all right again then, and watched Aileen come slowly down the road again with her head down, quite thoughtful like, very different from the way she went up. She didn't stop at the house, but walked straight down to the barn and came in at the door. I wondered what she would do when she saw my horse. But she didn't start, only said—

'You may come out now, Dick; I knew you were here. I saw you ride in just as Sir Ferdinand and the trooper came up.'

'So that's why you were making yourself so pleasant,' says I laughingly. 'I mustn't tell Starlight, I suppose, or we shall be having a new yarn in the newspapers—"Duel between Sir Ferdinand Morringer and Captain Starlight."'

She laughed, too, and then looked sad and serious like again.

'I wonder if we shall ever have an end to this wretched hide-and-seek work. God knows I would do anything that an honest girl could do for you boys and him, but it sometimes looks dark enough, and I have dreadful fears that all will be in vain, and that we are fated to death and ruin at the end.'

'Come, come, don't break down before the time,' I said. 'It's been a close shave, though; but Sir Ferdinand won't be back for a bit, so we may as well take it easy. I've got a lot to say to you.'

'He said he wouldn't be back this way till Friday week,' says she. 'He has an escort to see to then, and he expected to be at Stony Creek in a couple of hours from this. He'll have to ride for it.'

We walked over to the house. Neither of us said anything for a bit. Mother was sitting in her old chair by the fire knitting. Many a good pair of woollen socks she'd sent us, and many's the time we'd had call to bless her and her knitting—as we sat our horses, night after night, in a perishing frost, or when the rain set in that run of wet winters we had, when we'd hardly a dry stitch on us by the week together, when we had enough of them and the neck wrappers, I expect plenty of others round about were glad to get 'em. It was partly for good nature, for mother was always a kind-hearted poor soul as ever was, and would give away the shoes off her feet—like most Irish people I've met—to any one that wanted them worse than herself, and partly for the ease it gave her mind to be always doing something steady like. Mother hadn't book-learning, and didn't always understand the things Aileen read to her. She was getting too old to do much in the house now. But her eyes were wonderful good still, and this knitting was about the greatest pleasure she had left in the world. If anything had happened to stop her from going on with that, I don't believe she would have lived a month.

Her poor old face brightened up when she seen me, and for a few minutes you'd have said no thought of trouble could come anigh her. Then the tears rolled down her cheeks, and I could see her lips moving, though she did not speak the words. I knew what she was doing, and if that could have kept us right we'd never have gone wrong in the world. But it was to be, I suppose.

Mother was a deal older-looking, and couldn't move about as well as she did. Aileen said she'd often sit out in the sun for an hour together and watch her walking up the garden, or putting up the calves, and carrying in the water from the creek, and say nothing. Sometimes she thought her mind was going a bit, and then again she'd seem as sensible as ever she was. To-day, after a bit, she came round and talked more and asked about the neighbours, seemed more curious like, than she'd done, Aileen said, for many a long day.

'You must have something to eat, Dick,' says Aileen; 'It's a long ride from—from where we know—and what with one thing and another I daresay you've an appetite. Let me see what there is. Mrs. Storefield sent us over a quarter of veal from the farm yesterday, and we've plenty of bacon of our own. Mother and I live half our time on it and the eggs. I'm making quite a fortune by the butter lately. These diggings are wonderful places to send up the price of everything we can grow.'

So she got out the frying-pan, and she and I and mother had some veal chops, with a slice or two of bacon to give it a flavour. My word! they were good after a forty-mile ride, and we'd had nothing but corned beef in the Hollow lately. Fresh butter and milk, too; it was a treat. We had cows enough at the Hollow, but we didn't bother ourselves milking; bread and beef and tea, with a glass of grog now and then, was the general run of our grub.

We had a talk about the merry time at the Turon races, and Aileen laughed in spite of herself at the thought of Starlight walking down the ballroom to be introduced to her, and being taken up to all the swell people of the place. 'He looked grander than any of them, to my fancy,' said she; 'and oh! what a cruel shame it seems that he should ever have done what keeps him from going among his equals as he was born to do. Then I should never have seen him, I suppose, and a thousand times better, too. I'd give up every hope of seeing him again in this world, God knows how cheerfully, if it would serve him or help his escape.'

'I'm down here now to see you about the same escape,' I said; and then I told her about Jim's letter, and what he said about the mate of the ship. She listened for a good while patiently, with her hand in mine, like we used to sit in old days, when we were and happy and alive—alive, not dead men and women walking about and making believe to live. So I told her how we made it up to meet somewhere near the Queensland border. Jim to come up the Murray from Melbourne, and so on to the Darling, and we to make across for the Lower Bogan. If we could carry this out all right—and it looked pretty likely—the rest of the game would be easy; and once on blue water—O my God, what new creatures we should all be!

Aileen threw her arms round my neck and sobbed and cried like a child; she couldn't speak for a bit, and when she looked up her eyes seemed to have a different kind of look in them—a far-away, dreamy sort of light from what I'd ever noticed in them.

'It may come about,' she said, 'Dick. I've prayed whole nights through and vowed my life to the Blessed Virgin. She may accept the service of my years that are to come. It may be permitted after all the sins of our people.'

After this she dried her eyes and went to her room for a bit, while I had a quiet, easy sort of talk with mother, she saying a word or two now and then, and looking at me most of the time, as if that was enough without talking.

Then Aileen came out of her room with her habit and hat on. 'Run up my horse, Dick,' she says, 'and I'll take you over to see George Storefield's new place. A ride will do me good, and I daresay you're not tired.'

I caught her horse and saddled him for her, and off we went down the old track we knew so well all our lives.

I told her all about our lark with old George, and how good he'd been through it all; besides promising to give us a lift through his country when we made the grand start. She said it was just like him—that he was the kindest soul in the world, and the most thoughtful. The new Mrs. Storefield had been very civil and friendly to her, and told her she knew George's feeling towards her, and respected it. But Aileen never could feel at home in the grand new house now, and only would go to see old Mrs. Storefield, who still lived in the family cottage, and found it the best suited to her. So we yarned away till we got in sight of the place. When I saw the new two-storey stone house I was regular struck all of a heap.

Old George had got on in the world and no mistake. He'd worked early and late, always been as steady as a rock, and had looked ahead instead of taking his pleasure straight off when he got the first few hundred pounds together. He'd seen fat cattle must be dear and scarce for years to come. Noticed, too, that however cheap a far-away bit of country was held, sometimes bought for £200 or £300, it always rose in value year by year. So with store cattle. Now and again they'd fall to nothing. Then he'd buy a whole lot of poor milkers' calves about Burrangong, or some of those thick places where they never fattened, for £1 a head or less, and send them away to his runs in the Lachlan. In six months you wouldn't know 'em. They'd come down well-grown fat cattle in a year or two, and be worth their £6 or £8 a head.

The same way with land; he bought up all the little bits of allotments with cottages on them round Parramatta and Windsor way and Campbelltown—all the old-fashioned sleepy old places near Sydney, for cash, and cheap enough. The people that had them, and had lived a pokey life in them for many a year, wanted the money to go to the diggings with, and quite right, too. Still and all this land was rising in value, and George's children, if he had any, would be among the richest people in the colony.

After he'd married Miss Oldham—they were Hawkesbury people, her grandfather, old Captain Oldham, was one of the officers in the first regiment that came out—he didn't see why he shouldn't have as good a house as any one else. So he had a gentleman up from Sydney that drew plans, and he had a real stone house built, with rooms upstairs, and furniture to match, a new garden, and a glass house at the side, for all the world like some of them grand places in Darling Point, near Sydney.

Aileen wouldn't go in, and you may be sure I didn't want to, but we rode all round the place, a little way off, and had a real good look at everything. There wasn't a gentleman in the country had better outbuildings of all sorts. It was a real tiptop place, good enough for the Governor himself if he came to live up the country. All the old fencing had been knocked down, and new railings and everything put up. Some of the scraggy trees had been cleared away, and all the dead wood burned. I never thought the old place could have showed out the way it did. But money can do a lot. It ain't everything in this world. But there's precious little it won't get you, and things must be very bad it won't mend. A man must have very little sense if he don't see as he gets older that character and money are the two things he's got to be carefullest of in this world. If he's not particular to a shade about either or both of 'em, he'll find his mistake.

After we'd had a good look round and seen the good well-bred stock in the paddocks, the growing crops all looking first-rate, everything well fed and hearty, showing there was no stint of grub for anything, man or beast, we rode away from the big house entrance and came opposite the slip-rails on the flat that led to the old cottage.

'Wouldn't you like to go in just for a minute, Dick?' says Aileen.

I knew what she was thinking of.

I was half a mind not, but then something seemed to draw me, and I was off my horse and had the slip-rail down before I knew where I was.

We rode up to the porch just outside the verandah where George's father had planted the creeping roses; big clusters of bloom they used to have on 'em when I was a boy. He showed 'em to me, I remember, and said what fine climbers they were. Now they were all over the porch, and the verandah, and the roof of the cottage, all among the shingles. But Mrs. Storefield wouldn't have 'em cut because her old man had planted 'em. She came out to see us.

'Well, Ailie, child,' says she, 'come along in, don't sit there on your horse. Who's this you've got with you? Oh! it's you, Dick, is it? My eyes ain't as good as they were. Well, come along in, too. You're on the wrong road, and worse'll come of it. But come along in, I'm not going to be the one to hunt you. I remember old times when you were a little toddling chap, as bold as a lion, and no one dreamt you'd grow up to be the wild chap you are. Gracey's inside, I think. She's as big a fool about ye as ever.'

I very near broke down at this. I could stand hard usage, and send back as good as I got; but this good old woman, that had no call to think anything of me, but that I had spoiled her daughter's chance of marrying well and respectably—when she talked to me this way, I came close up to making a fool of myself.

We walked in. Gracey was sewing away in the little parlour, where there always used to be a nosegay when I was a boy, and it was got out again. There she sat as sober-looking and steady as if she'd been there for five years, and meant to be for five years more. She wasn't thinking of anybody coming, but when she looked up and saw me her face changed all of a sudden, and she jumped up and dropped her work on the floor.

"Why, whatever brings you here, Dick?' she said. 'Don't you know it's terribly dangerous? Sir Ferdinand is always about here now. He stayed at George's new house last night. Wasn't he at Rocky Flat to-day?'

'Yes, but he won't be back for a week. He told Aileen here he wouldn't.' Here I looked at them both.

'Aileen's carrying on quite a flirtation with Sir Ferdinand,' says Gracey. 'I don't know what someone else would say if he saw everything.'

'Doesn't he talk to any one when he comes here, or make himself pleasant?' I said. 'Perhaps there's more than one in the game.'

'Perhaps there is,' says Gracey; 'but he thinks, I believe, that he can get something out of us girls about you and your goings on, and where you plant; and we think we're quite as clever as he is, and might learn something useful, too. So that's how the matter lies at present. Are you going to be jealous?'

'Not a bit in the world,' I said, 'even if I had the right. I'll back you two, as simple as you look, against any inspector of police from here to South Australia.'

After this we began to talk about other things, and I told Gracey all about our plans and intentions. She listened very quiet and steady to it all, and then she said she thought something might come of it. Anyhow, she would go whenever I sent for her to come, no matter where.

'What I've said to you, Dick, I've said for good and all. It may be in a month or two, or it may be years and years. But whenever the time comes, and we have a chance, a reasonable chance, of living peaceably and happily, you may depend upon my keeping my word if I'm alive.'

We three had a little more talk together, and Aileen and I mounted and rode home.

It was getting on dusk when we started. They wanted us to stop, but I daren't do it. It was none too safe as it was, and it didn't do to throw a chance away. Besides, I didn't want to be seen hanging about George's place. There was nobody likely to know about Aileen and me riding up together and stopping half-an-hour; but if it came to spending the evening, there was no saying who might have ears and eyes open. At home I could have my horse ready at a minute's warning, and be off like a shot at the first whisper of danger.

So off we went. We didn't ride very fast back. It was many a day since we had ridden over that ground together side by side. It might be many a day, years perhaps, before we did the same thing again. Perhaps never! Who was to know? In the risks of a life like mine, I might never come back—never set eyes again upon the sister that would have given her life for mine! Never watch the stars glitter through the forest-oak branches, or hear the little creek ripple over the slate bar as it did to-night.

CHAPTER XLVIII

We rode along the old track very quiet, talking about old times—or mostly saying nothing, thinking our own thoughts. Something seemed to put it into my head to watch every turn in the track—every tree and bush by the roadside—every sound in the air—every star in the sky. Aileen rode along at last with her head drooped down as if she hadn't the heart to hold it up. How hard it must have seemed to her to think she didn't dare even to ride with her own brother in the light of day without starting at every bush that stirred—at every footstep, horse or man, that fell on her ear!

There wasn't a breath of air that night. Not a leaf stirred—not a bough moved of all the trees in the forest that we rode through. A 'possum might chatter or a night-owl cry out, but there wasn't any other sound, except the ripple of the creek over stones, that got louder and clearer as we got nearer Rocky Flat: There was nothing like a cloud in the sky even. It wasn't an over light night, but the stars shone out like so many fireballs, and it was that silent any one could almost have fancied they heard the people talking in the house we left, though it was miles away.

'I sometimes wonder,' Aileen says, at last, raising up her head, 'if I had been a man whether I should have done the same things you and Jim have, or whether I should have lived honestly and worked steadily like George over there. I think I should have done so, I really do; that nothing would have tempted me to take what was not my own—or to—to—do other things. I don't think it is in my nature somehow.'

'I don't say as you would, Ailie,' I put in; 'but there's many things to be thought of when you come to reckon what a boy sees, and how he's brought up in the bush. It's different with girls—though I've known some of them that were no great shakes either, and middling handy among the clear-skins, too.'

'It's hard to say,' she went on, more as if she was talking to herself than to me; 'I feel that. Bad example—love of pleasure—strong temptation—evil company—all these are heavy weights to drag down men's souls to hell. Who knows whether I should have been better than the thousands, the millions, that have fallen, that have taken the broad road that leads to destruction. Oh! how dreadful it seems to think that when once a man has sinned in some ways in this world there's no turning back—no hope—no mercy—only long bitter years of prison life—worse than death; or, if anything can be worse, a felon's death; a doom dark and terrible, dishonouring to those that die and to those that live. Oh that my prayers may avail—not my prayers only, but my life's service—my life's service.'

Next morning I was about at daybreak and had my horse fed and saddled up with the bridle on his neck, ready all but slipping the bit into his mouth, in case of a quick start. I went and helped Aileen to milk her cows, nine or ten of them there were, a fairish morning's work for one girl; mothering the calves, bailing up, leg-roping, and all the rest of it. We could milk well, all three of us, and mother, too, when she was younger. Women are used to cattle in Ireland, and England, too. The men don't milk there, I hear tell. That wouldn't work here. Women are scarce in the regular bush, and though they'll milk for their own good and on their own farms, you'll not get a girl to milk, when she's at service, for anybody else.

One of the young cows was a bit strange with me, so I had to shake a stick at her and sing out 'Bail up' pretty rough before she'd put her head in. Aileen smiled something like her old self for a minute, and said—

'That comes natural to you now, Dick, doesn't it?'

I stared for a bit, and then burst out laughing. It was a rum go, wasn't it? The same talk for cows and Christians. That's how things get stuck into the talk in a new country. Some old hand like father, as had been assigned to a dairy settler, and spent all his mornings in the cowyard, had taken to the bush and tried his hand at sticking up people. When they came near enough, of course, he'd pop out from behind a tree or a rock, with his old musket or a pair of pistols, and when he wanted 'em to stop 'Bail up, d— yer,' would come a deal quicker and more natural-like to his tongue than 'Stand.' So 'bail up' it was from that day to this, and there'll have to be a deal of change in the ways of the colonies and them as come from 'em before anything else takes its place, between the man that's got the arms and the man that's got the money.

After we'd turned out the cows we put the milk into the little dairy. How proud Jim and I used to be because we dug out the cellar part, and built the sod wall round the slabs! Father put on the thatch; then it was as cool and clean as ever. Many a good drink of cold milk we had there in the summers that had passed away. Well, well, it's no use thinking of those sort of things. They're dead and gone, like a lot of other things and people—like I shall be before long, if it comes to that.

We had breakfast pretty comfortable and cheerful. Mother looked pleased and glad to see me once more, and Aileen had got on her old face again, and was partly come round to her old ways.

After breakfast Aileen and I went into the garden and had a long talk over the plan we had chalked out for getting away to Queensland. I got out a map Starlight had made and showed her the way we were going to head, and why he thought it more likely to work than he had done before. I was to make my way down the Macquarie and across by Duck Creek, George's station, Willaroon; start from there with a mob of cattle to Queensland as drover or anything that would suit my book.

Jim was to get on to one of the Murray River boats at Swan Hill, and stick to her till he got a chance to go up the Darling with an Adelaide boat to Bourke. He could get across from there by Cunnamulla towards Rockhampton, and from there we were safe to find plenty of vessels bound for the islands or San Francisco. We had hardly cared where, as far as that goes, as long as we got clear away from our own country.

As soon as Jeanie got a word from Jim that he'd sailed and was clear of Australia, she'd write up to Aileen, who was to go down to Melbourne, and take mother with her. They could stop with Jeanie until they got a message from San Francisco to say he'd safely arrived there. After that they could start by the first steamer. They'd have money enough to take their passages and something handsome in cash when they got to land.

Aileen agreed to it all, but in a curious sort of way. 'It looked well,' she said, 'and might be carried out, particularly as we were all going to work cautiously and with such a lot of preparation.' Everything that she could do would be done, we might be sure; but though she had prayed and sought aid from the Blessed Virgin and the saints —fasting and on on her bare knees, night after night—she had not been able to get one gleam of consolation. Everything looked very dark, and she had a terrible feeling of anxiety and dread about the carrying it out. But she didn't want to shake my courage, I could see; so she listened and smiled and cheered me up a bit at the end, and I rode away, thinking there was a good show for us after all.

I got back to the Hollow right enough, and for once in a way it seemed as if the luck was on our side. Maybe it was going to turn— who was to know? There had been men who had been as deep in it as any of us that had got clean away to other countries and lived safe and comfortable to the day of their death—didn't die so soon either-- lived to a good round age, and had wives and children round them that never knew but what they'd been as good as the best. That wouldn't be our case; but still if we once were able to put the sea between us and our old life the odds would be all in our favour instead of being a hundred to one that we weren't placed and no takers.

Starlight was glad enough to see me back, and like everything he tackled, had been squaring·it all for our getting away with head and hand. We wanted to take everything with us that could do us any good, naturally. Father and he had made it right with some one they knew at Turon to take the gold and give them a price for it—not all it was worth, but something over three-fourths value. The rest he was to keep for his share, for trouble and risk. There was some risk, no doubt, in dealing with us, but all the gold that was bought in them days wasn't square, not by a lot. But there was no way of swearing to it. Gold was gold, and once it was in the banks it was lumped up with the rest. There was a lot of things to be thought of before we regularly made a move for good and all; but when you make up your mind for a dart, it's wonderful how things shape. We hadn't much trouble dividing the gold, and what cash there was we could whack easy enough. There was the live stock that was running in the Hollow, of course. We couldn't well take them with us, except a few of the horses. We made a deal at last with father for them. He took my share and Starlight's, and paid us in cash out of his share of the notes. All we wanted was a couple of horses each, one to carry a pack, one to ride.

As for dad, he told us out, plump and plain, that he wasn't going to shift. The Hollow was good enough for him, and there he was going to stop. If Jim and I and Starlight chose to try and make blank emigrants of ourselves, well and good. He didn't see as they'd have such a rosy time getting over to these new townships on the other side. We might get took in, and wish we was back again before all was said and done. But some people could never let well alone. Here we had everything that any man in his senses could wish for, and we wasn't contented. Everyone was going to cut away and leave him; he'd be all by himself, with no one but the dog for company, and be as miserable as a bandicoot; but no one cared a blank brass farden about that.

'Come with us, governor,' says Starlight, 'have a cruise round the world, and smell salt water again. You've not been boxed up in the bush all your life, though you've been a goodish while there. Make a start, and bring old Crib, too.'

'I'm too old and getting stiff in the j'ints,' says dad, brightening up a bit, 'or I don't say as I wouldn't. Don't mind my growling. But I'm bound to be a bit lonely like when you are all drawed off the camp. No! take your own way and I'll take mine.'

'Next Monday ought to see us off,' says Starlight. 'We have got the gold and cash part all right. I've had that money paid to Knightley's credit in the Australian Bank I promised him, and got a receipt for it.'

'That's just like yer,' says father, 'and a rank soft thing for a man as has seen the world to drop into. Losin' yer share of the five hundred quid, and then dropping a couple of hundred notes at one gamble, besides buying a horse yer could have took for nothing. He'll never bring twenty pound again, neither.'

'Always pay my play debts,' says Starlight. 'Always did, and always will. As for the horse—a bargain, a bargain.'

'And a dashed bad bargain, too. Why didn't ye turn parson instead of taking to the bush?' says father, with a grin. 'Dashed if I ain't seen some parsons that could give you odds and walk round ye at horse-dealin'.'

'You take your own way, Ben, and I'll take mine,' says Starlight rather fierce, and then father left off and went to do something or other, while us two took our horses and rode out. We hadn't a long time to be in the old Hollow now. It had been a good friend to us in time of need, and we was sorry in a kind of way to leave it. We were going to play for a big stake, and if we lost we shouldn't have another throw in.

Our horses were in great buckle now; they hadn't been doing much lately. I had the one I'd brought with me, and a thoroughbred brown horse that had been broken in the first season we came there.

Starlight was to ride Rainbow, of course, and he had great picking before he made up his mind what to choose for second horse. At last he pitched upon a thoroughbred bay mare named Locket that had been stolen from a mining township the other side of the country. She was the fastest mare they'd ever bred—sound, and a weight-carrier, too.

'I think I'll take Locket after all," says he, after thinking about it best part of an hour. 'She's very fast and a stayer. Good-tempered, too, and the old horse has taken up with her. It will be company for him.'

'Take your own way,' I said, 'but I wouldn't chance her. She's known to a lot of jockey-boys and hangers-on. They could swear to that white patch on her neck among a thousand.'

'If you come to that, Rainbow is not an every-day horse, and I can't leave him behind, can I? I'll ship him, if I can, that's more. But it won't matter much, for we'll have to take back tracks all the way. You didn't suppose we were to ride along the mail road, did you?'

'I didn't suppose anything,' says I, 'but that we were going to clear out the safest way we could. If we're to do the swell business we'd better do it apart, or else put an advertisement into the *Turon Star* that Starlight, Marston, and Co. are giving up business and going to leave the district, all accounts owing to be sent in by a certain date.

'A first rate idea,' says he. 'I'm dashed if I don't do it. There's nothing like making one's exit in good form. How savage Morringer will be! Thank you for the hint, Dick.'

There was no use talking to him when he got into this sort of humour. He was the most mad, reckless character I ever came across, and any kind of checking only seemed to make him worse. So I left him alone, for fear he should want to do something more venturesome still, and went on with my packing and getting ready for the road.

We fixed up to start on the Monday, and get as far away the first couple of days as we could manage. We expected to get a good start by making a great push the first day or two, and, as the police would be thrown off the scent in a way we settled—and a good dodge it was

—we should have all the more time to be clear of New South Wales before they regularly dropped that we were giving them leg bail for it.

The Sunday before Starlight started away by himself, taking a couple of good horses with him—one he led, and a spare saddle, too. He took nothing but his revolver, and didn't say where he was going, but I pretty well guessed to say good-bye to Aileen. Just as he started he looked back and says—

'I'm going for a longish ride to-day, Dick, but I shall be here late if I'm back at all. If anything happens to me my share of what there is I give to her, if she will take it. If not, do the best you can with it for her benefit.'

He didn't take Warrigal with him, which I was sorry for, as the half-caste and I didn't hit it well together, and when we were by ourselves he generally managed to do or say something he knew I didn't like. I kept my hands off him on account of Starlight, but there was many a time my fingers itched to be at him, and I could hardly keep from knocking some of the sulkiness out of him. This day, somehow, I was not in the best of tempers myself. I had a good lot on my mind. Starting away seems always a troublesome, bothering sort of thing, and if a man's at all inclined to be cranky it'll come out then.

Next day we were going to start on a long voyage, in a manner of speaking, and whether we should have a fair wind or the vessel of our fortune would be wrecked and we go down with it no one could say. This is how it happened. One of the horses was bad to catch, and took a little trouble in the yard. Most times Warrigal was quiet enough with 'em, but when he got regular into a rage he'd skin a horse alive, I really believe. Anyhow, he began to hammer the colt with a roping-pole, and as the yard was that high that no beast could jump it he had him at his mercy. I wouldn't have minded a lick or two, but he went on and on, nearly knocking the poor brute down every time, till I could stand it no longer, and told him to drop it.

He gave me some saucy answer, until at last I told him I'd make him. He dared me, and I rushed at him. I believe he'd have killed me that minute if he'd had the chance, and he made a deuced good offer at it.

He stuck to his roping-stick—a good, heavy-ended gum sapling, six or seven feet long—and as I came at him he struck at my head with such vengeance that, if it had caught me fair, I should never have kicked. I made a spring to one side, and it hit me a crack on the shoulder that wasn't a good thing in itself. I was in at him before he could raise his hands, and let him have it right and left.

Down he went and the stick atop of him. He was up again like a wild cat, and at me hammer and tongs—but he hadn't the weight, though he was quick and smart with his hands. I drew off and knocked him clean off his pins. Then he saw it wasn't good enough, and gave it best.

'Never mind, Dick Marston,' says he, as he walked off; and he fixed his eyes on me that savage and deadly-looking, with the blood running down his face, that I couldn't help shivering a bit, 'you'll pay for this. I owe it you and Jim, one apiece.'

'Confound you,' I said, 'it's all your own fault. Why couldn't you stop ill-using the horse? You don't like being hit yourself. How do you think he likes it?'

'What business that of yours?' he said. 'You mind your work and I'll mind mine. This is the worst day's work you've done this year, and so I tell you.'

He went away to his gunyah then, and except doing one or two things for Starlight would not lift his hand for any one that day.

I was sorry for it when I came to think. I daresay I might have got him round with a little patience and humbugging. It's always a mistake to lose your temper and make enemies; there's no knowing what harm they may do ye. People like us oughtn't to throw away a chance, even with a chap like Warrigal. Besides, I knew it would vex Starlight, and for his sake I would have given a trifle it hadn't happened. However, I didn't see how Warrigal could do me or Jim any harm without hurting him, and I knew he'd have cut off his hand rather than any harm should come to Starlight that he could help.

So I got ready. Dad and I had our tea together pretty comfortable, and had a longish talk. The old man was rather down in the mouth for him. He said he somehow didn't expect the fakement to turn out well. 'You're going away,' he said, 'from where you're safe, and there's a many things goes against a man in our line, once he's away from his own beat. You never know how you may be given away. The Captain's all right here, when he's me to look after him, though he does swear at me sometimes; but he was took last time. He was out on his own hook, and it's my belief he'll be took this time if he isn't very careful. He's a good man to fight through things when once he's in the thick of 'em, but he ain't careful enough to keep dark and close when the play isn't good. You draw along steady by yourself till you meet Jim—that's my advice to ye.'

'I mean to do that. I shall work my way down to old George's place, and get on with stock or something till we all meet at Cunnamulla. After that there ain't much chance of these police here grabbing us.'

'Unless you're followed up,' says the old man. 'I've known chaps to go a deuce of a way, once they got on the track, and there's getting some smart fellows among 'em now—native-born chaps as'll be as good at picking up the tracks as you and Jim.'

'Well, we must take our chance. I'm sorry for one thing, that I had that barney with Warrigal. It was all his fault. But I had to give him a hardish crack or two. He'd turn dog on me and Jim, and in a minute, if he saw his way without hurting Starlight.'

'He can't do it,' says dad; 'it's sink or swim with the lot of you. And he dursn't either, not he,' says father, beginning to growl out his words. 'If I ever heard he'd given away any one in the lot I'd have his life, if I had to poleaxe him in George Street. He knows me too.'

We sat yarning away pretty late. The old man didn't say it, but I made out that he was sorry enough for that part of his life which had turned out so bad for us boys, and for mother and Aileen. Bad enough he was in a kind of way, old dad, but he wasn't all bad, and I believe if he could have begun again and thought of what misery he was going to bring on the lot of us he would never have gone on the cross. It was too late, too late now, though, to think of that.

Towards morning I heard the old dog growl, and then the tramp of a horse's feet. Starlight rode up to the fire and let his horse go, then walked straight into his corner and threw himself down without speaking. He had had a precious long ride, and a fast one by the look of his horse. The other one he had let go as soon as he came into the Hollow; but none of the three would be a bit the worse after a few hours' rest. The horses, of course, were spare ones, and not wanted again for a bit.

Next morning it was 'sharp's the word,' and no mistake. I felt a deal smarter on it than yesterday. When you've fairly started for the road half the journey's done. It's the thinking of this and forgetting that, and wondering whether you haven't left behind the t'other thing, that's the miserablest part of going a journey; when you're once away, no matter what's left behind, you can get on some way or other.

We didn't start so over and above early, though Starlight was up as fresh as paint at sunrise, you'd thought he hadn't ridden a yard the day before. Even at the very last there's a lot of things to do and to get. But we all looked slippy and didn't talk much, so that we got through what we had to do, and had all the horses saddled and packed by about eight o'clock. Even Warrigal had partly got over his temper. Of course I told Starlight about it. He gave him a good rowing, and told him he deserved another hammering, which he had a good mind to give him, if we hadn't been starting for a journey. Warrigal didn't say a word to him. He never did. Starlight told me on the quiet, though, he was sorry it happened, 'though it's the rascal's own fault, and served him right. But he's a revengeful beggar,' he says, 'and that he would play you some dog's trick if he wasn't afraid of me, you may depend your life on.'

'Now,' says he, 'we must make our little arrangements. I shall be somewhere about Cunnamulla by the end of this month' (it was only the first week). 'Jim knows that we are to meet there, and if we manage that all right I think the greatest part of the danger will be over. I shall get right across by Dandaloo to the back blocks of the West Bogan country, between it and the Lachlan. There are tracks through the endless mallee scrub, only known to the tribes in the neighbourhood, and a few halt-castes like Warrigal, that have been stock-riding about them. Sir Ferdinand and his troopers might just as well hunt for a stray Arab in the deserts of the Euphrates. If I'm alive—mind you, alive—I'll be at Cunnamulla on the day I mean. And now, good-bye, old fellow. Whatever my sins have been, I've been true to you and your people in the past, and if Aileen and I meet across the seas, as I hope, the new life may partly atone for the old one.

CHAPTER XLIX

He shook hands with me and dad, threw his leg over Rainbow, took Locket's bridle as if he was going for an easy day's ride, and cantered off.

Warrigal nodded to both of us, then brought his pack-horse up level, and followed up.

'There goes the Captain,' says father. 'It's hard to say if we'll ever see him again. I shan't, anyhow, nor you either, maybe. Somehow I've had a notion coming over me this good while as my time ain't going to be long. It don't make no odds, neither. Life ain't no great chop to a man like me, not when he gets the wrong side o' sixty, anyhow. Mine ain't been such a bad innings, and I don't owe much to any man. I mean as I've mostly been square with them that's done me a bad turn. No man can say Ben Marston was ever back'ard in that way; and never will be, that's more. No! them as trod on me felt my teeth some day or other. Eh, old man?' Crib growled. He understood things regular like a Christian, that old dog did. 'And now you're a-goin' off and Jim's gone —seems only t'other day as you and he was little toddlin' chaps, runnin' to meet me when I come home from work, clearin' that fust paddock, and telling me mammy had the tea ready. Perhaps I'd better ha' stuck to the grubbin' and clearin' after all. It looked slow work, but it paid better than this here in the long-run.' Father turns away from me then, and walks back a step or two. Then he faces me. 'Dash it, boy, what are ye waitin' for? Shake hands, and tell Jim the old man han't forgot him yet.'

It was many a day since I'd felt father's hand in kindness; he didn't do them sort of things. I held out mine and his fingers closed on it one minute, like a vice—blest if I didn't expect to feel the bones grate agin one another; he was that strong he hardly knew his own strength, I believe. Then he sits down on the log by the fire. He took out his pipe, but somehow it wouldn't light. 'Good-bye, Crib,' says I. The old dog looked at me for a bit, wagged his tail, and then went and sat between dad's knees. I took my horse and rode away slowish. I felt all dead and alive like when I got near the turn in the track. I looked back and seen the dog and him just the same. I started both horses then. I never set eyes on him again. Poor old dad!

I wasn't very gay for a bit, but I had a good horse under me, another alongside, a smartish lot of cash in notes and gold, some bank deposits too, and all the world before me. My dart now was to make my way to Willaroon and look sharp about it. My chance of getting through was none too good, but I settled to ride a deal at night and camp by day. I began to pick up my spirits after I got on the road that led up the mountain, and to look ahead to the time when I might call myself my own man again.

Next day after that I was at Willaroon. I could have got there overnight, but it looked better to camp near the place and come next morning. There I was all right. The overseer was a reasonable sort of man, and I found old George had been as good as his word, and left word if a couple of men like me and Starlight came up we were to be put on with the next mob of cattle that were going to Queensland. He did a store cattle trade with the far-out squatters that were stocking up new country in Queensland, and it paid him very well, as nearly everything did that he touched. We were to find our own horses and be paid so much a week—three pounds, I think—and so on.

As luck would have it, there was a biggish mob to start in a week, and road hands being scarce in that part the overseer was disappointed that my mate, as he called him, hadn't come on, but I said he'd gone another track.

'Well, he'll hardly get such wages at any other job,' says he, 'and if I was Mr. Storefield I wouldn't hire him again, not if he wanted a billet ever so bad.'

'I don't suppose he will,' says I, 'and serves him quite right too.'

I put my horses in the paddock—there was wild oats and crowsfoot knee-high in it—and helped the overseer to muster and draft. He gave me a fresh horse, of course. When he saw how handy I was in the yard he got quite shook on me, and, says he—

'By George, you're just the chap the boss wants to send out to some new country he's going to take up in Queensland. What's your name? Now I think of it, he didn't tell me.'

'William Turner,' says I.

'Very well, William,' says he, 'you're a dashed good man, I can see, and I wish I could pick up a few more like you. Blessed if I ever saw such a lot of duffers in my life as there are on this side. I've hardly seen a man come by that's worth his grub. You couldn't stop till the next mob starts, I suppose? I'd make it worth your while.'

'I couldn't well this time,' says I; 'my mate's got a friend out north just from home, and we're tied to time to meet him. But if I come back this way I'll put in a year with you.'

'Well, an offer's an offer,' says he. 'I can't say more, but I think you'll do better by stopping on here.'

I got away with the cattle all right, and the drover in charge was told to do all he could for me. The overseer said I was as good as two men, and it was 'Bill' here and 'William' there all the time till we were off. I wasn't sorry to be clear away, for of course any day a trooper might have ridden up and asked questions about the horses, that were a little too good for a working drover.

Besides, I'd had a look at the papers, and I saw that Starlight had been as good as his word, in the matter of the advertisement. Sure enough, the *Turon Star* and a lot of other papers had, on the same day, received the same advertisement, with a pound note enclosed, and instructions to insert it four times.

NOTICE

To all whom it may concern

The Messrs. Marston Brothers and Co., being about to leave the district, request that all accounts against them may be sent to the Police Camp, Turon, addressed to the care of Sir Ferdinand Morringer, whose receipt will be a sufficient discharge.

For the firm,

STARLIGHT.

I couldn't have believed at first that he'd be so mad. But after a bit I saw that, like a lot of his reckless doings, it wasn't so far out after all.

All the papers had taken it up as usual, and though some of them were pretty wild at the insult offered to the Government and so on, I could see they'd most of them come to think it was a blind of some sort, meant to cover a regular big touch that we were going in for, close by home, and wanting to throw the police off the scent once more. If we'd really wanted to make tracks, they said, this would be the last thing we'd think of doing. Bit by bit it was put about as there should be a carefully laid plot to stick up all the banks in Turon on the same day, and make a sweep of all the gold and cash.

I laughed when I saw this, because I knew that it was agreed upon between Aileen and Gracey that, about the time we were fairly started, whichever of them saw Sir Ferdinand first should allow it to be fished out of her, as a great secret, that we were working up to some tremendous big affair of this sort, and which was to put the crown on all our other doings. To make dead sure, we had sent word to Billy the Boy (and some money too) to raise a sham kind of sticking-up racket on the other side of Turon, towards Bathurst way. He was to frighten a few small people that would be safe to talk about it, and make out that all the bush-rangers in the country were camped about there. This was the sort of work that the young villain regularly went in for and took a pleasure in, and by the way the papers put it in he had managed to frighten a lot of travellers and roadside publicans out of their senses most.

As luck would have it, Wall and Hulbert and Moran had been working up towards Mudgee lately and stuck up the mail, and as Master Billy thought it a great lark to ride about with them with a black mask on, people began to think the gangs had joined again and that some big thing, they didn't know what, was really on the cards. So a lot of police were telegraphed for, and the Bathurst superintendent came down, all in a hurry, to the Turon, and in the papers nothing went down but telegrams and yarns about bushrangers. They didn't know what the country was coming to; all the sober-going people wishing they'd never got an ounce of gold in Australia, and every little storekeeper along the line that had £100 in his cash-box hiding it every night and afraid of seeing us ride up every time the dogs barked.

All the time we were heading for Cunnamulla, and leaving New South Wales behind us hand over hand.

The cattle, of course, couldn't travel very fast; ten or twelve miles a day was enough for them. I could have drowned myself in the creeks as we went crawling along sometimes, and I that impatient to get forward. Eighty miles it was from Cunnamulla to the Queensland border. Once we were over that we'd have to be arrested on warrant, and there were lots of chaps, like us, that were 'wanted,' on the far-out north stations. Once we sighted the waters of the Warrego we should feel ourselves more than half free.

Then there was Jim, poor old Jim! He wrote to say he was just starting for Melbourne, and very queer he felt about leaving his wife and boy. Such a fine little chap as he'd grown too. He'd just got his head down, he said, and taken to the pulling (he meant working) like our old near-side poler, and he was as happy as a king, going home to Jeanie at night, and having his three pounds every Saturday. Now he was going away ever so far by land and sea, and God knows when he might see either of 'em again. If it wasn't for the fear he had of being pitched upon by the police any day, and the long sentence he was sure to get, he'd stay where he was. He wasn't sure whether he wouldn't do so now.

After that Aileen had a letter, a short one, from Jeanie. Jim had gone. She had persuaded him for the sake of the boy, though both their hearts were nearly broken. She didn't know whether she'd done right. Perhaps she never might see him again. The poor fellow had forfeited his coach fare once, and come back to stay another day with her. When he did go he looked the picture of misery, and something told her it was their last parting.

Well, we struck the river about ten miles this side of Cunnamulla, where there was a roadside inn, a small, miserable kind of place, just one of those half-shanties, half-public-houses, fit for nothing but to trap bushmen, and where the bad grog kills more men in a year than a middling break-out of fever.

Somewhere about here I expected to hear of the other two. We'd settled to meet a few miles one side or the other of the township. It didn't much matter which. So I began to look about in case I might get word of either of 'em, even if they didn't turn up to the time.

Somewhere about dinner time (twelve o'clock) we got the cattle on to the river and let 'em spread over the flat. Then the man in charge rode up to the inn, the Traveller's Rest, a pretty long rest for some of 'em (as a grave here and there with four panels of shickery two-rail fence round it showed), and shouted nobblers round for us.

While we was standing up at the bar, waiting for the cove to serve it out, a flash-looking card he was, and didn't hurry himself, up rides a tall man to the door, hangs up his horse, and walks in. He had on a regular town rig—watch and chain, leather valise, round felt hat, like a chap going to take charge of a store or something. I didn't know him at first, but directly our eyes met I saw it was old Jim. We didn't talk—no fear, and my boss asked him to join us, like any other stranger. Just then in comes the landlady to sharpen up the man at the bar.

'Haven't you served those drinks yet, Bob?' she sings out. 'Why, the gentlemen called for them half-an-hour ago. I never saw such a slow-going crawler as you are. You'd never have done for the Turon boys.'

We all looked at her—not a bad-looking woman she'd been once, though you could see she'd come down in the world and been knocked about a bit. Surely I knew her voice! I'd seen her before —why, of course——

She was quicker than I was.

'Well, Dick!' says she, pouring out all the drinks, taking the note, and rattling down the change on the counter, all in a minute, same as I'd often seen her do before, 'this is a rough shop to meet old friends in, isn't it? So you didn't know me, eh? We're both changed a bit. You look pretty fresh on it. A woman loses her looks sooner than a man when she goes to the bad. And Jim too,' she goes on; 'only to fancy poor old Jim turning up here too! One would think you'd put it up to meet at the township on some plant of that sort.'

It was Kate, sure enough! How in the world did ever she get here? I knew she'd left the Turon, and that old Mullockson had dropped a lot of his money in a big mining company he'd helped to float, and that never turned out gold enough to pay for the quick-silver in the first crushing. We'd heard afterwards that he'd died and she'd married again; but I never expected to see her brought down so low as this—not but what we'd known many a woman that started on the diggings with silks and satins and a big house and plate-glass windows brought down to a cotton gown and a bark shanty before half-a-dozen years were over.

Jim and I both looked queer. The men began to laugh. Any one could see we were both in a fix. Jim spoke first.

'Are you sure you're not making a mistake, missis?' says he, looking at her very quiet-like. 'Take care what you say.'

He'd better have held his tongue. I don't know whether she really intended to give us away. I don't think she did altogether; but with them kind of women it's a regular toss up whether they'll behave reasonable or not. When they're once started, 'specially if they think they've not been treated on the square, they can't stop themselves.

'Take care what I say!' she breaks out, rising her voice to a scream, and looking as if she'd jump over the bar-counter and tear the eyes out of me. 'Why should I take care? It's you, Dick Marston, you double-faced, treacherous dog that you are, that's got a thousand pounds on your head, that has cause to care, and you, Jim Marston, that's in the same reward, and both of you know it. Not that I've anything against you, Jim. You're a man, and always was. I'll say that for you.'

'And you're a woman,' groans out poor Jim. 'That's the reason you can't hold your infernal tongue, I suppose.'

Kate had let the cat out of the bag now and no mistake. You should have seen the drover and his men look at us when they found they had the famous bush-rangers among them that they'd heard so much about this years past. Some looked pretty serious and some laughed. The drover spoke first.

'Bush-ranger here or bush-ranger there,' he says, 'I'm going to lose a dashed good man among cattle; and if this chattering fool of a woman had held her tongue the pair of ye might have come on with the cattle till they were delivered. Now I'm a man short, and haven't one as I can trust on a pinch. I don't think any more of you, missis,' he says, 'for being so dashed ready to give away your friends, supposing they had been on the cross.'

But Kate didn't hear. She had fallen down in a kind of fit, and her husband, coming in to see what the row was about, picked her up, and stood looking at us with his mouth open.

'Look here, my man,' says I, 'your wife's taken me and this gentleman,' pointing to Jim, 'for some people she knew before on the diggings, and seems to have got rather excited over it. If it was worth our while to stay here, we'd make her prove it. You'd better get her to lie down, and advise her, when she comes to, to hold her tongue, or you might be made to suffer by it.'

'She's a terror when she's put out, and that's God's truth,' says the chap; and starting to drag her over to one of the bits of back bedrooms. 'It's all right, I daresay. She will keep meddling with what don't consarn her. I don't care who yer are or what yer are. If you knowed her afore, I expect ye'll think it best to clear while she's unsensible like.'

'Here's a shout all round for these men here,' says I, throwing a note on the bar. 'Never mind the change. Good-bye, chaps. This gentleman and I have some business together, and there's no bush-ranging in it, you may take my word.'

We all left then. The men went back to their cattle. Jim rode quietly along the road to Cunnamulla just like any other traveller.

I went down and saddled up my horse. I'd got everything I wanted in my swag, so I'd left the other horse at Willaroon.

'Never mind the settlement,' says I to the drover. 'I'll be coming back to the station after I've finished my business in Queensland, and we can make up the account then.'

The overseer looked rather doubtful.

'This seems rather mixed,' says he. 'Blest if I understand it. That woman at the pub seems half off her head to me. I can't think two quiet-looking chaps like you can be the Marstons. You've been a thundering good road hand anyhow, and I wish you luck.'

He shook hands with me. I rode off and kept going along the road till I overtook Jim.

When I'd gone a mile or two there was Jim riding steadily along the road, looking very dull and down-like, just the way he used to do when he was studying how to get round a job of work as he wasn't used to. He brightens up a bit when he sees me, and we both jumped off, and had a good shake-hands and a yarn. I told him about mother and Aileen, and how I'd left dad all by himself. He said Jeanie and the boy were all right, but of course he'd never heard of 'em since, and couldn't help feeling dubersome about meeting her again, particular now this blessed woman had dropped across us, and wouldn't keep her mouth shut.

'As sure as we've had anything to do with her, bad luck's followed up,' says Jim; 'I'd rather have faced a trooper than seen her face again.'

'She can't do much now,' says I. 'We're across the border. I wonder where Starlight is—whether he's in the township or not? As soon as we meet him we can make straight for the ship.'

'He's there now,' says Jim. 'He was at Kate's last night.'

'How do you know that?'

'I heard her mutter something about it just when she went into that fit, or whatever it was. Devilment, I think. I never saw such a woman; and to think she's my Jeanie's sister!'

'Never mind that, Jim. These things can't be helped. But what did she say?'

'Something like this: "He thought I didn't know him, passing himself off as a gentleman. Warrigal, too. Kate Morrison's eyes are too sharp for that, as he'll find out."'

'Think she'll give us away again, Jim?'

'God only knows. She mightn't this time, unless she wants to smother you altogether, and don't mind who she hurts along with you.'

'There's one good thing in it,' says I; 'there's no police nearer than Trielgerat, and it's a long day's ride to them. We made it all right before we left the Turon. All the police in the country is looking for us on the wrong road, and will be for a week or two yet.'

Then I told him about Aileen putting Sir Ferdinand on the wrong lay, and he said what a clever girl she was, and had as much pluck and sense as two or three men. 'A deal more than we've ever showed, Dick,' says he, 'and that's not saying much either.'

He laughed in his quiet way when he heard about Starlight's advertisement in the *Turon Star*, and said it was just like him.

'He's a wonderful clever fellow, the Captain. I've often thought when I've been by myself in Melbourne, sitting quiet, smoking at night, and turning all these things over, that it's a wonder he don't shoot himself when he thinks of what he is and the man he ought to be.'

'He's head enough to take us safe out of this dashed old Sydney side,' says I, 'and land us in another country, where we'll be free and happy in spite of all that's come and gone. If he does that, we've no call to throw anything up to him.'

'Let him do that,' says Jim, 'and I'll be his servant to the day of my death. But I'm afeard it isn't to be any more than going to heaven right off. It's too good, somehow, to come true; and yet what a thing it is to be leading a working, honest life and be afraid of no man! I was very near like that in Melbourne, Dick,' he says; 'you've no notion what a grand thing it was—when I'd done my week's work, and used to walk about with Jeanie and her boy on Sundays, and pass the time of day with decent, square coves that I knew, and never dreamed I was different; then the going home peaceful and contented to our own little cottage; I tell you, Dick, it was heaven on earth. No wonder it regular broke my heart to leave it.'

'We're close up to the township now,' says I. 'This wire fence and the painted gate ain't more than a couple of miles off, that chap said at the inn. I wish there was a fire-stick in it, and I'd never gone inside a door of it. However, that says nothing. We've got to meet Starlight somehow, and there's no use in riding in together. You go in first, and I'll take a wheel outside the house and meet you in the road a mile or two ahead. Where's your pistol? I must have a look at mine. I had to roll it up in my swag, and it wants loading.'

'Mine's a good tool,' says Jim, bringing out a splendid-looking revolver—one of these new Dean and Adams's. 'I can make prime shooting at fifty yards; but I hope to God I shan't want to use it.'

'There's no fear yet a bit,' says I; 'but it's as well to be ready. I'll load before we go any farther.'

I loaded and put her back in the belt. We were just going to push on when we heard the sound of galloping, and round a patch of scrub comes a horseman at full speed. When he sees us he cuts off the road and comes towards us.

There was only one horse that carried himself like that, even when he was pulling double. We spotted him the same second. Rainbow and Starlight on him! What in thunder makes him ride like that?

When he came closer we saw by his face that something was up. His eyes had the gloomy, dull fire in them that put me in mind of the first time I saw him when he came back wounded and half dead to the Hollow.

'Don't stop to talk, boys,' he sings out, without stopping, 'but ride like the devil. Head to the left. That infernal Warrigal has laid the police on your track, Dick. They were seen at Willaroon; may be up at any minute.'

'Where's Warrigal now?' I said, as we all took our horses by the head and made for a patch of dark timber we could see far out on the plain.

'He dropped when I fired at him,' says Starlight; 'but whether the poor beggar's dead or not I can't say. It isn't my fault if he betrays any one again.'

'How did it come out?'

'I was tired of waiting at that confounded hotel—not a soul to speak to. I rode back as far as Kate's, just to see if you had passed. She didn't know me a bit.'

'The deuce she didn't! Why, she broke out on me and Jim. Said something about you and Warrigal too.'

'Wonderful creatures, women,' says he, thoughtful-like; 'and yet I used to think I understood them. No time to do anything, though.'

'No; the nearest police station's a day off. I'd give a trifle to know who's after us. How did you find out Warrigal's doubling on me? not that it matters now; d—n him!'

'When I talked about going back he was in a terrible fright, and raised so many objections that I saw he had some reason for it; so I made him confess.'

'How did he do it?'

'After we'd passed Dandaloo, and well inside the West Bogan scrubs, he picked up a blackfellow that had once been a tracker; gave him a pound to let them know at the police camp that you were making out by Willaroon.'

'I knew he had it in for me,' said I; 'but I depended on his not doing anything for fear of hurting you.'

'So I thought, too; but he expected you'd be trapped at Willaroon before there would be time for you to catch me up. If he hadn't met that Jemmy Wardell, I daresay he wouldn't have thought of it. When he told me I was in such an infernal rage that I fired point blank at him; didn't wait to see whether he was dead or alive, and rode straight back here to warn you. I was just in time—eh, Jim, old man? Why, you look so respectable they'd never have known you. Why didn't you stay where you were, James?'

'I wish to God I had!' says poor old Jim. 'It's too late to think of that now.'

We hadn't over much time for talking, and had to range up

close to do it at all at the pace we were going. We did our best and must have ridden many a mile before dark. Then we kept going through the night. Starlight was pilot, and by the compass he carried we were keeping something in a line with the road. But we missed Warrigal in the night work, and more than once I suspected we were going round and not keeping a straight course.

We didn't do badly after all, for we struck the main road at daylight and made out that we were thirty miles the other side of Cunnamulla, and in the right direction. The worst of it was, like all short cuts and night riding, we'd taken about twice as much out of our horses as we need have done if we'd been certain of our line.

'This ought to be Murrynebone Creek,' says Starlight, 'by the look of it,' when we came to a goodish broad bit of water. 'The crossing place is boggy, so they told me at the hotel. We may as well pull up for a spell. We're in Queensland now, that's one comfort.'

It took us all we knew to get over; it was a regular quicksand. Rainbow never got flustered if he was up to the neck in a bog, but my horse got frightened and plunged, so that I had to jump off. Jim's horse was a trifle better, but he hadn't much to spare. We weren't sorry to take the bridles out of their mouths and let them pick a bit on the flat when we got safe over.

We didn't unsaddle our horses—no fear; we never did that only at night; not always then. We took the bits out of their mouths, and let them pick feed round about, with the bridle under their feet, stockhorse fashion. They were all used to it, and you'd see 'em put their foot on a rein, and take it off again, regular as if they knew all about it. We could run full pelt and catch 'em all three in a minute's notice; old Rainbow would hold up his head when he saw Starlight coming, and wait for him to mount if there was a hundred horses galloping past. Lucky for him, he'd done it scores of times; once on his back there was no fear of any other horse overhauling him, any more than a coolie dog or a flying doe kangaroo.

Pretty well settled it came to be amongst us that we should be well into Queensland before the police were handy. Starlight and Jim were having a pitch about the best way to get aboard one of these pearling craft, and how jolly it would be. The captains didn't care two straws what sort of passengers they took aboard so long as they had the cash and were willing to give a hand when they were wanted.

We were just walking towards the horses to make a fresh start, when Starlight puts up his hand. We all listened. There was no mistaking the sound we heard—horses at speed, and mounted men at that. We were in a sort of angle. We couldn't make back over the infernal boggy creek we'd just passed, and they seemed to be coming on two sides at once.

'By ——! they're on us,' says Starlight; and he cocks his rifle, and walks over quite cool to the old horse. 'Our chance, boys, is to exchange shots, and ride for it. Keep cool, don't waste your fire, and if we can drop a couple of them we may slip them yet.'

We hadn't barely time to get to our horses, when out of the timber they came—in two lots—three on each side. Police, sure enough; and meeting us. That shook us a bit. How the devil did they get ahead of us after the pace we'd ridden the last twenty-four hours, too? When they came close we could see how it was, Sir Ferdinand and three troopers on one side; Inspector Goring, with two more, on the left, while outside, not far from the lead, rode Sir Watkin, the Braidwood black tracker—the best hand at that work in the three colonies, if you could keep him sober.

Now we could see why they took us in front. He had kept out wide when he saw the tracks were getting hot, so as to come in on the road ahead of us, and meet us full in the teeth.

He had hit it off well this time, blast him! We couldn't make back on account of the creek, and we had double our number to fight, and good men too, before we could break through, if we could do that.

Our time was come if we hadn't the devil's own luck; but we had come out of as tight a place before, and might do it again.

When they were within fifty yards Sir Ferdinand calls out, 'Surrender! It's no use, men,' says he; 'I don't want to shoot you down, but you must see you're outnumbered. There's no disgrace in yielding now.'

'Come on!' says Starlight; 'don't waste your breath! There's no man here will be taken alive.'

With that, Goring lets drive and sends a bullet that close by my head I put my hand up to feel the place. All the rest bangs away, black tracker and all. I didn't see Sir Ferdinand's pistol smoke. He and Starlight seemed to wait. Then Jim and I fires steady. One trooper drops badly hit, and my man's horse fell like a log and pinned his rider under him, which was pretty nigh as good.

'Steady does it,' says Starlight, and he makes a snap shot at the tracker, and breaks his right arm.

'Three men spoiled,' says he; 'one more to the good and we may charge.'

Just as he said this the trooper that was underneath the dead horse crawls from under him, the off side, and rests his rifle on his wither. Starlight had just mounted when every rifle and pistol in the two parties was fired at one volley. We had drawn closer to one another, and no one seemed to think of cover.

Rainbow rears up, gives one spring, and falls backward with a crash. I thought Starlight was crushed underneath him, shot through the neck and flank as he was, but he saved himself somehow, and stood with his hand on Rainbow's mane, when the old horse rose again all right, head and tail well up, and as steady as a rock. The blood was pouring out of his neck, but he didn't seem to care two straws about it. You could see his nostril spread out and his eye looking twice as big and fiery.

Starlight rests his rifle a minute on the old horse's shoulder, and the man that had fired the shot fell over with a kick. Something hits me in the ribs like a stone, and another on the right arm, which drops down just as I was aiming at a young fellow with light hair that had ridden pretty close up, under a myall tree.

Jim and Sir Ferdinand let drive straight at one another the same minute. They both meant it this time. Sir Ferdinand's hat turned part round on his head, but poor old Jim drops forward on his face and tears up the grass with his hands. I knew what that sign meant.

Goring rides straight at Starlight and calls on him to surrender. He had his rifle on his hip, but he never moved. There he stood, with his hand on the mane of the old horse. 'Keep back if you're wise, Goring,' says he, as quiet and steady as if he'd been cattle-drafting. 'I don't want to have your blood on my head; but if you must——'

Goring had taken so many men in his day that he was got over confident-like. He thought Starlight would give in at the last moment or miss him in the rush. My right arm was broken, and now that Jim was down we might both be took, which would be a great crow for the police. Anyhow, he was a man that didn't know what fear was, and he chanced it.

Two of the other troopers fired point blank at Starlight as Goring rode at him, and both shots told. He never moved, but just lifted his rifle as the other came up at the gallop. Goring threw up his arms, and rolled off his horse a dying man.

Starlight looked at him for a minute.

'We're quits,' he says; 'it's not once or twice either you've pulled trigger on me. I knew this day would come.'

Then he sinks down slowly by the side of the old horse and leans against his foreleg, Rainbow standing quite steady, only tossing his head up and down the old way. I could see, by the stain on Starlight's mouth and the blood on his breast, he'd been shot through the lungs.

I was badly hit too, and going in the head, though I didn't feel it so much at the time. I began to hear voices like in a dream; then my eyes darkened, and I fell like a log.

When I came to, all the men was off their horses, some round Goring—him they lifted up and propped against a tree; but he was stone dead, any one could see. Sir Ferdinand was on his knees beside Starlight, talking to him, and the other saying a word now and then, quite composed and quiet-like.

'Close thing, Morringer, wasn't it?' I heard him say. 'You were too quick for us; another day and we'd been out of reach.'

'True enough. Horses all dead beat; couldn't raise a remount for love or money.'

'Well, the game's up now, isn't it? I've held some good cards too, but they never told, somehow. I'm more sorry for Jim—and—that poor girl, Aileen, than I am for myself.'

'Don't fret—there's a good fellow. Fortune of war, you know. Anything else?'

Here he closed his eyes, and seemed gone; but he wakes up again, and begins in a dreamy way. His words came slowly, but his voice never altered one bit.

'I'm sorry I fired at poor Warrigal now. No dog ever was more faithful than he has been to me all through till now; but I was vexed at his having sold Dick and poor Jim.'

'We knew we should find you here or hereabouts without that,' says Sir Ferdinand.

'How was that?'

'Two jockey-boys met you one night at Calga gate; one of them recognised Locket by the white patch on her neck. He wired to us at the next station.'

'So you were right, after all, Dick. It was a mistake to take that mare. I've always been confoundedly obstinate; I admit that. Too late to think of it now, isn't it?'

'Anything else I can do?' says Sir Ferdinand.

'Give her this ring,' he pulls it off his finger, 'and you'll see Maddie Barnes gets the old horse, won't you? Poor old Rainbow! I know she'll take care of him; and a promise is a promise.'

'All right. He's the property of the Government now, you know; but I'll square it somehow. The General won't object under the circumstances.'

Then he shuts his eyes for a bit. After a while he calls out—

'Dick! Dick Marston.'

'I'm here,' says I.

'If you ever leave this, tell Aileen that her name was the last word I spoke—the very last. She foresaw this day; she told me so. I've had a queer feeling too, this week back. Well, it's over now. I don't know that I'm sorry, except for others. I say, Morringer, do you remember the last pigeon match you and I shot in, at Hurlingham?'

'Why, good God!' says Sir Ferdinand, bending down, and looking into his face. 'It can't be; yes, by Jove, it is——'

He spoke some name I couldn't catch, but Starlight put a finger on his lips, and whispers—

'You won't tell, will you? Say you won't?'

The other nodded.

He smiled just like his old self.

'Poor Aileen!' he says, quite faint. His head fell back. Starlight was dead!

CHAPTER L

THE breath was hardly out of him when a horse comes tearing through the scrub on to the little plain, with a man on his back that seemed hurt bad or drunk, he rolled in his saddle so. The head of him was bound up with a white cloth, and what you could see of it was dark-looking, with bloodstains on it. I knew the figure and the seat on a horse, though I couldn't see his face. He didn't seem to have much strength, but he was one of those sort of riders that can't fall off a horse, that is unless they're dead. Even then you'd have to pull him down. I believe he'd hang on somehow like a dead 'possum on a branch.

It was Warrigal!

They all knew him when he came close up but none of the troopers raised their pieces or thought of stopping him. If a dead man had rode right into the middle of us he'd have looked like that. He stopped his horse, and slipped off on his feet somehow.

He'd had a dreadful wound, any one could see. There was blood on the rags that bound his head all up, and being round his forehead and over his chin it made him look more and more like a corpse. Not much you could see, only his eyes, that were burning bright like two coals of fire.

Up to Starlight's body he goes and sits himself down by it. He takes the dead man's head into his lap, looks down at the face, and bursts out into the awfullest sort of crying and lamenting I ever heard of a living man. I've seen the native women mourning for their dead with the blood and tears running down their faces together. I've known them sit for days and nights without stirring from round a corpse, not taking a bite or sup the whole time. I've seen white people that's lost an only child that had, maybe, been all life and spirits an hour before. But in all my life I have never seen no man, nor woman neither, show such regular right-down grief as Warrigal did for his master—the only human creature he loved in the wide world, and him lying stiff on the ground before him.

He lifts up the dead face and wipes the blood from the lips so careful; talks to it in his own language (or leastways his mother's) like a woman over a child. Then he sobbed and groaned and shook all over as if the very life was going out of him. At last he lays the head very soft and gentle down on the ground and looks

round. Sir Ferdinand gives him his handkerchief, and he lays it
over the face. Then he turns away from the men that stood round,
and got up looking that despairing and wretched that I couldn't help
pitying him, though he was the cause of the whole thing as far as
we could see.

Sudden as a flash of powder he pulls out a small revolver—a Der-
ringer—Starlight gave him once, and holds it out to me, butt-end
first.

'You shoot me, Dick Marston; you shoot me quick,' he says. 'It's
all my fault. I killed him—I killed the Captain. I want to die and
go with him to the never-never country parson tell us about—up
there!'

One of the troopers knocked his hand up. Sir Ferdinand gave a
nod, and a pair of handcuffs were slipped over his wrists.

'You told the police the way I went?' says I. 'It's all come out
of that.'

'Thought they'd grab you at Willaroon,' says he, looking at me
quite sorrowful with his dark eyes, like a child. 'If you hadn't
knocked me down that last time, Dick Marston, I'd never have done
nothing to you nor Jim. I forgot about the old down. That
brought it all back again. I couldn't help it, and when I see Jimmy
Wardell I thought they'd catch you and no one else.'

'Well, you've made a clean sweep of the lot of us, Warrigal,' says
I; 'poor Jim and all. Don't you ever show yourself to the old man
or go back to the Hollow, if you get out of this.'

'He's dead now. I'll never hear him speak again,' says he, looking
over to the figure on the grass. 'What's the odds about me?'

. . . .

I didn't hear any more; I must have fainted away again. Things
came into my head about being taken in a cart back to Cunnamulla,
with Jim lying dead on one side of me and Starlight on the other.
I was only half-sensible, I expect. Sometimes I thought we were
alive, and another time that the three of us were dead and going
to be buried.

What makes it worse I've seen that sight so often since—the fight
on the plain and the end of it all. Just like a picture it comes back
to me over and over again, sometimes in broad day, as I sit in my
cell, in the darkest midnight, in the early dawn.

It rises before my eyes—the bare plain, and the dead men lying
where they fell; Sir Ferdinand on his horse, with the troopers standing round; and the half-caste sitting with Starlight's head in his
lap, rocking himself to and fro, and crying and moaning like a
woman that's lost her child.

I can see Jim, too—lying on his face with his hat rolled off and
both arms spread out wide. He never moved after. And to think
that only the day before he had thought he might see his wife
and child again! Poor old Jim! If I shut my eyes they won't go

away. It will be the last sight I shall see in this world before—before I'm——

The coroner of the district held an inquest, and the jury found a verdict of 'justifiable homicide by Sir Ferdinand Morringer and other members of the police force of New South Wales in the case of one James Marston, charged with robbery under arms, and of a man habitually known as "Starlight," but of whose real name there was no evidence before the jury.' As for the police, it was wilful murder against us. Warrigal and I were remanded to Turon Court for further evidence, and as soon as we were patched up a bit by the doctor—for both of us looked like making a die of it for two or three weeks—we were started on horseback with four troopers overland all the way back. We went easy stages—we couldn't ride any way fast—both of us handcuffed, and our horses led.

One day, about a fortnight after, as we were crossing a river, Warrigal's horse stopped to drink. It was a swim in the middle of the stream, and the trooper, who was a young chap just from the depôt, let go his leading rein for a bit. Warrigal had been as quiet as a lamb all the time, and they hadn't a thought of his playing up. I heard a splash, and looked round; his horse's head was turned to the bank, and, before the trooper could get out of the river, he was into the river scrub and away as fast as his horse could carry him. Both the troopers went after him, and we waited half-an-hour, and then went on to the next police station to stop till they came back.

Next day, late, they rode in with their horses regularly done and knocked up, leading his horse, but no Warrigal. He had got clear away from them in the scrub, jumped off his horse when they were out of sight, taken off his boots and made a straight track for the West Bogan scrub. There was about as much chance of running him down there as a brumbie with a day's start or a wallaroo that was seen on a mountain side the week before last. I didn't trouble my head that much to think whether I was glad or sorry. What did it matter? What did anything matter now? The only two men I loved in the world were dead; the two women I loved best left forsaken and disgraced; and I—well, I was on my way to be hanged!

I was taken along to Turon and put into the gaol, there to await my trial. They didn't give me much of a chance to bolt, and I wouldn't have taken it if they had. I was dead tired of my life, and wouldn't have taken my liberty then and there if they'd given it me. All I wanted was to have the whole thing done and over without any more bother.

It all passed like a dream. The court was crowded till there wasn't standing room, every one wanting to get a look at Dick Marston, the famous bush-ranger. The evidence didn't take so very long. I was proved to have been seen with the rest the day the escort was robbed; the time the four troopers were shot. I was suspected of being concerned in Hagan's party's death, and half-a-dozen other things. Last of all, when Sub-Inspector Goring was killed, and a trooper, besides two others badly wounded.

I was sworn to as being one of the men that fired on the police. I didn't hear a great deal of it, but 'livened up when the judge put on his black cap and made a speech, not a very long one, telling about the way the law was set at naught by men who had dared to infest the highways of the land and rob peaceful citizens with arms and violence. In the pursuit of gain by such atrocious means, blood had been shed, and murder, wilful murder, had been committed. He would not further allude to the deeds of blood with which the prisoner at the bar stood charged. The only redeeming feature in his career had been brought out by the evidence tendered in his favour by the learned counsel who defended him. He had fought fairly when opposed by the police force, and he had on more than one occasion acted in concert with the robber known as Starlight, and the brother James Marston, both of whom had fallen in a recent encounter, to protect from violence women who were helpless and in the power of his evil companions. Then the judge pronounced the sentence that I, Richard Marston, was to be taken from the place whence I came, and there hanged by the neck until I was dead. 'And might God have mercy upon my soul!'

My lawyer had beforehand argued that, although I had been seen in the company of persons who had doubtless compassed the unlawfully slaying of the Queen's lieges and peace officers, yet no proof had been brought before the court that day that I had wilfully killed any one. 'He was not aware,' would his Honour remark, 'that any one had seen me fire at any man, whether since dead or alive. He would freely admit that I had been seen in bad company, but that fact would not suffice to hang a man under British rule. It was therefore incumbent on the jury to bring in a verdict for his client of "not guilty."'

But that cock wouldn't fight. I was found guilty by the jury and sentenced to death by the judge. I expect I was taken back without seeing or hearing to the gaol, and I found myself alone in the condemned cell, with heavy leg-irons—worn for the first time in my life. The rough and tumble of a bush-ranger's life was over at last, and this was the finish up.

For the first week or two I didn't feel anything particular. I was hardly awake. Sometimes I thought I must be dreaming—that this man, sitting in a cell, quiet and dull-looking, with heavy irons on his limbs, could never be Dick Marston, the shearer, the stock-rider, the gold-miner, the bush-ranger.

This was the end—the end—the end! I used to call it out sometimes louder and louder, till the warder would come in to see if I had gone mad.

Bit by bit I came to my right senses. I almost think I felt sharper and clearer in my head than I had done for ever so long. Then I was able to realise the misery I had come down to after all our blowing and roving. This was the crush-yard and no gateway. I was safe to be hanged in six weeks, or thereabouts—hanged like a dog! Nothing could alter that, and I didn't want it if it could.

And how did the others get on, those that had their lives bound up with ours, so that we couldn't be hurt without their bleeding, almost in their hearts?—that is, mother's bled to death, at any rate; when she heard of Jim's death and my being taken it broke her heart clean; she never held her head up after. Aileen told me in her letter she used to nurse his baby and cry over him all day, talking about her dear boy Jim. She was laid in the burying-ground at St. Kilda. As to Aileen, she had long vowed herself to the service of the Virgin. She knew that she was committing sin in pledging herself to an earthly love. She had been punished for her sin by the death of him she loved, and she had settled in her mind to go into the convent at Soubiaca, where she should be able to wear out her life in prayer for those of her blood who still lived, as well as for the souls of those who lay in the little burying-ground on the banks of the far Warrego.

Jeanie settled to stop in Melbourne. She had money enough to keep her comfortable, and her boy would be brought up in a different style from his father.

As for Gracey, she sent me a letter in which she said she was like the bird that could only sing one song. She would remain true to me in life and death. George was very kind, and would never allow any one to speak harshly of his former friends. We must wait and make the best of it.

So I was able, you see, to get bits of news even in a condemned cell, from time to time, about the outside world. I learned that Wall and Hulbert and Moran and another fellow were still at large, and following up their old game. Their time, like ours, was drawing short, though.

. . . . .

Well, this has been a thundering long yarn, hasn't it? All my whole life I seem to have lived over again. It didn't take so long in the telling; it's a month to-day since I began. And this life itself has reeled away so quick, it hardly seems a dozen years instead of seven-and-twenty since it began. It won't last much longer. Another week and it will be over. There's a fellow to be strung up before me, for murdering his wife. The scoundrel, I wonder how he feels?

I've had visitors too! some I never thought to see inside this gaol wall. One day who should come in but Mr. Falkland and his daughter. There was a young gentleman with them that they told me was an English lord, a baronet, or something of that sort, and was to be married to Miss Falkland. She stood and looked at me with her big innocent eyes, so pitiful and kind-like. I could have thrown myself down at her feet. Mr. Falkland talked away, and asked me about this and that. He seemed greatly interested. When I told him about the last fight, and of poor Jim being shot dead, and Starlight dying alongside the old horse, the tears came into Miss Falkland's eyes, and she cried for a bit, quite feeling and natural.

Mr. Falkland asked me all about the robbery at Mr. Knightley's, and took down a lot of things in his pocket-book. I wondered what he did that for.

When they said good-bye Mr. Falkland shook hands with me, and said 'he hoped to be able to do some good for me, but not to build anything on the strength of it.'

Then Miss Falkland came forward and held out her beautiful hand to me—to me, as sure as you live—like a regular thoroughbred angel, as she always was. It very nigh cooked me. I felt so queer and strange, I couldn't have spoken a word to save my life.

Sir George, or whatever his name was, didn't seem to fancy it over much, for he said—

'You colonists are strange people. Our friend here may think himself highly favoured.'

Miss Falkland turned towards him and held up her head, looking like a queen, as she was, and says she—

'If you had met me in the last place where I saw this man and his brother, you would not wonder at my avowing my gratitude to both of them. I should despise myself if I did not. Poor Jim saved my life on one occasion, and on another, but far more dreadful day, he—but words, mere words, can never express my deep thankfulness for his noble conduct, and were he here now I would tell him so, and give him my hand, if all the world stood by.'

Sir George didn't say anything after that, and she swept out of the cell, followed by Mr. Falkland and him. It was just as well for him to keep a quiet tongue in his head. I expect she was a great heiress as well as a great beauty, and people of that sort, I've found, mostly get listened to when they speak. When the door shut I felt as if I'd seen the wings of an angel flit through it, and the prison grew darker and darker like the place of lost souls.

CHAPTER LI

ONE day I was told that a lady wanted to see me. When the door of the cell opened who should walk in but Aileen! I didn't look to have seen her. I didn't bother my head about who was coming. What did it matter, as I kept thinking, who came or who went for the week or two that was to pass before the day? Yes, the day, that Thursday, when poor Dick Marston would walk over the threshold of his cell, and never walk over one again.

The warder—him that stopped with me day and night—every man in the condemned cell has to be watched like that—stepped outside the door and left us together. We both looked at one another. She was dressed all in black, and her face was that pale I hardly knew her at first. Then she said, 'Oh, Dick—my poor Dick! is this the way we meet?' and flings herself into my arms. How she cried and sobbed, to be sure. The tears ran down her cheeks like rain, and every time the leg-irons rattled she shook and trembled as if her heart was breaking.

I tried to comfort her; it was no use.

'Let me cry on, Dick,' she said; 'I have not shed a tear since I first heard the news—the miserable truth that has crushed all our vain hopes and fancies; my heart has nearly burst for want of relief. This will do me good. To think—to think that this should be the end of all! But it is just! I cannot dare to doubt Heaven's mercy. What else could we expect, living as we all did—in sin—in mortal sin? I am punished rightly.'

She told me all about poor mother's death. She never held up her head after she heard of Jim's death. She never said a hard word about any one. It was God's will, she thought, and only for His mercy things might have gone worse. The only pleasure she had in her last days was in petting Jim's boy. He was a fine little chap, and had eyes like his father, poor old Jim! Then Aileen broke down altogether, and it was a while before she could speak again.

Jeanie was the same as she had been from the first, only so quiet they could hardly know how much she felt. She wouldn't leave the little cottage where she had been so happy with Jim, and liked to work in the chair opposite to where Jim used to sit and smoke his pipe in the evenings. Most of her friends lived in Melbourne, and she reckoned to stay there for the rest of her life.

As to father, they had never heard a word from him—hardly knew whether he was dead or alive. There was some kind of report that Warrigal had been seen making towards Nulla Mountain, looking very weak and miserable, on a knocked-up horse; but they did not know whether it was true or false.

Poor Aileen stopped till we were all locked up for the night. She seemed as if she couldn't bear to leave me. She had no more hope or tie in life, she said. I was the only one of her people she was likely to see again, and this was the last time—the last time.

'Oh, Dick! oh, my poor lost brother,' she said, 'how clearly I seem to see all things now. Why could we not do so before? I have had my sinful worldly dream of happiness, and death has ended it. When I heard of his death and Jim's my heart turned to stone. All the strength I have shall be given to religion from this out. I can ease my heart and mortify the flesh for the good of my soul. To God—to the Holy Virgin—who hears the sorrows of such as me, I can pray day and night for their souls' welfare—for mine, for yours. And oh, Dick! think when that day, that dreadful day, comes that Aileen is praying for you—will pray for you till her own miserable life ends. And now good-bye; we shall meet on this earth no more. Pray—say that you will pray—pray now that we may meet in heaven.'

She half drew me to my knees. She knelt down herself on the cold stone floor of the cell; and I—well—I seemed to remember the old days when we were both children and used to kneel down by mother's bed, the three of us, Aileen in the middle and one of us boys on each side. The old time came back to me, and I cried like a child.

I wasn't ashamed of it; and when she stood up and said, 'Goodbye,—good-bye, Dick,' I felt a sort of rushing of the blood to my head, and all my wounds seemed as if they would break out again. I very near fell down, what with one thing and another. I sat myself down on my bed, and I hid my face in my hands. When I looked up she was gone.

. . . . .

After that, day after day went on and I scarcely kept count, until somehow I found out it was the last week. They partly told me on the Sunday. The parson—a good, straight, manly man he was— he had me told for fear I should go too close up to it, and not have time to prepare.

Prepare! How was a man like me to prepare? I'd done everything I'd a mind to for years and years. Some good things—some bad— mostly bad. How was I to repent? Just to say I was sorry for them. I wasn't that particular sorry either—that was the worst of it. A deal of the old life was dashed good fun, and I'd not say, if I had the chance, that I wouldn't do just the same over again.

Sometimes I felt as if I ought to understand what the parson tried to hammer into my head; but I couldn't do anything but make a jumble of it. It came natural to me to do some things, and I did them. If I had stopped dead and bucked at father's wanting me and Jim to help duff those weaners, I really believe all might have come right. Jim said afterwards he'd made up his mind to have another try at getting me to join with George Storefield in that fencing job. After that we could have gone into the outside station work with him—just the thing that would have suited the pair of us; and what a grand finish we might have made of it if we ran a waiting race; and where were we now?—Jim dead, Aileen dead to the world, and me to be hanged on Thursday, poor mother dead and broken-hearted before her time. We couldn't have done worse. We might, we must have, done better.

I did repent in that sort of way of all we'd done since that first wrong turn. It's the wrong turn-off that makes a man lose his way; but as for the rest I had only a dull, heavy feeling that my time was come,—and I must make the best of it, and meet it like a man.

So the day came. The last day! What a queer feeling it was when I lay down that night, that I should never want to sleep again, or try to do it. That I had seen the sun set—leastways the day grow dark—for the last time; the very last time.

Somehow I wasn't that much in fear of it as you might think; it was strange like, but made one pull himself together a bit. Thousands and millions of people had died in all sorts of ways and shapes since the beginning of the world. Why shouldn't I be able to go through with it like another?

I was a long time lying and thinking before I thought of sleeping. All the small, teeny bits of a man's life, as well as the big, seemed to come up before me as I lay there—the first things I could recollect at Rocky Flat; then the pony; mother a youngish woman; father always hard-looking, but so different from what he came to be afterwards. Aileen a little girl, with her dark hair falling over her shoulders; then a grown woman, riding her own horse, and full of smiles and fun; then a pale, weeping woman all in black, looking like a mourner at a funeral. Jim too, and Starlight—now galloping along through the forest at night—laughing, drinking, enjoying themselves at Jonathan Barnes's, with the bright eyes of Bella and Maddie shining with fun and devilment.

Then both of them lying dead at the flat by Murrynebone Creek —Starlight with the half-caste making his wild moan over him; Jim, quiet in death as in life, lying in the grass, looking as if he had slid off his horse in that hot weather to take a banje; and now, no get away, the rope—the hangman!

I must have gone to sleep, after all, for the sun was shining into the cell when I stirred, and I could see the chains on my ankles that I had worn all these weary weeks. How could I sleep? but I had, for all that. It was daylight; more than that—sunrise. I listened, and, sure enough, I heard two or three of the bush-birds

calling. It reminded me of being a boy again, and listening to the
birds at dawn just before it was time to get up. When I was a boy!
—was I ever a boy? How long was it ago—and now—O my God, my
God! That ever it should have come to this! What am I waiting
for to hear now? The tread of men; the smith that knocks the irons
off the limbs that are so soon to be as cold as the jangling chains.
Yes! at last I hear their footsteps—here they come!

The warder, the blacksmith, the parson, the head gaoler, just as
I expected. The smith begins to cut the rivets. Somehow they none
of them looked so solemn as I expected. Surely when a man is to
be killed by law, choked to death in cold blood, people might look
a bit serious. Mind you, I believe men ought to be hanged. I don't
hold with any of that rot that them as commits murder shouldn't
pay for it with their own lives. It's the only way they can pay for
it, and make sure they don't do it again. Some men can stand anything but the rope. Prison walls don't frighten them; but Jack
Ketch does. They can't gammon him.

'Knock off his irons quick,' says Mr. Farleigh, the parson; 'he will
not want them again just yet.'

'I didn't think you would make a joke of that sort, sir,' says I.
'It's a little hard on a man, ain't it? But we may as well take it
cheerful, too.'

'Tell him all, Mr. Strickland,' he says to the head gaoler. 'I see
he can bear it now.'

'Prisoner Richard Marston,' says the gaoler, standing up before
me, 'it becomes my duty to inform you that, owing to representations
made in your favour by the Hon. Mr. Falkland, the Hon. Mr. Storefield, and other gentlemen who have interested themselves in your
case, setting forth the facts that, although mixed up with criminals
and known to be present when the escort and various other cases of
robbery under arms have taken place, wherein life has been taken,
there is no distinct evidence of your having personally taken life. On
the other hand, in several instances, yourself, with the late James
Marston and the deceased person known as Starlight, have aided in
the protection of life and property. The Governor and the Executive
Council have therefore graciously been pleased to commute your
sentence of death to that of fifteen years' imprisonment.'

.   . .   .   .   .

When I came to I was lying on my blankets in a different cell, as
I could see by the shape of it. The irons didn't rattle when I moved.
I was surprised when I looked and saw they were took off. Bit by
bit it all came back to me. I was not to be hanged. My life was
saved, if it was worth saving, by the two or three good things we'd
done in our time, and almost, I thought, more for poor old Jim's sake
than my own.

Was I glad or sorry now it was all over? I hardly knew. For a
week or two I felt as if they'd better have finished me off when I was

ready and ha' done with me, but after a while I began to feel different. Then the gaoler talked to me a bit. He never said much to prisoners, and what he said he meant.

'Prisoner Marston,' says he, 'you'd better think over your situation and don't mope. Make up your mind like a man. You may have friends that you'd like to live for. Pull yourself together and face your sentence like a man. You're a young man now, and you won't be an old one when you're let out. If your conduct is uniformly good you'll be out in twelve years. Settle yourself to serve that—and you're a lucky man to have no more—and you may have some comfort in your life yet.'

Then he went out. He didn't wait to see what effect it had on me. If I wasn't a fool, he thought to himself, I must take it in; if I was, nothing would do me any good.

I took his advice, and settled myself down to think it over. It was a good while—a weary lot of years to wait, year by year—but, still, if I got out in twelve years I should not be so out and out broke down after all—not much over forty, and there's a deal of life for a man sometimes after that.

And then I knew that there would be one that would be true to me anyhow, that would wait for me when I went out, and that would not be too proud to join in her life with mine, for all that had come and gone. Well, this might give me strength. I don't think anything else could, and from that hour I made up my mind to tackle it steady and patient, to do the best I could, and to work out my sentence, thankful for the mercy that had been showed me, and, if ever a man was in this world, resolved to keep clear of all cross ways for the future.

So I began to steady myself and tried to bear it the best way I could. Other men were in for long sentences, and they seemed to be able to keep alive, so why shouldn't I? Just at the first I wasn't sure whether I could. Year after year to be shut up there, with the grass growin' and the trees wavin' outside, and the world full of people, free to walk or ride, to work or play, people that had wives and children, and friends and relations—it seemed awful. That I should be condemned to live in this shut-up tomb all those long, weary years, and there was nothing else for it. I couldn't eat or sleep at first, and kept starting up at night, thinking they was coming for me to carry me off to the gallows. Then I'd dream that Jim and Starlight was alive, and that we'd all got out of gaol and were riding through the bush at night to the Hollow again. Then I'd wake up and know they were dead and I was here. Time after time I've done that, and I was that broken down and low that I burst out crying like a child.

CHAPTER LII

The months went on till I began to think it was a long time since anything had been heard of father. I didn't expect to have a letter or anything, but I knew he must take a run outside now and again; and so sure as he did it would come to my ears somehow.

One day I had a newspaper passed in to me. It was against the regulations, but I did get it for all that, and this was the first thing I saw:—

STRANGE DISCOVERY IN THE TURON DISTRICT

A remarkable natural formation, leading to curious results, was last week accidentally hit upon by a party of prospectors, and by them made known to the police of the district. It may tend to solve the doubts which for the last few years have troubled the public at large with respect to the periodical disappearance of a certain gang of bush-rangers now broken up.

Accident led the gold miners, who were anxious to find a practicable track to the gullies at the foot of Nulla Mountain, to observe a narrow winding way apparently leading over the brow of the precipice on its western face. To their surprise, half hidden by a fallen tree, they discovered a difficult but practicable track down a gully which finally opened out into a broad well-grassed valley of considerable extent, in which cattle and horses were grazing.

No signs of human habitation were at first visible, but after a patient search a cave in the eastern angle of the range was discovered. Fires had been lighted habitually near the mouth, and near a log two saddles and bridles —long unused—lay in the tall grass. Hard by was stretched the body of a man of swarthy complexion. Upon examination the skull was found to be fractured, as if by some blunt instrument. A revolver of small size lay on his right side.

Proceeding to the interior of the cave, which had evidently been used as a dwelling for many years past, they came upon the corpse of another man, in a sitting posture, propped up against the wall. One arm rested upon an empty spirit-keg, beside which were a tin pannikin and a few rude cooking utensils. At his feet lay the skeleton of a dog. The whole group had evidently been dead for a considerable time. Further search revealed large supplies of clothes, saddlery, arms, and ammunition—all placed in recesses of the cave—besides other articles which would appear to have been deposited in that secure receptacle many years since.

As may be imagined, a large amount of interest, and even excitement, was caused when the circumstances, as reported to the police, became generally known. A number of our leading citizens, together with many of the adjoining station holders, at once repaired to the spot. No difficulty was felt in identifying the bodies as those of Ben Marston, the father of the two bush-rangers of that name, and of Warrigal, the half-caste follower always seen in attendance upon the chief of the gang, the celebrated Starlight.

How the last members of this well-known, long-dreaded gang of freebooters had actually perished can only be conjectured, but taking the surrounding circumstances into consideration, and the general impression abroad that Warrigal was the means of putting the police upon the track of Richard Marston, which led indirectly to the death of his master and of James Marston, the most probable solution would seem to be that, after a deep carouse, the old man had taxed Warrigal with his treachery and brained him with the American axe found close to the body. He had apparently then shot himself to avoid a lingering death, the bullet found in his body having been probably fired by the half-caste as he was advancing upon him axe in hand.

The dog, well known by the name of Crib, was the property and constant companion of Ben Marston, the innocent accomplice in many of his most daring stock-raids. Faithful unto the end, with the deep, uncalculating love which shames so often that of man, the dumb follower had apparently refused to procure food for himself, and pined to death at the feet of his dead master. Though the philanthropist may regret the untimely and violent end of men whose courage and energy fitted them for better things, it cannot be denied that the gain to society far exceeds the loss.

When the recesses of the Hollow were fully explored, traces of rude but apparently successful gold workings were found in the creeks which run through this romantic valley—long as invisible as the fabled gold cities of Mexico.

We may venture to assert that no great time will be suffered to elapse ere the whole of the alluvial will be taken up, and the Terrible Hollow, which some of the older settlers assert to be its real name, will re-echo with the sound of pick and shovel; perhaps to be the means of swelling those escorts which its former inhabitants so materially lessened.

With regard to the stock pasturing in the valley, a puzzling problem presented itself when they came to be gathered up and yarded. The adjoining settlers who had suffered from the depredations of the denizens of the Hollow were gladly expectant of the recovery of animals of great value. To their great disappointment, only a small number of the very aged bore any brand which could be sworn to and legally claimed. The more valuable cattle and horses, evidently of the choicest quality and the highest breeding, resembled very closely individuals of the same breed stolen from the various proprietors. But they were either unbranded or branded with a letter and numbers to which no stock-owners in the district could lay claim.

Provoking, as well as perplexing, was this unique state of matters—wholly without precedent. For instance, Mr. Rouncival and his stud-groom could almost have sworn to the big slashing brown mare, the image of the long-lost celebrity Termagant, with the same crooked blaze down the face, the same legs, the same high croup and peculiar way of carrying her head. She corresponded exactly in age to the date on which the grand thoroughbred mare, just about to bring forth, had disappeared from Buntagong. No reasonable doubt existed as to the identity of this valuable animal, followed as she was by several of her progeny, equally aristocratic in appearance. Still, as these interesting individuals had never been seen by their rightful owners, it was impossible to prove a legal title.

The same presumptive certainty and legal incompleteness existed concerning Mr. Bowe's short-horns (as he averred) and Mr. Dawson's Devons.

'Thou art so near and yet so far,'

as a provoking stock-rider hummed. Finally, it was decided by the officials in charge to send the whole collection to the public pound, when each proprietor might become possessed of his own, 'with a good and lawful title in addition— for 'a consideration'—and to the material benefit of the Government coffers.

So it was this way the poor old Hollow was dropped on to, and the well-hidden secret blown for ever and ever. Well, it had been a good plant for us and them as had it before our time. I don't expect there'll ever be such a place again, take it all round.

And that was the end of father! Poor old dad! game to the last. And the dog, too!—wouldn't touch bit or sup after the old man dropped. Just like Crib that was! Often and often I used to wonder what he saw in father to be so fond of him. He was about the only creature in the wide world that was fond of dad—except mother, perhaps, when she was young. She'd rather got wore out of her feelings for him, too. But Crib stuck to him to his end—faithful till death, as some of them writing coves says.

And Warrigal! I could see it all, sticking out as plain as a fresh track after rain. He'd come back to the Hollow, like a fool—in spite of me warning him—or because he had nowhere else to go. And the first time dad had an extra glass in his head he tackled him about giving me away and being the means of the other two's death. Then he'd got real mad and run at him with the axe. Warrigal had fired as he came up, and hit him, too; but couldn't stop him in the rush. Dad got in at him, and knocked his brains out there and then. Afterwards, he'd sat down and drank himself pretty well blind; and then, finding the pains coming on him, and knowing he couldn't live, finished himself off with his own revolver.

It was just the way I expected he would make an ending. He couldn't do much all alone in his line. The reward was a big one, and there would be always someone ready to earn it. Jim and Starlight were gone, and I was as good as dead. There wasn't much of a call for him to keep alive. Anyhow, he died game, and paid up all scores, as he said himself.

. . . . .

I don't know that there's much more for me to say. Here I am boxed up, like a scrubber in a pound, year after year—and years after that —for I don't know how long. How ever, O my God! how ever shall I stand it? Here I lie, half my time in a place where the sun never shines, locked up at five o'clock in my cell, and the same door with never a move in it till six o'clock next morning. A few hours' walk in a prison yard, with a warder on the wall with a gun in his hand overhead. Then locked up again, Sundays and week-days, no difference. Sometimes I think they'd better have hanged me right off. If I feel all these things now I've only been a few months doing my sentence, how about next year, and the year after that, and so on, and so on? Why, it seems as if it would mount up to more than a man's life—to ten lives—and then to think how easy it might all have been saved.

There's only one thing keeps me alive; only for that I'd have starved to death for want of having the heart to eat or drink either, or else have knocked my brains out against the wall when one of them low fits came over me. That one thing's the thought of Gracey Storefield.

She couldn't come to me, she wrote, just yet, but she'd come within the month, and I wasn't to fret about her, because whether it was ten years or twenty years if she was alive she'd meet me the day after I was free, let who will see her. I must be brave and keep up my spirits for her sake and Aileen's, who, though she was dead to the world, would hear of my being out, and would always put my name in her prayers. Neither she nor I would be so very old, and we might have many years of life reasonably happy yet in spite of all that had happened. So the less I gave way and made myself miserable, the younger I should look and feel when I came out. She was sure I repented truly of what I had done wrong in the past; and she for one, and George—good, old, kind George—had said he would go bail that I would be one of the squarest men in the whole colony for the future. So I was to live on, and hope and pray God to lighten our lot for her sake.

.   .   .   .   .

It must be years and years since that time as I last wrote about. Awful long and miserable the time went at first; now it don't go so slow somehow. I seemed to have turned a corner. How long is it? It must be a hundred years. I have had different sorts of feelings. Sometimes I feel ashamed to be alive. I think the man that knocked his head against the wall of his cell the day he was sentenced and beat his brains out in this very gaol had the best of it. Other times I take things quite easy, and feel as if I could wait quite comfortable and patient-like till the day came. But—will it? Can it ever come that I shall be a free man again?

People have come to see me a many times, most of them the first year or two I was in. After that they seemed to forget me, and get tired of coming. It didn't make much odds.

But one visitor I had regular after the first month or two. Gracey, poor Gracey, used to come and see me twice a year. She said it wouldn't do her or me any good to come oftener, and George didn't want her to. But them two times she always comes, and, if it wasn't for that, I don't think I'd ever have got through with it. The worst of it was, I used to be that low and miserable after she went, for days and days after, that it was much as I could do to keep from giving in altogether. After a month was past I'd begin to look forward to the next time.

When I'd done over eleven years—eleven years! how did I ever do it? but the time passed, and passed somehow—I got word that they that I knew of was making a try to see if I couldn't be let out when I'd done twelve years. My regular sentence was fifteen, and little enough, too. Anyhow, they knock off a year or two from most of the long-sentence men's time, if they've behaved themselves well in gaol, and can show a good conduct ticket right through.

Well, I could do that. I was too low and miserable to fight much when I went in; besides, I never could see the pull of kicking up rows and giving trouble in a place like that. They've got you there fast enough, and any man that won't be at peace himself, or let others be, is pretty sure to get the worst of it. I'd seen others try it, and never seen no good come of it. It's like a dog on the chain that growls and bites at all that comes near him. A man can take a sapling and half kill him, and the dog never gets a show unless he breaks his chain, and that don't happen often.

Well, I'd learned carpentering and had a turn at mat-making and a whole lot of other things. They kept me from thinking, as I said before, and the neater I did 'em and the more careful I worked the better it went with me. As for my mats, I came quite to be talked about on account of 'em. I drew a regular good picture of Rainbow, and worked it out on a mat with different-coloured thrums, and the number of people who came to see that mat, and the notice they took of it, would surprise any one.

When my twelve years was within a couple of months or so of being up I began to hear that there was a deal of in-and-out sort of work about my getting my freedom. Old George Storefield and Mr. Falkland—both of 'em in the Upper House—and one or two more people that had some say with the Government, was working back and edge for me. There was a party on the other side that wasn't willing as I should lose a day or an hour of my sentence, and that made out I ought to have been hanged 'right away,' as old Arizona Bill would have said, when I was first taken. Well, I don't blame any of 'em for that; but if they could have known the feelings of a man that's done a matter of twelve years, and thinks he might—yes, might—smell the fresh air and feel the grass under his feet in a week or two—well, they'd perhaps consider a bit.

Whatever way it came out I couldn't say, but the big man of the Government people at that time—the Minister that had his say in all these sort of things—took it into his head that I'd had about enough of it, if I was to be let out at all; that the steel had been pretty well taken out of me, and that, from what he knew of my people and so on, I wasn't likely to trouble the Government again. And he was right. All I wanted was to be let out a pardoned man, that had done bad things, and helped in worse; but had paid—and paid dear, God knows—for every pound he'd got crooked and every day he'd wasted in cross work. If I'd been sent back for them three years, I do r'aly believe something of dad's old savage blood would have come uppermost in me, and I'd have turned reckless and revengeful like to my life's end.

Anyhow, as I said before, the Minister—he'd been into the gaol and had a look once or twice—made up his mind to back me right out; and he put it so before the Governor that he gave an order for my pardon to be made out, or for me to be discharged the day my twelve years was up, and to let off the other three, along of my good behaviour in the gaol, and all the rest of it.

This leaked out somehow, and there was the deuce's own barney over it. When some of the Parliament men and them sort of coves in the country that never forgives anybody heard of it they began to buck, and no mistake. You'd have thought every bush-ranger that ever had been shopped in New South Wales had been hanged or kept in gaol till he died; nothing but petitions and letters to the papers; no end of bobbery. The only paper that had a word to say on the side of a poor devil like me was the *Turon Star*. He said that

'Dick Marston and his brother Jim, not to mention Starlight (who paid his debts at any rate, unlike some people he could name who had signed their names to this petition), had worked manly and true at the Turon diggings for over a year. They were respected by all who knew them, and had they not been betrayed by a revengeful woman might have lived thenceforth a life of industry and honourable dealing. He, for one, upheld the decision of the Chief Secretary. Thousands of the Turon miners, men of worth and intelligence, would do the same.'

The Governor hadn't been very long in the colony, and they tried it on all roads to get him to go back on his promise to me. They began bullying, and flattering, and preaching at him if such a notorious criminal as Richard Marston was to be allowed to go forth with a free pardon after a comparatively short—short, think of that, short!—imprisonment, what a bad example it will be to the rising generation, and so on.

They managed to put the thing back for a week or two till I was nearly drove mad with fretting, and being doubtful which way it would go.

Lucky for me it was, and for some other people as well, the Governor was one of those men that takes a bit of trouble and considers over a thing before he says yes or no. When he says a thing he sticks to it. When he goes forward a step he puts his foot down, and all the blowing, and cackle, and yelping in the world won't shift him.

Whether the Chief Secretary would have taken my side if he'd known what a dust the thing would have raised, and how near his Ministers—or whatever they call 'em—was to going out along with poor Dick Marston, I can't tell. Some people say he wouldn't. Anyhow, he stuck to his word; and the Governor just said he'd given his decision about the matter, and he hadn't the least intention of altering it—which showed he knew something of the world, as well as intended to be true to his own opinions. The whole thing blew over after a bit, and the people of the country soon found out that there wasn't such another Governor (barrin' one) as the Queen had the sending out of.

The day it was all settled the head gaoler comes to me, and says he, 'Richard Marston, the Governor and Council has been graciously pleased to order that you be discharged from her Majesty's gaol upon the completion of twelve years of imprisonment; the term of three years' further imprisonment being remitted on account of your uniform good conduct while in the said gaol. You are now free!'

I heard it all as if it had been the parson reading out of a book about some other man. The words went into my ears and out again. I hardly heard them, only the last word, free—free—free! What a blessed word it is! I couldn't say anything, or make a try to walk out. I sat down on my blankets on the floor, and wondered if I was going mad. The head gaoler walked over to me, and put his hand on my shoulder. He was a kind enough man, but, from being 'took in' so often, he was cautious. 'Come, Dick,' he says, 'pull yourself together. It's a shake for you, I daresay, but you'll be all right in a day or so. I believe you'll be another man when you get out, and give the lie to these fellows that say you'll be up to your old tricks in a month. I'll back you to go straight; if you don't you're not the man I take you for.'

I got up and steadied myself. 'I thank you with all my heart, Mr. ——,' I said. 'I'm not much of a talker, but you'll see, you'll see; that's the best proof. The fools, do they think I want to come back here? I wish some of them had a year of it.'

As soon as there was a chance of my going out, I had been allowed to 'grow,' as they call it in there. That is, to leave off having my face scraped every morning by the prison barber with his razor, that was sometimes sharp and more times rough enough to rasp the skin off you, particularly if it was a cold morning. My hair was let alone, too. My clothes—the suit I was taken in twelve years ago—had been washed and cleaned and folded up, and put away and numbered in a room with a lot of others. I remember I'd got 'em new just before I started away from the Hollow. They was brought to me, and very well they looked, too. I never had a suit that lasted that long before.

That minds me of a yarn I heard at Jonathan Barnes's one day. There was a young chap that they used to call 'Liverpool Jack' about then. He was a free kind of fellow, and good-looking, and they all took to him. He went away rather sudden, and they heard nothing of him for about three years. Then he came back, and as it was the busy season old Jonathan put him on, and gave him work. It was low water with him, and he seemed glad to get a job.

When the old man came in he says, 'Who do you think came up the road to-day?—Liverpool Jack. He looked rather down on his luck, so I gave him a job to mend up the barn. He's a handy fellow. I wonder he doesn't save more money. He's a careful chap, too.'

'Careful,' says Maddie. 'How do ye make that out?'

'Why,' says Jonathan, 'I'm dashed if he ain't got the same suit of clothes on he had when he was here three years ago.'

The old man didn't tumble, but both the girls burst out laughing. He'd been in the jug all the time!

I dressed myself in my own clothes—how strange it seemed—even to the boots, and then I looked in the glass. I hadn't done that lately. I regularly started back; I didn't know myself; I came into prison a big, stout, brown-haired chap, full of life, and able to jump over a dray and bullocks almost. I did once jump clean over a pair of polers for a lark.

And how was I going out? A man with a set kind of face, neither one thing nor the other, as if he couldn't be glad or sorry, with a fixed staring look about the eyes, a half-yellowish skin, with a lot of wrinkles in it, particularly about the eyes, and grey hair. Big streaks of grey in the hair of the head and as for my beard it was white—white. I looked like an old man, and walked like one. What was the use of my going out at all?

When I went outside the walls by a small gate the head gaoler shook hands with me. 'You're a free man now, Dick,' he says, 'and remember this—no man can touch you. No man has the right to pull you up or lay a finger on you. You're as independent as the best gentleman in the land so long as you keep straight. Remember that. I see there's a friend waiting for you.'

Sure enough there was a man that I knew, and that lived near Rocky Flat. He was a quiet, steady-going sort of farmer, and never would have no truck with us in our flash times. He was driving a springcart, with a good sort of horse in it.

'Come along with me, Dick,' says he. 'I'm going your way, and I promised George Storefield I'd call and give you a lift home. I'm glad to see you out again, and there's a few more round Rocky Flat that's the same.'

We had a long drive—many a mile to go before we were near home. I couldn't talk; I didn't know what to say, for one thing. I could only feel as if I was being driven along the road to heaven after coming from the other place. I couldn't help wondering whether it was possible that I was a free man going back to life and friends and happiness. Was it possible? Could I ever be happy again? Surely it must be a dream that would all melt away, and I'd wake up as I'd done hundreds of times and find myself on the floor of the cell, with the bare walls all round me.

When we got nearer the old place I began to feel that queer and strange that I didn't know which way to look. It was coming on for spring, and there'd been a middling drop of rain, seemingly, that had made the grass green and everything look grand. What a time had passed over since I thought whether it was spring, or summer, or winter! It didn't make much odds to me in there, only to drive me wild now and again with thinkin' of what was goin' on outside, and how I was caged up and like to be for months and years.

Things began little by little to look the way they used to do long and long ago. Now it was an old overhanging limb that had arched over the road since we were boys; then there was a rock with a big kurrajong tree growing near it. When we came to the turn off where we could see Nulla Mountain everything came back to me. I seemed to have had two lives; the old one—then a time when I was dead, or next door to it—now this new life. I felt as if I was just born.

'We'll get down here now,' I said, when we came near the dividing fence; 'it ain't far to walk. That's your road.'

'I'll run you up to the door,' says he, 'it isn't far; you ain't used to walking much.'

He let out his horse and we trotted through the paddock up to the old hut.

'The garden don't look bad,' says he. 'Them peaches always used to bear well in the old man's time, and the apples and quinces, too. Some one's had it took care on and tidied up a bit. There, you've got a friend or two left, old man. And I'm one, too,' says he, putting out his hand and giving mine a shake. 'There ain't any one in these parts as'll cast it up to you as long as you keep straight. You can look 'em all in the face now, and bygones'll be bygones.'

Then he touched up his horse and rattled off before I could as much as say 'Thank ye.'

I walked through the garden and sat down in the verandah on one of the old benches. There was the old place, mighty little altered considering. The hut had been mended up from time to time—now a slab and then a sheet of bark—else it would have been down long enough ago. The garden had been dug up, and the trees trimmed year by year. A hinge had been put on the old gate, and a couple of slip-rails at the paddock. The potato patch at the bottom of the garden was sown, and there were vegetables coming on in the old beds. Some one had looked after the place; of course, I knew who it was.

It began to get coldish, and I pulled the latch—it was there just the same—and went into the old room. I almost expected to see mother in her chair, and father on the stool near the fireplace, where he used to sit and smoke his pipe. Aileen's was a little low chair near mother's. Jim and I used to be mostly in the verandah, unless it was very cold, and then we used to lie down in front of the fire—that is, if dad was away, as he mostly was.

The room felt cold and dark as I looked in. So dreadful lonely, too. I almost wished I was back in the gaol.

When I looked round again I could see things had been left ready for me, so as I wasn't to find myself bad off the first night. The fire was all made up ready to light, and matches on the table ready. The kettle was filled, and a basket close handy with a leg of mutton, and bread, butter, eggs, and a lot of things—enough to last me a week. The bedroom had been settled up, too, and there was a good, comfortable bed ready for any tired man to turn into. Better than all, there was a letter, signed 'Your own Gracey,' that made me think I might have some life left worth living yet.

I lit the fire, and after a bit made shift to boil some tea; and after I'd finished what little I could eat I felt better, and sat down before the fire to consider over things. It was late enough—midnight—before I turned in. I couldn't sleep then; but at last I must have dropped off, because the sun was shining into the room, through the old window with the broken shutter, when I awoke.

At first I didn't think of getting up. Then I knew, all of a sudden, that I could open the door and go out. I was in the garden in three

seconds, listening to the birds and watching the clouds rising over
Nulla Mountain.

.   .   .   .   .

That morning, after breakfast, I saw two people, a man and a
woman, come riding up to the garden gate. I knew who it was as
far as I could see 'em—George Storefield and Gracey. He lifted her
down, and they walked up through the garden. I went a step or
two to meet them. She ran forward and threw herself into my arms.
George turned away for a bit. Then I put her by, and told her to
sit down on the verandah, while I had a talk with George. He shook
hands with me, and said he was glad to see me a free man again.
'I've worked a bit, and got others to work, too,' says he; 'mostly for
her, and partly for your own sake, Dick. I can't forget old times.
Now you're your own man again, and I won't insult you by saying
I hope you'll keep so; I know it, as sure as we stand here.'

'Look here, George,' I said, 'as there's a God in heaven, no man
shall ever be able to say a word against me again. I think more of
what you've done for me almost than of poor Gracey's holding fast.
It came natural to her. Once a woman takes to a man, it don't matter
to her what he is. But if you'd thrown me off I'd have not blamed
you. What's left of Dick Marston's life belongs to her and you.'

.   .   .   .   .

That day week Gracey and I were married, very quiet and private.
We thought we'd have no one at the little church at Bargo but George
and his wife, the old woman, and the chap as drove me home. Just
as we were going into the church who should come rattling up on
horseback but Maddie Barnes and her husband—Mrs. Moreton, as
she was now, with a bright-looking boy of ten or eleven on a pony.
She jumps off and gives the bridle to him. She looked just the same
as ever, a trifle stouter, but the same saucy look about the eyes. 'Well,
Dick Marston,' says she, 'how are you? Glad to see you, old man.
You've got him safe at last, Gracey, and I wish you joy. You came to
Bella's wedding, Dick, and so I thought I'd come to yours, though
you kept it so awful quiet. How d'ye think the old horse looks?'

'Why, it's never Rainbow?' says I. 'It's twelve years and over since
I saw him last.'

'I didn't care if it was twenty,' said she. 'Here he is, and goes as
sound as a bell. His poor old teeth are getting done, but he ain't
the only one that way, is he, Joe? He'll never die if I can keep him
alive. I have to give him corn-meal, though, so as he can grind it
easy.'

'I believe she thinks more of that old moke than me and the children all put together,' says Joe Moreton.

'And why shouldn't I?' says Maddie, facing round at him just the
old way. 'Isn't he the finest horse that ever stood on legs, and didn't
he belong to the finest gentleman that you or any one else looked at?
Don't say a word against him, for I can't stand it. I believe if you

was to lay a whip across that old horse in anger I'd go away and leave you, Joe Moreton, just as if you was a regular black stranger. Poor Rainbow! Isn't he a darling?' Here she stroked the old horse's neck. He was rolling fat, and had a coat like satin. His legs were just as clean as ever, and he stood there as if he heard everything, moving his old head up and down the way he always did—never still a moment. It brought back old times, and I felt soft enough, I tell you. Maddie's lips were trembling again, too, and her eyes like two coals of fire. As for Joe, he said nothing more, and the best thing, too. The boy led Rainbow over to the fence, and old George walked us all into the church, and that settled things.

After the words were said we all went back to George's together, and Maddie and her husband drank a glass of wine to our health, and wished us luck. They rode as far as the turn off to Rocky Flat with us, and then took the Turon road.

'Good-bye, Dick,' says Maddie, bending down over the old horse's neck. 'You've got a stunning good wife now, if ever any man had in the whole world. Mind you're an A1 husband, or we'll all round on you, and your life won't be worth having; and I've got the best horse in the country, haven't I? See where the bullet went through his poor neck. There's no lady in the land got one that's a patch on him. Steady now, Rainbow, we'll be off in a minute. You shall see my little Jim there take him over a hurdle yard. He can ride a bit, as young as he is. Pity poor old Jim ain't here to-day, isn't it, Dick? Think of him being cold in his grave now, and we here. Well, it's no use crying, is it?'

And off went Maddie at a pace that gave Joe and the boy all they knew to catch her.

.   .   .   .   .

We're to live here for a month or two till I get used to outdoor work and the regular old bush life again. There's no life like it, to my fancy. Then we start, bag and baggage, for one of George's Queensland stations, right away up on the Barcoo, that I'm to manage and have a share in.

It freshens me up to think of making a start in a new country. It's a long way from where we were born and brought up; but all the better for that. Of course they'll know about me; but in any part of Australia, once a chap shows that he's given up cross doings and means to go straight for the future, the people of the country will always lend him a helping hand, particularly if he's married to such a wife as Gracey. I'm not afraid of any of my troubles in the old days being cast up to me; and men are so scarce and hard to get west of the Barcoo that no one that once had Dick Marston's help at a muster is likely to remind him of such an old story as that of 'Robbery Under Arms.'

THE END